ISBN 978-0-276-44447-0

www.readersdigest.co.uk

The Reader's Digest Association Limited, 11 Westferry Circus, Canary Wharf, London E14 4HE

and in Canada
www.rd.ca

The Reader's Digest Association (Canada) ULC, 1100 René-Lévesque Blvd. West, Montréal,
Québec, H3B 5H5 Canada

of love & life

Three novels selected and condensed
by Reader's Digest

The Reader's Digest Association Limited, London, Montreal

CONTENTS

The Brightest Star in the Sky

Marian Keyes

I wanted to write a novel with a huge cast of characters, and to explore the way peoples' lives overlap and become entwined. I wanted to see what impact individuals in a community have on one another, sometimes without them even knowing it. And I certainly had a good few surprises along the way . . .

So here it is—The Brightest Star in the Sky. I do hope you enjoy it.

Marian

Day 61

June the 1st, a bright summer's evening, a Monday. I've been flying over the streets and houses of Dublin and now, finally, I'm here. I enter through the roof. Via a skylight I slide into a living room and right away I know it's a woman who lives here. There's a femininity to the furnishings—pastel-coloured throws on the sofa, that sort of thing. Two plants. Both alive. A television of modest size.

I appear to have arrived in the middle of some event. Several people are standing in an awkward circle, sipping from glasses of champagne and pretending to laugh at what the others are saying. A variety of ages and sexes suggests that this is a family occasion.

Birthday cards abound. Discarded wrapping paper. Presents. Talk of leaving for the restaurant. Hungry for information, I read the cards. They're addressed to someone called Katie and she appears to be celebrating her fortieth birthday. I wouldn't have thought that that called for much celebration but it takes all sorts, I'm told.

I locate Katie. She looks a good deal younger than forty. She's tallish and dark-haired and bosomy and gamely doing her best to stay upright in a pair of spike-heeled knee-boots. Her force field is a pleasant one; she vibrates with levelheaded warmth.

The man next to Katie, glowing with dark pride—the pride is in large part to do with the new platinum watch on Katie's wrist—is her boyfriend, partner, loved one, whatever you want to call it.

An interesting man, with a compelling life force, his vibrations are so powerful they're almost visible. I'll be honest: I'm intrigued.

Conall, they're calling this man. The more polite members of the group, at least. A few other names are hovering in the ether—Show-off; Flash Bastard—but remain unuttered. *Fascinating.* The men don't like him *at all*. I've identified Katie's father, brother and brother-in-law and not one of them is keen. However, the women—Katie's mother, sister and best friend—don't seem to mind him as much.

I waft past Katie and she puts a hand up to her neck and shivers.

'What?' Conall looks ready to do battle.

'Nothing. Someone just walked over my grave.'

Oh come now! Hardly!

'Hey!' Naomi—older sister of Katie—is pointing at a mirror that's propped on the floor against a cupboard. 'Is your new mirror not up yet?'

'Not yet,' Katie says, sudden tension leaking from between her teeth.

'But you've had it for ages! I thought Conall was going to do it for you.'

'Conall *is* going to do it,' Katie says very firmly. 'Tomorrow morning, before he goes to Helsinki. Aren't you, Conall?'

Friction! Zinging around the room, rebounding off the walls. Conall, Katie and Naomi volleying waves of tension against each other in a fast-moving taut triangle. *Entre nous*, I'm *dying* to find out what's going on but, to my alarm, I'm being overtaken by some sort of force. Something bigger or better than me is moving me downwards. Through the 100 per cent wool rug, past some dodgy joists, which are frankly *riddled* with woodworm—someone should be told—and into another place: the flat below Katie's. I'm in a kitchen. An astonishingly dirty kitchen. Pots and pans and plates are piled higgledy-piggledy in the sink, the lino floor hasn't been washed in an age, and the stove top sports many elaborate splashes of old food. Two muscular young men are leaning on the kitchen table, talking in Polish. Luckily, I discover I am fluent in Polish, and here's a rude translation of what they're saying:

'Jan, you tell her.'

'No, Andrei, you tell her. She respects you more.'

'No, Jan. Hard as it is for me, a Polish man, to understand, she doesn't respect either of us. Irish women are beyond me.'

Into the kitchen comes the object of their discussion and I can't see what they're so afraid of, two fine big lads like them, with their tattoos and slightly menacing buzz cuts. This little creature is *lovely*. A pretty little minx with mischievous eyes and spiky eyelashes and a head of charming jack-in-the-box curls that spring all the way down past her shoulders. Mid-twenties, by the look of her, and exuding vibrations so zesty they zigzag through the air.

In her hand she's carrying a pre-prepared dinner. (Greyish roast beef, in case you're interested.)

'Go on,' Jan hisses at Andrei.

'Lydia.' Andrei gestures at the, quite frankly, filthy kitchen. Speaking English, he says, 'You clean sometime.'

'Sometime,' she agrees, scooping up a fork from the draining board. 'But sadly not in this lifetime. Now move.'

With alacrity Andrei clears a path for her to access the microwave. Viciously, she jabs her fork into the cellophane covering her dinner, then she slams the carton into the microwave. I take this opportunity to drift up behind her to introduce myself, but to my surprise she swats me away as though I were a pesky fly.

Me! Don't you know who I am?

Andrei is giving it another go. 'Lydia, pliz . . . We hev made rota.' Feebly he waves a piece of paper at her.

'Good for you.' Oh, how white her teeth are!

'You livingk here three weeks. You hev not cleaned. You must clean.'

An unexpected pulse of emotion radiates from Lydia, black and bitter. Apparently, she *does* clean. But not here? Where, then?

'Andrei, my little Polish cabbage, and you too, Jan, my other little Polish cabbage, let's imagine things were the other way round.'

'The other way round?' Andrei asks anxiously.

'Say it was two women and one man living in this flat. The man would never do anything. The women would do it all. Wouldn't they?'

The microwave beeps. She whisks her unappetising dinner from it and, with a smile, leaves the room to look up something on the Internet.

'I hate when she calls us cabbages,' Jan says stonily.

But, eager as I am to see what transpires next, I'm being moved again. Onwards, downwards, through the health-hazard lino, through more porous timberwork, and I find myself in yet another flat. This one is darker. Full of heavy furniture too big and brown for the room. It features several rugs of conflicting patterns, and net curtains so dense they appear to be crocheted. Seated on a sturdy armchair is a dour-looking elderly woman. Knees apart, slippered feet planted firmly on the floor. She must be at least 116. She's watching a gardening programme and, from the furrow-browed expression on her face, you'd swear she's never heard such outrageous idiocy in her life. Hardy perennials? No such thing, you stupid man! Everything dies!

I float past her and into a small gloomy bedroom, then into a slightly bigger, but just as gloomy, second bedroom, where I'm surprised to meet a large, long-eared dog so big and grey that for a moment I think he's a donkey. He's slumped in a corner, his head on his paws, sulking—then he senses my presence and instantly he's alert.

You can't get away with it, with animals. Different frequencies, see.

Frozen with awe and fear, he growls softly, then changes his mind, poor confused fool. Am I friend or foe? He hasn't a notion.

And the name of this creature? Well, oddly enough it would appear to be Grudge. But that can't be right, that's not a name. The problem is, there's too much *stuff* in this flat and it's slowing the vibrations down.

Leaving the donkey dog behind, I flit back into the sitting room, where there's a mahogany roll-top desk. A modest pile of opened mail tells me that the crone's name is Jemima.

Beside the mail is a silver-framed photo of a young man, and with a flash of insight I know his name is Fionn. It means 'Fair One'. He looks like a prince from a child's storybook. It's all in the hair—which is fairish and longish and wavyish—and the jaw, which is square. He's wearing a leather jacket and faded jeans and is crouching down in a flowerbed, and he has a handful of soil, which he's proffering to me with a cheeky smile, *saucy* almost, like he's offering a lot more than—! God almighty! He's just winked at me! His photograph winked! I can scarcely believe it.

'I can feel your presence!' Jemima suddenly barks, scaring the living daylights out of me. I'd forgotten about her, I was so engrossed in Fionn the Prince and his winking.

'I know you're here,' she says. 'And you don't frighten me!'

She's onto me! And I haven't gone near her.

'Show yourself,' she commands.

I will, missus, oh, I will. But your time will have to be bided. Anyway, I appear to be off again, being pulled and stretched ever downwards. I'm in the ground-floor flat now. I can see the street through the living-room window. I'm sensing a lot of love here. And something else . . .

On a sofa, washed by the flickering light of the television (thirty-two-inch) is . . . is . . . well, it's a man and a woman, but they're clinging so tightly to each other that for a moment I think they are one and the same, some strange mythological, two-headed, three-legged thing. (The fourth leg is there, simply hidden beneath their bodies.)

The woman—Maeve—now that I can make her out, is blonde and rosy-cheeked, like an angel from a painting. There's a cheruby freshness about her because she was once a farm girl. This woman has no fear of mud. Or cow's udders. Or hens going into labour. (Somehow I sense that I've got that slightly wrong.) But this woman fears other things . . .

It's hard to get a look at the man—Matt—because they're interwoven so tightly; his face is almost entirely hidden. Funnily enough, they're watching the same gardening programme as Jemima one floor above them. But unlike Jemima, they appear to think it's a marvellous piece of televisual entertainment.

Unexpectedly, I sense the presence of another man here. It's faint but it's enough to send me scooting round the place to check it out. Like the other three flats in the building, there are two bedrooms, but here only one functions as an actual bedroom. The other, the smaller of the two rooms, has been turned into a home office-cum-skip—a desk and a computer and abandoned sporting goods, but nothing on which a person could sleep.

Whatever this extra male presence is, he doesn't live here. Back in the living room, I move up close to the angelic Maeve, to introduce myself—being *friendly*—but she starts flapping her arms, like someone swimming on dry land, disentangling herself from Matt. She breaks free of him and sits bolt upright. The blood has drained from her face and her mouth has opened into a big silent O.

Matt, struggling from the couch's saggy embrace to a seated position, is equally distressed. 'Maeve! Maeve. It's only about gardening! Did they say something?' Alarm is written all over him. Now that I get a better look, I see he's got a young, likable, confident face, and I suspect that, when he isn't so concerned, he's one of life's smilers.

'Sorry, Matt, I just felt . . . No, it's OK, I'm OK,' Maeve says.

They settle—a little uneasily—back into their clinging positions. But I've upset her. I've upset them both and I don't want to do that. I've taken a liking to them; I'm touched by the uncommon tenderness they share.

'All right,' I said (although they couldn't hear me), 'I'm going.'

I sit outside on the front step, a little disconsolate. One more time I check the address: 66 Star Street, Dublin 8. A red-bricked Georgian house with a blue front door and a knocker in the shape of a banana. (One of the previous occupants was a fun-loving metalworker.) Yes, the house is definitely red-bricked. Yes, Georgian. Yes, a blue front door. Yes, a knocker in the shape of a banana. I'm in the right place. But I hadn't been warned that so many people live here.

Expect the unexpected, I'd been advised. But this isn't the type of unexpected I'd expected. This is the *wrong* unexpected.

And there's no one I can ask. I've been cut loose, like an agent in deep cover. I'll just have to work it out for myself.

I spent my first evening in 66 Star Street rattling from flat to flat, wondering anxiously which one was mine. Katie's flat was empty. Shortly after my arrival her crew had departed, in a cloud of tension, to some expensive restaurant. In the flat below, while Andrei and Jan cleaned the kitchen, Lydia parked herself at the little desk wedged into a corner of their living room and spent long intense minutes surfing the Net. I descended yet another floor, to Jemima's. I took care to keep myself well clear of her; I didn't want her shouting abuse at me again. But I must admit that I got great entertainment out of toying with the dog, Grudge. I shimmered before him and he stared in paralysed amazement.

Then, finally, I returned to Matt and Maeve. It's where I'd wanted to be all along but, professional that I was, I'd thought I'd better explore every avenue. Well, they were explored for the moment at least so, with a clear conscience, I could rejoin the loved-up pair on their sofa, which, in my discombobulated state, was soothing.

A cynical type might suggest that it was all a little too perfect. But a cynical type would be wrong. Matt and Maeve weren't just acting the part of people who are Very Much in Love. It was the real thing because Matt's and Maeve's hearts Beat as One.

The moment that Matt fell in love with Maeve . . .

That moment had been coming for quite a while, to be honest, and it finally arrived on a bone-cold March morning, roughly four and a quarter years ago, when Maeve was twenty-six and Matt was twenty-eight. They were on the Dart, and they were with three others, all on their way to a one-day training course. The five of them worked at Goliath, a software multinational, where Matt headed up one of the sales teams.

Matt was a city boy, born and bred in Dublin. He'd never been within a hundred yards of a cow. But Maeve had lived on a farm in Galway for the first eighteen years of her life and had recently been 'down home' to help out with the calving. She was full of a life-and-death saga of a calf called Bessie who was born prematurely, then rejected by her mother. When Maeve got to the end of the tale and confirmed that Bessie was now 'thriving', Matt was surprised by how relieved he felt.

'Here, I've a photo of her in my wallet,' Maeve said, and pulled her wallet from her satchel, looking for the photo. But, in her enthusiasm, she accidentally opened her purse and, with an ominous flash of metal, a waterfall of change roared towards the floor of the Dart.

'Oh cripes!' Maeve stood up and laughed helplessly. 'There goes my change for the launderette.' As if she had a magnetic draw, all thirteen passengers raised their heads, and suddenly Matt saw the power she possessed. She never considered that the strangers around her wouldn't want to help—and her faith was repaid. Matt watched, transfixed, as nearly everyone in the carriage dropped automatically to their knees, scrambling for any coins that they could see. 'Thank you,' Maeve said, over and over, receiving the returned coins. 'God bless, thanks.'

This is the person I want to be with, Matt found himself thinking. This is—

My trip down Matt and Maeve's memory lane is interrupted by sudden activity from two floors above and I scoot up to check it out.

Andrei and Jan had equipped themselves with beer and Pringles and were watching television. They didn't hear Lydia enter the room. They only knew she was there when she asked, 'Boys, boys, why so glum?'

'What is glum?' Jan asked anxiously. Instantly, he was sorry he had spoken. Andrei's constant advice was, Do not engage with her.

'What is glum?' Lydia considered. 'Glum is unhappy, sad, downcast, low, gloomy, of little cheer.' She gazed at them with an expression that was intended to seem fond. 'Homesick, that's what Dr Lydia has diagnosed.' In a voice dripping with insincere sympathy she asked gently, 'My little dumplings, are you missing Minsk?'

Neither boy spoke. Over the past three miserable weeks, they had become familiar with this routine in which Lydia threw about city names ending in 'sk'.

'Minnnssskkkk!' Lydia savoured the sound. 'Missing it?'

This was too much for Jan, who, every waking moment he was in Ireland, yearned with desperate passion to be back home. 'Irishgirl, we are not from Minsk! We are from Gdańsk! Poles, not Belarussians!'

As soon as the words were uttered, Jan wanted to cut out his tongue. Deeply ashamed, he looked at Andrei. *I'm sorry. I'm not as strong as you.*

It's OK, Andrei replied silently. *You must not blame yourself. She could destroy even the bravest man.*

Lydia left, and after a silence Jan admitted, 'I am glum.'

Several seconds elapsed before Andrei spoke. 'I too am glum.'

Back on the ground floor, it seemed that Matt and Maeve were planning to pop out for a late-night jog. In their bedroom—an Ikean wonderland, the bedside cabinets slightly off-kilter because the assembly instructions in the boxes had been in Czech—they undressed, Maeve turning away from Matt as she removed her bra. Immediately, they proceeded to get dressed again, seeming to put on even more clothes than they had already been wearing. Maeve was now covered neck to ankle in grey sweats and Matt was kitted out in jocks, baggy jogging pants and a long-sleeved T-shirt. Then . . . bafflingly! . . . they got into bed! Why so swaddled? It was a warm night out there.

It suddenly occurred to me that perhaps they were about to play a sexy undressing game. But what was wrong with removing the clothes they'd already been wearing?

I was far from happy at the thought of witnessing whatever strange jiggery-pokery they were about to unleash but I forced myself to linger. I had no choice! It was important to get the lie of the land. Propped up on his pillow, Matt flicked his way through a car magazine; meanwhile, on her side of the bed, Maeve read *Pride and Prejudice* . . . and that's all that happened. I lingered until it became clear that no sexy undressing game was about to kick off.

I must admit to a little relief.

The only problem with Matt falling in love with Maeve four and a quarter years ago was that Matt already had a girlfriend . . . Yes, the lovely Natalie. Matt and Nat each headed up a sales team and, lovers though they were, they were also rivals.

So when Maeve joined as a trainee, it was no surprise that Matt, with his glossy girlfriend and his demanding job, barely noticed her until one night when he and Nat were leaving work. Moving in harmony, they powered through Goliath's massive double doors—taking a door each—passing Maeve, who was crouched low, unlocking her bike.

'Good night, lads,' she said.

With perfect synchronicity, Matt and Nat swung their smooth, perfectly shaped heads to see who had spoken and—as one—exploded into uncontrollable laughter.

'What?' Maeve asked. Realisation dawned and a smile spread across her face. 'Is it my hat?'

'Yes!'

Maeve's hat was an orange and pink Inca-patterned knitted helmet. A triangle of yarn covered each ear, woollen plaits fell to her chest and the top came to a sharp point, on which an orange pompom was perched.

'Is it very bad?' Maeve was still smiling.

'Very bad,' Nat said.

'But it's all the rage on the Machu Picchu trail and it keeps my ears warm.' This made all three of them laugh even harder. Then, with a rough rush of metal, Maeve liberated her bike from its chain, hopped onto the saddle and, moving fluidly, freewheeled out into the traffic.

'She's so sweet.' Nat sighed. 'What do you think about her and David? Is it the real thing?'

Matt hadn't a clue. He'd barely noticed Maeve until five minutes ago, much less known that she was going out with David.

'So much in common.' Nat smiled fondly. 'Seeing as they're both Galwegians.' (David was actually from Manchester—it wasn't necessary to come from Galway to qualify for Galwegian status. It was an umbrella term that implied fondness for felafels, frizzy jumpers, festivals and protest marches.)

The funny thing was that at the time, Matt coveted David far more than he coveted Maeve.

By 11.30 p.m. Star Street had fallen silent. I'd been waiting for Katie to come home and I realised she wasn't going to.

In her wardrobe, I compressed myself into a red-soled peeptoe shoe and accessed some of her memories.

How Katie met Conall . . .

Well, just like Matt and Maeve's story, this too happened at work. Katie was head publicist at Apex Entertainment Ireland. They called themselves Apex Entertainment because they wanted to seem twenty-first-century and multimedia, but basically they were a record company, the Irish outpost of a much bigger multinational. Katie had been there for five years, welcoming visiting rock stars to Ireland, organising their interviews, hanging around backstage wearing a laminated pass, then bringing them out on the piss. It was harder than it sounded, because she was the one who had to remain sober and coherent enough to sign for all the bottles of Cristal, get the artistes home, then show up at her desk at ten o'clock the following morning after four hours' sleep.

If you met her at a christening, you'd probably never guess she worked for a record company. Admittedly, she always wore high heels and sometimes tight jeans but she didn't take cocaine and her thighs were wider than her knees. Despite these impediments, Katie was popular with the visiting rock stars, who referred to her as 'Auntie Katie', which she didn't mind too much. Or 'Mum', which she did.

So yes, Katie was working away, not exactly happy but not exactly unhappy either, when a press release announced that Apex had been bought by Sony, who planned to keep it as a separate label. The relief engendered by this was short-lived because the next sentence said that Apex would be 'rationalised' by Morehampton Green.

'Who are they?' Tamsin asked. (Low-grade frequency. Not too bright.

White lipstick. Long legs, large breasts. Popular with visiting artistes.)

'Who cares?' Katie said. Her frequency was quivering with fear.

'Vultures,' Danno said, with contempt. (Danno, aged twenty-three. Shrill, fast-vibrating frequency. Always wore black. Could consume copious amounts of cocaine without any apparent ill-effects. Also popular with visiting artistes.)

'Morehampton Green descend on companies that are underperforming,' Danno explained. 'Strip them of their assets, sack most of the staff and leave nothing in their wake but shock and awe.'

'What's going to happen to us, Katie?' Tamsin asked.

'I don't know.'

Alerted by a swishing noise, everyone turned to the *Star Trek*-style automatic glass doors. It was Graham from human resources. Under normal circumstances he exuded smug, confident vibrations but today his life force was much reduced.

Silently, he gave a memo to everyone in the room: two brief lines that said a Mr Conall Hathaway would be making contact 'shortly'.

'Who's he?' Katie asked.

'The axeman sent by our new owners,' Graham said. 'He *is* Morehampton Green. He has number crunchers with him but Conall Hathaway makes all the decisions.'

'Why will he be contacting me?' Tamsin cried.

Graham bowed his head and said nothing.

'To let you know whether you still have a job or not,' Katie deduced. 'Am I right, Graham?'

Graham nodded, with resignation.

For two days nothing happened. Everyone continued working as normal, because until something occurred there was always a chance that it mightn't. But on the afternoon of the third day, Danno burst into the office, like he'd been spat from a machine.

'He has the cold dead eyes of a killer!' Danno declared. 'He got into the lift with me just now and, I swear, I nearly shat myself.'

'Who?'

'Slasher Hathaway. Conall the Barbarian. He's come to sack us all!'

'So soon?' Katie was alarmed. 'It's almost indecent.'

'We'll be toast before this day is out,' Danno warned.

Katie summoned Audrey. (A vibration that was so muted it was almost apologetic. Reliable, trustworthy, meticulous. Not as popular with visiting artistes as Tamsin or Danno.) 'Go and check on this Conall character. Be discreet.'

Within minutes, Audrey had reappeared, wearing her hangman's face. 'He's in with Graham. They're going through personnel contracts.' Then she added, 'He's eating chocolate.'

'What?'

'One of those massive bars you can only get in the duty-free. You know what, Katie? He's really good-looking. I think I fancy him.'

'Don't fancy him,' Katie said.

Her phone rang: the cars had arrived.

'OK,' Katie called. 'Danno, Audrey, saddle up—the cars are here.'

They were off to the Four Seasons to pick up Knight Ryders for tonight's gig. Knight Ryders were a 'metal' band, a quartet of hoary old rockers who'd survived addiction, divorces, bankruptcy, near-death heart failure, kiss'n'tells and more. Many of their audience, who paid the high ticket prices, came along not in order to hear their hits from the early seventies, but simply to marvel that all four of them were still alive.

The boys were on their eighth month of a nine-month world tour and they'd been in Ireland for two very long days. Katie's greatest worry was Elijah Knight, lead singer, living legend and proud owner of a secondhand liver (one careful previous owner). He'd been clean and sober for almost a year but whispers had reached Katie's ears that he was wearying of it all.

Katie or one of her team made it their business to be with him at all times—Tamsin was over there right now—and a 'bodyguard' kept watch at night outside his bedroom.

As Katie slid into the back seat of a blacked-out limo, she got a call from Tamsin. 'It's Elijah.'

'What's up?'

'It's time for him to start backcombing his hair, but he's just sitting there with his arms folded, like a child.'

'I'm on my way.' Katie crossed her fingers and said a silent prayer that tonight would not be the night that Elijah went back on the sauce. Not on her watch. If he could just wait until tomorrow, when he and his three big-haired, craggy-faced, liver-damaged *compadres* left for Germany, she'd be very grateful.

With Katie's kindly inveigling, Elijah obediently backcombed his hair until it stood a full eleven inches above his head; the Knight Ryders played an entire set and none of them had a stroke; they even bowed out of a gratis trip to Dublin's finest brothel.

This meant that when Katie got home at the unexpectedly early hour of 2 a.m. there was room in her head for the reality of her job situation to hit her. She was done for, she abruptly realised. She might as well face it: getting Elijah Knight home safely to bed might have been her last act as senior PR of Apex Entertainment.

It made sense to get rid of her—of the six PR staff, she was paid the most. Also, a more painful acknowledgment, she was the oldest, and the music business was a young woman's game. I'm thirty-nine, she said to herself. Thirty-nine! It's a miracle I've survived this long.

She had to go to sleep now. But how could she? Tomorrow she was going to be sacked and she would lose her flat and her car and her highlights and her personal trainer.

All of a sudden her thoughts veered off in an unexpected direction and she began to blame Jason. (Between the ages of thirty-one and thirty-seven, Jason had been her boyfriend. In their sixth year, just as they'd started trying for a baby, they had the tremendous shock of discovering that they were no longer in love. They faked it for almost a year, hoping to rekindle the flame, but they were kaput. Kyboshed. All washed up.)

If she and Jason had got married and had a baby, and if Jason wasn't marrying Donanda the Portuguese stunner instead, she wouldn't have these worries.

Her anger filled her chest, until she began having difficulty breathing, and even though she hadn't had an ounce of sleep, she had to sit up and turn on the light and get her de-bittering books off the shelf to stop herself from drowning in her own bile.

Gasping, she read a few lines of *My Happiness, My Responsibility*, but it did nothing. She cast it aside and hungrily scanned *The Spiritual Laws of Success*: nonsense, *rubbish*! She was starting to think she'd have to ring for an ambulance when she opened the next book and a line jumped out at her: 'The Chinese word for "crisis" also means "opportunity".'

That's what did it.

She felt as if she'd been hacking through dense jungle and suddenly found herself on top of a mountain where the light was clear and the air was thin. Yes, her life was over! Unemployed—indeed, possibly unemployable—but her crisis could become her opportunity. Surely she could do something else with her life? Live in Thailand and learn scuba diving? Or, better still, go to India and become enlightened, and when she came back—*if* she came back, ho-ho—she wouldn't mind being homeless and carless and having to wear terrible shoes and having to do her own motivation to go for a run.

It would all be OK.

Day 60

SIXTY-SIX STAR STREET remained silent until 5.30 a.m., when Lydia got up. She lurched into the bathroom, where she showered—there's only one word for it—resentfully. She reached behind her for her conditioner and her elbow dislodged Andrei's shower gel from the shelf. No! There was a slippery scramble as she tried to catch it but it leaped from her sudsy grasp and landed on the floor of the shower with an echoey three-bounce clatter. Irkutsk! She didn't want to wake Andrei or Jan. They were bad enough when they got a full night's sleep; they'd be even more stony-faced and grumpy if they were woken prematurely.

God, the miserable bloody pair were hard work. Not once in three weeks had she seen them laugh. And no one could say she hadn't made an effort, trying to jolly them along with good-humoured slagging, the kind she employed with all men.

And she was stuck with them: it was their lease. In fact, she wondered why they didn't just tell her to hop it, because it was so obvious that they hated her. Perhaps it was because her room was laughably small, barely more than a cupboard. Lydia suspected—correctly—that it had been turned down by many viewers before she had shown up. The bed was narrow and short, there was no dressing table and no wardrobe, so most of Lydia's clothes were kept in boxes under her bed. She also suspected—again correctly—that Andrei and Jan had expected she'd bring a woman's touch to the flat. They were, of course, mistaken. As soon as she was certain that the lads didn't *expect* her to clean, then she would fall into line.

Perhaps . . .

In the meantime, the rent was astonishingly reasonable, and the house was conveniently close to the city centre. And when she'd discovered that the lads hailed from Gdańsk, she had been alerted to the excellence of words ending in 'sk'. Gdańsk! She'd enjoyed saying it so much that she'd hit the Net, looking for similar city names. And there were loads of them! Tomsk and Omsk, Minsk and Murmansk. She used them a lot. She couldn't exactly say why, she just liked them. Gdańsk was a positive word, because it sort of sounded like 'thanks', but all the others, especially Minsk and Irkutsk, sounded like swearwords, only far hissier and snakier than the ones she usually called upon. Minsk! How pissed-off that sounded! Irkutsk! How riled you could seem if you put a bit of effort into the delivery. These were quality swearwords that had cost precisely nothing and, in her current, cash-strapped circumstances, she was grateful for free pleasures.

She stood before the bathroom mirror and poured large quantities of a serum designed to combat frizz onto her head. For no matter how impoverished her circumstances, she would never give up her hair.

She dressed quickly in jeans, trainers and a hoodie, then left.

Down in the street, the morning was sunny but chilly and Lydia made her way to a taxi. A taxi? What kind of flashy minx spurns public transport?

Well, what a surprise when she climbed into the driver's seat! One could be forgiven for thinking she was proposing to hot-wire the vehicle, but when she shoved a key in the ignition it became clear that she owned it and that she was a taxi driver by trade!

She did a screechy U-turn and headed towards town, the traffic lights changing to green just as she neared them. 'Gdańsk,' she said, with satisfaction, smacking her lips with the pleasure of saying it.

Back at 66 Star Street, people were stirring. Andrei had been awake since 5.35 when Lydia had deliberately dropped something on the bathroom floor. Since she had moved in, he and Jan had been in a state of shock. They had never met a girl like her and the only good thing about her was that she was small enough to fit into the tiny room.

Andrei stared wistfully into space, remembering the halcyon days with their previous tenant, a Ukrainian electrician-cum-accordion player named Oleksander Shevchenko. Life with him had been so harmonious—because he was never there. He'd spent every night at the much swankier digs of his girlfriend, Viktoriya, and his room at 66 Star Street functioned mostly as his wardrobe. Until Viktoriya had fallen for the charms of an Irishman, and Oleksander was thrown back on his own resources. He'd endured a succession of sleepless nights with his legs extending six inches over the end of his narrow single bed, then told Andrei he could take no more.

Lots of people, most of them Polish men, had come to view the room but without exception declared themselves too big to fit into the bed. So when Irish Lydia arrived Andrei and Jan had been so dazzled by her miniature proportions they entirely neglected to notice that she was an evil little pixie.

Now they were paying the price.

After washing and dressing, the boys descended to the street, where they extended the palms of their hands outwards and expressed sarcastic surprise that it wasn't raining. Then they went in different directions, Andrei east to an industrial estate and Jan north to a shopping mall.

Jan liked to say he worked in IT, which in a way he did. He was employed in an enormous supermarket, filling the online orders. His days were spent pushing a massive super-trolley device off which branched twelve baskets, representing twelve different customers, each with a separate grocery list. When he'd located every item on all twelve lists and put them into the correct baskets, he'd deposit the merchandise in the loading area, for the truck to distribute throughout Dublin, then he'd trudge to the printer to pick up another twelve lists. He lost track of how many times a day he repeated this exercise.

Andrei also worked in IT. Except that he really did. He drove round the city in a white van, fixing broken computers for office workers. The van itself took up a lot of his thoughts. He was a pragmatic man and it irked him terribly that he was obliged to return it to base every evening, where it idled for fourteen useless hours in a car park, when it could be used for his own purposes—specifically, picking up Rosie. He had been dating Rosie (an Irish girl, but in all other respects entirely different to evil pixie Lydia) for two months and eight days and thus far she had refused to surrender her virginity to him. Andrei, with his muscles and astonishing blue-eyed good looks, was accustomed to getting his way with the girls but he was genuinely impressed by Rosie's old-fashioned virtue and his lust had blossomed into something far more complex.

On the ground floor of 66 Star Street, Matt and Maeve were roused gently from their slumber and welcomed into the day by a Zen alarm clock, a plinky-plonky affair, which sounded like Tibetan goat bells. Not very Matt. He seemed more like a man who'd prefer an alarm that behaved like a defibrillator, issuing a discordant BRRRING to oust him from the bed. But Maeve wanted the chimes, so Maeve got the chimes. She also got a leisurely breakfast. Matt, I suspect, would have been happy to mindlessly scarf down a Snickers bar while rushing to work, but instead he made tea for Maeve, Maeve made porridge for him, then they sat at their kitchen counter, mirroring each other's actions, checking that the other had honey, orange juice and other breakfast paraphernalia.

On their kitchen windowsill, in a curlicued silver frame, was a photo of them on their wedding day. They glammed up well, the pair of them,

I must say. Maeve's dress was one of those deceptively simple numbers: a slender unadorned fall of heavy satin, from an empire-line bodice. An off-the-shoulder neckline revealed pretty, creamy-skinned shoulders, and a pearl headdress gathered her thick fair hair into a bun. Matt, clutching on to Maeve and gazing at the camera with the expression of a man who has just won the lottery, was kitted out in a dark, serious-looking suit. The kind of suit that people wear to sign peace treaties.

Maeve swallowed the last of her orange juice, Matt clattered his spoon into his empty bowl, they each took their vitamin tablet, knocking it back with a shared glass of water, and—finally—left the flat. Matt had a car, a sharp suit and a sharp haircut. Maeve had a bicycle and a pair of cords so unattractive (too big and a most unappealing shade of olive-green) that it seemed as if they had been chosen specially for their ugliness.

They kissed and said goodbye. 'Be careful,' Matt said.

Of what? I wondered. Anyone foolhardy enough to negotiate a bicycle through rush-hour traffic could expect admonitions from their nearest and dearest, but, all the same, I knew that coming a cropper at the hand of a careless car was not what Maeve feared. Oh, she was definitely scared, don't get me wrong, but I didn't know what of: she was blocking me. All I could tell from looking at her was that she had no fear of being mocked for her crap clothes. *Fascinating.*

In Jemima's flat, Jemima was trying to tempt the dog to the kitchen but he was playing hard to get. 'Grudge, Grudge, my lovely Grudge.'

Jemima had been washed and dressed since 6.15 a.m. She couldn't abide slugabed behaviour. She hunkered down, her knees cracking like pistol shots, until her face was level with Grudge's sulky one. 'Just because Fionn is coming doesn't mean I'll love you any less,' she said.

All became clear: Grudge was sulking because he'd discovered that 'The Fair One' was due to visit.

'Come and be fed.'

Within moments Grudge was dancing the Dance of Breakfast. A thin-skinned creature, slow to forgive, except when food was involved.

I kept my distance from Jemima. I didn't want to frighten her. Not unless I had to. Nonetheless, her thoughts reached me. She was pulsing on a strong, steady, strident vibration, which fought its way through the clutter of the flat and insisted on attention.

She was thinking about the word *grudge*. Such a splendid noun, she thought. So suitable for purpose: you couldn't possibly utter it without your face contorting itself into a sour prune of grudgingness.

Grudge was regarded by many as a strange name for a dog, but when people were crass enough to mention this, Jemima's answer was that he had chosen it himself. They'd told her at the pound that his name was Declan but he was no more a Declan than she was. She believed that he should be trusted to make the best choice for himself, so when she got him home—where he wedged himself tightly into a corner and sat, low and mournful, on his paws—Jemima reeled out a long list of high-esteem dog names. Champion? Hero? Rebel? Prince? She watched carefully for a positive reaction but, after each suggestion, Declan growled, 'Grrrrr,' followed by a short little bark that sounded like 'Udge'. Eventually, she heard him: Grudge it was.

They'd warned her in the pound that he was a highly strung, mercurial creature, who would require careful handling, but Jemima wasn't daunted. Her philosophy was that a well-balanced dog would always get a home, but it was the poor damaged ones who really needed it.

Entre nous, I'm wondering if I was too quick with my initial judgment of Jemima as a prickly old crone.

His breakfast consumed, Grudge stared at Jemima with melting Malteser eyes, then flicked a few anxious sideways glances around the room. He was a wonderful dog, Jemima thought with pride. More intuitive than most humans.

'Yes, I feel it too,' Jemima told Grudge. 'But we won't be bowed!' She whirled round 180 degrees and planted her legs wide, like a warrior woman. 'You hear me?' she said—nay, *demanded*—glaring hard (but into the wrong corner of the room, God love her). In ringing tones, she repeated, 'We won't be bowed!'

Keep your pants on, Jemima. It's not all about you.

Matt liked to get his daily Act of Kindness out of the way early. As he drove to work, he scanned the streets looking for a chance to do good. At the upcoming bus-stop a lone woman was waiting.

He opened the passenger window and called out, 'Would you like a lift?'

Startled, the woman looked up from her texting. 'With *you*? I can't get into a car with a strange man! Don't you read the papers, son?'

'I'm not a strange man, I'm a nice man.'

'Well, you're hardly going to admit you're an axe-murderer.'

'I'm married. I love my wife. I don't own an axe.'

'Kids?'

'Not yet.'

'I've four.'

'Hop in, you can tell me about them.'

'Yeah and you can show me your axe.'

'I sell software for a living.'

'So did Jack the Ripper.'

'He didn't!'

'Look.' She sighed. 'You might be a lovely lad, in fairness you look like a lovely lad, but I can't take the chance. My kids wouldn't even be able to remember what I was wearing to tell the police. On your way, son.'

Dispirited, Matt drove off. His daily Act of Kindness was like a mill-stone round his neck. It was harder than you'd think to be kind. There were all these rules (Maeve's). Buying the *Big Issue* didn't count: it was too easy. Giving money to a busker didn't count either. The AOK had to cost emotionally. It had to be something he really didn't want to do.

However, going to work didn't count. Funnily enough, Matt usually enjoyed his job at Edios (Easy Does It Office Systems). (He'd moved on from Goliath some time ago.) But this Bank of British Columbia thing was doing his head in. They were leading him a merry dance. Over the course of the last eight months, they'd flirted and teased and enjoyed innumerable outings at Edios's expense—and they still had given no indication whether or not they were going to buy the system.

He brooded resentfully for four seconds until his attention was caught by the radio and he snapped out of it. (Resentful brooding wasn't natural to him and he couldn't ever sustain it for long.) Boulders of ice had started to fall mysteriously out of the sky across Europe. One, the size of an armchair, had crashed through the windscreen of a parked car in Madrid. A week later, another, just as big, had burst through the roof of a house in Amsterdam. Experts had been brought in to examine the phenomenon but, to date, no one could say definitively what was causing the lumps of ice. Or where the next one might land.

Matt listened with enjoyment. He was so caught up in the story that he didn't notice that he'd got through two green lights in a row. Then three. It was only when the fourth light was in his favour that he saw what had happened. Four green lights in a row! During rush hour! Could that count as one of today's Trio of Blessings?

For a moment he mused on how unexpectedly his life had turned out, with Acts of Kindness and Trios of Blessings and suchlike. All down to Maeve, to the fact that she'd spilled her money around the floor of the Dart four and a quarter years ago and he'd realised, Christ, I'm in love. And it's not with my girlfriend.

He had tried to pretend it wasn't happening. He couldn't be in love with Maeve because he and Natalie were perfect, but Maeve kept taking up space in his head. She was his first thought every morning, and all day, every day, he was tormented by malign ghostly whispers: *You're living in the wrong life.*

And he suddenly woke up to the Maeve and David love story. Beady-eyed surveillance revealed that they were very much an item. Did Maeve love David? Matt concluded that she probably did because she wasn't the type to toy with people's affections. But even if she didn't, surely there wasn't a man alive who wouldn't want her for himself? He'd have to do battle with each and every one of them. Which he was willing to do. But a girl as worthy as Maeve probably despised him and his suit-wearing, car-driving, non-Galwegian lifestyle. He'd never even been tear-gassed! What if he failed to win her heart? How could he live?

Then his essential optimism reasserted itself. He had as much chance with Maeve as the next man, surely? He was Matt Geary, decent bloke. Maybe that would be enough for Maeve.

At 5.35 a.m., in Conall's obscenely comfortable bed, Katie had been woken by Conall kissing her goodbye. He was shaved and suited and fragranced with something sharp and citrusy. 'I'll ring,' he said.

'OK,' she mumbled, tumbling back down into sleep. She'd taken the day off work because she'd wanted to be able to drink as much as she liked at her birthday dinner. Of course, in a perfect world, no one would celebrate their birthday on a Monday night—and in fact it wasn't her actual birthday until Friday—but it had to be Monday night because Conall had to go to Helsinki this morning, to slash jobs and plant terror in the hearts of some unfortunate Finns, just like he'd done to everyone in Apex Entertainment Ireland ten months ago . . .

The morning after Katie's epiphany about her crisis being her opportunity to go to India, Danno greeted her by saying, 'The night of the long knives. Half of sales have been sacked. I hear Slasher Hathaway sold their desks on eBay overnight.'

'How much of that is true?' Katie asked. She was more focused on getting Knight Ryders out of Ireland. Once they passed into German airspace they were no longer her responsibility.

'He's sacked five of sales,' Danno said, a little sulkily.

Katie checked her emails: the plane to take the entourage to Germany had landed at Dublin Airport . . .

'Out of how many?'

'Thirty-seven.'

. . . Lila-May was at the Four Seasons, picking up Elijah and the boys. 'Not exactly half, is it?' Nonetheless, a thrill of fear ran through her.

Katie's phone rang. It was Lila-May. 'Elijah Knight's gone AWOL.'

Katie pressed her hand over her eyes. Living legends were such hard bloody work.

'OK, get them to search the hotel. Check all the bars.' She hung up and called out, 'Everyone, stop whatever you're doing. Elijah's done a runner.'

Appalled yelps rose into the air.

'George!' Katie said. 'Ring every journalist you know, every contact you have on gossip desks, in case people have rung in with sightings.'

(George's vibration was insubstantial; only a cold, steely seam of bitchiness kept him from dissolving into absolute nothingness.)

'We shouldn't try to contain this?' Audrey asked anxiously.

'No, we've no time.' In the midst of her panic, Katie noticed that a man—he had to be the lean and hungry Barbarian—had appeared by her desk. 'Splash it everywhere; we'll find him quicker.'

'I'm Conall Hathaway,' he said. 'And you are?'

'Katie Richmond.'

'What's going on?' He gestured around the room, at the panic that was almost visible.

'We've lost a lead singer. Elijah Knight.' With a sarcasm that was uncharacteristic, she added, 'He's with Knight Ryders, a metal band who are signed to Apex—'

'I know who they are.'

Her phone rang, interrupting their exchange. It was the tour manager, who wanted to know how long he should hold the plane. Katie clutched the front of her head and squeezed hard, seeking the right decision. Stay or go? Go or stay? The crew needed at least five hours to assemble the set. But what use was a stage without a singer? Then again, what use was a singer without a stage?

'Katie . . .?'

'Go now. Get the crew to Berlin. If I can't get Elijah on a scheduled flight later, I'll sort out a private charter.'

Conall Hathaway was still there, his eyes like gravel.

'If you're here to sack me,' she said to Conall, too fearful to be careful, 'it'll have to wait.' She whistled to Danno like she would to a faithful hound. 'You. Here. With me. And you too, Audrey.' To Conall Hathaway she said, 'Because I'm going out to look for Elijah.'

'Where will you look?'

'We'll start in pubs.'

'And if you can't find him there?'

'There are some ladies of the night . . .'

'And what if he's not with them?'

'I suppose . . . ah . . . I suppose'—Katie stared into the distance and began to feel the full weight of her sleepless night, her crisis/opportunity conundrum, and heard herself say—'I suppose it'll have to be an instrumental version tonight in Berlin. The fans will probably riot, eighty thousand dreams will be dashed, millions of euros will be lost and . . .'

'And?'

'And . . .' She shrugged her shoulders and smiled with relief because, for a moment, everything was clear. 'And I suppose one day we'll all be dead and none of this will matter.'

As it happened, it all worked out. Following a tip-off from a helpful member of the public, Elijah had been discovered in a snug in Neary's. Katie and Danno had bundled him onto a plane, flown with him to Berlin, deposited him with the German publicist, then flown straight back to Dublin. Elijah went on to sing as usual, but aftershocks from the debacle were still plaguing Katie a day later: what if they hadn't found Elijah? Or what if he'd been too drunk to perform? Of course, if she was going to be made redundant anyway, what did it matter? At lunchtime, looking for comfort, she decided to go to the local stationery shop. She liked to browse through the pens and notebooks, finding their colourful beauty had a healing effect on her bruised soul. She came across a journal that had dried pansies pressed into the paper. Beautiful. Admittedly, the pages were too lumpy to be of any practical use, but she didn't care, she was going to buy it and . . . Curses! Brooding by the coloured Post-its and unenthusiastically feeding square after square of Fruit & Nut into his mouth, was none other than Slasher Hathaway.

Why did he have to be here in her sanctuary? Instantly, she began to retreat. She'd go to a chemist instead; she enjoyed them just as much as stationery shops. She could lose hours browsing among the blister plasters, homeopathic remedies and hair bobbles. A chemist was a cornucopia of delight, a beacon of light in a world that was frequently dark . . . Too late! Conall Hathaway had spotted her! Their eyes connected.

'Katie. Hello. How are you?'

'Fine.' A silence opened up and with the reflex politeness of someone who worked in PR she asked, 'How's things?'

Conall shrugged. 'I'm not exactly flavour of the month in Apex.'

'Maybe you should have gone into a different line of work. If it's love you're looking for.' *Did I really say that?* To her further astonishment she added, 'The priesthood, maybe?'

India, she thought, looking into his startled face. India. Nothing he could do could hurt her. The worst travail he could visit upon her was to make her redundant and then she'd be off to India. Where she would be enlightened. Also, hopefully, where she would contract a water-borne digestive-tract infection and lose tons of weight.

'The priesthood?' Conall asked.

'Or perhaps a doctor who cures blindness?' she suggested. 'They probably get a lot of love.'

Conall stared wistfully after Katie as she strode from the shop maintaining admirable, straight-backed posture in her four-inch heels. Impressive girl. Not that she was really a girl, he acknowledged. She was older than his usual type—he'd read all about Katie in her personnel file so he knew her salary, her address, her *age*: thirty-nine. But he was forty-two and perhaps it was time he had a girlfriend who wasn't a decade younger than him, someone who remembered David Bowie from the first time round. And the second time round.

Conall Hathaway was badly smitten. It was that comment Katie had made yesterday: 'One day we'll all be dead and none of this will matter.' For a moment it had opened up a sliver of insight into an entirely different way of thinking. He was always so caught up in the extreme focus of his work, of the brutal choices he had to make, but suddenly all that anxiety had diminished and he saw his life as a small, unimportant thing, his decisions as essentially meaningless, and he was astonished by how free he felt. He was intrigued by Katie's originality, her courage and, most of all, her wisdom.

What was he to do? he wondered, staring balefully at a container of coloured drawing pins. He could hardly ask her out, then sack her. Or sack her and then ask her out. It was a hellishly awkward position he found himself in. Usually, when he wanted something, it was his. I'm Conall Hathaway, he thought, and I always get what I want.

Disconsolately, he picked up a slab of red heart-shaped Post-its and made his way to the till.

In the park, Grudge dreamed of being a steeplechaser. He sprang high and long, clearing invisible obstacles, while Jemima sat on a bench and inhaled the oxygen-rich, life-giving morning air. A man sat down beside her and watched Grudge's athletics with an interest bordering on fascination. 'Look at that dog,' he said.

'He's mine,' Jemima said briskly. 'And much beloved.' She said this in order to save the man from embarrassing them both by saying, 'Isn't he the maddest-looking article you've ever seen?'

'He's full of vim, that's for sure.'

Jemima got to her feet and whistled for Grudge. 'Must get on,' she told the man. 'My son, Fionn, is coming to stay.' She didn't really have to go home, she just wanted an excuse to say those delicious words: *My son, Fionn, is coming.*

Of course he wasn't really her son, he was her foster-son, but no need to tell the man that.

'He's a gardener.' She couldn't stop herself, the pride was simply too great. 'And he's just been given his own television show. For six weeks. Initially. But if it flies . . .' Yes, she checked with herself, *flies* was almost certainly the word Fionn had used. 'If it flies, they might recommission it.'

'Very good.'

'He'll be staying with me for the filming. They offered to put him up in a hotel but he said he'd prefer to be with me.'

'Very good.' The man shifted a little.

'There's a gap in the market for a good gardening programme. Last night I had the misfortune to watch something hosted by one Monty Don and, really, such balderdash . . .'

'But Monty Don is marvellous!'

'Hardly *relevant*, though, is he? My son's show will offer much more. The buzz words are *Fresh! Organic! Grow your own!*'

'Fair play.' The man got to his feet.

'It's called *Your Own Private Eden*,' Jemima called after him, as he hurried away. 'Watch out for it. Channel 8, coming soon.'

Maeve's journey to work was such a high-risk performance you could have sold tickets to it. She zipped like a streak of light through narrow canyons formed by buses and lorries, she zigzagged complicated patterns between nose-to-tail lines of cars and—most breathtaking of all—she hurtled through red lights and wove miraculous paths between the startled drivers who poured at her from both the left and the right. An adrenaline-riddled exercise that seemed quite at odds with her gentle, nerve-soothing alarm clock.

She no longer worked in a software company but was employed in the reservations department of Emerald, a smallish hotel chain.

Emerald's administrative staff were housed in the basement of their flagship hotel, the Isle. Maeve passed through the long office, nodding and smiling, and arrived at her desk, which was right down at the end.

She switched on her monitor, reached into her in-tray and began work immediately. All around her, her many colleagues were discussing what they'd each had for their dinner the previous evening but Maeve kept her eyes on her screen and tapped away diligently.

It seemed that Maeve didn't indulge in idle banter and chat. Everything perfectly civil, don't get me wrong, but Maeve kept herself to herself with her colleagues, which was surprising. As was the uncomplicated, unchallenging nature of her work—frankly, a well-trained monkey could have done it and it wasn't at all what you'd expect from a woman of her charm and ability. But why had she left Goliath? Perhaps, after Matt had spurned the lovely Natalie in favour of Maeve, things had become awkward and they had found it preferable to work elsewhere, and this was all she'd been able to find?

In many ways she and Matt were so different that it was mad they'd ended up together. But she'd always had a tenderness for him and she could still pinpoint the moment when she'd started to fall in love . . .

It was four and a bit years ago, a Saturday evening in April. Maeve was curled up in David's bed, half in, half out of a doze, when suddenly she jolted back into alertness. She grabbed his wrist to look at his watch.

'David, it's half eight. Get up! Who wants to go in the shower first?'

'Wait.' He dismissed her agitation. 'Slow down a minute.'

'But if we don't get going, we might miss the band.'

'Easy,' he soothed. 'Five or ten minutes won't make any difference.'

'OK,' she said, releasing all her anxiety in one long breath.

'OK.'

David and Maeve. Maeve and David. In a way, Goliath was like one big dating agency. There were over 200 employees, the vast majority of them under the age of thirty. Soon after Maeve had started her training at Goliath, she met David. They had plenty in common. Bicycles. Pints. Tuareg bands. Boogie-boarding in Clare. Hummous in the fridge. Barbara Kingsolver novels. Altruistic tendencies. David was the most principled person Maeve had ever met.

'Right, I'm getting in the shower,' Maeve said.

But David pulled her tightly to him and twirled one of her curls round his finger. 'Let's not go.'

'What? Where?'

'Let's not go out tonight.'

She was taken aback. 'What would we do instead?'

'I can think of plenty.'

But they'd spent the afternoon in bed.

'I've never seen Fanfare Ciocarlia,' she said. 'I want to go.'

'And I want to stay in with you.'

'We've paid for the tickets.' That would work, she thought. He didn't like waste of any kind.

'It's only money.'

'Yeah, but . . .'

'OK.' He sighed. 'You'd prefer to be with the people you work with than with me.'

'David—' But he'd left the bed and was on his way to the bathroom.

Then at the gig, who should she bump into, only Matt! He was dancing along madly with everyone else! It was a surprise because, other than Friday-night drinks, team leaders didn't tend to socialise with their staff. But it was a nice surprise because everyone loved Matt. His was the best team to be on. 'Matt!' Maeve yelled over the music. 'I didn't know you liked this sort of thing.'

'Neither did I, but it's fecking mighty!'

'Where's Nat?' she shouted.

'Not here. Not for her.'

Fair play to him for coming without her, and what made him even more endearing was that he was such a bad dancer, but flinging himself around like a puppy and no fear of being laughed at. It was cute. With a heart softened by his sweetness, Maeve thought, *Matt . . .*

This popping in and out of their memory pools—I'm able to do it but it's not clean. I can't just jump into their pasts, find what I want and hop out again, leaving everything as it was. I'm already causing ripples, disquiet, upsets. I'm weaving my way into their lives, showing up in their dreams, haunting the edges of their thoughts. In the days and weeks afterwards, everyone will admit they'd felt this was on its way. That they knew.

Up in the top-floor flat of 66 Star Street, I've noticed that Potent Conall never came this morning to hang Katie's mirror before he went to Helsinki. It's still sitting on the floor. This makes me unaccountably nervous. Trouble will ensue—of this I am confident—if the mirror is not smiling down from the wall when Katie comes home.

Oh God, and here she comes . . .

She dumped her bag and shucked off her boots; then she went straight to the living room, looking for her mirror.

First—perhaps naively?—she looked on the wall, and when she couldn't see it there she turned her gaze to the floor. There it was, exactly as it had been the last time she'd seen it, propped against the cupboard looking, if this could be possible, apologetic for its layabout status.

Katie didn't get angry often but she was angry now.

I didn't want a platinum watch, she was thinking. It had made everyone else's presents look like jokes (her mother had given her a breadbin). She hadn't wanted Conall to pay for last night's dinner for all ten of them, because every male member of her family had a chip on his shoulder about Conall being rich. All she'd wanted for her birthday present was for Conall to make good on his seventeen days of promises and put a thing in the wall so she could hang up her new mirror. She'd shown him where she wanted it, she'd marked the spot with a Biro, and he'd said with great believability that he'd nip over in the morning before he left for Helsinki and do the job. Five minutes it would take, he promised her.

Conall could have organised a man to do it, a joiner or a handyman of some sort—when she'd bought the mirror, that's what he'd offered—but she stuck to her guns. Her mirror was to be hoisted onto her wall by the efforts of Conall and Conall alone. She wanted a gesture from him, a gift of his time and energy, something that money couldn't buy.

She lunged at her phone and clicked off a rapid-fire text: Mirror, mirror on the wall. Whoops, no. Mirror, mirror, still on the floor.

She was very incensed, oh very incensed indeed. Conall is a selfish liar, she was thinking, Conall is an unreliable bastard. All the promises Conall had broken were whizzing around like multicoloured flying saucers and it was herself she was most angry with. She should never have agreed to go out with him in the first place.

Eight working days after Conall first arrived at Apex, he requested a meeting with Katie.

'I have news,' he said.

'You're going to sell me on eBay?'

'No. I have reports from the artistes. They're fond of you. They say you mother them. You get to keep your job.'

'How about my team?'

'They get to keep their jobs too.'

'*All* of them?'

'All of them.'

'Same salary packages?'

'Same salary packages.'

She watched him suspiciously.

'There's no catch,' he said. 'New employment contracts are being drawn up. Now, can I take you to the ballet?'

She jerked her head up. 'God, no. I find it so tedious I want to cry, and when they go up on their pointes I get an excruciating pain in my big toes in sympathy.'

A smile touched his face, perhaps the first ever smile she'd seen from him. 'Pains in your big toes?' He gazed at her as if she was both rare and fascinating. 'I see. How about the opera? Would you like that?'

'No, no, no. I can't stand it. I hate it all.'

'All of it?' He seemed astounded. 'I love opera.'

'Well, I like silence.'

'Silence?' He shook his head with wonder. 'You don't like the ballet, you don't like the opera. What do you like?'

She thought about it. 'Eating. Sleeping. Drinking wine with my friends and discussing celebrity meltdowns.' The days of lying to a man to make herself sound fascinating were far in the past.

'Eating? Sleeping?' Again his face was radiant with admiration.

She'd had no idea that she was so interesting.

'Especially eating,' she said.

'You don't look like you love to eat.'

If only he knew the battle she fought with her appetite.

'I have a personal trainer,' she admitted.

'So do I,' he said.

'Mine's called Florence. She takes me out running in the rain and makes me do star jumps in Tesco's car park.'

'Mine's called Igor. We go to the gym.' He paused. 'Are you free next Saturday?'

'Why do you want to go out with me? I can't be your usual type.'

'You're not. But I'm . . .' He shook his head. 'I'm, ah, you know, can't stop thinking about you.'

She looked at him beseechingly. This was very difficult.

'Just one date,' he said.

One date. It wasn't as if he was asking her to marry him. Once upon a time she'd wanted the ring and the dress and the babies—so shoot her. There were lots of things she had wanted once upon a time: to be a size 8; to be fluent in Italian; to hear that Brad had got back with Jennifer. None of those things had come to pass but she'd survived.

'What were you doing in the stationery shop?' she asked, with sudden urgency. 'Remember one day, I met you—'

'I remember. I was just . . . looking at stuff . . .'

'You mean, you didn't go in to buy something specific? You were just browsing?'

'Browsing?' He tried out the word. 'I suppose you could say that. I guess I . . . *like* . . . stationery shops.'

Her heartbeat quickened: they had a common interest. 'How do you feel about chemists? Do you ever just browse in them?'

'I *like* them,' he said cautiously. 'But what I really enjoy is a good hardware shop. You?'

'Well, they're useful,' she acknowledged with the same caution he had employed. She couldn't abide hardware stores, they were always so cold. But she was prepared to show willing.

'Saturday?' he said, sensing that she'd softened.

What about the people he had sacked? Then again, you only got one life and one shot at happiness . . .

'Do you have any chocolate?' she asked.

He looked surprised. 'Yes.'

'I mean on you, right now?'

He patted a pocket. 'Yes.'

'Do you always have chocolate with you?'

'Um . . . yeah.'

A man who always had chocolate on him? It would mean the kiss of death for her battle with food. But how could she not be charmed— even a little—by a man who loved what she loved?

'OK,' she said. 'Saturday.'

Day 59

JEMIMA HAD LIVED in her little flat for five years and she adored it. Her now-deceased and much-missed husband, one Giles, had been an architect who had designed an award-winning example of 'High Modernism', which was built (due to vocal objections from residents in almost every other part of Ireland) in County Monaghan. 'High Modernism' meant glass, lots and lots of glass. Acres of the stuff. Jemima used to have nightmares that she'd been charged with the task of cleaning all the windows in the world and her only tools were a small bottle of Windolene and an old newspaper. Then she would discover that she was not, in fact, asleep.

In addition to the constant daily round of window-cleaning, Jemima had never felt entirely comfortable in attending to her private needs. For example, if she was overtaken by an irresistible basic need—as can happen to all human beings—such as to scratch her bottom, she was obliged to check first that three or four bored locals didn't have their sights trained on her. That was the main trouble with where she lived: there was absolutely nothing to do in Pokey, and spying on the oddball Protestant in her ludicrous glass cube was accepted as a hobby.

When Giles shuffled off his mortal coil, Jemima felt his loss with shocking impact but she wasted no time putting the Glass House on the market. To the almost-orgasmic pleasure of the agent, she said she was prepared to throw in all the lightweight titanium furniture, which had been specifically designed for the house. They were welcome to it, she thought. She was off to Dublin, armed with great plans to trawl auction rooms, seeking dark, heavy stuff, furniture of substance. She wanted minimal housework, no window-cleaning and—most liberating of all—no wretched garden with its need for perpetual upkeep!

The move was not without its upheaval. Fionn was the issue. She would miss him terribly and, of course, he would miss her. But she wouldn't be alive for ever. Time to cut the apron strings.

Right from the very first time Katie had gone out with Conall, the warning signs were there.

It had been such a big deal, the first date. Conall had actually presented her with a travel folder. 'Tomorrow a car will pick you up from home at twelve. You're flying to Heathrow at two.'

'We couldn't do something small and normal, like going round the corner for something to eat?'

He'd laughed; he'd thought she was joking.

'What am I meant to wear for this magical mystery tour? Because if it's sturdy boots and a hat with earflaps, I'm not coming.'

He laughed again. He was still finding her every utterance absolutely enchanting. 'Formal dress. High heels. A small pointless bag.'

She finally decided on a severely tailored (black, of course) dress, cut with hip-narrowing, stomach-flattening deftness. For the flight she covered it with a roomy jacket and a certain amount of resentment: it was embarrassing having to get on a plane—alone—in a sexy dress and

sexy shoes in the middle of the day. People might think she was a delusional type, like those mad old duchesses who went to the dry-cleaner's
in their tiara and dressing gown.

When she exited the plane at Heathrow, a man was waiting with a
whiteboard featuring her name. He took her away down some secret
steps, put her into a big fat car and drove her a short distance to—what
was this?—a helicopter. 'Where am I going?' she asked.

'I don't know. You could try asking the pilot, I suppose.'

But the pilot was too caught up in making sure she put on her head-
phones and a safety harness.

'Where are we going?' she asked.

'Pull that a bit tighter.'

'It's tight. Where are we going?'

'Glyndebourne.'

And Katie was thinking, *Glyndebourne?* Opera. But perhaps other
things besides opera happened at Glyndebourne. Because she detested
opera and Conall knew she detested opera, so he was hardly going to
bring her on a date to something she detested.

When the chopper came in to land Conall was standing waiting,
wearing a dark suit and looking like a handsome undertaker.

With her hand on her head, she ran across the asphalt and said,
'What on earth—'

He smiled, appearing very happy, and said, 'Just one favour. Don't
ask questions yet. Trust me. You look beautiful, by the way.'

Trust him. But they were at the opera place. Conall led her into an
auditorium. The lights dimmed, the curtain went up and the next thing
was there was a load of fat people on the stage, singing their fat
pompous heads off. Yes, *opera*. She was so stunned she didn't know
what to think. For a thrilling instant she considered standing up and
pushing her way to the exit, but she envisioned a sniper with night-
vision goggles killing her with one shot to the head. Interruptions were
frowned upon at the opera; you couldn't even cough.

After an epoch of screeching elapsed, an interval finally came.

'Well?' Conall said, as the lights went on.

'Are you having a laugh?' Katie asked, getting to her feet.

'What?' He looked stunned.

She turned to face him, as people streamed past them. 'It's opera.
Yes? I told you I couldn't abide opera. Didn't I?'

'I thought if you heard good stuff you'd change your mind.'

This, his apology, actually incensed her further. 'What? You thought that I was so . . . *uncultured* that I couldn't have an informed opinion?'

'No, I—'

'You didn't listen to me.'

He looked pale and chastened. 'I was wrong. I'm sorry. Because I love it, I wanted to share it with you. I wanted to surprise you.'

'Oh, you surprised me all right.' Even though she worked in the music business and was exposed on a daily basis to gigantic egos, she'd never before met such a selfish, self-willed megalomaniac.

'I'm so sorry.'

'I want to go home now.'

'I'll ring the chopper.'

Lydia was having a right old Irkutsky day of it. Each fare was more annoying than the previous. The traffic was appalling. She was caught by red lights, roadworks, pedestrian crossings and, worst of all, lollipop ladies. When she finally knocked it on the head for the day, she hoped the lads wouldn't be at home.

But the lads were at home. Jan too had had a bad day. A woman in Enniskerry had got tarragon vinegar when she had ordered white wine vinegar, while a woman in Terenure had received the white wine vinegar. It was a disaster and it was all Jan's fault.

Jan was sorrowfully recounting the scolding he'd received when Lydia came in, cranky and exhausted.

'Love of God!' she declared. 'A more miserable-looking pair I've never seen. What's up?'

'We are glum,' Jan said, almost happily. What a useful word this *glum* was. Glum, glum, glum.

'Why?'

'I mix up order. I give wrong vinegars to womans. I get bollocked.'

Lydia looked at him in surprise. 'My God, Jan, your English is really coming along.'

'Thenks.' He smiled with shy pride.

'So, Andrei, why are *you* so glum?'

He shrugged. 'I did not come to this country to be happy. I came to earn money for my family. I do not expect to be happy.'

'That's no way to live.' Mind you, she was a fine one to talk. She was working seventy hours a week but was too afraid to buy new clothes.

'I am strong,' Andrei said. 'I will endure.'

'Yeah, me too.' She sighed extravagantly. Then, without warning, the itch was upon her: she had to go on the Net. She had to check again.

Maybe this time it would be different. She pulled the stool up to the little plastic desk and started bumping and battering the mouse.

Behind her Andrei asked, 'You goingk out tonight?'

'You'll be happy to hear I am.'

The boys were indeed happy. They had plans to plonk themselves in front of *The Apprentice* and take detailed notes.

'You goingk out with Poor Fucker?'

When Lydia had first moved in and mentioned she had a boyfriend, Andrei hadn't been able to hide his disbelief. 'You hev boyfriend?'

'Of course I've a boyfriend!' The nerve of him.

Andrei thought his heart would burst, so great was his pity for this unknown man. There was no Polish phrase that adequately expressed the extent of his misfortune so Andrei was obliged to utilise English. 'Poor Fucker.'

'Yes. And don't call him that. His name is Gilbert.'

So! Gilbert! What kind of man was he? Surely he'd have to be someone fairly special to handle Lydia. (And was he the mystery person she cleaned for? The reason she refused to wash the pots in her own flat?)

Gilbert was to be found in a small, dark pub, almost a shebeen, in a side street on the north side of the city, gathered round a table with four other men, going at it hot and heavy in Yoruba. Originally a native of Lagos, Nigeria, he had made Dublin his home for the past six years.

When Lydia came through the door, the argument among the men was so intent that it sounded as though they were planning a coup.

Suddenly, they noticed Lydia and the conversation ceased abruptly.

'Baby,' Gilbert said. He was, like Lydia, a taxi driver, which was how they'd met—at some café frequented only by taxi drivers and only in the middle of the night.

A man evidently partial to fancy clothing, Gilbert. Tonight he sported a pair of midnight-blue winkle-pickers that were—if one were to speak frankly—a little girlie. More worrying still was his jacket. There was something *very odd* about the waist region: nipped-in, almost like a corset.

Lydia seemed like the kind of person who would make extravagant fun of those who took their look too seriously, but she snuggled into Gilbert like a cat and no mockery ensued.

I, unlike lesser beings, am not swayed by appearance but by vibrations, and Gilbert's spiky life force alerts me to his tendency to secret-keeping. I don't entirely trust him, but I cannot help but like him.

'Hi, guys,' Lydia said to the four men. She knew them well; they were all taxi drivers. 'What's going on? What were you shouting about?'

Eventually, Abiola spoke. 'It's Odenigbo.' At this, Odenigbo exploded into heated Yoruba, then so did everyone else. Lydia picked up the occasional English word—lemon meringue, rainstorm—and she held up a hand, silencing the men. Irritably, she said, 'Little trees? Again? I'm sick of this conversation.'

Unlike Lydia, who owned her own car, the Nigerians shared three taxis between seven drivers. One man's choice of Little Tree air freshener had consequences for everyone.

'We've been through this a million times!' Lydia said. 'Forest Floor is fine, so is Spice Market, the rest are gank! End of. Now, who wants to buy me a drink?'

There was a strong connection between Gilbert and Lydia and they were well-attuned physically but—mark me here—their hearts did NOT beat as one. However, that didn't mean that they wouldn't at some stage. There were no obvious impediments . . .

Matt and Maeve enjoyed a leisurely evening during which they ate a large dinner followed by a variety of confectionery, all the while entwined tightly on the couch, watching home make-over shows. It was an uplifting demonstration of two people very much in love—and yet now and again there was that faint whiff of a third party, the presence of some man curling his way, like cigarette smoke, through the flat.

At 11 p.m., Matt and Maeve retired to their bedroom and I was keen to see what would happen this time. Just like the first night, they got undressed *and then got dressed again*, as if they were about to go jogging. But instead they got into bed. They read for a while, then Maeve opened a bedside drawer and I braced myself for furry handcuffs, blindfolds and other sexy folderols. But instead of sex toys Maeve produced two notebooks, one with a glossy photograph of a red Lamborghini on the cover, the other bearing a reproduction of a Chagall painting.

With a certain amount of gloom, Matt accepted the Lamborghini notebook and a pen. At the top of a blank page, he wrote, *Today's Trio of Blessings*. Then he seemed to run out of inspiration.

With a gold-coloured pen, Maeve wrote, *I saw a green balloon by a green traffic light.*

On the next line she put, *A little girl smiled at me for no reason.*

And her third blessing? *Matt*, she wrote, and shut the notebook.

Matt was sucking his pen; he hadn't produced a single word. Then! Struck by sudden inspiration, he scribbled:

A mysterious lump of ice didn't fall on my car.
A mysterious lump of ice didn't fall on my flat.
A mysterious lump of ice didn't fall on my

. . . on my . . . Stumped, he looked around the room. What else was he glad that a mysterious lump of ice hadn't fallen on? What did he value? Well, Maeve, obviously. He picked up his pen again.

. . . *wife.*

There! He tossed the notebook back to Maeve. That was a good list. Sometimes Maeve inspected his list of blessings just to make sure he was doing it right, but he was entirely confident with what he'd written today.

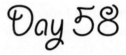

Day 58

FIONN DIDN'T LIKE DUBLIN. Even though he'd lived there until the age of twelve and it could be called home, there were too many unhappy memories. He waited until everyone else had climbed off the bus—the Monaghan Meteorite—before he stood up and descended into the chaos of the bus station.

He needed to find a taxi. Excellent Little Productions were expecting him for a meeting and he hadn't a clue how to get there. He straightened his back, squared his already square jaw, threw his bag over his shoulder and sauntered towards the taxi rank. He was twenty minutes late and counting.

Three miles away, in a converted mews house, Grainne Butcher, the director of Excellent Little Productions, paced in the light-flooded greeting area, watching for the taxi. Mobile in hand, she hit redial for the seventh time and once again got Fionn's voicemail.

'Who turns off their mobile?' she asked, incredulous. She turned to Alina, who was cowering behind the blond-wood reception desk.

'Don't know,' Alina mumbled. As the lowest of the low, she ultimately got all the flak.

'And he hasn't rung?' Grainne Butcher asked again.

'No,' Alina whispered. 'No, he hasn't rung.'

Mervyn Fossil, the owner and producer of the company, and Grainne's husband, hurtled into the hallway. 'Where? The hell? *Is he?*'

'Coming,' Grainne muttered. 'Go on, go away, keep making calls. I'll tell you when he's here.'

Mervyn, a short fake-tanned tyrant, stared at Grainne, his mouth curled into a sneer.

'Go *on*,' she said.

With a silent but deadly glare, he returned to his office. As soon as his door shut, Grainne started pacing again.

'Here he is! Thanks be to Christ!' A taxi had drawn up outside. Grainne strode out, thrust a tenner at the driver—'Keep the change!'—then hoicked Fionn from the car. She clicked open the boot and stared at the emptiness. 'Where's your stuff?'

Fionn indicated the one medium-sized bag on his shoulder.

'That's all you have? For a whole month?'

'What do I need?'

Then Grainne remembered why she'd fallen under his spell in the first place. Who would have thought that in the miserable hole that was Pokey she'd have stumbled across the likes of Fionn?

She'd been sitting at her sister-in-law's kitchen table when Fionn had shown up to do Loretta's garden. Grainne took one look at the hair, the jaw, the big spade-like hands, and got that tingly feeling—so rare and so cherished.

'What planet has he come from?' she asked Loretta.

'He's local.'

Watched by Loretta, who was aghast at her brazenness, Grainne marched right out into the garden to talk to Fionn.

'I'm Grainne, Carmine's sister. So you love being a gardener, do you?' she asked. He didn't know it but he was being interviewed for a job.

'Love it! I couldn't imagine doing anything else.'

'Why?'

'Flowers, plants . . . they're like miracles. You put a gnarly little bulb in the ground. All around it everything dies, then lo and behold, two or three or five months later, Lazarus flowers start poking up through the soil. Back from the dead.'

'Go on . . .' The way his face lit up! She could just see how the camera would catch it. Televisual gold!

'And it's not just about making the world beautiful; you could grow your own food.'

'*I* couldn't. My garden's the size of a matchbox.'

'You don't need much land. This here'—Fionn swept his hand around Loretta's quarter acre—'this could be your personal Garden of Eden.'

Grainne almost doubled over with the painful perfection of it all: *Your Personal Eden*! That's what they'd call the show! Or perhaps *Your*

Secret Garden, which had delicious sexual overtones, so handy with Fionn being astonishingly handsome. Her head began firing with ideas and when she took them back to Excellent Little Productions they argued the toss for a long time: *Your Private Eden? Your Secret Garden? Garden of Eden?* Days were spent searching for the best title, but they weren't wasted days because, in television, once you had the name right, the rest was easy.

'Let's get going,' Mervyn Fossil said, hooshing people towards the meeting room. 'We've wasted enough time waiting on . . .' He caught a warning look from Grainne: don't openly insult the talent. Reluctantly, he swallowed back the words *this fool*. 'Let's get to work.'

On her bike, Maeve came within inches of having her back wheel clipped by a car, but the car swerved just in time and she was grand. It made her think of some line she vaguely remembered from *The Great Gatsby* about it being OK to be a reckless driver because everyone else would be careful. Not that she was actually driving, of course. Because she couldn't drive.

No, four years ago she'd failed her driving test, and she often wondered whether, if she had passed it instead, things would have turned out the way they did.

four years ago

'WELL?' At least ten expectant people were waiting at Maeve's desk and she sensed a celebratory card, a cake, maybe even a bottle of fizz.

Maeve dipped her chin. 'I failed.'

'Ohhhh!'

No one had expected that, not really. Of course, everyone had horror stories about driving tests, but in her soft, easy-going way, Maeve was quite the achiever.

Quickly, David rallied. 'Everyone fails the first time,' he said.

'Absolutely!'

'We got you a cake,' David said, and Roja produced it from behind her back. The cake was iced with a big loopy 'Congratulations'.

'Obviously, that's "Congratulations on not passing",' David said.

'We also got you a bottle of fizz,' Tarik said.

Humbled, Maeve shook her head. 'I work with the nicest people in the world.'

The cork was eased off and cups were passed round. 'To failure!'

Fatima, distributing slices of chocolate cake on napkins, asked, 'Do you want to talk about it?'

'Sure, OK.' Maeve was feeling better now. The first sting of humiliation had passed. 'Well, the most important piece of advice I can give anyone hoping to pass their driving test is, do not do your practice on your dad's tractor! It was no preparation for the real thing. But you know what's really at me? My dad has a car.'

'So why didn't he let you practise in it?' Franz asked. 'Did he think you'd crash it?'

'No,' Maeve said gloomily. 'The opposite. He says that anyone can drive a car but it takes real skill to drive a tractor. He thinks I'm brilliant, he thinks I can do anything. It's a real scourge.'

Into the laughter, interrupting Maeve as she was saying, 'But at least I can plough a field—' came Matt's voice.

'I just heard!' he said. 'I was in a meeting and I just heard!'

He moved with purpose towards Maeve and a clear path leading directly to her opened up as, instinctively, people moved out of the way.

'Driving-test bastards! Tinpot tyrants.' Matt took Maeve into his arms in a comforting embrace, laying her head on the shoulder of his dark suit. Matt was clearly sincere in his sorrow for Maeve's humiliation. How kind he was, everyone thought. What a great guy he was. Then came the first prickles of alarm. The embrace should have broken up by now. It had lasted a second longer than was acceptable. It was time for it to stop.

Break away now and no harm will have been done. Smiles were freezing and falling from the watchers' faces. They stood like statues round the two-becomes-one figure and exchanged fearful, questioning looks— although no one looked directly at David.

Emotion radiated like heat from Matt and Maeve, moving beyond the immediate circle and out into the furthest parts of the office, where it reached Natalie. *Something is wrong.* She got to her feet and made her way to the cluster round Maeve's desk.

Finally, to the giddy relief of the audience, there was movement. Maeve lifted her head. But, for the aghast witnesses, things only got worse. Matt also lifted his head, and the moment when his eyes met Maeve's, a jolt of energy passed between them with a crackle that was almost audible. With faces stunned with wonder, they gazed at each other, exchanging souls. Everyone around them knew that it was unseemly, being present at this moment of extreme intimacy, but no one could tear their eyes away.

It wasn't how Matt had planned to tell Nat that he no longer loved her, but she got the message anyway. Dignified as ever, she departed the compelling scene, left the office, drove into town, sat in her car in a multistorey car park and sobbed. Then she got six inches cut off her hair, ate eleven macaroons, quite large ones, and felt ready to move on.

David's white face was the first thing Maeve saw when she emerged. It was the face of someone she'd known a long, long time ago. In the course of forty-seven seconds, her whole world had shifted.

What happened? his eyes asked.

I don't know.

I love you.

I know.

And I thought you loved me.

I thought I did too.

You've humiliated me.

I didn't know this was going to happen . . .

Around them, everyone except Matt had melted away.

'David, I—' But Maeve could think of nothing to say. 'I'm sorry,' she whispered. She couldn't bear the look in his eyes, the shock, the grief, the anger. 'I'm really sorry.'

'You're not good enough to lick her boots,' David said to Matt, his voice trembling. 'You're nothing but . . . but a *suit*.' He turned his fiery-eyed gaze to Maeve. 'As for you, I don't know what you're doing and I don't think you do either. This isn't over yet and don't for one minute think that it is.'

Day 57

'I'M NOT NORMALLY a dog person, but you're different. You're in a category of your own. I suppose I trust you and I don't trust easy. Can I get you anything? What are these things here? Dog biscuits. Have a couple, I insist. You deserve it.'

From her bedroom Jemima could hear Fionn in the kitchen attempting to sweet-talk Grudge. A mighty battle of wills. Grudge, a paranoid, vengeful creature who felt under extreme threat, loathed Fionn. But Fionn had to make everyone, even dogs, love him. If they didn't at first, he would stop at nothing; he would chip away with smiles and compliments and simply erode a person until they surrendered and wearily agreed to love him. But considering what he'd come through, poor soul, he'd turned out very well.

Jemima could still remember when Fionn, aged twelve, had arrived in Pokey with Angeline, his mother. Their arrival had taken the town by storm. Only on television had the townsfolk seen the likes of Angeline, with her glamorous, hollow-eyed, breathless beauty, and her stunning mini-me daughter. (Because of his tousled, shoulder-length blond locks and pretty, pouty face, it took about six months for people to realise that Fionn wasn't a girl.)

The story was that they'd moved from Dublin 'for the climate'. Naturally, this was accepted as a euphemism. Was Angeline on the run from the law? Because who in their right mind would move to Pokey for the weather? Indeed, who would move to Pokey *at all*?

Angeline got a job, working in the pub, and lost it almost immediately. She found alternative employment in the chip shop but got the sack within the week. A stint as a cleaner didn't last long either. The problem was that Angeline was often 'sick'.

Lazy, was the consensus. Or drunk. *A lazy drunken Dubliner. Who wears too much make-up. And gives our men the glad eye.*

Drugs, someone else whispered, behind their hands. *And no father for that ladyboy.* They loved talking about Angeline. Endlessly, relentlessly, they watched and talked and lost any interest in spying on the oddball Protestants in their preposterous glass home. Angeline's beauty, her kohl-rimmed eyes, her murky past—she was better than a soap opera.

No one could believe it when she died.

It turned out that she'd had emphysema. Her story about coming to Pokey for the climate was true. She'd been seeking fresh air to mend her poor damaged lungs when what she'd really needed was medication.

Everyone assumed that Angeline had been an amoral floozy with no idea who'd fathered her child, but Fionn produced details and one phone call from the Pokey gardai was enough to conjure up Pearse Purdue. A fisherman, Pearse had spent his life working the trawlers up and down the west coast. Fionn had been the result of a short-lived but very passionate marriage with Angeline, and although they hadn't stayed together, relations had remained cordial. Pearse loved Fionn but acknowledged he was incapable of parenting him.

He'd have to be fostered.

Which is when Jemima and Giles stepped in. They were aghast at

Angeline's death. 'How could we have let it happen?' Jemima asked Giles.

'We weren't to know,' Giles said, kneading her shoulders. 'We weren't to know. But we can give him a home now.'

'He'll be a handful,' the man from Social Services warned Jemima. 'He's inherited irresponsibility from both sides of the family. A double hit. He hasn't a hope. And he looks like a girl.'

'Giles and I aren't daunted,' Jemima said. 'A well-balanced child will always get a home, but it's the poor damaged ones who really need it.'

Today is Katie's actual birthday.

A small delegation of staff approached her desk. 'Happy birthday, Ms Richmond,' Danno said. They presented her with a card and a gift-wrapped parcel. 'It's only small, we could never compete with Slasher's loot, but we put a lot of thought into it.'

It was a fortieth-birthday diary. On the cover it said, 'Life Begins . . . A guide to what's left of your life.' At the top of each day was an uplift-ing thought.

'But this is divine.' Katie flicked through it. 'Let me read out today's message. "Dance joyously every day of your life. But don't let anyone else see you, not at your age." That's beautiful. You shouldn't have, guys.'

'Slasher Hathaway's here!' announced Danno. 'I thought you said he was in Helsinki?'

'He was.'

'He's waiting downstairs. Eating chocolate, as usual, trying to push down all that guilt he must be carrying. He's keen to see you.'

She took her time. She made the four phone calls she'd been planning to make before Danno had announced Conall, then proceeded to the Ladies and put on all the make-up she could find in her bag. Only then did she get the lift downstairs. There, as Danno had said, was Conall, clicking away on his BlackBerry, deep in thought and looking grim.

As she approached, he lifted his head and his entire demeanour softened. He jumped to his feet. She let him kiss her, not a full-on super-snog—they were in her working environs, after all, *and* he hadn't put up her mirror *or* replied to her text—then she pulled away.

'Happy birthday,' he said, his eyes shining into hers.

'What happened to Helsinki?'

He shrugged, still smiling. 'It's your birthday.'

'You mean, negotiations briefly broke down but you're going back there tomorrow?'

'Yeah.' He sighed. 'I can get nothing past you. I don't even know why I try. Can I take you to lunch?'

She waited. She thought about her mirror. 'Probably.'

'Then will you take the afternoon off and spend it in bed with me?'

'I've got a press conference.'

'I've missed you,' he said softly.

'I've got a press conference.' She set her jaw.

He was unhumanly persuasive. He didn't even have to speak to exert his will; all he had to do was look at her with those gravel eyes, eyes that said he was an unhappy man and all that made life bearable for him was Katie.

It was a measure of just how persuasive he was that, after the terrible first date at Glyndebourne, Katie ever went out with him again. She was adamant that she would have nothing further to do with him, but somehow he talked her into giving him one more try.

On the second date, which was entirely different from a trip to the opera but probably as risky, Conall took her to meet his family. It was his nephews' birthday, Laddie and Hector, fourteen-year-old identical twins with an identical absence of interest in Katie when she was ushered into their small sitting room. Only at Conall's instigation did they grunt a greeting.

Katie was mortified. No one but a headcase would think this was a good idea. But Conall's brother, Joe, a balding sandy-haired man, was friendly enough, as was his wife, Pat. Then a little girl bowled into the room and declared, 'I like your shoes. They're wicked.'

This was Bronagh, Conall's seven-year-old niece, who looked so astonishingly like Conall that Katie actually laughed.

'I know,' Joe said. 'You'd think the missus was diddling me brother behind me back, but she swears she wasn't.'

Pat rolled her eyes. 'I'm mad but I'm not that mad.' Too late, she realised what she'd said.

'Thanks, Pat,' Conall said. 'Like I'm not having enough trouble trying to convince Katie I'm normal.'

'Show us the new motor!' Joe said, kick-starting a stampede to the front door. Even the Surly Twins were roused from their torpor at the idea of test-driving Uncle Conall's new Lexus. They piled out of the house and Pat melted away to the kitchen, leaving Katie alone with Bronagh, who sighed extravagantly. 'Boys and their toys. Give me a try on of your shoes and I'll paint your nails silver.'

By the time the men returned, Katie had been ferried upstairs by Bronagh, who confided that she had taken to her.

Conall's risk had paid off: the warmth of his family had convinced her that he might just be semi-sane.

In the restaurant, Katie asked, 'My mirror—'

'It's on the wall.'

'Since when?'

'Since . . .' He took a look at his watch. 'Since an hour and forty-four minutes ago.'

'Jason's wedding?'

'I'll be back for it. I swear on my life.'

She exhaled slowly, wondering if it was OK to relax.

'I'm sorry,' he blurted out. 'For your mirror. For the way I am. I know you're holding back on me . . .'

She was startled. Yes, she'd taken care not to fully surrender her heart and her hope and her future to a man who mightn't be capable of caring for them. But she hadn't realised he'd noticed.

'Who knows what's going to happen with us,' he said. 'But whatever it is, it won't work if only one of us is into it.'

He'd never been so forthright before and she wasn't sure how to reply. 'But, Conall, you're a workaholic. It makes you unreliable.'

He flinched. 'I'll change. I'm trying. I turn off my phone when we're together, haven't you noticed?'

She had but . . . She took a risk and jumped into virgin territory. 'I've been heartbroken before. I really don't know if I have the energy for it again.'

'Who's to say that that's what would happen?' He was earnest. 'You could just as easily get sick of me.'

'Maybe,' she acknowledged.

'Please don't.'

He sounded unexpectedly anguished and suddenly the word LOVE was hanging in the air, looping them together, garlanding them with flowers and hearts and lovebirds and pink mist. I love you. It was there, all that was needed to breathe life into it and make it real was for one of them to utter it. I love you. But Katie wouldn't.

Even though she had fallen in love with him. It was up to him.

He looked at her, an eyebrow raised questioningly. She presented a bland face to him and he watched her for a little too long. 'OK.' He sighed. 'Let's order.'

Lydia had just pulled in to eat her lunch, a strawberry yoghurt and a banana, when her phone rang. It was a County Meath number, one that she didn't recognise—then she did! Shite.

'Lydia? It's your mum's neighbour Flan Ramble here—'

'Hello, Flan.' A low, dready feeling swamped her. He only ever rang with bad news. In fact, he seemed to delight in it. 'What's up?'

'If I was to say the words *a small house fire*, would you get my drift?'

'A fire? In the house? A small one?'

'Got it in one! A pot was left on the ring too long, the curtains went up, blew out the windows. No real damage, but you'll have a fair old job dealing with the scorch marks.' He chuckled. 'You'd better get down here pronto with your paintbrush.'

'I'm in Dublin.'

'I've tried to get hold of Murdy or Ronnie, but I can't run either of them to ground.'

Irkutsk, Irkutsk, Irkutsk.

'OK, thanks. I'm on my way.'

No time for lunch now. She switched off her FOR HIRE light, agonised about losing half a day's income, and headed for home. While she drove she rang Murdy, who, to her surprise, answered.

'I thought you were the bank,' he yelped. 'I'm in crisis here! They've stopped my credit line.'

He hung up on her! She was used to him doing that but this was different. A fire. Flames. Burnt curtains. Serious stuff.

Immediately, she rang Ronnie, who—to her disbelief—refused to get involved. 'You're making a drama out of a crisis,' he said.

'The house went on fire!'

'If you're that worried why aren't you here?'

He—too—hung up on her. *Ssskkkk!* This was mad stuff. Why was she the only one . . .? With shaking fingers, she rang Raymond but his phone was switched off.

She tried to decide which of her brothers she hated the most. Murdy was obviously a total gobshite, you only had to look at him. He'd shaken off his taxi-driving roots and gone on to head up a bathroom-fittings empire. He lived in a mansion on the outskirts of Boyne, with a blonde wife and two discontented children. Ronnie, Lydia's second brother, was different. He lived from hand to mouth, was secretive, mysterious and had at least two unknown women on the go. Then there was Raymond, who'd run away to Stuttgart as soon as he was old enough. They were a selfish, useless crowd.

Her final call was to Gilbert. The phone rang for a long time and eventually his voicemail kicked in.

'I won't be round tonight. Maybe not tomorrow night either. Call me,' she said. But she had a feeling he wouldn't. He'd probably sulk, in a childish attempt to punish her for abandoning him at such short notice.

At times she had her doubts about Gilbert.

Maeve had a regular appointment on Friday evenings. It was a good night for it because Matt was out too, on the jar with his team for their end-of-week wind-down.

On the dot of six, Maeve finished up and began cycling through the bright evening, heading south. After eight minutes of pedalling, it suddenly hit her what date it was. Hard to believe that she'd only remembered it now, considering she'd spent her entire day working with days and dates. She spent a few shocked seconds just coasting, then made an abrupt U-turn. She was moving with purpose down towards the river, to the docklands. The roads got narrower, but she zigzagged her way through them, bumping over cobbles, like a woman who knew exactly where she was going. She stopped in a side street, propped her bike against a wall and fired off a quick text: Sorry. Sik. C u next week.

Half hidden by a building, Maeve peeped out at an office complex across the road. No Brainer Technology. An IT company, yet another one; this city was overrun with them. People were streaming out through the front door, nearly all of them young and casually dressed.

Maeve watched and watched and her face displayed no emotion, even though she'd bent her right ankle until it was facing the wrong way, as if her leg had been put on backwards. It was an agonising manoeuvre, by the looks of things, but she was feeling no pain, even her breathing had almost stopped. And then she was ablaze with a cocktail of emotion. She released her ankle and it spun round, back to its correct alignment. Some bloke had just emerged from the building. Long and thin and handsome in a dishevelled, unkempt fashion, he had the demeanour of a poet. He was walking away from where Maeve was secreted, but something stopped him in his tracks and made him look back over his shoulder. He saw her. Their eyes locked and a cable of white-hot energy snaked forth to unite them. It pulsed for some seconds, sparks and stars fizzing; then he dropped his head and stumbled away.

This was the man who was present in Maeve and Matt's flat. *This* was the person who had inveigled his way in, corrupting the perfect two-of-this and the perfect two-of-that.

All of a sudden Maeve was desperate to be somewhere, *anywhere* else, but her legs were shaking so much she couldn't trust herself to cycle. Slowly, placing her feet carefully on the uneven streets, she wheeled her bike and wheeled her bike until the trembling left her.

Day 55

ANDREI WAS IN BED, crying softly. The combination of homesickness, the comedown from the weekend of heavy drinking and it being Sunday evening, the worst night of the week, was just all too much.

When he heard the key in the door, he was surprised because he wasn't expecting Jan back from Limerick until the following morning. But he wasn't expecting the evil little pixie either. She always spent Sunday nights with Poor Fucker. But it was definitely her; he could hear her, moving lightly around. He buried his face in his pillow, trying to stifle his sobs. The pixie must not hear him.

Lydia wasn't exactly on top form either. Drained and depressed by the weekend, she was facing a five-thirty start in the morning followed by a seventy-hour week. And from the grumpiness that pervaded the air, at least one of the Poles was home. Andrei probably.

Gilbert would fix her. She'd missed him this weekend. She rummaged for her phone, hit redial and irritation rose as she got his voicemail—again. He'd blanked her since Friday, obviously pissed off by her abrupt disappearance. Weekends were their time together. They both worked Friday and Saturday nights, usually finished up around 3 a.m., then spent Saturday and Sunday together, luxuriating in Gilbert's big bed.

'Stop sulking,' she said. 'I'm home and I want to see you.'

It was a bright summer evening and she was going mad at the thought of being trapped in this flat. Desperately, she fired off a few texts but no one would come out to play. Shoane was nursing a hangover, Sissy was on a date, and Poppy was sitting before a spreadsheet, trying to do a seating plan for her wedding. Apparently, it was complicated, with various members of the family not speaking to other members and having to be kept well apart from each other.

'Come on out tonight. A few drinks will relax you.'

'Lids, I can't.' There was an edge of hysteria to Poppy's voice.

'I could come and help you with your plan.'

'But you wouldn't help me. You'd tell me I'm a madzer to be getting married at twenty-six, and that Bryan is boring—'

'I never said Bryan is boring—'

'Steady! You said he's steady. That's the same thing as boring.'

'I like Bryan!'

'But you don't want me to marry him.'

'I do, Poppy, I do, I do, I do. Really, I do. Look, I'll go now, leave you to it. Good luck and all.'

She hung up, hugely relieved to have extricated herself from that downward spiral. Getting married sent people *mad*.

Gloomily, Lydia decided to get drunk and if it had to be alone, then so be it. She went out and bought savoury snacks and a bottle of wine and lined them up on the kitchen counter.

For her starter she'd have the Sour Cream and Onion Pringles, and for her main the Texas BBQ Sauce Pringles . . . *What was that?*

Strange noises. She strained to listen. Coming from the Poles' room. A sort of a quiet whimpering. She moved closer to the door.

Was someone having sex in there? But who? Jan was away and there was no way Rosie would have dropped her kecks for Andrei unless there was a ring on her finger. Lydia took a moment to savour her hatred of Rosie. She couldn't abide her and her ironed clothes—she was only twenty-one, what twenty-one-year-old ironed her clothes?—and her neat ponytail and her fake air of injured innocence and the very *uninnocent* way she used sex as a bargaining tool . . . Then she heard the noise for what it was: crying! Andrei (or possibly Jan, but for some reason she suspected Andrei) was crying! Well, it was too funny for words. This she must see.

She knocked on the door and opened it before Andrei (or possibly Jan) could shout at her to go away.

It was Andrei, who, aghast at her presence, jerked round to face the wall, wiping his eyes furiously.

'You're crying.'

'Not.'

'You are. I heard you. What's up? Did Rosie break it off with you?'

'No.' That really would have been reason to cry.

'Get up. Come out. I'm bored.'

'No.'

'It's got to be better than boohooing in here on your own, like a girl. Come on, I've got wine and crisps.'

He wasn't going to get any peace. She would keep at him and at him until he caved in. Reluctantly, he swung his feet onto the floor.

'So why were you crying?' Lydia asked.

He shrugged. 'I wish I could live in my own country.'

'I wish you could too.'

He lifted his head. Was she being kind? No.

'It was a joke,' she said, almost in amazement. This had gone on for too long. 'Don't you have jokes in Poland?'

'Of course!' They had everything in Poland and all of it much better than what was provided in this benighted country. 'But you . . . when you say it, it is not funny.'

'Right back at you, crybaby.'

With great dignity, he surrendered the four Pringles he held in his hand and got to his feet. 'I'm going back to bed.'

'Stay where you are. This will cheer you up: I'm going to tell you about my weekend.'

Well, he cried again. He was in a teary mood and it was all very sad. And he saw Lydia with new eyes.

'So this is why you are this terrible person!'

'Ah, yes . . . I suppose.' Was she that terrible? 'So what's your excuse?'

Day 53

'JEMIMA, WHAT'S KEEPING YOU?' Fionn called. 'The car is here.'

'I'm coming.' She was struggling to close the button on the waistband of her skirt. How infuriating. Her skirt had unaccountably become too small. But she had no plans to purchase a new skirt, not at this stage of her life. She didn't indulge in squanderbug behaviour: she was eighty-eight years of age and, although she came from excellent stock, she was unlikely to get forty years' wear out of a new skirt before she died. Which, incidentally, she had no intention of doing anytime soon, regardless of that wretched presence hanging about.

Nor did she intend to go on a reducing diet. Since the age of seventeen, she'd been a stringy ten stone—except for a short spell four years ago, when she'd dropped to nine and a half stone during a clash with cancer, in which the cancer came off as the definite loser and had to limp away bruised and humiliated—and she did not intend to alter now, no matter what this recalcitrant button was trying to tell her—

'Jemima, are you all *right*?' Fionn called.

How entertaining! Fionn, the most unreliable creature alive, chivvying Jemima Churchill, who had Punctuality Is Next to Godliness running through her bone marrow, like a message through a stick of seaside rock.

Her hands slippery with effort, she forced the button into its hole and exhaled with triumph. But the enthusiasm of this breath proved too much for the waistband and the button pinged from its moorings and shot across the room like a bullet.

'Jemima!' Fionn roared. 'Grainne's after ringing. We have to go!'

Jemima had to smile. Grainne Butcher ran a tight ship. This was only the second day of Fionn's television career and already the early starts and long hours were taking their toll on him. He wasn't used to having to be places at a certain time and then having to stay there once the novelty had worn off. Nevertheless, experiencing a schedule with a certain amount of rigour might do him some good.

Jemima smoothed her cardigan down over her gaping waistband and picked up her ancient brown handbag. Fionn was pacing in the hallway, looking cranky but so dazzlingly handsome that it lifted her game old heart just to look at him. Grainne Butcher's stylist had brought pressure to bear so that he had washed his hair, his jeans and his many-pocketed jacket. He was a prince, thought Jemima, a beautiful clean prince.

Today is a very special day for Fionn. Except that Fionn doesn't know it. Not consciously, anyway. Several layers down in his subconscious, continental plates are starting to shift, creaking apart, clashing, promising forthcoming upheaval.

Today Fionn has been alive for 36 years and 128 days. He is a day older than the age his mother was when she died. He has outlived her. Up until this day, Fionn has had to work at keeping himself alive. So much energy had to be put into protecting himself that there was none left over to give to another.

But today marks a new dawn.

Today, for the first time in his life, Fionn is free to fall in love.

Frankly, I'm on the edge of my seat . . .

Like a greyhound out of the traps, Fionn was. Not a second to waste in this new exciting phase of his life. He hurried down the stairs, Jemima and Grudge, who were accompanying him on today's shoot, bringing up the rear. He opened the front door . . . and a few feet away, standing in a pool of yellow light, was the most exquisite woman he'd ever seen. Stunned, he came to an abrupt halt, Jemima and Grudge tumbling into the back of his legs. He gazed at this woman's succulent rosebud mouth, her pink and white skin, her tumbling blonde curls, her freshness, her innocence, her bicycle, her—

Alerted by the intensity of his gaze, the woman lifted her head sharply and an expression of frozen awe appeared on her face.

Fionn bounded down the last few steps to the street, his hair flashing golden in the early-morning sunlight. 'I'm Fionn Purdue.' He extended his hand to her.

The woman ignored Fionn's hand. She remained silent and motionless and continued to stare at Fionn as if she'd been turned to stone.

A man appeared from nowhere. 'Matt Geary,' he said.

Once again Fionn thrust his hand forward, but once again it was ignored.

'And'—Matt leaned much closer to Fionn and bellowed these next words—'this is MY WIFE.'

'What's your name?' Fionn asked the beauty. But she didn't answer.

Fionn turned to Matt, his radiant face eager for knowledge.

Seconds ticked by, then Matt admitted with reluctance, 'Maeve.'

'Maeve,' Fionn said, with wonder. *Maeve.* What a beautiful name. 'Maeve, the warrior queen. I'm your new neighbour. I'm on the first floor, with Jemima Churchill. Do you know Jemima?' Frantically, he flapped his hand, urging Jemima to step forward. 'Come and say hello to Maeve!'

'I already know *Matthew*. And Maeve,' Jemima said politely.

'I'll be living here for a while.' Fionn addressed this solely to Maeve. 'A couple of months or thereabouts.'

The beeping of a car horn interrupted his reverie. 'Fionn, would you come on!' It was Ogden, the driver. 'Grainne's going mental!'

All of a sudden, Fionn was delighted to be making this television show. 'I'm starring in my own gardening show,' he blurted eagerly. 'Called *Your Own Private Eden*. Channel 8.' He half noticed that Jemima had grasped his elbow and was determinedly leading him to the car. 'Thursday nights,' he called over his shoulder to the vision, who remained rigid and mute. 'Coming soon! Watch out for it!'

Doors slammed shut, Ogden floored the accelerator, and Fionn gazed in rapture out of the back window until they turned a corner and he could no longer see her.

'Who was *she*?' he asked Jemima.

'Leave her alone.' Jemima sounded uncharacteristically sharp.

Fionn laughed happily. 'You've nothing to be jealous of! I'll always love you the best. What can you tell me?'

Jemima's lips tightened. She didn't engage in scuttlebutt. Although she wished she did. She yearned to have what women's magazines called 'A Good Gossip'. To learn a secret gave her a pleasure rush that was almost alarming in its intensity and to pass it on was even more enjoyable. But she couldn't indulge in tittle-tattle. Good-living people didn't. However, there were times, she thought wistfully, when she wished she hadn't been brought up as she had been, when she wished she wasn't so good.

Matt left work ten minutes early. His morning meeting with the Bank of British Columbia hadn't brought about any conclusion. They'd been friendly and had asked more questions and said they'd be in touch.

Back in the office, he spent his lunch hour alone reading *Top Gear*. When he'd finished that—and it seemed to end far too soon—he found himself grabbing the paper and, in a kind of frenzy, doing the three sudokus, one after the other. He refolded the pages, and, as he did, he noticed a short paragraph about the random lumps of ice falling from the sky. He narrowed his eyes as he realised that the locations where the ice had landed were all capital cities. Had any of the experts clocked that? What were the chances of one of these ice boulders landing in Dublin? And if so, where would it land? Whose car would it squash or whose roof would it damage or—daring thought—whose life would it end? For a moment, the image was so delicious that he closed his eyes, to savour it even more.

But resentment curdled this glowing vision. It would never happen. There was no justice. None. None at all.

He was unable to do any work. He should be tracking down new business, pestering more companies to buy Edios's software, but right now he had no heart for it.

He was having a bad day; everyone had them sometimes. Maybe tomorrow would be different, but he might as well give up on today.

'Gotta go. Dentist appointment,' he said casually.

Matt got in his car and shot out of the car park—but he didn't drive towards home. I followed his route, trying to make sense of it. For a moment I wondered if the dentist story had been true and not just a pretext to spring him from the office early. Then I noticed that he was headed for the docklands. Did this mean what I thought it meant? It did.

In the same side street where Maeve had parked her bike four days earlier, Matt parked his car. He put enough money in the meter for two hours, then stood directly opposite the main doors of No Brainer

Technology—brazenly, not hidden like Maeve had been—and watched the people leaving, just like Maeve had.

And here came the bloke, loose shirt tails and long, uncombed hair, a satchel with a fraying strap stretched across his long torso. When he saw Matt, fear pulsed from his ashen face but almost immediately his equilibrium was restored and he laughed—*laughed*—at Matt. The chuckling sound floated across the road, and rage roared from Matt's centre, pushing and swelling into every cell in his body. Lanky-boy ambled away with exaggerated insouciance and Matt wanted to punch a wall.

He got back into his car and pummelled himself five times in the gut and felt a bit better: his anger had reduced and he had hurt himself. Which was appropriate, because this was all his fault.

There's no point asking me: I'm all at sea.

'**W**hat am I to wear?' Conall asked, when he called from Helsinki. He checked in most nights before Katie went to sleep.

'Your Tom Ford suit and that shirt I bought you.'

'The pink one?'

'It's not pink, it's lavender. Very pale lavender. Almost white.' Not really; it was full-on girlie lavender, which paradoxically made him look extra manly. 'And I've left out the tie I want you to wear. It's on your bed.'

'And I'm to pick you up at one?'

'That's my flat at thirteen hundred hours, just so we're clear. Is your car clean?'

She detected a hesitation. 'It will be. We could always go in yours.'

No, they couldn't. Her car was nice but not impressive. Not like his Lexus. Call her shallow but this was her ex-boyfriend's wedding they were attending. She was happy that Jason was happy and all that blah but *nevertheless* . . . she didn't want to look like it was hurting.

'And your flight?' she asked. 'Finnair, is it? Gets in at ten fifteen on Saturday morning?'

'Ten fifteen.'

'You couldn't come on Friday night, just to make sure you'll be here?'

'I will be there. I promise.'

A moment of silence.

'I promise. I will not let you down on this.'

Very obviously changing the subject, Conall asked, 'Now, what's the thought for today?'

'Hold on.' Katie reached for the diary Danno and the others had given her for her birthday. She flicked to the right page. 'Today's uplifting thought is, "Love your body exactly as it is. You think it's imperfect and you're right, but it's only going to get worse."'

'Your body is perfect,' Conall said softly.

Katie snorted, but he'd got her.

After she'd hung up she wondered if he'd know which shoes to wear. Should she ring him back? Maybe not. He was unreliable but he was well dressed and perhaps she'd hounded him enough about this wedding.

Instead, she decided to put her bin out.

Fionn stood up.

'Where are you going?' Jemima asked sharply.

'I think I'll stretch my legs.'

'They're long enough already. Sit down.'

'I need to get out, Jemima. A country lad like me, I'm no good cooped up in a small flat. I need a stroll.'

'It's ten o'clock at night. The streets will be littered with scofflaws and stumblebums.'

'Just for a few minutes . . .' He was already at the door.

'She's married,' Jemima said, in ringing tones.

'Who?'

'You know who. Maeve.' Jemima was trying to shame him into forgetting about Maeve, but he would not. He could not! He was stunned by the intensity of his feelings for her. She'd been in his head all day, an unbroken background hum. It was the first time a woman had affected him in this way and, if he was to be really honest, he didn't care that she was spoken for. He wanted her and he was going to get her.

Less than ten feet below Fionn, Matt and Maeve were at their usual lark, twisted around each other on the couch, watching some home-improvement programme. They were very much creatures of routine. When the clock struck eleven, they put on several layers of clothing, went to bed and wrote their Trio of Blessings in their notebooks.

They were made for each other, Matt and Maeve.

The irony was that even though David—like Maeve—was a Galwegian and Matt was, to quote David, nothing but 'a suit', Maeve had far more in common with Matt than she'd ever had with David. She laughed with Matt, she laughed a lot. Something that hadn't happened much with David, who found the world so outrageously unjust that laughter seemed like the act of an insensitive and frivolous person.

But even though she and Matt were made for each other, she was eaten up with guilt about David. All he had ever done was love her and be good to her, and she was appalled and ashamed by how publicly she'd humiliated him.

She was desperate to explain things to him, to somehow take away his hurt, but David wouldn't permit Maeve to 'explain' anything. Mind you, Maeve acknowledged, she'd have her work cut out. She hadn't a clue how it had happened. One minute David was her boyfriend and she'd been vaguely fond of Matt and the next she was violently in love with Matt and David had been relegated to a bit player.

She tried to get David to meet for some sort of talk, but it was impossible. He hung up on her phone calls, bounced back all her emails and took to crossing the road when he saw Maeve coming.

Matt's innate optimism insisted that David would get over Maeve and soon move on to someone new, but Maeve wasn't so sure. David felt things deeply, and the traits she had once so admired about him, like his passionate objection to all injustices, suddenly seemed like impediments.

Natalie was a different story. With admirable pragmatism, she accepted the new Matt'n'Maeve configuration almost overnight. 'You guys'—she waved a smooth brown hand at them—'just look at you: you're the real deal, you're meant to be together. I didn't like it at first, but what could I do?'

'What should we do about David?' Maeve asked Natalie.

But Natalie was from the same optimistic school as Matt. Airily, she advised, 'Just give him time.'

So a month passed, then two months, but David remained cut up and Maeve remained riddled with guilt, and all in all it made work a little awkward. And, indeed, their leisure time also. Matt was keen to be with Maeve at all times; he was happy to fall in with her usual pursuits, but Maeve couldn't do it to David. She'd hurt him so much, it was only fair that he get custody of their friends and their social life.

Hopefully, it wouldn't be for ever and, in the meantime, she and Matt forged a new path, finding a middle ground between their two different lifestyles. She made him read a Barbara Kingsolver book and he persuaded her to spend a weekend in a hotel with a spa, even to partake of a couples massage. And although she'd been sure she'd feel guilty about the demeaning work the poor masseuse had to do, she found that giving a hefty tip went a long way to clearing her conscience.

In fact, she had to admit that she found the whole weekend delightful. As Matt did the Barbara Kingsolver. But then again, they found everything about each other delightful, so it was hard to be sure.

Katie, dressed in pyjamas and high heels, was returning from putting out her bin. The ability to do everything in life in four-inch heels was a gift similar to having a beautiful singing voice. If she lost her gift, if she began to tilt forward and go over on her ankle and complain about the balls of her feet killing her, she'd feel like she'd lost a part of herself.

She was running up the stairs and had almost reached Lydia's flat, when she heard Jemima's door open below her.

Curses! Like any normal person, she lived in dread of having to speak to her neighbours, but she was too near to Jemima's flat to escape. With huge misgivings she turned, bracing herself for a few minutes of polite nocturnal chat with the old woman. But, to her great surprise, it was not Jemima who emerged into the hallway, but the most stunning-looking man. A golden god, with long hair and perfect bone structure and a jaw set with purpose. A phrase of her mother's spoke in her head: his beauty would take the sight from your eyes.

Who was he?

Though she was frozen to the spot and openly gaping, he didn't see her—proof that she'd become invisible now that she was forty. Fascinated, she leaned over the banister and followed his glowing progress as he tiptoed furtively downstairs and slipped a note under Matt and Maeve's door.

What was the story there?

Then, assailed by a mild reeling in her head—the heels—she realised she'd topple over the rail if she wasn't careful. She pushed herself back into a vertical position and continued upwards.

Day 52

MATT WAS STUMBLING and yawning along the hall on his way to make the tea—he always got up before Maeve—when he noticed the piece of paper lying on the floor. It was immediately obvious it wasn't a flier; it was a handwritten note and it had to be from one of the neighbours. He was mildly curious. What had they done? Had their telly on too loud? Then he read it, and even as a boiling rage lit up his every cell, he stepped into the kitchen and closed the door to protect Maeve from the strength of his feelings. Such *disrespect*!

Would he tell Maeve? Like fuck he would! He thrust the note into the compost bin, where it belonged, where it would rot with vegetable peelings and discarded food.

When he brought Maeve her tea, she was still in bed, lying flat on her back and looking particularly leaden. 'Matt . . .?'

'Mmm?'

'I feel . . . like someone is watching me.'

For the second time in ten minutes, Matt was assailed by emotion. A dense lump of doom hurtled into him and at high velocity pulled him towards the centre of the earth. He was appalled at his own reckless-ness: that detour he'd made yesterday, what had he been thinking? He should have left well alone. He'd stirred stuff up; he'd drawn your man on them. Unless it was that Fionn bloke . . .?

'Watching you how?' he managed to ask. 'Through the windows?'

'No, more like . . . this sounds mad, watching me through the walls.'

'Through the walls?' *Through the walls?*

'I don't know, Matt. I'm sorry. I just feel it.'

They had their showers, prepared their porridge and poured their honey but Matt couldn't eat. His throat was so closed he could barely force down his vitamin pill.

Eventually, they leave for work, but I stay in the flat. I'm looking for something. But what? Nothing awry with their tea bags; their underwear drawer holds no secrets; and in the bathroom, an unopened cellophane-wrapped box of Coco Chanel body lotion is cov-ered with a thin coating of dust, which strikes me as sad but not exactly revelatory. Then I return to the kitchen cupboards and entre nous *I'm actually quite ashamed. I've been watching Maeve and Matt for over a week and it's taken me until now to notice that their daily vitamin pill is not, in fact, a vitamin pill. It's an antidepressant.*

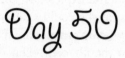

Day 50

'WELL, EXCUSE ME.' Lydia barrelled into the bathroom in her nightdress (actually, a T-shirt, an old one of Gilbert's that he'd been about to give to the charity shop and she'd rescued) and collided with Andrei, who was cleaning his teeth.

She'd overslept. How, when she'd lost so much work lately, could she have overslept? She needed to shower and get moving *fast* but there was a half-naked Pole in her bathroom. There he was with his bare chest and his muscly arms and nothing but a small towel wrapped tightly round his narrow waist. The . . . the *cheek* of him.

'What are you doing here?' she asked, flapping her arms impatiently.

He raised an eyebrow: what did she *think* he was doing?

'Whatever,' she said. 'Just get out. I'm late. I need to shower.'

But why should he get out? Andrei asked himself. He too had a job. He too had ablutions to perform. And—not to be childish about things—he was here first.

'Outttt,' she repeated, with menace.

Surprising them both, Andrei reached out his right arm, his shoulder shifting like there were ropes under his skin, and pulled her to him. Her feet resisted, but he was too strong for her and she found herself pressed against his bare chest.

Speechless at his audacity, that he'd had the nerve to touch her, she moved her eyes past his smooth pectorals to gaze up at him. Frozen in the moment, he gazed down at her. His minty breath was fresh on her face and his eyes blazed blue. She was close enough to see that he hadn't yet shaved.

Heat blossomed between them and they both became aware of a growing hardness beneath the towel; then she shook herself free and he gave her one last, puzzled look, before turning away.

Maeve was crouched over on herself, her hand in front of her mouth. 'I just keep thinking . . .' she said, then meandered off into silence.

Dr Shrigley gazed calmly at her.

Dr Shrigley was a psychotherapist. A calm, intellectual lefty, she wore no make-up, had no time for any silliness.

As Maeve contorted herself into a miserable-looking pretzel, Dr Shrigley presented a wonderful expression: concerned but not patronising. She gave the impression she could wait all day, or at least until the hour was up, and that it wouldn't matter a whit if no one said anything. But if Maeve *did* open her mouth, well, then she'd be delighted to hear whatever she had to say. No wonder people have to study for so long to be therapists; it could take years to accomplish that look.

After some time, Maeve spoke. 'I always thought the best of people. I thought the world was a good place. But now . . .'

'Your trust has been violated and recovery takes time.'

'But how much longer? It's taking so long!'

Dr Shrigley tried to smile reassuringly but her mouth trembled a little. 'This is your journey, Maeve. It's hard, but you are doing it. Putting one foot in front of the other, moving forward.'

'Will I ever feel OK again?'

'Yes. But there's no time frame.'

'I'm still doing my daily Act of Kindness and I write my Trio of Blessings every night. I've been doing it for months now. That's got to count for something, right?'

Dr Shrigley nodded. She feared that Maeve put too much faith in those practices, but it probably didn't do her any harm. 'That's certainly one way to try to regain your faith in the goodness of the world.'

Maeve nodded.

'Time's up now,' Dr Shrigley said. 'Same time next week?'

Maeve nodded again.

'And your cancellation last week . . .? You were just not feeling well? That was all?'

Maeve couldn't make eye contact. 'That was all.'

Day 49

KATIE HAD SPENT a fortune on her dress. And a fortune on her shoes—gold sandals, Dolce & Gabbana, very glamorous. And a fortune on her hair. And now she was having a de luxe pedicure. Conall was picking her up in an hour, which gave her plenty of time to get home, change into—Her phone double-beeped and she *knew*: he was cancelling on her. Still in Helsinki. Emergency. Very very very sorry.

She read it again, wanting it to say something different, then she swallowed hard and her throat tightened with the onset of angry tears. She wanted to kick something but her toenails weren't dry and she wasn't going to risk her pedicure. He wasn't worth it. If she had to go to her ex-boyfriend's wedding on her own, at least she could hold her head up, secure in the knowledge that her feet were second to none.

As it happened, the pedicure was a godsend, especially during the church bit. It took her mind off the radiant beauty of Donanda, the sincerity of Jason's vows and the pitying sidelong glances from those who'd been friends of Katie'n'Jason but who had backed the winning side after the split.

However, when she got to the restaurant, her poise faltered: the room plan revealed that she was seated at TST—the Shit Table.

She gave herself a pep talk, counselling against paranoia. She and Jason were fond of each other; why would he insult her? But her table was at the back, with a wall on two sides—one beside her, one opposite her. The other guests, all Portuguese, clearly part of Donanda's family, were four ancient, black-clad women and a burly man in his fifties who sported a magnificent moustache and a shirt opened to mid-chest. They didn't speak a word of English. Yes, undeniably the Shit Table.

· With exaggerated gallantry, the man with the moustache moved into Conall's vacant place so that he was beside Katie.

'Ohhh-hooooh!' All the doting old women egged him on.

He hit his chest and said, 'I, Nobbie.'

'Katie.'

'You har bee-oodiful kwoman.'

'You have a magnificent moustache. You must be very proud of it.'

'Donanda great-aunt.' One of the women pointed at herself. Then she indicated the other three women. 'Great-aunt, great-aunt, great-aunt.'

Katie poked a finger at Nobbie and said, 'Great-aunt?'

Well, how they laughed!

'Oncle, oncle,' Nobbie said, in his deep, macho voice. 'You?'

'Ex-girlfriend of Jason's,' she explained, as if they spoke perfect English. 'Probably the love of my life.' The Portuguese people nodded politely. 'We decided it was time to have a baby and it was only when we had to have lots of sex that we discovered we didn't fancy each other any longer! Terrible, as you can imagine.' The Portuguese people were starting to look nervous. But, in fairness, Katie thought, they *had* asked. 'Then Jason met Donanda.'

'Donanda.' They nodded to each other, relieved to understand something. 'Donanda.'

What was she like? These poor people were only trying to make conversation. She had been a far nicer person when she was in her thirties. Instantly, she resolved to be extra-polite and kind but making small talk across a language divide was hard work and it was a long reception. Now and then she'd stick her foot out and admire her toenails: they were still nice. Then she'd get up and go to the Ladies. On one of her excursions, Jason lunged at her.

'Is your table OK?' he asked. 'Because your boyfriend speaks Portuguese we thought it would be a good idea . . .'

Conall spoke Portuguese? News to Katie.

'Yes, Jason, Conall is accomplished at many things.'

Most of all *lying*.

'I must be off now. Enjoy being married to someone other than me.'

Day 47

CONALL TOOK IT HARD.

'But, Katie, I love you.' It was the first time he'd said it.

'You don't.'

'I do. I'm sorry about Helsinki. I'm sorry about Jason's wedding. I know how much it meant to you. But we couldn't get the takeover signed off without losing another twelve staff—'

'I don't want to know.'

'I will work less.' He grasped her hands. 'I will. I promise you.'

'No.' She pulled her hands away from his. 'You're too unreliable and I don't want to do it any more.'

The strange thing was that she meant it. She wasn't playing games. Conall was sexy, he was powerful, he was rich, he had a beautiful mouth, he smelled delicious, he had perfect skin, he had stubble, he was a good kisser—and it didn't matter. She could no longer do the dance of Conall, one step forward and one step back, and she'd never felt this way before: sad but certain she was making the right decision.

Was this what turning forty did to a person? Removed your tolerance for bullshit? Did people run out of patience? Could it be that you only get so much in a lifetime and hers was all used up?

'I'm serious,' she said.

From his stunned expression, he was starting to realise that, actually, she was. 'But what will I do without you?'

'Try a younger woman,' she said.

He was aghast. 'I don't want a younger woman. I want you.'

'A girl in her twenties.' She carried on as if he hadn't spoken. 'They usually can't tell the difference between challenging and fucked up.'

She should know. She'd wasted her twenties.

'But what happened?' he asked. 'What changed?'

'I just . . . can't be bothered any longer.'

'Can't be *bothered*?'

'Conall, I've always believed in love, that love would conquer all. But it doesn't. Because here I am, at forty, and love has conquered nothing. Except my common sense over two and a half decades.'

'But, Katie . . .'

'Please go now. And remember what I said: a girl in her twenties.'

Conall's and Katie's heart vibrations are no longer in harmony. Something has jolted Katie's heart off course—it could be that bloody milestone birthday—and Conall's heart knows this. It's all over the place, trying to latch on to the new beat, trying to find the way back.

Day 45

'GILBERT, I SLEPT . . .' Lydia paused. If she was going to tell the truth to Gilbert, she might as well do it properly. 'I had sex with Andrei.'

She waited for thunder to fill his face, but apart from a little flicker behind his eyes Gilbert's expression remained blank. After staring at her for some moments he asked, very politely, 'Which Andrei? Your flatmate?'

'Yes.'

'The one you dislike so much?'

'Ah . . . yes.'

'Perhaps,' he said, in his dark-chocolate voice, 'you will have the courtesy to tell me what happened.'

She opened her mouth, then closed it again. It was very hard to say. 'There was this pot,' she started.

'A pot?'

'You know, a saucepan. We were in the kitchen. He wanted to use it but I hadn't washed it. He was annoyed. Is he ever any other way?'

She wondered how best to describe what happened next. Andrei had banged the saucepan down hard on the kitchen counter and he'd glared at her, his eyes burning blue, a muscle working in his jaw, and she'd glared back at him, and suddenly—and quite genuinely she was at a loss to describe how it started—they were kissing frantically, ferociously, and it was such a relief. Then she was tearing at his clothes, desperate for more of him, and he was steering her to his bedroom and, locked in his steely embrace, she tumbled onto the bed, and he was muttering endearments in Polish and distributing small frenzied kisses along her hairline. And despite the narrowness of the single bed and the fact that she disliked Andrei so strongly, it was the best sex of her life.

But she couldn't tell Gilbert any of that.

'It meant nothing.'

'"It meant nothing"? You sound like a man.' Gilbert's face was cold.

'It meant *nothing*. It will never happen again. I don't even like him . . . and I like you very much.'

'So, Lydia.' He tapped his long, elegant fingers on the table. 'I am asking myself a question: why are you telling me this?'

'Because it's right. I have to be honest. I respect you, Gilbert.'

'You respect me? You sleep with another man and show me disrespect by telling me?'

'No! I sleep with another man, *by accident*, I might add, and I respect you enough to tell you the truth.'

'When did this *accidental* event take place?' Gilbert asked.

Lydia looked at her watch. 'An hour and . . . thirty-seven minutes ago.'

'You have come straight from his bed?'

'I had to tell you.' She'd felt that every second that had passed without Gilbert knowing was a further insult to him, although he was so angry that now she wasn't sure.

'You think you have been my only woman?' Gilbert asked softly.

She swallowed a lump in her throat. 'Yes,' she said. 'Actually, I did.'

'But you were not.'

She swallowed again. 'Grand. I see. Right.' She heaved a huge breath from deep in her gut. 'Just as well we're having this little chat, then, no?'

'But these other women'—with a triumphant glint, he sarcastically mimicked her earlier words—'it meant nothing.'

'It meant nothing? Just like mine meant nothing? But funnily enough,' she said, as she got up to leave, 'the last thing you sound like is *a man*.'

Day 40 (early hours of)

KATIE WAS HELPING Keith Richards put his socks on—'That's the boy, that's it, now the other foot'—when stumbling, scuffling noises at her front door woke her from the dream. She lay on her side, frozen in her sleep pose. It was 5.29, according to the red devilish numbers on the alarm clock, and she was being broken into. She listened hard. Louder noises this time—her front door was being pushed and shoved—then came the most frightening sound of all: the metallic scratching of a key seeking the lock.

Had someone stolen her key and had it copied?

There was one other explanation for this person at her door.

It could be . . . Conall.

With a click and a shove, the door opened and the person, whoever it was, was in her hallway.

'Katie?' she heard Conall ask in an urgent whisper. 'Katie?'

Should have changed that stupid lock.

He knocked on her bedroom door. 'Katie. Are you asleep? Wake up.'

Should have made you leave your key

The light clicked on, nearly blinding her. Conall, looking dishevelled, was swaying at the side of her bed. 'Katie, I'm going out of my mind.'

'Why?'

'Because I love you. Sorry for this.' He waved his hand to encompass him standing in her bedroom at five thirty in the morning. 'I should have rung, but it's so late. Or maybe it's too early.'

'So you thought it was better to come in person.'

'Absolutely!'

He was, she realised, quite drunk.

'Katie, I want to marry you.' He dropped to one knee and wobbled slightly but managed to maintain his balance.

She stared at him, wondering if she'd actually woken up, or if she'd simply moved sideways into one of those dreams where you dream you're awake.

'Is this a proposal?'

'Yes.'

She was electrified with sudden insight. This was one of the most important moments of her life. Yes, she thought, she would be the wife of Conall Hathaway and live with all of the pleasures and unhappiness that that would guarantee if, *and only if*, he had brought a ring with him.

'A ring?' she prompted.

It would be a sign that their week apart had altered him, that he would be more amenable to making concessions in their future.

Conall patted one jacket pocket then another and rummaged around in his trouser pockets, then admitted the unpalatable truth. 'I didn't bring a ring . . .'

Well, that was it. The decision was made for her and the vision of her life as the wife of Conall Hathaway dissolved and disappeared.

'I would have got one but I came over here in such a rush—'

'It's not a proper proposal if there's no ring,' she said.

'I can get one.' Already, he had his mobile out. 'Trevor, Conall Hathaway here. Did I wake you? My apologies. Listen, I need a diamond ring. Right now. Open up the shop. I'll make it worth your while.'

Conall put his hand over the speaker and asked Katie, 'Is it diamonds you want?' Like he was ordering a takeaway.

She shook her head.

'Emeralds, then? Sapphires. Anything you want, just say.'

She shook her head again. He couldn't buy his way out of this.

'Trevor, I'll call you back.' Conall was confused. 'Katie, what *do* you want?'

'Nothing.'

'But . . .' He was stymied. 'I thought this was what you wanted?' He couldn't make sense of this. There could be only one explanation. 'You've met someone else?'

'No . . . I . . .' Of course she hadn't met someone else, but for whatever reason, a picture of the golden-haired man from downstairs appeared in her mind's eye—and Conall, being the astute machine he was, felt it.

'You have!' he declared, appalled.

'I haven't.'

But it was enough for Conall.

A taxi was approaching. A gift from the gods, he thought, and stuck his hand out. It pulled up beside him and he tugged at the handle of the door and climbed into the front seat.

'Get out,' the taxi driver said. 'I'm off duty.'

'Take me to Donnybrook. Quick as you can.'

'I'm finished for the night. My light's off. Get out.'

'So why did you stop for me?'

'I didn't. I was parking.' With an efficient screech forward, then a perfect reverse curl, she—for the driver was a she—had manoeuvred the taxi into a tiny space, in one of the neatest pieces of parking he'd ever seen. 'There we are, parked,' she said. 'Out you get.'

He reached for his wallet. He had to get away from this terrible place, the site of his shame. For the second time in five minutes he said, 'I'll make it worth your while.'

'I'm not for hire, I'm actually asleep with my eyes open, I shouldn't be on the road, I'm a danger . . .' Then she looked at him carefully. 'What's up with you?'

'Nothing.'

'There is. Your tie is crooked and your hair is a mess.'

'I don't need your sympathy.'

'You're not getting my sympathy. Put your fat wad away. I'll drive you metered rate if you tell me what's going on. I'm always uplifted by the misery of others. Where to?'

'Wellington Road.'

She tightened her mouth and put the car into gear. 'That was a good spot, the best I'll ever get, and it'll be gone when I get back. This'd better be good. Is it to do with the sexy schoolteacher?'

'Who?'

'The woman with the knockers and the shoes? Your girlfriend?'

'Do you mean Katie? How do you know her?'

'I live in the same house. The flat below hers.'

'You do? Number sixty-six? But she's not a schoolteacher.'

'Governess, then? So she's dumped you, yes? Why?'

'Because I work too much.'

'Why? Short of money? Saving up for when your mother turns into a nut bar and you've to stick her in a home?'

'No.'

'Demanding boss?'

'I work for myself, essentially.'

'So, *essentially*, you work too much because you like it?'

'No, not *like* . . .'

'Because you need to keep proving yourself?'

'I guess. That's what my girlfriends keep telling me anyway. How did you know?'

She waved her arm, airily. 'I'm always driving the likes of you. Emotionally crippled overachievers. Gdańsk.'

'But I'm going to change.'

'If I had a euro for every time I heard that, I'd probably live in Wellington Road, next door to you. Gdańsk.'

'Why do you keep saying "Gdańsk"?'

'I like to say "Gdańsk".'

'Why?'

'The beginning is cheery, it sounds like "G'day", but the end has the "sssskkkk" sound. I love the "sssskkkk" noise. It's like the beginning of "skedaddle". You can say it to get rid of people. Like this.' She turned her attention away from the road and hissed at him with venom, 'Ssssskkkk!'

Conall recoiled.

'Now do you see?' she said. 'It's a great word. Gdańsk! If you want to use it in your own life, work away. It's my free gift to you.'

Conall was looking at her with sudden interest. What a funny, acerbic little creature she was . . .

'You'd probably charge people for the use of it,' she said. 'I suppose that's why people like me are living in Dublin 8 and people like you are living in Wellington Road.'

. . . and now that he looked at her properly, he saw how very pretty she was, those flashing eyes, that sexy mouth, the mass of curls . . . and out of nowhere, he was remembering the advice Katie had given him . . . and Katie's advice was always on the money.

Slowly, he asked, 'What age are you?'

'Not that it's any of your business.'

'Not that it's any of my business.' He was liking her more and more.

'Twenty-six.'

Day 39

'WHAT FILM HAVE you got us?' Lydia's mum asked.

'*Pirates of the Caribbean.*' Lydia was up to her elbows in sudsy water.

'I've seen that before. A musical.'

Lydia paused in her scrubbing. 'I think you must be thinking of something else, Mum. It's not a musical. It's got Johnny Depp in it.'

'Johnny Depp. He's lovely. Tormented. I do like a tormented man.'

Lydia agreed grimly. She had a couple of men in mind and, as far as she was concerned, the more tormented the better. Suddenly, she realised that this particular pot was done for: no amount of effort was going to shift the burnt-in food. She hauled it out by the handle, shook off the worst of the bubbles and made for the bin.

'Lydia, what are you doing with that pot?'

'Throwing it out, Mum. It's done for.'

'That's a good pot.'

'It's burned to fuck.'

'Do you kiss your mother with that mouth?'

'Ha-ha.' Lydia lunged, her tongue extended, and her mum beat her back.

'Get away, you filthy creature.'

Lydia picked up another saucepan and clattered it into the sink. She'd been scouring till her shoulders hurt for the past twenty minutes and the mountain of food-soiled cookware hadn't seemed to diminish at all. It was like the Mad Hatter's tea party—as soon as one pot or plate or cup was used, her mum simply moved on to the next clean one, washing nothing, and when she'd worked her way through everything, she began using and reusing at random.

'How will I cook a dinner if you keep throwing my saucepans out?'

For a moment Lydia considered chucking them all into the bin. No pots meant no cooking meant no smelly, stinky pile awaiting her every time she arrived from Dublin. It also lessened the risk that the curtains might go on fire again.

But it would unsettle Mum too much if all her pots suddenly disappeared. And Lydia was still determined that she could force Murdy and Ronnie, the lazy bastards, to do their share.

'We'll get a takeaway tonight, Mum. Chinese, you like Chinese.'

'Do I? And then will we go out dancing?'

'We've got a DVD. Remember? We're watching a movie.'

'What movie?'

'You know what movie.' *Please know.*

'How would I know?'

'*Pirates of the Caribbean.*'

'I don't like musicals.'

Lydia swallowed. 'It's not a musical; you're thinking of something else. This is good, it's got Johnny Depp.'

'Johnny Depp! I like him. Soulful. I feel he couldn't be happy if you put a gun to his head, do you know what I mean?'

'I do, Mum.'

'When will you be finished with the washing-up?'

Lydia surveyed the horror of the kitchen, the precarious-looking heaps of plates and pans and half-eaten food. 'I'll be a while yet.'

'I'm hungry,' Ellen declared.

'OK, I'll order the takeaway soon.'

'Are we getting a takeaway? Goody!'

'I'll just put on a machine-load of laundry first.'

After clearing the laundry basket in the bathroom, she carefully made her way back down the narrow stairs. Ellen was sitting in the chair exactly as she'd left her. She glared at Lydia. 'This is no life for the pair of us. Sitting in on a Saturday night.'

'It's Tuesday.'

Her mum jumped to her feet in a girlish fashion. 'We should *do* something.' She twirled round, her arms outstretched. 'Don't you feel it, Sally? Oh, Sally, life is out there. We're letting it slip away from us!'

Lydia spent a lot of time on websites, inputting her mum's symptoms—confusion, forgetfulness, abrupt abandonment of all housekeeping duties—and looking for a disease that would fit.

'Sally, do my hair.'

Should she? Helpless and frustrated, Lydia didn't know if it was best to humour her or guide her back to reality. No one would tell her. No one would even admit that Mum had become a bit of a madzer.

'Put it up for me on top of my head.'

Ellen's hair was short and had been for as long as Lydia could remember, so that made the decision.

'Mum, you know I'm not Sally, don't you?'

Ellen studied her cautiously. 'You're . . . Lydia?'

'But you keep calling me Sally.'

'Sorry, love, it's just you look so like her.'

'Ah, Mum!' She couldn't stem the rush of tearful exasperation.

'Eat up,' Mum urged.

'Yeah, OK.' Lydia shoved another forkful of fried rice into her mouth.

'It's delicious!' Mum exclaimed.

It wasn't. It wasn't revolting either, just all a bit bland. But when the double-chocolate ice cream also tasted a bit nothingy, Lydia acknowledged what she'd already known: it wasn't the food, it was her. The flavour was gone from her life.

Without Gilbert, there was nothing to look forward to. Idly, she picked up her phone to see if Gilbert had left a message—even though she knew he hadn't. Just like she wouldn't.

'Oh, Mum!' Chocolate ice cream was smeared all over her chin, dripping onto her skirt. Lydia reached for a tea towel. 'Here, let me wipe your face.'

Her mum twisted away, slapping her hands at Lydia's. 'Stop treating me like a *child*. And why did you come to see me if you're not going to watch the film with me?'

'I am!'

'You're not. You're thinking about other things.'

You see. There were times when Mum made some sort of sense, and in those moments Lydia told herself that maybe there was nothing wrong with her at all.

Quickly, Lydia deleted Gilbert's number. There! Gone, now. Even if she got scuttered, she wouldn't be able to ring him.

She ousted Gilbert from her head, then stretched out her legs and put them in Mum's lap, and gave Johnny Depp her full attention for the next two hours. Even Mum stayed agog until the credits began to roll.

'Did you like that, Mum?'

But Ellen fixed her mouth into a sullen line.

'What's wrong, Mum?'

'You said we were having a takeaway. When are we getting it?'

Day 38

FIRST THING IN *the morning, I popped in to see how Matt and Maeve were getting on and, yes, I admit it was my fault. Maeve was lying in bed, waiting for Matt to bring her tea, and I suppose I got a little too close, just trying to see if I could get in there, you know? Maybe winkle something out of her, find out some of her secrets, because of all the people in Star Street, she was the one putting up the most resistance to me, and it was driving me mad. I swirled my way round her head—and she felt me . . .*

Suddenly everything in Maeve was going at ten times its normal speed. Her heartbeat went into overdrive and her blood was pumping hard and fast through her arteries. Her body was flooded with adrenaline and her skin was prickling with the need for fight or flight. She clambered to a sitting position, her back against the wall, her head jerking from corner to corner, her eyes scudding wildly, trying to see everywhere at once, patrolling for all possible danger. She began to sob with terror. It was happening all over again. Something was wrong with her chest, a terrible weight pressed on her lungs and she could barely breathe. Air was being pulled in through her open mouth, making an awful creaky sound, and her eyes bulged with fear. She had to call for Matt, who couldn't be far away, he'd only gone to the kitchen, but she was paralysed, held in a never-ending spasm, like one of those nightmares where you know you're sleeping but you can't wake up.

'Wake up and smell the—Oh Christ!' Matt dumped the two cups on a shelf and rushed to Maeve. 'Breathe,' he urged. 'Just breathe. You're OK, you're not going to die. It's just a panic attack. Just breathe.'

He squeezed his arm round her shoulders, so she could have the comfort of physical contact but without her airways being blocked. 'In through the nose, out through the mouth, that's it.'

After ten minutes of inhaling and exhaling, Maeve said, 'I think I'm OK now.' Then she promptly burst into tears. 'Oh, Matt, I'm so sorry.'

'It's OK, it's OK, don't be sorry.'

'It's been ages since the last one. I thought I was better.'

'It's probably just a one-off,' Matt said.

'You think?'

'I do.'

He didn't.

Day 37

'COME IN, COME IN, come in!' Dr Buddy Scutt greeted Lydia and Ellen with what Lydia considered to be unprofessional bonhomie. (Ellen and Buddy played on the same team on Thursday night's table quiz at the Condemn'd Man.) Buddy dragged a chair round to the public side of his desk and the trio sat in a little circle. Way too pally for Lydia's liking.

She cleared her throat and tried to create a more sombre atmosphere. 'I'm sure you heard, Dr Scutt, about the guards having to bring Mum home in the middle of the night.'

'Sleepwalking,' Ellen said. 'Buddy, I went sleepwalking.'

Buddy nodded at Ellen, flashing a message: *Let's humour the little missy; then I'll make short work of her.*

'But there's other things. She puts the milk in the microwave, she forgets conversations—'

'And you're perfect, are you?'

'No, but—look, sorry, Mum,' Lydia said. She didn't know if Ellen minded being humiliated like this but it was a surprise to find that it was killing her to do it. Unfamiliar emotions—compassion, a tender painful love—were squeezing the breath out of her. 'Could you refer her for a scan?' Lydia's Internet research recommended it. 'An MRI scan?'

'What for? MRI scans cost a fortune and there's nothing wrong with your mother.'

'I'll pay.'

'That's not how it works. You can't go having MRI scans willy-nilly.

There's a huge demand for them. Only sick people should have them.'

'But she *is* sick. Sorry, Mum!'

Buddy Scutt shook his head. 'There's not a bit wrong with her. I've known this woman all my life.'

'So if you've known a patient all their life, they can't get cancer?'

'Have I cancer, Lydia?'

'That's not what I meant, Mum. You're just a bit . . . well, senile or something.'

'Senile, my jumper!' Buddy interjected. 'Let's ask the woman herself. Ellen, are you worried?'

'Ah sure, I'm just getting old,' Ellen said.

But Lydia saw the little flicker. Ellen knew that something somewhere was gone a bit wonky, but like everyone else—Murdy, Ronnie, Raymond, Buddy here—she didn't want to know what it was.

'You heard your mother. I've a waiting room out there full of real sick people so don't be wasting my time. See you Thursday night, Ellen.'

Lydia walked away. A doctor with decades of experience had said that Mum was OK. But she knew he was wrong. What else could Lydia do, though? Wait until Mum got worse, then try again?

And lo and behold, Mum got worse. She had always been house-proud and germ-aware but, overnight, she abandoned all cleaning duties. And Ronnie and Murdy did nothing—nothing!—to help. It was amazing to her that they would let their mum live in this squalor. But what was worse was that Mum didn't mind. She didn't even notice.

To prevent an outbreak of bubonic plague Lydia drove down from Dublin every five or six days and cleaned like a fury.

Fury is right. Now I understand why she wouldn't wash up after herself. Which hardly seems fair to poor Andrei and Jan. Not that I'm here to judge. Or am I . . .?

Ellen stopped paying her bills. Because she stopped being able to write her signature. Because she was no longer convinced about who she was. ('Is that my name, Lydia? It doesn't feel right.')

Lydia brought each new set of problems to her brothers and laid them at their feet like a cat with a dead crow, and they responded to each offering with a variety of deflections: that Lydia was a drama queen; that Ellen was menopausal; that care of the sick was women's work.

'You should come home and mind her,' Raymond said. 'You're the only one with no ties.'

'Ronnie has no ties!'

But Ronnie was a man.

As soon as Mum had started to go offside in the head, Lydia had been seized by fear, and she found that underlying every other fear was the fear of not having enough money. What if Mum had to go into residential care? Someone would have to pay for it and, unlike other families, the Duffys had nothing.

Lydia had started planning for catastrophe. She'd launched into working flat out, she'd stopped buying herself cute trainers, she'd moved into a cheaper place. She now spent most of her waking life being eaten up by corrosive rage. She was twenty-six, she wasn't meant to have these sorts of worries. She was the baby of the family, the only girl; her brothers were meant to be sappy and dotey about her. Bastards.

Katie turned the page of the storybook and kept reading and, in her cot, Vivienne sighed with sleepy pleasure.

'. . . and the king of the fairies said to Killian, "You have succeeded in your task. You may have your wish. You can become all-knowing."

'"Now I will leave this place," Killian said. "And show everyone my great knowledge."

'The king said, "Not so fast."'

Katie stopped reading and looked doubtfully at the cover of the book. *Celtic Myths*, it alleged. Something called *The Man Who Knows Everything*. Not a story she'd ever encountered before tonight.

Vivienne stirred in her cot—why had the story stopped?—and hastily Katie continued reading.

'"Only as a spirit can you be all-knowing. You must surrender your life."

'Killian was angry. "You have tricked me," he said. "And how come, if I am all-knowing, I did not know about this?"

'The king of the fairies was compassionate. "You did not read the small print. Never was it said that you would know everything. It was said you would have *the ability* to know everything—but you would have to work for it."'

This was the oddest story, Katie thought, looking again at the cover. But she might as well finish it. Vivienne seemed to be enjoying it.

'"Let me live."

'In sorrow, the king said, "The time for that is past; your life is claimed. You may choose to be born into a new life, but when you become mortal again all your knowledge will vanish. What do you choose? Knowledge or Life?"

'Killian considered, but the choice was an easy one. "Life."

'"You may decide whom you wish to be born to. Use your great knowledge. Choose wisely."'

'There were many people, the length and breadth of Ireland, whom Killian could choose from. He visited the north, the south, the east, the west. But his heart led him to one couple, humble, good people, who loved each other deeply, so much so that their souls had merged and become as one. "This man and this woman have the purest hearts in all the land. They have endured much sorrow but I could make them happy."'

'When Killian's spirit had become housed within his new mother, the king of the fairies tapped Killian on the head. "With this touch, I retrieve your knowledge and gift you with innocence in order that you may be born again."'

'Killian began to tingle and spark. Like an incoming tide washing away traces on the sand, he disappeared little by little, clearing the way for his soul to be rewritten by a brand-new person.'

'And the man and woman, humble, good people, kind and loving companions who shared the one soul, who had endured many sorrows in their lives, were full of heart and restored to happiness and love when they learned that their baby had finally been sent to them.'

And that was it. How . . . *odd*. Despite the strangeness of the story, Vivienne had fallen asleep. Katie tiptoed from the room and hurried to the kitchen, ready for her glass of wine.

'*The Man Who Knows Everything*?' she said to her best friend, MaryRose. 'It was weird.'

'Never heard of it. She has so many books in there.'

'Nothing like what we were told as kids.'

'Because we were told the one about the good girl with long hair who gets rescued by a prince with a Lexus and a job in the finance sector.'

Katie's face crumpled and slowly she lowered herself into the sofa.

'Have wine, have wine.' Anxiously, MaryRose thrust a glass at her.

'I was doing OK, you know.' Katie looked up beseechingly. 'I was doing grand. The first few days I was downright blasé. I'd got so sick of being let down, I was *certain* I was doing the right thing. But I hadn't thought it through. Every morning, no matter where he was, I used to read out my thought for the day from my diary . . . and now I can't.'

'Here's my phone. Ring him. Just say yes.'

She'd told MaryRose about the proposal. She'd told everyone because she wanted them to talk her into it.

'But he was jarred. If I'd said yes, we'd have gone right back to me being number five or six on his priority list. Wouldn't I?'

'Maybe he's learned his lesson.'

But what if he hadn't? 'I'd have had to go through all this again at some stage. I've already done ten days of agony. I can't waste them. I just have to keep going.' Katie managed a watery smile. 'When you think about it, my life is so good. I have my friends and my sister and my job—'

'And shoes! You have such beautiful shoes.'

'Yes—'

'And cake! Not much in life that can't be fixed by cake.'

'Cake, yes, cake.'

But after an uneasy pause, Katie toppled forward until her forehead was almost on her knees. 'I'm always going to be the childless woman who has to read bedtime stories to other people's kids.'

'You could have a baby! If that's what you wanted.'

'It's just that now there's no chance of . . . anything.' Katie addressed her lap. 'I might as well be dead.'

'But you don't have to be childless or dead—Conall asked you to marry him! He loves you, he's serious about a future with you.'

'But what if he isn't, MaryRose? What if I'm just fooling myself? Oh God, I don't know *what* to do!'

Day 36

LATE FOR WORK, Katie galloped down the stairs, trying to text Danno at the same time. Then, probably because she had the phone in her hand, she addressed head-on the thoughts that had burgeoned and grown more real over the last couple of days.

Conall has learned his lesson, he loves you, he's serious about a future with you. She'd been too harsh, insisting that he had a ring on him there and then—it was a spontaneous act. And what she kept coming back to was this: he had asked her to marry him. And he had said he loved her . . .

Maybe she'd just ring him, have a conversation, see what came out of it and—Hold on a minute! She knew that van! The one that was parking outside her house and that she'd expected never to see again. It was Cesar, the flower-delivery guy.

Oh, Conall.

Cesar jumped out of his seat. ''Morning, Katie.' Conall had sent so many bouquets over the past ten months that she knew Cesar well.

Cesar went round to open the back of the van and Katie followed. Her heart was rising, rising, rising. Just how big would the bunch be? she wondered. The size would be an indication of the seriousness of Conall's intentions.

With much crackling of cellophane, Cesar drew out the bouquet and it was a monster, right enough. But there was something odd about it; it was made up of strange spiky blooms, sharp, almost aggressive. Was that . . . *a thistle* . . . lurking in the middle of it? Conall usually sent lilies—stargazers, tigers, callas, elegant and fragrant. Why was he sending these ugly, pointy things?

With some misgivings, Katie stretched out her arms to accept the thorny-looking bundle. But Cesar was consulting his clipboard. 'Have you moved flats?'

'No.'

'But this is for flat three.'

'It must be a mistake. I'm flat four.'

'This is for flat three. It says it here.' He indicated his worksheet.

'It's just a mistake, Cesar.' She had a thought. 'Unless they're not from Conall.'

'They're from Mr Hathaway, all right.'

'Then they're for me.'

'Hold on a minute.' Cesar had his mobile out. 'I'll just check.'

After a short conversation, he snapped his phone shut. 'It's for the taxi-driver girl who lives in the flat below Katie Richmond.'

'Oh.' Katie couldn't think of anything else to say so she said it again. 'Oh.'

All the breath had been knocked out of her. What was Conall up to? How did he know Lydia? How did he know she drove a taxi?

'I'll, ah . . . just . . .' Cesar indicated that he needed to get past to reach the doorbell—in order to give the flowers to the right person. He looked a little mortified. 'Right, ah . . . Good luck, Katie, have a nice day.'

'Yes, ah, Cesar. Yes, right, you too.'

Lydia tumbled into the flat, every sense on red alert, seeking Andrei's presence. Or rather, hoping not to seek it. She stuck her head round the sitting-room door and there he was. Shite. The first time she'd seen him since . . . Since nothing. Since the thing that hadn't happened.

'Where's Jan?'

'At work.'

'When will he be home?'

'After ten.'

'Are you in for the evening?' Maybe he'd be going out with Rosie.

'Yes.'

Minsk.

'Rosie is coming over,' he added.

Oh no! Worse and worser!

'Andrei, how long before you go on your summer holiday?'

'Four weeks, six days and sixteen hours.'

Further away than she'd thought. Much further. Shite.

'You see your mum?'

She gave a curt nod.

'Sad?' he asked.

Feck off with your sad, *you love-wrecker. Gilbert would still be my boyfriend if it wasn't for you.*

Naturally, she was prepared to take the rap for whatever part she'd played in herself and Gilbert being banjoed but, come on, when you thought about it, it was all Andrei's fault.

She went into the kitchen and came to an abrupt halt. Instantly, she returned to the living room. 'What's with all the bunches of flowers?'

'They are for you.'

'Ha-ha.'

'Truly. They are for you.'

'For real?' She'd assumed he had bought them to give to Rosie. 'Who are they from?' Then she had a dreadful thought. 'Not from you?'

'Ha-ha. Funny joke.' His sarcasm was quite impressive.

She returned to the kitchen and gazed with confusion and irritation. There were four bundles of blooms, each of them humungous. One in the sink, one lying on the draining board and two standing upright on kitchen chairs, looking like they were about to tuck into their dinner. Even then she knew they weren't from Gilbert. He wasn't that type of man, and just as well he'd slept with other girls because this sort of cheesy gesture would send her right off him.

Cautiously, she approached the bunch in the sink. There was a little white envelope on a stick, in the middle of the foliage. As she reached for it, something stung her. 'Ow! Christ!' What happened there? Were those green fronds . . . *nettles*? They fecking were! In fact, all the plants—you couldn't really call them flowers, they were mostly thistles and thorns—were spiky and aggressive and dangerous-looking. They were held together by a neat little bow, very cute, except that it was made of barbed wire. She tore open the envelope and written on a little white card was, *I saw these and thought of you.*

It was so unexpected that she actually laughed. But the card wasn't signed so she reached into the heart of another bouquet, this time the one lying on the draining board. Large, closed, flesh-coloured buds crowded together, sinister-looking, like they could open their jaws and savage you with serrated teeth. Horrible yokes. She whipped the card out quickly before they came to life and snapped her hand off . . . *and these . . .*

Love of God!

She rounded on one of the bundles on the chair. A cluster of pointy, orange things, as long as razor shells and just as sharp, it bristled with malign energy . . . *and these . . .*

The last bouquet was different. It had proper flowers: round smiling blooms in vibrant yellows and reds and pinks—like a child's drawing . . . *and these. Conall Hathaway. Give me a call.*

Who? Aha! She had it! Mr Wellington Road. The old rich guy. She'd been so tired doing that drive she only half remembered it. But she remembered that he'd asked her out.

'*Out* out?' She'd been gobsmacked.

'Yeah. On a date.'

Then he'd asked her if she liked stationery shops. Or chemists. He was weird. She didn't think she'd ever been in a stationery shop in her life.

'No, thanks,' she'd said.

'Why not?'

Why not? She'd turned to stare at him. 'You're not my type.'

'I'm fucked up,' he'd said enticingly.

Perplexed, she'd asked, 'Since when was that a good thing?'

'I'm told that's what the girls like. The young ones, anyway.'

'Look, just pay up and get out of my car.'

'How much do I owe you?'

'Eight euros forty. I'll call it eight if you'll just get out.'

He'd handed her a tenner. 'Keep—'

'—the change? No, thanks. Here's your two euros. Please get out. I've to go and see my mum.' She'd looked at her watch. 'I need a kip first.'

'One of my girlfriends, the one before Katie, parked outside my house for sixty-seven hours when I broke up with her.'

'I would never go out with someone like you. You're too old. You're too . . . You'd bore me senseless . . . Look! You're upset about the sexy governess, but she'll take you back; her type always does.'

'I'm Conall Hathaway. I like you. Expect to hear from me again.'

Fionn was outside on the front step, the blue door swinging open behind him. He was pretending to study the stars while trying to catch a glimpse of Maeve through the gap in her sitting-room curtains. But all he could see was Matt sitting on the floor, steadily eating his way through a box of—Fionn couldn't be certain, it was too far away—but it looked like a box of blackcurrant flapjacks.

'What are you up to, son?' A duo of passing policemen interrupted his beady-eyed squinting.

'Standing outside my own dwelling place looking at the stars.'

'Stars are that way.' The bigger of the two pointed at the sky and only when Fionn turned his face upwards did they lumber on.

Fionn gazed up into the royal-blue dusk, waiting for the boyos to disappear, resenting every second that he wasn't keeping tabs on Maeve. And it wasn't like he could even properly see the stars, not in this city, which blazed artificial light everywhere and dimmed the wonder of nature. *Arm-wrestling with nature.* He liked that phrase. He wondered if Grainne would let him use it. She might, you never know. Then again, she might not and Grainne was a tough nut . . . Something compelled him to turn his head, and through the dim light he saw a female creature walking along Star Street towards him. All at once his vision filled with comets and stars, colours and spirals—Fionn had fallen in love again.

Like someone who'd discovered a new skill, perhaps like making pancakes or riding a unicycle, Fionn was keen to keep trying it out. Even as he was stunned with love for this new woman, this bandbox-fresh little delight, he was kind enough to consider Maeve and he knew he would always think fondly of her, his first love. But, all of a sudden, Maeve seemed raw and dishevelled—*What was with the baggy cords?*—and the type of woman a youngster, inexperienced in the ways of love, would fall for. This new emotion was different, infinitely more sophisticated, because Fionn was more mature now, more of a man.

He fastened his loving gaze on the vision's swinging skirt, her narrow waist, her swishing ponytail. An expression that Fionn didn't even know that he knew spoke in his head: *matchy-matchy.* Shoes, belt, handbag. An embroidered blouse. A modest girl, like something from the olden days.

Fionn stepped forward to impede her progress along Star Street. He was powerless to stop himself. 'Hello,' he said.

She stopped. 'Hello.'

'I'm standing here looking at the stars,' he said.

'We all have to have a hobby.'

'See that one.' He pointed towards a pinprick of intense light. 'That's the planet Venus. It's not actually a star at all.'

'Would you credit it? It looks just like a star. Only brighter.'

'The brightest star in the sky. They call it the planet of love.' Was he going too far? 'I'm Fionn Purdue.'

'Pleased to meet you, Mr Purdue.'

Oh, the modesty, the sweetness! 'Fionn, Fionn, Fionn. And what do they call you?'

'Rosemary Draper.'

'Rosemary,' Fionn murmured. God, it was beautiful.

'My friends call me Rosie.'

'May I . . .?'

'Are you my friend?' Oh, flirting! Flirting from the little madam who looked like butter wouldn't melt.

'I'd like to be.'

'Oh, stop that now, you brazen pup!' But she smiled. A prim little smile, somewhat lacking in warmth, but a smile nonetheless.

'What do you do for a crust, Rosemary?' He was planning to land it on her that he was shortly to be a star of the small screen.

'I'm a nurse. Now, if you'll excuse me.'

Rosemary—dare he call her Rosie?—made to get round Fionn. She seemed to be aiming herself at the open doorway.

'You're coming in! You live here too? I'm on the first floor!' What was it with this house that it was riddled with beautiful women? Sirens! Temptresses!

'I'm visiting my boyfriend. Andrei Palweski.'

'You have a boyfriend?' It was a blow.

'I have a boyfriend.'

But of course she did. Never mind. He'd make short work of that arrangement.

'What hospital do you work at?' he called, as she climbed the stairs away from him.

Her legs—all he could see of her—hesitated. Then the magic words floated down to him. 'St Vincent's.' And her legs began to climb again.

'I've no food in and I'm starving,' Lydia said. 'Do you mind if I eat some of your funny Polish bread?'

'No problem; but it is old.'

'Stale. Can I eat some of your funny Polish cheese?'

'For sure.'

She slapped some white cheese and two slices of stale bread together, then flung herself on the couch. Amazing what tasted nice when you were starving. Some programme was on, about a house being exorcised.

She flicked a glance out of the corner of her eye, just to see if Andrei was showing signs of effing off to his room. As if he felt her eyes on him, he turned and looked at her and they exchanged a moment of hearty mutual dislike. Naked antipathy. Then one of them, probably Andrei, she decided afterwards, made a small movement and everything went blurry. They both moved, a twist of the body towards each other, and then they somehow launched themselves at one another, kissing and pulling and tearing, caught in a frenzy of want.

It was like the previous time, except that now she had the pleasure of anticipation. She knew how fabulous it was going to be. She knew how his skin would feel—hot and cold and smooth and rough—against hers. She knew how he would press her hips flat against the bed, his biceps bulging. She knew she would arch herself upwards to meet him.

Harmonious heart currents? It's all such a wild, lustful flurry, everything beating in such a frantic, deafeningly loud cacophony that it's impossible to tell. On paper, Andrei and Lydia don't look like the perfect match, but you've got to stay open-minded, no?

Rosie knocked softly on the door of flat three, then stood back and smoothed her skirt and fixed a sweet smile to her face.

But the moments passed and the door remained unanswered and she was surprised. Vexed, in fact. Obliging her to knock for a second time was . . . well, it felt disrespectful. As she rapped once again, a frosty persona began to steal over her, one that Andrei would have to work hard to jolly her out of. And still—astonishingly—no one appeared. How unexpected. Andrei and she had arranged that she call at 8.30 and here she was now, 8.50.

She considered simply flouncing away down the stairs. She was wearing a good skirt for it. But a flounce was no good if there was no man to suffer from seeing you do it.

She rapped once more, quite angrily this time. The seconds ticked by and the door remained impassive. This was unacceptable. Rosie Draper was not the kind of girl you left standing outside an unanswered door.

This wasn't a deliberate snub; Andrei had the total dotes for her. Something must have happened with his job or the van or that cretin

Jan to derail his plans. Nevertheless, if Andrei couldn't organise his life adequately, in order to fulfil his obligations to her, a price had to be paid. She would make it very clear that this slight had added several more weeks to the endurance period before—indeed, *if*—she went to bed with him. Already his longing for her had him unravelling with despair, and to tighten the screws further would be fun . . .

Gosh, she was still outside the door and it still hadn't been answered. It seemed that he actually really wasn't here. She could phone him. But she would not. She, Rosemary Draper, making calls, trying to track down a man? I don't think so!

On the floor below, she heard the Fionn hunk going into his flat and calling out, 'I'm back.' Fionn must have had his fill of stargazing.

A dreamboat, no one could deny it, one of the most handsome men she'd ever seen. Quite full of himself, though.

But Andrei had seriously blotted his copybook and Rosie was a great believer in safety nets, Plan Bs and contingency arrangements.

She reached into her handbag and fetched out a pretty little notebook, the pale yellow pages patterned with buttercups. With the matching yellow pen, she wrote:

Dear Andrei, I called at your flat like we arranged but you're not here. I can't understand what I have done to you that you would need to humiliate me so badly.

She tore the page out and shoved it under the door, then skipped down a flight of stairs and reached once again for her notebook. Neatly, she printed her name and work number, eased the page out carefully, folded it tidily and slid it smoothly under Fionn's door.

Day 34

KATIE STUCK HER HEAD round the sitting-room door. 'Hi, Dad.'

Energised by the sight of her, Robert Richmond dusted the newspaper off his lap and onto the fireside rug. 'How's Miss Havisham?'

'Do you mean . . . me?'

'Ah, Katie, Katie, what were you at? He arrives in the middle of the night, jarred by all accounts, gets down on one knee and you think he means it?'

Silently, Katie cursed herself for having told anyone about Conall's middle-of-the-night visit. Especially her bloody sister, Naomi!

'I didn't think he meant it.' She kept her voice steady. 'I didn't say yes.'

'I hear he has his eye on some young one now,' Robert said, almost cheerfully. 'Naomi said he sent her flowers. And you're all upset.'

Robert and Penny Richmond had worked hard to instil a powerful value system in their children: getting ideas above your station could only end in tears. Low expectations were the key to happiness.

Penny darted in from the kitchen, a vision of domesticity in a Simpsons apron. Clearly, she'd been listening. 'You should never have gone near him.'

'Why not?'

Katie's mother stretched her neck to ten times its normal length and reared back in shock. 'Are you raising *your voice* at me?'

Robert, never one to miss an opportunity to take offence, rose halfway out of his chair. 'Are you raising your voice at your mother? In her own house? While she's cooking you Sunday lunch?'

A long, tense stand-off ensued. From the kitchen Katie heard Naomi ask, 'What's going on in there?'

Nine-year-old Nita answered, 'I think Auntie Katie raised her voice at Granny.'

And Ralph's voice said, 'Oh Christ, Naomi, your family. Where's the wine?'

Penny glared at Katie, her mouth trembling with woundedness.

'Why shouldn't I have gone near him?' Katie heard her voice quiver. Then she answered her own question. 'Because I wasn't good enough.'

'I don't know what's got into you.' Penny stared at Katie.

'Don't mind her, love,' Robert urged his wife. 'Just get on with the lunch.'

Rain beat against the windows and the only sound throughout lunch was the clinking of cutlery on plates. Penny Richmond maintained her martyred air for over an hour and even Naomi's kids, Nita and Percy, were silenced by the toxic atmosphere.

As soon as the torturous meal ended, Naomi pulled Katie out into the garden.

'I told you not to tell her,' Katie said.

Naomi made an apologetic face, but they both knew that when Penny Richmond sensed a story, no one could withstand the interrogation.

'You could kill that thing with the taxi-driver girl with one call,' Naomi said.

'Why would I do that?' What would be achieved? In her heart of hearts, Katie had known she shouldn't ever have taken Conall's 5 a.m. proposal seriously. She'd tried to talk herself into believing it, but she'd always known. Nevertheless . . .

'Why did he have to pick someone *where I live?*'

Naomi narrowed her eyes. 'He's one vicious bastard.'

'He's just clueless. But it's all gone so messy. In the beginning it was a neat surgical strike; now the wound has become infected.'

'You do love a medical analogy. So what you need is a painkiller.' Naomi thrust a cigarette at Katie. 'Take this, would you? I'm after lighting it for you.'

'For a clever man he can be really stupid—Would you stop with that thing? I don't smoke.'

'You do today.'

Katie accepted the cigarette. TLC at the Richmonds'? This was as good as it got.

'Don't let her see us,' Naomi said.

'You're forty-two.' Katie inhaled. 'What age do you have to be before your mum will let you smoke?'

In silence, they sat on wet garden chairs and listened to the raindrops dripping from the branches.

'Death by Sunday lunch,' Naomi said moodily.

'Fecking torture.'

'How does Charlie get out of having to come to these bloody things?'

Katie paused, afraid that the secret she knew about Charlie would just tumble out of her mouth; then she carried on. 'He's got a stronger sense of survival than either of us. He knows Mum will make him feel like shit, so he won't put himself through it.'

'Yeah.'

'I hate her,' Katie said suddenly. 'I hate them both. Why couldn't we have had parents who told us we were great?'

'Well, you chose them.'

'Excuse me?'

'This book I'm reading. It's one of yours, actually. Louise L. Hay. I took it off your shelf the night of your birthday. It says we choose everything we get in life. Even our own parents.'

'We *choose our own parents?* Before we're born?'

'Before we're conceived, actually.'

'But how could we do that? That's just . . . *shit.*'

'I know. They're all shit, all those self-help books. I'm only saying.'

Day 32 (very early in the morning)

THEY ALL LOOKED the same, those tall, posh Georgian houses. Lydia parked outside number 11 and reached for her mobile. She refused to get out of the car and ring the doorbell because it was drizzling and she had her hair to think of. 'Taxi for Eilish Hessard.' Lydia left a message on the mobile contact. 'I'm waiting outside.'

Over the years she'd discovered that there was no pattern to where she could be taken by the forces that governed taxis. She might never have visited a road and then she could find herself driving there five times in the one week . . . so to find herself picking up on Wellington Road could be a meaningless coincidence.

But she didn't really believe it. Not after those bloody flowers. And it wasn't much of a surprise when the passenger door was wrenched open and the rich old guy, whatever his name was, jumped in beside her. ''Morning, Lydia!'

'Out,' she said. 'This is Eilish Hessard's car.'

'She's my assistant. Subterfuge. I booked you. Did you get the flowers?'

'How did you track me down?'

'I thought at the very least I'd get a call thanking me for the flowers.'

'I didn't ask for them. There should be a law against sending things to people that they don't want. So how did you book me?'

'Very easy. Luckily, there aren't many girls who drive taxis. Eilish rang all the taxi companies.'

'You got your assistant to ring?'

'Because she's a woman. I didn't think your controllers would be too keen to hook you up with a man.'

They were nothing like as noble as that, Lydia thought.

'Eilish said you'd driven her and that she'd liked you. The guy seemed to find it hard to believe but . . . Joke, Lydia.'

'I'm doubled over laughing. So where to?'

'Nowhere. I just thought we'd sit here and talk. Why don't you come in for some breakfast?'

'The neck of you! I've a living to earn. I'm not your . . . plaything.'

'I'll pay you.'

'I don't want you to pay me.' She shuddered. 'This is really creepy. You're turning my stomach. Please get out.'

He stared at her, aghast. 'I've handled this all wrong,' he muttered. 'How can I make it better?'

'By getting out of my car and never contacting me again. That way I won't press charges.'

'When's your next day off? What would you like to do? Say anything you want. Anything, and I'll go along with it.'

'Yeah, grand, so. I'd like you to drive me to Boyne in County Meath, help me clean a really manky kitchen, humour my not-very-well-in-the-head mum, and threaten one of my brothers. I don't mind which one. I've got three, so you can have the pleasure of choosing.'

'Wouldn't you prefer something more . . . you know? We could drive down to Powerscourt and have lunch at—'

'Don't start negotiating. It's my day off; that's what I'm doing.'

'When?'

'Tomorrow.'

'Tomorrow? I've to go to work tomorrow.'

'So go to work. I couldn't give a shite.'

Conall rolled his eyes. 'What time will I pick you up?'

'No time. You're not coming. Get used to it. Go into work, make another million quid.'

'I'm coming. I reckon you'll want to leave at about ten o'clock. You won't want to go any earlier because of the traffic. But any later and too much of the day will have gone.'

If he was doing this to anyone else, then it might even work. But it wouldn't work with her.

'So . . . see you at ten?'

'See you at ten,' she repeated, with great sarcasm.

She'd go at nine.

Day 31

CONALL HATHAWAY HAD to circle the block four times before he found a parking space with a good view of the front door of 66 Star Street. He switched off the engine and reached gratefully for his BlackBerry. The red light was flashing. Lovely. New emails. Seven in total and nothing exciting in any of them, but still, communications were like oxygen to him.

He flicked through the radio stations and watched the blue front door and shifted in his seat and looked at his BlackBerry and wished the red light would start flashing again. He was feeling edgy. He couldn't remember the last time he'd rung Eilish and said the words *I won't be in today*. Naturally, he'd been absent from his desk many, many times, but only because he was sitting at another desk in another company, in the process of taking it over. And he went on corporate jollies, champagne-soaked days in Monaco or Ascot, but that was in order to stay on the inside track with those shadowy figures in the financial markets who knew when a company was failing long before the company itself knew. It was still work.

He'd never before just called Eilish and said he wasn't coming in because . . . well, he just *wasn't coming in*. It didn't feel good, it didn't feel right, but it had to be done.

He'd been fond of Katie, very fond if truth be told, and he hadn't been at all prepared for them breaking up. A woman finishing with him was a radical mutation in his pattern of romance. It had shaken him.

Worse than Katie dumping him was that she refused to be won back. He'd offered her the ultimate prize—marriage—and she'd spurned it. Spurned *him*. But instead of wasting time in hand-wringing regret, he asked himself what he could learn. That always worked when things veered off course in his job. He'd devised his own formula, 'The Three As and the One M':

> **Assess** the situation.
> **Acknowledge** where control had been compromised.
> **Adapt** with a new, more appropriate response.
> **Move** forward.

He wished it was a catchier slogan. Four As would have been ideal. The first three were perfect but he just couldn't find an A that encapsulated the last point.

With Katie, he'd Assessed the situation and wasn't afraid to admit he'd made a mistake—it was what made him so good at his job—and he was man enough, in his opinion, to Acknowledge that being dumped was *his fault*.

Now it was time to Adapt: he'd have to become more flexible about his devotion to the job. He didn't believe in fate but he believed in maximising opportunities, so when Lydia appeared and challenged him to take a weekday off work, he Moved on it. Give it a go, see if the world ended; and if it did, well, he was always on the BlackBerry.

He stared at the door of number 66 and eyed its banana-shaped knocker with irritation. He'd never liked it. Now that he and Katie were kaput he wouldn't have to look at it ever again. Unless, of course, things worked out with Lydia . . .

He couldn't explain why but he was extremely taken with her. Her beauty wasn't the first thing you'd notice because she was so angry but, actually, she was a doll. He liked seeing her, small and furious, behind the wheel of her taxi. He liked her 'Gdańsk!' and 'Outttt!' and all that mad stuff. She was a one-off.

And she was the right age. Katie was spot-on: a girl in her twenties would suit him.

It was coming up to 8.30 and if Conall had read Lydia right, she'd exit the house soon, looking to put many miles of road behind her before he showed up at ten o'clock. But he was already here!

Get up, Katie urged herself. *On your feet and face the world.*

She'd just emerged from one of the worst night's sleep of her life, the genesis of which could be traced back to last night, at a launch, when she'd jettisoned all pretence of professionalism and attached herself to the free bar. She drank grimly and with purpose until the hard edges slipped off life.

Somehow she'd got home and tumbled way down into a drunk, dreamless coma. Then, in the dead of night, she'd jerked awake. She'd been having a terrible nightmare in which she had landed on a deserted planet, a lump of barren, grey rock, swept by howling, perishing winds. Alone, all alone, stranded for eternity.

She waited for the terror of the nightmare to disperse, but it didn't— because, she realised with a terrible thud, it was all true. She *was* alone, all alone, stranded for eternity. No one would love her ever again.

She got up and puked and crawled back into bed, desperate for sleep to release her from her tormented thoughts. At some stage she passed into a light, anxious doze, and when her alarm started beeping at 7.30 she wanted to slit her own throat.

Make-up wasn't helping. She painted epic quantities of concealer under her eyes and still she looked like Sylvester Stallone. Eventually, furtive and jumpy, already anticipating pain, she was ready to bolt from the building (she was so frightened of bumping into Conall romancing Lydia that, whenever she had to leave her flat, she sprinted down the three flights of stairs and into the street with her eyes closed and her breath held).

But it had been five days since he'd sent the horrible flowers—they'd come on Friday and now it was Wednesday. She'd seen no sign of him over the weekend and a tiny bud of hope, like a snowdrop after an unforgiving winter, broke through: maybe it had been a one-off.

She was out of the front door; the gallop was over. She could open her eyes; she could inhale. Then she remembered that there was no point jingling her car keys because there was no car. Her ride was still in the car park at work. But hey! There was Conall's car. Right there! Just parked, waiting! Without thinking, she made for it.

'Conall?'

He looked up from his BlackBerry. Jesus Christ, it was Katie! Standing there in the street! He clambered out from the car and reached down to kiss her politely on the cheek.

'What are you doing here?' she asked.

'Ah . . . waiting for someone.' He was very, very embarrassed. He should have known this might happen. *Unless, of course*, a little voice prompted, *unless he had known*.

Her face tight and closed, Katie backed away on her high heels. All of a sudden, the door of 66 Star Street opened and a large donkey-like dog bounded out, followed by the old woman who lived on the first floor, and then came this . . . *man* and it was the man who caught Conall's attention. He was alerted by a sense of threat. This blond-haired, sloppily dressed, idle-looking . . . *gobshite* was the one who had replaced him in Katie's affections.

Katie was still backing away from Conall; then she collided with your man. Speedily, she turned round and Conall heard her say, 'Sorry,' and your man said, 'No, *I'm* sorry,' then came the sounds of laughter, then more conversation, too low for Conall to hear properly, followed by more laughter, then Goldilocks lifted Katie's hand and kissed the back of it with fulsome tenderness. *Prick.* The dog, the old woman and the man piled into a Merc and sped off, Katie walked away into the distance and Conall was left alone.

With great contempt Grudge watched Fionn gaze through the rear window as they drove away from Katie. 'Now,' Fionn asked, 'who was *she*?'

Jemima rested her head back and closed her eyes. 'Fionn, dear heart, truly I find I'm quite wearied by your wayward affections.'

'Ah, Jemima!'

Fionn was sparkly-eyed and skittish and Grudge shook his hairy head in disgust.

'First poor Maeve, then Rosie . . .'

Grudge attempted to tut but his tongue was too thick. That had been an appalling episode, the little nurse sliding her phone number under the door of the flat and urging Fionn to call her. Jemima had become terribly distressed, beseeching Fionn to stay away from girls who were spoken for. 'She and Andrei are a good match.' But Fionn had disregarded Jemima's distress and rung Rosie anyway. An assignation had been arranged for this very evening, but would Fionn proceed with it now that his attentions had been caught by Katie?

'Katie? Is she married?' Fionn pressed. 'Or what?'

Jemima exhaled. 'Not married. That dark, brooding creature in the Lexus was in attendance for many months, but I sense there has been a sundering recently.'

'So she's single!' Fionn rubbed his hands together in glee.

'Don't they have women where you come from?' Ogden eyed Fionn in the rearview. 'I never met such a randy article.'

'Ogden makes a good point, Fionn. Perhaps you should consider returning to Pokey. I fear you're finding city life rather overstimulating.'

Just as Conall had anticipated! Only 8.55 and here was Lydia, leaving earlier than she'd said, just to avoid him.

He stepped out of the car, into her path. 'Going somewhere?'

First she looked incredulous; then a thunderous rage appeared on her little dial. 'Right, that's it,' she said. 'I'm calling the police.'

He couldn't stop laughing. 'Lydia, I just want to go on a date with you.'

'You're stalking me!'

'I'm wooing you.'

'What kind of stupid word is that?'

'I mean, I like you, I'm trying to get you to come out with me. Since when was that a crime?'

Lydia pressed a couple of buttons on her phone. 'It's ringing.'

Alarm overtook him. 'You've the police on speed dial?'

'I'm a taxi driver. Me and the cops are in regular contact.'

'Hang up, Lydia.' Their gazes were locked. Fire burned in her eyes but his will would prevail . . . 'Hang up, Lydia!'

'Love of God!' She snapped her phone shut. 'What is it you want?'

'One chance. The day you suggested. We go to that town in Meath, I clean a dirty kitchen, talk to your mother and put the frighteners on your brother.'

'But I don't want you to come.'

'We'll go in my car. I'll drive you.'

She wasn't happy but it was the offer to drive that swung it in his favour. His consummate skill was in finding a weak spot and he'd assessed, correctly, that she was sick of being behind a wheel.

I'm Conall Hathaway and I always get what I want.

Danno missed nothing. Katie hadn't even opened the office door fully before his eyes locked with hers. 'What?' he asked.

'Nothing.'

He unfolded himself from his chair. She watched his snake-hips cross the office floor and she was powerless to stop him.

'Go back to your desk, Danno. Do what you're paid to do.'

'What's Slasher done now? Did he *hurt* you?'

It was Danno's concern that broke her.

'I think . . .' She shouldn't be telling Danno. She was his boss and he already did everything in his power to ignore hierarchy. 'I think Conall is seeing the girl who lives in the flat below me.'

George gave a theatrical gasp and placed his hand on his chest. '*That's* a bit close to home.'

'Katie, what makes you think that?' Danno asked.

Without inflection, Katie related Friday's events with the flowers, then finding Conall waiting in his car outside the house this morning.

'It could be just a coincidence.' Audrey had crept closer to Katie's desk. They all had, like little woodland creatures emerging from their hidey-holes.

'No coincidences in Slasher Hathaway's life,' Danno said. 'But something else happened?'

Katie hadn't been expecting that. 'How do you know?'

'Because you look so . . . something.'

'I met a man.' Even to her own ears, she sounded faint and strange.

'Ooooh.' She had the rapt attention of all her staff, something that didn't happen often.

'No, not like that. Not like, *I met a man.*' Their faces were baffled. Kindly, but baffled. 'I don't mean like a potential boyfriend.'

'No, no, bit old for that now.' Danno chortled.

'I bumped into him,' Katie said, unable to stop herself from talking about Fionn. 'I was backing away from Conall's car and smacked into him and he was so nice—' She stopped. The expression on Lila-May's face said, *Pathetic,* so she definitely couldn't splurge how she really felt: that Fionn had healed her pain. The shock of seeing Conall waiting for another girl, the agony of her jealousy, the aching, gaping sense of loss—it was as if she'd been in red-hot torment with a toothache and suddenly, with Fionn smiling and speaking, the pain was wiped clean and she was flooded with its absence, like it was a force in itself.

'He must live near you if you bumped into him,' George said. 'Maybe on the same road.'

'Same road? He lives in the same house as me. Two flats below.'

'What's going on in that house?' Lila-May asked sharply.

'What do you mean?'

'Something's happening. Something weird. That's too much of a coincidence. Slasher's new girl, your new man.'

'You read too much Stephen King,' Danno said.

'He'll only be living there for a couple of months. He says he's making some gardening programme.'

'It's not that guy?' George widened his eyes. 'Finn something.'

'Fionn Purdue.'

'Yes! Google him!' George stood up. He was actually shrieking. 'Google him. Google him. I saw him in the paper. Google him!'

They clustered round Katie's screen and watched in awe as Fionn's picture appeared, pixel by pixel.

'Is he that beautiful in real life?' Tamsin asked.

Katie swallowed. 'You probably won't believe me, but this isn't a great picture of him.'

They studied Fionn's square jaw line and golden glow, trying to decide what, if any, colour he had in his hair when a twinkle of light sprang from the screen and the five of them reared back.

'Did he just . . . wink?' Danno asked faintly.

No one spoke.

'Power surge or something.'

'Yeah. Power surge.' A little bit rattled now, the exodus back to their desks began. They needed to put some distance between themselves and Katie's freaky goings-on.

'He said he's coming to see me tonight.'

'What the hell . . .' Lila-May furrowed her forehead. 'Why you?'

'I honestly have no idea.'

Maeve was sitting on the steps of the Central Bank, eating her sandwich, alert for AOK opportunities. It was the bag she noticed first, a colourful embroidered mini-rucksack. It was attached to a girl, a slight little thing, with short black hair, ordinary-looking in every way except for the air of isolation that surrounded her. She was alone, very alone, glowing her way darkly through the aimless shoals of shiny people, and the rigid immobile cast to her face was one that Maeve recognised. Though she wasn't close enough to see the girl's eyes, she knew what she'd find if she looked in there. *This* was today's act and Maeve so didn't want to do it. She'd rather lug twenty buggies up twenty flights of stairs than this. But what choice had she? Suddenly aware of Maeve's scrutiny, the girl twisted her head, and when their gazes met Maeve forced herself to smile. Really smile, right from the heart. The girl looked puzzled—she was wondering if she knew Maeve, because why would a total stranger be smiling at her with such warmth? Maeve kept smiling, kept sending out love, but the girl looked at her in alarm, almost fear. *Keep smiling, keep smiling.* Then Maeve's mouth began to wobble and she had to look away. When she looked back again, the girl had gone, and Maeve felt worse than she would have thought possible. Acts of Kindness were meant to make her feel better, not plunge her into despair. What was the point of doing them? The panic attacks were back; she'd had another one this morning.

She might stop the Acts of Kindness and Trios of Blessings, she decided. They weren't working. But how would she break it to Matt?

Conall pulled in outside 74 Star Street, an impressively adjacent parking spot for number 66. How did he manage it? Lydia wondered. How did people like him always get what they wanted?

'Today went quite well,' Conall said.

She already had her seat belt off and her hand on the door but she paused. 'I hate the way you do that. Always assessing things and putting values on them.'

'So what'll we do for our next date?'

'Bye.'

'Describe your perfect night.'

'Have you gone deaf?'

'Go on. Your perfect night.'

'You're unbelievable. OK, I'd love to go to Float. It's this club with a swimming pool on the roof and—'

'I know it.'

'But you have to be a member—'

'I'm a member.'

'*Mr* Hathaway! Are you really? Savage!' Her face was transformed with a luminous smile.

'We can go there, no problem.' He looked happy to have pleased her.

'With Poppy, Shoane and Sissy.'

'Who are they?'

'My friends.'

'So . . . what? I come too? And pay for everything?'

'Thanks very much, Conall. We like pink champagne.'

He watched her, without comment.

'Oh.' She furrowed her forehead and shook her head sadly. 'Mr Hathaway no happy? You asked me what my ideal night was. I told you. Simple as.'

He shrugged and wouldn't meet her eyes.

'Are you *sulking*? At your age? You wanted my perfect night to be something you wanted to do too. But I'm different to you, Hathaway. You can't *make* people want the same stuff as you.'

Something in her words . . . Suddenly, he was hearing echoes from the past, from the day he'd taken Katie to Glyndebourne.

Adapt! Adapt in order to survive! 'OK. Bring your friends. When do you want to go? Tonight?'

'God, no. We need time to look forward to it.'

'Saturday, then?'

'Saturday!' Such scorn. 'Every gobshite goes out on Saturday. We'll go on Monday—that's when the cool people go out.'

Monday wasn't ideal. He was meant to be going to Milan on Tuesday. Maybe he could change that to Wednesday. 'Right, Monday.'

'And, Conall?' she said softly.

He looked at her, ready to accept her gratitude.

'You'll be the oldest of us by about sixty years. Just so long as you're cool with that?'

Katie knew how these things worked. Television: they did long hours. Fionn hadn't said what time he'd visit her but it could be as late as nine. Maybe even later, depending on where they were shooting.

She dressed in casual, hey-just-hanging-out stuff. It took several attempts before she got the right combination and even then she worried about her feet. She couldn't wear her gold sandals because who wore four-inch heels at home? But when she put on her flip-flops, she had to take them off immediately, appalled at how stumpy they made her legs look.

The lovely pedicure she'd had for Jason's wedding had worn off and the hard skin on her soles had crept back, but she'd done nothing about it. Just let it happen!

By the time I've scrubbed my feet raw with my diamond foot-smoother, he'll be here.

She knew Fionn would come. She was certain. There had been something strong and sure between them that she couldn't explain.

'You can depend on me,' he'd said, when they'd had their first conversation this morning. 'You can depend on me for your life.' And although it was a frankly ridiculous thing for one stranger to say to another, she knew it was true.

The balls of her feet were pretty smooth but he still hadn't arrived, so she scrubbed a bit longer then she stopped. She wouldn't be able to walk tomorrow if she continued eroding her soles like this.

She paced between the living room and the bathroom, checking her make-up, checking it again.

A quick flick at her watch. It was suddenly 9.45, and dread began a slow slide inside her.

He wasn't coming.

She was a cretin to have thought he would. That's it, then! Cleanse, tone, moisturise and into bed! She turned off her light and, almost instantly, noises started up in the downstairs flat. Grunting and the slap of wood against something. Were they moving furniture? So late? . . . Oh no! It was people having sex!

An unbearable thought struck her: it wasn't Conall, was it? With little taxi-driving Lydia? That would finish her off entirely. There was no way on earth she could endure hearing Conall having sex with someone else. She listened hard. She didn't recognise the grunting. Conall *was* a grunter, but a different kind. This must be one of the Polish guys, she reckoned. What was his name? She couldn't remember . . .

'Andrei! Oh, Andrei, Andrei!'

'Thank you,' Katie yelled at the floor. 'I wouldn't have slept a wink trying to remember!'

Angrily, she thrust ear-plugs into her ears, and eventually she fell into a troubled but deep sleep.

You're breaking up with me? On our first date?'

'The thing is, Rosemary, I've met someone else.'

'How? You only met me five days ago.'

Fionn shrugged helplessly. How could he describe how he felt about Katie? Unlike the first time he'd seen Rosie, with Katie there had been no spirals and colour. Instead, he'd had an abiding, irresistible sense of safe harbour. Of docking. Of everything—*everything*—clicking into place. He was powerless over it and his short-lived fancy for Rosie had immediately seemed silly and skittish.

'Sorry,' he said, hoping he could go now. It would take him for ever to get back to Star Street and Katie.

Rosie had chosen a spot far, far across the city for their first date. A pub in Greystones overlooking a little harbour. Very scenic. Also— Fionn suspected—handily placed so that it was unlikely she would bump into anyone she knew.

Fionn hadn't wanted to go. Now that he'd met Katie, what would be the point? But the only number he had for Rosie was the one at the hospital (cagey creature that she was, she hadn't given him her mobile), and she wasn't on duty. He had no way of cancelling and he couldn't simply abandon her to sit in the Harbour View in a pretty lemon-coloured cotton dress, sipping her West Coast cooler all by herself, looking up hopefully every time the door opened. He'd loved her once.

'This is not acceptable.' Rosie quivered with affronted dignity.

'Rosie, you're a lovely girl,' he said. 'I'm sure you're a great girlfriend.'

She nodded. 'I'm a prize, Fionn.'

'And I'm sorry if I misled you—'

'Misled me?'

'—but I'm not sure this is working out.'

That's when she realised what was happening. But she didn't slink off in humiliated tears. She sat up straighter, seething with righteous indignation. 'You can't do this. I'm not the type of girl you play games with.'

Great alarm rose in Fionn. Was she going to insist on a relationship?

'Do you think I make a habit of giving my phone number to men? And meeting them in Wicklow? I've risked things for tonight. I have a boyfriend!'

'You still have him?'

Reluctantly, she nodded. Far too canny to dump one prospect before the other was a dead cert, Fionn realised. Thank God for that.

'Go back to your boyfriend, Rosie. Forget me.' Fionn remembered a line that had sometimes been yelled at him as a parting shot. 'I'm a fucking eejit. I'm not worth it.'

Fionn bounded up the stairs to the top floor of 66 Star Street, but there was no response to his urgent knocking. Was Katie asleep? Or ignoring him? It was imperative that he see her. She had to know that he wasn't a flake. Or a . . .? He summoned further insults from past breakups.

A lightweight. A chancer. A messer. An immature moron. And most popular of all, by a long chalk, a fucking eejit.

But he was no longer any of those things; he was a man now, a man whose intentions were serious, and it was very important that Katie knew. But she wasn't answering the door.

A note. He'd write her a note and explain everything. His pockets yielded up a leaky pen and a few pages of the previous day's shooting schedule.

Dear Katie, I'm sorry I didn't get here until now.

But he didn't own a watch, so he didn't know when *now* was.

I would like to see you. I will call again. Depend on it.
Yours, Fionn

But words were frustratingly inadequate. He had to *prove* his regret. He searched his pockets for something and brought forth an ear of sage. No. What good was wisdom? Or grey pebbles? Or a torn Orbit wrapper? A deeper rummage unearthed a withered, dark green sprig. What was that? Then he identified it. Well, *perfect*! It was rue. Rue was very much a statement herb—God almighty, he was starting to think like Grainne Butcher's scripts—as it was bitter, poisonous stuff. In times past, people threw it at weddings, when their loved ones were marrying another.

Please accept this gift as a token of my rue.

He wasn't sure if that was grammatically correct, but it was from the heart, and Grainne kept saying that if it was from the heart, it would work. Then he folded the sprig into the note and tried to shove it under the door—but it wouldn't go. Katie's door had something like a short sweeping brush fitted to the bottom of it. (A draught-prevention measure, but he wasn't to know, undomesticated animal that he was.) Reluctantly, he left the note outside and anxiously descended the stairs to Jemima's flat.

This evening Fionn had learned that not all women were like the ones in Pokey, who, in retrospect, were sweet, malleable creatures, always cutting him plenty of slack, despite the insult-fest that usually signalled the end of their dalliance. Katie might be as tough and unforgiving as that Rosie.

Katie might never speak to him again.

You're right, Fionn, she mightn't.

Day 30

As Lydia had expected, Conall had been completely bloody clueless about cleaning. He'd emptied nearly a whole bottle of washing-up liquid into the sink and Ellen, Lydia and himself had almost been carried off in a wash of foam.

But other than that, Lydia had to admit that he'd done quite well. Ellen had liked him.

'Are you Lydia's boyfriend?' she had asked him, as he'd pawed through the bubbles, trying to locate the sink somewhere beneath him.

'Ah, not yet, maybe. But working on it.'

A sound at the door made the three of them turn round. It was Ronnie. Lydia couldn't remember the last time she'd clapped eyes on him.

'What's going on here?' Ronnie spoke softly and with terrible menace.

'Oh, you know,' Lydia said. 'Cleaning a manky house, taking care of our mum because—'

Ronnie ignored her and focused on Conall. 'And who might you be?'

'Conall Hathaway.' Conall wiped his sudsy hand on his jeans, pulled himself up to his full height and squeezed Ronnie's hand hard enough to hurt. Neither man spoke, but so much hostility passed between them that Ellen gazed anxiously at Lydia.

The deadlock was broken when a noise beyond the house made Ellen look out through the window. 'Murdy's here!'

'It's like a sitcom,' Conall said.

Ellen laughed with pleasure. 'You should visit more often. Usually, the lads avoid Lydia like the plague.'

There was a startled silence at the astuteness of this observation. Even Ronnie seemed surprised.

'If you stay long enough'—Ellen's eyes twinkled—'Raymond will be getting on a flight from Stuttgart.'

Murdy hurried in and fixed Lydia in his sights. 'Flan's after ringing about the fancy car with the Dublin reg. Have you bought a Lexus?'

'No, it belongs to my friend here.'

'Conall Hathaway.' Conall fixed Murdy with a flinty smile.

'Good to meet you.' Murdy was smiley and overeager. He always went a bit mental when he smelled money. 'Any friend of the sister's and all that. Do you work together, or is it more of a personal thing?'

He bombarded Conall with probing questions. He was desperate to piece things together: how much was Conall worth? How much power did Lydia have over him? What could he, Murdy Duffy, get out of it?

'What's brother number three like?' Conall asked Lydia, in full hearing of Ronnie and Murdy.

'Raymond? Great fun. Full of hilarious stories.'

'I hate him already,' Conall drawled.

Katie didn't want to wake up. She didn't want to go to work. Everything was shit. If it wasn't for poor Wayne Diffney's career relaunch, she wouldn't bother.

When she saw the note lying just outside her front door, she deduced it was from Fionn but her heart didn't bother to lift. Her heart would never lift again. She unfolded the piece of paper and ignored the small, dark green sprig that floated from it.

I'm sorry.

Yeah, right.

I will call again. Depend on it.

I don't think so.

Please accept this gift.

Another Conall, thinking he could buy his way out of things. Anyway, what gift? Casting a glance around the landing, she could see no flowers or chocolates, no box of flimsy, ridiculous underwear.

She crumpled the note into a ball and threw it over her shoulder into her flat, then locked her front door behind her.

There was a weed on the floor by the stairs. She should pick it up and bin it, but instead she flattened it to a pulp with the red sole of her Louboutin.

Why had she told everyone at work about Fionn? They'd be dying to hear how she'd got on with him. She couldn't handle the thought of their pity, so she decided she'd lie. Lie and be vague and airy. Yes, he called in, she'd say. Yes, he was very good-looking. No, he was a bit of a fool. No, she didn't sleep with him. No, she wouldn't see him again.

No special make-up tonight. All Katie wore on her face was an expression of lemon-sucking disappointment.

Shortly after nine, frenzied knocking started up at her door. It could be a balaclavaed man with a harpoon in his hand and evil in his heart, but Katie opened it anyway. What did she care? Invade her home, violate her person . . . she no longer gave a shite. Nevertheless, she wasn't exactly surprised to discover Fionn, golden and radiant, smiling a full beam of love right into her upturned face.

'I got delayed,' he said.

By twenty-four hours and twenty years, she thought.

'Can I come in?'

'No. You could have come in last night, but sadly you didn't avail of that opportunity.'

'Last night,' he said, 'I had something to do and it took longer than I thought it would. But did you get the rue?'

'The what?'

'The rue.'

Yes, that's what she thought he'd said.

'It's a herb. I left you a sprig last night.'

She remembered the weed that she'd crushed with her shoe this morning.

'I don't know where it came from,' he said urgently. 'I don't grow it, it's poisonous. But when I was desperate last night, trying to write how sorry I was, it appeared in my pocket. You must forgive me.'

Tosh. 'You're a flake.'

'Yes! And a chancer, a messer, an immature moron and, most of all, a fucking eejit. But I'm ready to change. Because of you.'

She was silenced. This was a really impressive apology. Way more anguished and convincing than anything Conall had ever rustled up.

'Please forgive me.'

Day 26

CONALL WAS READING his BlackBerry. Idly, he scrolled down through assets tied up in foreign banks . . . then something made him look up. A young woman was being led to his booth. It took a moment for him to recognise Lydia. In her short skirt, high heels and heavy eye make-up, she was a totally different person. Sexier than he could have imagined.

He abandoned his screen and sat up.

Lydia was trailing three other girls, all of them shiny and fragrant and giggly, but none as sexy as her. Behind them were a couple of drab men, who barely registered.

'Mr Hathaway. Your guests.' The hostess smiled and withdrew.

Conall leaned forward to kiss Lydia on the cheek but she had twisted her head round, deep in an assessment of how their booth measured up compared to every other one in the club. He watched her scanning the room, noticing their lofty vantage point above the dance floor and their proximity to the stairs for the pool.

'This is a good table,' she concluded.

'The best in the place,' he said. Because he'd requested it. And paid for it. No point leaving that sort of thing to chance.

Then she seemed to remember the other people she was with. 'Oh yeah, Poppy, Shoane, Sissy, Conall.'

They were sweet but showed little interest in him—very different from any other occasion when he'd met a girl's circle of friends for the first time. He'd be presented and paraded like a prize bullock, his girl-friend so proud of him and so desperate for him to like her friends. This couldn't be more different. He was just a handy fool who hap-pened to be a member of Float.

Lydia summoned the two lads forward from where they'd been lurk-ing behind the girls.

They were cautious, even nervous. 'This is Steady Bryan.'

'Pleased to meet you, Steady Bryan.'

Steady Bryan looked pained at being thus addressed.

'And this is Jesse, Sissie's boyfriend.'

'Good to meet you, man.' Jesse was bright-eyed and eager. He sounded South African.

'Get in there,' Lydia said, and there was an eager stampede into the booth. It was only thanks to some nimble footwork by Conall that he managed to insert himself in front of Shoane and thereby next to Lydia.

A hovering waitress, a tall blonde girl with a yard of tanned leg on display, murmured, 'Should I open the champagne now, Mr Hathaway?'

He smiled his assent.

In silence, they watched the ritual of the champagne being removed from the ice bucket and opened and poured.

Glasses were seized. 'A toast,' someone cried.

'To Lydia for getting us in here!'

'No, what's your man's name?' Conall heard Steady Bryan ask.

'Conall Hathaway,' Lydia said, as though she wasn't sitting right beside him.

'To Conall Hathaway!'

'OK! To Conall Hathaway!'

Conall smiled. He knew when he was being mocked.

Conall fingered his BlackBerry in his pocket. Could he . . .? Just a quick look? Would it be so bad? After all, there was no one there to care. There was no one but him in the booth: everyone had peeled away. Within moments he was openly answering emails.

He hadn't seen Lydia in about an hour. She, Jesse and the other three girls had swept off to dance and although he hadn't planned to dance himself—he had some dignity—Lydia had pressed her hand firmly against his chest and said, 'You stay here and talk to Steady Bryan.'

But Steady Bryan wasn't a scintillating conversationalist. He seemed so freighted by his forthcoming marriage that he could barely speak. He muttered something about a cigarette and that was the last Conall had seen of him.

'How are you doing for drinks here?' The waitress was back.

'Ah . . . another bottle, I suppose,' he said.

'Sure thing.'

As soon as she'd disappeared, Conall started to have serious doubts. It was so long since he'd seen Lydia, she and her friends could have left for all he knew.

He'd had enough. He didn't like it here. He was a member of every club in Dublin, but he didn't normally frequent them and this place seemed worse than most. He'd noticed he wasn't the only man in Float with a posse of much younger women; the only difference was that his girls weren't Russian. All of a sudden, Conall felt foolish and exploited and exploiting, and really quite miserable. He was almost unable to consider failure but his heart wasn't in this. You choose your battles and he no longer cared about winning this one.

Out of nowhere, he thought of Katie.

Katie leaned forward in her seat as the opening sequence of *Your Own Private Eden* appeared on screen. Loads of them were crowded into the tiny edit suite: Jemima, Grudge, Grainne Butcher, Mervyn Fossil, Alina, and any number of techies and runners. They were all squashed together on the couch, almost sitting on top of each other. This was just a rough cut—music still had to be added—but it was fairly momentous because until now no one other than Grainne had seen a full show.

And there was the first shot of Fionn! Standing on a hill gazing moodily at the horizon. Katie squeezed his hand, which was sweaty with nerves.

Rigid with concentration, Katie carefully watched the monitor, praying that the programme wouldn't be shite. What if it was? What would she say? *Brave*, that was a good word. *Astonishing*, that was another.

Anxiously, she had to admit that the camera didn't do Fionn justice; he was far more beautiful in real life. And the piece about starting your own compost heap wasn't really for her. But when they moved to the next segment—Fionn rambling through a farmers' market, talking through seasonal produce, the screen filled with plenty of close-ups of him slowly handling and rubbing phallic vegetables with his big hands—Katie felt some interesting sensations.

'Wow,' she murmured, and Fionn looked at her gratefully.

Now and again the camera cut to scenes of Fionn spontaneously producing pebbles or herbs or crystals from his pockets and gifting them to random passers-by. The reaction of the recipients was variously startled, receptive and interested, and often the random gift would be curiously appropriate in their life. These little human vignettes became a recurring motif throughout the show, and when Fionn once again reached into his on-screen pocket, Katie found she was actually excited. What was going to emerge? What would it mean to the person?

'That jacket should have its own show,' Katie said, and the room exploded with good humour.

You couldn't fake that. From her own job, Katie could tell the difference between hype and genuine belief in a product. To her, *Your Own Private Eden* felt right. Obviously, its success would all depend on viewing figures, which depended on time slots, which depended on advertising, which depended on viewing figures. A chicken-and-egg kind of thing. It was very tricky to make a success of a television show. So much came down to luck.

A home-improvement programme. I mean, Matt thought afterwards, with some acrimony, if that's not safe, then what is? She wasn't even particularly attractive, the presenter, Rhoda Stern. Well, obviously she didn't have two heads either but her shtick was plain-talking advice, where she spelled out every mistake people had made in their home decorating.

Matt and Maeve were lying on their couch, watching with some sympathy as a young couple—not dissimilar to themselves—had their bedroom decor mocked by Rhoda.

'I don't think it's so bad,' Maeve said. 'The curtains are nice.'

'But!' Rhoda shouted. (Because presenters always shouted in those shows.) 'There *is* something that saves this room from being a total disaster!' The camera panned back to show a super-king-sized bed. 'Mmmm'—Rhoda licked her lips—'I know what I'd like to do in that bed.' She gave a suggestive sidelong glance at the camera. 'I'd like to sleep for twelve hours straight.'

But it was too late. Something in that suggestive glance had awoken the beast. All of a sudden, Matt was aware of stirrings. *Down there.* In his groin. *Stop*, he ordered himself. *I command you to stop.* But it carried on, like it had a mind of its own. He shifted slightly so that Maeve wouldn't notice, but that just gave it more room to expand and it began to jut against his underwear, making a bid for freedom.

Interest rates, Matt thought desperately. *Root-canal surgery.* Anything to stop his body from betraying him like this. *Mouse droppings. Gangrene* . . .

Beside him, he felt Maeve tense up. She'd noticed. Then she twisted herself round to see into his hot face.

'Matt . . .?' She looked almost confused.

Without another word, she slid from the couch, taking care that no part of her body came into contact with his region then, moments later, he heard the rushing of taps in the bathroom.

'I'm just going to have a bath,' Maeve called, in a fake-cheery voice.

'Enjoy it,' Matt called back, forcing similarly upbeat tones.

He heard the bathroom door being shut firmly, and he slumped back onto the couch, feeling quite hopeless. I am a man, he thought. I'm an animal. I'm programmed to respond in certain ways to certain stimuli. I can't help it. I've no control over it.

I've no control over anything.

I've just come to a shocking realisation: Matt's and Maeve's heartbeats are in perfect harmony, but nothing of a sexual nature has happened between them for a long, long time.

Sitting on the loo, Lydia stared at her phone. Eight missed calls. Four messages. All from Flan Ramble.

Bollocks. Just when she was enjoying herself.

But no, she wasn't going, not this time. Murdy could deal with it. Ronnie could deal with it. *Mum* could deal with it. After all, if there was nothing wrong with her, there was no need for Lydia to leave Float and rush down to Boyne in the middle of the night. Anyway, she was way too pissed to drive. Let them try to manage without her for once. Let them find out that she, Lydia, was right and they were all wrong . . . Pleasantly adrift in her little reverie of self-righteous self-pity, she got a fright when her phone rang.

Flan Ramble again. But no, it wasn't. It was—

'Mum?'

'Lydia?'

'Are you OK?'

'Um . . . no.' Her voice was small and pitiful. 'I did something and I don't remember doing it and the guards are here and I'm scared.'

'Oh God, Mum. You didn't kill someone, did you?'

'No. No.' She sounded less than certain.

'OK, I'm on my way.'

Conall was still in the booth. Sending emails, by the look of things. What a tool. 'I've got to go,' she said. 'Something's after happening. Thanks for tonight.'

'Wait, wait, what's going on?'

'It's Mum.'

'Is she OK?'

'Yeah. But, like . . . upset.'

'You don't need to go. Two of your brothers are right there.'

'You saw what they're like.'

'You're not planning to drive?'

'I'll get a taxi. One of the lads will do me a favour.'

Conall stood up. 'I'll drive you.'

'You? Aren't you over the limit?'

'Pink champagne isn't my thing. Do you want to say goodbye to your friends?'

Lydia thought about it for a moment. But they were all so drunk, and the whole Mum thing—they'd never really got it.

'No, let's just go.'

Day 25

'SO! YOUNG MR GEARY! How close are we to finalising the deal with your Bank of British Columbia?'

Matt had been summoned to the Office of Fear, to account to Kevin Day, the MD, for all the money he'd spent trying and failing to flog a system to the Bank of British Columbia.

The trio of Edios bigwigs—the MD, the finance director and the chairman—were gathered in Kevin's office and they were keen to talk to Matt. No warning had been given.

'You've shelled out a fair few bob,' the finance director said, tapping a page in front of him and fixing Matt with an assessing stare.

'Gotta spend it to make it.' Could they see the sweat on his face, gleaming beneath the harsh overhead lights?

'How soon will it close?' Kevin Day asked.

How soon? It was over ten days since anyone at the bank had even returned his calls. 'I reckon,' Matt said, gazing up at a ceiling corner. 'I'd say we should have it wrapped up in the next week.'

'You do, do you?' More shrewd looks from the finance director. Matt's bowels spasmed. God, he was afraid. He should have been expecting this; he didn't know why he hadn't prepared himself.

'Good, good, within the week. Excellent,' the chairman said. 'Tell me, Matt, how's morale?'

Morale was rock-bottom. Matt and the team had poured boundless energy into this deal without any sign of a return, yet they hadn't been cut loose to lick their wounds and move forward.

'Morale?' Matt flashed a cheesy grin and felt a line of sweat trickle down his back. 'Morale is great!'

The perfect prospect was right there in front of Matt. An elderly man was all goofed up with the automatic till in Tesco. He couldn't get his bar codes to scan and he didn't know he had to weigh his apples. He looked confused and quite frightened by the hostile vibes from the arsey queue that had built up behind him. Absolute bloody godsend. Matt could go in and gently point out the apples on the screen and show him where the bar code on his biscuits was.

But he kept right on going and waited for another till.

No Act of Kindness today. Or ever again. No point. Fucking things didn't work. And he was going to tell Maeve. When he got home tonight she'd ask, like she always asked, what today's Act of Kindness had been and he would tell her he hadn't done one. Just like that. No explanations, no anxious apologies. He'd make it way clear that he'd had a tailor-made opportunity and he'd walked right past it. Spurned it. See what she had to say to that.

'How was your day?' Matt asked Maeve.

'Oh, you know.'

Go on, ask me, ask me.

He was ready, he was braced, he was pumped.

But she didn't. Nor did she offer details of her own AOK and that was strange too. Things got stranger still when the time came for bed and they got into their sleeping clothes and she didn't produce their Trio of Blessings notebooks out of her drawer.

No explanation was offered and in the end Matt cracked. He had to know what was going on. 'Er, Maeve, no Trio of Blessings tonight?'

'Nope.'

'Are we giving it up?'

'Yip.'

'Why?'

'It's not working.'

And then he was really scared.

Conall pulled into a service station on the outskirts of Boyne. 'We'll get some stuff for the drive home to Dublin.'

They hadn't eaten properly all day, had just drunk endless cups of tea in Ellen's kitchen. The place had become Crisis HQ and had been over-run with people—Buddy Scutt and Flan Ramble and various guards, as well as Murdy and Ronnie.

Lydia had urged Conall to leave, had told him that she'd make her own way back to Dublin, but he'd said he had such a good signal on his BlackBerry that he'd stay. So she let him. She couldn't help but notice— and it was fiercely annoying—that everyone was taking her far more seriously now that Conall was hanging around.

He clicked away on his BlackBerry and nobody said he was rude; then, when Ellen went to the bathroom, he made an announcement to the full room. 'Listen up. An MRI scan. That's what Ellen needs. That'll give a better idea of how things are.'

'What's that you said? An MRI scan?'

'What does that do?'

'It gives a photo of her brain,' Lydia said tightly. No one had listened when she'd asked for it, but because a rich man who drove a Lexus sug-gested it, suddenly everyone was all ears. 'It'll show up the damaged parts and then she can get treatment.'

'How do we get one of them?'

'Her GP refers her.'

'Except he won't,' Lydia said.

'Can you sort her out with an MRI scan?' Ronnie narrowed his eyes at Buddy Scutt.

'Aaaah.' Buddy shifted in his chair. 'I suppose I could.'

'Why didn't you do it before now?' Ronnie hissed.

'Yeah,' Murdy sneered. 'Why didn't you?'

'I didn't think there was anything wrong with her. Neither did you.'

'We could sue you for this,' Murdy said.

'Boys, boys, less of the handbags.' Conall shook his head. 'You're all to blame. Lydia's the only one who's tried to help.'

'I can fight my own battles,' Lydia said hotly.

But, obviously, she couldn't.

Conall had dozed off in an armchair and slept away the afternoon, and only when the evening shadows began to fall did Lydia wake him.

'We're going home,' she said.

'OK.' A bit dazed, he stood up.

They'd driven less than a mile when he pulled into the service station. Lydia, still in her short skirt from the night before, attracted a lot of attention as she prowled the aisles, gathering up smoothies and bags of popcorn.

At the till she rejoined Conall, who was trying to control an armload of ice creams and sweets.

'Give me them,' she said. 'I'll pay. Least I can do.'

They sat, parked in the forecourt, eating their Magnums.

He crunched briskly through his, shattering the chocolate coating without a second thought.

'I like to eat mine slooowww.' She flashed a glance from under her lashes—then she stopped. It wasn't right to torment him. 'Thanks, you know, for this. Driving me down and staying all day. How did you know about MRI scans?'

'I got Eilish to find out. Didn't take her long. Your mum should have had one months ago. I don't know why she didn't.'

'Because her doctor is a gobshite and my brothers didn't want to know.'

'They know now.'

'Yeah, well . . . thanks for saying it. And thanks for last night.'

'Did you like Float?' Conall started on his second Magnum.

She thought about it. 'Not really. It was sort of sleazy. I just wanted to go because I couldn't.'

'We always want what we can't have.'

'Like you with me.'

He laughed but didn't answer.

'You've money, you've a house in Wellington Road, you're . . . you know . . .' She waved a hand up and down his body. 'For an old bloke, you're not bad-looking. You could get plenty of girls. Why are you hanging around, pestering me?'

'You're nice-looking.' He paused. 'Very nice-looking. And even though you're not pleasant, you're interesting.'

'When will it all go weird and I'll suddenly be mad about you?'

'Actually, I would have thought it would have happened by now. Most girls . . . me coming to see their sick mother. And rescuing you, doing the middle-of-the-night drive. That stuff is normally pretty effective.'

'So when will you go off me?'

It was starting to happen already. Last night in Float—had it only been last night?—had shown him how mismatched they were. 'When I've had sex with you.'

She laughed. At least he was honest.

Eventually, she spoke. 'All right.'

'All right what?'

'Sex. Let's do it.'

'You fancy me?'

She hesitated. 'I think I might. A bit.' She paused again. 'I guess I'm curious. I think.'

Suddenly, she was being pulled towards him and his mouth lowered itself to meet hers. He smelled different. More grown-up. Gilbert had been a great man for statement aftershaves, ones that surrounded him like a pungent cloud. Andrei smelled of man-body and sweat and lust. But Conall smelled of . . . sophisticated lives. He smelled of money. And ice cream, but only briefly.

Their heart vibrations are not in harmony. Lydia's beat is a nanosecond behind Conall's, so the start of hers bites off the end of his. But it's an interesting, edgy, overlapping one-two rhythm that in many ways is more seductive than harmony. Fascinating.

Day 24

'Big night last night, Matt?'

'What?' Matt realised that Salvatore was talking to him.

'Where's my smile?'

'What?'

'Why the long face? One too many amarettos last night?'

'Nothing's up. Eee-yargh!'

Matt waited until Salvatore went back to his own desk, then let his face sink down again, until it was as gloomy as his feelings.

Doing the AOKs had been a pain in the arse, but Maeve nixing them was far more unsettling. Everything was moving in the wrong direction. Things were supposed to be getting better, but they seemed to have doubled back on themselves and started getting worse. He wasn't sure he could do this again.

He picked up a newspaper that someone had left lying around and his heart lifted slightly when he read that another lump of ice had come crashing to earth, this latest one in Lisbon. Lisbon. See? Another capital city. The very strange thing was that—as yet, anyway—no one had been hurt by these massive ice boulders. They came hurtling out of the sky and made shit of cars and roofs and public monuments, but no human being had strayed into their path. If—no, *when*—Matt told himself hopefully, *when* one landed in Dublin, it would definitely land on a person, a particular person, and it would knock the living bejayzus out of them. If there was any justice. Which, of course, there wasn't. The descent back into despair began again and intensified when he read that scientists were investigating the phenomenon and they'd concluded that the icy missiles definitely weren't the opening salvos from a hostile alien race. The theory the boffins liked best was that the lumps of ice were coming from planes flying overhead.

Matt's phone rang and his nerves flared. With his heart banging in his throat, he spoke. 'Edios. Matt Geary.'

'Matt?' It was Natalie. 'Are you leaving Edios?'

'No. Why?'

'I've been head-hunted.'

The lizard part of his brain, the old instinctive response that alerted him to life-threatening danger, suddenly kicked into action.

'By Edios,' she said. 'Heading up the sales team, chasing new business, conducting negotiations until they sign.'

'That's my job.'

'That's what I thought. Sorry, Matt.'

They were sacking him; there was no other explanation. They wouldn't be bringing Nat in to head up a second sales team, not in the current climate when there was barely enough work for one. Suddenly, Matt understood that yesterday's summons to the Office of Fear had been for the gruesome threesome to settle their heads on the matter.

It all came back to that Bank of British Columbia thing, Matt realised. Everything that had gone weird and wrong could be blamed on that. It was his own fault. He'd been affected by a perplexing paralysis whereby he didn't have the strength of will to bend the bank into buying and he didn't have the guts to call their bluff, and because of that everyone was stuck.

Christ, though. To be sacked. He'd never before been sacked. It was always the other way round; employers loved him, and whenever he'd tried to leave they always begged him to change his mind. A sacked Matt? He didn't know that person.

Money. Without an income, what would he and Maeve do? Maeve's salary was a joke, like pocket money. He'd have to get another job but, for the first time in his life, he felt he wouldn't be able to. He wasn't the person he used to be. There was no way he could go into a room, the way he had once upon a time, and face down an interview board and convince them that what their business needed was him, Matt Geary.

It wasn't just the money that was a worry. It was Maeve. This would be the finish of her. She saw disaster in everything; one piece of bad luck was a sign that their life together was cursed.

He had a terrible sense that all control had long disappeared, that he and Maeve were heading towards some terrible dark finale. Goodness and happiness were gone for ever and nothing could be retrieved. This was going to end, and end terribly. The last three years had been spent trying to dodge their fate, but it was rushing up to meet them.

His phone rang. Feeling like he was in the middle of a bad dream, he answered and . . . oh, the irony . . . it was head of procurement at the Bank of British Columbia. They were buying the system.

It was too late. He'd taken too long. He'd spent too much money on the chase. But for the sake of the team he had to go through the motions. Yell. Punch the air. Shout, 'Ouff,' many times. 'For a minute there I thought the bastards were going to bail on us!' He had to pick up Salvatore and twirl him round. Send Cleo out to buy champagne. And at least when he started crying, heaving out some awful feelings from his solar plexus—and for a few petrifying moments, being simply unable to stop—it had been put down to tears of relief.

It was almost five thirty before the call came: he was to present himself at the managing director's office a.s.a.p. The old Matt would have made some quip to the others: 'I may be some time.' But the old Matt was no more. He said nothing to anyone. He'd never see them again; he wouldn't be allowed back into the office to say his goodbyes; he'd be escorted from the building without his special mug and his picture of

Maeve. But it didn't matter. It was only stuff; they were only people.

At least, thanks to Natalie, he knew what was coming. Without her call he might be skipping off to the Office of Fear, thinking he was going to get a pat on the back for landing a big sale. And yet, as his legs moved forward without any input from him, it was impossible to believe that things had got so bad.

He'd arrived. He knocked, the door was opened and in he went. Serious faces all round. Matt bowed his head and waited for the executioner's axe to fall.

But it was worse than he'd expected. Oh, far, far worse.

Matt wasn't being sacked. Oh no. Matt was being promoted.

Day 10 (two weeks later)

LYDIA'S PHONE RANG. It was Conall.

'Where are you now?' she asked.

'Vietnam.'

She laughed out loud. 'No? For real?' In the last two weeks he'd gone from the company's HQ in Milan to its operational centres in Kuala Lumpur and Manila in Southeast Asia. 'Where's next?'

'Phnom Penh, then Cambodia.'

'You lucky bastard.'

'It's not as nice as it sounds.'

'Yeah, right. Flying first class, staying in hotels, getting room service. I *love* room service.'

'When I come back, we could go someplace with room service.'

'Whatever.'

'So what's going on?'

'The results of Mum's scan tomorrow. Buddy Scutt will explain all.'

'Good luck with that. Let me know.'

'Will do.'

Jemima tossed and turned in her bed, trying to find a position that didn't hurt. Grudge clambered up beside her and lay his head on her stomach. The heat he emitted was a great painkiller, so Jemima frequently told him. But she wriggled and couldn't settle and he wasn't surprised when she said, 'Forgive me, my darling Grudge, but I'm finding the weight of your head quite uncomfortable.'

Not surprised, no. But wounded, oh yes, very wounded. He bounded off the bed and stalked, rigid-necked, from the room to nurse his grievance in his basket. Then he tensed. Fionn! So finely tuned was Grudge's hatred that he could sense him even at a distance.

Fionn was down in the street with Katie. They were getting out— nay, *tumbling* out—of a taxi and trying to get their key into the front door; and here they came, padding up the stairs, giggling and mumbling. Coming home with the milk, to use a phrase of Jemima's, which Grudge didn't understand. Fionn and Katie didn't bring milk. They didn't bring anything, only sadness to his poor old mistress. Grudge shook his woolly head in disgust.

Until now, he had liked Katie—well, as much as he was able to like anyone—but her dalliance with Fionn showed a regrettable lapse in taste and judgment.

Trying to curl his lip in contempt, Grudge listened to the sniggering and whispering as the loved-up pair ascended the stairs in their stocking feet. Lots of 'Sssh's and stifled laughs. Unseemly.

They tiptoed past Grudge, hidden behind Jemima's door, growling softly. Now they would go into Katie's flat at the top of the house and have noisy relations.

Fionn hadn't slept a night in Jemima's flat for almost three weeks. He was practically living with Katie. This development had thrilled Grudge to his angry marrow—not only did he have Jemima all to himself again, but he could indulge in long sessions of sanctimonious disdain. What a fickle, feckless creature Fionn was. What a disloyal ingrate. Jemima had taken care of him through his vulnerable years but he had dropped her like a hot potato when he took up with the fragrant, large-bosomed Katie.

Poor Jemima tried to pretend she wasn't sad. 'Katie is such a sweet girl. So sensible. Although how long will she stick with Fionn? That's the question.'

Nowadays, they only saw Fionn when he called in to pick up his invitations to glamorous events. The first few times he'd pretended that it was a real visit; then Jemima had got wise. Now, she had taken to stacking the large, coloured, exciting-looking envelopes in a neat pile on the escritoire, and when Fionn breezed in he'd make straight for it and start tearing things open.

Grudge blamed Fionn's new glamorous life on that horrible pushy Grainne Butcher. She'd given Fionn's details to every PR agency in the country and told him to get his face 'out there' because the countdown to the first episode of *Your Own Private Eden* was under way. Only twelve days to go now and she wanted to build a 'buzz'.

Grudge couldn't bear the waiting. He just wanted the show to air and for it to get the slagging it so richly deserved. He'd seen the rough cut of the first episode and everyone—idiots!—had seemed to think it was good. It beggared belief! It was meant to be a gardening show, and instead there was some gobshite going round with a dirty jacket, producing weeds and stones from his pockets!

Your Own Private Eden would fail. It *must* fail.

Day 9

'MAEVE?'

'Mmm?'

Tell her, tell her, tell her. 'Ah . . .' *You useless plank, would you just tell her.* '. . . nothing.'

Head of international sales, that's what Matt was now. At least, that's what it said on the stiff new business cards he'd been presented with in the Office of Fear, the day the Bank of British Columbia had said they were buying the Edios system. A storm of congratulations on his promotion had rained down on Matt from the Edios bigwigs. His hand had been shaken by the finance director, he'd been clapped on the back by the chairman and he'd tried to keep his despair off his face as a stream of enthusiastic information flowed from Kevin Day, the MD. 'Fighting fire with fire, that's the way to deal with this recession. You know what "international" means, don't you, son? That's right—lots of travel! All those lovely new markets out there in the Far East, just waiting to be conquered, and who better to lead the raiding parties than our very own Matt Geary?'

No hike in pay, naturally. 'A recession on, son, but you can't beat the prestige and, of course, *lots of travel.*'

Maeve would have a total freaker. When he told her.

But two weeks had passed and he still hadn't said anything. Nat was working out her notice in Goliath; there were only ten more working days before she showed up to oust Matt from his desk.

Every night he went to bed weary with the weight of another day having elapsed without him telling Maeve, and every morning he knew with sick dread that he had to do it *right now*. Then a minute would pass, then another and another, and then somehow, amazingly, it would be bedtime again and the words would still be locked inside him.

Turning down the new post had never been an option—it was a done deal, his old job was in the past, it had been taken from him and given to someone else—yet he couldn't possibly accept it either, and there was no way, absolutely no way, out of the bind.

Today stretched ahead of him and he knew he wouldn't say anything and he'd go to bed tonight and he'd wake up tomorrow and he wouldn't tell Maeve and the day would pass and end and a new one would start and new days would keep on starting until Nat showed up in Edios and a plane would be waiting at Dublin Airport ready to fly Matt to China, and what would happen then?

Katie gazed into her bathroom mirror, inspecting the damage. It was amazing really, she thought, that she didn't look more wrecked. She'd been getting by on no more than four hours' sleep a night. Her skincare regime had gone to hell. She was eating crap at all the wrong times: chocolate biscuits for breakfast, cheese on toast at four in the morning. And she wasn't lifting a finger in exercise. Apart from sex and, to be fair, she was doing an awful lot of that.

'Is there no milk?' Fionn called from the kitchen.

'Where would it come from?' She leaned on the doorjamb and watched him foostering with a tea bag. 'You've been with me since I finished work yesterday. Unless I went out in the middle of the night to buy it.'

'I'll just nip down to Jemima and get some.'

'Don't.' It wasn't right to treat her like a shop.

'Why not? She won't mind.'

She might, though. She just wouldn't let Fionn know. 'Drink it black; it won't kill you.'

'We'll have to get stuff.' Vaguely, he waved a hand in the direction of the empty breadbin. 'Food and that.'

'How about tonight? Quiet night in?'

He frowned. Was she serious? Then they both burst out laughing. Every single night there was something. There was nothing—*nothing*—in Dublin that Fionn didn't get invited to: movie premieres, birthday parties, car launches, hotel openings. He kept all his invitations stuck in the frame of Katie's mirror and often he stood before it to admire them. 'I spent all those years in the back-arse of nowhere,' he'd say. 'Look at what I was missing.'

Dementia. There it was, in black and white and shades of grey, a digital photo of Ellen Duffy's brain, showing clearly that she had multiple-infarct dementia.

'So she doesn't have Alzheimer's?' Murdy asked.

'No.' Buddy Scutt latched on to the one piece of good news.

'Actually, she might.' Lydia knew everything about it from the hours she'd spent trawling the Net. 'Sometimes multi-infarct can coexist with Alzheimer's. It could even trigger it.'

'So what's this multiple-infarct thing when it's at home?' Ronnie asked Buddy Scutt.

'She's had a ton of mini-strokes,' Lydia said.

'She did not have a stroke,' Murdy said. 'We'd know about it.'

'Mini-strokes, mini-strokes! They're only small—the clue is in the name—but they've damaged the flow of blood to parts of her brain.'

'Is that right?' Ronnie addressed Buddy Scutt, who was sitting on the far side of his desk, looking cowed and embarrassed. As well he might, Lydia thought darkly.

Buddy cleared his throat. 'Multiple-infarct dementia results from a series of small strokes, which damage the flow of blood to parts of the brain.'

'Sis just said that.'

'You'd better fix that so.' This from Ronnie. Just because he spoke softly didn't make him any less menacing.

'We can certainly ensure that it no longer happens. We'll start her immediately on medication to thin the blood and end the seizures.'

'And you'll fix the damage, Doc?' Ronnie was quite insistent.

'Ah, you see'—Buddy Scutt twisted miserably in his chair—'the damage already caused is irreversible.'

'Irreversible?' Ronnie spoke even more quietly. 'Dear me, no, that won't do at all.'

'Believe me, Ronald, if I could fix your mother, I would.'

'Sis here came to you nearly a year ago looking for a scan and you sent her packing. A whole year of Mum having them multiple things and her brain getting more and more damaged.'

'We'll sue the arse off you!' Murdy declared. 'That Beemer for starters.'

'Shut up,' Lydia said wearily. 'We're not going to sue him.'

'He should be struck off.'

'But he won't be. They stick together, doctors and whoever are meant to strike them off. The likes of us don't stand a chance.'

'We might be able to arrange a little extrajudicial punishment all the same,' Ronnie said, almost as if he was talking to himself.

'You shut up too. Forget about revenge.'

The brothers were so on-side now it was almost sickening. All in the gang together: Operation Madzer Mother. Only Raymond, cushioned from the worst of things in Stuttgart, was still keeping his distance.

'What are we going to do, to take care of Mum?'

'Aaaahhhh . . .'

'What does Hathaway have to say about all this?' Ronnie asked.

'He really should get down here for a parlay,' Murdy said. 'So we can put a plan together. When's he back from Vietnam?'

'He still has to go to Cambodia,' Lydia said shortly. Love of God! *Hathaway?* He was nothing to Mum, no one, yet this pair were behaving like he was her saviour.

'Why don't we try putting a plan together ourselves?' Lydia suggested sweetly. 'And we can run it by Hathaway when he gets back.'

'Right.'

So there it was, Lydia thought, as she drove back to Dublin, finally alone to absorb the news. She'd known something terrible was wrong with Mum. She'd long passed the point of hoping she was imagining it, but to have it made official . . .

She'd been right. And everyone else had been wrong, and, although it wouldn't make Mum better, it was nice to be right.

But the waste, the awful, shameful waste. A whole extra year of Mum being eroded from within. Poor Mum.

And poor Lydia, she suddenly thought. Her mouth opened and she found herself howling, crying like a little girl, like her heart was breaking. She took one hand off the steering wheel and put it over her mouth, trying to stifle the shocking noise of her own grief. Tears poured down her face and blurred her vision and she kept on driving, because what else could you do?

three years ago

TWO DAYS AFTER Maeve returned from her honeymoon she met David in the corridor at work. Guiltily, she braced herself for him to hang his head woefully and sidle past her with dramatic sadness, as he had done every time their paths had crossed in the previous months, but this time, to her surprise, he advanced towards her, smiling.

'Welcome back, Maeve, or should I say Mrs Geary?' he said cordially. 'Nice honeymoon?'

'Um . . . yes . . .'

'Sorry I didn't show on the big day . . .'

'No! Please! Don't worry, I get it. Did you mind being invited? It was like if we don't invite you, you'll be pissed off; if we do invite you, you'll be pissed off.'

'Yeah, I know, I know.'

'I didn't mean to hurt you, David.' Fiercely, she said, 'You meant a lot to me. You're a good man. It was the last thing I ever wanted to do.'

'I know that.' Almost shamefaced, he said, 'I got you guys a wedding present.'

'Oh, David . . .'

'But I don't want to show up here with it. I'd feel a bit . . .'

'I know! Of course.'

'You could pick it up from my place.'

'Sure, like, whatever suits you.'

'Tonight?'

'Sure, why not?'

Actually, tonight suited her perfectly. Matt was going out for dinner with potential clients. Out of nowhere, a little voice in her head piped up that it might be best if she didn't tell Matt about this. Obviously, he'd know after the event, with a brand-new wedding present sitting in the middle of their flat, but was there any need to tell him in advance? He might tell her she shouldn't bother, that David was in the past. But this was her chance to mend fences with David, to lessen her load of guilt.

Day 8

SOMETHING HAD HAPPENED. Before Katie had even got her key out of her bag, her mum had wrenched open the front door. Penny was quivering with rage. 'Your photograph was in the *Herald*,' she hissed. 'With your new boyfriend. What a thing to do to your father on his birthday.'

'Oh really?' Katie was excited. Over the course of her career, she'd been in the paper disappointingly few times. Considering the number of launches she went to and the high-calibre celebrity of people she worked with, you'd think it would happen more often. 'Was it nice?'

'No, it was not nice. You looked boss-eyed. And you're late. We're already sitting down.'

Katie swung into the dining room. They were all there: Naomi and Ralph and the kids, Dad at the head of the table. Even Charlie had turned up.

'God!' Katie recoiled dramatically. 'Haven't seen you since . . .?' Since her birthday. Ages ago.

'Happy birthday, Dad.' She slung him his present. 'Right! Show us this photo.'

'There are only two times in her life when a lady should appear in the press,' Penny said. 'On her marriage and on her death.'

'Is that a real rule?' Katie asked. 'Or did you just make it up?' Yet another way to make them all feel shit? 'So come on. Where is it?'

'We threw it out,' Penny said.

'You didn't?' Suddenly, she was quite riled. She'd be able to get a copy of it at work, but she wanted to see it now. 'What did you do that for?' Mean old cow.

Penny looked speculatively at Katie. 'Are you feeling all right?'

'Never better,' Katie said breezily. It was Fionn, he was her painkiller. Nothing could burst her bubble, not work, not a bitterly angry mother, nothing.

'And why, seeing as the entire country now knows about this romance, haven't we met this man?'

'It's just a fun, temporary thing.'

'Fun?' Penny's brows furrowed in alarm. 'Temporary?' She couldn't decide which was worse. 'Katie, please remember that a woman's good reputation is all she has.'

'I don't mean to be picky but I also have a flat, a car, a television—'

'Too small to matter,' Charlie interrupted.

'—thirty-eight pairs of shoes, a Lucy Doyle painting and two hundred euros in the bank.' And credit-card debts that ran to thousands but no need, no need *at all*, to get into that now.

'None of them count for anything if you've got a name for yourself. And he's a gardener? A manual worker? A lot younger than you?'

They must have given Fionn's age in the paper—some age, anyway: it could have been anything.

'Katie, you're a professional woman! How much does he earn?'

'Feck all,' Robert said, thinking of how much he and Penny paid their own gardener. 'At least Conall Hathaway had a proper job. Instead of being a young wastrel who's only with you for your money.'

'Fionn's making a television show.'

'A media whore.' Penny had obviously come across the phrase only recently. 'And Naomi says he lives with that old woman in your building? But he's not her son? Her grandson?'

'No. He's her foster—'

'Well, there it is, then,' Robert declared. Fionn clearly made a habit of attaching himself to wealthy older women.

'And he's living there rent-free?' Charlie asked.

'We don't actually know that—'

'Just pokes the oul' wan from time to time to keep her sweet,' Charlie said.

'Careful that he doesn't get you to change your will in his favour,' Ralph said, his first contribution to the conversation. 'And watch out for tea that tastes of bitter almonds.' He winked. 'Arsenic poisoning.'

'This is no laughing matter,' Penny said. 'Katie could be taken advantage of.'

'Basically, you all think that Fionn seduced me for my money and I'm so old and loveless and vulnerable that I think he really loves me?'

'Seduced?' Penny said anxiously.

'Seduced.'

The word hung in the air and Ralph muttered, 'You've done it now.'

'Mum.' Katie smiled. 'I have sex. I have done for many, many years. And Naomi smokes twenty cigarettes a day. And . . .' This was it, the moment she'd been waiting for, to reveal the secret that had come to her courtesy of Conall some months ago, to drop the bomb that would blow the whole respectable, rancorous family set-up wide open. Could she do it? '. . . and Charlie has a little boy that none of us are supposed to know about.'

three years ago

'WHERE'S EVERYONE?' Maeve asked, stepping into David's flat and noting the silence.

'Not home yet, I suppose. Go on in.' He gestured to the sitting room. 'You know where it is.'

Nothing had changed—the rough woven throw on the couch, the Tibetan tapestry hanging on the wall, the Moroccan rug on the old wooden floor, the beanbags, the peasant ceramics, the lava lamp, the guitar in the corner. Stuff and dust and loose tobacco everywhere.

'Have you still the same—'

'—flatmates? No. Marta went back to Chile and Holly went travelling. Two guys from Turkey now. You might meet them later.'

She wasn't planning on staying longer than an hour; but why talk about leaving when she'd only just arrived? He was so bright-eyed and happy to see her.

'Drink?' he asked.

'OK. Tea, thanks.'

'No, no. No. A *drink* drink. Not every day my ex-girlfriend gets married. Beer.'

He produced two Dos Equis and clambered beside her onto the couch. 'To old friends.' He clinked bottles.

'Old friends,' she repeated.

They drank in silence. 'Good honeymoon?' he asked.

'Oh, amazing!' Immediately, she wished she hadn't been so enthused.

'Malaysia, I hear. Tell me.'

'Well—'

'An obvious military police presence?' David prompted.

'I didn't see any sign of it,' Maeve said truthfully.

'Didn't you?' He sounded surprised. Disappointed, actually.

'But Islam's in the driving seat?'

'God, I dunno, David. Some of the women were veiled, some weren't.'

'Interesting.' Thoughtfully, he drummed his fingers on his chin. 'It'll come back to bite them, but for the moment Malaysia's doing a canny job of walking that line.'

She knew what line he was talking about, the one between American cultural imperialism and fundamentalist Islam. She cared about world politics too, but suddenly she understood that David had no interest in positive interpretations; it was like he wanted everything to be as bad as it could possibly be.

'I've missed you, Maeve.' He reached out his hand and began to twirl his fingers in the curls at her neck. She sat very still. This felt wrong, but she'd been so cruel she couldn't add to the hurt by asking him to stop.

'I hope that we can be friends, David.'

'Like the old days?'

'Like the old days, exactly! And when you get to know Matt properly, you'll love him—'

With an unexpected move, David was right in front of her and, to her shock, she realised he was about to kiss her. Quickly, she turned her head so that his mouth landed on her ear. 'David, sorry, you know we can't do this.'

He nuzzled at her neck and she said, 'I think I'd better go.'

'But you haven't seen your wedding present.'

She stood up. 'Don't worry about it. Give it to me some other time. Sorry, but I'm going to go.'

'There's nothing to be scared of.' He seemed surprised and wounded. 'After what you did to me, I just want to give you a wedding present.'

'I know, it's just—'

'Come on, come and see it.'

'Why? Where is it?'

'In there.' He pointed towards his bedroom.

'Oh . . . no, David,' she said haltingly. 'Just bring it out here.'

'I can't, it's too big. Just come in.'

'Sorry, David, I don't feel right . . .'

He sighed heavily. 'Have you any idea how this is making me feel?' He looked at her with injured eyes. 'I'm not going to hurt you. Come on, it's cool, you'll love it.'

'OK.' This was David, *David*.

As he opened the bedroom door, he said, 'Close your eyes.'

She felt the weight and heat of his hands on her shoulders, guiding her forward.

'Such a big deal.' She laughed. 'This'd better be worth it.'

Day 6

ROSIE HAD HER EYES tightly shut. She heard the whizzy sound of jeans being taken off, then the rustle of cotton (that must be his shirt going). She lay, naked and rigid, wondering what would happen next, and when Andrei's cold hand landed on her stomach, she jumped.

'Is OK,' he crooned. 'All OK, beautiful Rosie.'

He was kissing her, her face, her mouth, her throat. Somewhere out there was his . . . *thing*. She knew what an erection was like; she'd done six months on the geriatric ward, where dementia-riddled men playing with themselves were ten a penny.

She had always feared her life would come to this, ever since the age of six, when she'd watched *Grease* and seen that Olivia Newton-John had to become a bad girl to keep her man.

You better shape up . . .

Being virtuous and ladylike didn't seem to be keeping a hold of Andrei, so she was gambling her virginity and going for broke.

Her eyes still closed, she could feel Andrei *at* himself. Probably putting on the condom.

It's six days too soon but could I jump the gun here? It's the best chance I've had so far. Never mind the condom, that could be dealt with, no bother. A couple of brave little sperms could leak; all you need is one, after all. But, entre nous *and forgive me for being picky, I don't really like Rosie. Andrei's grand, a bit intense, God love him, but a decent man at heart. I wouldn't mind him. But not her.*

Rosie screwed her eyes up tighter. In a moment, Andrei would clamber on top of her and he'd plunge it right in. Her entire body tensed at the thought. It would be awful, but worth it and . . . What was taking him so long? She was starting to get chilly. 'What's happening?'

'I don't know,' Andrei said. Something was wrong.

She opened her eyes. 'What?'

'I don't know . . .'

She sat up, leaned on her elbows and looked down. What was that shy, floppy, pink and white marshmallow thing?

Andrei turned and buried his face in his pillow. 'I'm sorry, my Rosie.' His voice was muffled but there was no mistaking his anguish.

Rosie went cold with horror. This was the worst possible thing she could have done, showing up at Andrei's flat and undressing herself and lying on his bed like a haddock on a slab. He wasn't that sort of man.

'I understand,' she said, trying to radiate calm and retrieve what she could. With men, you must never show fear. Not real fear. *Fake* fear, obviously, when it was called for, to make them feel like the big man. But at a time like this you must take control. 'You have too much respect for me.'

Pertly, she hopped off the bed and began to dress herself. Andrei's face was still plunged into his pillow.

'I'll pop the kettle on,' she said brightly. 'And I'll see you out in the sitting room.'

Conall tumbled onto the wide hotel bed and eased his shoes off. Better book an alarm call before he fell asleep. He could set his phone but he didn't know what time it was here in Manila. Then he had a terrible thought and groaned out loud: he'd forgotten to buy a shirt and under-wear today. It was over two weeks since he'd started crisscrossing Southeast Asia and his carry-on case barely held the basics. He'd run out of clean clothes for ever ago, but he wasn't in any place long enough to get his laundry done so since Jakarta he'd been buying and discarding as he went.

He'd have to ring the concierge. He'd have to make nice.

'Concierge desk. How may I help you, Mr Hathaway?'

'I have a special request.'

'Certainly, sir!'

Your man was thinking, *Girls!* Conall realised. He didn't want a girl. He had a lovely girlfriend at home. A vague impression of bosoms and feminine fragrance comforted him. Katie. No, not Katie. A new one now. Lydia, yes, his hard, shiny little diamond.

'I need a couple of shirts and some underwear.'

'Certainly, sir. Anything else, sir?'

'Well, actually . . .' Bronagh had sent an email reminding him of her birthday.

As you are my uncle, my godfather and the only millionaire in the family, I'd like a good present.

'Could you get a birthday present for a little girl?'

'What age?'

'Seven.' Or was it eight? One of those ones.

He woke with a terrible start. Where was he? A hotel room . . . could be any one of millions. Someone was knocking, that was what had woken him. Smacking his tongue against the roof of his mouth, trying to scare away the appalling dryness, he opened the door. It was a helpful young lad bearing Conall's new shirts and jocks and a pair of sapphire earrings for Bronagh. Conall pawed around in his pocket and found currency of some description, with which he despatched the youth.

He looked at the clock. Nearly 5 a.m. Might as well make phone calls now that he was awake and it was some sort of time in Ireland.

'Happy birthday, Bronagh!'

Bronagh sighed elaborately. 'Conall. A day late and a dollar short. As usual. My birthday was yesterday.'

'I'm in Asia. Today is tomorrow.'

'Then you're two days late.'

Christ, she was right.

'I'm eight years of age. You're my uncle and my godfather. I reminded you, I made it easy for you, and still you disappoint me.'

Holy Christ. This was too reminiscent of too many other phone calls.

'Better go now, hon. See you when I'm back.'

Quickly, he rang Lydia.

'Hathaway?' she said briskly. 'Are you home?'

'In Manila.'

'Again?'

'Yeah, I had to come back. A problem arose with the Cambodian—'

'Lalalalala. I can't hear you. Oooouuuuuuh!' She ceased wailing and asked cautiously, 'Is it safe? Have you stopped?'

'Yeah.' She'd told him not to talk to her about his work, that it was too boring. He could describe his hotel room to her, though, anytime he felt like. Or the breakfast buffets, especially the hot plates where they made the pancakes.

'When are you coming home?'

'Sometime next week.'

'You said it would be this weekend.'

'Like I said, things changed. The situa—'

'Whatever.'

Day 5 (early hours of)

ANDREI TURNED HIS PILLOW over again. For a few blessed moments, the cool cotton gave relief to his fevered face, then it wore off. He'd never known a night so long. He shifted and thrashed, unable to find escape from his tormenting thoughts. This was the issue: he had no idea if his marshmallow-textured failure was a mortifying one-off or if he was doomed for it to recur. He was so frightened of discovering the situation was ongoing that he wasn't sure he could chance having sex ever again.

Not that Rosie was likely to insist on any such thing—even if he could win her back, she was evidently repulsed by the sexual act . . . What a virtuous little flower she was. Such modesty was rare, yet she had offered herself up to him like a sacrifice on an altar. All of a sudden he was so humbled by how a good woman had gone bad in the name of love that he wept into his overheated pillow.

Oh! If only daylight would come.

But as the sun began to rise, Andrei's shame at failing to consummate the deed with Rosie began to soften and blossom into a new and unexpected emotion: gratitude. Of course he couldn't have committed such an abomination on his little petal! Not until they were married.

Or engaged, at any rate.

As pearly, early-morning light began to slip under his curtains, hope, beautiful hope, lifted him, and a course of action revealed itself, a daring but clear imperative. There could be no more Lydia. He needed to put himself beyond her reach for ever. As this vision became a convincing possibility, his load became light, almost airborne. Quietly, in order to not wake Jan, he extracted a roll of banknotes from a sock on the floor of the wardrobe. He showered, dressed and drank two cups of coffee, and he was actually in the hall, almost gone, almost safe, when the rattle of a key in the lock made his heart plunge. Lydia was home from work. The door pushed open and she landed into the hall. She looked at him, he looked at her and a whiplash of sex crackled around them.

'No,' he called, in terrible anguish. He threw himself at the open doorway. He had to escape, before she lured him in and ruined all his plans. He plunged headlong down the stairs, down, down, down; then he was in the street, walking fast until he was well beyond her reach.

He moved with purpose. He knew where he was going: a jeweller's in South Anne Street. He and Rosie had looked in the window one night, pointing out rings they liked, like people in a seventies soap opera.

He had a certain amount of time to kill—the shop didn't open until 9 a.m. and it was now only 6.35—but he remained clear-headed and focused, and by the time the jeweller rolled up the metal door guard, he was more sure than ever of the rightness of his path.

Andrei knew precisely which ring Rosie wanted. But he couldn't afford that. So he bought another one, the second cheapest in the shop. It was a simple band with a single diamond: sweet and humble, like Rosie herself. Then he made his way to her house, where he rang the bell and got down on one knee.

In answer to his prayers, it was Rosie and not one of her housemates who answered the door.

'Rosie,' he said, blind to the relief that rolled behind her eyes as he proffered the small velvet box. 'Will you marry me?'

'You're not going to believe it.' Fionn stalked into Katie's flat and threw a fax onto the kitchen table. 'Look at that.'

Katie smoothed out the crumpled page and gleaned the salient facts.

Channel 8 had put Fionn's show back by four weeks. They'd just managed to buy the rights to *DOA*, a hot US crime show, and had decided to run that in the slot they'd earmarked for *Your Own Private Eden*.

'Oh, poor Fionn.'

'There's heat around me,' Fionn said, obviously quoting Grainne. 'I'm on fire right now. But we've to wait another four weeks. And then it might be too late.'

Katie couldn't think of a thing to say. Once a network began messing with transmission dates, it was usually an indication of a lack of confidence and a reshuffling of their priorities. Even if they still had complete faith in the show, the trajectory of success was interfered with; something was lost that could never be retrieved.

'And what am I meant to do? We finish filming on Friday.'

Katie understood exactly what he meant: until the show aired, Excellent Little Productions had no idea whether or not it would be recommissioned. Should Fionn hang around and see what happened? Or should he go back, temporarily, to Pokey, to hold on to his customers? Katie's stomach lurched as she realised that uncertain times loomed. For Fionn's bank account. For Fionn's ego. Perhaps for Fionn's romance?

Day 4

'*Dzien dobry*, Andrei.' Jemima liked to greet those poor Polish boys in their native tongue. A small pleasantry that cost her nothing and might put a gloss on their day.

'*Dzien dobry*, Jemima. *Dzien dobry*, dog.' Andrei dropped to his knees and began wrestling happily with Grudge.

'My dear, you seem positively joyous.' *For once.*

'I'm gettingk married.'

'Congratulations! The lovely Rosemary?'

Andrei nodded and reddened with evident pride. 'We are lookingk for own place.'

Jemima said, with interest, 'I may be able to help you there. Shortly, my flat will be coming free.'

'You are movingk out? When?'

'In a week or so, I would imagine.'

'Good timingk. We are all going to Gdańsk on Friday, Jan, Rosie and I. When we come back, Rosie and I, we could move in then.'

'You're bringing Rosie to meet your family? How delightful. Now, you'll like the flat, but there is a condition attached.'

Well, Andrei thought sadly, wasn't there always?

'You must take care of my dog.'

'That's condition? That's all? You cannot take dog to new place?'

'Regrettably, no.'

'And your Fionn man? He will be moving out also?'

Yes, he just hadn't realised it yet.

'Fionn and Grudge don't see eye to eye, I'm afraid. Fionn is a grown man. All things considered, it's clear that Fionn will also be moving on.'

'I like this dog.' Andrei beamed. 'Rosie too will like. She like everyone.'

'Just one thing. You're quite sure you and Rosemary wouldn't like a fresh start in an entirely new location? Far away from Star Street?'

Jemima lifted her chin and maintained steady eye contact with Andrei. Oh yes, she had heard himself and Lydia 'at it'. Many's the time. She might be hard of hearing but not even the stone deaf could have missed their enthusiastic yelping and groaning.

Not that she was passing judgment. That was not the way of the good-living person. But she would like to be sure that Andrei knew exactly what he was doing. She watched as countless emotions flickered across his face, a cocktail of shame, self-examination, absolution, fortitude and, finally, something approaching happiness.

'Thenk you for concern,' Andrei said, also lifting his chin and matching Jemima's steady eye contact. 'But Star Street is good. Handy for bus. When we have babies, we will need bigger place, but for moment is good. How long will lease be? Six months? A year?'

'For as long as you like, my dear.'

The Poles were going! They were going—and not coming back!

They were off on their summer holidays on Friday, which was excellent enough in itself. But big changes were afoot. Jan was returning to live in Poland and—in a shock move—Andrei had got engaged to Rosie, the last virgin in Ireland, and they were moving in together.

Jan related all of this to Lydia with no small amount of smug triumph. 'Good girl wins,' he said. So he had known about her and Andrei.

'If Andrei's the prize, you can keep it.'

'We will pay you two months' rent,' Jan said, which even she couldn't find fault with. 'Lease is yours if you want.'

She might keep it on, she thought; the location wasn't bad. But she might move somewhere else. She didn't have to live in her cupboard any longer because everything had changed. The catastrophe with her mum was still real but, with Murdy and Ronnie on-side, she was no longer carrying the burden alone. And now that she wasn't so afraid she saw how laughable her money-saving efforts had been. She could never have afforded to pay for a home for Mum, not even if she'd lived under a bridge.

And here came Andrei.

'The groom-to-be,' she said. 'I hear congratulations are in order.'

He looked a little shy but undeniably proud.

'You went down on one knee, I believe?' she said. 'The last of the great romantics.'

They eyed each other with mutual dislike and there was a pinprick of time when a lunge was possible. Everything froze, the universe hovered on a knife-edge, not a breath was taken . . . then they both turned away.

Now that it's all calmed down, their individual heartbeats have separated out, and mother of God, what a disaster. They're so mismatched, it's like they're talking two different languages.

Day 3

'KATIE? KATIE!' She barely recognised Fionn's voice, he sounded so distraught. 'Have you seen today's *Irish Times*?'

Katie looked around. They got all the papers in the office. 'Danno. Bring us the *Times*.'

'Page sixteen,' Fionn said.

Katie leafed through the pages and . . . *Curses*.

The headline shouted, 'GARDENING? THE NEW ROCK'N'ROLL?' It was accompanied by a quarter-page photo of a tousle-haired, unshaven sex god, smiling a big dirty smile and rubbing a courgette with his big dirty hands. *But that man was not Fionn.*

Instead, it was one Barry Ragdale, the star of *Diggin' It*, a new gardening programme on RTE, which would commence its run in two weeks' time. The gimmick was that Barry had once been a bass player in a band and would play out the closing credits every week.

At once, Katie saw the worst-case implications. For Fionn. And for her.

'Is that why Channel 8 moved me?' Fionn asked.

It could be. They'd probably got wind of RTE's show and either they hadn't had the nerve to go head-to-head with the state broadcaster or they were watching to see how it played out. If it was a disaster, they wouldn't bother running their version; if it was a flier, they could coat-tail on Barry Ragdale's success.

'I'll tell you something, Katie'—Fionn's voice was trembling—'I'm sorry I ever got involved in this whole lousy caper. I was happy in Pokey. Now, I'm jealous and insecure and I hate everyone.'

Katie forced steadiness into her voice. 'Fionn, listen to me. There are always going to be other artistes, other people in competition with you. It's a fact of life and even more so in something as cut-throat as television. You've got to play the long game. Wait and see. This Barry Ragdale could crash and burn spectacularly and you'll be ready to step into his place.'

'Really?'

'Oh yes.' She was good at this. After all, it was her job, calming down artistes. 'And Channel 8 haven't pulled *Your Own Private Eden*. It's still full steam ahead for Sunday three weeks, right?'

'But what if they do pull it? Then it's all over for me here and I'll have to go right back to Pokey.'

'Fionn, you're jumping several guns. Look at it this way: it's actually a compliment, another good-looking gardener getting his own show. It shows you're tapping into the *Zeitgeist*.'

'Oh, right, I hadn't thought of that.'

'It's all good.' *Well, who knew whether it was or it wasn't?*

'You're right, Katie, it *is* all good, especially because if I hadn't come to Dublin, I would never have met you.'

Day 2

AT FIRST, it seemed like Matt was simply looking for an alternative route home. After twenty-three and a half frustrating minutes, inching along in traffic that was a smidgen speedier than a total standstill, he abruptly pulled a U-ee and sped off in the opposite direction. Any minute now, he'd do a sharp right turn, then another one and once again he'd be heading towards home. But he didn't. He put further and further dis-tance between himself and Star Street, and before long he was driving by the river, making for the docklands. He pulled in off the quay, zigzagging through streets that became narrower and narrower, and soon enough he was bumping over cobbles.

He threw the car into the first space he saw, unconcerned that he was on a double yellow—clamp the car, do what you like, he didn't care—and took up his lookout post outside No Brainer Technology.

Thirty-seven minutes elapsed before the lanky, unkempt, poetic-type bloke appeared, rushing down the steps. He was hurrying after a slender girl with an attractive gap between her front teeth. 'Wait!' he called, placing a hand on her shoulder, halting her progress. 'Steffi, wait!'

Like a dam had been opened, rage roared through Matt.

But wait a minute, I recognise the poet-bloke from Maeve's memory pools! He's—

'David!'

Yes, David. Maeve's old boyfriend, from before Matt. It's only now that Maeve is letting me in fully and I can get to know all the details of her past.

'David!' The gap-toothed girl's voice floated over to Matt. 'You scared the life out of me!'

David said something that Matt couldn't hear; then he flung his arm round the girl's waist, gathered her close and snogged her energetically.

So now he had a girlfriend, Matt thought. And he could go over there right now—seven or eight strides would do it—and in a few choice sentences screw it all up for them. He could tell the girl a thing or two about David that would have her hightailing it in the opposite direction.

And then it was happening. He was walking with purpose and David, with the instinct of an animal sensing danger, saw him. He flickered with something—fear, Matt hoped—but Matt ignored him and focused all his attention on the girl. 'I need to talk to you.'

She shrank away and he realised his intensity was frightening her. 'Look, sorry—Steffi, is it?' She nodded fearfully and he swallowed hard, as if that would stem the despair. 'My name is Matt Geary.'

'Maeve's husband?' Steffi said.

This was the last thing Matt had been expecting. Incredulously, he asked, 'You know about me?'

'David told me.'

Matt turned to look at David, who was smirking smugly; then he looked back at Steffi. 'But he didn't tell you the truth. Listen, Steffi—'

'Hey,' David said. 'You can't simply rock up here and start—There are laws against that sort of thing.'

Laws. *Laws.* That was what did it for Matt. Suddenly, it all left him, every bit of impetus just drained to nothing, leaving him emptier than he'd thought a human being could be.

He limped away, as if he'd been physically injured. At his departing back, David yelled, 'Get some self-respect, man—and get *over* it.'

Conall gazed out of the plane window, blind to the housing estates of Dublin circling below him. He'd finally identified the uncomfortable sensation that had been clawing at his gut for the past ten days.

He should have let the Cambodian arm of the Milan company go. It was wildly inefficient, riddled with corruption and cursed with atrocious local infrastructure.

That one mistake had pinballed off myriad other situations and each of them had unleashed a chain of events, fanning out like falling dominoes, and what Conall had ultimately achieved was a bodge job.

He was famed throughout his industry for his slick, surgical work. When he chopped up a company, then put it together again, the scars disappeared fast, and very quickly the taut new version began to seem like the only possible one. No one would have believed that the old, saggy, bloated configuration had ever existed, never mind functioned.

But this time was different. What kept rising to the surface of his mind was that this scaled-down company would never entirely convince. He felt like a plastic surgeon who'd done a breast reduction and forgotten to sew the nipples back on.

He'd let the personal get in the way of the practical. He hadn't wanted the Cambodian directors to get thrown in chokey, and that reservation had hobbled the fluid blue-sky thinking that was his talent. He'd eventually come up with a solution but, now that the job was done and he was almost home, he was hit with a bout of painful perspective.

He'd . . . he tried out the word; it was a new one for him . . . well, he'd *failed*.

Failed. No one else had guessed, his paymasters in Milan seemed happy enough, but Conall himself knew. And word would get out eventually. Conall Hathaway's lost it. Burned out. No longer reliable.

Now that failure had happened once, he knew it would happen again. His unbroken chain of successes had been interfered with, and he had a superstitious conviction that the direction of his life had been altered and that he had to go where the new path took him.

Adapt! Adapt, adapt! That's what he needed to do: adapt to survive. And another chunk of awareness floated to the surface. He needed—wanted—someone to help him at work. Only now that this job was over and he was almost home was it safe to admit just how hard he'd found it. All those flights, those time-zone changes, the lack of sleep, the information overload . . . Too many times in the last three weeks he'd been seized with the ice-cold conviction that he simply wasn't able for it. Admittedly, he found every takeover frightening, it's what had made him so good—that level of fear had produced lots of adrenaline—but this had been different. It was madness to have attempted it on his own. An operation as big as that needed several Conalls.

A deputy. There, he'd said the unsayable: he needed a deputy. Someone to share the workload, to bounce ideas off, to assume some of the responsibility. He realised he even had a few candidates in mind, people younger than him, possibly even more cut-throat than he'd been at his prime, and already he was wondering which one he'd choose. But who said he had to have just one deputy? He could have two, even a team, a whole group of outside-the-box thinkers. Together they'd be terrifying.

But the more effective they were, the more it meant that Conall Hathaway, lone trouble-shooter, was no more. That person was gone. Whatever the future brought, and it could be all good, it still meant that he was a failure.

Finally, the plane was on the ground. Conall unfastened his seat belt and switched on his phone before he was told he could. He stood up and stretched elaborately, almost hoping that the steward would berate him, then hit Lydia's number.

'Hathaway?'

'I'm home. My bed, forty-five minutes.'

'If you want me, come and get me. I've been driving all day.'

Entre nous, *I'm delighted he's back in the country especially if, as seems to be the case, Andrei is off. I have big plans for Hathaway.*

Day 1

'WHAT TIME WILL YOU be home?' Maeve asked.

'Could be quite late,' Matt said.

'Oh, Matt.'

'You know what it's like.' He smiled apologetically. 'Potential clients, private room, tasting menu, expensive wine. These things drag on.'

'Friday night's a funny one for that sort of do.'

'Only night we could all manage. But you'll be grand. You've got Shrigley, right?'

'Mmm. And there's a leaving do at work.' She didn't know why she'd said that. It wasn't as if she'd go.

'You could go to it after Shrigley. Then you wouldn't be on your own here for so long.'

Maeve paused, a spoonful of porridge halfway to her mouth. Matt didn't usually try to persuade her to go out with her work colleagues.

'Half an hour, maybe,' he said. 'You never know, you might find you're enjoying yourself.'

'But, Matt . . . even normal people don't enjoy leaving parties.'

'Maeve, look.' She saw desperation in his expression. 'We've got to keep trying.'

She dropped her eyes. No, no more trying. He was on his own with that particular mission.

'Maeve?'

She had to say something. 'What restaurant are you going to?'

'Ah . . . Magnolia.'

'I thought that had closed down.'

'Ah . . . no, it hasn't.'

Matt snapped two antidepressants out of their foil package and rolled one over to Maeve. 'Like I say, I'll be late, so take your time.'

Maeve threw the pill into her mouth and chased it with a gulp of water. She passed the glass to Matt. 'I'll just brush my teeth and we'll get going.'

She left the room. Matt tensed and listened hard. When the buzzing sound of an electric toothbrush reached him, he threw himself on her satchel, rummaged through it, produced a bunch of keys, clattered them into the cupboard under the sink, dumped the satchel down on to the floor and shoved himself back in front of the breakfast counter.

I've just noticed that something's wrong, something's terribly wrong. Matt and Maeve, well, their shared heartbeat . . . I can't feel it any more. It's gone and I realise it's actually been dead for a long while. What I was feeling was something like a recorded message, an echo from the past. Like the light that reaches us from a long-dead star.

Lydia threw herself onto the floor, flat onto her stomach, to check there was nothing left under either of the beds. She wanted every last microfibre of the lads out of here. A couple of dust balls were rolling around, but other than that, nothing. The packing had been thorough; the last few days had been a frenzy of activity.

'That looks like it.' Andrei did a last sweep of the bedroom.

'If you've forgotten anything, you can pick it up when you come back,' said Lydia.

She hadn't cared even when she'd discovered that Andrei's new billet was just one floor away. He was an engaged man now and that operated like a repellent force field for her. That messy business was all in the past, a baffling little dabble, over for good.

She was so cheerful about getting rid of them that she'd helped carry the last of their boxes down to the van.

'Goodbye. Goodbye.' Now that they were leaving, she felt almost sentimental. 'Safe journey, all that.'

As she watched the van disappear up the street, her phone rang. 'Hathaway?'

'Tonight?'

'Cleaning. I'm moving into my lovely new big room. Sissy's calling over when she's finished work to help me kick over the traces. You can come too, seeing as you were such a dab hand at the cleaning down in Mum's. Not.'

'I'll come. I can help.' He sounded a little huffy. 'Then do you want to come to my brother Joe's? To give Bronagh her birthday present?'

'Who's Bronagh?'

'My niece. I told you about her.'

'Oh yeah.' No, no memory. 'The answer would be no.'

'No?'

'I hate kids and kids hate me.'

'But she's a laugh!'

'Believe me, Hathaway, not to me she won't be.'

'Ah . . . all right. I'll go there on my own and then come over to you.'

'So then I flew back to Manila again and—'

'Yeah?' Joe said, drinking his tea and staring around his kitchen.

Suddenly, Conall realised that he sounded like he was boasting. His brother had never been to Southeast Asia; he never *would* go there; it was just a faraway foreign part of the world that might sometimes be mentioned on the news. Conall abruptly shut up.

Without speaking, they drank their tea, Conall slurping energetically to demonstrate that he hadn't lost touch with his roots.

'Where's my present?' Bronagh's appearance broke the tension.

Conall reached into his pocket and produced the little box.

'Wicked,' Bronagh breathed, unknotting ribbons and unpeeling silver paper. 'This is a *proper* present.' Reverentially, she removed the lid and gazed at the winking sparkling jewels.

'Are they . . .? What are they?' Bronagh asked.

'Sapphires.'

'Ah, for Jayzus—' Joe said.

Bronagh was wide-eyed. 'Are they real?'

Conall nodded.

'She's eight, bud.' Joe sounded angry. 'Her ears aren't even pierced.'

'Adopt me, Conall.' Bronagh held the sapphires to her ear lobes. 'Make me your ward. Rescue me from these smelly peasants.'

'Ah, ha-ha-ha.' Conall flamed with embarrassment. God, he'd messed this right up. Sweating with the need to fix things, he grabbed Bronagh and said, right into her eyes, 'My brother is the best da you could have.'

'You could be a good da too, if you didn't work so hard,' Bronagh said. 'But then you mightn't have the money to buy sapphire earrings. Hmmmmm. Tricky choice.'

'I'll tell you something, Conall,' Joe said hotly. 'You might be going to the Philippines and all them places but I never have to leave the house. Having kids, that's the greatest adventure of them all.'

'You're right, bud. Bang on. I'm beginning to think that way.'

Joe's face softened. Then froze. 'Oh no, Conall, bud. Having kids, it's not like buying a motorbike. You can't give it back when you get bored.'

All my ducks are in a row for tomorrow. I think I'm going for Hathaway and Lydia. I know she says she doesn't like kids, but when it's her own baby, it'll be different. And Hathaway, he's ready. Well, he's fast coming round to the idea. By the time I arrive, I'll be welcome. Just in case things go unexpectedly skewwhiff, I've got Katie and Fionn as back-up. But as for Matt and Maeve, I'm afraid we'd need a miracle.

'Anyone mind if I shoot off early today?' Matt asked. 'Got my packing to do.'

Good-natured, office-wide jeering sparked up. 'Only ten past five and he's out through the door already! That's international sales for you.'

'Nothing left for me to do in homeland sales.' The new name that had been given to the department selling systems within Ireland. 'No point me hanging around.' He grinned, pale and sweaty. 'So, see ya.'

'What time?' Salvatore asked.

'Say seven o'clock? At the Aer Lingus check-in?'

Salvatore and Matt were due to fly to Shanghai on Monday morning.

'Good stuff. So see you at the airport!' Salvatore whooped. The start of a new venture, an exciting business.

'Yip,' Matt said cheerily. 'See you Monday morning at the airport.'

Does Maeve know anything about this?

'**H**ow are you, Maeve?' Dr Shrigley asked.

'OK.'

But she was far away, inside her head. She couldn't shake an image of herself being tossed up in the air, light and limp as a rag doll. The pictures were becoming more and more elaborate. She kept seeing it, the moment of impact, as a car hit her bike and she was sent flying, her skull shattering like an eggshell as she landed on the road, and the light suddenly vanished from her eyes. The thought of the pain didn't concern her; she was so numb that she couldn't imagine feeling any.

She'd had four panic attacks in the last few weeks and with each one she'd felt the presence of death. She'd been afraid at the time, but she wasn't any longer. She was looking forward to it all being over.

This was her last visit to Dr Shrigley. She didn't know how to tell her, so she wouldn't bother. Dr Shrigley would figure it out when Maeve stopped showing up. It didn't matter. None of it mattered.

She cycled home, fast and carelessly. When she got to Star Street, she hopped off the bike and wheeled it the last few yards to the front door. It was amazing to her that she was still alive. I mean, what do you have to do to get killed around here?

For once she was glad that Matt wouldn't be home for a few hours. That way he wouldn't know that she hadn't gone to the drinks yoke at work. Although he couldn't have thought there was any real chance she'd go. Poor Matt. He wanted evidence that she was getting better, when everything indicated that she was getting worse.

She flicked a quick look over each shoulder to check that no one was lurking behind her; then she reached into her satchel for her keys. But she couldn't find them. Her hand clawed and closed, but she came up with nothing.

Carefully setting her back against the front door, so she could keep an eye on all passers-by, she emptied the bag onto the step. No keys. Definitely, no keys. Her purse was there. Why would someone take her keys and not her purse? Creepy. Unless, maybe the keys just fell out. But wouldn't she have heard them jingling?

Of all the nights to lose her keys. She fired off a quick text to Matt: Come home.

There was no point calling on any of the neighbours. None of them had a spare key. She didn't trust anyone with her keys.

Four men passing along the street stared at her, sitting on the step. She couldn't stay here, advertising her vulnerability to all and sundry. She should at least get into the communal hallway.

She hesitated about ringing the old woman because Hungry Fionn was living with her. What if he answered? She couldn't chance Katie in the top flat either because she and Fionn were an item. The only option was to ring the flat on the second floor. She was nervous of the Polish guys who lived there, but then she remembered that they were moving out when she was on her way to work this morning.

She pressed the buzzer and someone, probably the impatient taxi-girl, said, 'Hathaway?'

'This is Maeve from—'

The door clicked open. 'Thanks,' Maeve said to dead air, wheeling in her bike and leaning it against her door.

She sat on the bottom stair, gazing at her phone. Why hadn't Matt texted her back? What was keeping him? After a while, she rang him and it went straight to voicemail. He never turned his phone off. Why, today of all days? Sod's Law.

A jingling of keys at the front door had her sitting up hopefully, but it was Katie. She tumbled into the hall, followed by Hungry Fionn. They were both in convulsions at something.

'Oh, sorry!' Katie laughed. 'Didn't mean to nearly stand on you there. Maeve, isn't it? Are you all right?'

Maeve didn't want to tell, not with Fionn standing there.

'Are you locked out?' Katie asked.

Why else would she be sitting on the fecking stairs?

'Come on up to our place,' Fionn invited.

Maeve suppressed a shudder.

'Do,' Katie said. 'We're going out in about an hour but you can stay as long as you like.'

'I'm OK. My husband will be home soon.'

'Do you need to ring him?' Already, Katie was reaching in her bag.

'He's on his way.' Maeve displayed the little phone in her hand. 'Thanks. I'm grand.'

Matt still hadn't texted her back. It was weird. It had been ages. She checked the time on her phone—nearly fifteen minutes—

A voice spoke behind her. 'Still sitting here?' It was Fionn.

She scrambled to her feet. Her heart was suddenly pounding like the clappers and every instinct was telling her she was in mortal danger. Fionn bounded down the last few steps. He seemed almost amused. She was remembering the way he used to look at her, like he wanted to eat her. Devour her. Kill her.

'Come on up and wait in Katie's,' he said.

She shook her head, unable to speak. Blood was roaring in her ears and fear was building, building, building in her chest, filling up the cavity, stopping her from breathing.

'There's nothing to be scared of.'

He stepped nearer and reached out. 'I'm not going to hurt you. Come on.' He closed his hand round her arm.

She hadn't screamed the last time—that was her biggest mistake and she wouldn't make it again. 'Stop! Please!'

Something was happening at the front door. Someone was out there. The buzzer sounded.

'Matt!' she shrieked. 'Matt!'

But it wasn't Matt, it was that big, dark man. Conall, she thought his name was. Katie's boyfriend. At least he used to be.

'What the hell?' Conall asked, looking from Maeve to Fionn, at Fionn clasping Maeve's arm, at Maeve pulling away, trying to get free.

Conall stepped forward and Maeve's struggling and shrieking intensified. 'Don't! Oh, please! I'm begging you.'

Immediately, Conall stepped back and Maeve became vaguely aware that other faces had appeared on the stairs, looming over the banisters—Katie, snappish Lydia, some other girl and the old woman.

'Leave her alone,' Conall said to Fionn. 'You're scaring her.'

'Me? I'm helping her.'

'She's terrified of you. And me. Right?' he asked Maeve.

Conall and Maeve locked eyes. She nodded.

'She can't breathe,' Conall said. 'Someone get her a paper bag.'

No one moved. Everyone was frozen as if the pause button had been pressed on a big action scene, so, without taking his eyes off her, Conall reached into his pocket and produced a big bag of Liquorice Allsorts. He tipped them onto the letter table, then handed the empty bag to Maeve. 'Breathe into that.' He looked up the stairs at Katie. 'Does it matter if it's plastic?'

'I don't know. I don't think so.'

'Can someone tell me what's going on?' Conall asked.

'She's locked out,' Katie said. 'Her husband isn't here and none of us has spare keys.'

'Do you know where he is?' Conall asked Maeve. 'Matt? Is that his name?'

'He's on his way home from Magnolia.'

'*Magnolia?* I thought that closed down,' Conall said, looking at Katie.

'It did. About a month ago.'

'That's what I thought,' Maeve whispered.

An uncomfortable silence ensued.

'We could try to pick the lock for you,' Conall offered.

'How?' Maeve looked out from dazed eyes.

As if by a powerful force, the collective gaze was drawn to one point: Lydia.

'Why's everyone looking at me?' she asked. 'Oh . . . *all right.*'

She ran upstairs and returned with a metal coat hanger, straightened it out and slid it into the keyhole, manoeuvring carefully. Suddenly, she stopped. She whipped out the wire. She'd gone quite pale.

'It's locked from the inside. Key is still in it.'

'He's in there?' Sissy mouthed.

'Matt's in there?' Conall asked Lydia.

'What do you mean, he's in there?' Maeve struggled for breath.

Conall banged on the door. 'Matt? Matt?' He turned to Maeve. 'Did you try the buzzer?' Mutely, she shook her head, so he opened the front door and stepped out to press the bell for Flat 1, long and hard. When no voice came from the intercom and Matt didn't appear to open the door, Conall said to Maeve, 'Ring him. The land line.'

Maeve handed him her phone. 'It's under "Home".'

Conall tapped a few buttons then through the door came the sound of a phone ringing. They were all holding their breath, and when they heard the answering-machine message start up there was an unspoken understanding that they had somehow found themselves in the middle of a tragedy.

Conall was removing Maeve's bicycle from where it was leaning against her door. 'Stand back.' To general shock—how had things got so serious so quickly?—Conall threw himself, shoulder first, at the door and bounced violently off it. (Jemima saw Fionn fail to suppress a smirk.) Conall tried again and the rebound wasn't quite so intense second time round.

'What's going on?' Maeve whispered. 'I don't understand.'

The third assault was accompanied by the sound of wood splintering. Two more onslaughts from Conall's shoulder and the door was swinging free of the lock.

'Right,' he gasped. He looked around at the sea of faces. No one wanted to go in. It would have to be him. He perched in the doorway, like a man about to dive into a crocodile-infested river; then he took the plunge. For some moments a terrible silence prevailed; then they heard him. 'Katie! Katie!'

White-faced, Katie disappeared, following his voice, and almost immediately returned full of orders. 'Lydia, ring an ambulance. Fionn, go in, he needs you to help lift him. Jemima, stay with Maeve.' As she was speaking, Katie was pulling up her skirt and pulling down her tights. She stepped out of them and ripped them in two at the weakest point, the crotch. 'Tourniquets,' she said.

Jemima put her hands on Maeve's shoulders. 'This is not the time for advice, but we may not get another chance. Listen to what I have to say, it is very, very important. Your body belongs to you. Not to that man, whoever he was. Take it back from him.'

Maeve's eyes were black and stunned-looking. She was stupefied, almost drugged from shock. 'How do you know?'

'I'm very old. I've seen a lot. Your fear of men, your unrevealing clothing, it seemed clear to me—'

'Ambulance is here!'

'That was fast,' someone said.

Lydia watched as Matt's lifeless body, dripping red water and trailing sheer black nylon from both arms, was stretchered out of the flat and up into the ambulance. She cornered Conall. His dark suit was wet and his white shirt was splashed with what looked like blood. He was on the phone to Eilish Hessard, organising a new door for Maeve's flat. As soon as he hung up, she asked quietly, 'What happened?'

Conall flicked a look at Maeve, checking that she wasn't listening. 'In the bath. Cut his wrists.'

One of the ambulance guys, a short, stocky bloke, was back in the hall. 'Which one of yous is coming? Be quick about it.'

'This is Matt's wife,' Conall said.

'She can come in the bus, but there's no room for the rest of yous.'

Maeve shrank into herself. 'I can't,' she said. 'They're men.'

'You must go, dear heart,' Jemima said. 'You must be with Matthew. But we will follow.'

Katie draped her arm round Maeve's shoulder and Maeve allowed herself to be led to the ambulance.

'I knew death was here.' Jemima gazed at the ambulance doors as they slammed shut. 'I've felt it for weeks. I was so sure it had come for me. Far better me than this young man.'

For crying out loud! I'm not death. I'm the very opposite.

'Is your man, Matt, is he—actually, like, dead?' Sissy swallowed.

Conall looked pained. 'I don't know. He didn't look too alive.'

The sound of a siren made them all jump and the ambulance pulled away.

'Someone needs to go to the hospital to be with Maeve,' Jemima said.

Lydia looked at her feet. This wasn't her sort of thing. You have to play to your strengths and she was no TLC merchant.

'I'll go,' Katie said.

'I'll go if you think it'll do any good,' Conall said.

'I would like to go,' Jemima said. 'If none of you object and Fionn will escort me.' Fionn opened his mouth, then seemed to crumple to the inevitable. Jemima might be ancient, Lydia acknowledged, but she had a will of iron.

Fionn went upstairs to change out of his wet, bloodstained clothes; then he and Jemima left, leaving Lydia with Conall, Sissy and Katie.

'Maybe we should get a drink,' Sissy said.

'OK,' Conall said, and raised his eyebrows at Katie. 'Any suggestions?'

'Flying Bottle?' she said. 'It's handy. And they won't object to a man with blood on his shirt.'

'Practically obligatory.' He gave a weak smile.

'Flying Bottle?' Lydia asked, her mouth awash with something bitter.

'You know, the pub just down the road there, whatever it's called,' Conall said.

'There was a fight one night when we were there,' Katie said to Lydia. 'Hence the nickname. But it's early now, we should be grand.'

'Grand,' Lydia said. *Grand.*

If it was anywhere else except the Flying Bottle; their appearance might have caused a few comments. Lydia and Sissy in grimy sweats and trainers, Katie in a classic little black dress and high heels, and Conall in a dark grey Brioni suit, accessorised by splashes of blood that were already turning black.

'I'll go to the bar,' Conall said, as Sissy tried to find four stools that hadn't been knifed open and had their foamy stuffing hanging out. 'What'll you have?'

'Vodka and Red Bull,' Lydia said.

'Me too,' Sissy said.

'Katie?'

'Oh? Sorry!' Katie looked waxen and dazed. 'Brandy, I think. It's meant to be good for shock.'

Lydia waited until Conall was standing at the bar with his back to them. 'So,' she said to Katie. 'You know all about first aid?' Something was telling her that the answer to this question was important.

Miserably, Katie shook her head. 'I'm just a keen amateur. I like getting spray and ointment from the chemist's, all the new stuff, every time they bring out a new type of Savlon, I get it, but when it comes down to it, like it did with Matt, I know nothing.' Her hands were shaking and she looked on the verge of tears.

'You knew about tourniquets.'

'That's only from watching cowboys films. And what if it was too late? What if he was already . . .?'

Katie's phone beeped and she looked at the screen. 'It's Fionn. Matt is still alive. He's getting a transfusion.'

'So does that mean he's OK?' Sissy asked.

'I don't know. He doesn't say. Maybe no one knows yet,' Katie said.

three years ago

As HE OPENED the bedroom door, he said, 'Close your eyes.'

She felt the weight and heat of his hands on her shoulders, guiding her forward.

'Such a big deal.' She laughed. 'This'd better be worth it.'

'It will be.'

She had crumpled and hit the floor before she knew what was happening. Her understanding was two or three seconds behind events. She felt a sharp pain in her hipbone and a ringing in her skull before she realised that he'd put all his weight into his arms and pushed her downwards, that her knees had buckled neatly and she'd banged against the wooden floor. While she was still piecing this together, David had climbed on top of her, his knees on her shoulders, the full weight of his body on her torso.

No breath was going in or out of her; she'd been so busy falling and banging that she'd forgotten to inhale, and as soon as she tried, her chest couldn't expand because David's weight was crushing her.

In the confusion, she'd thought it was an accident. But David was on top of her; his face was red and smiling. Obviously, he'd meant to do this. Taking small sippy gasps, she said, 'David. Get off me. I can't breathe.'

Desperately, she pressed her palms against the floor and shifted and wriggled beneath him, hoping to topple him off her, but his weight pinned her so perfectly to the ground that her movements were tiny.

He looked weird, like a stranger. She couldn't read the expression on his face, but alarm bells were ringing. She was alone with him. No one knew she was here. And he was bitter and angry—she knew now that she'd been way wrong to think he'd forgiven her.

She couldn't even lift her head, so when she felt rather than saw him fiddling for the button on her jeans, genuine panic kicked in.

'David, what are you doing? David, no! This is crazy. You're hurt, you're pissed off, but this has gone too far. Stop it now!'

But he'd done it, the button was open. She'd always thought you could do something to protect yourself, you could scratch, you could kick, you could bite. But there was so much weight on her shoulders and upper arms that the nerves in her hands weren't working, they'd turned to sand, her feet were too far away from him to do any harm and her head was pinned to the floor.

Now he was unzipping her jeans.

Was he planning to . . . rape . . . her? It couldn't be true, because . . . Why not? Because things like that didn't happen to people like her.

He was shifting about on top of her, redistributing his weight as he pulled down her jeans. 'Please, David, don't, David.'

I should yell. There might be people in the other flats; maybe they'd hear her. Bizarrely, she was almost embarrassed at the melodrama of shrieking, 'Help!' After all, this was *David*. But when she opened her mouth, it was a shock to discover how weak the scream was—she was flat on her back, there was no power to it.

Awkwardly but methodically, he was managing to pull down her knickers, first one side, then the other, tug by tug.

My God, he's really going to rape me.

He moved, to position himself for entry, and for a moment his weight was off her shoulders. This was her opportunity. She struggled to sit up and she let forth a proper scream this time, shrill and ringing.

He shoved her back down onto the floor, banging her head smartly against the wood, then lay his forearm across her throat and pushed.

Not even that hard. Immediately, she began to choke. He leaned a little harder. Terrified, struggling, desperate to breathe, she saw how easily he could kill her. It happened all the time. Women got raped and killed and it was happening to her. Her vision was going black at the edges and instantly she became silent and floppy. She had to live through this. That was the only thing that really mattered. Anything else . . . well, she'd deal with it afterwards, but she couldn't die.

He began to move back and forth and it felt raw and terribly wrong. *I am being raped. This is what it's like.*

For the first time since he'd brought her to the bedroom, he spoke. 'Is it good for you?'

Mutely, she gazed at him; then she had the strangest sensation, of leaving her body, of spiralling away through the crown of her head. She was gone; she was waiting outside herself until it was over. She could see herself, rigid on the floor, her eyes tightly shut, tears leaking from beneath her lids; she could see him lying on top of her, thrusting and shoving and, strangest of all, whispering words of love. 'You're beautiful.' 'I love you.' 'You really hurt me.'

After a long time, he climaxed. Pregnancy, she thought. Chlamydia, she thought. Evidence.

Cold metal. An internal examination. Swabs and photos. An STD test. An AIDS test. Too soon, of course, to do a pregnancy test. Matt holding her hand. Checks for bruising, tearing, internal bleeding. A whole world that she'd known nothing about.

After David had finished with her, he'd rolled off and lay on the bedroom floor. She had lain rigid, wondering what he was going to do to her next. But, as the seconds had ticked by and nothing happened, she'd scooted away from him, and in a sudden frenzy of activity she'd been pulling up her knickers and jeans, still expecting him to stop her, to wrestle her back down onto the floor and start it all over again.

Downstairs, she'd unchained her bike. She hadn't been able to ride it, but she couldn't leave it there. She had to take away every part of herself; she could leave nothing for him. So she'd set off half running, wheeling her bike a distance of over two miles, and the next moment, so it seemed, she'd arrived at her own front door.

She hadn't rung Matt; she hadn't wanted to disturb his evening. Instead, she'd sat, small and cold, on her sofa, waiting for him to come home. And when he did, he was confused, at least initially, but he believed her.

Two guards, a man and a woman, took her statement. 'You can do DNA, prove it was him?' She hadn't had a bath, she hadn't washed away any evidence; she was proud of that. She'd gone home and waited for Matt, and though she'd felt like she was dreaming it all, she'd intuitively known that she shouldn't even change her clothes.

'We're getting a bit ahead of ourselves here,' the man guard said. Vincent, his name was. 'We don't know yet that it was non-consensual.'

Maeve looked at him blankly. 'But it was.' She looked at Sandra, the woman guard. 'But it was,' she repeated. She looked at Matt. 'But it was.'

'I know,' Matt said.

Calmly, Sandra eyeballed them. 'Let's start at the beginning. What were you wearing?'

'Those clothes.' Maeve indicated the polythene evidence bag containing her jeans and underwear. Once again, she'd done exactly the right thing: she'd known her clothes would be taken from her, she'd known to bring a spare set.

'Not very provocative, are they?' Matt said, with a flash of defiance.

'It would be better if Mrs Geary just answered the questions,' Sandra said. 'Maeve, you weren't wearing a dress?'

'What does that mean?'

'It's no easy job to pull down someone's jeans while restraining them.'

'Yes, but . . . he did.' How could she explain David's dead weight, his strength?

'How would you describe your relationship with Mr Price?' Sandra asked.

'Who—Oh, David. He used to be my boyfriend. Before I met Matt.'

'You went to his flat earlier this evening.' Sandra checked her watch. 'Still today, just about. Why didn't your husband go?'

'He had a work thing,' Maeve said at the same time that Matt said, 'She has a right to her own life.'

'But your husband approved of this visit?'

'He didn't know,' Maeve had to admit.

'But I wouldn't have minded,' Matt said.

'You didn't tell him that you were going to visit Mr Price? Why was it a secret?'

'It wasn't a secret. It was just something I didn't tell him.'

'You and Mr Price had a drink together? Would it be fair to say that your inhibitions were lowered due to alcohol intoxication?'

'I had one beer. I didn't even drink it. Look, I didn't even want to see him but he said he wanted to give me a wedding present.'

'A wedding present?' Sandra raised her eyebrow and Maeve realised how sleazy the phrase sounded.

'I have to ask you this, Mrs Geary, because, if this case gets to court, you will be asked the question again: when you were the girlfriend of Mr Price, did you have sexual intercourse?'

She swallowed. 'We did, but this was different.'

'You've been examined thoroughly. You display no bruising or internal injuries.'

'There must be bruises. I banged my head on the floor and he put his arm across my throat and tried to choke me.'

'Your clothing isn't torn, you're not cut, there's no evidence of a struggle.'

'But I did struggle.'

'Any meaningful bruising would be visible within minutes. It's over four hours since the alleged incident.'

'I did struggle but I was afraid he'd kill me.'

Again that raised eyebrow. 'Kill you?' she asked, writing something down. 'Wow.'

The two guards left the interview room.

'What do you think is happening?'

'They'll be talking to . . . *him.*'

'And what, they'll arrest him? He'll go to prison . . . like, tonight? Is that how it works?'

'I don't know. He might get bail. Like, until the trial.'

Trial. Court.

'Matt? I feel like I'm dreaming.'

'So do I.'

'This time three days ago we were on our honeymoon.'

'We'll get through this.'

With sudden urgency, she said, 'Matt, don't tell Mam and Dad. They couldn't take it. They're so . . . innocent.'

'It's OK. We'll keep it to ourselves, just you and me.' They'd wrestle this horrible thing into a box; then they'd bury it and hide it for ever.

Hours passed. Propped up against each other's shoulders, they waited while everything was being fixed and they could go home and back to normality. 'I wish someone would just tell us what is happening,' Maeve said, trying to keep her voice steady.

'They will soon. It'll all be grand.'

Eventually, they both nodded off, and just after four in the morning, a sound at the door made them jerk into dry-mouthed wakefulness. The man guard, Vincent, had come back. He pulled up a chair and said, 'Right, this is the situation. We've interviewed Mr Price. He admits you had sexual intercourse. He says it was consensual.'

Fear, sour and sticky, flooded into Maeve's mouth. 'But it wasn't.'

'It's your word against his. Look.' Vincent leaned closer to her. 'Are you sure you didn't just, you know, get a bout of the guilts? One last go, for old times' sake, then got afraid that hubby there might get wind.'

'I'm sure.'

'Are you sure you want to go ahead with this? Taking it further?'

'I'm sure.'

'Because it'll ruin his life, you know. Just so as you know.'

Eight days later, Guard Vincent called to their flat. 'The DPP isn't going ahead with the prosecution. They think there isn't enough evidence to get a conviction.'

'So . . . does that mean, like, there won't be a court case?'

'That's right. No court case.'

She'd been dreading it, she knew they'd probe her about her sex life and they'd try to make out that she was a slut; but now that it wasn't going to happen she felt as if she'd gone into free fall. They needed to go to court. How else could things be put right?

'Why not?' Matt's jaw was clenched.

'The DPP doesn't have to give reasons.'

'You mean, you think David is innocent?' Maeve felt so dizzy she wondered if she might faint. 'You think I made it up?'

'I mean that the DPP doesn't think there's enough evidence to get a conviction.'

'So . . . so, like, nothing will happen to him?' Matt's face was white.

'Innocent until proven, and all that.'

'But how can it be proved if it doesn't go to court? Maeve and I, we work in the same place as him. You're saying he'll just carry on with his job and everything like nothing happened?'

'In the eyes of the law he's done nothing wrong.' The guard left.

No one believed her.

She confided in Yvonne, her best friend from school. 'David raped me.'

'How could he rape you? He used to be your boyfriend. You already had sex with him.'

She confided in Natalie. 'David raped me.'

'David doesn't need to rape anyone. He's a nice guy.'

She stopped confiding in people.

But she was going back to work. At the start of next month. When her two-month certificate ran out. After the summer.

The panic attacks started. The first time it happened, she didn't even know what it was. All she knew, with absolutely certainty, was that she was about to die. Her heart was spasming in her chest, no air could get in or out and she didn't think she could survive the intensity of her fear. The same fear she'd felt on the floor of David's bedroom, his forearm lying so easily across her throat. The expectation of imminent death.

She became terrified of men, of their height, their strength, even a casual look in her direction.

She overate, both she and Matt did, shoving down the feelings with butter and sugar and sweetness. She put on weight, but not as much as she would have liked. She wanted to disappear into a roly-poly body, to become invisible in it, so that no one would fancy her ever again.

She couldn't be naked, not even alone. The touch of another human being, even Matt, stopped her from breathing. The last time she and Matt had had sex was on their honeymoon.

Fear was the only thing she felt. Otherwise, nothing. It was as though, when she'd spiralled outside her body that evening on David's floor, she'd never come back in again.

They had no one except each other. All of their friends—*all* of them—had fallen away because they thought that Maeve had gone so weird, with her strange rape accusations, her drama-queen antics, the gasping and rocking and clutching her chest. Like, in *public*.

The social life that Matt shared with his male friends came to a halt because Maeve couldn't spend an entire night at home without him.

Burning them both up was the thought that David was walking around a free man while they were in prison.

Matt discovered things he'd never before thought about: that only one in ten reported rapes make it to court; that out of them, only six in a hundred result in a conviction. And what about all the rapes that are never reported, because the girl is too scared. Of her rapist? Of the police? All those rapes unacknowledged, unavenged. It was enough to drive him mad. How was the world as normal as it was? How was all that rage and injustice and grief and fear contained?

When Matt saw that Maeve would never return to Goliath, he left too.

As for David, there was no evidence of remorse or guilt. He never spoke directly to Matt but the smirk in his eyes said it all. *You took her from me and I fucked it up on you.*

Matt left Goliath and went on to bigger and better at Edios. Evidently, he could still do his job.

Both Matt and Maeve started taking antidepressants; then they began weekly appointments with Dr Shrigley until Dr Shrigley tried to get Matt to admit that sometimes he'd doubted Maeve's story, so Matt stopped going.

But he did doubt Maeve. Sometimes. How could he not? Everyone else doubted her and he was only human. At times he hated her. He'd feel irrational rage that she'd got raped, that she'd ruined everything.

It was almost two years before Maeve got a job, a tiny, tame little thing, gifted to her because she was the only applicant who would agree to the very low salary. A routine was the way to go, she realised. That would keep her safe. She kept things very small and very pre-dictable, and sometimes she caught a glimpse of all that she had lost. Had she really been that light-hearted innocent who'd approached the world with a wide-open heart, as if life were a great, big, juicy red apple, just waiting for her to bite into it?

They kept track of David. But Matt didn't know that Maeve did and Maeve didn't know that Matt did. Now and again, independently of each other, they showed up outside No Brainer, in the hope that David might be showing signs of remorse, but they always came away feeling worse.

'Time wounds all heels,' Matt sometimes said to Maeve.

But somewhere along the way, three years had passed and they were still wounded and waiting.

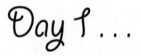

CONALL HUSTLED LYDIA up the stairs and into his bedroom. He was des-perate for her.

'What did you think?' Lydia shimmied out from under his grasp. 'When you saw Matt in the bath?'

Conall tightened his lips. He didn't want to talk about it. When he'd opened that bathroom door, he'd been rooted to the spot with horror.

He kept seeing it again: the bath filled with Matt's blood; the waxy, lifeless face lolling on the taut red water line.

'I thought he was dead,' he said.

As he'd hovered in the doorway of that bathroom, the world felt like it had stopped turning, and battling with his horror was grief, a mesmerising sense of loss at the waste of the young man's life.

'You thought he was dead?' Lydia said. 'Nasty.'

'It's over now.' He reached for Lydia, but she backed across his enormous bedroom. He followed her.

'Why did you call for Katie?' Lydia asked. 'To come and help you?'

'Because . . . she was the obvious person.'

'What way obvious?'

'She knows about first aid.'

'Owning seven different versions of Savlon doesn't make you a paramedic. I asked her in your so-called Flying Bottle—thanks for that, by the way. Really rub it in, your private joke, why don't you? Anyway, she knows zip about first aid.'

Conall looked quizzical. 'Your point?'

'You were scared, really scared and Katie was the one you wanted.'

Elaborately, he rolled his eyes.

'You're not getting it, are you?'

He gazed at her, then something changed behind his eyes. 'You're . . . breaking up with me?'

'Took you long enough. I can't believe your nerve, bringing me back here to have sex, when it's Katie you want.'

'I don't want her. I want you.'

'Love of God.' She shook her head. 'You haven't a clue. You'd want to cop onto yourself or you'll never be happy.'

She disappeared into the bathroom and reappeared with a cluster of bottles—shampoo and things—and threw them into her bag.

'What are you doing?'

'Getting my stuff.'

'Why?'

'Because I'm going, thick-arse. In case you have to explain to people what's after happening, here it is: I've broken it off with you. And no, we can't be friends. You don't really do friends, do you? Another thing you'd want to sort out.'

She cast one last contemptuous look around the room, checking that she had everything, before thundering down the stairs.

The house shuddered when she slammed the front door behind her. Automatically, Conall reached for his BlackBerry. What was Lydia's problem? She was too much of an attack dog, that's what it was. How could you reason with someone like her? Katie had been the obvious person to call for. She was capable, she was an adult, she understood things, she was . . . well, simply obvious.

Four new emails had arrived, and he read them hungrily, clicking quickly from one to the next, but none of them did the trick. He didn't feel so good; everything seemed slightly surreal. Sort of nasty.

He lay on his giant bed, staring at the far wall. Time passed and, after a period of nothingness, he wondered if he should ring Katie. Just to find out what was happening with Matt.

Then he realised that Lydia was the one he should be ringing—apologising, explaining, all that. There were rules, Conall knew. You weren't supposed to prefer your ex-girlfriend to your current one. But he didn't *prefer* Katie. It had been an emergency: someone was dying, things needed to be done and done quickly. Katie had been the right person.

Or maybe Lydia was right, he admitted reluctantly. Maybe she was the one he should have called for. But she was so hard and what he'd needed, in those moments when it had seemed like the horror was going to overwhelm him . . . what he'd needed right then, was soft.

'Into the pillow,' the nurse said. 'Or you'll have to leave.'

Maeve looked up. Her face was hot and sore with salt and her eyes were so swollen she could barely see. Another surge of uncontrollable feeling rushed up through her.

'Pillow!' the nurse said. 'There's other people here. They're upset too.'

Maeve doubled over and buried her face into the pillow, which had appeared from somewhere, and shrieked, 'How could you do this to me? How could you leave me here all alone? I will *never* forgive you.'

When she'd finally understood what Matt had done, she'd landed with an almighty bump back in her body, back in Maeve. It was like that suddenly present, super-real sensation when your ears pop on a plane. She was alive and in agony and blind with fury.

A red-curtained screen-on-wheels had been wrapped round Matt's trolley, in an attempt to give them some privacy from the rest of A & E. Maeve sat beside him on a hard hospital chair. His wrists had been stitched, taped and swaddled in bandages; he'd been given four litres of blood and two litres of electrolytes. Wires connected him to drips and green beepy monitors. He looked at death's door but he was going to live.

'You must really hate me to do that to me!'

His eyes were closed, he looked unconscious, but she thought he was faking it.

'As soon as they let you out of this place, you get yourself straight round to our flat and move your stuff out. I don't care *where* you go.'

'Pillow!'

Fionn paced up and down in the hospital car park. A & E was like the waiting room in hell, with its clusters of injured people crying and wailing. Someone had given Jemima their chair, but there was nowhere for him. Not that he was able to sit, he was too agitated. He was feeling bad. Angry, actually. First with Jemima for insisting that he escort her to the hospital, leaving Katie with that territorial Conall. And, secondly, with Maeve for treating him like the Antichrist. Somewhere during this evening's dramatic events, he'd realised that the emotion that used to light up Maeve's face at the sight of him wasn't awe. It was fear. Terrible paralysing fear. He felt foolish, really quite *sore*, that he'd thought she was mad about him. And why wasn't she? Everyone else loved him.

They'd been here for hours. He wasn't sure how long but it was properly night now, good and dark.

He'd had enough of this.

He stomped back in through the polythene doors. Someone was shrieking like a banshee. It was Maeve, still at it. She'd end up being sectioned if she didn't watch it.

'What did I miss?' he asked Jemima. 'Did he die or something?'

'No, you'll be delighted to hear he's going to survive.'

'So why's she still shouting and that?'

'She's distressed.'

'Can't they give her something?'

'Why ask me? I'm afraid I don't have medical training.'

Well, tetchy! 'Jemima, let's go.'

'Maeve needs someone with her.'

'She doesn't even want you here.' Earlier, Maeve had slapped Jemima away when she'd tried to comfort her.

'What Maeve wants and what Maeve needs are two very different things.'

'Does she even know you're still here?'

'*I* know I'm here.'

God, Jemima could be infuriating.

'When the storm passes, which it will, she may be glad of my company. But you go home, Fionn. I'll be fine. Thank you for escorting me.'

'Could you not knock off the do-gooding, Jemima? Like, at this hour of your life?'

Jemima gave a little smile. 'I may not have many more chances.'

'You?' He snorted. 'You'll outlive us all.'

'I may not, dear heart.' She paused. 'Fionn, remember when I had that little brush with cancer?'

'That was years ago.'

'Four—'

'And you're better now.'

'Well, the thing is, I—'

'Look, if you're sure you're not coming, I'm going to head off.'

Taking the stairs three at once, Fionn bounded up to Katie. There were already men at work fitting a new door to Matt and Maeve's flat. That Conall, Mr Make-it-happen, he'd make you boak.

Katie was waiting at her open door. 'Well?' She had been crying.

'He'll live.'

'Thank God, oh, thank God for that. And how's Maeve?'

'Tell me something.' His wounded emotions erupted. 'What did I ever do to her? What's her problem?'

Katie was staring at him. 'Something happened to her. Obviously. Something to do with a man or men. We think that maybe she was . . . raped. You can't take it personally.'

'Yeah, I suppose.'

'She was just as scared of Conall.'

He had to close his eyes. 'You're comparing me to him?'

Silent seconds elapsed, then Katie took him by the hand and led him into the living room. 'Fionn, come on. It's been a bad few hours. We're all rattled.'

'Yeah, OK,' he muttered. 'So what did I miss?'

'Very little. Had a quick drink in the Flying Bottle with the others.'

'What others?'

'Conall, Lydia and Sissy.'

'Hold on a minute. You went with Conall?'

'And Lydia and Sissy.'

'Why?'

'Because we were upset. Because we wanted a drink.'

'And you thought it was OK to go with him, even though he's your ex-boyfriend? And even though he did his best to make me look like a . . . a *woman-pesterer* in front of everyone?'

'Fionn . . .' She wrapped her arms round him. 'It's been a weird, horrible evening. Come and sit down. Come on. Listen, is Jemima OK?'

'Jemima? Never better.'

He let himself be guided to the sofa but, as soon as he was sitting, he felt trapped. 'Let's go out.'

'What? Tonight?'

'Yeah. Now. There's a thing on in the Residence. Some launch.'

'I don't want to go out.' Katie sounded shocked. 'I couldn't.'

'Why not?'

'Because someone almost died and we were there. I'm in the horrors. I wouldn't be able to be happy and chatty. I need to be quiet.'

'You were happy enough to go for a drink with Conall.'

'Fionn.'

'So you're really not going to come out tonight?'

Katie tilted her head to one side and gazed at him. He tried to read what she was thinking. She looked scared. She looked confused. She looked—unexpectedly—sad. Then she looked calm and he knew he'd got her. But when she spoke, her words didn't match her look. 'No, Fionn,' she said. 'But you go. Have a good time.'

Christ alive. Their heart currents have gone right to hell. They had become as one, a perfect smooth union, but this thing with Matt has sent them flying and they've bounced and broken apart, like a peanut tumbling from its shell. And whatever way they landed, it's altered their heart currents. Fionn's has speeded right up, beating an anxious, urgent tattoo, leaving Katie's for dust.

I'm in the soup now, rightly in the soup. They've all split up, all three couples, and I've less than a day to go.

Day zero (early hours of)

5 hours remaining

'Sorry,' Matt croaked, startling Maeve into wakefulness.

'Oh, you're alive,' she said. 'Sorry about that. Saving your life, and all, but it wasn't up to me. I'd have let you die.'

'Maeve, I'm really, really sorry.' His tears were flowing freely and he was the very picture of a broken man. 'But I wasn't able to help you.'

'Don't blame me.'

'I was just a reminder to you of what had happened. And I wanted to kill him all the time. I was bursting with anger every minute of the day and I was knackered from it.'

'And what? You think I enjoyed it?'

'I shouldn't have done it. I didn't see it that way when I was doing it. I was at the end of my rope. I didn't feel like I was any use to you.'

'You're not. You're going to be allowed out of here at seven o'clock. Come to the flat. I'll have made a start on packing your stuff.'

'Where will I go?'

'What do I care? You were all set to die on me so don't be asking me to find you somewhere to live.'

'How will I get home?'

'Get the bus. Get a taxi.'

'A moment, dear heart!' Jemima managed to apprehend Maeve as she stalked from behind the red curtain shielding Matt. 'Are you leaving?'

'Yip.'

'Without Matthew?'

'*Matthew* tried to kill himself. *Matthew* has made it clear that he doesn't want to be with me.'

Sarcasm didn't become her, Jemima reflected.

'It is imperative that we speak, Maeve. You are mired in anger and betrayal, but it's vital that you are apprised of some facts. To wit: with men, the most common method of suicide is hanging. In other words, it's almost certain that Matthew wanted to be found.'

Maeve stared stonily into the middle distance. 'I'll never forgive him.'

'Really, dear heart, such melodrama. When one thinks about it, he had to do *something*. How many more years were you going to spend lying on your sofa, watching the wretched gogglebox and eating cake?'

Maeve's face became luminous with shock.

'Yes. The truth is painful, Maeve. But you were stuck. Something needed to happen. And don't tell me that the notion of ending it all didn't occur to you also.'

'But! How do you . . .?'

'You were in despair,' Jemima said. 'It's what happens to human beings in despair, when all doors are locked and escape seems impossible.'

With curiosity, Maeve asked, 'Have you felt suicidal?'

'Me? Oh no, dear. But I've certainly had my sorrows in my time. Giles and I longed for babies of our own but they were gifts that we were never granted. Despair would have been an appropriate response, but no, I just soldiered on. Made soup for the deserving poor, that sort of thing.' She fell into a short reverie, before snapping back to the present and clapping her hands together. 'Now, you and Matthew! You must have a baby.'

After a long, almost hostile stare, Maeve asked, 'Why?'

'Any *number* of reasons. Relations between you would have to be rekindled. You would feel the power of your body instead of its lamentable vulnerability. You would have someone to love, apart from each other. A baby will reclaim the innocence that was stolen from you both.'

Maeve took a while to answer. 'And that'll, like . . . exorcise everything that happened?'

Young people? Wherever did they get the notion that life operated in such absolutes?

In a gentler tone, Jemima said, 'What has happened has happened. It can't unhappen. You are different, Matthew is different, but you must simply get on with it. You have a choice here, Maeve. You can go under or you can come out fighting—' A sudden spasm of pain in the region of Jemima's liver sent her eyes rolling into the back of her head.

'Cripes!' Maeve exclaimed. 'What's up? Are you OK?'

'Perfectly fine. A tummy ache. Probably all the excitement.'

'D'you want to sit down?'

'No, thank you, you are kind. I must go home now. But I beseech you to wait for Matthew. It's four thirty and he'll be permitted to leave in two and a half hours. Can't you wait that long?'

Maeve bit her lip. She didn't want to do anything for Matt ever again, but Jemima having that pain in her stomach had shifted the moral high ground in Jemima's favour.

'I assure you,' Jemima said, her breath emerging as a pant as another spasm of pain took a grip. 'I assure you, Maeve, that one day you will be happy again. Your life will get better.'

'Back to the way it used to be?'

Jemima sighed. 'One can never go back. You know that. Perhaps you could . . . try going forward.'

4 hours remaining

KATIE WOKE WITH a terrible bump, her mind racing like a speeded-up film through the atrocities of the previous evening: the key still in the lock; the door splintering and breaking; Conall disappearing into the hall; him calling her name and—the most terrible part of all—her first sight of Matt floating lifelessly in the red water. Although it couldn't have been more than a few seconds, it felt as though she'd stood in the doorway for hours, trying to make sense of the macabre scene before her. Matt? *Matt*? Young, cheery, smiley Matt, *that* Matt? What was he doing, drained of all colour and life, bobbing in a bathful of his own blood . . . *The bath*, she realised, with a bang to her heart. That's what had woken her.

Was the bath water still in it? If so, it had to be emptied and cleaned, and the bloodied towels that had been abandoned on the floor needed to be washed before Maeve got home. She swung her feet onto the floor—and then it hit her: Fionn wasn't here. He'd gone out and obviously he hadn't come back. There was a chance that he might be downstairs in Jemima's but even that would be a bit of a death knell; he hadn't slept there for weeks.

Real life had finally caught up with them, that's what had happened. For weeks they'd led it an effervescent dance, skipping and laughing, gleefully outpacing it, having a blast. But, all along, she'd been preparing herself for something like this. She'd predicted that his show would be a success and it would go to his head, or his show wouldn't fly and he'd go back to Pokey. Things hadn't played out exactly as she'd thought: the success hadn't occurred, but it had still gone to his head. And all it had taken was one unpleasant event to reveal how little comfort they were to each other.

She couldn't wipe away the memory of Fionn's disregard for Jemima or his lack of empathy for Maeve, but, still, she couldn't dislike him either—at least she didn't at this very moment; who knew how she'd feel in an hour or a day or a week? Too much had happened to him too quickly. You'd have to have a rock-solid sense of self to remain unaltered in the face of all the attention he'd recently been showered with.

A hoodie was lying on her chair and she pulled it on over her pyjamas and slipped into a pair of her mid-height heels—she was feeling a little too fragile for the full four-inchers. From the cupboard under the sink, she gathered bathroom cleaner, rubber gloves and a couple of sponges, then slipped downstairs to the ground floor. In the light cast by the street lamps, she saw that a temporary door of raw plywood had been fitted to Matt and Maeve's flat. There were two super-shiny keys on the hall table.

All she had to do was pick one up and let herself in, but suddenly she was reluctant. Then the oddest impulse came over her. She decided to open the front door, the one to the street, because Conall Hathaway would be waiting outside.

She turned the knob, she swung the door and standing on the step was . . . 'Conall?'

'Katie?'

'It's five in the morning,' she said.

'Quarter past.' He checked his watch, then fixed his eyes on her in utter astonishment. 'I was just going to buzz your flat to let me in. Look.' He demonstrated his hand. 'I was just about to touch the thing that says your name. And you just . . . materialised.'

'I must have heard your car or something,' Katie said faintly. 'Are you looking for Lydia?'

'Out working.' Well, she might be; her car was nowhere to be seen. He wasn't getting into the breakup stuff with Katie. 'I woke up, like, half an hour ago, just bolt upright, and my first thought was, *The bath.*'

'Me too.' Katie indicated her cleaning stuff. 'I didn't want Maeve—'

'—coming home to that horror—'

'—so I thought I'd come down and—'

'—empty the bath and—'

'—clean up a bit.'

They chanced a wobbly smile at each other. 'I like your shoes,' he said.

'Standards must be maintained. And what's that you're wearing?' She touched the tips of her fingers to his black jumper. 'Cashmere? To clean up blood?'

'I haven't a clue what it is,' he said. 'I needed to wear something and who cares if blood gets splashed on it?'

She nodded sombrely. 'I know what you mean. Kind of puts things in perspective, all right. But he's going to be OK. Fionn says they've given him four litres of blood and he'll be getting out in the morning.'

Conall nodded. 'I thought Maeve might be home already.'

'Fionn said she was still at A & E at midnight—'

'—and the keys are out here—'

'—so I suppose it's safe to go in—'

They let themselves into the silent flat and made their way down the short hallway to the bathroom. Conall pushed the door with his fingertips and it swung open and there it was, the bathful of blood. Redder and even more shocking than he remembered.

Conall swallowed noisily. 'Better pull the plug.'

They exchanged a look.

'I'll do it,' Katie said.

'No, I'll—'

Two steps from Katie, the plunge of an arm, an efficient hoist and immediate gurgly draining noises. 'There.' She tried to smile. 'Done.'

'Ah . . . thanks. You're magnificent.' He handed her a towel to dry her arm.

She shrugged, half embarrassed. 'Nothing to it.'

'*I* didn't want to do it.'

'Don't suppose anyone would actually *want* to do it.'

'I thought he was dead,' Conall said, his voice husky. 'When I first came in. It was horrible. I'll never forget it.'

'The weird thing was that I didn't know what I was looking at,' Katie said. 'I couldn't make sense of it.'

'I know what you mean.'

'Like, why was the water so red?'

'Yeah, and why did he look so . . . you know? Nothing prepares you for something like that.'

'Nothing.' She was emphatic. 'It was the worst thing I ever saw.' Noiseless tears began to slide down her face.

'Don't cry!' Tentatively, Conall put a hand on her shoulder and, when she continued to cry, he gathered her awkwardly to him. 'He's going to be OK.'

'But it's so sad.' She allowed herself to fall against him, just for a moment, against the softness of his jumper. It was such a comfort to let go. 'What must they have gone through? To get to that point?'

He rested his chin on her head and she cried into his jumper. When the tears had passed, she pulled herself away. 'I'm all right now.'

'Sure?'

'Grand. Thanks.' But being held by him had felt good and right and she had the unexpected thought that maybe herself and Conall would be friends after this.

'Let's get cleaning.'

'OK.'

Together they scrubbed the bath and the floor and washed away the red splashes that decorated the walls and tiles, erasing all evidence. They worked in silence until the task was completed. 'That's it, I think. All done.' With a final flourish of her sponge, Katie sank to the floor, leaning her back against the bath. 'God, that was hard.'

'Satisfying, though.' Conall joined her on the floor, propping himself against the opposite wall.

'That too.'

Buoyed up by the strange, almost celebratory mood, Katie decided to take a chance. 'Conall. Can I ask you a question? Something I've been dying to know.'

'Work away.'

'Can you speak Portuguese?'

'Ah, you know. Enough to get by.'

'How did Jason know about it?'

'Let's see . . .' Conall drummed his fingers on his lips as he thought. 'Oh yeah! I met him at some yoke for the Portuguese Trade Board. His fiancée, wife now, I suppose, is Portuguese—sure you know that.'

'Nice to know that you didn't lie about absolutely everything.'

He turned his head, looking aghast at her.

'Oh, come on! Don't give me that look!'

With great urgency, he said, 'Katie, I'm different now.'

'Lucky Lydia. Didn't I always tell you it would be the girl after me who reaped the benefits of my hard work?'

'Yes, but, Katie—'

'I *thought* I heard voices.'

Conall and Katie jerked their heads round. Jemima, looking every one of her eighty-eight years, was standing in the bathroom doorway.

'I was anxious that evidence of Matthew's foolhardiness be cleared away before Maeve brings him home. But I see you pair of ministering angels have beaten me to it.'

2 hours remaining

JEMIMA, HAVING PERSUADED Maeve to wait at the hospital until 7 a.m. to accompany Matt home, had one last good deed to do and, really, this charming set-up here, with Katie and Conall having toiled side by side, simply couldn't be better. Life was all about timing. As indeed was death.

She placed the back of her hand against her forehead and permitted herself a neat little collapse, folding herself up like an accordion.

'Christ!' Conall leaped to his feet and caught her before her knees hit the floor. 'Are you all right?'

Well, hardly, *dear. I've just done a picture-perfect swoon.*

'I think you'd better lie down.' He looked for confirmation to Katie, who nodded.

'Jemima, if Conall carries you, can you make it upstairs to your place?' Katie asked.

'I think so,' Jemima said faintly. What a sensible creature Katie was. It would be a very unpleasant homecoming indeed for Matthew and Maeve to discover a sick old woman prostrate on their sofa. And Jemima had plans of her own, which she would prefer to carry to fruition without interruption.

Conall insisted on carrying Jemima in his arms up to her own flat, where he expertly negotiated all the heavy furniture crowded into the front room and gently arranged her on the divan. Grudge skittered around anxiously, like a fussy old woman.

'I do apologise,' Jemima murmured. 'So much drama.'

'We're all a bit wobbly since last night,' Katie said.

'What can we get you?' Conall asked. 'A glass of water? Are there tablets?'

'Goodness me, no,' Jemima said. 'I don't need a thing. Except . . .'

'Except?' Katie said. 'You'd like Fionn?' Concern passed over her face, her expression saying, *But I don't know where he is.*

'No need for Fionn, wherever he is.' Much as Jemima loved him, she had other fish to fry. 'But could both you and Conall bear to sit a while with me? It won't be for long, I assure you.'

'Of course we will,' Katie said.

'Sure,' Conall chimed in.

Katie was such a sweet girl, Jemima thought. She'd known that she would stay. And naturally Conall would do whatever would please Katie.

Jemima pulled some hairpins out of her bun. 'Digging into my skull,' she explained. 'I've endured daily discomfort for at least eighty years and I find I've had enough.'

'You're letting your hair down,' Conall said.

'Precisely, dear!'

'It's never too late.'

'Hold that thought, Conall, as they say in those American shows. Now . . .' Jemima settled herself back on the divan, looking small and wan, the effort of yanking out the hairpins having taken its toll.

Katie knelt by the divan, a heavy, carved mahogany table behind her and an elaborately floral armchair at her side. 'Would you like me to hold your hand?' She felt that Jemima needed some sort of comfort, but you never knew with posh Protestants. They could be gravely offended at any offers of affection.

'Would you, dear heart? That would be *such* a consolation.'

Her face creased into a grateful smile and she extended a bony hand.

'I could hold your other one,' Conall offered.

'Conall!' Jemima said. 'That would be entirely delightful.'

Surprised, Katie looked at him. Since when had he started being kind to old ladies? He gave a shrug that said, *Why the hell not?*

Why the hell not, indeed.

Grudge took up the middle spot, between Katie and Conall, his woolly head on Jemima's lap, and all Katie could think about was how very, very weird it all was. Her! And Conall Hathaway! In Jemima's apartment, holding her hand! How had they ended up in such a bizarre triangle?

'Might I . . .' Jemima said tentatively, 'might I . . . that is, would you think badly of me if I asked a small favour?'

'Anything,' Conall said.

'Could you tell me? I've always wanted to know an item *of gossip.*'

1 hour remaining

RAW, BARE PLYWOOD. Maeve was angered at the sight of their new door.

'Look,' she said to Matt. 'See what you did.'

'God.' He stared at the bare wood, working out what must have happened. He looked sick.

'I suppose these must be the keys.' Maeve snatched a set of keys from the hall table and Matt held out his hand, expecting she'd give them to him, but she was already slotting one into a lock.

She was furious again. Jemima's lecture had calmed her, she'd felt hopeful for a short while, but now the rage was back and all her senses were lit up with it. It was so long since she'd felt anything and everything had come rushing at her at once; she was struggling to contain it.

It took her trembling fingers a while to get the hang of the new lock. When it finally clicked, she gave the door a good, hard, enjoyable shove. The first thing she noticed was the clean, fresh smell in the flat. One of the neighbours must have come in and disappeared away the evidence of Matt's . . . she didn't know how to describe what he'd done.

It was decent of whoever had come in. Probably Katie, she decided. But her rage couldn't help leaking out even at that act of neighbourly goodness. It would have done Matt no harm to see more evidence of what he'd done.

'Do you want tea or something?' she asked ungraciously.

'I'd love a cup.'

She put the kettle on, then went into the bedroom and wrenched the big suitcase out from under their bed. The last time it had been used was on their honeymoon; a Malaysian Air baggage tag still fluttered from it. She took the case in her arms and hurled it with force onto the bed, where it bounced a few times; then she clunked the lock and, sweeping her arms wide, flung it open.

She'd start with his shoes. There they were, lined together neatly on the floor of their wardrobe, and she began picking them up and lobbing them one by one towards the bed. Sometimes they landed in the case and sometimes they didn't, bouncing on the bed, clanging off the radiator, clattering against the window.

It was almost like a game, actually quite enjoyable, and she was sorry when she ran out of shoes.

The kettle was probably boiled by now anyway, so she went into the kitchen and made tea. Matt was sitting on the sofa in the front room, looking small and ashamed. 'Tea.' She thrust the mug at him. 'I've started packing your things.'

His face spasmed.

'Oh?' she asked. 'You didn't think I meant it. But I do.'

'How will you live on your own?'

'You weren't thinking of that when you ran yourself that bath yesterday, were you?'

He hung his head. 'I shouldn't have done it.' His voice choked. 'I wish I could take it back.'

'I'll manage on my own. It'll be better than living with you and waiting for you to try to top yourself again.' While she'd been sitting beside his trolley in A & E, she'd thought it all through. Kicking Matt out of the flat was just for show, an attempt to hurt him for the way he'd hurt her, because she was going back to live with Mam and Dad. Her life was over anyway, it had ended three years ago, and living in the back of beyond couldn't make it any more over. And if the screaming despair down on the farm got too terrible, well, she could always hang herself in a barn or mess around on the edge of a slurry pit or get too close to a combine harvester. Spoiled for choice.

She'd been thinking about being dead for so long, she was very comfortable with the notion. Admittedly, she hadn't quite got to where Matt had got to, but she didn't want to go on living. She hadn't been exactly sure how to die. But she'd have got there.

30 minutes remaining

LYDIA WAS SO SHATTERED she felt sick. The high jinks of last night had taken their toll and she was fit for nothing. Not even sleep. Was that possible? she wondered. To be too tired to sleep? Telly, that's what she needed. She flung herself full-length on the couch and pawed around for the remote. Thank God it was Saturday and she didn't have to endure the usual weekday, early-morning shite: fatso make-overs and diets and cookery. First she found a programme about Botswana, then she found one on Cuba. She luxuriated in her indolence, half awake, half asleep, dreaming of foreign lands. God, this was great. She could drift off right here without fear of disturbance from grumpy Poles. It was *fabulous* living on her own.

When the doorbell rang, rudely interrupting her paradise, she was outraged. No! Nohhhhh! I'm not bloody well going.

It rang again.

Love of God! Stomach-first, she vaulted from the couch, like a high-jumper clearing the bar, stomped noisily into the hall and pressed the buzzer. Ten seconds later someone knocked on her door and she wrenched it open. '*What?*'

Standing there was a man with dark eyes and longish hair, a touch of wildness to him. Selling mops, she assumed. But, to her horror, she saw that he had some sort of musical instrument in a case under his oxter. A door-to-door busker? When did that lark start?

She said, 'I'll give you money if you promise *not* to sing.'

He looked confused. 'I em Oleksander. Oleksander Shevchenko.'

'Who? Oh! The person who was here before me.' Not a roving entertainer! Her face lit up with relief.

'And you?' he said. 'You are new tenant? You live now in little room?'

'Yes. You're here for your letters? I suppose you'd better come in.'

'**A**nd no one in your family had any idea about Charlie's secret love child?' Jemima was incredulous.

'Not a clue,' Conall said, with some smugness, glad to be able to contribute such a juicy item of gossip to Jemima. 'Only Katie. Only because I knew, and it was pure chance that I found out.' Conall had come by the information when he'd been 'rationalising' a company and a young woman had begged to keep her job because she had a child to support and wasn't receiving a penny from the dad—who'd transpired to be Charlie Richmond, younger brother of Katie.

'But why would your brother neglect to tell your parents?' Jemima was struggling to understand. 'Surely they would be delighted to discover they had a grandchild?'

'Because Katie's mother is a—' Conall paused and looked at Katie.

'What?' Katie asked.

Choosing his words with evident care, Conall said, 'She's a . . . an unfulfilled woman who . . . ah . . . undermines all her children.'

Katie dropped her eyes and smiled to herself. 'You never said.'

Conall's eyes lit with indignation. 'As if, Katie. I made a lot of mistakes with you, way too many, but I wasn't a total idiot.'

'I must say,' Jemima said happily, 'that really is a choice morsel of gossip. Well worth waiting a lifetime for.' She shifted herself beneath the weight of Grudge's head. 'Not there, my darling hound. Too painful.'

'Oh?' Katie asked, just as Jemima had intended she would.

'I had cancer four years ago.' With an airy wave, Jemima dismissed it as being barely worse than a stubbed toe. 'The wretched thing has returned.'

Katie and Conall exchanged a look.

'How do you know?' Katie asked cautiously. 'Have you had tests?'

'No need. I can feel them. Tumours. One on my liver. Quite large. I can no longer button my skirt. Most vexing.' She smiled. 'When one's skirt no longer fits, it's time to go.'

'Ah . . . we can get you a new skirt,' Conall said, trying to hide his mortification beneath a veneer of jolliness. 'A whole new wardrobe.'

'Most kind. But that wouldn't banish the cluster of bumps under my left arm. Or those behind my knees.'

That wiped the fake smile off Conall's face good and proper. He gazed anxiously at Katie. Was Jemima serious? Katie returned Conall's beseeching look and gave a small shake of her head: she hadn't a clue what was going on.

'I see I have embarrassed you,' Jemima said. 'For that I apologise. And I see that you doubt me, but I assure you I am deadly in earnest.'

'I see . . .' Conall sounded stumped. 'So how can we help you?'

'You can't.'

'No such word as can't.' Conall began rummaging for his phone. 'I'll find a doctor.'

'He really is quite the Mr Fix-it.' Jemima smiled at Katie, who wasn't finding this at all amusing. 'He'll be ringing that long-suffering Eilish, I'll wager. Find a new door, Eilish! Find a cancer specialist, Eilish! Poor woman. Conall, put that confounded contraption away. I'm beyond the help of a doctor.'

She reached out to touch Conall's BlackBerry and, as she did, her body twisted, lifting her skirt and revealing alien-like clusters of lumps and bumps, like mini-mountain ranges, behind each knee.

Jesus Christ, Katie thought. Jemima certainly wasn't exaggerating.

She stared at Conall and the look on his face said that he had gone beyond shock. 'Right! That's it!' Conall knew when he was in over his head. 'I'm ringing an ambulance!'

'Absolutely not,' Jemima said, in ringing tones. 'Absolutely not! I forbid you.'

To his great surprise, Conall found he was afraid to defy her.

'It's far too late, dear heart,' Jemima said.

'We can't *do nothing*.' He thought he would burst with frustration.

'Yes, we can,' Jemima said. 'A good lesson for you to learn, Conall. Sometimes nothing is the very best thing one can do.'

'But why didn't you do anything before now?' Katie exclaimed.

Jemima looked ashamed. 'Would you think me a coward if I admitted a reluctance to endure chemo again? It was deeply unpleasant. I'm eighty-eight, and it's been a good life, except for the dearth of gossip.'

'But what about the pain? Aren't you in pain?' Conall asked.

'Oh, pain,' Jemima said dismissively. 'Everyone is so frightened of pain. But how else is one to know one is alive? Conall, please put away your phone and hold my hand again—I was so enjoying that.'

Reluctantly, Conall settled down again on the floor and Jemima extended her hands to be held.

'Is there someone, people, you'd like us to ring?' Katie chose her words carefully. Jemima was clearly very sick, and she wasn't showing signs of getting up off the divan anytime soon: how appropriate was it that herself and Conall were the ones by her side? Jemima knew Katie fairly well, but Conall was practically a total stranger. 'To be here with you?'

'You're the two I want.'

Why? 'Well'—and Katie had to force herself to be brave—'at the very least Fionn should be here.' That meant Katie would have to try to find him, and she didn't want to because she might bump up against all kinds of painful stuff.

'I sought opportunities over these past few days to tell him, but we were always interrupted.'

'You mean . . .?' Jesus Christ. *Fionn didn't know.* 'Conall, quick, give me your phone, mine's upstairs.'

With fumbling hands, Conall passed it over and Katie left a quick, terse message for Fionn. 'You need to come home right now. It's urgent.'

'**I** wanted to kill myself too,' Maeve said suddenly.

Matt looked aghast. 'Why didn't you tell me?'

'Why didn't *you* tell *me?*'

Matt stared up at her, his shoulders bowed, his eyes dead. 'Christ, what a shambles,' he said, with terrible weariness. 'You wanted to kill yourself. I actually tried to. I suppose the real miracle is how we managed to keep going for so long.'

'It's been . . .' Maeve had to stop. 'I can't think of the right word. A nightmare wouldn't describe it, it wouldn't come close.'

'Nightmares end.'

'And this just went on and on. Sometimes, when I was a kid, I used to think about my life and wonder what was going to happen, because they always said that bad stuff would happen to everyone at some stage. But I never thought about this. I never thought I could be raped. And I never thought I'd feel so . . . so . . . I had no idea that anyone could feel this bad for so long.'

'Sweetheart . . .'

'And I'm sorry, Matt. It was very hard for you, I know that. You just got caught up in someone else's stuff. You didn't bargain on any of this when you married me.'

'I loved you.'

'It was too much for us, though. We're only human. Both of us suicidal, that's not a good sign.'

He gave a weak smile.

'How do you feel now?' Maeve asked. 'Still not able to go on?'

'Not the way we were.'

'Me neither. Come on, you can help me pack your stuff.'

In the bedroom, Matt slowly gathered his shoes from all the places they'd landed and lined them up on the floor.

'It's probably better if the clothes go in first,' he said.

'Grand.' She opened one of Matt's drawers, gathered an armload of clothes and dumped them in the case. And the memories hit her. It was the smell, she realised. A cloud of it had risen from the impact of the clothes. She could smell their honeymoon—sea salt and sandalwood and moist, fecund air—as if they were there right now. Wasn't it unbelievable that the residue had survived so strongly for three long years? Dried rose petals were still strewn in the bottom of the case and she picked out a couple.

'Remember these?'

'Oh, I do.' Matt's eyes sparked briefly at the memory. 'It was every night after dinner, wasn't it?' They'd come back to their room and find that some mysterious person had used handfuls of rose petals to draw a big red heart on their duvet.

'And in the beginning we thought it was so romantic.'

'Ah no, I always thought it was cheesy.'

'No, you didn't, Matt, you loved it!'

'Well–ll, I guess I thought it was nice that someone would go to the trouble.'

'But then we started getting ungrateful, d'you remember? And we'd be saying that the hearts were getting smaller and more crooked.'

'And the petals would get into the bed—'

'—and we used to be finding them in all kinds of places,' she said.

'*All* kinds of places,' he repeated.

'And do you remember the bath the butler bloke ran us?'

'No . . . Oh yes! That's right. More bloody petals!'

'And we were covered with them and we couldn't get them off us—'

'—and they'd gone black from the water so we looked like we had Kaposi's sarcoma.'

And even that hadn't put them off drying each other with elaborate care and having sex for about the hundredth time. It was amazing, really, Maeve thought, just how much sex they'd had during those two weeks. Almost as if they'd known it was all going to come to a sudden stop and that they'd better make hay while they could.

'We were so happy,' Maeve said. 'Like, we really were, weren't we?'

'I felt like the luckiest man on the planet. You were everything I ever wanted . . . No, it's more like you were everything I hadn't even known I'd wanted and I was so scared that I'd never get you.'

'And look at how it ended up. Three years later you try to kill yourself.'

The shock of it hit her afresh and a storm of crying overtook her.

'Maeve, please, it was only because I thought you'd be better off without me. I thought I was no use to you.'

'Yeah? Well, you were.'

She snatched hold of him and held tightly to his body, pressing herself against the solidity, the realness, the warmth, the life in it, feeling his heartbeat and her own.

'Don't ever do that to me again,' she whispered. 'It was worse than anything else that's happened in the last three years. Miles worse.'

'Come on, come in, your letters are in the kitchen. I've no time for chat, I'm in the middle of watching—'

Softly, Oleksander Shevchenko asked, 'And do you find my bed comfortable?'

Lydia had almost turned away, but at this impertinence she twisted back to him, a sharp put-down in her mouth. The *neck* of him.

'My bed . . .?' he insisted, his expression full of sauciness. 'To your likingk?'

'Actually'—Lydia stared him in the eye—'your bed *is* to my liking.' She could more than hold her own with random sauce-merchants.

Wait a minute! Their heart currents are going berserk, right here on the doorstep, with flashing lights and the sound of applause, like a fruit machine when someone hits the jackpot.

But is it enough? Is there time? Can they fall in love and have sex in the next twenty-two minutes? Because that's all I have left. If I could just steer them towards the bedroom . . . Lydia wouldn't give me any crap about not sleeping with a man less than ten minutes after they'd first met. For spontaneity, for catching life by the balls, she's my girl.

20 minutes remaining

THE ONLY SOUND in the room was the ticking of a big wooden clock. Jemima's eyes were closed in peaceful silence and Katie, Conall and Grudge lovingly watched over her. The room was so still and tranquil that Katie began to eddy down into a pre-sleep state and was brought back to the now when Jemima spoke.

'I've had a good and happy time on earth,' she said.

'What more can you ask for, really?' Conall said.

'Death is only sad if one hasn't lived one's life.'

Death? *Death?* Katie and Conall looked at each other.

'I'm entirely ready to go.'

Did she mean she was planning to die now?

'Yes, dears.'

Right now? Right *here*?

'In the next few minutes. And I want to be here, in my own home, with both of you with me.' Katie and Conall shared another look.

I say we should let her have her way, Conall's eyes said.

'This hasn't come upon me suddenly,' Jemima said. 'The presence of death has been in this house for weeks.'

That's when I realise that, actually, she hasn't got the wrong end of the stick; there has been a presence here. Other than mine, I mean. The Grim Reaper, the old buzz-wrecker himself.

It's often the policy: one in and one out.

In quiet harmony, Maeve and Matt filled the suitcase with Matt's clothes. Oddly, the longer they packed, the less likely it seemed that he was leaving.

'I'll be back in a second,' he said to Maeve.

'Where are you going?'

'I'm a bit cold.'

'If you will go cutting your wrists . . .'

'I'll never do it again.'

'You'd better bloody well not.'

'I know it's August but do you mind if I put on the heat?'

She thought about it. 'Let's get into the bed for a while. It's probably warmer there.'

They shoved the suitcase to the floor and most of the things they'd packed fell out; then they lay fully clothed on the bed and threw the duvet up in the air, letting it fall and wrap itself softly about them. Maeve twined her legs tightly round Matt and briskly rubbed his back, his shoulders, his arms. 'Any warmer?'

'Yes.'

'Good.'

'Listen, I've an idea!' Matt said suddenly.

'What is it?'

'We could get a kitten. Or a puppy.'

'A puppy?' Maeve said slowly. 'No, it would be jealous.'

Lydia handed Oleksander a small bundle of envelopes. 'Tell me where you live now, give me your address.'

He tilted his head and gazed at her with quite naked sauce. 'So you can visit and see my new sleeping place?'

Lydia wore an expression of polite irritation. *I'll see your naked sauce,* her look said. *And I'll raise you a provocative stare.*

'So I can send your stuff on,' she said. 'And stop you calling round, interrupting me watching Michael Palin.'

Now, now! Do it now, get on with it now! Sex and plenty of it! My life depends on it!

15 minutes remaining

'BE KIND TO EACH OTHER,' Jemima murmured, closing her eyes.

'Who?' Conall asked. He just wanted to be sure.

'You two. You and Katie.'

'OK.'

Jemima's breathing became quieter and the fall and rise of her chest softer and weaker until it became invisible. Conall was—well, he didn't know exactly how he felt, except that he was no longer scared, the way he had been a while ago when Jemima had revealed how sick she was. He no longer needed to make phone calls or organise the unorganisable or run away. He was prepared to sit on this violently patterned rug, sit here for as long as it took, holding the hand of a dying woman.

How weirdly coincidental that, for the second time in two days, he was right up against the thin membrane that divided life and death. But this time was different, this time felt strangely beautiful.

Oleksander leans closer to accept the letters. His face is so close to Lydia's that he'd barely have to move to kiss her.

I'm telling you, the air is hopping with sex! One kiss and they'd be overtaken by passion; there's so much of it fizzing and popping between them. One kiss, that's all I'm asking for and the rest will take care of itself.

But Oleksander laughs softly, then lounges out through the door and down the stairs.

He'll be back. But not in time for me.

Bollocks.

'**S**o your man Conall actually broke down the door?' Matt asked.

'And took complete charge. Shouting orders left, right and centre and everyone hopping to it. Are you warm yet?'

'No. Keep rubbing.'

'We'll have to do something to thank him.'

'We will. Any ideas?'

'Yes.'

'Ah . . . feel like sharing them with me?'

'We'll call our baby after him.'

'What baby?'

'We're going to have a baby.'

'Are we?' Matt pulled back from Maeve, in order to look properly into her face.

'The wise old woman upstairs says we are.'

'But . . . how are we going to manage that?'

'Like this.' Maeve wrenched her T-shirt over her head and wriggled out of her cords and knickers. 'Will you . . .?'

His eyes locked on to hers and, wearing an expression almost of panic, as if he was afraid she'd change her mind, Matt pulled off his clothes, then slid his arms round her and carefully gathered her fullness to him. For the first time in three years, he felt her soft naked body next to his, thigh against thigh, chest against chest, the bliss of his hand on the smoothness of her hip bone.

Tears spilled down her face and he kissed them away.

'Will I stop?' he asked.

'No, no, no.'

'Is this OK?' Gently, he touched her.

She nodded.

'And this?'

'All of it, Matt, all of it's OK.'

5 minutes remaining

CONALL SLIPPED his spare hand into Katie's and she looked at him and smiled.

And would you credit it! Can you believe it! Their heart currents are in perfect harmony again.

It was now or never. Conall had to speak. He had something very important to say. 'Katie, I—'

A noise at the door made them both look up.

'Fionn!' Katie exclaimed.

No! No, no, no!

Fionn was staring at Jemima on the divan, at Grudge whimpering quietly, at Conall's hand in Katie's.

Then, more gently, Katie spoke again and clambered to her feet. 'Fionn . . .'

It was only when Grudge threw back his head and began to howl that Conall realised what had happened.

Gently, slowly, patiently, his gaze never leaving her face, Matt let himself be guided by Maeve and, at the moment his body merged with hers, he paused and the look they shared was one of triumph.

'Cripes! We've done it,' she said. She could barely believe it.

'You're right, we've done it.' This was real. It was actually, really happening. With Maeve, his beautiful Maeve, who bewitched total strangers into collecting spilled coins from the floor of the Dart. 'We've done it together, the two of us.'

'Matt, don't cry.'

'Am I?' So he was. But why, when he was so happy? 'Anyway, you're a fine one to talk.'

Tears were spilling from the corners of Maeve's eyes. 'I thought this would never happen again.'

They were laughing, they were crying, with joy, with relief. They'd been lost to each other for such a long time, lost, they'd been so sure, for ever. But they'd found their way back to each other, they'd found their way home.

And just in the nick of time . . .

Here I go . . . I've had the tap to the head and it's happening, I'm dissolving, I'm already starting to forget. But . . . I'm in! I exist! Matt and Maeve's baby. I was always on my way to them but I must admit there were times when I wondered if I'd ever get here. Am I a boy or a girl? Not that it really matters because I'm finally in and . . . ooh, it's just like what happened to Killian in the story, everything's gone tingly and sparkly and, like the incoming tide washing away traces on the sand, I'm disappearing little by little, clearing the way for my soul to be rewritten by a brand-new—

And the man and woman, humble, good people, kind and loving companions who shared the one soul, who had endured many sorrows in their lives, who had lived through times of fear and loneliness and despair, were full of heart and restored to happiness and love when they learned that their baby had finally been sent to them.

Epilogue (four months later)

It's a Saturday afternoon, at the end of November, and I'm flying over the streets of Dublin, looking for Star Street. Number 66, to be precise. My mission is to find my future parents. According to my information—which, by the way, isn't half as detailed as I'd like—at least one of them will be living there. Another pregnancy happened there four months ago, to a pair called Matt and Maeve, so it looks like a fertile sort of a spot.

But we're off to a bad start. It takes me ages to find the place and time is of the essence. There are—count 'em—not one, not two but *three* Star Streets in Dublin. The first Star Street showed up in jig time, but number 66 turned out to be a taxidermist's showroom. So I set off again, but the second 66 Star Street was an office block, all locked up because it's a Saturday.

Anyway, my travelling companion, who is killing time with me—he's always killing something, that same fellow—said he knew exactly how to get to the elusive third Star Street. He keeps going on about what an experienced traveller he is, always down here, he says, ending people's lives when they least expect it. So I put it up to him and said, all right so, show us this other Star Street, and he said, grand, I will, but I can't show you right now because I've got *my* mission to carry out, and it's very time-specific and you might as well come with me.

I was worried. Some in my situation get days, weeks, even months to identify their prospective parents, but I'd been given less than twenty-four hours—just the luck of the draw. Whatever was going to happen for me, it was going down today, and I wanted to get the lie of the land in 66 Star Street as soon as possible. On balance, though, I thought I'd be better off sticking with someone who actually knew how to get there. Waste some time to gain some time, as it were. So, swept along on my companion's self-important coattails, we arrive in the centre of Dublin. I suppose you could say we're an odd couple, me about to give life and him about to take it away. But we aren't such an unlikely pair as we seem; life and death often work together, matching each other hit for hit.

We're in a wide street where some public rally is underway. I start reading the banners and listening to the chants and it appears to be a protest against the low conviction rate for Irish rapists and, as you might expect, the crowd is mostly women. Like, you wouldn't expect turkeys to be campaigning for extra Christmases.

Fast worker, my knowledgeable friend—in no time, he's spotted his mark: a lanky, unkempt-looking yoke, name of David, one of the few men present. No surprises, David is with a girl; you wouldn't get too many lads going along to a rape protest on their own. And a lovely girl she is too: tall and slender, with a gap between her front teeth that doesn't look like she needs to go to the dentist for a brace, but just makes her all the better-looking, if you get me. Steffi is her name. And this David seems to be well aware of how lovely Steffi is, because his arm is clamped round her waist like a vice, like he's afraid she's going to do a legger.

Now, wait till I tell you something weird. David's vibrations are muted and harmless-seeming, but I'm picking up distress from Steffi. She doesn't want to be at the march. *She's only there because David was so insistent!* And she doesn't like the way he's holding on to her so tightly. All of a sudden she can't take it for one more second and she pops herself out from the rigid hold and he gives her this *look* and she says, sort of apologetically, 'Too tight.' And he gives her another look, very wounded, like; then he grabs her hand and squeezes it until it hurts.

My know-all companion is watching the sky, then eyeing the protesters, then watching the sky again. You wouldn't describe him as anxious, exactly, but attentive. His job, as he keeps telling me, calls for a lot of precision. Well, so does mine, as a matter of fact.

And then he's all smiles. 'Ah, here it is.'

Far above us, a plane has entered Irish airspace and its flight path is going to take it over the centre of Dublin. I'm not liking this one bit. What has he lined up? A bomb? A crash? How many innocent people will be killed in order to take out this one individual?

'No.' My companion laughs darkly (he does most things darkly; it's his way). 'Nothing like that. It's quite ingenious, actually.'

He points at the sky. 'Up there, about a mile above us, a lump of ice is coming loose from the underside of the plane. Any second now it'll start to plummet to earth and it'll land right on top of me boyo here.'

I'm impressed. I gaze upwards, then back at the unkempt David, who hasn't a *clue* that he's living out his final seconds. Anyway, a short way back in the march, he's just seen a couple of people he recognises—a blondey-haired cheruby woman and a smiley man . . . Actually, hold on a minute, it's Matt and Maeve. From 66 Star Street.

David has been hoping they'd be here and now that he's spotted them he lights up like a Christmas tree, but the kind they'd have in hell. Badness, blackness, that sort of thing.

Aha! David is thinking. *I'll go back there and taunt the pair of them. I'll introduce them to Steffi. I'll say that it's a crime that so many Irish rapists walk away free. It'll kill them!*

'Steffi! There's someone I want you to meet.'

'Who?' Christ, you never saw anyone looking as miserable as her.

'My ex-girlfriend Maeve. Come and meet her.'

Steffi's confused and afraid and, God, she *really* doesn't like him. 'Why would I want to do that?'

'Just come on, would you?'

'No, David.'

He tugs at her arm, pulling her with him, and she digs her heels in, so he gives her another hoick, much harder this time, and she wrenches herself backwards, breaking free of him, and people are starting to look at him.

'Suit yourself,' he says. Then he adds, 'You bitch.' And a cluster of banner-carrying girls—strangers, like—gasp in shock. You can't be going around calling your girlfriend a bitch. But David doesn't care. He just steps forward, all business, and everyone around him scoots back and gives him space, because they know he's a bad hat.

Meanwhile, Matt and Maeve have spotted him and are presenting expressions of defiance. With a nasty little laugh, David walks one large pace, then another, deaf to the faint whistling sound that has suddenly started above his head, and oblivious of the breeze that's interfering with his already very messy hair.

'Now watch this,' my companion murmurs to me.

And the very next thing, a smallish boulder of ice hurtles from the heavens and collides with David's head, sending him toppling to the ground. His head, shoulders and chest are covered with the jaggedy frozen ball and, from the way his blood is oozing out from under the ice, there's no doubt that he's dead.

There's a long silence and then everyone starts howling and yelping and running and tearing their hair and putting their arms protectively over their heads and gazing horror-struck at the sky and staring, their eyes bugging out of their heads, at the ball of ice, with the lower half of a body sticking out from under it.

However, and full credit to my companion here, in spite of all the hoo-ha, no one else is hurt, not even a scratch from a stray ice chip.

'See,' he says, swaggering around like the big man. 'Talk about a precision strike.'

'They'll be upset, though,' I say. 'Some of them will have nightmares and have to go on Valium. Look at poor Steffi here.'

She's rooted to the spot and her mouth is wide open, trying to suck in oxygen. One of her hands is on her chest and the other is on her throat, and she's staring at her boyfriend's legs and at the blood that's oozing from beneath the boulder of ice. She's in profound shock. But, all the same, you can't miss the thick waves of relief that are coming off her.

'Steffi'll be grand,' my companion says airily. 'She's been trying to break it off with him for ages. They'll all be grand. Bit of counselling and Bob's your uncle.'

'What about Matt and Maeve? She's pregnant. We don't want her going into shock and losing the baby.'

My companion finds this amusing. 'Take a look at them,' he says.

Somehow, Matt and Maeve have fought their way to the front row of onlookers around David's body and their faces are luminous with some strange emotion—that isn't shock.

'Is he dead?' Maeve asks Matt.

'Sure looks like it. I fantasised about this. When I read about the balls of ice falling out of the sky, I wanted it to happen to him.'

'Cripes, did you really?'

'And now look.'

'It's enough to restore your faith.'

'Right!' my companion says. 'Job done. And a lovely neat one, if I may say so. Off we go to Star Street. We'll be there in five.'

Five hours, more like. He was nothing like as familiar with the layout of Dublin as he'd given me to think and it took us *ages* to find the place. Anyway, I'm here now. Number 66, blue front door, knocker in the shape of a banana (no room for doubt). In the ground-floor flat a throng of people are drinking beer and punch and eating sausage rolls. Matt and Maeve's leaving party, would you believe? They're departing Star Street and moving to a bigger place because of their forthcoming baby. So I start wafting myself around the crowded flat, finding out what's what.

To my relief, neither Matt nor Maeve is showing any sign of delayed shock from the afternoon's icy events. On the contrary. They look wildly happy, chatting away to all their guests. Everyone asks about the baby. They already know it's a boy and they're calling him Conall, and although there *is* a Conall present at this party for whom the baby is being named, he is *not* the father.

In a quest for answers, I focus more on Conall, a fine, big, hunky specimen of a man, and suddenly I get a powerful tingling feeling: *he's the one.* He looks like a daddy; his dark hair has a neglected quality that bodes well, because daddies don't have time to be foostering around with moulding wax and the like. And he wears the right kind of clothes—jeans and a dark blue fleece—like he'd hoist you up on his shoulder and burp you and not care if you puked on him. His vibrations are decent, loving and humble (although I feel that the humility might be a fairly new addition to his bundle of characteristics). Most of all he's *ready.* In fairness, he'd want to be: he's forty-three.

Conall is watching the door, alert to each new arrival. Then there's this rush of energy, a spiky, barby sort of a thing: Lydia has arrived. Apparently, she once had a short-lived fandango with Conall, but you'd never know. They exchange a glance, but there's not a zing, not a flash.

Lydia is trailed by a flashing-eyed, wild-haired musician, one Oleksander Shevchenko. He's a handsome devil, even if he is wearing an embarrassing scarf-meets-cravat type thing.

You know what? This pair are worth considering. They *are* Very Much in Love . . . But, on second thoughts, I don't know . . . I'd be good-looking, no doubt about it, coming from that gene pool, and conception would be no bother (they do nothing except have sex), but Lydia has a lot of living in her yet. No way is she ready for me and I want to be wanted.

She seems to be making her way across the room to chew the fat with Conall, but no, she's only getting herself a drink. But they're so close to each other that she realises she can't ignore him.

'Howya, Hathaway. What is it? Dress-down Saturday?' Making some scornful reference to his jeans.

'Hello, Lydia,' he says calmly. 'You're looking well. How's Ellen?'

'Doing all right. Taking the tablets. She's not the full whack, obviously, never will be again, but she's not getting any worse.'

'Murdy and Ronnie? Doing their duty?'

Lydia laughs. 'Well, Murdy's *wife* does a lot. And Ronnie's produced a girlfriend from somewhere, and she's a dab hand at housework. But Mum's being taken care of and that's the main thing.'

'And Raymond?'

'Still hiding out in Stuttgart. Ronnie wanted to send in a crack squad to kidnap him, like the SAS do, and bring him back to face the music, but . . .' She shrugs. 'You can't win every battle.'

'Very wise. And Ellen's still living in her own house?'

'Still living in her own house. She asks about you sometimes. I'll tell her I saw you.'

'Do. Do. And your brothers as well, tell them I said hey.'

'They ask after you too. They took it very hard, me breaking it off with you. A lot harder than you did.'

'Aaah, Lydia . . .'

Just one thing I've realised about Conall: he's not very happy. In fact, he's throbbing with a red-hot, long-last ache, like an ear infection, but of the heart . . . And something else: Conall doesn't *live* at 66 Star Street. So unless I can hook him up with a woman who resides here, it can't be him.

That starts a panic in me. I scoot to the top of the house, where a woman called Katie lives. She's sitting facing a handsome prince called Fionn. Their knees are touching, their heads are bent towards each other, there is a profound connection. OK, she's no good for Conall but, if I'm stuck, she and Fionn would do.

The next floor down is where Lydia and Oleksander live. And the flat below that one houses a married couple, Andrei and Rosie. Mad-looking place. There's all this gloomy, heavy furniture but it looks like it's being edged out by a flood tide of bright, spriggy, yellow neatness.

The woman of the house, Rosie, is small, prim and pretty— *immensely* powerful. She's responsible for all the yellowness and she has plans for much more of it. And Andrei? To be quite honest, I couldn't tell you the first thing about him because he has surrendered himself body and soul to this domestic dynamo.

In a basket in a corner, a great big donkey-like dog crouches, a left-over from the previous, dark-wood occupation and when Rosie is done with her decorating, he is all that will survive. Like Andrei, the dog adores Rosie. *Adores* her.

Andrei and Rosie are about to leave for the party and I follow them downstairs.

Just before Rosie knocks on Matt and Maeve's door, she taps her watch and says to Andrei, 'An hour and fifteen minutes, we leave here at five past nine, not a second later. You can have two beers. Any more and there will be trouble.'

Andrei nods. He's very happy. He likes to know what's what. Then Rosie smoothes her already smooth cotton shirtwaister and summons up a sweet smile before rapping on the door.

And what I'm thinking is, No, not her. She's way too joyless. Andrei might be in the running if I could extricate him from Miss Prissy-knickers but I don't give much for my chances.

Maeve opens the door and Rosie hands over a little gingham-wrapped basket of homemade muffins and then they're in. Andrei's heartbeat steps up. He's on the alert, twisting his neck like a periscope, looking for Lydia—and then he sees her, poking her finger contemptuously through the sausage rolls. She must feel his eyes on her because she looks up sharply. Their gazes lock. Andrei is in bits, in so much panic that he thinks he might have a heart attack. As far as he's concerned, that lunacy with Lydia was the worst mistake he's ever made and he lives in terror of Rosie finding out. Automatically, he accepts a beer from Matt—one of his allotted two—and his panic starts to abate. And when all his fear has subsided, nothing else remains. As for Lydia, her eyes slide right over Andrei, like he's not even there.

Not them, so.

And now it transpires that it's two gay lads who are moving into Matt and Maeve's! They're at the party, meeting their new neighbours. A likable pair, all smiles and banter and fashionable clobber, but neither of them is much use to me for conceiving a child with Conall.

Which means . . . there's no spare woman in this house for Conall.

What the hell. Make lemonade. It'll have to be Katie and Fionn.

Back up on the top floor, there's no denying the bond between them. They're very close.

But something is off . . . They're close, but they're not together. They *were* together for a short time, but Fionn slept with someone called Alina the night Jemima, his foster-mother, died; and Katie found she didn't give a damn, so then the whole thing was banjaxed. But they've stayed very fond of each other, all credit to them.

Fionn was knocked sideways by the death of his foster-mother. He's saddled with a ton of guilt because he wasn't there for her, and Katie's been good to him.

Which means—all becomes clear—which means that Katie is available! Free to be with Conall! Katie's standing up. Because Fionn's leaving. He doesn't live here. He did for a spell, while he filmed a television show but it was never shown, and now he's gone back home, to some faraway rocky, rural place called Pokey. He was only in Dublin today to pick up bits and pieces that used to belong to his foster-mother.

'Are you sure you won't pop in with me?' Katie asks, making for the door.

Fionn shakes his head. 'Maeve doesn't like me.'

Katie was trying to sympathise while simultaneously keeping them moving forward. 'Don't be a baby.'

Fionn stops in his tracks and gives a thousand-yard stare. 'I'm not really a party person.'

That makes Katie laugh good and hard.

'OK,' Fionn admits. 'I was for a short while. But that wasn't who I really am. I'm a loner by nature.'

'I know. Come on, out.'

Katie locks her door and they go down a flight of stairs, and as they start going down the next one, Rosie and Andrei's dog tenses in his basket, then races out to his hall, barking and throwing himself with violence at the door. 'Let me at him,' he roars. 'Let me at the yellow-haired prick. I'll have the shagging *leg* off him.'

In response, Fionn gives the door a good hard kick and the lock rattles. 'He's a headcase,' Fionn says to Katie.

'So you say, but it's Andrei's door now; you shouldn't be kicking it.'

'Can you believe Jemima actually left the flat to him? In her will?'

'I'm sure she had her reasons. What use is it to you? You hate Dublin.'

Katie's anxious. Katie wants to keep things in motion because she wants to get to the party before—

Conall's leaving! Down on the ground floor, he's said his goodbyes to Matt and Maeve, he's coming out of their door and now he's in the communal hall, and Fionn and Katie are still standing outside Andrei's flat, chinwagging away about Jemima's will like they have all the time in the world. Like *I* have all the time in the world. Which I haven't.

'It was just a surprise, is all I'm saying,' Fionn said.

'You can hardly complain. She left you all her money.'

Come on. Come ON! Downstairs, downstairs!

'And sure, what interest have I in property?' Fionn said.

'None at all. You're a man of the land.'

'Speaking of which'—Fionn starts foostering in the pocket of his manky old jacket—'I've probably got something for you.'

Oh, sweet suffering Jesus! Would you COME ON! One flight of stairs, that's all you have to do. Fourteen steps. It's not going to kill you.

But Conall's opened the front door.

'Katie?'

Down in the hall, Conall's spotted Katie on the landing above him.

'Conall!' Katie's face blazes whiteness. She hasn't seen Conall since Jemima's funeral.

Followed by Fionn, who sticks close to her, she comes down the stairs. Walking slowly and oddly, because her legs are shaking.

'Fionn.' Conall nods stiffly.

'Conall.' Fionn nods back, just as stiffly.

Conall's emotions have gone haywire. His terrible heartache is puls-ing and pounding, each squeeze of his heart, each breath that he takes, more painful than the previous one. He's wild with relief at the sight of Katie, but seeing her with Fionn is like being wounded in the guts with a spear. Warmth, wound, joy, pain: a right old emotional stew. 'Were you at Matt and Maeve's?' Katie asks him.

I love you. 'I was just leaving.'

'Back to work? At eight thirty on a Saturday night? Some things never change.'

I love you. 'Katie, I'm not going to work.' He's keen to splurge as much information as he can because he doesn't know how much time he has before Fionn sweeps her away. 'That's all changed. I've taken on two partners and I'll be getting more. Things are different. I haven't left the country in'—he counts in his head—'nearly nine weeks.'

'God. What are you doing with your time?'

Thinking about you. Nonstop. 'Dunno. Over with Joe and Pat a lot. Bronagh asks about you.'

'So if you're not going to work, why are you leaving the party?'

Conall opens his mouth, then closes it again. He's not sure what he should say, especially with Fionn standing at her shoulder, glowering possessively, but he came here today because he couldn't take the pain of not seeing her, so he might as well do what he set out to do. After all, he's a fighter, isn't he? Or is he? He's no longer sure. 'I thought you weren't coming. I gave up waiting for you.'

Katie screws up her face in a question. 'You were waiting for *me*?'

He nods, his eyes dark, all his intensity on her face.

'Why?'

'I wanted to see you.'

This is too much for Fionn. 'Excuse me interrupting,' he says, with savage sarcasm, 'but I have something for Katie.'

'Sorry, Fionn.' Katie looks a little stunned. 'What is it?'

'I don't know yet, do I? I was just about to find out when your man here started shouting up to us.' Fionn rummages around in his pocket and emerges with a dark green sprig. He doesn't seem happy.

'What is it?' Katie asks.

'Ah . . . bridewort. It's, er, the herb of love. Historically, the most pop-ular strewing herb at weddings.'

'Who's getting married?' Katie asks.

'You, according to the magic pocket. It must be a mistake. Hold on, I'm sure I can find you something better.' A quick rootle produces another sprig. Fionn stares at it. 'Ivy.' He crumples it into nothing.

'But what does it mean?'

'Fidelity. There must be something better in here.' He delves again, deeper this time, and finds a tiny seed. He swallows hard. 'Liquorice.'

'And?'

'Fidelity and passion to a sexual union. I'll try another pocket.' Once again, his hand dives to the depths.

'This one?' Katie looks at the wilted leaf that emerges.

'Elderflower.'

'And?'

'Brings blessing to a married couple.'

Well, there's a silence, of a type you can't even start to describe. Conall looks confused and Katie looks perplexed, while Fionn glares from one to the other, then back again.

'I'm going home!' he announces. He steps out into the street, and over his departing shoulder he throws back, 'I hope the two of you will be very happy together.'

'Fionn!' Katie hurries after him.

'Hey, look,' Conall says, embarrassed, 'I'll leave you—'

'No!' Katie places her hand on Conall's chest and hisses, 'No, you stay right there. This won't take long.'

'Fionn!' Katie catches up with him. 'What is it?'

'You always loved him. That gobdaw Conall Hathaway.'

What can she say? Yes, she has always loved him. She still loves him. The closeness she and Conall shared the morning that Jemima died felt intensely meaningful, like it was the beginning of a different sort of love, a solid, steady one. But, in the days afterwards, Conall didn't contact her and more days passed and then they were into weeks, and around the two-month mark she made herself admit that she must have imagined the intimate trust they'd shared. The pain was atomic, quite a surprise really. She thought she knew all the different kinds of heartbreak but this was a new one, a crushing sadness, an appalling knowledge of lost chances, of the life she and Conall could have had together if both of them had been just a little bit different, if he'd been less work-obsessed, if she'd been more willing to compromise.

She could have contacted him, a breezy text, a casual email—he was no longer with Lydia, no one could miss Lydia's antics with

Oleksander—but she didn't, because . . .? Because she wasn't starting that old thing again, begging for scraps of his time.

And then he turns up in her hallway, saying he only came to the party so he can see her. She was barely able to walk down the stairs, the way he was watching her. What was going on . . .?

Fionn is still waiting for an answer. Quickly she says, 'I loved you too, Fionn.'

'I was just a bit of fun to you.'

'Nothing wrong with fun. And we'll always be friends.'

'Yeah.' He looks a little contrite. 'Sorry. Look, go back in to him. You're meant to be together.'

'Ah, come on, Fionn—'

'No, *you* come on, Katie! Look at what my magic pockets were saying. Fidelity, love, union. The magic pocket never lies.'

The magic pocket is far more of a hit-and-miss phenomenon, in Katie's opinion, but it is sort of weird that everything Fionn produced had to do with love.

'They mightn't have broadcast *Your Own Private Eden*, but there's no denying I've still got that old razzle-dazzle.' Considerably cheered up by his own brilliance, Fionn strikes out in the direction of the Luas. 'I'll ring you,' he calls back to her.

'Grand.' She watches him go; then she steps back into her hall.

Conall is sitting obediently on the stairs, just as she left him. There's something wrong, a certain bareness to the picture. She finally identifies it. 'Your BlackBerry?' she says. 'Where is it?'

'Oh . . .' He pats his jeans pockets. 'Here. Do you need it?'

'No. It's just that I think this is the first time I've seen you doing nothing. Just sitting staring into space.'

'I'm telling you, Katie, I'm different.'

'So what goes on in your head now that you're not thinking of work all the time? Like what were you thinking while you've been sitting here?'

'I've been saying prayers.'

'*Prayers?*' She'd known this was too good to be true. He'd swapped workaholism for religion.

'Praying that you'll come back to me.'

'Oh!' Well, maybe those sorts of prayers were OK.

'Look.' She's suddenly sombre. 'What's going on, Conall? I don't hear from you for four months and now you show up, talking about prayers.'

He puts his face in his hands, breathes deeply, seems to make a decision and sits upright. 'All right, here's how it is. I've nothing to lose at this stage. I love you, Katie. I can't stop thinking about you. I never have, not since I first met you. But that morning, with Jemima, you and I being there when she died, I felt so much love for you, such a . . . an attachment. But you have a boyfriend, so I didn't know what to do.'

'That doesn't sound like you.'

'Because I'm not me, not any more. I'm different, Katie. All of that stuff happening at the same time, Matt trying to kill himself and Jemima dying and work going weird, it was no longer doing it for me; then when I heard about Maeve getting pregnant . . . I felt, I don't know, like a miracle had happened, and . . . you know?' He shrugs. 'I thought you wouldn't meet me if I asked you to, but I was hoping to bump into you at the party.'

Katie says nothing. She's been hoping that she'd bump into him too. She thought Fionn would never leave.

'I haven't,' she says.

'Haven't what?'

'A boyfriend.'

'But Fionn?'

'That's all over. It's been over since the night of Jemima.'

'You're not serious.' Conall slumps into himself. 'All that time . . . I don't *believe* it. I thought I was going to have to fight him for you today.'

'You're making a lot of assumptions, Conall. Does my opinion count for nothing?'

'It counts for everything, as it happens. I've a question for you.' Conall gets to his feet and clears his throat as if he's about to make a speech. 'Katie Richmond, I love you with all my heart and I will do my best to make you happy for the rest of your life. Will you marry me?'

'Well, I don't know, now that you've given up your job . . . Will we be poor?'

'Not at all. Haven't you a job? We'll be grand.' More seriously, he says, 'No, we won't be poor.'

'Have you a ring?'

'Yes, I have a ring.'

'No!'

'What? You think I was going to make the same mistake twice?'

'Show me.'

He produces a little box and flips it open and white light blazes at them. 'Diamonds,' Katie remarks.

'Unless you'd prefer emeralds?' Another box appears, containing a deep green stone in an antique setting.

'You're not serious.'

'Or sapphires?' And out comes another box.

'Stop, please. Conall, you haven't changed that much!'

'I just wanted to get it right.'

'God.' Katie presses her hands over her eyes. This was all too much. 'Stop asking me things.'

'For how long?'

'A while.'

Five seconds pass. 'That's a while,' Conall says. 'So what's it to be?'

'Ah . . . the diamonds.'

'Christ! Is that a yes?'

'Yes.'

'Yes?'

'Yes. It's a yes.'

It's Lydia who discovers them. Us, I suppose you could say. She's highly indignant. All she's trying to do is get up her own stairs, but her way is *impeded* by Hathaway and the governess snogging the face off each other. Disgusting. And *selfish*! Blocking public thoroughfares.

'Take it somewhere else!' she commands, curling her lip at their evident happiness as she stomps on up the steps.

When they hear the door of her flat slam behind her, Katie murmurs, 'She has a point.'

'You mean . . .?' Conall says.

'I do.'

And the next thing, they've grasped each other's hands and they're running upstairs and I'm all swept up and enmeshed in their magical energy. And when we arrive at the top floor, the three of us tumble into Katie's apartment and we fall onto the bed and, and, and . . .

. . . I'm waiting for my moment, and . . . and . . .

. . . any minute now . . .

. . . and . . . aaaannnndddd . . . here we go! Hold on to your hats. I'm going in.

Marian Keyes

Marian Keyes was born in Limerick, in the west of Ireland, in 1963, and brought up in Dublin. 'When I left school I went to college, got a law degree, then put it to good use by going to London and getting a job as a waitress. Eventually I upped and got respectable and took a job in an accounts office, where I worked (I use the term oh-so-loosely) for a long, long, long time. I thought I'd be there for ever, that I'd end up as a grumpy old woman with forty cats, and that small boys would throw stones at me. What I certainly had no notion of doing was becoming a writer.'

However, during this period, Marian was battling a life-long low-self-esteem problem that developed into a drinking problem. 'By the time I was thirty it had all come to a terrible head and, after a suicide attempt, I was lucky enough to get into rehab. (Mind you I didn't feel lucky at the time! I thought my life was over.) However, I've been one of the fortunate ones and I've stayed sober and—more importantly—happy about it, ever since.

'I began writing short stories four months before I finally stopped drinking, and after I came out of rehab decided to send them off to a publisher. So that they'd take me seriously, I enclosed a letter saying I'd written part of a novel. Which I hadn't. I had no intention of so doing, either—I was much more into the instant gratification of short stories. But they wrote back and said, "Send the novel," and for once in my self-destructive life I didn't shoot myself in the foot. I wrote four chapters of *Watermelon* in a week, and was offered a three-book contract on the strength of it.' Since then, Marian has taken the publishing world by storm and sales of her novels exceed five million copies in the UK alone.

Her latest best seller, *The Brightest Star in the Sky,* was inspired by Alexander McCall Smith's *44 Scotland Street* series. 'I loved the way he wrote about the massive cast of characters and the way we all intersect, and the impact we have on other peoples' lives without even knowing it.' Marian's characters live in the four flats at 66 Star Street, Dublin, and are introduced by a mysterious narrator whose identity is not fully revealed until close to the end of the story. 'Most people don't guess until a good way in. They think: Is it death? Is it an angel? Is it a ghost? What can it be?'

Her previous novels have touched on some pretty bleak subjects—domestic violence, addiction and bereavement—and the characters in her latest book are given some dark struggles to overcome. Marian highlights the devastation of rape, and spent time with the Dublin Rape Crisis Centre. She also focuses on the sadness of watching a beloved parent cope with the onset of dementia. But this talented author also blends comedy and humour with her exploration of the darker elements of life, and insists her stories must have happy endings. 'In my experience the best comedy is rooted in darkness. All my books are different but they share a common theme of people who are In The Bad Place, and who achieve some form of redemption. I've been In The Bad Place myself many a time, which wasn't very pleasant while it was happening, but has since come in very handy when writing about it. I write for me and I need to feel hopeful about the human condition and so there is no way that I am going to write a downbeat ending. And I have this feeling that, you know, sometimes there are happyish endings or hopeful endings and it's not entirely ludicrous to suggest that things might work out for the best. I've always used humour as a survival mechanism and it's what I like to write about.'

For the moment, Marian is caught up in an altogether different kind of addiction. She absolutely adores *Strictly Come Dancing* and also follows the after-show gossip on *It Takes Two*. On a recent promotion tour for *The Brightest Star in the Sky* in London, she was invited to join the Friday-night panel of *It Takes Two*, which meant that she got to meet one of her 'girl crushes', Claudia Winkleman, in person. 'I chose my outfit with painstaking care because I nurture the pitiful ambition that if my shoes are impressive enough, Claudia might befriend me.' Well, they must have done the trick because after the show 'Claudia invited me and my pals to her dressing room to admire *her* shoes and the array is nothing short of magnificent'.

The Good Luck Girl

by Kerry Reichs

Lots can happen when, as an author, you load a girl who's

determined to change her luck into a temperamental

1978 Plymouth Road Runner called Elsie and let her

drive across country. Especially when the girl's beloved

rattletrap breaks down in Unknown, Arizona, and she

starts to feel very much at home among the quirky

characters who live in the town.

I really hope you enjoy my new novel about finding

yourself—after finding yourself in the middle of nowhere!

Kerry

Chapter 1: Fired Up

I CAN HONESTLY SAY I didn't *intend* to be bad. It's just that I have rotten luck. I was nine and on a camping trip. Four suburban families with expensive tents that didn't get out of the garage much, and Coleman stoves that the fathers couldn't really figure out but which required hours of happy tinkering while the women gossiped and made burgers. A dozen kids charged about in OshKosh B'gosh overalls.

We were marshalling forces for the day's excursion. I was instructed to stay put while the adults debated Grandfather Mountain versus Blowing Rock. A nearby trailhead tantalised. I begged to explore. My father gave me permission to go for ten minutes, not a minute more.

But the lure of each new bend of the trail was too much for me. I *had* to see what was round the corner. And the next. And the next. By the time my father caught up with me an hour later, I got a bare-bottom spanking right there on the trail. My punishment was to sit in the tent and 'think about things'. What I thought about was how great that trail had been and how I wished I'd got to the end of it. Back then, I was different. Back then, I was fearless. It was much later that the death of my best friend made me dread things I couldn't see coming.

I've always been restless. I can't seem to settle on anything. That's probably why it took me seven and a half years to finish college. I finally graduated at the ripe old age of twenty-five with a major in Anthropology and a minor in Film Studies. I had no idea what I wanted to do and a lot of time on my hands. That was the situation four weeks ago. That was when the trouble began. That was when I discovered Facebook.com.

'**W**hat're you doing?' I asked my brother, Brick, over the phone as I lounged on the sofa. I was looking for a diversion.

'Screwing around on Facebook instead of studying.' Brick was in college, following a normal four-year plan.

'What's Facebook?' I picked at my nail polish.

'It's a social networking web site, and death to productivity.'

I perked up. Oliver, my cockatiel, ruffled his feathers in annoyance. I'd disturbed his perch on my head. I ignored him. The possibility of a time-sucking web site was far more appealing than figuring out what I was going to do for the rest of my life. Normally a reader, lately I was into short-attention-span diversions like the Internet and TV.

'Let me get a pen . . .' I said.

An hour later, I'd posted a photo, established a Super Wall and was diving into the Cities I've Visited application. It involved sticking virtual pins into a world map of all the exotic locations you'd been to. Unless Frying Pan Landing, North Carolina, counted as exotic, it was going to be a short diversion for all of us. I hadn't ventured far from my home town of Charlotte. Not that I had many people to impress. So far I had one friend in my network, and it was my brother. My interest was waning when a message popped up: a friend request!

'It's a movie producer,' I predicted to Oliver. 'Who wants to make me a movie star after seeing my photo.' It *was* a fetching shot, and I was wearing my favourite polka-dot knee socks. You can't see them in the picture, but the right socks are essential to total appearance.

'Are you thinner?' squawked my bird, as he did at least once a day. One of my more successful projects. I grinned as I clicked open the request, and stared at the face of a stranger named Laura who wanted to be my friend. Was this how it worked? Random people became your friends online? I hesitated. Something about the name nagged at me. Laura Mills. I frowned in concentration, then immediately stopped and rubbed my forehead. A wrinkle between your eyes is so unattractive, and our family was prone to the Connelly divot.

Suddenly I remembered. Laura Mills had lived across the street and been my best friend when I was eight, but then her family had moved to Texas when I was eleven and I never saw her again. I examined the photo. There was no doubt about it. Eleven-year-old Laura was looking out from behind the glamorous make-up of my new future friend. I had no idea how she'd found me after fifteen years, but Facebook was officially the coolest web site ever. I clicked 'Accept', bracing myself for a flood of long-lost acquaintances.

Two hours later, I slid behind the bar at Gin Mill as unobtrusively as possible. 'Maeve? Are you here?' shouted my boss Joe from his office. His voice was followed by his stocky frame, sporting folded arms and a forehead crease big enough to hide a body.

'Hey, Joe,' I tried. 'I was taking out the trash.'

'Maeve, you're an hour and sixteen minutes late!' Rats. My typical luck he'd noticed. Some days he never left the office.

'I'm sorry, Joe. It was traffic.' I really was sorry. I didn't want to lose another job.

'Look, Maeve, I like you. I really do. But from four to eight, I count on you to handle the bar. Between you and that unreliable car, I spend half your shifts at the bar myself.' My car Elsie was an ancient 1970 Plymouth Road Runner prone to breakdowns.

'I'm sorry, Joe. It won't happen again.' I hung my head, long blonde braids drooping penitently.

He considered me. 'Not again, Maeve,' he relented, before lumbering back to the office.

I thought about the last message of an afternoon emailing with Laura. She lived in Los Angeles and worked as something called a First AD, which meant she worked on the Fox Studio lot, met all kinds of famous people, and got to see movies before they were released:

> You should *totally* come visit. Los Angeles is awesome, I see celebrities *every day*. Last week I sat next to George Clooney at a screening. You could crash with me as long as you needed, and get a job at the studio. We'd have so much fun.

It sounded a lot better than wiping down a dirty bar counter in Charlotte.

The next day started well—I'd savoured the arrival of spring during my three-mile run, and returned to read the details of Laura's morning with actress Katherine Heigl. I wished I had the money to take her up on her invitation. The fantasy of life in California was delicious but the reality, for me, was the picture I'd spotted on Facebook of an old boyfriend, arm slung round the shoulders of a petite redhead, matching happy smiles. It'd been a blow, but I knew the cure for a foul mood. I glanced at my watch; I had plenty of time before work.

'Road trip. Don't forget the bird,' chirped Oliver as I put him in his cage.

'Next time, pal,' I promised. Elsie grudgingly started. My car was sunshine yellow with a black stripe across her hood. Unlike 'collector-quality' Plymouth Road Runners, Elsie had done over 150,000 miles and was limping through her golden years. I loved her.

Twenty minutes later, I was happily browsing Nordstrom's shoe section. From forty feet away I felt the jolt you get when you first lay eyes on the boots you know will shortly be yours. I sprang towards them like a lioness on an antelope.

'These.' I waved the red suede boot at a clerk. 'Size eight.'

As he glided off, I glanced at the $225 price tag. Ouch. I thought of the ignored bills stacked on the kitchen counter. I'd already charged dinner at the club to my parents' account six times this month. Or had it been seven?

When the shoe salesman returned, I wrestled with myself. Maybe I shouldn't try them on. I could get attached. But they *were* gorgeous.

'This is your lucky day,' he said. 'They're twenty per cent off.'

'Fantastic.' I grinned as I reached for the box. God did love me.

Fifteen minutes later, back in Elsie, I doubted God's love as I fumed at the traffic. Four twenty-three. Shit. I should be at work. I crept along Fairview Road. What the hell was going on?

I spotted red and blue lights flashing and groaned. An accident was narrowing traffic to one lane. It would take fifteen minutes to get past. I banged the steering wheel. Elsie responded with an ominous rattle.

'I'm sorry, Elsie,' I repented, patting the console. 'Please don't die.' I glanced at the gas gauge. The last thing I needed was to run out of gas.

I ran out of gas. I leaned forward in my seat, as if shifting my five-foot-nine, 140-pound frame would give the 4,000-pound car momentum, and willed Elsie to coast. Still pissed about the steering-wheel thing, she rolled to a stop a mile from the Texaco.

'How much bad luck can one person have?' I moaned, reaching for my cellphone to call Joe. At least I had a bona fide excuse, I thought virtuously.

I flipped open my phone. I had No Service. How come I had no service in the middle of town? I had a text message, so I opened it curiously as I stepped out of Elsie. I froze.

Your Sprint mobile phone service has been suspended for nonpayment. Payment of your outstanding balance in full is required to reactivate phone service.

I couldn't believe it. I was *sure* I'd paid the bill. I recalled the stack of bills on my counter. Hadn't I? I frowned, then smoothed the groove between my eyes. Nothing for it but to trudge to the gas station.

It was close to six when I pulled into the Gin Mill parking lot. The place was packed. I mean, *really* packed. I could see Jules's long, dark ponytail flying as she whirled to grab bottles of beer. Next to her, Joe was sloshing something pink into shot glasses. My heart plummeted. Today was our inaugural Young Professionals happy hour.

I dashed to the bar. The look Joe gave me would have made a frailer woman faint, but now wasn't the time to explain. I started taking orders and slinging beer.

By eight, most of the crowd had moved on and we could draw a breath. Joe was back in the office. 'That was crazy, daisy!' I said. 'Jules, I'm so sorry. I ran out of gas.' When she laughed, I protested. 'No, really, I did!'

Jules shook her head. 'You don't have to convince me, girl. I'm fine with it.' We'd been friends since junior high. She was used to forgiving me. 'Joe was pissed off, though.'

I hesitated. 'How pissed off?'

'Well—'

'Maeve!' Joe's holler cut her off. 'Get in here.'

'Good luck, little camper.' Jules patted my shoulder as I passed.

Joe's look was black. 'Shut the door,' he instructed. I did, and sat in the uncomfortable chair that wobbled.

'Today was unacceptable—' Joe began.

'Joe, there was an accident, and then I ran out of gas . . .'

Joe sighed. 'I'm sorry, Maeve. But I gotta let you go.'

'But—'

Joe held up his hand to cut off my protest. 'It don't matter whether it was traffic or running out of gas. The bottom line is that you're regularly late and other people aren't. So, you're off the schedule.'

I blinked rapidly at the welling tears. I would *not* cry, I vowed.

Joe's gaze softened. 'Maeve, I know you're sorting things out . . .'

I sprang from my seat. I didn't want his pity. 'Mail me my cheque.'

'Maeve . . .'

I ignored him and strode out with a wave and a chipper 'Thanks, Joe.'

Behind the bar, I hugged Jules. 'I'm off.' I radiated cheer. 'Sorry again about tonight.'

'Did he fire you?' She looked worried.

'It wasn't working out.' I was vague. 'This is for the best.' I fluttered my fingers and practically skipped to my car to show how carefree I was.

It was only when the door was shut and locked behind me that the tears came. 'Elsie, what am I going to do?' I whispered, the thought of my unpaid bills making me queasy with fear. What was wrong with me? I used to have a plan.

I needed spaghetti. If my mother was cooking spaghetti, my luck would change, I told myself.

'**M**aeve!' My father's face lit up when I walked into the kitchen. He was leafing through the mail, still in his suit. 'Joining us for dinner?'

'Yep.' I received one of his excellent hugs. I was feeling better already.

'Hello, dear.' My mother popped up from behind the counter. 'You're in luck. I'm trying something new tonight. A curry chicken.'

I wobbled, but rallied. No big deal. I'd already had my daily dose of bad luck.

'Hey.' My attention returned to my father. 'You're looking at your mail.' My father looked at mail only on Sunday, when it was guaranteed that no more would arrive while he was sorting it.

He gave me a rueful look. 'Your mother has insisted on some *reforms* since she finished the Spirit Square project.' He winked, and headed upstairs.

'Ah.' My mother, a sculptor, alternated between periods of complete oblivion when she was immersed in a project, and ruthless organisation when she emerged and tried to make up for lost time.

'Speaking of mail,' said my temporarily Type A mother, 'there's a letter for you, Maeve. It's from Cameron's parents.'

I got the panicky feeling I got whenever I thought about Cameron.

My mother continued, her voice gentle. 'I believe they plan to do something to commemorate the anniversary of her passing.'

I met her eyes. 'I don't think I can,' I said.

She opened her mouth to say something more, then thought better of it. 'No need to decide right now. Let's sit and wait for your father.' She kicked off her Birkenstocks and sat cross-legged on the bench. I sat on the 'grown-up' side of the table, in a normal chair. 'Have you given any thought to what you'd like to do now that you've graduated?' Her tone was careful.

'I don't know.' I hesitated. 'I don't know what I'm good at.'

My mom squeezed my hand. 'Maeve, you're good at so many things.'

'You have to say that. You're my mother.'

'It's the truth. Look at what a good bartender you are!' Not encouraging words. I grimaced. 'What about photography? You did a remarkable job taking pictures of my sculptures.'

'I don't think you can make a living—'

'Maeve!' My father's bellow echoed down the hallway. He strode into the room, deep crease between his eyebrows, waving a sheaf of papers. 'What the hell is this?' He thrust the sheets under my eyes and I winced. The country-club bill had arrived. I couldn't believe it. The *one* day this month I needed to be far away from home happened to be the day I got fired, dropped in unexpectedly, and Dad uncharacteristically opened his mail before Sunday. Talk about bad timing. 'Care to explain?'

'Um.' I looked at the bill. Had I really eaten at the club *nine* times?

'We don't begrudge you the occasional meal, Maeve,' my father chastened. 'But four massages? A new tennis racket?'

Dad's outrage deflated at the sight of my hunched frame. 'Your mother and I understand that you've had a hard time. Harder than most. We've been patient, allowing you time to figure things out. But now you must take responsibility for your life. You're a bright girl, you've got your degree. You need to start thinking about your future.'

I stared at them aghast. My future loomed impossibly large and intimidating. I had no idea how I'd fill the chasm.

'You have to curb your tendency to spend beyond your means,' my father lectured in a gentle voice. 'You can't buy something every time you're upset.' He paused, as if afraid of his own words, then plunged in. 'I'm going to require you to repay us for the massages and the tennis racket. You can take as long as you like, and of course we won't charge interest. But you need to learn responsibility. The way you live now is,' he waved his hands in the air, 'flibbertigibbety,' he pronounced.

'Flighty,' my mother affirmed.

'I am *not* flighty.' I adopted a haughty tone. 'I graduated with a 3.5. I take excellent care of Oliver.' I wanted to say more, but the fact that I never missed an episode of *Bones* didn't seem quite right.

'I'll help you work out a payment plan.' My father seemed happy to sidestep the debate. 'We'll look at your shifts at Gin Mill and your current expenses and create a budget for you.'

'Then you can decide how long you want to keep bartending, and if you want to try something else.' My mother sounded hopeful.

My stomach turned. 'Um . . . Isortoflostmyjob . . .' I mumbled.

'What was that?' Mom's confusion-divot mirrored Dad's anger-dent. My forehead was doomed.

'I'm not working at Gin Mill anymore,' I said. 'I ran out of gas so I was really late for work.'

'Joe fired you for being late?' My father looked confused.

'It wasn't just the once,' I confessed to my plate.

My mother rubbed her face tiredly. We sat there for a moment, mutely staring at cooling curry chicken. Then my parents' eyes met, and my father voiced a decision I suspected they'd prearranged.

'Maeve, I won't require you to repay the club bill, but, from now on, you're on your own. Your mother and I will start you out with next month's rent and utilities. That gives you a month and a half to find a job and become self-supporting. After that, consider yourself cut off.' They both looked stricken as he spoke. 'We want what's best for you, and being extreme seems to be the sole way to get through.'

'How is it whenever someone tells me they are doing what's best for me, it ends up hurting me?' I demanded, fighting tears.

'Maeve, you cannot be dependent on your father and me for ever.' My mother's eyes were serious. 'The only thing holding you back is you. We haven't helped matters by enabling your inertia. I recognise that. But it's time to take the next step in your life.'

A wave of anger doused my panic, and drove me to my feet. I was *not* some basket case. I had a wicked bad-luck curse. How many people get fired and cut off by their families because they bought a pair of boots? *On sale?* Something was out of kilter in the universe, but it wasn't me. I had a vision of palm trees.

'I am *not* a flake,' I squeezed out of a tight throat. I fought tears as I grabbed my purse and ran-walked to the door. 'And I'll prove it.'

I drove away with the window down, hoping the cold March air would blow my head clear. I dug in my purse for a bottle of charcoal tablets and popped two—my stomach was roiling. I hoped I wasn't getting a virus. I cursed myself for forgetting to take Emergen-C that morning. I fumbled for my car supply of echinacea and popped one of those too.

I'd already gone for a run today, but I needed more, like a hit. I steered Elsie towards the university track. I parked and stretched for only a nanosecond before I was sprinting. My feet pounded rhythmically along the track in a steady alternation; I lost myself in the physical exertion of repetitive motion. Of my body obeying me. Of the rare moment when I was in total control. I wanted to crush my parents' pity and the look on Joe's face beneath my pounding feet. I was *not* someone to be pitied. Look at me, see how I *run*. I can push myself. I have discipline. I *would* prove them wrong. I would elude my rotten luck if I had to run all the way across the country to do it. In fact, that sounded like just the trick. I was ready for Hollywood.

To: LALola@neticom.net
From: Maeveyourday@gmail.com
Sent: March —

Subject: LA Here I Come!

Laura, guess what? You've talked me into it. I've decided to come to
California. I'm still working out the details but I'm thinking sooner rather
than later. Why wait for Paradise, right?
Give me a call at 704-555-1881 to talk about details.
Can't wait to see you in person!
Later gater, M

'**A**re you sure about this?' my older sister Vi asked me.

'Never more.' I used my shoulder to hold the phone in place while
I refreshed my computer. Still no reply from Laura. I squelched a
twinge of anxiety. When she was running round the lot, she didn't have
email access. Anyway, how hard could it be to find her? I'd drive until
the ocean stopped me.

'It's an awfully big move without a *plan*,' Vi pressed.

'I have a *plan*, Stan.' I mimicked her tone. I was in high spirits.

Vi snorted. 'What, drive west until the ocean stops you?' She had an
uncanny ability to read my brain. But nothing could dampen my conviction that moving to California was the solution to my problems.

'Laura invited me. Remember Laura Mills?'

'Laura Mills from when you were ten?'

'We reconnected.' Vi let it go. I was grateful. Laura was the unknown
variable in the plan. I was counting on being able to crash with my old
friend while I got sorted. Still, there was no reason to think Laura's
invitation wasn't sincere.

'A marathon, huh?'

'Yep. The Los Angeles Marathon.' The first step towards a new me
was a personal goal. I would train over the summer and the fall
marathon would literally be the starting gun for my new life.

'It just seems so . . . far. From all of us. If anything happened . . .'

'Nothing's going to happen. I need to make a change. Here, I don't
know, I feel trapped in, well, in *before*. I want to prove that I am a completely responsible and capable person. It'll be good for me,' I assured
her. 'I've got to go, Vi.'

She sighed. 'I know. But let me help. I'm sending you a cheque.'

I wanted to say no, but I was stony-broke. 'Not much,' I capitulated
after embarrassingly little inner struggle.

'Trust me.' She laughed. 'I'm buying peace of mind that you won't end up stranded in the middle of the desert with no gas or cell service in a town named Skeleton Junction with a population of four people and one tooth. Promise you'll call before you leave?' It made my departure sound so definite I caught my breath. I almost recanted it all as a big joke. Instead, I assured Vi I'd call her and hung up.

I explored my instinct to retract from the trip. Was I doing this because I wanted to or because I wanted to prove people wrong?

No, I decided. I *did* want to make a real change. I'd been living down to everyone's (low) expectations of me. In their eyes I was Maeve the Clown. I made people laugh. It's a truism that we respond to people's perceptions. I'd lazily adopted the Maeve-is-a-slacker notion as my own. But not anymore. If I went far enough away, I could be anyone. I assembled my morning vitamin regimen as I pondered, absently lining up vitamins A through D, a woman's multi, ginkgo biloba, manganese, flax oil, selenium and the other dailies. I made a note to pick up ginseng and coenzyme Q10 to counteract the increased stress of travel. If I was going to do this, I needed a battle plan, supplies.

My eye fell on a Post-it that read: *Before you can arrive where you want to be, you have to know where you are going.*

The first thing I needed was a SuperMap . . .

I spend hours studying maps. They fascinate me. Riding back from the beach one weekend with Jules, studying a map, I'd noticed a nearby town called Half Hell, North Carolina. I'd insisted she detour, and my passion had been born. I'd organised day trips all over the state to visit Toast, Erect and Whynot, occasionally crossing the border to visit Ninety Six or Sugar Tit, South Carolina. I loved capturing the curves of the road and the quirks of the towns on film. For me, it was like that trail when I was nine. I couldn't rest until I'd reached my destination.

I liked to snap an Elsie centrefold from each destination, and developed quite a collection of my car in front of one-of-a-kind town signs. I meticulously categorised my scrapbook. First you have just plain peculiar names, like Peculiar, Missouri, or Goofy Ridge, Illinois. Second you have 'I was here' places, such as Hell, Michigan; or It, Mississippi. Third are the great imitators: Milan, Ohio; or Moscow, Idaho. Fourth you have superlatives, such as Best, Texas; or Top of the World, Arizona. Best, Texas, is not to be confused with Veribest, Texas. I fully intended to stop by both on my drive across. I wanted to photograph America from the inside out.

Elsie couldn't handle the high speeds of the Interstate, so I happily planned a back-roads course wending between these alluring designations. Back roads would extend my trip, but I was in no hurry. The marathon wasn't for months. Only, the longer the journey, the more money I'd need. That *was* a problem, since I didn't have any.

Affordable camping would figure heavily in my trip, and I'd chosen the southwestern route because southern states not only had some crazy town names, but the warm, dry weather would be best for camping. Food would be a bigger problem. I pondered. Hard-boiled eggs kept well, travelled easily and are a good source of protein. I'd throw in trail mix and cheese sticks for variety. And oranges. I lived in constant fear of scurvy, so oranges were essential. I'd reserve my cash for necessities, like Diet Coke and water. You want to take lots of water when you drive through the desert.

That left the last hurdle. Cold, hard cash.

The phone rang. It was Jules.

'Can I borrow your ladder?' she asked without preamble.

A year ago in a fit of DIY that petered out almost before I got home from Lowe's, I'd blown $300 on a ladder. It now served as the world's most expensive drying rack for my delicates. Well, second most expensive. Maybe third. My road bike and treadmill were also costly clothes lines. The only time the poor emasculated ladder was used for its intended purpose was when I loaned it to friends. Jules regularly borrowed it to change the seasonal fairy lights in her apartment. As it was April, I suspected illuminated mini-bunnies were going up.

'For a hundred dollars you can keep it,' I joked.

'For real?' she demanded. ''Cause if you mean it, you're on.'

'Really?' I was surprised. A hundred bucks was a lot for something as boring as a ladder. But Jules took her seasonal decorations very seriously.

'Hell, yeah. Save myself the hassle of driving to your place and back every month. And that's over half off.'

My eye fell on my new, troublemaking tennis racket, tag still on. 'Do you play tennis?' I asked Jules.

'No. Why?'

'Never mind.' An idea was forming. 'You know my turquoise BCBG pumps you love?' Jules and I wore the same size of shoe.

'Of course.'

'I'll sell them to you for another hundred dollars.' I held my breath. It seemed like an outrageous sum to ask of a friend. But the shoes had cost me $160 and I'd worn them in only two battles before the pain in my toes won the war. Jules wore them much more often—she has a commendable tolerance for pain when it comes to shoes.

'Seriously? Hell, yes! I love those shoes.' Jules jumped at my offer. I couldn't believe it. I'd made $200 just like that. My brain raced.

'Jules, if you help me organise a yard sale, I'll give you an employee discount on all my shoes.' I barely listened for her response as my eyes flicked from item to item round the room: treadmill, bowling ball, tennis racket, chess set, television, sofa, yoga ball, juicer, waffle maker. I was going to California for a fresh start. I'd sell it all.

'Sure. I'd help anyway.' She was quiet for a moment. 'So I guess you're really leaving. I'll miss you.'

I thought of her bright eyes and easy laugh. I wanted to say something in return, but it was hard for me. I said, 'When I leave, I'm giving you my yellow suede Fiorinas as a memento, pimento.'

'Girl, I can't get you out of town fast enough.' Jules laughed.

When I hung up, I hoped she knew I'd really been trying to say thanks for being a friend.

I was fidgeting anxiously as I stared at my possessions arrayed in an eclectic contents sale. 'Do you think we're charging enough for the dartboard?' I asked Jules.

'Yes.' She ignored me as she arranged my DVDs, having spent days wrestling me to relinquish my attachment to superfluous inventory. I'd capitulated on everything but my treasured collection of books and my classic Pentax 35mm camera. Now I wasn't so sure.

I twitched watching people handle my things. A girl wearing a purple scarf over an orange sweater picked up one of my silver Marc Jacobs peeptoes. I jolted. Oh no. She could *not* have those shoes.

'Maeve!' exclaimed my mother, quick eyes taking in the scene. My father, crowding in behind her, was beaming. When I'd told them over dinner about my plan, they'd been delighted, proud of my sacrificial initiative. In return, they'd been more than generous in discharging my debts. Dad had even given me a gas card with $200 to get me started.

'We've come to help!' bellowed my father.

'Great!' Jules beamed. 'Here—wear this.' She produced a sticker that said 'Ask me for help!' and handed it to my dad. I looked at her suspiciously. Funny that she'd had that lying around.

'Okey-doke. Jules can tell you what to do.' My gaze returned to Tacky Girl. She'd slipped on the Marc Jacobs. They fitted. I jumped. 'I have to . . .' I started towards her.

'Actually,' my mother looped her arm through mine, 'your father's going to stay and help so that you and I can spend some mother–daughter time together. We thought you'd need a little break.'

'I don't think . . .' Tacky now had the box tucked under her arm. 'Oh.' I reflexively reached an arm towards the shoes, but my mother was herding me helplessly towards the door.

Jules and my father waved as if I was off to my first day of school, and, while I went from a person who had everything to a girl with a moderate wad of cash and only ten pairs of shoes, my mother distracted me with lunch. I never did have a good attention span.

We ordered our salads, and discussed my planned route.

'We're quite proud of you,' my mother said. 'It's very brave to start over like this. But it's not too late for you to reconsider postponing your departure a few weeks for Cameron's memorial service. Her parents would love to see you.' My best friend's birthday was approaching. She would have been twenty-eight.

'I can't,' I said. 'They don't mean it. Seeing me only reminds them. Best to leave it and move forward.'

'Sometimes you have to move through something before you can move forward,' she ventured.

'Mom, I'm leaving soon, and who knows when I'll be able to come back for a visit. Can we make this about me and *not* Cameron?'

A flicker crossed her face, but all she said was, 'Of course. Tell me more about this marathon.'

We talked about everything and nothing. The bill came, and I reverted to a child, not even pretending I'd contribute.

'Before we go, I have one last thing for you. A kind of Connelly road map,' she said, extracting a bundle from her bag.

Jules and I were collapsed on folding chairs in my barren living room, Oliver hopping about the apartment in an agitated manner, cataloguing empty space. Jules had sold almost everything. Anything left in the apartment would either go home with her or be packed in my car bound for Los Angeles. The boxes of books were stowed in my parents' attic.

'Thanks, Jules. I really mean it.'

'No problem. Beer?'

'Let's get boozy, Suzy.'

She handed me a can. We resumed our study of eight small statues perched on an empty box in front of us.

'So what are they again?' Jules asked.

'My mom made them for my trip.' I was touched that she'd paused work on her current sculpture commission for me. 'She called them "kachinas". I'm supposed to leave them along the way.' The eight figures were partially anthropomorphised, happy, round animal-Buddha-type figures, each about the size of a pool ball, incorporating a combination of animals, or animal and human.

'What do you mean?'

'I'm supposed to spend time getting to know each one and identifying it with . . . something. Whatever I feel when I contemplate the kachina is its chakra. When that chakra is evoked, either because of how I'm personally feeling or because of how a place makes me feel, I'm supposed to commit the kachina to that place.'

'Sounds complicated.'

'See, like this one, it's a knot of intertwined leaves and stems, like new shoots, and what looks like a hummingbird in there. It makes me think of new growth. So maybe I'd take it to my first day of my new job or leave it in the yard of my new apartment or something.'

'And you can't keep them?'

'I think it's a metaphor that I shouldn't regret selling my shoes.'

'I don't know,' mused Jules. 'It sounds pretty cool. Letting go of things. You can make them mean anything—fear, loss, a bad guy, a bad time—and then you leave them behind—'

'Maybe.' I cut her off. I was feeling good and forward-looking. I didn't want to dwell on past missteps. It didn't help that the first kachina was a girl intertwined with a crab, looking backwards. I had a good idea what that one meant. 'I'm supposed to keep the last one.'

'That one?' Jules gestured towards a statue.

'Yes.' It was a combination of a plump female mother-figure and an owl that resembled my favourite stuffed animal. My protectors.

Jules finished her beer. 'Well, I can't have another or I won't be able to get home. And I'm stalling anyway. I guess it's time to say goodbye.'

I nodded. 'Take care of the bar,' I said. 'And make sure Joe doesn't have a heart attack.' Translation: I'm going to miss you and Joe, but I can't admit it and I refuse to cry.

'You too, girl. Be careful driving, and call me. We're going to miss the hell out of you.' Jules was much more in touch with her emotions. She hugged me so hard I thought my ribs would crack. Since she initiated it, I let her. We were both blinking.

'You call me, kid.' She didn't look at me as she gathered together her bags of my former stuff. We both knew I wouldn't get in touch often. It wasn't really my thing. But, for her, I would, once in a while.

Jules stopped at the door. 'You know, bad luck isn't really a thing. It's like weather. It happens, but it doesn't follow you round specifically. But frame of mind, now that stays with you for ever.'

We held gazes for a moment. Then she smiled and said, 'Come home soon.' And she was gone. Seconds ticked by. I ran to the back of the room, then whirled to dash after her.

Her car was pulling out when I hit the sidewalk. 'Jules,' I screamed. She hit the brakes and I ran to the driver's-side window.

'I forgot . . .' I gasped, breathless from my sprint. 'I forgot to give you these.' I offered the box.

Jules looked confused, then understanding. She took the brand new pair of prized red suede boots that didn't hurt my feet even a little bit.

'You didn't have to,' she smiled, 'but I'll take them. Love you.' She paused, then smiled more broadly. 'And I know you love me back.' And she drove off, one hand fluttering out the window.

I waved back, goodbye to my friend, goodbye to my boots, and goodbye to the small kachina I'd tucked into the box. It was one of an egg intertwined with what looked like a tadpole, and it was the first one I'd had an immediate reaction to. My reaction had been gratitude. To Jules, for putting up with me, for understanding me. And most of all, for being around to say goodbye to me. I was down to nine pairs of shoes. My journey had begun. I went to bed, ready for my new adventure to arrive.

Chapter 2: Road Trip, Don't Forget the Bird

MY FIRST ADVENTURE SUCKED. I stared at Darryl, a mechanic from Okay, Oklahoma, in disbelief. 'You're kidding, right?'

'Nawp.'

I rubbed a hand over my face, praying it was a dream.

The trip had started out fine. Our routine was set from our first night camped outside Sweet Lips, Tennessee, I in my tent, Oliver cosy in a little birdie fleece-lined Snuggle Hut that hung from a hook at the peak of my tent, so I didn't roll on him in my sleep. We'd followed back roads across North Carolina, Tennessee and Arkansas, snapping stylish pictures of Elsie in front of landmarks. I ate a lot of boiled eggs. After a few days of pouting silence, Oliver adapted to the new routine and started complimenting me again. Elsie guzzled gas. Our journey had been adventure-free. Until today.

We woke in Toad Suck, Arkansas. The day was hot and sunny, and I was eager to keep going. After forcing down a heavily salted egg, we visited Paris, Arkansas, before pointing Elsie towards Okay, Oklahoma. Leaving Charlotte farther and farther behind felt miraculous. Freedom. Savouring it, my foot unconsciously pressed the gas pedal too far, causing Elsie to wobble precariously as she picked up speed. I eased up.

'Sorry, old girl.'

Nothing could shake my optimism. On either side of the deserted country roads were endless fields of something agricultural. Instead of finding the unchanging landscape boring, I found it soothing. As had become my routine, I didn't play music in the first hours of the day, preferring to let my mind wander. Mostly, I let it wander into wholly unrealistic but highly entertaining fantasies of my new life in California.

John Mayer was just bending on one knee to propose, when Elsie started wobbling in earnest. I frowned at the speed gauge. She shouldn't be wobbling at 45 mph. I slowed again. As long as I held it to 40 mph, there didn't seem to be any problems.

I considered this. I considered Elsie's history of 'surprises'. I considered the endless rows of unidentified plants and complete lack of humans surrounding me. I made a decision. After consulting the map, I decided that Okay was a suitably sized city. Which brought me to here, now, with Darryl at Okay Body.

'You're telling me I have suicidal front tyres?'

'Guess so.' Darryl wasn't big on pronouns.

I closed my eyes. 'How much?'

'Cain't just replace two. Ya gotter change all four.' Spit. 'Cain't have two new tares and two old tares. Getcher wobblin' that way. An's hell on th' axles. Gotta replace all four.'

'How much?' I repeated, bracing myself. When he said three hundred and twenty dollars, I started breathing very fast.

'Installation's 'nother two-hunnerd-fitty.'

'Five hundred and seventy?' That was half of what I had left.

Darryl's eyes softened. 'Got a deal goin' where if ya buy three tares ya get the fourth free. Save ya eighty bucks.'

'Oh.' I exhaled with relief, nodding. It wasn't much, but it was something. 'Let's do that.' I even managed a smile.

''Course, gotter order 'em. Take ya 'nother three days, mebbe.'

Three days in this town. I had a thought. 'If I'm going to be here three days, can you give me some work? I'm a hard worker. And honest. I can pitch my tent right here, and I can clean, I can work a register . . .' I trailed off as Darryl shook his head.

'Crystal does all that.' He said it as if I was supposed to know who Crystal was. 'Place up the road could use some 'sistance, Rico at the Okay Burrito's always lookin' for day labour.'

My face fell. 'Oh. I can't get around. No car.'

'Reckon ya can borrow the bike. Can pitch yer tent here if ya want to, too.'

I loved him. 'Thanks.' I beamed. 'Thanks a lot.'

'No worries.' Spit. 'Want them tares, then?'

I set up my tent on a charming piece of asphalt behind the garage, fragrant with diesel. Darryl took a shine to Oliver, so his cage was installed in the Okay Body office. As I pedalled off on Darryl's bike, Oliver was wooing Crystal with compliments about her hair and figure. It turned out she and Darryl were sister and brother. She was charmed right to the roots of her blue rinse; I was assured Oliver was in good hands.

Okay Burrito was a generic-looking place with a big marketing challenge convincing people the food was better than the titular-proclaimed average. It was run by a short Hispanic man sporting the most precise middle parting I'd ever seen and a trim moustache. When I explained why I was there, Rico's face split into a huge grin.

'You start now?'

It was three o'clock. 'Sure.'

'Good, good.' He actually rubbed his hands together. And then he disappeared, leaving me alone in the restaurant. I was startled. I'd at least expected a lesson in how to make a burrito, and maybe an apron to put on. I was studying the menu when Rico reappeared.

'Yes, yes. You're just the right size. You can try on in back. I'll stay here.' And then he handed me a donkey suit.

'What . . .' When I hesitated, he shook it at me.

'You pass out these.' He pointed to a stack of flyers. 'You get customers into the restaurant. You work all day, fifty dollars cash. No tax. And burrito for lunch and dinner.'

I grabbed the donkey suit. It looked like it would fit just fine.

After an all-egg diet, the burritos were heaven on earth. The work was not. I was sweating my ass off. I refused to think of my sweaty predecessors. Instead I smiled at passers-by and tried to force flyers they didn't want into their hands.

At 9 p.m. Rico locked the front doors and handed me thirty dollars and a burrito. 'You come back tomorrow. You make good donkey.'

The shop was closed when I got back. Through the window I could see Oliver sleeping in his cage. I pressed my hand against the glass as if it would bring us closer. It was the safest place for him, but I felt very cut off. My phone was dead—I needed Elsie to charge it—and I was separated from my bird. Tears threatened to leak out of the corners of my eyes. But with resolute hands I wiped them away and straightened. 'You did good today, kid,' I told myself, and went to get comfortable on my asphalt bed.

It took another five days rather than three to get the tyres delivered and installed, but the $280 I earned made it all worthwhile. And I'd come to care for Darryl, Crystal and Rico. Their quiet kindness reassured me that I could venture out into the world and make a new start, that there'd be help along the way. That and my new business plan.

I felt a twinge of guilt as Okay diminished in my rear-view mirror. The mirror also reflected the ear of a large donkey. Rico was expecting me at work, and instead I'd slunk off in the early-morning light with a newly shod Elsie and his donkey suit. I intended to repay him and return the suit when I was done. I hoped the kachina I'd left on the counter holding down my IOU note made up for it. To him, the little statue resembling a fox and grapes would be an odd form of security deposit. To me, it meant ingenuity.

Bonnie Bunn, of Bunn in the Oven, stared at me blankly. 'What?'

I gave her my most engaging smile. 'I have this donkey suit, see.' I displayed it. 'And you sell burritos. I'd attract customers. People would think Bunn, and crave a burrito.' It was a thin argument. Burritos occupied a wafer-thin slice of Bonnie's menu, which was heavier on baked goods than sandwiches, never mind Mexican entrées. I'd had better success at Loco Taco in Loco, Oklahoma, and Bell-A-Burrito in Uncertain, Texas. But Bonnie offered the only burrito in Ding Dong, Texas, so I had to give it a shot. I was a little desperate. Given the distance between west Texas towns, I didn't want to leave Ding Dong without plenty of money stockpiled. It was a long way to Noodle.

Bonnie wasn't convinced. 'You mean like the guy who used to walk around in the cellphone suit in front of Hank's place?'

'Used to?' I said.

'Haven't seen him in a while.'

'Where is Hank's exactly?'

Five days later my guilt as I drove off in the middle of the night with Hank's cellphone suit was eased by the fact that I'd lured fifty people into his store. More importantly, I had enough gas money to get to Truth or Consequences, New Mexico, which had both a Mexican restaurant and a cellphone store.

I tapped my pencil against my teeth as I studied the map. Unknown, Arizona, looked pinprick-tiny. I was seasoned at route-planning now, triangulating desired towns, available campsites and potential burrito, cellphone and (after Sunshine, New Mexico) chicken restaurants. The small towns were the trickiest. I'd arrived at faded crossroads 'towns' to find they no longer existed. It shook my self-assuredness that something as seemingly substantial as a town could fade just like that. If we couldn't keep a town alive, how vulnerable was something fragile like me? I reapplied SPF70 sunscreen.

I could go the lower Arizona route, entering at Portal and passing through Paradise and Tombstone, to Greaterville before reaching Unknown. Beyond the irresistible Unknown was the equally alluring Why, Arizona. My other option was the northerly route from Eager, through Superior, Carefree, Surprise and Nothing. There was also the appeal of a little town named Brenda near the California border.

It was a difficult choice. I called my sister.

'It's early, cruel wench,' Vi mumbled into the phone.

I looked at my watch. Oops. 'Sorry. I've driven across three time zones in two weeks, including states and Native American reservations that don't observe daylight savings. The actual time can ricochet wildly within sixty miles, so my understanding of it has devolved to "diner open" or "diner closed". I'm in a diner.'

'Diners allow birds?' Oliver was talking up a storm.

'This one does.' 'Diner' was a strong word for the folding chair I occupied in the back of the local Texaco store, but the pancake breakfast was good.

'So what's up?'

I explained my dilemma.

'Brenda is tempting,' she agreed. 'You could see if the residents wear funny outdated hats. But Eager, Superior, Carefree, Surprise and Nothing denote a negative emotional trend from vain purposeless to unanticipated emptiness. It sounds like bad feng shui to me. In contrast, Portal, Paradise, Tombstone, Greaterville, Unknown and Why all tap into the fundamental questions of life, the afterlife and why we're here. You could actually drive through a version of heaven on earth.'

'Philosophical genius,' I complimented her. 'There's an Eden around there too.'

She laughed. 'Call me if you find the Fountain of Youth.'

It might not be heaven on earth, but the drive from Tombstone towards Unknown was gorgeous. The sky was blue and impossibly large, the road a ribbon of asphalt snaking across the wide golden prairie. In the distance the grasslands met sloping brown hills.

As I headed south, the distant hills became more pronounced, pushing upwards to fully fledged mountains and jutting cliffs. I was driving through the cradle between the Santa Rita Mountains to the west and the Huachuca Mountains and Canelo Hills to the east. Cattle and the occasional cluster of deer roamed the high desert scrublands. I felt like I'd stepped back in time to the cowboy era.

'Howdy, pardner,' I said to Oliver as we cruised past the occasional ranch, with gates proclaiming Circle Z or Lazy Bar.

'Carrot,' said Oliver.

'Howdy, pardner,' I repeated, waiting for him to catch on.

Silence. 'Carrot. Squaaawk. Are you thinner?'

A few miles ahead, a road travelled off to the east. I consulted the map. It looked to be the turnoff for Unknown. I took it, looking at the sky to assess the time. Not that I had any tracker skills. I couldn't tell time from the sun but I'd learned that the sun dropped fast in the west. From about four, the sun's rays slanted noticeably with a day-is-ending feeling. When it began to set in earnest, you had about an hour before it dropped like a stone and everything became as dark as ink. At that point you wanted your tent up for the night.

As I was mentally counting my remaining pairs of clean socks, Elsie emitted an ominous clunk and rattle. A horrible grinding noise came from under the hood and the car bucked once before all momentum ceased. We coasted to a stop on an unnamed road in the least populated place I'd ever been.

For a moment I sat there, my mind not grasping our predicament. Stupidly I looked at the gas gauge, but I wasn't out of fuel. Next most stupidly, I looked at my phone. I hadn't had a signal since this morning. Besides, who would I call? I looked at Oliver. He looked at me.

'Howdy, pardner,' I said.

'Oh shit,' Oliver said.

I opened the door and stepped out. My pulse thumped triple time. I looked up the road, stretching without variation to the east. I looked down the road, stretching without variation to the west. I felt the impending presence of bad news, like a long-ago waiting room.

Cameron had not been doing well. Her family had asked me to wait outside her room for a bit. A white-coated doctor stepped out. He conferred with a nurse, and she pointed. They both looked at me. He started in my direction, shoulders weighted with news I didn't want. The room pressed around me, and I wanted to escape, to run away from that white coat that was going to ruin things.

I looked up the road again, and broke into a run. I sprinted for all I was worth, sneakers blurred with motion. I raced against panic, running hard. I ran until I thought my lungs would burst, then stumbled to a stop, doubled over, gasping. I let out a yell that came from deep within, expelling all my frustration. It felt good, so I did it again, straightening.

'Dirty rotten luck, you won't always win!' I shouted at a sky that calmly absorbed my rage into its wide, unwavering depths. Then I turned and jogged slowly back to my life.

Calmer this time, I realised I had to figure out what to do.

First, ascertain the level of hopelessness. I slid behind the wheel and tried the ignition. Nothing. I shifted the car into neutral and got out, then put my shoulder into it and pushed. It was slow, sweaty, exhausting going, but I eased the car over to the side of the road.

Next, I considered Oliver. I hated the idea of leaving him. The sun was setting now, promising cool temperatures, but who knew when I'd get back tomorrow? It could get hot. Roasty, even. No, I'd have to take him with me. Thank God I'd had his wings clipped right before we left.

'Want to go for a walk, buddy?' I gently extracted him from his cage.

'Road trip. Don't forget the bird!' he chirped happily.

'Yeah, this is all fun and games to you,' I chided as I secured a loop round his right leg that connected by a long cord to a bracelet on my wrist. I perched him on my shoulder. He promptly clambered up my braid like a rope ladder to settle on top of my head. I slipped his Snuggle Hut inside my jacket. When it got cold, he could nestle in it.

I removed extra sweaters and socks from my overnight backpack, and replaced them with my sleeping bag, my current book and essentials from my purse. I tied my tent to the bottom loops. I tested my head-lamp: no telling how far I'd be walking in the dark. Finally I grabbed two large bottles of water and stuck a boiled egg in my pocket.

With a last pat for Elsie, I locked the door and started walking.

Fifteen minutes after I set out, the landscape was unchanged and the sun abandoned me. Soon after, the darkness was impenetrable and I was dependent on my headlamp. I prayed that Unknown still existed.

I sat down after a while to rest and put on an extra sweater. Oliver clambered down my arm to my wrist, not liking the cold either. I tucked him into his Snuggle Hut and put both into my jacket as he gave a happy 'tut'. I resumed walking. I hadn't seen a single car in three hours. It was only around nine but I was getting tired.

After half an hour, the road did something funny. I swept my head-lamp from side to side, but the night gobbled its puny effort. As far as I could tell, the road split round an island of land. I stepped off the road and advanced cautiously. After picking my way several hundred yards, my headlamp caught a picnic table. I wilted in relief. It must be some kind of camping or roadside facility. I would stay here.

I pitched my tent beyond the picnic table, moving carefully so as not to jostle Oliver. I hung his hideaway from the hook on the tent ceiling, and undid my braids, combing my fingers through my long hair. I debated shucking my jeans in favour of more comfortable sweats but decided against it. It was cold. I alternated between worrying about Oliver and my conviction that my own glands were swelling with the onset of an aggressive sore throat.

I slid tiredly into my sleeping-bag. 'Tomorrow will be a better day, pal,' I murmured to my sleeping bird, before I dropped off myself.

I was being abducted by aliens. Bright lights were flooding the tent in a swirl of colours. Some red, some blue, but mostly a penetrating white light. The entire tent was illuminated. My brain struggled to understand.

A car door slammed. Wait a minute. There was nothing supernatural about that, unless the aliens drove a truck. I heard booted footsteps crunching towards my tent, accompanied by another beam of bobbing light. Fully awake now, alarm dissipated my confusion. Oh God. I was going to be murdered by some isolation-deranged cowboy.

'Knock, knock,' drawled a pleasant, twangy voice. 'Care to come on out here, li'l camper? I can see ya in there.' The voice sounded amused.

I remained immobile, frozen with indecision.

'Howdy, pardner!' My bird introduced himself.

There was a disembodied chuckle. 'Howdy back atcha. Whadda ya say ya come on out and make our acquaintance proper like?'

Resigned, I unzipped my bag and crawled out of the safety of my tent. I stood blinking at the light shining on my face.

'Wall now, ya are a young thing, ain't cha?' the amused speaker pronounced. 'And prettier than ya sound.'

Was this some weird kind of hillbilly courtship?

'Road trip, don't forget the bird!' Oliver chirped, anxious at being left alone. This is why people get dogs, I thought.

'That a 'tiel in there?' My assailant's question surprised me. 'My ex-wife had one a them. Damn thing had a mouth like a sailor.'

I squinted, trying to make out my extraordinary visitor while his beam was directed towards Oliver. I could only distinguish impressive height and breadth before the light returned to me. I winced.

'Sorry.' The light went out. 'Guess you musta been sleepin'.'

I faced him again, but he was backlit by the headlights of what I guessed was a sizeable dual-wheel SUV truck, and all I could ascertain was his considerable bulk.

'Care to share your name, missy?' he asked, not unkindly.

I shifted in my socked feet. Should I tell him?

'Tell you what. Seein' as you mebbe warn't expectin' me, I'll go first. My name's Lawrence Perry. I'm the sheriff here in Unknown. People mostly call me Bruce.' The light clicked on again, this time shining at a bronze star on his chest. The beam then angled up, revealing a thick dark moustache, round cheeks and deep eyes surrounded by appealing crinkles. He looked like an amiable Bavarian barber.

The light clicked off. 'An' you?'

'Maeve,' I said. 'Maeve Connelly.' It registered that I might be saved.

'Wall, Maeve Con'ley, what're you doin' camping in the middle of my town square?' were his astonishing next words. My jaw must have dropped wide open because Lawrence Perry chuckled. I looked around, and sure enough I could make out faint building outlines in the truck headlights.

'Is it . . .' I hesitated. 'Is it a . . . ghost town?'

His chuckle turned into a guffaw. 'No, Unknown's a full-on thrivin' little town with enough colourful characters for a serial TV show.'

'How many people?' I asked.

''Bout eight hundred or so, give or take.'

'But I didn't even know it was there,' I protested. 'There are no lights.'

'Wall now, you're right there. You picked quite a night to visit. Ronnie Two Shoes was being a doofus as usual when trimmin' his old cottonwood, and one of the branches snapped the power lines clean through. It's a miracle he didn't fry hisself up like a chicken nugget.'

'I thought I was in the middle of the woods.'

'A hundred more feet and you'd be bunking in the community centre,' he said. 'That your Plymouth Road Runner 'bout ten-twelve miles back?'

I nodded.

'You walk all that way in the dark? With a bird?' Another nod.

'Wall, I can't let ya stay in the square, I'm 'fraid. And I can't put ya in the jail without ya bein' under arrest.' I was pretty sure I was glad on that one, though his regret seemed genuine. 'But I might be able to help. You break down your little campin' site while I make a call.'

I did as he said. I perched on the picnic table with all my worldly goods in a backpack and a Snuggle Hut until Bruce returned.

'Looks like you're in luck. Follow me.' When we got to the truck, it was 'Climb on up.' I was too tired to ask where we were going.

In the cab of the truck, blessed heat seeped into my bones.

'Lawrence,' I said. 'Why do they call you Bruce?'

'Wall, I reckon it's because I like Monty Python so much,' he answered obligingly, leaving me as mystified as before.

After a short trip we pulled up to a long, low adobe house. The truck headlights lit up attractive pink walls and a doorway framed by some kind of flowering tree. Bruce ignored the front door and followed a path to the left through an archway cut into the long wall. Beyond appeared to be a courtyard garden. I could see candlelight flickering through double glass doors to the right. Bruce went through them, and I followed him into a beautiful and spacious kitchen. A welcoming fire flickered in the hearth. Bruce wiped his feet on a colourful rag rug and stepped in, pulling off his sheriff's hat. I remained his dutiful shadow.

'Hello, Bruce. How you doin', Bruce? All right there, Bruce?' squawked a voice from beyond a darkened doorway to the left.

Oliver, on my shoulder now, began hopping agitatedly, lifting one foot then the other, a cockatiel sign of anxiety.

'Lulabell, hush your beak,' said Bruce.

'Quiet, Lulabell,' mimicked the squawk. 'Right, Bruce!' said Lulabell.

It was too much for Oliver. He released a torrent of sounds. 'Squawk. Carrot. Are you thinner? Howdy, pardner. Oh shit.'

Silence from the other room.

'Yours's just as bad as Lulabell for the potty mouth,' Bruce observed.

'Oh, no,' I rushed to assure him. 'He almost never says that.'

'Oh shit,' repeated Oliver.

Sigh. 'That's his only bad word. I have no idea where he got it.'

'It won't be for long,' Bruce foretold.

On cue, from the next room: 'Fuck me. Legs up, toots.'

Bruce rolled his eyes. A tiny woman hurried into the room. She wore her greying hair in two long braids and I instantly tumbled in love. 'Don't you mind Lulabell,' she said. 'She spent too much time in the sheriff's office when she was young listening to foul-mouthed criminals and even fouler-mouthed deputies.' Here she shot Bruce a dirty look. He managed to look abashed. It clicked that this was his ex-wife.

It was hard to make out detail by candlelight, but she was clearly no more than five feet tall. At five foot nine, I towered over her. And Bruce towered over me. What a funny couple they would have been. I didn't realise I was transfixed until she demanded, 'Well, are you two going to sit or am I going to need neck surgery from looking up at you?'

We sat. Bruce cleared his throat. 'Maeve, this here is Ruby. Ruby, this is the gal I was tellin' you about,' he said.

'It would be a remarkable feat if you managed to come up with a substitute stray girl in the fifteen minutes since you called, Lawrence,' Ruby said. She examined me in the candlelight.

'I'm Maeve Connelly,' I said. 'This is Oliver.'

'Howdy, pardner.' He focused on Ruby, on his best behaviour.

'Howdy yourself.' Ruby returned the greeting seriously. I plummeted even further in love. Her level gaze returned to me. 'I'm Ruby Ransome. I understand you've had car trouble.'

There was another squawk. We all looked confused, because it didn't come from Oliver or Lulabell. It emanated from the vicinity of Bruce's stomach.

'Bruce? Bruce, you there?' It was a walkie-talkie.

Ruby rose fluidly. 'Lawrence, you're needed. Go back to the station. I'll handle it from here. Call me tomorrow at ten o'clock with information on PIGS and Barney's schedule.' I had no idea what she was talking about. Bruce bent and kissed her cheek.

'You're a good woman, Ruby.' To my surprise, Ruby blushed. To me he said, 'I'll be seein' about your car.' Then he was gone.

'Maeve, you'll sleep in room number 1.' Too exhausted to think, I didn't question her choice to identify her rooms by number rather than function. 'Oliver can bunk with Lulabell.'

I froze, panic blooming. 'No. I'm sorry, it's just . . .' My voice trailed away. How to explain that I couldn't be parted from my bird? My life was topsy-turvy. Oliver was the only thing tethering me to myself. I looked at her helplessly, mute. 'He might get scared,' I finally said.

Ruby's eyes told me she knew exactly what I meant. 'I don't want bird poop all over my bedroom,' was her logical position.

'I have this Snuggle Hut, see.' I held it up. 'I can wrap him in it. He won't be roaming free. And he was just clipped,' I pleaded.

Ruby relented. 'Your bird can stay with you. Follow me.'

She lifted a candle and I followed her through a glass door and down a covered adobe walk. We stopped in front of a door with a brass numeral affixed. Room number 1. Ruby opened the door.

'I trust you'll be comfortable. There are towels in the bathroom. I'll expect you for breakfast at eight thirty. I know it's early considering your night, but that's when I do business.'

I nodded. She took my hand and gave it a squeeze. 'Sleep well. Everything will sort itself out. Or we'll get it sorted.'

When the alarm dragged me awake in the morning my eyes flew open and I bolted upright. My eyes leaped to the clock. I wilted in relief when I saw it was only eight and I hadn't missed meeting Ruby. I rubbed my temples and surveyed the room.

Coral adobe walls met ochre tiles, accented by sage-green window trim. White curtains flanked windows on both sides of the room. I pushed back thick feather-filled covers and stepped out of bed. My dusty backpack was on an antique dressing table that matched a wardrobe and bedside table. Ruby must have brought it in. I retrieved a clean sweater and underwear. After some deliberation I decided on my favourite parrot-adorned knee socks. I hoped Ruby would like them.

Showered and dressed, I collected Oliver and left the room. My door opened onto a passage flanking a square courtyard. To my left was the door we'd exited last night. I went through it. Daylight revealed a beautifully decorated house with a Native American motif. Through an arched doorway on the left was a sunken living room, with more doors beyond. On the right I could see a comfortable social room with a number of small tables and a television. I kept walking. Ahead was presumably the front door we'd ignored the night before. Before reaching it, I turned into the kitchen, pulse accelerating out of nervousness.

Ruby Ransome was sitting at the long table, perusing a paper. She didn't look up when she said, 'There's coffee.'

I helped myself to a cup from the carafe on the sideboard, loading it with milk, and listened absently to the low murmur of talk radio. As I tried to decipher what the programme was discussing, I realised that it wasn't the radio, but human voices. The fireplace dominating the far wall was a through and through, another hearth opening into the room opposite. The voices were coming from that room.

I sat across from Ruby, curious. Three minutes passed then, with meticulous movements, she folded the paper and placed it aside. 'Good morning.' She assessed me. 'Did you sleep well?'

'Yes, ma'am, thank you,' I said.

'No more ma'am,' she said.

'Sure,' I said. There was a burst of laughter from the other room. 'Is this a hotel?' I worried about paying her.

'A boarding house. People live here,' she said. 'Tell me your plans.'

'I'm driving to California,' I said. 'Or I was. I've been on the road a few weeks, but it should take only a few more days now. I'm going to Los Angeles. To start over.' I mentally groaned. Why had I said that last bit?

'What are you starting over from?' Ruby pounced.

'I needed a change,' was all I said. What else was there to say?

She nodded. 'You're going to have some setbacks, I'm afraid. Unknown's mechanic, Barney, is out of town for a bit. You just missed him. He wasn't supposed to leave until tomorrow, but when that fool Ronnie put the lights out, Barney decided to leave early.'

I nearly laughed out loud. Could my luck have been worse? 'A bit?'

'Yes. You never know how long with Barney and these trips. Sort of depends on his luck at the tables. Simon Bear will drive over from Sierra Vista with the tow truck and bring your car to PIGS in a few days, but Barney could be gone anywhere from a week to a month.'

'PIGS?' I ignored her last statement. No way he'd be gone a month.

'The Politically Incorrect Gas Station.'

'But . . . surely there's someone else.'

Ruby looked at me. 'How many towns did you pass on your way from Tombstone?' she asked.

'One,' I answered, dreadful awareness sinking in. 'If it counted as a town. It was more like an intersection.' I recalled Sonoita.

'It counted. Round here you won't find a stoplight until Nogales.'

My mind raced. There had to be a way out. I was desperate to get to California. Maybe I could rent a car. Or catch the Greyhound. Or . . . As my brain churned, my heart conceded. I wasn't going to abandon Elsie. First of all, I loved her. Second, I couldn't afford a new car. Hell, I had no idea how I was going to pay for the repair . . .

'I don't have the money to stay here,' I confessed. 'I just have my tent and enough gas money to get to California. I don't know what to do.'

She regarded me some more. It was like she could see everything. 'You seem healthy.' I was, but I felt irrationally guilty and furtive, as if a remainder of every sick day was germinating within me.

'Yes.' My answer was breathless. 'I am.'

'Then I see no reason why we can't work out an arrangement.' She folded her hands, neat on the tabletop. 'For some time I've been chafing at the demands of the boarding house, as I've wanted to spend more time on other pursuits. You can manage those requirements for me, in exchange for room and board. Number 1 is empty.'

I was speechless. She was offering to let me stay in this oasis. I wondered if it was too much charity to accept.

'It isn't charity, mind you.' Ruby read my thoughts. How was it everyone could do that? 'You'll do what's needed when it's supposed to be done. I won't be paying you, so you'll have to discover other ways to earn the money you need to pay Barney. The schedule here is plenty flexible to allow for that, and I suspect you are a resourceful girl.'

'What on earth makes you think I'm a resourceful girl when I'm broke and stranded in the middle of nowhere?'

'Unknown, Maeve. You're in Unknown. Nowhere is in Oklahoma,' Ruby admonished. 'A young lady who gets herself this close to California on a shoestring and boiled eggs in a 1970s relic while taking care of her bird is resourceful in my book. Not to mention walking twelve miles in the dark and managing to pitch a tent in the middle of the town square during a blackout.' She broke into a wide smile.

I said the only thing there was to say. 'I accept your offer, Ruby. Thanks. Um, how did you know about the eggs?'

'Your things are in the common room. We retrieved the keys from your rucksack and Lawrence brought them by this morning. I took the liberty of discarding the last egg. It looked a little forlorn. Not that eggs are a bad idea. You could stand to gain five pounds,' Ruby added as an afterthought. 'Now follow me.' She stood and eyed Oliver, who had been docilely sitting on my head the whole time. 'I expect it's about time we introduced your young man to Lulabell.'

I followed Ruby through the door to the left of the hearth into a large common room. A collection of tables was arrayed in front of double French doors opening onto the courtyard. Two women were having breakfast at one, the source of the chatter I'd heard earlier. In the corner was a kitchenette. A large roll-top desk hugged the far left wall, along with a sofa and armchair grouping centred round a television.

Next to the door was a palatial birdcage. Inside was an inquisitive-looking pearl cockatiel. Oliver came to attention. I scooped him down to my hand as a precaution.

'This is Lulabell,' Ruby pronounced. 'She's very friendly. Normally she's free to wander, but since your man is human-bonded, I thought we'd see how they got on for a bit first.'

Oliver's cage had been set adjacent on the cabinet. I slipped him inside, and we both stepped back to watch. Lulabell didn't move, affecting an uninterested air, though following Oliver's every move with her eyes. Oliver hopped from one perch to another, muttering to himself. He didn't seem perturbed, so I stopped worrying.

'Great hair,' he finally squawked. I was impressed at his savvy choice.

Lulabell just eyed him.

'Are you thinner?' Oliver tried again.

Lulabell tilted her head.

'Pretty,' Oliver repeated.

'Show some tits.' Lulabell was won over, and the two of them began madly chirping back and forth.

'Lord knows there'll be no peace now,' growled one of the ladies.

Ruby smiled. 'Maeve, let me introduce you to the Cowbelles.' We walked over to the two women who could have been a hundred and looked to have another hundred in them each. 'April War Bonnet.' Ruby gestured to a tiny Native American woman with long, still-dark hair, and a brown face as wizened as a crab apple. 'And Busy Parker.' Busy's skin was powdery pale, every wrinkle emanating the essence of smiling, framing snapping blue eyes. 'This is Maeve. She's going to be staying for a while.'

April considered me. Busy stood and embraced me.

'Welcome, welcome,' Busy fluttered, all bonnets and tea services. 'Don't mind April. That's just her way. She's a total bitch.'

I was surprised into a belt of laughter.

'Better that than a stranger-hugging nincompoop,' April retorted in a gravelly voice. She shook my hand in a firm clasp.

'Let's go a little easy on Maeve on her first day,' Ruby said.

'What's a Cowbelle?' I gave in to my curiosity.

'Back in the forties, a group of ranch women was organised to foster social interaction among women living on isolated ranches. They called themselves the Cowbelles. April and I are the last founding charter members of the Santa Cruz County Cowbelles,' Busy explained. 'We still have regular meetings.'

'At eight o'clock here for breakfast, at noon over there for lunch, and at five on the sofa for sherry.' Ruby's tone was dry.

'Bite your tongue, Ruby,' April growled. 'Sherry my ass. It's Scotch. And mind we don't run out. The bottle's light.'

'That's Maeve's job now,' Ruby said. 'I'm about to show her the ropes.'

And just like that, I became a boarding-house manager.

Chapter 3: The Girl Who Could

AN HOUR LATER, my head was swirling. My job was to clean the common areas and Ruby's kitchen, do dishes, laundry, and keep the cupboards full of clean sheets and towels. Ruby provided breakfast supplies and household basics, so I was in charge of stocking those things. It was definitely a good deal, but I had to figure out how to make some cash to pay for the tow and repair of Elsie.

I scribbled throat lozenges on the grocery list, as my throat was sore and scratchy after my nocturnal adventures, and stepped outside. I followed Ruby's directions from our address on Emerald Street to the centre of town. It wasn't far. Unknown consisted of a handful of streets, named after the colours of the rainbow. No stoplight. There was a centre square, on which I'd pitched my tent. All of the commerce existed on Main Street and Red Road; it was an eclectic mix. There were several local artisan craft stores, the Guess Who's Coming To Diner, and two clothing stores. The Wagon Wheel Saloon boasted that it was Unknown's original cowboy bar. The Velvet Elvis offered pizza, several doors down from a shuttered PIGS. Up Market was your only bet for groceries and sundries.

'So it's fancy stuff, then?' I'd asked Ruby.

Her look was quizzical. 'No, it's quite normal. It's owned by Patrick and Jenny Up.'

I was heading in that direction when I was arrested by a store called The Little Read Book. The sign featured a grass-skirted Hawaiian dancer and Chairman Mao both reading red tomes. Unable to resist a bookstore, I pushed open the door. It was perfect. The hardwood floors creaked just right. There was a table for staff picks and favourites. Comfy chairs occupied sunny nooks, and café tables invited people to linger over coffee. The sound of grinding beans drew me to a café within the store, where a beautiful woman worked an espresso machine. She was exotically unique, with almond eyes and long dark hair.

'*Aloha!*' A beatific smile accompanied her greeting. 'What can I do for you?'

I developed an enormous girl crush. My second in two days.

'I'm Maeve,' I said.

'Tuesday,' she said, in response to my non-answer, smile widening.

I frowned. It was Thursday, I was pretty sure.

'Coffee in five days?' I asked.

She giggled as if I'd told the funniest joke in the world. 'No, silly. Tuesday's my name. You're funny.'

'I just got here,' was my inane response.

'Cool.' Her nod supported my decision. 'I live on Purple Street. My car is the one with the sticker saying "I'd Rather Be Doing the Hula".'

'Mine is the one sitting outside PIGS waiting for Barney to get back to town and fix it.'

'Ah. A compulsory visit.' Tuesday laughed.

'Kind of,' I admitted. 'That's why I came in. I'm looking for work.'

'Oh, yay!' Tuesday beamed at me. 'I need more time off.'

My heart burst. I'd found a job. In a bookstore! 'I love your shop.'

'Yeah, it's good. But it isn't mine. I teach hula and dance. I help out only when Noah's in a bind. Grouchy owner extraordinaire.'

'Want to be my best friend?'

'Sure!' Her laugh was rich. 'Where are you staying?'

'Ruby Ransome's boarding house.'

'Oooohhh, I love Ruby. Lulabell is the bomb.'

'I have a bird. He's learning dirty words from Lulabell as we speak.'

'Tuesday!' A bellow interrupted me. 'Tuesday!'

She sighed. 'Guess you'll meet the man himself now.'

A man appeared from around a book shelf. He was tall, very tall, maybe six four, with dark-brown hair and startling green eyes. And a frown. I'd never allow a furrow that depth on my forehead.

'Did you see where I put the receipts from the Decatur Book Festival?' As he spoke, he sighted me and did an unexplained double take, before refocusing on Tuesday.

'Nope,' she said with a wide smile. He looked perplexed.

'I swear I put them somewhere special.'

'I'll bet you did!' Tuesday chirped. 'Remember the Monkey Flower special orders? You put them on the top shelf of the cookbook section.' She winked at me. 'We found them two years later.'

'But I never lose things.' More divot. My hands itched to rub it out.

'Only when you put them in special places,' Tuesday agreed.

'Helen came in,' Noah explained. 'Looking for a copy of *The Book of Murder*.'

'Ah.' Apparently this made sense to Tuesday, as she nodded. 'You'll find them. You always do. You're the most organised person I know.'

'Apparently not.' He gave a rueful laugh, then turned distractedly to me, extending a hand. 'Sorry. I'm Noah. Glad to have you here. Travelling in the area? Anything I can help you find?'

I took his hand. It was strong and knew how to shake properly. In fact, all of him was fit. Long and lean, with defined features. I'm a sucker for killer cheekbones, and Noah had them like razors.

'Maeve Connelly.' I felt a little fluttery. 'In town temporarily.'

'Nice socks,' he said. 'I like socks with birds on them.' I gripped the coffee-bar counter to keep upright. His attention returned to Tuesday. 'Well, crap,' he said. 'So I've lost them.'

'I'm very organised,' I piped up. They both looked at me. 'I keep great track of things.' It was true. I might not always deal with my paperwork, but the stacks were meticulous.

'Noah, Maeve's looking for work,' Tuesday said.

Noah assessed me, then turned away. 'I'm sorry. We're not hiring.'

'What?' Tuesday and I yelped in unison.

'Noah, I need help!' Tuesday wailed.

Noah's green eyes evaluated me. 'Do you have bookstore experience?' I hated answering. 'No.'

'And you're looking for a temp position?'

I wanted to lie, but it was true, so I nodded.

He shook his head. 'I'm sorry. This is a bookstore, not a summer job fair. My staff have to be knowledgeable about books, and intend to stick around more than three weeks.'

'I've spent legions of time in bookstores, as an avid customer.'

'I'm sorry. We're the only bookseller in a fifty-mile radius, and people come here because we know literature. You look more like a . . . a . . . model, or something, than a book geek.'

He looked uncomfortable, and it was probably common sense not to hire anyone who wandered in off the street, but he was pissing me off. 'You don't look like a creepy evil child-toucher, but I'm reserving judgment. The neighbours always say you'd never have guessed.'

'Don't take it the wrong way.' He held up his hands. 'I take matching people to books seriously.' Pause. 'And I'm not a child molester.'

'Well, not a good one, at any rate,' I snorted. 'You don't have any kind of children's section to speak of.' I pointed. 'If you had a genius like me working here, I'd shift those shelves over and turn that corner into a kid-friendly section called The Little Read Picture Book or The Little Little Read Book, and offer Saturday story time.'

'Noah.' Tuesday's eyes widened at my suggestions. 'She isn't Gina.' I caught her eye and she mouthed, 'Tell you later.' To Noah, she said, 'Ruby trusts her. She gave her a room.'

'It wouldn't be responsible to hire an unqualified person.'

I faced him. 'Test me before you decide I'm unqualified.'

'I've hired walk-ins before. It doesn't work—even if they have charming braids and funky knee socks. I'm being realistic.'

'Try me. You're the customer, I work here. Ask me a literary question I can't answer. If I can answer five toughies, I get the job.'

'What are you reading now?'

Easy. '*The Bean Trees*, Barbara Kingsolver. I'm being regional.' *The Bean Trees* was set in Tucson.

'Who wrote *Dubliners*?'

I fought back my eye-roll. This was almost insulting. 'James Augustine Aloysius Joyce. Who also wrote *Ulysses*, *A Portrait of the Artist as a Young Man*, *Finnegans Wake* and some mediocre poetry. My favourite short story from *Dubliners* is "The Dead".'

'His middle name was Aloysius?' Tuesday giggled.

'OK.' Noah squinted. I knew it was going to get harder. 'I like the classics. I've read most of them. I'm looking for something I haven't yet discovered. What do you recommend?'

I racked my brains. '*I Capture the Castle* by Dodie Smith or *Good Behaviour* by Molly Keane are excellent choices.'

He shifted his feet. 'I like thrillers but don't want garbage. What's an intelligent new release?'

'I think the new Jack Reacher novel by Lee Child is at the top of the chart,' I said. I'd spied it on the best-seller shelf when I'd walked in.

'I'd like something for my son,' Noah persisted. 'He's thirteen.'

I paused. I didn't want to give the obvious Harry Potter answer. I pondered a moment, then nailed it. '*The Boy Who Could Fly*,'

I announced. 'It's not that well known but it's a wonderful book, where a boy who loses his father escapes into his imagination as a superhero while he struggles to take care of his mother and sibling.'

'You are *so* hired.' Tuesday burst out laughing.

Noah looked uncomfortable. And oddly distressed. Too bad.

He caught Tuesday's eye. Then, 'Ruby took you in?' Clipped.

'Uh-huh.'

They exchanged glances. She nodded.

Finally, 'Fine.' His tone was terse. 'You can help out a few days a week. Come on Monday at ten. Tuesday, you'll train her.'

'Sure.' Tuesday's head bobbed.

Noah walked away, then paused. 'But we don't recommend *The Boy Who Could Fly* here,' he said, before disappearing through a door.

I was confused, especially as Tuesday's giggles amplified.

'He wrote it,' she said. 'He wrote the whole series. He's N. E. Case.'

And my jaw hit the floor just like that.

I was bubbling over. I had a job, and I was thrilled with the movie and dinner date I'd planned with Tuesday. We'd agreed that after my first day of work, we'd order pizza and watch *Juno*. I talked to Oliver as I tidied the breakfast area. 'And I met the guy who wrote *The Boy Who Could Fly*, and *The Boy Who Could Walk Through Walls*, and *The Boy Who Could Stop Time*. All of them—he's not that much older than me, but he's written this whole series. The actual guy! He's my new boss!'

'Nice tits!' said Oliver. I had to move his cage away from Lulabell.

'And I have a new best friend,' I said. 'Well, besides you. Her name is Tuesday. She's half Hawaiian, half Chinese. We have a date.'

After Noah had conceded to hiring me, I'd spent the afternoon hanging around Tuesday like a teenage sycophant at a lifeguard stand, and she'd explained his odd behaviour.

'You're blonde and she was brunette, but, otherwise, the resemblance is strong. Gina wore long braids and had this great smile. The problem was that she was a *criminal*.'

'What'd she do?' I marvelled.

'Destroyed Noah's trust in mankind,' she exaggerated. 'We'd always had good luck with short-termers, then Gina came along. She told Noah she wanted temp work to be near a grandmother who'd broken a hip, so of course he couldn't say no. He's a big old softie. We were glad for the help. It gave me more time to teach dance and him more time to write. After a few weeks, I went to Tucson at the same time Noah flew to New York for a meeting and we left her in charge. When we got back, the store was dark and the register had been cleaned out. She even stole some knick-knacks from Noah's office.'

'She was a con artist?' I was shocked.

'Totally. Noah was heartbroken. It wasn't the financial loss—he makes his money from the books. He was wounded to the core that a person could be so calculating and callous. Plus she pinched his favourite stuffed monkey.' I didn't ask. Tuesday sighed. 'He feels things too deeply. He hasn't hired anyone since.'

A violent sneezing fit yanked me back to the present. The ferocity of the attack alarmed me. I'd been sneezing quite a bit since arriving in Unknown, and my sore throat hadn't improved. With my luck it wasn't just a cold. I recalled an article I'd seen on incurable spore infections in the rural southwest. 'Oh my God,' I said to Oliver. 'I have pneumonitis.'

'Better go see Dr Samuel Looking Horse,' growled April War Bonnet. I jumped. She'd been silent, her diminutive frame completely concealed by the large armchair she occupied.

'What?'

'Dr Looking Horse, over at the clinic on Blue Street. He'll put you right.' April's eyes had a gleam, and I wondered if she was setting me up for trouble. My few days' acquaintance had taught me caution. I'd already endured a near heart attack over the dried llama foetus she'd left on my bed, a good-luck token from a Bolivian witch doctor.

'Is he a real doctor? Not like your witch-doctor friend.' I hadn't been able to get rid of my 'lucky charm' fast enough. I'd rather stay cursed.

'Phffft. Native Americans can be real doctors, you know.'

Horrified, I protested, 'I didn't—'

She cut me off, enjoying herself. 'He is. Plus, he's the only doctor in town.' That sealed it. I was going.

'And steal the lobby magazines for me.' Ah. That explained the gleam. Up Market carried only a few out-of-date periodicals.

An hour later, I was sitting in a paper gown in an examination room, my backpack stuffed with clinic magazines. My life of crime was getting out of control, but the alternative of disappointing April promised retribution, probably in the form of my make-up glued to the dressing table. I'd been delighted to find a cheery little health centre, rather than a larger, impersonal hospital. I didn't like hospitals. Waiting for Dr Samuel Looking Horse, I envisioned a kindly, wizened old Native American. That's not who walked in.

Dr Looking Horse was in his early thirties, well over six feet tall, and chiselled like a dusky-skinned shirtless lothario sweeping up a feisty beauty on the cover of a book called something like *Savage Native Love*. April's twinkle became understandable. I was ready for my exam.

'I have my charts.' I handed him a sheaf of folders.

'You carry your charts around?'

'Mmm-hmm.' I was noncommittal. It was a time-saving measure.

His eyes met mine after he scanned the first file.

'I had a sneezing fit, and my lungs feel a little swollen.'

'A sneezing fit?' Bemused this time.

'It could be spores.' I was earnest. 'I'm new to the area. Not adapted.'

'I see.' I suspected I wasn't being taken seriously. Still, he was a professional. 'Let's have a look. Cough for me.' He placed his stethoscope to my chest. Coughing had never been so much fun.

It took less than twenty minutes for Dr Looking Horse to pronounce me perfectly healthy. 'There's absolutely nothing wrong with you. I'll write you a prescription for a multivitamin if that will make you feel better about acclimatising to our spores.'

I squinted at him. 'Uh, no thanks, I have loads.'

He faced me again, expression serious. 'Ms Connelly, there's no reason to worry about such minor discomforts. It's very unlikely—'

'Are there things a newcomer to the area would need to be concerned about?' I persisted, this time with a new agenda. Why take home a prescription if you could take home the doctor? 'Spores, poison oak? Maybe you should give me a primer. Over dinner.'

'I . . .'

The door opened and a nurse with violent pink lipstick popped her head in. 'Dr Looking Horse? Liz Goldberg is here—it's an emergency. Tommy fell out of a tree and broke his arm.'

'I'm sorry,' he said to me. His regret looked genuine. 'I must go.' Then he smiled. 'I imagine you'll survive any Unknown hazards just fine.' And with that he was gone.

On Monday morning, I bounced down Red Road to The Little Read Book, eager to embrace my new job.

No one was in the shop when I entered, all the lights were off.

'Hello,' I called, walking to the register. A note on the counter read: *IOU. I got that book. Ronnie Two Shoes.*

'Hello?' I repeated. I wondered if there was another power outage, but when I flipped the lights they came on. I walked towards where

Noah had disappeared on my first visit. I found him in his office, but hesitated in the doorway.

N. E. Case was playing with dolls. Specifically, he was sitting on the floor, swimming an action figure through a tub of water, muttering to himself. He looked up, confused, a thousand-mile stare.

'I'm Maeve,' I reminded him. 'I'm starting work today?'

'Oh.' He looked distressed. 'I don't have time to train you. Is Tuesday here?' He seemed torn between the toys and me.

'Nice dolls.' I couldn't resist.

His expression became haughty. 'They are *not* dolls. They are creative visualisation devices. They help me when I'm blocked. Anyway, I'm sorry I can't train you, I need—'

'You need a shower, no more coffee and some sleep.' Tuesday bustled in, and cut him off with authority. Noah looked back at his tub.

'I'm close. I think. I mean . . .'

'I didn't see your car all weekend, which means you've been here and are probably sugar-deprived, which makes you cranky, which makes me cranky. It is therefore in my self-interest to feed you and send you home. Up, up, up.' Her hands under his armpits were firm as she lifted him to his feet and propelled him out into the café. I trailed after them as Tuesday got to work behind the coffee bar.

'I have to finish ten chapters of *The Boy Who Could Breathe Underwater* by Friday,' he protested. 'How does he get back? Does he . . .'

'Noah, you were playing with your toys, which means you're stumped. I'm making you breakfast then sending you home.'

He capitulated. 'I could use some sleep. Will you be OK? The reorder is due today.'

'I'll be fine,' she assured him. 'I've got Maeve.'

'Sorry.' Noah looked at me, tugging a hand through his nest of hair. 'Not much of a welcome. I've been working all weekend.'

'When I have a hard time focusing, I find that picking the right socks can help.' He looked dubious, so I rushed on. 'I mean, not *literally*, like the socks themselves do anything, but organising your thoughts to choose the right pair can put you in the proper mind set.' I showed him my favourite bookworm socks. 'I wore these to start my new job.'

'I appreciate the effort,' he said. 'Those are nice socks.'

'Eat this.' Tuesday dropped a plate of scrambled eggs and a sliced tomato in front of Noah. 'Then go home. Maeve, let's get this place operational. Can you please fire up the register, while I try to figure out which book Ronnie Two Shoes walked off with?'

I didn't see Noah until the next day. I showed up promptly at 9.45 a.m., key in my hot little hand. Tuesday had a performance in Tucson, so she wasn't coming in. I'd got up early to run, eager to start work on time. I hoped I remembered everything she'd showed me. I knew she'd had to cajole Noah into trusting me alone in the front, and he'd only conceded because of his deadline.

'When Noah's on deadline, he doesn't do anything but write,' Tuesday had explained to me. 'And I mean anything—he can forget to eat, sleep, change clothes. Forget about helping you in the store. You'll probably want to bring him a sandwich around lunch. It might seem like the secretary fetching coffee, but, trust me, low blood sugar equals cranky equals not fun. It's in your best interest.'

I was feeling confident. It was pretty basic register operation and sandwich-making, nothing I hadn't done in past jobs. Traffic was light. In the absence of customers, I busied myself dusting the front table. Then I busied myself changing it. No one was going to buy *War and Peace* unless they already intended to, no matter how prominently it was displayed. It was a waste of prime real estate. I replaced it with *Run* by Ann Patchett.

At 11.38 exactly, I could resist no longer. It was *almost* noon. I sidled into Noah's office. He was sitting at a large desk drumming his fingers. He looked less demented. And very attractive.

'Knock, knock, J. Alfred Prufrock,' I called.

He looked up, surprised. 'Oh, hello.' Back to drumming.

'I was wondering if there's anything you don't like on your sandwich?'

'Hmm?' Absently. 'Oh, whatever.' Then he came to himself. 'Oh, you don't have to do that. I can make my own lunch.' He didn't move.

'It's no problem,' I assured him. I hesitated. 'What's got you blocked?'

His office was tasteful wood and leather; only the numerous 'creative visualisation devices' belied the perfect image of a gentleman's study. A polar bear, a male action figure and what looked like Nemo the fish lay on the desk. I bit my lip.

'I don't know how to balance underwater time and land time.'

I pondered. 'Maybe he can breathe both water and air, but, to preserve his ability, he has to return to an aquatic environment at various intervals. It would add a race-against-the-clock element. And show his ingenuity—like the length of time he can spend on land can be prolonged if he goes somewhere with lots of humidity.' My Southern roots inspired me.

Noah's jaw dropped. He turned his back without a word and started typing madly into his laptop. I slipped out to fix the most delicious sandwich ever. When I slid it onto the desk, he didn't look up from his rapid key-pounding.

Shortly before closing, I surveyed the new arrangement of shelves in the rear-left corner, wiping my brow. I was reconfiguring the area to put the chairs where there was the most light. A voice in my ear made me jump out of my skin.

'The boy has universal consciousness of, and can communicate with, all sea life. How would it apply to animals that spend time on land *and* water, like sea lions and polar bears?'

I thought. He waited, stare intense.

'Can he push his telepathic powers to the higher land creatures by finding that element of their brain that dates to their ancestors' time in the ocean? Whether you believe in the Bible or Darwin or Native legends, at one point the earth was entirely covered in water and our genetic origin was aquatic.'

'I like it. It's a good way to slip in some science to educate my readers as well.' He turned towards the office. I was buoyant. He paused. 'What do your socks look like today?' was his surprising question.

I hesitated, embarrassed to expose my fascination, but tugged my jeans to show him the fishes, sea horses and aquatic creatures decorating my favourite undersea knee socks.

'Interesting.' He gave a thoughtful smile, then was gone.

I was brewing coffee, when Tuesday came in the next morning.

'You're early! How'd it go yesterday?'

'It was divine.' I glowed. Tuesday did a double take.

'I rearranged the Religion section,' I covered. I didn't want to disappoint her yet by telling her that soon I'd be spending all my time huddled in the back office collaborating with Noah, inspiring and educating kids everywhere. 'How was the show?'

'It was good, but I wish I'd had someone to take pictures. People kept asking me.'

'I'm pretty handy with a camera,' I offered. It was the one hobby I'd stuck with. I loved the permanence of pinning something as fleeting as an expression or a shadow to paper.

The bells on the door sounded before Tuesday could answer. Her expression plummeted. 'Gotta run. Back in a sec.' She disappeared.

I looked up to see a human bollard in front of me. The woman's short

stature combined with her grey wool coat created the impression of a
cement postbox. It also begged the question of why she was wearing
a grey wool coat when it was seventy degrees.

She marched over to me. 'Helen Rausch. I need a book on poisons.'

'Oh. OK. I'm Maeve.'

'I'm uninterested. Poisons?'

I blinked. 'Sure. Do you want a history of poisons, an encyclopedia
of poisons, an Agatha Christie novel . . .'

'I want to know how to cause death by poison.'

Use your face, I thought. What I said was, 'Plants, then? Or pests?'

'Liz Goldberg.'

Two blinks this time. 'Um.'

'Are you developmentally challenged? I. Want. To. Poison. Liz.
Goldberg.'

'Helen, how lovely you're looking today.' Noah, at my side, was the
epitome of gallant. 'Now, I understand you're looking for a book.' He
placed a hand on her shoulder and guided her to the gardening section,
head bent.

'Is she gone?' Tuesday hissed from where she was crouched below
the counter. I nodded. 'Thank God. Helen Rausch. Trundling proof that
not everyone in Unknown is likeable. Sorry I had to dash, but Noah
has strict orders that he handles Helen. What did she want?'

'To poison Liz Goldberg.' I admired the way Noah deftly rang up a
Thai cookbook for Helen only ten minutes later, and saw her out before
returning to his office.

Tuesday snorted. 'Those two have been feuding since a ranch bound-
ary dispute between their great-great-great-granddads. Liz keeps
threatening to shoot Helen. I wish she would. Oh!' She bounced back
to me. 'Can you really photograph my student recital on Thursday? If
you do it, I'll treat you to dinner.'

'Will do, cockatoo.' I was impatient for the coffee to brew. I'd take
Noah a cup and see if he needed any help. I was surprised he hadn't
stopped by after Helen left.

A tall, blonde woman entered the store, having just stepped from the
Lacoste advertisement where she lived. I'd never seen a more perfect
embodiment of pink-cheeked Midwestern beauty. The only thing keeping her out of the Colgate toothpaste ad was the lack of smile.

'Hey, Beth,' Tuesday greeted her.

'Is he here?' Beth dispensed with hello.

'Yeah, you know.'

Beth rolled her eyes. Apparently she did know, and wasn't charmed. 'He left the sink running when he left this morning.' She turned to me. 'Hi, I'm Beth Watson, Noah's girlfriend.'

I shot the coffee pot I was gripping out of its cradle and hot liquid ran down the back of my hand. 'Shit!' I jerked my burned appendage out of harm's way. 'Sorry!' I apologised to Beth. 'My language! Too much time with Lulabell. I'm Maeve.'

'Are you OK?' asked Beth, as Tuesday exclaimed, 'Oh, honey!'

'Sure, sure. It barely got me.' My hand was throbbing.

'Listen.' Beth turned to Tuesday. 'Can you remind Noah that I'm going up to Tucson for work? I'll be back on Friday. Oh, and remind him we have dinner with my brother and his wife on Saturday, and I don't care what his deadline is, he'd better be there physically *and* mentally.'

'I'll try!' Tuesday's cheerful reply sounded forced.

Beth turned back to me. 'You should be more careful. I think there's aloe vera cream in the bathroom for that burn. Noah wouldn't like it if you claimed workman's comp as a result of your own clumsiness.'

I didn't know why I was disappointed. Had I really thought I'd become writing partners with Noah and spend the rest of my life in Unknown, Arizona? Hell, no. It didn't affect me that he had a girlfriend. I'd barely have time to get to know him before I left.

'I think Beth is right.' Tuesday pulled me from my thoughts, with a sly grin. 'You should do something about that hand.' I looked at it. It was angry-red and hurt like hell. 'But I don't think aloe vera's gonna do it.' She winked. 'You'd better see a doctor.'

I responded with a broad smile, 'I think you may be right.'

I looked round the Velvet Elvis pizzeria. 'Early Elvis or late Elvis?' I asked my companion.

Samuel looked thoughtful a moment. 'Early Elvis. As a doctor, I can't condone how he abused his body at the end.' He flashed his white grin.

'Uh-oh,' I said. 'I'm late Elvis all the way. I love the idea of the come-back. And "A Little Less Conversation".'

'We'll have to see if we can overcome this seemingly insurmountable obstacle,' Samuel said. I didn't think we'd have a problem.

'Thanks for fixing me up this afternoon.' I waggled my bandaged hand.

'Yes, well, before you continue a course of self-injury, you should tell April that she's perfectly able to subscribe to magazines herself. I had to put out my medical journals after your last visit, and self-diagnostic hysteria skyrocketed. Everyone thought they had lupus.'

I blushed. 'You noticed.'

'Don't worry. Happens every time Busy comes in for her heart medication.' His smile was warm. It was hard to imagine him being angry.

Samuel was a charming and attentive companion. I was fascinated by his stories from the reservation.

'I'd love to see it sometime. I really like Arizona,' I said. 'It's the opposite of anything I've known. North Carolina is lush and verdant. Maybe that's why I find the barrenness of the desert so striking. When I get my car back,'—a wistful pause for Elsie—'I'd like to photograph more of it.'

'You like photography?'

'Yep. I'm covering a recital for Tuesday on Thursday.' It sounded silly, so I giggled. Samuel grinned.

'The Bitty Bees Touch Their Knees? I'll be there too. Last year Celia Sweet danced right off the bandstand, so now we have a doctor on call just in case.' He was thoughtful. 'My grandmother turns ninety next week. What do you think about coming to the party and taking pictures? You're a lot alike. You both have a bright light.'

I caught my breath. 'I'd love to.'

'It should be quite a party. No one cooks like my *ama' sa' ni* and her sisters. There are eleven Nizhoni sisters. None of them ever left the res.'

'Did you grow up there?'

'Yes and no. My family home was there, but I went to an off-reservation boarding school. I always wanted to be either a doctor or a vet. I didn't get into vet school, but someone slipped up at the University of New Mexico medical school, so doctor it was.'

'Yeah, I struggled between subparticle physics and sandwich-making myself. Did you ever think of moving back?'

'Not really. Health care on the res is terribly underfunded. Pay for providers isn't lucrative. I struggled with a sense of obligation to go back, but I had to pay off my med-school loans. My compromise was a split— private practice here, and one day a week I provide non-emergency medical services at an Indian Health Services Clinic on the res. Mostly I treat diabetes management. Long-time residents aren't made to process the high-concentrated-sugar foods introduced from the outside. Speaking of sweets,' he asked, 'would you like dessert?'

What was sweet was when he covered my hand as we shared a sundae. He kept the hand as we strolled back to Ruby's.

'Well, thanks for walking me home,' I babbled when we got to her door, suddenly shy. 'You really need to come back in the daylight and see the garden. And you can meet Oliver. His language skills have significantly expanded since he met Lulabell. Though it's not really—'

Samuel interrupted. 'Maeve. How about a little less conversation?'

'Hound dog,' I whispered, before I shut up and did something else with my mouth.

'**W**ell?' demanded Tuesday when I danced into work the next day. I swooned.

'Dr Samuel has *excellent* bedside manners.'

'Ay-yi-yi! I'm so jealous. He is soooo hot.'

'I know,' I said smugly. 'We're going to your recital together tonight and out to dinner tomorrow.' I shivered at the memory of Samuel's kisses.

'You should treat yourself to a new pair of socks. Go remind Noah he has to write you a cheque tomorrow.'

I found Noah leaning back in his chair, crossed ankles propped on his desk, bouncing a ball against the wall. 'Howdy,' I said.

He turned and broke into a wide smile. 'Hello, little muse!'

I had to stop from shuffling my feet and saying 'Aw, shucks' like a country bumpkin. 'Tuesday says to remind you to pay me.'

'I sent ten chapters to my editor, so I've rejoined the living,' he announced with satisfaction. 'I'll write your cheque now. Look.' He hitched up his trouser legs to reveal bright blue socks covered in polar bears. My laughter satisfied him. He swung his legs to the ground and wrote the cheque. He stood, but when I reached for my salary, he held it beyond my grasp.

'First you have to agree to put *Grapes of Wrath* back on the front table.'

He'd noticed. I groaned. 'It's so *depressing*.'

'It's also the book-club selection this month. Promise,' Noah demanded.

'Fine,' I grumbled. 'But only for the month. Then I'm replacing it with *The Coroner's Lunch*.'

'To higher learning.' He held up his hand for a high five. I jumped to slap his palm, and toppled onto him.

'If you wanted to dance, you only had to ask,' he teased as he caught me. He spun me in a twirl. I was astonished at his rock-solid frame, considering he typed for a living. The man had a chest. He led me in a little waltz round the office. Then, arms pointing, we tangoed cheek-to-cheek out into the store, where he dipped me dramatically.

'Where do you go dancing?' I asked.

'Bitty Bees Touch Their Knees.' He righted me. 'Tuesday's having a recital tonight.'

'I'm already going. I'm taking pictures for Tuesday.'

'Great! We can go together and get something to eat after.'

'Um. Actually, I'm going with Samuel. Dr Looking Horse. He's picking me up here.'

Noah's smile vanished. 'Ah. That was fast work.'

I started to get mad. Who was he to judge? Men with girlfriends shouldn't be waltzing other girls round their store anyway.

'I'd invite you *and Beth* to join us, but it doesn't sound like you and Samuel get along.' My tone was sharp.

Noah turned away. 'Samuel's a great guy. I like him. I'm not sure about Beth tonight.' I was pretty sure he meant that literally. He didn't know where Beth was.

'She's in Tucson,' I said. 'For work. She said to remind you that you're having dinner with her brother on Saturday.'

'Oh, right. Well, here's your cheque. I'll see you at the community centre later.' With that he disappeared.

'**R**eady?' said Samuel.

I wondered if it was unprofessional to hold hands in front of my boss, but it felt good when Samuel took mine, so I didn't really care. When we stepped outside, Samuel pulled me close for a kiss.

'I've been waiting to do that again,' he said, then reclaimed my hand.

We headed to the town square. The site of my aborted camp-out was a pleasant rectangle flanked by Main Street and Red Street, filled with trees, picnic benches and lawn. At one end was the community centre, and at the other a bandstand. Tonight, the bandstand was decorated with fairy lights and a rainbow of paper rosettes, and was surrounded by rows of folding chairs.

The park was crowded. The whole town had turned out. News of my arrival preceded me, and I was surprised at people's eagerness to get acquainted, and their warm reception.

'It's the most tasty salad—basically green beans and peas,' Liz Goldberg said, as she scribbled the recipe for me on a crumpled receipt.

'Great, thanks. I'm planning to introduce more vegetarian items on to the lunch menu at the bookstore. Maybe I'll call your salad The Liz.'

'Maybe you should ask the boss,' said Noah.

'Maybe I'll call the turkey sandwich The Noah,' I said.

The arrival of a pert blonde about my age prevented his retort.

'Sandy Irwin from the nail salon,' she introduced herself. 'You have to come to the Wagon Wheel for a beer sometime.' She scribbled her number and the details on to the back of the nail salon's card. As soon as Sandy moved on, Jenny Up wandered over and struck up a 'casual' conversation about the sanitary (read: unsanitary) nature of pet birds visiting grocery stores. It was almost a relief when Helen Rausch approached, with muttered invective that I'd best watch out before eating anything Liz Goldberg recommended because 'that hussy is pure poison'.

When the music cued, Helen rushed to get the middle seat of the first row before one of the sneaky Goldbergs did, and Samuel went to claim our seats. I lurked round the bandstand as unobtrusively as possible, snapping shot after shot. The show was an unintended work of comic genius, as Tuesday tried to shepherd the children of Unknown through various routines. It was like herding cats. Little Bloom Tarquin stomped on Frieda Watson's foot when Frieda stepped upstage of her. Frieda ran off in tears, Tuesday scurrying after her, as Bloom pirouetted prettily alone centre stage. But it was Patrick Up Jr who stole the show when his lederhosen came undone and the short pants fell to his ankles, revealing Spider-Man Underoos.

I burned through film; I didn't want to let Tuesday down.

Even once Celia Sweet had danced safely offstage after the last number, I continued to shoot. Liz Goldberg with Tommy, arm in a sling, telling the story of his fall to Jenny Up, with elaborate hand gestures. Helen scowling at them. Click. Click. I loved the sound the shutter made as I stole this part of Unknown. The permanence of photography left me in awe. Click. Tuesday flushing with pleasure as she accepted accolades. Click. Ronnie Two Shoes, thumbs hooked into belt loops, chatting up Sandy. Click. The setting sun highlighting the planes of Samuel's throat as he laughed. Click. Samuel turning towards me. Click. Samuel reaching to tug the camera away from my eye.

'Aloha? Where are my people?' I heard Tuesday demand. 'Maeve, Samuel! Let's go eat!' She waved us over, and it was my turn to flush. I was her people. I happily fell in with the crowd bound for dinner.

Later, stuffed with chile rellenos, Samuel and I meandered back to Ruby's. Inside, I noticed that Oliver had taken up residence with Lulabell. They were snuggled up on her perch.

'Look,' I whispered to Samuel. 'They're in the same cage.' Samuel murmured. And without another word, I took his hand and led him to number 1.

'You need to see Child,' April rumbled. We were contemplating the pile of film on the table.

I was worried about the cost of developing. My cheques from Noah were minimum wage, and I was still paying off Simon Bear for towing Elsie. I wondered how I could barter. 'What child is that?' I asked.

'Child Sugar. He develops the pictures here. In the back of the print shop.'

'The octagonal building?' I was interested. I'd seen it on my runs.

'Yep.'

A picture-perfect model for cardigan sweaters looked up when I walked into the print shop an hour later. When he saw me, he smiled. 'I'm guessing you're Maeve Connelly,' boomed his rich bass.

'How did you know?' We'd never met.

'Ruby mentioned that a young lady wearing knee socks might be by today, most likely with a barter scheme at the ready.'

I laid the eleven rolls of film on the counter. We eyed them.

'Will Noah let you work for me on Mondays from four to eight o'clock in the evening? Mondays are my late night—everyone wants his or her weekend images ten minutes ago—however, I dislike missing *The NewsHour with Jim Lehrer*. I'll instruct you in the operation of the machines. You may develop your own film after the paying customer orders are complete. You will be required only to compensate me for the cost of the paper if you rely on your own labour.'

'Absolutely,' I said, with no idea what Noah would think.

'Let us be civilised.' Child gestured to two armchairs and I sat. He pressed a button on an electric kettle, and in less than a minute loose tea was steeping in an Aurora Royal Patrician bone-china teapot. Child settled in his chair. 'Tell me about yourself, Maeve.'

I froze. Child was the first person to ask me about my past. Most of the time, I peppered people with questions, got them to talk instead.

'Not much to tell, really. My car broke down and I'm earning the money to fix her up. Are you originally from Unknown?'

'My family comes from Pittsburgh. I am sorry for your car misfortunes. Where is your family?' He poured the tea.

'North Carolina. How long have you lived here?'

'I moved to Unknown in 1988. Did you attend university in North Carolina?' Most people can be conversationally diverted with ease: you ask them something about themselves. Child was unshakeable.

'Mmm-hmm. I bet Unknown hasn't changed much. Is it pretty much the same as when you arrived?'

'They offer an excellent book on the history of Unknown at the artisan shop on Red Road. What did you study?' It was like fencing.

'Oh, lots of things. How did you get into prints?' The walls were hung with beautifully framed antique maps, old posters from something called the Monkey Flower Festival, and intricate line drawings. The shop felt like a Victorian parlour except for the photo-processing machines behind the oak table serving as a counter.

'I studied art history. What did you do after college?' *Riposte*.

'This and that. I haven't really decided on a career.' *Parry*.

'When did you complete your studies?' His gaze was level.

'December. When did you open the shop?'

'Ten years ago. So photography is a career interest for you?' *Redoublement*.

'Career? I don't know. I like taking pictures.' I decided to give him something. *Retraite*.

'Tell me what you like about it.'

'Capturing people as they really are. My goodness, is that the time?' *Feint*. 'I have to get to work.'

After agreeing to meet on Monday, I fled.

'These are incredible, Maeve! A million *mahalos*!' We were looking at the photos from Tuesday's recital. 'This one of Bloom Tarquin is precious!' I'd caught her mid-pirouette, tongue at the corner of her lip in concentration. I was anxious for Tuesday's approval. Child had carefully tutored me in operating the sensitive developing machines, but it'd taken more than a couple of rolls to get a feel for them. My first set of prints came out completely black. My second split images over two sheets. With the third I managed to centre the images and produce a roll where Bruce's camping photos were only slightly orange.

'I'm sorry, Child.' I'd pushed back sweaty hair, hot with frustration. 'I'll pay for these.'

'Don't be silly. Training is a cost of business. You'll get it.'

And eventually I did. It was 3.30 in the morning when Bruce's image of a pheasant taking wing emerged crisp and clear. No one was there to hear me whooping, but Child must have known, because when I showed up unscheduled at closing time on Tuesday, he didn't seem surprised.

By Friday all he said was, 'Remember to lock up.' He'd given me keys when it became apparent that my nocturnal fervour showed no sign of stopping. It was worth it. After mastering the machines, I'd cleared the backlog of customer orders (and learned a few things about Ronnie

Two Shoes), and had turned to my own film. My pile of rolls had grown as I continued to take images of Unknown and its citizens.

'I can use these for promotional cards.' Tuesday fanned out pictures of herself dancing, and hugged me.

'What are those?' Noah pointed to another folder.

'Oh.' I shrugged, embarrassed. 'Nothing.'

I reached for it but he was quicker, flipping it open and spreading the candid photos. Tuesday doing the hula behind the coffee bar when she thought no one was watching. April War Bonnet whispering new dirty words to Lulabell. I worried that they looked invasive. These subjects didn't know they were being captured.

'Maeve, these are amazing.' Tuesday's voice was hushed.

Noah paused at one of himself. Beth was talking to him, but he wasn't listening; he was looking past her, directly at the camera. He looked at me again now. 'You've captured the town well.'

I liked that he used my word, *capture*. I was grabbing moments. 'You can keep things from disappearing,' I said.

'But you're not in any of them.'

'What?'

'Where are the pictures of you and Tuesday gossiping when you should be working? Or you running down the back roads, braids flying?' I was embarrassed at his awareness. I preferred to stay below the radar. He tapped a photo of Ruby, Bruce, Samuel and Tuesday walking over to the Wagon Wheel Saloon. 'You should be in this.'

'How can I take the picture if I'm in it, silly?'

He gave me a look. 'That's exactly it. Why were you behind taking the picture and not walking with everyone else?'

'I was catching up.'

'Or hanging back?'

I had the same uncomfortable feeling I'd had with Child. Like being rebuked, but I wasn't sure what for. 'I'm a tourist here,' I said breezily. 'Strictly observer status.'

'Don't remind me.' Tuesday groaned. 'It feels like you've always been here. You belong in Unknown. I hate the idea that you'll leave.'

Anxious tickle. California waited.

Noah considered me, then said, 'We'll display your pictures in the store. You can sell prints for Elsie.'

'No one'll want to *buy* my pictures,' I protested.

'I think you'll be surprised. How much for this one?' He tapped a shot of him and Beth walking, heads bent together.

'Five dollars unframed.' I named a ridiculous price.

'Fine.'

'Kill me for vanity, but I'll take these two.' Tuesday waved two pictures of herself dancing. I felt guilty for overcharging.

They both handed me money and, just like that, I was Maeve Inc.

Chapter 4: Snapping

IT WAS MY BAD LUCK that Jenny Up decided to buy new cookbooks as soon as the store opened. Some days we sold nothing but lunch, but the day I was late, we had customers at the unlocking of the door. It figured. Noah smiled pleasantly at Jenny as he rang up her purchases, but his right eyebrow was drawn down so I knew he was steaming. When the door closed behind her, he snapped, 'You're late.'

'I'm sorry.' I was still breathless. I really was late.

'How am I supposed to write if I'm tending customers while you loll about in bed? God help us if someone needs a doctor.'

I was offended. 'I was not lolling in bed! I was in the darkroom.' Truth was, I'd barely seen Samuel all week, except for our daily lunches. And I'd completely neglected my marathon training.

Last Monday, Child did not pass me on his way out, as usual, but was waiting. 'Come with me.' He had led me out the front door and round to the back of the octagonal building to a small room painted black, counters covered in trays, machines, filters and bottles.

'This is my darkroom. The photographs you've been taking are wasted on automated printing. How would you like to learn to develop negatives and print by hand?'

'I'd love to.' I breathed in a chemical smell that wasn't offensive.

Clipped to a clothes line were 8" by 10" black-and-white prints of pueblo life. They were flawless, capturing snapping eyes in a wrinkled face, a profile half in shadow, colourfully garbed dancers.

'Did you take these?'

'My wife.' His voice was heavy with sadness. I remembered that Child was a widower.

Loss makes you selfish enough to think that you alone know what it feels like. You don't. Child had reminded me what we shared. 'My best friend died,' I surprised myself by offering. 'She loved to draw. The last picture she gave me means the world to me now.'

Child gave a brief nod. I was relieved he didn't ask *how* Cameron had died. I hated recalling my last images of her, stretched gaunt by an illness that didn't understand the rule that the young don't die. I hadn't taken any photos then. I didn't want to preserve the disease.

Time disappeared as Child taught me. For a week, I spent every free moment in the darkroom, and the rest of the time in a semi-daze, smelling faintly of chemicals. I saw everything through the frame of the lens. I couldn't admire sunset without itching to photograph leafy shadows. People became subjects. I started to view Samuel as a collection of planes and angles. I wanted a still image to portray Ruby's precise way of moving. Or Ruby's precise way of informing me that the bareness of the linen cupboard, breakfast bar *and* refrigerator yesterday was unacceptable.

Which brought me back to my present predicament.

Noah looked mollified to learn I hadn't been late because of morning delights with Samuel, but not defused. 'It is completely unacceptable that you're over an hour late. I have a deadline *today*.'

'I'm sorry, Noah. I really am.' I wasn't. The man could ring his own register once in a while. I was doing important work. People *valued* it.

'Stock hasn't been put out, sales reports never got generated last week, and you put peanuts in the salad instead of walnuts. We're lucky no one went into anaphylactic shock.'

'You're not an infant, you know,' I snapped. 'You own the shop. The buck does not stop with your minimum-wage slave. It stops with you.'

'Yes, and I'm the one *paying you* to work for me. Forget the basics— this place is a wreck with your half-finished projects. We have shelves in disarray for some imaginary future children's nook. We have half a vegetarian menu. And now we have only half the best sellers in stock!'

'And the store is half again as appealing as it used to be. I've worked hard.' I shouted over the little voice that said he was right.

'Until you lost interest.'

'My career has no value?' I elevated my hobby on the spot. His jab went to my anxious place. 'I'm supposed to tiptoe round your creative brilliance and not do anything for myself?'

'Interacting with humans wouldn't be a bad idea. It beats running away from everyone or hiding in a darkroom.'

'Working in the darkroom is *art!* It takes time. I'm doing hired *jobs*, I'll have you know. I am not *hiding*.' My protest felt oddly like a lie.

'Right. You're so focused on your *career* that you don't replace sold prints? There aren't any left. My store is naked.'

That stopped me. 'We sold them all?' I hadn't noticed. The bookcases now sported only forlorn nails. I felt a pang of guilt.

He was yelling now. 'You aren't doing even the basics of your job. You've become unreliable.'

My bravado left me. He couldn't see me as that girl. I wasn't careless Maeve. I was reliable Maeve. Talented Maeve. Desirable Maeve. New Maeve. I needed Noah to see that.

'I . . .'

At my expression, he stopped, his own face becoming stricken. He ploughed a hand through his hair and dropped into a chair.

'Damn, I'm sorry. I should not be taking my stress out on you.' He rested his forehead in his hands. He looked exhausted.

I fidgeted, but he didn't say anything. 'Have you eaten?' was the closest I could come to 'Sorry'.

'Forgetting my morning coffee is no excuse to be rude. I'm a grown man. It's not your job to fill my cup.'

'We could both use some.' I set about making a pot.

'I like having you around the shop,' he said as he watched me. 'And you have good ideas.' I felt awful.

'I *am* sorry.' This time it was easier to use the word. I meant it. 'I like being here. I'm not sure why I got so obsessed with the photography.'

'Who am I to talk? You've seen me work. A lot of being able to create is stepping out of your life into someone else's. I love it, but I'm no good at straddling two worlds. When I'm in the not-real one, it makes me dependent. You make it easy to count on you.'

'You *should* count on me,' I protested. 'As long as this is my job, I should be doing what I'm paid for.'

'Your photography is beautiful, Maeve. I don't want you to stop that.'

Squelching my flush of pride, I poured two cups of coffee and pulled up a chair. 'Been playing with your toys?'

He rose to my bait. 'They are *not* toys. They're—'

'I know, I know. What's the problem?'

He sighed. 'I think it's wrong to have an environment where every-one coexists happily. That doesn't happen. My setting is full of joyful frolicking sea creatures. There needs to be threat within the society.'

'Make an evil sea creature.' The answer seemed logical.

'It's not that simple. I'm afraid to characterise anything as a bad element. You should see the angry letters I received from third-graders when I painted warthogs in a negative light.' He grinned.

I thought a minute. 'How about jellyfish? No one likes jellyfish.'

We talked until the lunch crowd arrived. Afterwards I spent the afternoon catching up on my paperwork, and diagramming how I wanted Bruce to rearrange the tall shelves. I was shamed when I saw how much I'd let slide. I had to put limits on my darkroom time.

'**S**till no Barney?' Vi asked. 'How long has it been?'

'I don't know. A little while.'

'A little while? It's been over two months!' Vi exclaimed. 'How can you not notice? You're stuck in the sticks!'

'There's a lot going on,' I defended. 'I'm training for the marathon, taking hula lessons, and Tuesday and I started a book club. And I spend lots of time in the darkroom.' But still. Where had two months gone?

'The pictures you sent are amazing, Maeve.' The sincere admiration in my sister's voice took my breath away.

'It's hard to take a bad photo here.' I went for casual. 'I've been getting lots of jobs. I've got my first wedding in two weeks.'

'I'm impressed.' Vi said. 'How's Samuel?'

'He's like a male version of you—he watches what I eat, he slathers me with sunscreen, he makes sure I don't train every day, he turns on a light when I read. He takes good care of me.'

'I like to hear that!' she said. 'Why don't you stay?'

I frowned at the phone. I couldn't stay in Unknown. 'Because I'm going to California,' I insisted. 'I have the marathon.'

'Plans change.'

'Stopping halfway would definitely qualify as flaky,' I protested. It occurred to me that I hadn't emailed Laura in over a week. We had been in regular contact, but recently I'd let the correspondence lapse. 'I want to go to California. I'm making the best of a bad situation.'

'Really? It sounds to me like you're having the time of your life.'

I was seething.

'I couldn't resist,' Beth had exclaimed. 'Aren't they great?'

They were four framed prints depicting pastel scenes of Victorian children playing on beaches. They were *not* great. They were tacky.

'They'll be *perfect* in the children's nook,' her narcissistic rant had continued. She'd paused and given me an assessing look. 'It's just that,

Maeve, well, with your taste . . .' Her gaze had swept from my Converse low-tops to my *That's How I Roll* T-shirt. 'You're what, Maeve? Thirty? Thirty-one?'

'Twenty-six,' I'd ground out.

'Oh.' Delicate brows had arched. With a bemused shake of her head, she'd walked out, French manicure smoothing a blonde tress.

I tried to conceal my fuming, but couldn't help thumping books down harder than necessary as I muttered.

'The Little Read Picture Book is *mine*.' Thump, thump. '*I'm* the one who dragged those heavy-ass shelves all over, and lost brain cells painting them rainbow colours. Who does she think she is, foisting ugly-ass mass-produced art on me?' Thump. The cheap prints were a far cry from the classic children's book covers I'd planned to frame. Slam.

'Hey, easy on the furniture.' Noah appeared behind me after I banged the cabinet. 'What's up?' His eye fell on the pictures. 'And what in God's name are those awful things?'

My mood lightened a tad. I told him.

'Oh, no. No. Those things are not hanging in my store.'

I blew out my fringe in relief. 'I thought we could use children's book covers. You know, framing the books in shadow boxes.'

'Sure. You can grab some from the back.'

'I thought maybe used copies with the original cover art. I've been finding them on the internet.' I reached under the counter and pulled out the vintage copies. 'I have a stack of them.'

Noah lifted an old copy of the first volume of the Hardy Boys series almost reverently. 'Why didn't you go down to the used-book store in Nogales?'

His question sparked my ire over another sensitive subject. I turned my back on him. Slam. Thump.

'I. Can't. Go. To. Nogales. Because. You. Don't. Give. Me. The. Six. Days. Off. I'd. Need. To. Walk. There.' I bit out my words. Since Vi's call, I'd been chafing at my utter inability to leave Unknown's confines.

'You've been here what, two months?' Noah stared at me. 'And you haven't been out of town? You must be going stir crazy. Let's go. Road trip.'

'Don't forget the bird,' I said automatically.

'What?'

'Never mind. We can't just go in the middle of the day,' I protested.

'Despite the way you fan about the place, last I checked, I still own it. Which gives me the authority to close it. Even in the middle of the day.'

I was already halfway to the door.

Ten minutes later we were heading south. Only half an hour later we pulled into the good-sized city of Nogales, on the border of Arizona and Mexico. It was bustling with traffic and humans.

'Lunch first, or bookstore?' Noah asked.

After the sleepy tempo of Unknown, I was a little overwhelmed by the activity. 'Um . . .'

Noah read my face. 'Lunch,' he pronounced. 'With beer. Let's go to Mexico.' He turned left.

'Noah! I can't go to Mexico!'

'Why not?'

'I don't have a passport, sport.'

'You don't need one. Got a driver's licence?'

'Ye-es. Are you sure?' I found the idea of casually strolling to another country for lunch unsettling. It should be more complicated. The high walls and dangerous-looking fencing supported this.

'Maeve, I do this all the time. A friend of mine has a place.' He took my hand, and tugged me. I felt a tingle shoot up my arm. Then I got mad at myself. Why was I breathless around Noah? Samuel was a marvellous boyfriend and no slouch in the bedroom. I was satisfied.

Noah's voice recalled me to the scary-looking border-crossing chute we were poised to enter. 'Let's see your licence.'

I handed it to him without thinking. Perhaps I should ask the guard, just to make sure. The area seemed weirdly abandoned. The few men in white shirts, apparently US Border Patrol, looked anything but military.

'Nice do,' Noah teased. 'Rocking the Sinead O'Connor look?'

I snatched my licence back from him. I was completely bald in the picture. 'It was an ill-judged impulse. My stylist assured me I had a "shapely skull".' I laughed it off.

'I prefer it this way.' He tugged a tress and smiled at me. 'I'm getting attached to those braids of yours.' For a moment we held like that, eyes locked. When he tugged my hand again and said, 'The taqueria awaits,' it felt like I could safely follow him anywhere. And just like that, I became an international traveller for the first time.

'I have enough to decorate the whole nook now,' I gloated as I hugged my bag of books. 'That place was the mother lode!'

'Ah-ha.' Noah laughed. 'A convert!' It was true; he had practically had to drag me back across the border. I *loved* Nogales, Sonora. Stepping through the gate had literally been a portal to another world. My mind was aswirl with the chaos and colour of the town. I'd run out of film. In addition to my books, I boasted a fabulous turquoise ring, a brightly woven belt for Tuesday, a pottery bowl decorated with chillies for Ruby, a deliciously full stomach and a slightly sunburned nose. I was having a perfect day. I didn't want to go home.

'I don't want to go home,' Noah said. 'I'm having too much fun.' He slung a casual arm over my shoulders.

'What's in mind, partner in crime?' I masked my overdelight with a bland tone.

He looked round. 'How about we get inked?' he said. For a moment I thought he'd said 'naked' and my pulse shot into my mouth. Then I spied the tattoo parlour next door and felt like an idiot.

'Got any?' Noah asked playfully. He pulled on my jeans belt loop and pretended to peek down my backside. 'Anywhere interesting?'

'No.' I giggled, swatting him. 'You?'

'I think it's time. Today's the day. Let's get you a tramp stamp.'

'Where's yours?'

'My treat, baby. Whatever you want.'

'You avoided the question. Again.'

'How about a butterfly? No, not a butterfly. How about a Jolly Roger?'

I faced him, hands on hips. 'You're the Roger Dodger. You totally have a tattoo. Confess.'

He looked away. 'I have one. I got it a long time ago.'

'Really? What is it? Where is it? Where were you doing when you got it?' I was fascinated that relatively straight Noah had this racy secret.

His look was superior. 'That's very personal. A gentleman never tattoos and tells.'

I felt oddly cheated that Noah had a tattoo and I didn't. 'I always wanted one.' I was serious. 'I still do.'

'Why haven't you got one? Afraid of the needle?'

'Lord, no. I couldn't decide what to get. What would I love enough to live with for the rest of my life? I'm not exactly great with commitment.' Noah knew enough of my history.

A tiny frown line appeared on his forehead. I put a finger on it. 'Watch that,' I warned. 'You'll get a dent. Not a tattoo I'd want for ever.'

'So what *would* you want for ever?' he persisted. I had a feeling the conversation wasn't about tattoos anymore. I didn't want to go there.

'What's next?' I changed the topic.

'We could get something to eat.' Noah caved in.

I rubbed my belly. 'I'm not sure I could. I'm still full of tacos.' I spied a seedy bar across the street. 'Let's go there.'

'Two Sols,' I ordered, feeling ultra-Mexican. We clinked. 'Cheers, big ears. Thanks for a great day.'

'The pleasure was mine.' His look made it the truth. 'If I thought I had to crowbar you out of Mexico, that was nothing compared to the bookstore. Considering you work in mine, I was a little offended they had to close to get you out of there.'

'Books are my friends. A bookstore is kind of like a reunion for me.'

His look was dubious, eyebrow cocked like a Sherlock Homes actor.

'It's true! I had a hermit period. I dropped out of school and didn't know what to do with myself. Books were better than people.'

'I know what you mean.' He became serious. 'For me it was writing. After my dad died, things were tough. Mom worried all the time. It was like she was eroding before my eyes. I took care of my kid sister, and escaped into stories about a boy who could do everything.'

'Weren't you a kid, too? Who took care of you?'

He considered me. 'I took care of myself.' I opened my mouth, but he beat me. 'So who were your best friends? Of the bound-page variety? If you were stranded on a desert island, which three would you take?'

I mused. '*Pride and Prejudice*, because it's the greatest romance ever written. *Catch-22*, because its satire gives you perspective on what's really crazy. And *A Bear Called Paddington*, because no matter how many times I read it, it makes me laugh every time.'

Noah waited, but I was done talking about books. Instead, I launched into one of my favourite games. 'Would you rather only drink water for the rest of your life, or never see the ocean again?'

'Would you rather . . .' lasted us through the drive home. I was deciding whether I wanted to eat only hamburgers for the rest of my life or live for ten fewer years when we pulled up to Ruby's.

'Really?' Noah demanded. 'Ten fewer years?'

'Of course! I love food. Living for ever is overrated. Why cling to life when you can't eat or enjoy yourself?' I thought of how hard Cameron fought to live when she couldn't do either, and got flustered. Fortunately Noah was getting out of the car and didn't notice. I slid out of the truck and looked up at him. His head blocked the porch light, giving him a halo and obscuring his features. He leaned towards me.

'Maeve.' Ruby's voice cut the tableau. Noah stepped back and I turned, refusing to wonder what he'd intended.

'Ruby! I went to Mexico! I got you a bowl!' I babbled.

'How thoughtful. I have good news. Barney has returned. He will look at your car tomorrow.'

'Oh.' The news didn't feel like I'd thought it would.

'I can see you're pleased,' Ruby said. I squinted at her unreadable expression. 'Noah, Beth was looking for you. Something about tickets to the ballet. Maeve, come along. It's high time we discussed the Monkey Flower Festival. October is nigh upon us.'

'I'm off,' Noah said with a casual wave. 'See you tomorrow, Maeve.'

'Right.' I matched him. 'Hey, Ruby, what's the Monkey Flower Festival? We're in June, right? Isn't today still in June?' I followed her into the house, shutting the door firmly behind me.

'**N**ice ass!' If a bird could holler, that's what Oliver did. I'd brought him along to separate him from Lulabell, but so far Project Wash Your Mouth wasn't going well. The ass that was facing us stilled, then slowly backed up, extracting its attached person from under Elsie's hood.

'Hi! You must be Barney. I'm Maeve.' I stuck out a hand.

He shook with a filthy paw. 'Barney.' He was a bear of a man, in denim overalls, with bushy red facial hair.

'*Quero otra bebida alcolica, por favor.* I'd like another alcoholic drink, please,' requested a soothing female voice. I spotted a dusty cassette player on Elsie's roof.

'Learnin' Portuguese,' Barney explained. 'Quite a car you got here.' He patted Elsie. I warmed to him. He had good taste.

'*Onde fica o putalheiro?* Where is the nearest brothel?'

Barney hastened to stop the tape player.

'Legs up and give me some, toots,' Oliver chimed in.

Equally shamed, Barney and I focused on Elsie. He started speaking. It might as well have been Portuguese. I extracted the salient double-whammy from his explanation.

'How much?' My inner masochist asked him to repeat the sum.

'If'n I get that part, be around two thousand seven hundred dollars. If'n I don't, you'd need a whole new engine. At that price, be better to get a new car.'

I decided not to torture myself with minimum-wage calculations yet. 'Can you get the part?'

'Miss Elsie here's no spring chicken, so those parts aren't just laying around like one-legged beggars.' I winced. Politically Incorrect Gas Station was right. 'It's gonna be hard to find, and it'll cost you.'

'But you can find one?'

'If'n anyone can it's Carla. She's my parts gal over at Tucson Auto. But you'll need cash up-front. She won't order till it's paid for.'

'If she finds them, how much time will I have?' It was a lot of money.

'You don't want me to guess. Way my luck's going, I'd bet wrong.'

Normally I'd commiserate, but despite the magnitude of Barney's bad news, the prospect of more time in Unknown was not as distressing as it should have been. Still, I cursed myself for the money I'd blown on children's books, pizza with Tuesday and photo paper. I'd forgotten my agenda. What on earth was I doing on a committee for the town festival the same month as my marathon? I needed to get back on plan. It could take me weeks to order the part, pay Barney and have enough to get to LA. With that thought, I hurried back to work.

I was surprised to find Ruby at the café when I arrived.

'I sent Tuesday on her way and brought you some lunch,' she said. Bruce waved from a table set for three with chicken salad, fruit and iced tea. 'I suspected you might have received bad news.'

My shoulders slumped even as my heart warmed. 'It's going to be a lot of money.'

'Howdy, gal!' beamed Bruce as we joined him. 'I hear you're going to chair the publicity committee for the Monkey Flower Festival.'

'Oh. I . . . I . . .' The festival was four months away. The marathon was four months away. I visualised LA in October, but couldn't conjure the sandy beaches as clearly as I used to. I could see a perfect meadow shot that would work for a Monkey Flower poster. 'Tell me more about the festival,' I asked.

'Wall, it's 'bout the biggest thing that happens in Unknown all year. There's a parade and booths sellin' food and art, a stage for singin' and performances, and fireworks at night. There's drinkin' and dancin', too. Someone always ends up in the tank. It commemorates the first bloom of a flower the Navajo have relied 'pon for many purposes.'

'Actually, it's not just one flower. There are hundreds of monkey flower varieties,' Noah chimed in from behind me. My pulse jumped. 'Ruby, is that your famous chicken salad? Who's sick?'

'No one's sick. I thought perhaps Maeve could use some cheering up after seeing Barney this morning.'

'How did it go?' Noah pulled his chair close to mine.

I sighed. I couldn't very well do my ostrich routine with bad news if these people kept asking me about it. 'It's going to cost a ton, and it may take ages to find the parts.'

Noah's face lightened. 'Bummer,' he said cheerfully, then continued blithely, 'We do events here at the store. You know, the festival would be a great time to inaugurate The Little Read Picture Book.'

'I could teach the hula!' Tuesday swooped in. 'Ruby, is that your famous chicken salad? What's the occasion?'

'Maeve's stuck here,' Noah announced. 'The car repair will take for ever and cost a ton!' He made it sound like I'd won the lottery.

'Yay!' Tuesday pulled up a chair. 'I always do a performance at the festival. This year the Cowbelles want me to teach them something.'

'I'll get some great pictures!' I said, then remembered I'd be in LA. I pushed the thought away. I could always come back.

'Maeve, you have to help me with the Bitty Bees float,' Tuesday said. 'You saw how hopeless my paper flowers were at the recital.'

'I see I missed the invitation to the party.' If she was teasing, Beth didn't quite pull it off. The mood at the table dimmed. 'Tuesday, you don't have to make paper flowers. You can buy them off the Internet.'

Tuesday looked chastened. 'You're right, I guess. It's just not as fun.'

'Beth, would you like some chicken salad?' Ruby offered.

'Oh, no. I don't eat mayonnaise.' Beth wrinkled her nose in distaste.

'Twat,' said Oliver.

For some reason I found this hysterically funny and erupted into laughter. Within seconds the entire table was roaring. I couldn't remember when I'd been happier.

Chapter 5: The L Word

THE SUN SLANTED through the front window, highlighting the planes of Noah's face and the bulge of his forearm muscles below rolled-up sleeves. Forearms that were crossed in anger as he glared at me.

'Maeve, The Little Read Book is not that kind of store. We are a bookstore. We sell *books*. We do *not* sell trash.'

'That's the *Economist*.' I pointed at the brand-new magazine rack at the front of the store, the cause of Noah's ire. 'It makes you smarter.'

'This is *Us Weekly*.' He shook it at me. 'I'm less intelligent just for holding it. I can't believe you did this behind my back. I take one day off, and this is what happens. We are a *book*store, not a news stand. We do *not* sell magazines!'

'You've actually been selling them like crazy,' Tuesday interrupted mildly from where she was arranging the staff picks.

We both stopped and looked at her.

'In one day Barney bought *Popular Mechanic* and *Sports Illustrated*, Ruby bought *Traveler*, and Bruce bought *Cooking Light*. April War Bonnet picked up copies of *Oprah, Newsweek, Glamor, Cosmo, Self, Ebony, Golf Digest, GQ , Road & Track, Men's Health* and *Forbes*. She requested that next week you get in *Mad Magazine* and *Garden & Gun*.'

We continued to stare. She shrugged.

'I didn't ask. In contrast, you sold only one book yesterday. Liz Goldberg bought the latest R. L. Stine *Goosebumps* for Tommy.'

Noah's brow wrinkled. 'We don't carry *Goosebumps*. Kids Tommy's age should be reading R. L. Stevenson, not R. L. Stine.'

I looked away guiltily, to see Samuel coming through the door. I welcomed the distraction. Noah, for some reason, looked even more peeved. 'Samuel!' I smiled and waved. He gave me a harried look as he came over.

'And what is this emergency that requires me to leave the clinic and run over here while actually sick patients are waiting for me?' His cross words were tempered by the fact that Samuel couldn't be abrupt if he tried. Underneath his sceptical look was concern.

I remembered the rash I'd discovered that morning. 'Oh, see, look.' I worriedly lifted my shirt and showed him the outbreak along my abdomen. He stared in disbelief. I started to feel foolish. Perhaps I had overreacted. 'Um, it could be Omenn syndrome or Rickettsialpox . . .' My voice trailed off. Noah and Tuesday busied themselves stacking books.

'Maeve.' Samuel looked at me kindly. 'I doubt you've been bitten by mice mites.' That was how you got Rickettsialpox.

'Well, I'm not a doctor,' I snapped. 'How would I know?'

'Maeve,' He cupped my face with his hands. 'It's not bad luck. And it's not the leukaemia. You're in remission. You're healthy now.'

I felt like I'd been punched. I couldn't breathe. My eyes filled, and I couldn't see either. Tuesday gasped, then silence hit the room like a bomb. I stared at the blurry outline of Samuel, aghast. How could he? He'd said the L word out loud. No one did that around me.

'What the hell?' said Noah. 'Maeve?'

I blinked hard. The room spun. I felt Noah staring, mouth hanging open, while Tuesday gnawed at her lip. I felt dizzy and hot. The room was pressing in. The white coat was walking down the corridor towards me. Cameron was in a box. I was . . . I was . . .

'Maeve,' Samuel beseeched. I shook my head and backed away. He reached for me, but I turned and dashed out of the door. I broke into a run. I ran as if my life depended on it, past the post office, past the market and up the hill, stumbling on the rough dirt track. I ran and ran even after my side was stabbing with pain. Now that the word had been spoken, it permeated the air and I might breathe it in. It could catch me unless I stayed ahead of it. I kept running, until a stone caused me to roll my ankle, and took me down hard. I lay gasping, until my gasps turned to sobs.

I'd pretended to leave it behind. It was part of college. It was part of Charlotte. It was part of the past. But it wasn't. Leukaemia was part of me and it was constantly lurking, waiting for me to let my guard down.

The first time I lost a clump of hair, it'd been a good day. The chemo had been gentle on my body that week and I felt well. Vi was taking me out for pizza to celebrate. I would manage only a fraction of a slice, but it would be fun to be partaking in such a normal activity.

That day, I was feeling good as I brushed some colour across my cheeks. I surveyed my reflection as I ran a hand through my long blonde hair. A thick clump of strands came along with it, tangled among my fingers. It was a sharp kick to the gullet. A reminder that even on the days I felt good, the cancer was still winning. It was April 22. I was eighteen years old.

Strong hands on my shoulders brought me back to the present. Samuel rolled me over and eased me up against his solid shoulder, brushing the tangled hair from my face. 'It's going to be OK, Maeve.' He placed a soft kiss on my forehead, then slid his arms under my knees and shoulders, carrying me to where Noah was waiting in his truck. I didn't even care that I looked a wreck. Now that everyone knew I was rotten on the inside, what did it matter what I looked like?

Samuel settled me onto his lap in the front seat. Noah looked concerned. He started the truck, and turned round on the dirt road, pausing once to encircle my ankle for a squeeze so brief and private I might have imagined it. Then he put the truck into drive and took us home.

Ruby was waiting at the door, and led us to my room with her precise steps. I buried my face in Samuel's neck, ignoring everyone. He started to speak, but Ruby gave a shake of her head. He nodded, and after laying me down, gave me another gentle kiss and left the room. Noah followed Samuel. When we were alone, Ruby gently washed my face.

'You'll sleep now.' Her voice didn't invite contradiction. She pulled the shades on the afternoon sun, then faced me in the gloom. 'A closet isn't scary in the daytime, Maeve. It holds clothes, not monsters. Whatever is scaring you, bring it into the light. Its strength will fade.'

My first reaction was that she didn't know how strong cancer was. Then I figured Ruby wasn't talking about cancer itself being my monster in the closet, but its memory. It was a nice idea but, almost three years later, I still looked over my shoulder, fearful. Ruby pressed her palm gently on my forehead and held my eyes with hers. As if she'd drawn something out of me, I relaxed, lashes fluttering down, and sighed. Perhaps I could sleep, just for a bit.

When I woke, it was fully dark. For a moment I was confused. Then memory flooded back. I tensed. Then, slowly, relaxed. A part of me was relieved. It'd been getting harder and harder to hide my secrets.

At home, people knew I'd been sick, but by my dictate no one talked about it. We pretended I ate normally. We pretended everyone took nine million vitamins. We pretended that seven and a half years of college was about average.

In Unknown, no one knew better. I'd refused to spoil their untainted image with the truth. I couldn't bear the pity creeping back into my life. But it had begun to chafe. How could I make new friends if I couldn't trust them enough to be myself? Samuel was like heaven. I'd cut him short when he'd tried to discuss my medical records, but he knew everything all the same. Maybe because he was a doctor, or maybe just because he was Samuel, he'd been perfect. God, it was nice to have, to *want*, sex once more. Samuel made me feel human again.

'Cancer' is a word like 'rape'. It's irretrievably tainted, and I dreaded becoming an untouchable in Unknown. I knew how people changed towards you. You even change towards yourself.

Being told you have cancer alters everything. I used to think my body and I were partners, together against the world. We acted in sync. We were a team. With that word, our relationship broke. Who was this stranger, full of cells out to destroy me? We became two separate things, me and my body. I'd catch myself staring at an alien-looking hand, thinking, whom do you belong to? I distrusted my body. I could discipline it, and make it run, but I always worried what it was doing behind my back.

In the dim light, I saw that Ruby had laid clean jeans, a T-shirt and my favourite Rainbow Brite striped knee socks on the chair by the bed. I was fairly certain those socks had been in the dirty laundry this morning.

I pushed back the bedcovers and sat up. My secret was out now, so no help for it but to face them. And maybe . . . I looked at the clean socks. Well, just maybe. I smiled as I pulled them on.

Tuesday was sitting with Ruby at the kitchen table, talking over mugs of tea. I tensed walking in but, for once, the conversation didn't stop, replaced by guilty looks and fake, overbroad smiles, when I entered the room. Instead, Tuesday said, 'Hey there, Sleeping Beauty. I brought over Season Three of *Bones*.' I remembered it was date night, and felt guilty for assuming she was there to cluck over me. 'I'll cook 'cause you've had a rough day,' she continued matter-of-factly. 'Do you want cereal, salad in a bag or frozen pizza?' I laughed at my choices.

'Don't you want to hear about the cancer first?' I surprised myself by saying. No one gasped, no glasses shattered.

'If you want,' said Tuesday. 'There's time.' Her response astonished me more than my offer. *There's time,* so nonchalantly. The presumption that you could get to something later was novel. I turned it over in my mind. Could you be happy doing half a trail because you could go back and do the rest another time? The idea was like a new green shoot poking through the dirt. The kettle whistled, and Ruby prepared more tea.

'You're good now?' Tuesday met my eyes straight on. It was alarming but pleasing.

'I like the way you ask. The first time someone asked if I was in remission yet it took the wind out of my sails, like if I said "No" I'd somehow failed. But I am—about two and a half years.'

Tuesday nodded. 'That's excellent.'

I stuck to the facts. 'I was diagnosed with acute lymphocytic leukaemia in the spring semester of my freshman year of college. I had chemo and radiation treatment for two years. I dropped out of school and moved home. I was pretty sick most of the time.' I'd never spoken about it to someone who didn't already know. I wasn't sure where to go. Tuesday sensed I was a little lost. She was, too, but she did her best.

'Did you lose your hair?'

'Every strand. That wasn't the worst, though. It's the things you aren't expecting that get you the most,' I said. 'I knew my hair would fall out. My sister Vi and I bought hats and scarves and pretended it was fun. It was when the hair fell off my arms that I lost it. It was an inconsequential thing—I can honestly say that prior to its absence, I'd never appreciated arm hair to any degree. But when it was gone, I felt like I couldn't live without it.' Both Tuesday and Ruby contemplated their forearms. I did too, covered now in fine blonde hair.

I remembered the day sharply. I'd felt the loss so keenly I'd slid bone-less to the bathroom floor. All my sorrow over the chapped lips and cold sores and baldness, all the stuff you were supposed to be brave and stoical about because that was a part of having cancer, had poured into my naked arms, and I had sobbed and sobbed.

'But the treatment worked,' I said. 'After two years, I was in remission. My hair grew back, I returned to school. I was fine for a while.' No point in being suspenseful about the hard part. I reflexively rubbed at the furrow on my forehead. 'I relapsed a year and a half later.'

'That must have been hard,' Tuesday said.

There is absolutely no way to tell someone how it feels to be racing to get to your sister because if you're alone when realisation sinks in, you'll drive your car at maximum velocity into a wall. That instant when choosing your own death seems better than it taking you against your will.

'Mmm-hmm.' I avoided eye contact. 'It was tough for my family. I dreaded telling them more than I dreaded being sick again. I couldn't bear the fear returning to my father's eyes.'

'Is it different when you relapse?' Tuesday asked.

'The second time, we caught it early. The treatment was nowhere near as bad. They'd made a lot of advances, and I needed a much less severe regimen.'

We were quiet for a moment. Then Tuesday said, 'Well, from now on I'll remember not to tug your braids so hard in case they fall off. So what do you want to eat?' And I snorted tea out of my nose, I was laughing so hard.

When Samuel came over later, we didn't talk.

'I'm sorry,' he whispered, as he settled me against him in bed.

'I'm sorry, too,' I said, 'for putting you in that position for so long. And I promise we can talk about it. But not now, OK?' I was worn out. He held me close, stroking my hair until I fell asleep.

It was the most ordinary day. I was in the hospital and we were waiting, because that's what you did. Even though it was Wednesday, everyone was there.

'Another game of Uno?' asked Vi.

'No.' I was sullen. The doctor was late.

She picked up Us Weekly. 'Leonardo DiCaprio and Kate Winslet are doing another movie.' She tried again.

'Maybe they'll both drown this time.'

My dad looked up from his Sudoku. 'Don't worry, Maeve. I'm sure you'll be able to come home today.'

'You're sure? Really? Sure like Johnny-Depp-is-a-hot-piece sure? Or more pork-bellies-are-the-way-to-go sure?' The words lashed out. Everyone froze. I wilted. 'Sorry,' I muttered.

'How about some iced tea? Lemonade?' My dad stood carefully, his expression controlled. 'We could all use some refreshment.'

'I'll have unsweetened iced tea,' said my mother.

'I'll take a beer,' said my brother.

My dad thumped him. 'Call me when you're twenty-one, kiddo.'

There was one of those shock freeze moments in the room where the air went still and everyone's heart stopped for a beat. A single, unacknowledged stutter of time. Casual references to events far in the future were to be avoided. Ba-boom. One beat. Shimmer. Then life resumed.

'Be right back.' My father escaped.

'You know what? I want something after all.' Vi hurried out.

'Having cancer doesn't make you noble,' I said to my mother. In the movies they don't show you too fretful for another stupid game of Uno.

'It doesn't make you excused either,' my mother said.

'It's hard,' I whined. 'There's so much *waiting*. If I'm not vomiting, I'm waiting.'

My mother levelled me with her look. 'We're waiting, too.'

And with that I felt their pain. Shame washed over me. They were there for me and I was being a bitch. I resolved to be better.

When the knock came, I turned off the safe light and admitted Child to the darkroom. 'I thought I might find you here,' he said. No surprise there. For days I hadn't been anywhere else.

'I gave myself the week off work,' I said.

Child examined the hanging prints. 'Nice work.'

'I'm not in any of them,' I said. It wasn't self-pity, it was a question. I remembered Noah's earlier comment. How could I be expected to be in the picture if I was taking it? Was it strange to love being behind the camera? It didn't mean I didn't want to be with people, too.

Child didn't answer right away. 'I think you're in all of them,' he said finally. 'Your eye, your world, how you see things. Anyone looking at these is closer to you than to the subjects.'

He tapped a picture of Samuel sitting alone, eyes closed, meditating. 'This is how you look at someone with affection.' Then he tapped a picture of Bruce with Ruby. 'This is how you look at someone with love.'

I frowned.

'And this.' He chuckled. 'Well, don't let Beth see this.'

'What do you mean?' It was just a picture of Beth sitting in the Wagon Wheel, looking like . . . Beth.

'Trust me.' Again the chuckle. 'I was thinking you could assist me in developing some prints. It's just one roll.'

'Sure.' I didn't know Child took photos.

He turned out the lights. I heard him pop the film canister open. 'The night my wife died wasn't special.' Child's disembodied voice prompted a jolt of adrenaline. 'I'd cooked a pot roast. Janie did most of the cooking, but I chipped in where I could.'

'Her name was Janie?'

'Janie Sugar, sweet as candy. I ate my dinner and put the rest away. I figured she'd got caught up in Tucson and could reheat something when she got home. I was watching *Prime Suspect* when the state trooper arrived. She loved that show.'

'What happened?'

'She hit a deer. They gave me a box of her things. She never went anywhere without her camera. The lens was shattered in the crash, but the film was safe.'

It didn't normally take Child this long to thread negatives. 'What was on it?'

'We're about to find out.'

I took in a breath. 'Child, when did Janie die?'

'Six years ago. I was afraid to know the last thing she saw. What if she'd spent her last day immersed in disappointment or injustice? I wasn't ready for her final impressions of the world.'

'Why now?'

'For six years no one's used this room, or stepped into Janie's shoes. You unfroze things, Maeve. It's like we all got pulled in the wake of your forward motion. Watching you work images reminded me that no matter what's on this film, Janie loved her craft.'

We were quiet. 'No one talked to you about it?' I asked.

'Some of the widows tried, but I wasn't interested.'

'When I had leukaemia,' I said, then paused. I tried to recollect how many times I'd spoken those words. Not many. 'I met this girl, Cameron. We were on the same treatment schedule. We became best friends. It was stupendous to have someone who understood. But then she got sicker, and I felt guilty because treatments working for me were failing her. I got scared too. My "treatment twin" faded and died in front of me. At the funeral, being alive felt like a brand—my family a bubble of toxic happiness among her family's pain. After that, I put space between myself and other patients.'

'Seems to me you keep the healthy world at arm's length as well.'

'Once you tell people, they change towards you. A guy I was dating broke up with me because he thought I might be contagious. Can you believe that?' I shook my head.

'Most people don't appreciate how lucky they are until they aren't.'

'My cousin told me I was unfairly lucky, because she'd been dieting for years and I lost tons of weight just like that. She said I looked like I'd been in a famine like it was a good thing. I told her she looked like she'd caused one. There should be an etiquette guide for cancer.'

Child chuckled. 'They need an etiquette guide for loss, too. I had a fellow tell me I was lucky to be able to date again, that he was stuck with his old lady for the rest of his life. I remember thinking I'd trade half of my remaining days to have Janie back, and the other half to shove the guy into a sack and stow him on a plane to Uzbekistan.'

'I detest the hijackers that turn your diagnosis into their drama. One friend was so overcome she had an asthma attack and had to be rushed to the emergency room. I had cancer cells and I was breathing fine.'

'I recall a widow that wanted to hold hands and weep together over our loss. I wanted to stuff her in a sack bound for Uzbekistan, too.'

'Some people, no matter what I say, they're visualising the chisel on my tombstone.'

'It's real nice to have you talk with me, Maeve.'

'People make it hard to keep to yourself here,' I said. 'Folks want to talk about stuff. I'm surprised they left you alone.'

'Even widows run out of steam eventually. Though if I never see another casserole with Fritos on top it'll be too soon.' Child chuckled.

'I hate cut flowers,' I said. This time my mind spun away.

'**L**ook at what you got,' Maria sang, as she brought a gorgeous arrangement of lilies and hydrangeas into the room. My mother and I were sitting quietly, reading. Maria had the body of a sand-filled balloon tied about the middle with a rubber band. She called me sugar, her hugs were squishy and her smile never wavered. I loved her.

'They're beautiful!' my mother exclaimed. 'Who are they from?'

'A florist,' I said.

'Sugar, you crack me up!' Maria's laugh sounded like bells. She read

the card. 'It's from your Aunt Leigh. It says "Happy Birthday, Maeve".'
Maria looked at me over the card. 'Maeve! Did you have a birthday?'

'At least once,' I said.

'Last week.' My mother swatted my legs under the blanket.

Maria's laugh rippled. 'But how'd I miss your birthday, sugar?'

'It was your day off, Maria. Cecile was here,' my mother explained.

'I'm bringing you a balloon and a cupcake later,' Maria said. 'Now . . .'
She hefted the flower arrangement. It really was gorgeous. We admired
them a moment. '. . . where shall we send them?' Flowers aren't allowed
in cancer wards. Patients are too sensitive to smell.

'Can you find someone elderly? Someone who doesn't get visitors?
Tell them it's a secret admirer,' I instructed.

Maria beamed at me. 'That's why you're one of my favourites.' She
headed for the door. 'Sweet girl,' she called back to me.

I didn't feel sweet as I watched the flowers depart. I loved Maria but
I didn't really want to be a hospital favourite. I wanted to go home and
be someone no one ever thought about sending flowers to.

'I think I'm ready.' Child brought me back. 'Let's see what we've got.'

Janie's pictures were beautiful. She'd stumbled on a community
picnic. Her camera caught women sharing mangoes covered in hot
sauce, children chasing one another, men squinting through cigar
smoke. Each one drew you into Janie's eye, and I understood what
Child had meant earlier when he said he could see me in my photos.

Child interrupted my thoughts. 'You're not responsible for other
people's happiness, Maeve, just as I wasn't responsible for Janie's last
day. Let yourself believe that. Figure out what makes you tick. Don't
wait as long as I have.'

'I'm trying, I guess. It's like a split path. I used to love chasing a
curved trail, and now I'm stuck at a fork. My *It'll never happen to me* is
gone for ever. I can't go back, but I'm unsure how to go forward.'

'All I can assure you is that nothing will happen if you spend your
time alone in a darkroom. Or in front of *The NewsHour with Jim Lehrer*.
The sun is shining, Maeve. Let's go outside and share some lemonade.
I love the taste of cold lemonade.'

'If you'll let me give you something,' I said. The third kachina was
the organic twining of leaves, new shoots rising round the hummingbird with its strong heart. Healing.

'It seems a fair bargain.'

And so we did.

When I got home, I slipped through the yard to avoid April and Busy. I felt the need to burrow into a book.

My foot kicked something as I stepped into my shaded room. There was a large envelope with my name on it on the floor.

I extracted a slim volume, heavy pages bound between beautiful handmade covers. I turned it over gently. It was a children's picture book, each page framing its words in beautiful watercolour drawings filled with a boy, a girl, a bird and lots of tall trees. It was inscribed to me. I began to read.

THE GIRL WHO COULD
for M.

Once upon a time there lived a Boy and a Girl. They were about that age where they were curious and just starting to understand things—a little older than you and a little younger than me.

The best way to see curious things was to climb very high. The Girl was an excellent tree-climber. The trees were very tall. The Girl wore knee socks to protect herself.

The Boy did not like to climb. He was afraid of heights. He would stay at the bottom and write down what the Girl saw. He had excellent penmanship.

One day a branch the Girl was sitting on broke. It wasn't her fault but she fell a long way. Even though she was wearing knee socks, she got a bad cut on her knee.

The Girl went to the best doctor and she gave her a special bandage. Time went by, but she refused to take off the bandage.

'Does it hurt?' asked her mother.

'No,' said the Girl.

'Are you bleeding?' asked her father.

'No,' said the Girl.

'Why won't you take the bandage off?' they asked.

'I'm afraid,' said the Girl. 'The bandage stays.'

The Girl decided to go where there were no trees. She walked a long way and came to a fence. On the other side was a vast open space with no trees. She went through the gate and walked to the middle. 'How large do you think this space is?' the Girl asked. No one answered her because she was alone. The Girl thought about writing it down, but she had forgotten a pencil. It didn't matter. No one could read her handwriting anyway.

The Girl sat down. 'I'll be safe here.' She sat for a long time.

Nothing happened. She began to fidget. There wasn't much to look at. The Girl decided to go home. It wasn't any fun with no one to talk to. When she got to the fence, the gate was locked.

The Girl sat down. The moon kept her company all night, even when the lights went out in the town.

In the morning, the Boy walked up to the gate. 'What are you doing?' he asked.

'I'm stuck on this side of the gate,' she answered.

'Why don't you climb over?' he asked.

'I can't,' she said. 'I might get hurt.' The Boy went away.

The next day the Boy came back. 'I brought you some knee socks,' he said.

'I wore my knee socks and I still got hurt,' she said.

'These are special knee socks,' he said.

She took the socks.

'Well?' asked the Boy.

'I'm thinking about it,' said the Girl. She was getting lonely and tired of the vast open space with no trees.

'Maybe I'll try the knee socks on,' she said. She put on the right sock. It fitted perfectly. She put on the left sock. It wouldn't fit over her bandage, no matter how hard she tugged.

'Take off the bandage,' said the Boy.

The Girl wanted to wear the knee socks. She liked curious things better than vast open spaces. She took off the bandage.

They both looked at her knee. There was nothing there. Not even when they looked really close.

'I guess you can climb over now,' said the Boy.

'I guess so,' said the Girl.

And she did.

The next day, the Girl woke the Boy up early. They found a very tall tree. 'What do you see?' called the Boy. He didn't hear anything. 'Have you made a discovery?' asked the Boy. There was no answer. 'How can I know what's there if you don't tell me?' shouted the Boy.

Something floated down from the tree. It was a knee sock. A second one followed the first.

The Boy paced back and forth. Then he sat. Then he paced some more. There wasn't much to look at down there.

Maybe I'll just try the socks on, the Boy thought.

And just like that, the Boy and the Girl were sitting side by side on the highest branch, admiring the view.

Noah looked surprised when I walked into The Little Read Book. I was suddenly shy. 'Hi,' I said.

'Hi,' he said. 'That dress looks pretty on you.' I was wearing a lilac dress that floated when I twirled.

'Thanks.'

We ran out of ideas. Silence stretched. I broke it. 'I love my book.'

'I'm glad.' He walked to a table and held out a chair. I sat. He sat. Without a word, he reached out and grasped my hand, hard. 'You could have told me.'

A minute passed. 'A lot of having cancer,' I forced out the word, 'is worrying about the people around you. There's an overwhelming need to take care of the recipient of your bad news. It's exhausting.'

He nodded, holding my eyes.

The door tinkled, and I realised we were still holding hands. Embarrassed, I withdrew. Beth's arrival made me more flustered.

'Oh. Hello, Maeve! How. Are. You. Doing?' She spoke slowly and overenunciated. Did she think my illness had rendered me deaf and slow? Noah's frown matched mine.

'Fine.' I stood. Oliver was right. She *was* a twat.

'I just came by to drop these off, honey. You left them on the counter.' She handed Noah his sunglasses. 'Gotta run.' She bolted from the store.

I frowned. Noah mistook the cause.

'You're not going back to work. Let's get out of here,' he commanded. 'Wagon Wheel. I'm buying you a beer.' He strode to the front, flipping the sign to CLOSED as he held the door for me. Twenty minutes later, we were the only patrons at the bar at one in the afternoon.

'You from round here?' I teased, with the hackneyed pick-up line.

'I grew up on the Gulf coast of Florida.'

'Really?' Noah didn't strike me as a beach-volleyball type.

'Yep. First bookstore I worked in had a defibrillator on hand, in case any of the elderly clientele got too excited about the new releases. I did like the clowns, though.'

'Clowns?'

'It was the winter training ground for the Ringling Brothers Circus. Growing up, we were forbidden to hang around the circus people, so naturally every kid in the neighbourhood spent every waking minute watching them practise.'

I was fascinated. 'Can you juggle? Show me.'

'Hey, Vic, throw me a couple of limes,' Noah called. The bartender complied, and Noah expertly tossed the fruit.

I applauded when he was done. 'All I can juggle is credit-card debt.'

'You're falling behind.' Noah indicated the full pint stacked up behind my half-finished one. I drained my glass and clutched the full one.

'Don't hug the glass!' Noah chided. 'It's the first sign of alcoholism.'

'I have a reputation for abuse.' I laughed. 'Half my college dorm thought I was on drugs. I was pale, not eating, losing weight, skipping class and sleeping all the time. One day, a classmate walked in as I was about to shoot up an injection to help me produce white blood cells.'

'You stayed in school when you were sick?'

'Not long. I was the loser who moved back in with my parents to sleep under my old Michael Jackson posters. They put everything on hold to take care of me, and I acted like a petulant teenager.'

He squinted at me. 'I'm trying to imagine you whispering down the phone, and telling your dad to mind his own beeswax.'

'Oh, I can tell you to mind your own beeswax with the best, buster.' I did my best impression of a snotty teenager. '"Where are you going?" "Out." "Out where?" "Out*side*."'

'Scarily accurate.'

'That's probably why the hospital sent me home.'

He signalled the bartender. 'Vic! Two more.' I closed my eyes to check if my head was spinning. Not bad. Only mild spin.

Vic delivered our beers. And two shots. 'Upgrade,' he said.

I was dubious.

Noah tossed back his shot. 'Chicken?'

Not a chance. 'Prost!' I downed mine, and slammed the glass upside-down. My enthusiastic gesture tipped me off the stool and onto Noah, pinning his beer between us. 'Don't hug the glass,' I sputtered.

'I'm too busy hugging you.' He didn't hurry to put me aright. I didn't rush to pull myself off. When I did, our eyes caught.

Confused, I shoved my face in my beer. 'How come you left Florida?'

Noah finished his beer, and waved at Vic. 'My dad died in a plane crash. His Cessna went down in the Florida Gulf during a storm. They never found a body. After that, I detested the sight of the ocean. As soon as my sister started college, I moved to the desert.'

'When I started having nightmares, my doctor told me cancer patients often suffer post-traumatic stress disorder. They used to think only combat veterans suffered from it, but now they say any traumatic event can cause it. One of the characteristics is wanting to avoid places that remind you of your trauma.'

'Dr Connelly, did you just diagnose me with PTSD?'

I rolled my eyes. 'How old were you when your dad died?'

'Eleven.'

I thought of something. 'Your first book was about a boy who could fly.'

'My sister Lily was only eight when Dad died. Mom was working all the time and Lily started getting in trouble. I made up stories to keep her in line. She wouldn't get to hear the next chapter if she didn't behave. I wrote about a boy who could fly because I wanted her to know that just because something bad happened to Dad didn't mean that it would happen to everyone. It was rotten luck.'

'Now you're writing about a boy who can survive underwater.'

He shrugged. 'Just because I occasionally escape into stories doesn't mean I don't try to tackle my demons.'

'Just because I run doesn't mean I always run away,' I offered. We smiled at each other. More beers arrived.

Noah toasted. 'Be not afraid of wastedness: some are born wasted, some achieve wastedness and some have wastedness thrust upon them.'

'To pee or not to pee. That is the question.' I hopped off the stool.

'Is that a stagger I see before me?' Noah called after me as I wobbled to the bathroom.

When I got back, I struggled to remember what we'd been talking about. 'Your sister. Where is she now?'

'If you can believe it, Lily flies mail planes in Alaska. She's the one that sent *The Boy Who Could Fly* to an agent. It never occurred to me.'

'I think it's great that you do what you love.' I was a little envious.

'What about you? What do you want?' Noah's smile was naughty.

'All I want is a warm bed, a kind word and unlimited power.'

'It's good to have goals.'

'It's good to have beers!' I toasted.

'Right. That's it. It's game time. BarOlympics are *on*,' he said.

Half an hour later, we were clutching the bar and laughing hysterically. 'A hundred thousand sperm and *you* were the fastest?' I gasped.

'I beat you,' he reminded me, panting. We'd been doing sprints between the bar and the jukebox.

'It doesn't matter whether you win or lose. It's whether *I* win or lose.'

We'd competed in sprints, speed-drinking, breath-holding, thumb-wrestling, hopping on one foot and handstands. Vic had nixed the mustard toss. The final game was bar football.

'She shoots! She scores!' I flicked the folded paper football through the goalpost Noah had created with his hands. 'I won! I won!'

'Beginner's luck,' he dismissed.

'How're you guys doin'?' Vic called.

'No more.' I shook my head. 'I'm done. This little athlete is retiring.'

Noah nodded. He tossed Vic a credit card, and waved off my effort to contribute. 'The boss can pay for the company meeting.'

We tumbled out of the Wagon Wheel into bright sunshine. We lingered, looking at each other. Noah had just opened his mouth when I ripped a loud hiccup. I fell apart into giggles.

'Good night, good night! Parting is such sweet sorrow,' Noah said with a grin. 'Now get thee to a nunnery.'

'To sleep, perchance to eat ice cream,' I responded as I turned away. I carried his smile with me as I staggered home. I needed a serious nap to sleep it off before my date with Samuel.

Ready?' Samuel asked several hours later. I hadn't shared my afternoon's escapade, but that wasn't what he was asking about. Tonight's outing to an open-air movie was my first public appearance post-Cancergate. I didn't feel anxious, though. I felt floaty and happy.

'Yeppers.' I giggled. He gave me an odd look. I wiped off my smile. Proper ladies didn't go boozing in the middle of the day. I concentrated on walking a straight line to the door.

The square was a chequerboard of blankets on which picnics were being consumed. We saw Tuesday waving and headed in her direction.

'Oh, Samuel,' Liz called. 'Tommy got into poison oak this afternoon. I was wondering . . .'

Samuel was already extracting a bag from his pocket. 'Ruby mentioned it,' he said. 'I brought some samples. If this doesn't work, come see me.' She accepted the package gratefully.

'And Maeve, thanks so much for agreeing to baby-sit next week.' Liz looked so appreciative, I hid my wince. Minding Tommy was like caring for ten Ritalin-deprived demons. 'No problem,' I lied.

'I imagine watching him will make cancer seem like a walk in the park.' Her smile was rueful. I appreciated the casual acknowledgment.

'Don't be so sure,' I joked.

We moved on. 'It's polite to arrive no later than six so that you don't trample over more considerate people's blankets,' Helen sniped as we passed.

'But then you would have trampled on ours,' was my logical retort.

'Don't think that just because you were sick you get special treatment, missy. You don't.'

Samuel hustled me on. We were almost at our destination when we reached a seamless row of blankets. There was no way across without stepping on one. The dirtiest one, next to April and Busy's blanket, was unoccupied. I was hopping gingerly towards the middle to vault to the other side, when I tumbled into a heap.

April was doubled over in fits. Busy's breathy giggles accompanied her. Samuel reached down and helped me stand. I'd stepped into a hole, covered by the blanket.

'Sleep with one eye open.' I managed my threat through gritted teeth.

'Haw, haw, haw.' April's deep honk sounded over and over as she delighted in the success of her trap.

We reached Tuesday's blanket as April reassembled her joke.

'Yay!' Tuesday smiled and wiggled when we arrived.

'*Mahalo*,' I said, ready to sit. I was starting to feel a headache coming on, and I was famished. 'Ruby, is that your chicken salad?'

She passed me a plate, while Samuel poured us wine. I was scouting a place to dump some of my wine discreetly when April's guffaw sounded again, accompanied by an enraged shriek. We looked over to see Beth, hair askew, panties flashing, taking an unexpected tumble. Noah and Bruce skirted the trap and reached to help.

'Goddamnit, April,' Beth screeched. 'I could have been seriously injured. Noah, *do something*.' Beth's pitch was glass-shattering.

'Like what? You want me to fight April?'

'No! Yes! Aaargh! You are so passive! It's like dating goddamn Gandhi!' She grabbed Noah's arm and hauled herself upright. 'Drunk-in-the-middle-of-the-afternoon Gandhi, that is.' I flushed at that. 'I'm going home,' Beth announced, and stomped out of the square.

Noah started after her, but stopped when she snarled, 'Don't follow me! I strongly suggest you give me some space for a good while.'

'She's always had a temper,' Ruby observed. 'Chicken salad, anyone?'

Noah looked unsure.

'Don't worry, Noah,' I said. 'You're not smart enough to be Gandhi.'

He made a face at me and sat on the blanket next to ours.

'She's a handful,' Samuel said.

'She prefers it when I say "piece of work",' Noah joked. 'She thinks I mean masterpiece.'

Dark clattered down in a Monty Python instant, the way it did in southern Arizona, and we looked towards the screen set up against the back of the community centre. I'd faced the town and it hadn't been bad at all. They knew I'd had cancer and it didn't change a thing.

Chapter 6: Bell Pepper

EATING A FRESH, COLD bell pepper on a hot, sunny Sunday afternoon is like a religious experience. Since I didn't go to church, it was as close as I was going to get, at any rate. I settled onto the edge of the picnic table, legs dangling. I tore off the top of the pepper and crunched into it, loving the cool crispness exploding in my mouth, feeling the hot sun, the dusty planks under my butt. I was a girl sitting in the sun, enjoying a pepper. I took another bite.

'I remember this,' rejoiced the inner voice that did the movie narration for my life. I caught my breath. This was the sort of thing I didn't think. I forced myself to relax. 'Yes,' I said out loud. 'I remember this. I liked this. I *like* this.' I felt a scary delight in articulating the words as if acknowledging my pleasure would alert someone to take it away from me. I took another bite.

'I wonder what else I can remember,' I challenged the empty yard. The yard didn't do anything. 'Well, if no one is going to stop me . . .' I wondered if I hoped someone was going to stop me. But of course no one did. No one ever had. Only me.

'Honeycomb cereal,' I pronounced. 'Eating an entire watermelon with a knife while reading a trashy novel. Watching a dog chase sticks.'

After a while I stopped speaking aloud. I let my mind wander wherever it wanted for a change, reacquainting itself with all the simple pleasures I'd walled off because to admit they mattered would be to suffer if I lost them, and apprehension slowly, slowly released its talons. Holding hands. First dates. Clean sheets. As my thoughts roamed, I lightly held the kachina of the girl entwined with the crab, Cancer, warming it with my hands. I knew my mother had made it for the moment when I decided to let it go. I hadn't been in the grip of bad luck, but had myself been the crab, clutching the past tight with my claws. I rose and settled the fourth statue among the raspberry bushes. I sat back down to continue my musings, a fraction lighter. Relaxing outside on a sunny day. I sat there a long time. A girl, just like any other girl. Enjoying her pepper.

I woke gasping for air. My disorientated mind struggled. My last memory was the beast sidling outside my periphery, angling to burrow back in, scuttling claws poised for damage. 'A leukaemia cell is a blood cell that transforms into a malignant cell capable of uncontrolled growth,' my doctor had explained. My imagination saw a dark, evasive creature, not dissimilar from its crablike namesake.

The nightmare loosened. The sound I'd attributed to dragging claws became Samuel's deep, easy breathing. I lay back, shaken. My experiment earlier in the day had had consequences. *Everything* I'd blocked for so long was flooding back, good and bad alike.

'It's like school,' my mother said.

'Sort of.' Dr Gerber played along. 'A two-year course of radiation and chemotherapy. We like to follow the same schedule every week, but of course we adjust for specific conflicts.'

'See,' my mother said. 'Like a class schedule.'

'Do I get *CliffsNotes* before the exam?'

'That's what I'm for.' Dr Gerber smiled. 'Induction is the first step, reducing the cancer and evaluating reaction to treatment; consolidation is the intense phase, to eliminate all leukaemic cells; and maintenance delivers lower doses over a longer period to destroy strays and outliers.'

I liked the preset regimen. It spared me the worry on adult patients' faces as they dissected the meaning of adjusting treatment schedules. I didn't have to decipher the import of every radiation session. Radiation meant it was Thursday. Thursday happened every week.

'We like Thursday so you can have the weekend to recover,' Dr Gerber explained. He meant you had the weekend to collapse.

Back in bed in Arizona in the dark, my heart rate slowed to normal. I had expelled cancer from my blood, but it continued its grip on my mind. When was it over? When did 'remission' become 'normal'? What 'normal' would I go back to? I didn't know who cancer-free Maeve would have been. She didn't exist.

Except we both liked bell peppers. And . . .

'Samuel,' I whispered, shaking him. 'Samuel, wake up.' There was something else that we both liked.

'Congratulations, graduations!' I sang to my brother.

'Thanks,' Brick's voice was gruff, pleased, but too cool to admit it.

'I'm sorry I'm going to miss your graduation ceremony.'

'Mom and Dad said they'd pay for the ticket if you want to fly back.'

'I . . .' I couldn't find the right words.

'I understand.' He cut me off. 'You're not ready to come back yet.'

'No,' I admitted. 'Thanks for understanding.'

After I hung up, I sat for a moment looking at the kachina in my hands. It was the fifth one, a ring of small creatures, maybe squirrels, maybe possum, maybe bear cubs. They were a team, the cluster supporting each other. It made me think of my family, and their support. I wanted my brother to know that all the family's attention wasn't sucked up by me. We'd join forces to hold protection over him his whole life, too. The comforting statue was hard to part with, but I carefully packaged the kachina for its trip to my brother on his big day.

'Maeve, sweetheart, would you be a dear and pick up some sherry for me? You know I like a little nip before bed,' Busy intercepted me on my way out.

I did indeed. Her 'little nip' amounted to two or three bottles a week. 'Okey-dokey, smokey. April?'

'Copy of *Family Handyman Magazine*.' I stopped and faced her, hands on hips. No way was I putting ammunition for mayhem into her hands.

'I'll get you a nice gardening magazine if you untie the lines round my desktop items by the time I get back.' I'd been poised to pull out the chair when I'd spotted the fishing line strung between the legs and my desk set, prepared to tumble it all to the floor when the seat was pulled out. April's face fell as Busy's giggles followed me to the kitchen.

Oliver and Lulabell were in her cage on the table.

'Road trip! Don't forget the bird!' said Oliver.

I paused. I hadn't really had much Oliver time. He preferred Lulabell to my shoulder these days. 'You want to come, buddy?' Jenny didn't really like it when he came to Up Market, but she'd get over it. Oliver hopped onto my finger, and I settled him on my shoulder.

'Howdy, pardner.' He looked expectantly at Lulabell. 'Nice hair!'

Lulabell mirrored Oliver. 'Howdy there! Howdy!'

'You want to come, Lulabell?' I'd never taken her on an outing before, but I didn't see the harm. I was getting Jenny's dirty looks anyway. Lulabell hopped onto my other shoulder.

I walked towards the square, considering whether to stop by Barney's. So far, he hadn't made any real progress on Elsie. We were still in limbo, waiting for that missing part. His Portuguese was improving, though.

It was when Oliver bit my ear that I noticed the clouds. They were coming in fast. One thing I continued to marvel at about Arizona was the rapidity with which the weather changed. What had been a sunny day looked to be a humdinger of a storm. I knew enough to realise that I'd better get inside. Oliver didn't like storms; I'd hole up in the book-store until it passed. Oliver was pressed so close to my neck that he was practically in my ear. Lulabell was rocking anxiously. As I stepped into the square, thunder sounded like a crack. And Lulabell flew away.

My jaw dropped. Lulabell could fly. Cockatiels were clipped not to fly, but Lulabell could fly, and I had taken her outside.

'Lulabell!' I called, frantic. Thunder cracked again, and I saw the flutter of a terrified bird. She was thrashing among the treetops and I was petrified she would hurt herself. I was also horror-struck at the possibility that she would fly away. 'Lulabell!' I cried again, but my voice was drowned out by the commencement of falling hail.

I started shaking. My bird was freaking out, and Lulabell was flying farther and farther away. Never taking my eyes off her in case I lost her, I cupped Oliver in my hands. Think. How did you get a free-flight bird down from a fifty-foot tree in a hail storm?

'Maeve, what's the matter with you? I've been calling. Get inside!'

I didn't even look at Noah. 'Take Oliver.' I held out my hands.

'Are you crazy? Come inside!'

I chanced a quick look. 'I can't.' My voice cracked. 'Please. Look after my bird.'

He stared. Without a word, he took Oliver and hurried back to the store. Within minutes he was back, shaking a jacket over my shoulders. Rain mixed with the hail.

'What is it?'

'Lulabell.' I pointed. 'Give me your phone,' Noah handed it to me and I dialled. 'Bruce? I have an emergency and I need you to do some-thing.' I forced my voice to be calm.

After giving him instructions, I hung up and focused on the bird. Lulabell fluttered agitatedly from branch to branch. I made clucking and calling noises. When Bruce arrived fifteen minutes later, Noah and I were both soaked to the bone. Bruce'd brought what I'd requested. Noah unloaded the ladder and rope, while Bruce extracted Lulabell's cage. I kept my eyes glued to the bird. Without a word, I tied one end of the rope round the cage handle, and the other into a thick knot. 'Once I'm up there, throw me the knotted end of rope.' I was already on the ladder.

Bruce started to object, but I gave them both a look. They shut up.

I climbed past the top of the ladder into the branches, then turned to catch the rope. I caught it on the first try, then hefted the cage. I balanced it on a branch, and began pulling myself from branch to branch, lugging the cage after me. When I'd climbed as high as I thought I could go, I found a good branch and hung the cage, door open.

'Lulabell,' I called. I sat on a branch to wait. I almost cried with relief when the panic-stricken bird flew to the safety of her haven as soon as she saw it. I closed her inside and made more soothing noises. I carefully reversed my course out of the tree.

When I handed the cage down to Bruce, and Lulabell was safe, I started shaking. I had to pause at the top of the ladder for some deep breaths before I climbed all the way down.

Bruce shut Lulabell in the truck, and squinted at the sky. 'I don't like this storm. Too much rain too fast.'

'I'll bring Oliver home,' said Noah. 'Ride with Bruce. Go get dry.'

I shook my head. 'I'd like to walk,' I said. The rain had all but stopped, and I wanted to collect my thoughts.

'Don't tarry,' Bruce advised. 'Rain could start again at any time.'

I nodded, and set off on foot. My pace was rapid as I berated myself.

At the doorstep I gathered my courage, then stepped into the kitchen to face Ruby. Her back was to me, as she packed a bag at the kitchen table at a greater speed than her normal high efficiency. She turned.

'There's been an accident. We'll need your help. Please gather as many extra blankets as you can find in the hall closet. Hurry now.'

I did as I was told. I changed into a dry sweatshirt and rain jacket, and grabbed all the blankets I could carry. When I returned, she was loading her Volvo wagon with Thermos flasks and jackets. She collected and tested an enormous flashlight, with a radio and siren built in. We got into the car, and she turned north.

'Where are April and Busy?' I asked.

'The rain this afternoon flooded Harshaw Creek and weakened the banks at the bridge. The seniors were returning from a trip to Sonoita in their bus when one of the banks gave out and the bridge collapsed, probably from the vehicle's weight. The bus is in danger of falling into the flooded water.' Ruby's white knuckles on the steering wheel belied her even tone. 'I don't know more than that. April, Busy, Helen Rausch, Elsa Morrow, Diane Wall, Lupe Ortiz and Henrietta Mankiller are trapped on the bus, along with Liz, who was driving.'

A shiver ran down my spine as icy as flood water. My knuckles were as white as Ruby's when we pulled up to the collection of flashing lights and vehicles clustered at the south end of the bridge.

It was a disaster scene in miniature. The creek wasn't wide, but it was wider than the bus. The bridge had failed on the north side, and now angled from the south bank straight into the water. The bus was tilted, tail in the water, nose pointing up at a hypotenuse angle. The fierce current of the swollen creek was tugging at the tail and the west-facing side of the bus. The immediate threat was obvious. The south bank sustaining the bridge, and the bus, looked dangerously unstable as currents buffeted the saturated mud and the dangling concrete.

Ruby hurried over to where Samuel stood, a few feet from the bank.

'Everyone is still on the bus, and they seem unharmed aside from bumps and bruises.' He answered her unspoken question. 'But Helen . . .' He pointed. I squinted. There were six frightened faces that I could see, sitting very still in the first two rows of the bus, and Liz in the driver's seat, but Helen was tumbled at the bottom of the bus, clinging to one of the bench seats. From her knees down she was submerged in the filthy water swirling round the rear door.

'The impact with the side of the bridge must have jarred open the door.' Ruby's voice was tight. 'Can we get blankets down to them?'

'Too risky,' Samuel said. 'We don't want Liz to open the door in case the water rises. Also, we can't risk adding any weight or getting too close to the edge of the bank until Barney secures the tow rope.'

Bruce and Barney were deep in conversation. Barney was shaking his head. 'The weight is likely to cause the whole bank to collapse. I'm afraid to get too close.'

'Can we come at it from the other side?' asked Bruce.

'I called Simon Bear. He's driving in from the north with John Buell, but it'll take them twenty minutes to get here. Even then, it'll be a trick trying to attach the tow rope. That water's fierce even for those guys and the tail of the bus is farther from the bank.'

'What about the ladder from the extension fire truck over at County? Can we stretch it out over the bus and harness them ladies to safety?'

'Mebbe. Fire truck can be farther back, but it's heavier. Could collapse this bank jes' like the other. That'd be bad.'

'Work with me, Barney. We've got to do something,' Bruce begged.

Rain started to fall again as Noah and Tuesday pulled up. Right behind them came an ambulance and the county ladder truck. Bruce hurried to stop the vehicles well back from the edge of the creek. More people arrived, prepared to help however they could.

'What can we do?' panted Tuesday. Ruby raised her hands helplessly.

Barney took off his cap and smoothed his hair, then replaced it. 'Mebbe we could extend the tow cable and get Ronnie to climb down. He's pretty nimble and the lightest. Not ideal with the tow back that far, but lower risk of stressin' the bank.'

'I'll do it, Chief,' Ronnie said.

'There are life jackets on the ladder truck,' Ruby said. 'Can you make a harness out of one with a rope? Then he's attached, and has a life preserver on, just in case.'

'Good idea, Ruby,' Samuel agreed, as Bruce nodded.

Samuel and Noah fashioned a harness for Ronnie, while Bruce and Barney debated how close they dared back up to the creek bank. Tuesday and I watched Barney back the tow truck within ten feet of the bank. We held our breath as Ronnie struggled with the tow cable towards the lip of the creek. He attained the front of the bus and rolled onto his back to hook the cable round the axle.

'I need more cable,' he yelled.

Barney put the truck in reverse and backed up inch by cautious inch.

'I got it!' Ronnie shouted, and everyone started to cheer, when there was a horrible grinding sound. A section on our side of the bank gave way, and the near-right lip of the bridge shuddered and slipped a foot, tilting precariously and causing the rear of the bus to fishtail downstream. Barney put his truck in drive, wheels spinning without traction. Under increased pressure, the collapsed cement piling up on the far upstream side crumbled further. Without its support, the bottom of the bridge sank another three feet into the relentless current. The back door of the bus was torn open completely, and Helen Rausch lost her grip and was washed out, arms flailing.

'Get the truck!' 'Get the ambulance!' 'Throw a life preserver!'

Voices cried all round me, but I knew there was no hope for that. Helen was bobbing away quickly and the fields were too rutted for any vehicle. I wasn't good at much. I couldn't even take care of a pet bird. But I could run. I grabbed a life preserver off the pile and started sprinting. I could sense people running after me, but I quickly outpaced them. Weeks of practice made me sure-footed on the uneven ground. I kept my eyes glued to Helen. My feet ate the ground, and soon I overtook her. I looked ahead to a bend in the creek, and sited my target entry. There was an S-curve in the creek, leaving a shallow beach and protected spit on the far side. I launched over the lip of the bank, grabbing an overhanging tree branch with one hand and dangling above the water. For once, luck was on my side, and Helen passed the curved spit of land close enough for me to grab hold of her.

The weight of her body combined with the pressure of the water almost snapped my wrist. The one clutching the tree strained as well. I was strong, but both the water and Helen were fighting me.

'Stop thrashing!' I yelled, but she was like a wild animal. I wasn't going to be able to hold her with one hand. I let go of the branch. The freezing water took my breath away, but I didn't have time for shock. If I went into deeper water with Helen, we didn't stand a chance. The little peninsula was providing a limited barrier against the churning water. I thrust my feet into the silty bottom for traction and used both hands to haul Helen to my chest. Inch by inch I used the creek bed, branches, anything I could, to move us farther into the lee of the spit. At last the water released its suction and I heaved us onto the beach. I lay gasping for air on my back, Helen crushed against me.

'Over here!' People descended. Several hands rolled Helen from my chest. 'Bring the stretcher! We need blankets!' The scene was chaos.

'Are you insane?' Noah shouted. 'You could have killed yourself!'

'Noah, hush. She saved Helen's life,' Ruby chided. To me, 'That was something, Maeve.' She reached for my hand to help me up, and I cried out. Samuel was there in an instant.

'Let me see.' His gentle fingers probed my wrist.

'I'm fine.' I used my other hand to push myself to my feet.

'Stretcher!' Samuel and Noah shouted at the same time.

'No,' I protested. 'I can walk.' I couldn't stop beaming. 'I can *run!*'

'You sure can.' Bruce voiced admiration.

My smile faded. 'The bus . . .'

'It's secure on the cable. Firemen are getting everyone off.'

'Let's get back.' Noah's tone was impatient. 'You'll catch your death.'

We crossed the field back towards the road behind paramedics portering Helen on a stretcher.

'Samuel,' I said. 'You need to go.'

He shook his head. 'Her vitals are stable. They'll take her to the hospital and keep her overnight to be sure. There's nothing for me to do. I need to get you to the clinic and X-ray that wrist.'

I wanted to protest, but common sense dictated that my wrist needed seeing to. We reached the road in time to see a fireman handing a cable-clipped Liz from the bus to a waiting fireman on the safety of the road. The rest of the seniors were bundled in blankets, clutching Thermos flasks. Everyone looked shaken but unharmed.

'I think you're going to have to take them all in,' Ruby said.

We piled into various wagons and trucks to be chauffeured to the clinic. Despite Samuel's objections, I made him see the seniors first. Other than bruises and Busy's elevated blood pressure, my hairline wrist fracture was the only injury of note. Samuel wrapped it tightly. When he was done, we headed for the door. I was starving. To my surprise, the waiting area was packed with people. Everyone was there. When they saw me they began to clap and cheer. I was surrounded by well-wishers, congratulating me and patting me on the back.

As one creature, we migrated out of the clinic and down to the Wagon Wheel. Within minutes, plates of potato skins and pitchers of beer appeared. Tuesday handed me a beer, and cried, 'To Maeve!'

'Hear! Hear!' everyone shouted, even Liz Goldberg.

I couldn't stop smiling. I went to the bar and ordered a cheeseburger. 'Make it the size of my head,' I instructed. I was ravenous.

'That's on me.' Noah appeared at my elbow.

'Naw, man, it's on the house,' said Vic.

Noah looked me over. 'I'm sorry I yelled,' he apologised. 'I thought I was going to have a heart attack when you jumped into the river. Breathing underwater is only for made-up people.'

'Excuse me,' a voice interrupted. 'Chuck Hall.' He introduced himself. 'Are you Maeve Connelly?' At my nod, he said, 'I'm with the *Daily Dispatch*.' He named the regional paper. 'We'd like an interview, if you're up for it. We want to do a feature on the rescue.'

We sat at the table surrounded by everyone, and I tucked into my burger. I answered the reporter's questions, frequently interrupted or corrected by other witnesses.

When we were done, he said, 'We'll need a picture. You got a local guy?'

'Oh. It's me, I guess,' I said.

'I can do it!' Tuesday trilled. 'Who's got a camera?' Someone handed her a digital camera. She beamed at me. 'What do I push?'

Chuck had me pose surrounded by everyone raising his and her beers. Tuesday snapped the shot and promised to email it to Chuck.

A wave of tiredness hit me. Samuel saw it happen, and stood. 'All right, folks. Time to get Wonder Woman home.'

'Spoilsport,' I managed round my yawn.

He insisted on driving me home, and I didn't protest. I blew him a kiss and headed to my room. I registered as I passed that Lulabell seemed no worse for wear, and that Oliver had been returned and was sharing the safety of her cage.

When I woke, I was sore all over. I groaned and swallowed two painkillers as soon as I was upright. Then I headed to the bookstore. It was early, but I couldn't wait to see the paper.

April called after me on my way out. 'Hold up, Atalanta. We're coming too.' She, Ruby and Busy fell in.

We arrived to find Bruce, Liz and little Tommy chatting on the step. 'Look, Tommy,' Liz said. 'Maeve has a wrap on her wrist, like you.'

'Did you fall out of a tree?' Tommy asked.

'She saved Helen Rausch from drowning in the river yesterday.'

Tommy looked baffled. 'Why?'

By 9.30 a.m. there was a crowd sipping coffee. When it seemed like everyone in town was crammed into the store, Helen walked in with Samuel, who bore a rare look of irritation.

She marched up to the counter. 'Half caf, half decaf vanilla cappuccino with two per cent skimmed milk, and I want that milk piping hot.' She looked round at everyone staring. 'What?' She swung back towards me. 'If you think you get some kind of special treatment or thank you from me, you've got another think coming,' she snapped. Brushes with death do not, apparently, have the same effect on everyone.

The entrance tinkled again. The newspaper deliveryman was not expecting a stampede, and dropped the bundle of papers on his foot in alarm when the crowd surged towards him. He staggered out in a hurry, leaving it to Bruce to cut the ties and disseminate papers.

We scanned for the article. It wasn't hard to find. Right on the front page was the headline: **Local Girl Saves Unknown Woman**.

I cut out a copy of the article and mailed it to my family.

Ruby was in the kitchen having tea that night when I got home from work. I sat down. She set homemade coffee cake before me.

'Maeve, I owe you an apology. In all the excitement yesterday I never acknowledged it.'

My mouth dropped as she beat me to the words I'd been forming. Didn't *I* owe *her* the apology?

'I should have attended to clipping Lulabell's wings some time ago. She is not accustomed to free flight. I overlooked the proper care of my bird as I pursued my attempt at playwriting.'

'You're writing a play?' It was the first I'd heard of it.

'One of the projects I've been able to undertake with your assistance around the house. It turns out that I do not have a talent for it. The world shall live in wonder over the founding mothers of Unknown.'

I didn't know what to say to that. It was hard to imagine Ruby not accomplishing whatever she set her mind to in a fluid manner.

'Ruby, do you believe in luck?'

'I believe that birds fly away because their wings have not been clipped, not because they are in the company of someone afflicted with bad luck. I also believe it is reasonable that girls who have had bad things happen through no fault of their own might believe in bad luck.'

I looked off. 'When I first got sick, I walked in a cloud of anger with a chance of rage. I'd see people smoking cigarettes or eating fried eggs on cheeseburgers and couldn't understand it. Axe-murderers and rapists were perfectly healthy and I, who had never done anything to anyone, was fighting for my life. What had I done to deserve it?'

'You could conjure a variety of explanations where you internalise responsibility for becoming ill, but they would all be incorrect. Our own worst enemy is often ourselves. I would hope that yesterday demonstrated to you your own capabilities.'

'I'm good at one thing, at least,' I said. 'I can run.'

'We all have the potential to be good at anything we choose. Have you heard of deliberate practice?' Ruby asked.

I shook my head.

'It's a way of thinking about achievement. Researchers suggest we've historically been incorrect in our belief that talent is integral to success. It's not that talent doesn't exist, but, rather, that it may be irrelevant.'

'So what causes success?'

'Carefully designed hard work and always stretching beyond your abilities. Continually focusing on your weakest elements and trying to improve them. Those who persevere are high achievers.'

'So I'm not born a violin prodigy?'

'You could become a violin prodigy without innate talent if you wanted it badly enough. The key lies in knowing what you deeply want.'

'So you can make your own luck?' I considered my quest for the Maeve that could have been. I liked the idea that if I figured out what I *wanted* to be, I didn't have to settle for the mess I had.

'Why not?'

'So what you're saying is, if I don't have any talent for playwriting, but engaged in deliberate practice of the craft, my community might be able to see the story of our founding mothers performed at the Monkey Flower Festival?' I said, my smile sly.

Ruby looked surprised, then laughed. 'I suppose I am.'

The phone rang so many times I thought she might not answer. Part of me was relieved. I'd struggled with my preference to send an email, but it wasn't right. Deliberate practice.

'Hello?'

'Jules! Happy birthday!'

'Who's this?'

'It's me. Maeve!'

There was quiet. Then, 'You're shitting me. Damn, girl, I haven't heard from you in for ever,' said my closest friend in Charlotte.

'I'm sorry I haven't called.' I meant it.

'How's LA?'

I laughed. 'I don't know. Elsie broke down in this place called Unknown, Arizona.'

'All this time? That's crazy!'

'The funny thing is, I kind of like it here. It's like *Northern Exposure* in Arizona. *Southern Overexposure*, SPF90 required.'

'So you're gonna stay?'

I puckered my brow, then rubbed out the dent. 'Of course not. I'm going to LA as soon as Elsie's operational.'

'Well, good, because I'm still planning to come and visit. Though you might have to make room for two . . .' She giggled.

'Tell me.' She radiated new-love euphoria.

'He's awesome. His name is David. He's this sexy cowboy with crazy sideburns and he drives a motorcycle and plays the sax. I'm nuts about him. You know that feeling when it zings into your soul that this could actually be a person you spend the rest of your life with?' I did know that feeling. Unbidden, an image popped into my mind, but it wasn't Samuel. I frowned again, then rubbed irritably at my forehead. Jules continued gushing.

'It gets better the more time I spend with him. He's funny, smart, sexy, and he makes *me* feel funny, smart and sexy . . .'

I let Jules ramble. I was thinking. Really, I should be interrupting, talking over her to share my own passion for Samuel, but I didn't. I couldn't match her exuberance.

'I'm really happy for you, Jules,' I said at last.

'Thanks for remembering my birthday, pal. And thanks for that little doll you put in the shoe box. That was really cool. Love you, babe.'

'Love you back.' I was surprised at how easily it came. Maybe I *was* getting better.

'But if you wait until next year to call me again, you can stick it.'

The candlelight played on the planes of Samuel's face. We were back at the Velvet Elvis. We'd made a special date to talk. We hadn't yet discussed what had happened. I'd needed a little time.

'I'm sorry, Maeve.' He repeated his apology. 'It wasn't my place to tell people.'

'It's OK.' I meant it. 'Part of me was relieved.'

'It was torture watching you torment yourself. The old folks say you can't kill emotion. You might squash it flat, but it doesn't lose mass—it will spread wide, seep through the cracks, find a way.'

'Turn into rashes on my tummy?'

He smiled. 'You're my favourite hypochondriac.'

'Maybe I was trying to get face time with the hot doctor.'

'You didn't have to work that hard. Is there anything you want to ask me?'

'No. Yes. Maybe.' I hesitated. I'd asked Dr Gerber all the questions back in the day. *Am I going to die? Will I be able to have children? Why me?* But there *was* one thing. The risk was if I didn't like the answer.

'Do I . . .' I stopped. Count to three. Try again. 'Does it feel *different* when we . . .? You know, my body. Can you tell I was sick?'

'No. I'd say "Absolutely not, that's the silliest question ever", but I'm afraid you'd throw a breadstick at me.'

I threw a breadstick at him, looking away to hide my relief.

'The most rapidly dying and regenerating cells are the ones most impacted by chemotherapy,' Dr Gerber had explained. 'That's why you're getting sores in your mouth. Vaginal skin is like that too. Think of it as another mouth,' he had suggested.

But it wasn't another mouth. I'd stopped feeling desirable or female. There were times I thought I'd never want sex again. Until Samuel, who knew everything and wanted me just the same.

He grabbed my hand now. 'Maeve, your body is beautiful. Inside and out. Ah, perfect timing!' He looked up to see the waitress approaching with a cake and candles. Behind her were three others. When they reached the table, they broke into a chorus of 'Happy Birthday'. Soon the entire pizza joint was singing.

I let them serenade me, blushing and sending Samuel filthy looks.

'Thank you! Thank you!' I waved to everyone as the entire restaurant clapped, and blew out my candle. 'Just so you know,' I hissed, 'it's *not* my birthday!'

'It is for part of you. Healthy cells are being born by the hundreds as we speak. Today is *their* birthday. Instead of pretending nothing happened, why don't we celebrate what *did* happen. In many ways you're a miracle.' His look got earnest. 'Today could be your *re*birth day.' He reached down and pulled out a thick folder and two oblong packages wrapped in bright paper.

'What is it?' I was curious.

'It's a rebirthday gift. It has three parts. This first.' He flipped open the folder. 'Here. This is a study about cancer recidivism. And see here, these are your last blood-test results. Now do you see how when you relapsed . . .' I stared in wonder as Samuel patiently and carefully showed me just how healthy I was, with charts and diagrams and medical records. My heart constricted.

'So you see,' he said at last, 'there is no reason you won't live a long and healthy life. At this point you're no different from anyone else.' He smiled. 'Except your cells are younger and sexier.'

'Are you getting fresh with my plasma?'

'Beauty is only skin deep.' He pushed the first package towards me. I opened it. It was a beautifully framed image.

'Your last scan,' he explained. 'I had it framed so you won't forget.' It was oddly beautiful, the radioactive tracer injected in my veins lit up to provide a colour-coded picture of my body. 'Now this one.' He pushed over the second package. It was a leather-bound *Harrison's* medical dictionary, like the ones in his office. This one was inscribed. It read: *A book full of things that don't apply to you. Trust me, I'm a doctor. Samuel.*

'Every day you're supposed to look up something you don't have.'

I flipped to a page near the beginning. 'Ankylosing spondylitis. A form of chronic inflammation of the spine and the sacroiliac joints.'

'Excellent choice.' He beamed at me.

This was fun. 'Can I do another?' I asked.

'I don't know,' he answered. 'There are only so many entries in the book and you have a lot of mornings left. Maybe you want to go slow.'

I looked at the voluminous tome and thought about having more days than it had entries. What would I do with them all? It was a little terrifying. In that, I was no different from anyone else.

I looked across the table at Samuel, blinking back tears. His thoughtfulness was overwhelming. I felt warmth. And affection. That was all.

'Samuel,' I said.

He met my gaze, and nodded. Then he covered my hands. 'We're friends.' His eyes were sad.

That was it exactly. 'I think you're wonderful. Thanks for taking such good care of me.'

His smile was rueful. 'I did too good a job, I'm afraid. I don't think you want someone taking care of you anymore.'

'But I want more for both of us. Passion, crazy climbing-all-over-you need and joy. And we're . . . we're like a warm bath.'

'I know.'

'Thank you,' I said. 'For being you.'

He squeezed my hand and grinned. 'Break-up sex?'

'Cheque, please!' I smiled back.

Chapter 7: The Curse of the Alien Hand

ALIEN HAND SYNDROME *A neurological illness in which a sufferer's hand acts independently of the other and of the patient's wishes.*

After my morning run, I hurried into The Little Read Book, anxious to be there before Noah. I wanted to see his face when he came in. He'd flown to New York for a meeting with his publisher, and Tuesday, Bruce and I had worked round the clock to finish the children's nook in his absence. The book shelves were painted bright primary colours; there were kid-sized chairs and tables, and the café now offered juice boxes. I'd stayed until 2 a.m. to hang shadow box frames displaying our collection of classic children's books. It was perfect.

By the time he walked in at 12.47, I was vibrating with impatience. The sight of him sent a jolt through my system.

'Oh, are you back already?' The most erect posture of my life belied my casual tone. Noah gave me an amused look.

'Careful, or I'm going to think you missed me.'

'Tcha. Name one person in the history of time who misses the boss when he's away.'

'Monica Lewinsky. You're wearing your favourite rainbow socks.' He had me there. I was wearing my most happy socks.

I was about to retort when he said, 'I missed you.' And there I was, mouth hanging open like a fish. He laughed, eyes holding mine.

'Did I miss it? Rats!' Tuesday's bracelets jangled more than the doorbell as she bounded in. 'Well?' She turned a shining face towards Noah.

'What?' He looked confused.

'Oh goody! I'm not too late!' Tuesday clapped.

'Close your eyes.' I smiled. He did as he was told. I led him to face the corner nook. 'OK, open.'

He did. I waited. He didn't say anything. For a long, long time. I felt an anxious wiggle. Did he hate it? Was it too unserious? Noah was very serious about books.

He looked at me, tone controlled. 'You did this?'

Oh God. He was upset. He hated it. I blinked so he couldn't see I was fighting not to cry. I battled an urge to run, feet twitchy. How had I got it so wrong? I managed a nod, looking down.

'This is . . . by far . . . the most . . .' I peeked up and noticed he was blinking too. Kind of like me. And his eyebrow wasn't drawn down like it did when he was upset. He was staring at the mural on the far wall.

'Tuesday did it.' I relaxed. He was looking at a large painted image of a girl with long braids and a boy wearing knee socks sitting in a treetop. 'There's even a shelf for your toys.' I pointed. '*If* you feel like sharing.'

'They are not toys,' came his lofty refrain. 'They are visualisation facilitators.' He ventured farther in. 'It's amazing.' His smile was huge. He tugged a braid. 'I could get used to you being around.'

I took an involuntary step backwards. Part of me wanted to take care of Noah so badly I dreamed of snatching him under my arm and running far away to shove him in a warm nest and feed him soup. But with my luck, I'd trip and drop him into poison ivy, where he'd break an arm. I was still too unsure of myself.

'Hey, man, don't cry or anything. It's just a shop.' I looked round for Tuesday, but she'd vanished. It was a trick she perfected when Noah and I bickered.

He caught my shoulder. 'It's not just a shop. It's perfect. Thank you, Maeve.' He hugged me tight. I didn't want him to let go, but this was exactly the problem. I was trying to be a new girl. One who could take care of herself. Not one who overhugged another girl's boyfriend.

I pulled back—and Beth walked in.

'Hello!' she sang. 'Welcome back!' She flung her arms round Noah.

The smile he returned seemed forced.

'Have you got anything to say to me?' Her tone was coy.

His 'Of course' was clipped. 'Happy anniversary.'

'You didn't forget!' She kissed him on the mouth. Air left my lungs.

'I did not,' he said. 'We're going to Bella Mia in Nogales.'

My blood pressure shot like mercury in a thermometer. I realised I was staring, and bolted for the café. What was the matter with me? I'd seen them kiss before. Samuel and I kissed in the store all the time. Or we had, I corrected.

I shoved napkins in the dispenser in irritation. As if I'd conjured him, Noah appeared. I registered Beth dancing out of the store.

'So, tell me what happened while I was gone.' His smile was genuine.

'Not much.' I shrugged, remaining behind the counter. I didn't mention my breakup. It struck me how pathetic it might look, if he mistook my motive in fixing up the store. 'We had a good week in the café.'

'The store stayed open, then?' he teased. 'You didn't float off to take pictures of dust motes or something?'

My blood pressure pounded again. How could he take a frosted tart like Beth seriously and treat me like a piece of fluff? 'How much time do you think I took off, Noah?' I demanded. 'You were only gone for three days. You think that Little Read Picture Book sign, the murals and the shelves all painted themselves?'

He looked startled. 'Maeve, I . . .'

'And considering you forgot to pay me before you left, technically I've been working for free, so if I wanted to take off and photograph naked baby bottoms, I'd be perfectly entitled!'

His face was stricken. 'I'm sorry. I'll pay you right now. I didn't mean . . . Getting ready to leave . . . I was distracted . . . I just . . .'

'Forget it,' I snapped. 'Include it in next week's cheque. But try not to forget that most people don't have their jobs for kicks. And for the record, taking care of you is a lot more work than you think.' I turned my back, hating myself but unable to stop my mouth. I sensed rather than saw him disappear into the office. I was relieved.

It was when I was in remission and eased back into school that I started running in earnest. I felt most in control when I was running. I made good grades. I didn't date.

Ten days before Christmas, I stopped by Dr Gerber's office a week after my regular blood tests to pick up some antibiotics. The flu had been going around, and I didn't want to take any chances. I was impatient in the waiting room. Vi and I were going Christmas shopping, and I couldn't wait. It didn't register when the nurse led me to the doctor's office instead of handing me a prescription. When he started talking, I frowned. I needed to decide whether to get my mother new clogs or gardening tools for Christmas.

'You mean I have the flu?' I asked stupidly.

'Your white blood cell count is thirty-eight thousand.' He waited.

My needle went off the record. 'No,' was all I said. 'No.'

'I'm sorry, Maeve. We need to begin treatment right away.'

It was the first Christmas I'd had to spend in the hospital.

Twenty minutes past closing time, I hadn't moved to lock the doors. The store was empty. I sat on a sofa watching the light change.

'Maeve?' Noah. Hesitant. He held out a cheque. 'My New York trip went really well. So I'm giving you a raise. You deserve it.' He looked away. 'I know I'm a little difficult.'

'No.' I shook my head. 'I don't know why I said that.'

'Is everything OK?' He sat down next to me.

'It will be.' I said the truth. 'Anyway, it wasn't you.'

'What *was* it, Maeve? Why did we fight today? Did I do something wrong?' His earnest face made me want to cry.

I felt sick as I recalled Dr Gerber saying, 'People with post-traumatic stress disorder may act like they are under threat, becoming suddenly irritable or explosive even when not provoked.'

'No,' I said. 'You didn't. You're a good man, Noah. And an excellent friend. I'm grateful you put up with me. I can be a moody, bossy creature!' I forced a laugh.

His relief was evident. 'I'm glad. I really value our friendship.' He looked at his watch. 'Are you OK to close up? I have to get Beth. You know women and these anniversary things.' He unfolded his tall body. He gave my shoulder a quick squeeze. 'I love the nook. Every time I turn round, things get better here because of you.'

I watched him walk out, reflecting that it was unfair that a man's legs could look that long and sexy in jeans, and knowing two things. I was in love with Noah Case, and I had to get the hell out of town because of it. It would kill me to moon over him from a distance, and I never, ever wanted to make him look that vulnerable again.

'Clapp Cement.'

'May I please speak with Clem Clapp?' It felt like asking for a venereal disease.

'You got him.' The voice was brusque. I hoped I hadn't guessed wrong. I looked at the web site. No, this was my guy. I was sure of it.

'Is this *the* Clem Clapp, editor and CEO of *Plymouth Road Runner: The (Good) Times*?' I poured all the admiration I could into my question.

His voice warmed. 'That'd be me. Who am I speaking to?'

'Sir, it is an honour. You are speaking to Maeve Connelly, 1970 Plymouth Road Runner N96 Air Grabber Coupe, 727 auto transmission, yellow black stripes.'

'That's a rare beauty, that one. I have one of those myself, Moulin Rouge, no wheel covers.' Satisfaction radiated from his voice.

'383 CID rated at 335 bhp and 425 torque?' I carefully read Barney's notes.

'426 CID Hemi rated at 425 bhp—that's 317 kW—and 490 torque.' Perfect. It was engine-compatible.

'Is it true, Mr Clapp, that you have *six* Plymouth Road Runners, sir?'

'Call me Clem. There's no better vehicle than the Road Runner. It's a personal privilege to ensure these American icons never become extinct. What would the road be without them?' Bingo. 'And how can I help you, Miss Connelly?'

'Call me Maeve. Clem, I couldn't help but be impressed at *Plymouth Road Runner: The (Good) Times*. That's quite a publication for a man as busy as yourself.' I had the latest issue up on the Internet. It looked like a third-grade newsletter. You could almost smell the glue.

'Well, thank you kindly.' He sounded chuffed. Time to go for the kill.

'I noticed you don't publish on a regular schedule. I found myself so eager for more after reading the last issue that I wanted to find out when the next edition will be available.'

'That's a good question. My wife doesn't quite share my passion so I do most of the work myself. With running a company, my time is limited. There's only so much one man can do.'

'I might be able to help you out.' I started to talk. Clem became excited.

'Maeve, your dedication to the Road Runner does you credit. I like the way you think. But that's a lot of work you're proposing to take on. Now tell me, if you do this for me, what can I do for you?'

I couldn't hold back my smile. 'Actually . . .' I laid out my proposal.

'So he went for it?' Vi asked.

'Uh-huh.' I crunched a celery stick.

'And what exactly do you have to do?'

'When I told him how Elsie and I got to Unknown, he was laughing so hard I was afraid he'd have a heart attack. I promised to help him modernise the newsletter and to write a regular column about my various road trips, and feature pictures of Elsie in all the small towns I've visited, the car troubles we've had, and how we fixed them.'

'That sounds like a pretty sweet deal.'

'Not exactly.' Clem hadn't been a total mark. 'I also have to help him with his company newsletter, *Cement Times: Solid Facts.*'

'In return you get the part.'

'Yep. One of his six Road Runners will be Elsie's organ donor while both Clem and I keep looking for replacements. If Barney finds one first, I send Clem back his parts. If Clem finds one first, I help him out with his various newsletters until I've worked off my debt.'

'Ingenious. But wouldn't it be easier to buy the part off Clem and avoid the newsletter business?'

I cleared my throat, with slight shame. 'I don't think I could afford it.'

'But you've been working for ages! And selling your pictures!'

'Yeah, well, there were things . . .'

'What kinds of things?'

'Oh, I put some money into projects for the store. And it was Ruby's birthday. Then there was the DVD player for the house, some hula skirts for Tuesday, a yoga mat for Samuel, some rabbit ears for my in-room TV, new running shoes. You know, *things.*'

Vi was quiet. 'Maeve, has it ever occurred to you that maybe you don't want to leave Unknown? Maybe there's a reason you're not saving more efficiently. I know how determined you are when you set your mind to something.'

I opened my mouth. I closed it. I tried. 'Have you ever stayed up all night picturing someone who wasn't there?'

She sighed. 'Noah?' Somehow she knew I was nodding over the phone. 'Are you sure it's hopeless?'

'Yes.'

'Are you sure it's hopeless because he has a girlfriend or because you don't think you're good enough?'

Her words were a shock. At my silence she went on. 'I don't know if I'll say this just right, but you got a second chance, didn't you? And the thing about second chances is that they aren't worth beans if you don't do anything about them.'

'But . . .'

'Get out of your own way, Maeve.'

'**A**y-yi, I can't believe you're leaving us!' Tuesday wailed.

True to his word, Clem had delivered the parts to PIGS, and Barney was performing the transplant. I was giving notice at the bookstore.

Noah's face was expressionless. 'When do you expect to leave?'

'Next week.' I had enough to pay Barney for his time and get to Los Angeles.

'Noooooo . . .' Tuesday wailed. 'But you'll be back for the Festival?'

'We'll see, Tuesday,' I demurred. I didn't want to make promises I couldn't keep. For all I knew, once I got to Los Angeles I might never want to leave. Work might be demanding.

Noah cut in. 'I don't suppose you can be any more specific than "Next week", can you? It's not very professional notice.'

I might've laughed, if it wasn't so sad. Even Noah's Angry Eyebrow (fully on display now) was dear to me. 'I'm leaving on Monday,' I said gently. 'Barney will be finished on Friday. Sunday night Ruby's having a farewell dinner for me. I hope you'll both be there.'

'You bet I will! I'm going to call Ruby right now. We'll send you off with a *mino'aka*—that's a smile.' She twirled, dance infusing her movements. 'We'll need fairy lights and paper flowers . . .' She talked to herself all the way out the door, forgetting it was my day off and she was scheduled to work.

I turned back to Noah, *mino'aka* playing on my mouth as I pulled off my jacket. Looked like I was staying. The smile faded at his expression. 'Well?'

I was ready. 'I've filled out the café and stockroom order forms for the next four weeks. They tend to be predictable. All you have to do is fax them in on Mondays. You'll have the books and food you need. I've also asked Beth to come by and help out for the next few Thursday mornings until you get into the new routine. She can put out the stock.'

'Beth?' He frowned. 'The last book Beth read, the title began with *CliffsNotes*. She has no idea . . . and . . . well . . . never mind.'

'No problem,' I soothed. 'We'll ask Ruby. It only entails putting out new stock. I ordered the titles. Anyone can do it.'

'So you're just anyone?' His anger dissipated.

'No. I'm the girl who's spent the last seven years of her life in neutral, who needs to get back on course.'

Noah sat heavily on the couch. I joined him.

'Careful,' I mimicked. 'Or I'll think you're going to miss me.'

He stood abruptly. 'I'm sorry, but I need to go through the office so I can prepare for this rather abrupt departure.' He wasn't going to make this easy. He headed towards the back. 'Oh, just curious.' He turned, tone caustic. 'What socks are you wearing today?'

We both looked at my naked toes in flip-flops for a moment, and then he strode to his office and shut the door without a word.

Ruby laid hands on my shoulders. 'Come along. Everyone is here.'

'Everyone?' I tried to sound casual. I hadn't seen Noah since I'd told him I was leaving.

Ruby sensed my question, but she also sensed I didn't want it acknowledged. 'I'm sure there'll be stragglers,' she reassured me. 'But at the moment, your farewell party has quite a crowd already.'

I followed Ruby to the yard. It was an enchanted place. There were lights strung along the walls and trees: what Tuesday lacked in paper-flower expertise, she redeemed in fairy lights. Though the paper flowers were there too.

Bruce, Child, Barney and Ronnie Two Shoes were at the grill, preparing kebabs. Male imperative. April and Busy were tippling and bickering about sherry versus Scotch. I had a vision of transporting Busy to bed later. Ruby was laying cutlery down in precise settings, as Tuesday was cluttering the table with scattered napkins. Sandy and Liz prepared a salad, while Patrick and Jenny Up laid out pies.

Samuel pressed a brown paper bag into my hands. 'It's vitamin samples. Obscure ones like bilberry extract and selenium.'

I hugged him. He was a gift I'd miss.

When the kebabs were ready, we gathered for chicken, pineapple, onion and tomato treats on sticks.

'Tuesday, give us an interpretational dance about how you feel about food on sticks,' I demanded, not caring that her kebab would get cold.

As I'd known she would, without a thought, she did, leaping up and dancing in the yard. It got better when Busy told Tuesday she'd got the pineapple wrong and jumped up to do her own version.

Candlelight lit the faces of those who'd gathered. I laughed along as Samuel exaggerated stories of his favourite Maeve Hypochondriac Moments. Clearly they were exaggerated. April brayed a little *too* loudly at some. But I'd already unscrewed the top of the saltshaker closest to her. April liked salt on prickly pear pie, which we happened to be having for dessert. Heh.

I didn't dwell on the fact that Noah didn't appear. Beth didn't show either. It was better that he didn't come. I wanted to enjoy my own party, and Noah would have strained things. I took what he'd told me about missing me and put it in my vault.

We ate and laughed and drank for hours. April and I carried Busy to bed at midnight. Liz and Sandy, Patrick and Jenny faded away shortly after. Ronnie Two Shoes was hot after Sandy, so he left within minutes to escort her belatedly home. Soon, it was down to the hardest. Child

clasped my hands. 'Maeve, it would be a privilege if you would continue to share your images.' He hugged me. When he pulled away at
the natural conclusion of the embrace, it was me that still clung.

'I'll treasure my carved memory,' he whispered about the kachina I'd
given him, 'though it won't replace the giver.' With that he was gone. It
was like saying goodbye to Jules times ten.

I was grabbed and squeezed. 'I can't,' said Tuesday. 'Breakfast?'

'Breakfast,' I agreed. 'Wagon Wheel?'

'No. I can't bear a public farewell. I'll cook.'

I laughed. 'Salad in a bag?'

'*I'll* cook,' offered April. We all looked at her in fear.

'No, *I'll* cook.' Ruby rescued us. Everyone exhaled.

Tuesday sniffed. 'Ruby, the dishes tonight . . . I can't . . .' She fled.

To me April growled, 'Sleep with one eye open,' and departed. The
salt trick had worked. I tried not to contemplate the repercussions.

'You look after yourself, gel,' Bruce gave me a bear hug.

'Don't touch the dishes,' Ruby ordered, as she left. 'They'll be there in
the morning.'

That left Samuel and me. We held hands companionably as we
walked to the gate. 'I'll miss you,' he said.

'I'll miss you, too. And if you don't date Primrose Tarquin after I leave,
you're a nincompoop,' I teased, naming Bloom's attractive older sister.

'We'll see.' From his blush, I could tell it was already in the works.

As we approached the gateway, Samuel swung me close and hugged
me tight. He kissed the top of my head. 'Be good, Maeve. Believe in
your capacity. You're not going to get sick again.'

'Thank you, Samuel.' I held on to his comfort. 'You're the best thing
that happened to me here.' Even as I said it, my mind was a cheater.

Something caught my eye in the dark and I fantasised it was Noah's
shadow in the door archway. I squinted, but there was nothing.

Samuel cupped my face in his hands. 'It's been a pleasure.'

'I'll stay in touch,' I said, hoping I would.

With an amicable hug, we said goodbye. And if I was weepy when
I went to bed, it wasn't because I hadn't had the perfect parting from
my friends. I had. It was because of the one that hadn't happened.

'**S**o you're really going?' he asked.

'No, I thought I'd load all my things into Elsie and then unload them
for fun.' I was being glib, but I was afraid if I looked at him I'd break
down and cry or beg him to leave Beth or something equally foolish.

Plus I was still angry he'd blown off my going-away dinner. 'Well, that's it.' I backed out of the car. We were packed. Oliver was sulking in his cage. I'd said goodbye to Tuesday over breakfast. The last stop was for my final pay cheque. I'd be in LA the day after tomorrow.

Noah crossed his arms. 'Do you know where you're going?'

'I managed to get here, I guess I'll manage to get out.' I hated being snarky, but if he was kind I'd come unstuck. My throat was tight as it was. I'd already bawled once this morning when I realised April had glued my shoes to the floor.

'Why this sudden rush to leave?'

'Elsie's ready, my debts are repaid. Why would I stay?'

'What about The Little Read Picture Book? Your plans for story time and book events for kids? And the Monkey Flower Festival events?'

'It offends you that I'm pursuing my own projects rather than spending all my energy on yours?'

His eyes narrowed. '*You* begged *me* for your job.'

'I'm releasing you from the burden of your charity.'

'Are you being deliberately difficult?'

'Are you? Buy some more knee socks—you won't even miss me.'

'It's not about me, it's about you! You're always running. You're going to end up exhausted. What's there in LA for you?'

'What's there for me in this no-stoplight village?'

He flinched. 'And how long before it's off to the next place? Are you capable of settling down?'

I flipped. 'Yes, I am!' I yelled. 'But I'm not settling for less. You're a self-absorbed, highly strung prima donna who expects he can drop out of life whenever he wants and have a cadre of women cater to his every whim. I'm not interested in being a water-carrier.'

'At least I finish what I start,' he thundered, hitting my tender spot.

'I *am* finishing what I started. My trip to LA. I'm finishing it *right now!*' I yanked open Elsie's door to climb in.

Before I could, Noah grabbed my shoulders and turned me to face him. His expression was contrite. 'Wait, Maeve. I'm sorry. I'm sorry.'

I stepped away from his touch. He noticed. He dropped his hands.

'I'm sorry I missed the party. I thought I'd be back in time.'

'Oh? Weren't you there?'

'I have something for you.' Abrupt. 'It's the reason I went to Tucson. It wasn't ready, so I had to wait. By the time I stopped by Ruby's last night, it was too late.' He looked off. 'It was always too late.' I frowned, not understanding. When had he come to Ruby's?

'Here.' He handed me a small box. 'You didn't give me much notice.' I opened it. Inside was a chain and round silver locket. Affixed to the front was a miniature silver Paddington Bear, in his duffle coat and hat, holding his suitcase. On the back was etched, *Please look after this bear.* I opened it, and was confused.

'It's microfiche.' Noah explained the negatives inside. 'I had *A Bear Called Paddington* scanned onto microfiche, so if you ever get trapped on that desert island, you'll have it with you.'

My throat closed entirely, my mouth forming a perfect 'O'. This was no match for the sixth kachina I'd hidden on his office shelf among the 'toys'. It was an ascending swirl of birds taking flight, a thing to lift your heart. To me it meant potential, attaining great heights. Noah's heights would not include me, but it meant a lot to know that a part of me remained with him, a potentially undiscovered talisman. But it didn't hold a candle to the talisman he'd just given me.

I struggled to make a sound, and failed. What could I say when all I wanted was for him to grab me, to kiss me. I wanted it badly.

'Maeve . . .' His voice was low, and he reached towards me.

Do it, I willed him. *Just do it. Say it's me you want.* I couldn't take my eyes off his mouth. I could almost feel his lips on mine. I swayed slightly. Then a burst of light caught my eye. We both glanced as Beth's silver BMW pulled onto Main, sunlight flashing off her windshield as she headed south. In truth, he'd never acted other than amicably towards me. Anything more was my imagination. Shame and humiliation washed over me. What the hell was I doing? It *wasn't* me that he wanted.

'Take lots of pictures of the Monkey Flower Festival.' I stepped back.

His right eyebrow creased down and his look darkened. '*You* should be taking the pictures.'

'Hollywood calls.' I affected a careless air.

'So this means nothing to you?' Angry now. 'You don't care about Unknown or the people here counting on you?'

'Of course I care! But you knew I never intended to stay,' I defended myself. He wasn't being fair. 'What do you want from me?'

'I want you to tell me why you're leaving.' His eyes penetrated mine.

So I don't die inside when I see you look at Beth with those dark-green eyes, I thought. 'Because I'd rather be there than here.' I broke what was left of us with my answer. 'I have to go.'

This time he didn't try to stop me as I clambered into Elsie. When I was safely out of town, I pulled over, put my head on the steering wheel and sobbed until even Oliver took pity and told me I was a hot fuck.

Chapter 8: Being Wrong

TAKOTSUBO CARDIOMYOPATHY A sudden temporary weakening of the myocardium (the muscle of the heart). Because this weakening can be triggered by emotional stress, the condition is also known as broken heart syndrome.

It wasn't until I was staring directly into the perfect round ball of the sun heading towards the sea that it hit me I was in Los Angeles. The jittery feeling I'd had since leaving Unknown abated for the first time, replaced by a blossoming euphoria. I forgot about kachinas and a bookstore, and sat in wonder. I'd *done* something.

I called my mother. 'Guess what I'm looking at?'

'I couldn't possibly know, dear. A cow's butt?'

'I'm in LA, Mom! I made it!' I was actually teary.

Silence again. 'I'm so happy for you, Maeve.' Her voice was tender. I waited, aching with my need. She delivered. 'We never doubted you for a minute. I've always been in awe of your strength.'

Her statement took my breath away. *My* strength?

'I'm talking about your tenacity. I honestly don't know if I could have endured what you did. Maeve, you dug deep for resources many of us never need. I thank God every day you had enough. After it was over, perhaps your fields needed to lie fallow for a while. Now it's time to start using all the wealth you possess again.'

'Thanks, Mom.' I blinked back tears.

'If I could give you one gift, Maeve, it would be to see yourself as I see you.' She paused. 'And if you could give me one gift, it would be a chunk of George's Clooney's lawn. But don't get arrested.'

I hung up, images of verdant fields, sunny beaches and palm trees swirling in a kaleidoscope of colour behind my eyes.

It was four in the afternoon and Laura wasn't expecting me until eight. We'd planned to meet at her place, but I knew she was at work. She wasn't answering her phone. I decided to head to Fox studios. I knew she worked in Building 100, so I figured I could track her down. If the shoot was really demanding, maybe I could help. My trip had proven that an ability to sell on my feet worked. My mother's words buoyed me with a new kind of confidence.

After consulting my map, I headed north and spotted a public park across the street from the studios. The weather was perfect—Oliver would be fine. In the rear-view mirror I glimpsed the box filled with crimson paper flowers Tuesday had given me to decorate my new home, and smiled. It would do nicely.

'I'm sorry, girl, I don' see your name,' the guard apologised.

'Well, hell's bells.' I recovered. 'What'm I supposed to do with five hundred paper flowers?' I find a Southern accent useful from time to time. I blew out my fringe for effect.

'You say Laura Mills? That the gal, with, you know, the *clothes*?'

'Sure is,' I agreed, having no idea.

He gave a conspiratorial giggle. 'Lord, I don' know how that girl keeps her job. You know what I'm sayin'?' I rolled my eyes in response. 'Tell you what. I don' want that girl to lose her job a cause a me. This ain't the first time she done forgot to send someone's name up.' He tapped his keyboard and a badge spat out of his printer. 'Don' be steal-in' no golf carts, hear?'

'Thanks, man.' I stuck the badge on my T-shirt.

I consulted the map he'd given me. Building 100 was easy to find. I saw that Stage 5 was closer. I decided to try there first.

Stage 5 was an enormous pink stucco building with no windows. The street out front was cluttered with golf carts and trailers. Teamsters, grips and electricians lounged, smoking cigarettes. Double doors led into a lobby devoid of anything but a serious-looking red light bulb to indicate when filming was in progress. I bypassed the lobby in favour of the enormous bay doors beyond. Shooting must've been on a break, because the doors were open, and people wearing utility belts scurried about the cavernous space. Others stood round drinking coffee.

I observed a moment, then approached a bear of a man whose belt had more coloured rolls of duct tape, notebooks and tools than the others.

'Hey there,' I chirped.

He looked at my box of flowers. 'What are those?'

'Um, not sure. I'm supposed to find Laura Mills.'

His confusion increased. 'Laura Mills?'

'She works here?' My certainty wavered.

'Aaron!' he bellowed. 'You know a Laura Mills?'

'Never heard of her,' floated back a reply.

'I think she's that Lola girl,' said a grungy guy. He wiggled his eye-brows at Bear. 'You know, with the *clothes*.'

Bear's face lightened. 'Ohhhhhh. *That* Laura. Well, you won't find her here. She'll be in Building 100.'

I was beginning to get a bad feeling about Laura's illustrious career. I followed the map to Building 100, a squat white building, identical to Building 101 and Building 102. Its sign proclaimed *Black Angus*. Laura either worked for the show, or served steak.

The unattended reception fed into a horizontal hallway. I could hear activity. My choices were right or left. I hovered. The door opened and a Greek god walked in.

No, really. Colin Cantell had played a Greek god in *Athens*. And here he was, larger than life (at least his chest was), three feet away. Sadly not in a toga. I vaguely remembered that he played a detective on a TV show.

'Hi.' He looked harried. I worked on keeping my jaw hinged, and managed a small squawk. He didn't notice. Must happen a lot. He hurried off to the right. Decision made, I followed.

'Joel!' he called in a high-pitched whine. 'I need to talk to you!'

'Oh joy.' The disgruntled answering voice indicated this was not a shared need. 'What now?' Colin Cantell followed the voice, and I almost trailed him right into the producer's office until I stopped short.

'It's the script. It needs to be rewritten. All those scenes need to be taken away from Kate and given to Angus. The show is called *Black Angus*.'

'That's because you insisted we change the name. Hold on. Where's my script? Why the fuck isn't the script ever where it's supposed to be?' His voice became a roar. 'Lola! Lola!'

I stepped out of sight. A second later Laura tottered down the hall looking tense. And looking like Cyndi Lauper and Posh Spice got into a fight and both lost. The tottering was due to bizarre heel-less platform boots, requiring her to balance on the ball of her foot. These accompanied mesh tights and an extremely short pleated kilt. She didn't notice me as she wobbled into the office. She looked almost green when she wobbled out. If someone had directed that language towards me, I'd be green too. The only non-invective was the word 'intern', which amplified my bad feeling.

The voices in the office dropped to murmurs. I tiptoed after Laura. The hallway drained into a large room filled with desks. Laura was nowhere to be seen. 'Excuse me,' I asked that-guy-who-tries-too-hard-with-the-skinny-tie. 'Did you see where Laura went?'

'Laura-Lola, Fashion Icon?' His signature was sarcasm, naturally.

'That's the one.'

'Copy machine.' He sniggered at the paper flowers. 'Those all the flowers you could afford?'

'That all the tie you could afford?' I followed the sound of the copier.

Laura was muttering over the machine, collecting pink sheets as it churned them out. 'God, please let the final be pink.'

'Hey, Laura,' I ventured.

'For the last time, it's *LOLA*,' she snarled as she turned. Then her mouth dropped open. 'What are *you* doing here?'

'Surprise!' My announcement was weak. 'I got in early.'

A big smile replaced her shocked look, and she gave a theatrical shriek before hugging me, box and all. 'Maeve! Wow! How'd you find me?' She sounded genuinely glad. I relaxed.

'From your emails.'

'Wow,' she repeated. She gave a little hop, then regained her balance. 'You're here! How fun! Yay! We're going to have all *kinds* of—'

'*Scriiiipt!*' A bellow reverberated down the hall. Laura jumped.

'Shit. Hang on a sec.' She grabbed the pink pages and lurched off. I stayed where I was and studied the chart above the machine that indicated that all final scripts were to be printed on green paper.

Laura returned shortly. Joel was either colour-blind or just happy to have a script. She led me to an impossibly cluttered desk. She made a face. 'I have to share with the other in—I mean another staffer.'

What does a First AD do?' I asked.

Laura looked shifty. 'This and that,' she hedged. Then you could almost see the light bulb pop over her head. She adopted a superior tone. 'So much is *confidential*. But I'm *so* outta here. I've got a connection with this new cop drama, *Badge Attitude*.' I was pretty sure I heard a snort from Skinny Tie.

Laura seemed to recall the golden halo she'd painted over her current job. 'Not that this place is *bad*. I mean, I've learned *a lot*. But I've grown as much as I can here and it's time to move on.' Another snort. I was starting to forgive him. 'I mean, *really*, a tough male/strait-laced female crime-solving duo? It's sooooo formulaic. *Badge Attitude* is totally going to be ground-breaking. They're tough cops, but they don't have guns. Just *badges* and *attitudes*.' She opened her eyes really wide at me.

'Oh,' I said. A tiny frown appeared. '*Amazing*.' I ramped it up. She smiled, satisfied.

'Where's the intern?' a female voice called from an office somewhere out of sight. 'Colin needs a ride back to Stage 16.'

Laura gave an exaggerated sigh and addressed me in a martyred tone. 'Oh, *I'll* do it. Colin and I are *so* close. Then I've *got* to focus on *my* work. So much to do! I'll see you tonight?' It was a dismissal.

'Sure. Is there a trick with the keys or an alarm or anything?'

'Keys?'

'To the house?'

'I need the keys so I can drive home, silly.' Her tone was impatient.

'You could separate the house key,' I pointed out. 'I'll wait there.'

'Hmm, yeah . . . I suppose. Listen, there's a café near my place called the Sidewalk Café. They'll let you sit there for hours. They don't mind. I'll call when I'm on my way home, 'kay? See ya.'

I watched her wobbly departure, trying to check my disbelief. My excitement about LA threatened to come crashing down. A miniature, weepy me was inside my head somewhere, curled up in a ball, homesick for Unknown and—but I shut her down. That girl was pathetic. This one wasn't. I pulled myself up, clutching my box.

As I passed Skinny Tie, I paused.

'What's a First AD?'

'An assistant director. She preps the episode, oversees the shooting schedule, and runs the set, coordinating cast and crew. She's the director's right hand.' He pointed to a pretty blonde with a walkie-talkie, a crowd round her, and the biggest tool belt of all. 'Nina's our First AD.'

I must have looked confused, because he winked and said, 'In some cases, as it applies to *interns,* for example, it can mean Abysmally Dim.'

'Actuality Deficit?' I grinned.

'Absolute Diarrhoea,' he agreed. 'Speaking of which, I'd better get back, or Appalling Disaster will mix Wite-Out with toner ink and blow up the office. Joel would be displeased.' He patted my shoulder. 'She's not a bad egg. She merely occupies a . . . unique state of reality.' He handed me a card. 'If you need anything.' His name was Clark.

My vision of waltzing onto the lot and heroically pulling the Nikon lens free from the legendary stone in which it was embedded, fulfilling the prophecy to become the Chosen Image Taker, was ludicrous. Los Angeles wasn't Unknown. I wouldn't be talking my way into a job here.

It was 9.30 p.m. when Laura found me drooping into my tea. Waiters had begun to give me the eye. I was desperate to put my head down somewhere designed for sleep.

Laura looked frazzled. 'What a day!' She plopped down. 'You're lucky, you've been kicking back.'

I blinked at her. I'd got up at six to break camp. 'Let's go lay like vegetables on the couch.' I voiced my wish.

'Hmm? Yeah, for a minute. Minka's coming at ten.' She looked at her watch. 'Oh Gawd! I barely have time to change!' She jumped up.

'Change?' Laura was halfway out the door.

She smiled over her shoulder. 'I can't wear this, silly!'

'Wear that where?' I trailed after her.

'It's Wednesday! Wednesdays are Buffalo Club.'

'A club?' My mind struggled. 'Wait . . . my car,' I remembered.

'We'll get it tomorrow.' Laura didn't pause.

'But I have to get Oliver.'

'Oliver?' That stopped her.

'My bird,' I reminded her.

'You brought your bird?'

I frowned. 'Of course. What else would I do with him?'

'Oh. I dunno. Leave it or give it away.' My mouth dropped open. She registered it. 'OK, OK, we'll get your car.' She followed me to where I was parked, muttering, 'Minka's gonna be pissed if I'm not ready . . .'

We drove down an alley in Venice Beach and parked by a dilapidated entrance to a more dilapidated unit in a dirty stucco building. It didn't look promising. Laura hurried in and disappeared into another room. I would learn it was 'the' other room. The apartment was filthy. A biscuit-sized living room held a battered mustard sofa, an ancient TV and a scarred coffee table piled high with *Us Weekly, Star, OK!* and *In Touch* magazines. Volcanoes of clothing and pizza boxes obscured the dismal putty-coloured carpeting. The adjacent kitchen was stocked with appliances from 1952. I peeked through the only doorway to see Laura's back half sticking out of a closet in an even smaller bedroom. I looked back at the sofa and decided I was going to become quite acquainted with the water stain on the ceiling above it. I blocked an image of Ruby's downy bedspread. This wouldn't be for long.

I returned after retrieving Oliver and my case from the car to find Laura decked out in a tulle-swathed costume that would have been rejected by *Swan Lake*. She was considering an array of beads when an equally exquisite vision pranced in. Her dress looked like a belted garbage bag designed by Spock.

'Those pink go-go boots are *darling*.' The Minka creature stuck to script. 'It's soooo *Lola!* Perez Hilton is gonna love them!'

'Do you think so?' Laura squealed. Oliver squawked in protest. This brought their attention to me. Silence fell. 'You can't wear that.' Laura spoke first.

'Oh.' I regarded my perfectly normal jeans and T-shirt. Then saw my easy out. 'I *know*. I'm *soooo bummed*. Everything I have is all packed and wrinkled. I *can't* go like *this*. You guys go ahead.' Big sigh. Sad face. 'Really—you guys go. I'll be ready next week!'

'Next week?' Minka giggled. 'Tomorrow is Villa!' With that and twiddled fingers they were gone and I was left with blessed calm. I opened the fridge and found some withered carrot sticks and half a lemon. The freezer held a dozen Lion bars, two bottles of vodka and the aura of an eating disorder. I took a Lion bar. Laura hadn't given me a key, so a food foray was out. I gave Oliver a wilted carrot.

'At least we can get some sleep,' I said.

'Fuck me.' He turned his beak up at the limp vegetable. Too tired to argue, I shook out my sleeping-bag. I didn't want direct contact with the couch. I tried not to think about mould spores. My eyes strayed to my pack. I rooted in it and gently withdrew the story. *My* story. I curled against the cushions, already soothed as I started to read about a girl who loved to climb trees.

Within two weeks, life in LA had settled into a pattern. Naturally, the studio job offers that Laura had promised never materialised. After a few conversations that felt like trying to capture mist in a box, I gave up pressing her. Clark set me straight. No past experience, no rich uncle, no dice. He'd keep an eye out, but I wasn't hopeful.

Unworried, I'd hit Main Street, starting with the Italian restaurant closest to Laura's place. You could always get a job waiting tables. Except, apparently, in LA. In a town teeming with aspiring actors, service jobs were gold. Surprisingly, Laura was unconcerned. 'Don't sweat it,' she said. 'It took me a while too.' Living with her wasn't terrible. For a while, she and Minka dragged me around the party circuit, where we were invariably turned away from the first venue we attempted, ending up in a second-choice joint, with Minka and Laura whispering how much better it was than the first, heads on constant swivel for celebrities, of which there were none (presumably enjoying the venue that wouldn't let us in). I mostly sat mute until I could beg off and go home. After a while, Laura stopped protesting when I elected to stay in, and I spent most of my nights reading or watching movies.

In the mornings I would feign sleep while Laura pulled herself together for work. Then I would rise, release Oliver, and start my day of rejection at local restaurants and cafés. When I spiralled into the inevitable panic, I would stave off hyperventilation by going for longer and longer runs.

The marathon was going to be a snap. It was pretty along the board-walk, but unchanging. The sky was blue, the sun shone, the sand was white and the waves rolled. Even the boardwalk characters were pre-dictable: the guitar player, the bodybuilder, the mime, the tumbling crew, the man with no legs. We'd nod in recognition as we passed, day after day, each the same except for my socks. In Unknown, the mead-ows were constantly changing; the only variation in the California scenery was whether I ran north towards Malibu or south towards Manhattan Beach. Either way, I clocked the end of my run by the same landmarks—the giant statue, the pizza sign, the hookah café. I would slow to a walk in front of my favourite tattoo parlour, Do You Tattoo, and study the tattoos through the window, feeling further from perma-nence than ever, a dandelion fluff with no home, no job, no tattoo. If I ran and never stopped, it wouldn't matter to anyone but Oliver.

'You can't get a tattoo through the glass.' A voice made me jump one day.

'Christ! You scared me!' I accused. The speaker was a tattoo-covered Mr Clean in a sleeveless Hannah Montana T-shirt.

He shrugged. 'No scarier than watching you lurk outside every morning. I'm guessing about sixteen to eighteen miles today?' My mouth dropped open. He laughed and tapped the window. 'It's glass. You can see in, we can see out. C'mon in. I'll make tea.'

I followed him. The shop was empty but for a Gothic-pale skinny man in black jeans and a black T-shirt with a Lite-Brite skull on it. He squealed when he looked up. 'The little chicken came in!'

'Be nice,' Mr Clean said. To me, he said, 'This is Jacob. I'm Marion.'

'Maeve,' I said. 'Are you hiring?'

'Nope. But there's no charge for hanging out.' And, just like that, my routine expanded to include Marion and Jacob. I still had no job, but now I had something to do in the afternoons, drinking tea and pester-ing them to let me try my hand at tattooing.

Friday night I was stir crazy, so I joined Laura and Minka, preferring their chatter to isolation. We were at a dive called the Dime, having been turned away from Hyde (again). I was at the bar buying the drinks. I bought a lot of drinks. Freeloader's guilt. It also let me escape from the minutiae of revisiting every word expelled by gossip blogger Perez Hilton, Laura's personal barometer for where to go (and be turned away), what to wear (clearly misinterpreted) and whom to stalk (Score: Laura—0; celebrities—infinity).

'Did you invite all these people? I thought it was going to be just the two of us,' a voice said. I turned to face an attractive blond man. 'My friend over there sent me. He wants to know if you think I'm cute.' He grinned.

I did. His roguish smile was appealing. I didn't think too hard about why I liked it, of whom he reminded me. 'Maeve.' I stuck out a hand.

'Bill.' His touch was lingering.

'So, Bill, are you somebody?' I leaned on the bar facing him.

He laughed, blue eyes bright. 'I'm an accountant.' There went my stereotypes about accountants. 'And you?'

'New in town,' I said. 'The possibilities are endless.'

He settled himself more comfortably against the bar. 'I'm all ears.'

Where to begin? 'I'm sort of on a trip of self-discovery,' I said. 'I decided to pack up all my stuff and my bird and drive across country to change my life. See, I had cancer in college, and I sort of froze, you know? Just when I was finding my independence and growing up, wham! Perpetual adolescence. Other people did all my thinking and I showed up on time. Kind of like a stereotypical 1950s housewife— smile at everyone, do what you're told, worry about nuclear annihilation, buy Forever Fuchsia lip gloss from the Avon lady. Except make-up on a cancer patient looks as garish as earrings on a monkey. Obviously I made *some* decisions. Like what movies to rent—anything with Julia Roberts . . .' I was word-vomiting, and Bill's smile was long gone. I tried to reclaim my point. 'But I didn't make any decisions about my future. I mean, if you might not have one, what's the point? Better living through denial, I always say!' The words spewed faster, tripping over each other as they poured out of my mouth. 'So I just floated along, then I was twenty-six and hadn't made a single choice about what to do with my life. And I need to because I'm totally healthy . . . I mean, healthy like a normal person, I get coughs and colds, of course . . . but anyway, I have to do something. So I drove across country in Elsie—that's my car— do you like old cars? I like old cars. Elsie's a 1970 Plymouth Road Runner . . . And I love the desert . . . am I rambling? I'm rambling. So here I am, ready for adventure . . . a new LA girl.' I smiled brightly. 'Maeve Somebody, work in progress.'

Bill had straightened, alarm stamped on his face. I'd misstepped.

'So, who is Bill Somebody?' I tried.

It was a no-go. 'Hey, listen, I'm really sorry about the cancer,' he said, like apologising for dirty dishes in the sink. 'But you look great now! Um, that's my buddy waving. I'd better get back. Have a great night!' With a cheery wave and a fake smile, he stepped away faster than you could say 'contagious', leaving only the memory of an attraction.

I ducked into the bathroom. I rested my forehead on the mirror, cheeks burning. Idiot. He didn't want to hear about cancer. No one did.

I called Vi.

'It's two a.m.,' she mumbled.

'Shit, sorry. I forgot the time difference.'

'Where are you?'

'In the bathroom at a bar.'

'Tell me.'

I did.

'I'm proud of you,' she said. 'It's a big step.'

'He ran faster than drug-store pantyhose,' I protested.

'Forget about him. What's important is that you shared. It was the first time. Of course you overdid it. It's like a first date after a breakup. It's a cardinal rule that you don't talk about your ex, but it's all you can think about, and you're word-vomiting before you know it. Then you never hear from the guy again. Everyone does it. The problem isn't the sharing. The problem is being emotionally slutty—too much, too soon. It's no different from sex, really. You have to figure out when the time is right.'

'So you're saying I shouldn't have given Bill an emotional blow job during our first conversation?' I was feeling better.

She laughed. 'I'm not a hundred per cent sure about cancer chats round the water cooler. You may have to defuse some kinds of assumptions. Ease into it. Telling someone you're a survivor or that you detest broth because you overdosed during treatment is first-base kind of stuff. Busting out with your struggle to come to terms with a fear of death is more home-plate material.'

I sighed. There was a lot to learn about this communication business. No wonder I'd avoided it for so long.

'It was a disaster,' I moaned. 'Can you tattoo a verbal diarrhoea shock collar onto a person? Otherwise I'll never meet Mr Right.'

'I read something once that said love isn't about finding the right person, but about finding the right wrong person.' Marion was concentrating on the design he was drawing.

'Is this the beginning of an Abbott and Costello routine?'

'Why don't you listen instead of talking for a change and you might learn something.'

I listened.

'By the time we're mature enough to have a relationship, it's because we're all a little wrong. We've got our quirks and issues and know what they are. That's essential for a real connection. If you don't know yourself, you don't know what works with you. When you've figured out *how* you're wrong you can find a mate who complements that.'

'I thought you were supposed to end up with the person who thinks you're perfect.'

'Sounds exhausting and impossible to me. Can't change what you are, and you can't go back to who you were before life stamped some problems on you. It's like a tattoo—once you got it, you got it. Even if you remove it, there's a different kind of mark.'

'Know thy scars?' I was intrigued. 'So we're looking for someone who fits nicely against our unsolvable problems?'

'Zactly. If I don't know my true shape . . .'

'Try barrel-shaped, with an accent of pear,' Jacob called.

' . . . then I can't find the shape that fits with me. Though if I look for a string-bean-shaped num-num-head in a tiresome eighties Goth T-shirt, I might be close.'

It made sense to me. 'I'm looking for Mr Wrong.'

'Not just any Mr Wrong. The one you look at with love and think, "This is the problem I want to have for the rest of my life, that I want to be my first and last problem of every day."'

'I'm touched,' Jacob said.

Marion and I were wandering around Costco when it happened. I'd begged him to take me along. I loved Costco. You could dine on a buffet of samples, and return home with supersized vitamin bottles. Marion had been lured into the clothing section by a giant pack-o-undies, so I wandered to the vitamins. My health seemed to be holding just fine, but I thought I'd replenish. Laura's apartment was a breeding ground if ever I saw one.

I rounded the aisle, and froze. In front of vitamin C bottles bigger than my head stood a fragile creature, probably in her late thirties, scarf poorly concealing her baldness. She had the vulnerability of a newborn—a flightless baby bird. I took in her careful movements, her pallor, her fatigue. I guessed today was treatment day, and she'd steeled herself to stop on the way home to collect what she needed before losing all her remaining energy. I'd never had to do that alone.

I walked up. 'I like the Nature Made.' I nodded towards the vitamin C. 'It bothers me less when I take it on an empty stomach.'

She looked up, too tired to be surprised.

I smiled. 'Today's Thursday, huh?'

Comprehension flashed. 'You?' she asked.

'A long time ago. I got better.' I wasn't sure how she'd react.

She nodded. 'I'm glad.'

I put my hand on her shoulder. 'Can I help you?'

She nodded again. I knew that exhaustion. I took her basket, and said, 'I'm Maeve.' And it was true. Not Old Maeve or New Maeve. Just one Maeve, as wrong as she was.

I was irritable as I jogged back to Laura-Lola's (as I now thought of her) place. My run had been very unsatisfactory. My heart had jerked alarmingly no fewer than three times as the corner of my eye saw one man with a back identical to Noah's, another with Noah's stride, and a third driving Noah's truck into a parking lot.

'This is ridiculous.' I cursed. 'Why am I obsessing about someone six hundred miles away who drives me mad?' It'd been over a month. I tried to recapture the outrage I'd felt pulling out of Unknown, but it eluded me. I couldn't even remember the reason I'd been angry, which, of course, made me angry. I'd worked myself into an excellent state by the time I walked in the door.

Laura-Lola, it seemed, had too. Hers appeared to be one of exuberance. She was hopping excitedly round the living room. 'You're not going to believe it! I just found out that Perez Hilton is going to be at the Lisa Kline spring-line launch party tonight at her store on Robertson, *and I'm going to be there too!* Minka got us on the list through her uncle!'

'Oh.' I struggled for a response. Laura-Lola's brow began knitting together. '*Wow.*' I upped my tone.

'*I know!*' Good humour restored. 'Maeve, this is it. I know Perez and I are meant to be.' She sighed, her eyes in a far-off place I hadn't seen since she'd been on hold with KROQ to win front-row concert tickets to Justin Timberlake. 'Once we meet, Perez will instantly recognise the depth of our connection. It's going to be beautiful.'

I boggled over Laura-Lola's disconnect with reality. Perez Hilton was so openly gay that Elton John was jealous. 'You're talking about Perez Hilton, the *Queen* of Media,' I explored. It's true. Even I read his blog.

'Yes. He is so *insightful* about celebrities and how they really feel. He insults only the ones who are shallow and mean or on drugs.'

'Mmm-hmm. Doesn't he out a lot of gay actors as well?'

'He's committed to honesty in the industry.'

I wasn't getting anywhere with reality. 'Let's get you ready, Betty. You've got a big night out.'

'Oh, yeah, about that,' Laura-Lola said, without any real concern. 'You need to find someplace else to crash tonight. I don't know Perez's situation so we could end up coming back here.'

I boggled again. 'Are you serious?'

She frowned. 'Of course I'm serious. It's *my* house, isn't it?'

'I've got nowhere to go.' Desperation tinged my tone.

'Can't you go visit Madelynn or whoever?' Her tone was un-interested.

'It's Marion, and I can't just show up asking to stay!'

'Why not?' She threw over her shoulder the genuinely surprised look of the sublimely selfish.

'Laura, Perez Hilton is gay,' I yelled.

Laura-Lola froze. Slowly she turned, face like a raptor.

'My . . . name . . . is . . . *Lola*,' she pinched out. 'And I would expect better from you than petty jealousy and character slurs, Maeve.'

I swallowed a hysterical giggle. 'Lola, I'm sorry. But please. I have nowhere to go. I'll sleep in the bathtub!' I begged.

'I think you should leave now. In fact, since you can't be nice about Perez, I think you need to leave your key. There's no telling how long he'll stay and I can't risk you being rude to him tomorrow. You can come back tomorrow night.'

'Road trip, don't forget the bird,' said Oliver, the tension in the room making him anxious. My personal alarm multiplied.

Laura-Lola sensed my near-hysteria and rolled her eyes. 'Don't worry about your bird. I kind of like him. He's always telling me I look thinner.'

'Are you thinner?' Oliver dutifully mimicked.

My agitation subsided. Oliver's safety being settled, my temporary homelessness didn't seem like that big a deal. I'd slept in Elsie before.

I left before the horror of Laura-Lola's party outfit materialised, stowing my camping gear in Elsie just in case. It was after six when I hit the boardwalk and wandered down to Do You Tattoo to see Marion. Maybe today I might be able to convince him to give me a tattoo lesson. But I skipped up to a dark store and a dismissive 'Closed. We Went Camping' sign.

I sucked in a breath. Despite my protestations to Laura-Lola, I *had* been going to see if I could inveigle a sleepover invitation from Marion and Jacob. I was all bravado about sleeping in Elsie. I didn't want to. There were lots of weird people who lurked round Venice Beach.

I turned away, stalking off to . . . where? I didn't know. I turned east towards Main Street and passed O'Brien's Pub. The patio was rollicking with happy, lively people; they annoyed me. The World Café, Joe's Diner, even the Coffee Bean were hopping. The Library Alehouse seemed less packed so I braved my way in. I spotted one lonely stool at the bar. I elbowed through and grabbed it.

'Waiting for someone?' gleamed the bartender-actor, or 'bactor'.

'Johnny Depp will be here any minute.' I pasted on a fake smile. 'Can I have the Racer 5 IPA?' I ordered my favourite beer.

He winked good-naturedly and turned to get my drink, making me feel like a jerk. LA people were really happy. Maybe it wasn't the place for me.

'Aren't people in LA so fucking happy you can't stand it?' said the guy next to me.

I checked him out. He was about my height, skinny, and had a face you liked. Open brown eyes and a grin that said, 'I get it and I was about to make the same joke.'

'To tell the truth, it sort of makes me feel inadequate that I'm not happy all the time. What are *they* drinking?' I demanded.

'Well, it sure as hell doesn't have calories or taste like this.' He raised his pint of beer. On cue, Smiley-Muscles-Bactor-Man returned with mine. I clinked my new friend.

'I'm Judd Wooten.'

'I'm Maeve. My delusional room-mate kicked me out for the night because *she* thinks *she's* going to seduce Perez Hilton at the Lisa Kline spring-line launch party.'

Judd let out a guffaw. 'You new to LA?'

'A month,' I admitted.

'In town for good?'

'I expect to be here a while, but I'm not generally that good.'

'God, I'm glad you're sitting next to me.' He clinked my glass again. 'Does she seriously think she's going to pull Perez Hilton?'

'Dude, she seriously thinks he's going to fall in love with her.'

'Ah, the myopia of young dreams,' Judd sighed, signalling Smiley. 'TJ, another Alaskan Amber for me, and whatever the lady is drinking. Why did you come here?'

'I had cancer.' The words came out. 'I had leukaemia when I was in college. It surprised everyone when I beat it. I thought it'd be easier to start over somewhere far away.'

Judd assessed me. 'Your hair is long.'

I ducked my head in shame. 'Yeah, I'm not at all heroic. I took a long time.' Was this word-vomiting?

'Kudos to you, kid,' he said seriously. 'I lost my dad to cancer.' He vaulted into the club. 'It's nice to meet a survivor. How long have you been in remission?'

'Two years, seven months,' I whispered.

Judd grinned widely. 'You're cured!'

'No.' I shook him off. 'Not quite. Five years is just a number. I've been part-dead since the day I accepted that I might die.'

'That's not true.' Judd was all confidence. Then he looked sad. 'My dad's remission was for a year and eleven months before it came back. The two-year benchmark means a lot.'

I was having this conversation in a bar after evading survivors' groups for so long. Judd signalled Smiley for his bill and I felt anticipatory loss for my new-found friend.

'So what do you do, Maeve?'

I slouched. 'Nothing. I thought I had a job when I got here, but it fell through. At the moment, I run on the beach, take pictures and try to figure out what the hell I'm going to do.'

'What kind of pictures?' Judd looked interested.

'Oh, you know, just people doing what they do. That's what I used to do in Unknown—where I stayed for a bit on my way here. Only there I got paid for it.'

Judd signed his credit card receipt. 'You like taking pictures?'

'I love it.' I was getting confused.

'You want to shoot, you call me.' He slid me a card. 'I run a company that photographs special events. It's not for the starry-eyed. It's hard work and seriously-less-than-famous.' He smiled. 'I'd love to have you on board, purely because I like the way you think and I'm partial to long braids.' He tugged one, but it didn't feel predatory. This was the first person in LA other than Marion who seemed to be himself. 'Organise a serious portfolio and I'll pitch you to my partners.'

I looked at his card. It was professional, Woot Prints Photography.

'Wow, Judd. Thanks!' was all I could manage. Was it possible that for once, timing had worked in my favour, planting me next to this guy?

Judd stood, slinging a camera bag from the floor over his shoulder.

'I've got to go. I've got to cover a fashion event party at Lisa Kline tonight.' He winked as my mouth dropped open. 'I'll try to get some good ones of the seduction for you.'

I was still there an hour later when I had a brainstorm. I'd see a movie. Genius. Happy now, I hopped off my stool and headed down Main Street towards the Santa Monica Promenade. I'd only been walking for a minute when my cellphone rang.

'Maeve?'

I sucked in my breath, frozen. After phantom sightings of Noah all day, the real one was saying my name. Repeatedly.

'Maeve? Are you there? Hello? Maeve, can you hear me?'

I smiled at his impatience. 'What's up, duck?'

'Oh, there you are.' His voice was relieved.

'I'm here, Big Ears. How the hell are you?' I forced casual cheer.

'At the moment, hungry and in need of a drink.'

Huh. Well. OK. 'Too far away to help, I'm afraid.'

'Actually, I'm in Santa Monica. At the Loews Hotel.'

My heart stopped. Then started like a bird trying to fly out of my chest. He'd come for me! Noah was here to take me home!

'I'm in town for an independent booksellers' conference.'

His words shot the bird like an arrow. But my happiness was only slightly diminished. He was *here*. Near me.

'So I was hoping you'd meet me?'

'You betcha.' I tried not to sound overly enthusiastic. 'There's this great little dive right there called Chez Jay—or if you want swish, we can go to the poolside bar at the Viceroy. For Irish pubs we have Finn's and O'Brien's. Or there's—'

Noah's voice had an unseen smile when he interrupted my verbal flow. 'Why don't you come to the hotel? If it's not too far for you.' Always courteous.

'Sure, sure. I'm close. Ten minutes?'

'I'll be at the bar.'

I hung up and took a few deep breaths. I was a little hurt that he'd apparently been in town for a few days at the conference and hadn't called me, but I pushed it away. He'd been busy, and he'd called me now. Feet light, it was less than ten minutes before I was smiling at the doorman as I stepped into the Loews lobby. It exuded understated luxury and the scent of expensive floral arrangements. I located the bar and headed towards it, trying to maintain a measured speed.

I spotted his back instantly, and felt the same jolt as earlier in the day. Only this time it *was* his back. Inhale. Exhale. As if feeling my presence, he turned. His face split into a wide smile, and something warm flooded my body. I crossed the distance as he slid off his stool and stepped to me, meeting in a hug that increased from tight to bone-crushing.

'You look great.' His green eyes were warm. I grinned back.

'You should've warned me to wear sunglasses, pasty,' I joked.

'I've been trapped inside a store.' He shook his head, face rueful. 'I just can't keep good staff.' Now my smile spread, and we beamed goofily at each other like awkward teenagers. Noah recovered first.

'My lady.' Ever the gentleman, he assisted me onto a bar stool. 'I was about to order something to eat. Will you join me?'

My stomach's loud rumble would have overpowered a sonic boom, much less Noah's words. He started, then laughed. Without a word, he gave my braid a tug, and turned to the bartender. 'We'll have one fillet, medium, please, and one of the halibut, miso broth on the side, peas steamed with no butter. And a bottle of your Cambria Pinot Noir.'

'But . . .'

'And we'll start with the crab cake appetiser.' He looked at me. 'You like crab cakes, right?' He didn't wait for an answer. He knew I did.

I felt a little panicky at the thought of the cost. 'Noah . . .'

'Maeve, allow your old boss to buy you dinner. You brought me sandwiches often enough when I was on a deadline and forgot to eat.'

I gestured to the lavish surroundings and raised an eyebrow. 'This is pretty swish for an independent bookshop. Dipping a hand into the till, are we? Wait until the boss finds out. You're canned.'

He laughed, but his right eyebrow did the thing where it creased. There was something he wasn't saying. 'So, tell me about—' he began.

'You first.' I wasn't having it. 'Tell me about this independent booksellers' conference.'

His gaze flicked away. 'Nothing very exciting. Room full of people looking worried.' Definitely. There was definitely something he was withholding. I pondered it. Then horror flooded my body.

'You got married,' I accused, feeling sick. I felt miserable. And stupid. 'You and Beth are on your honeymoon.'

His eyes flew back to mine, astounded. 'What? Maeve, no . . . that's just ridiculous. Preposterous, even. Beth and I—'

'There's something you're not telling me,' I interrupted. I didn't want to hear about Noah and Beth. 'You have the worst poker face, Noah.'

He was smiling again. He tapped my hand on the bar and began to absent-mindedly play with my fingers. 'It's not that big a deal.' He gave a laugh, embarrassed. 'I've been flown out by a studio. They're interested in *The Boy Who Could Fly*. They've optioned the rights to make a film. They're trying to impress me Hollywood style, hence the hotel.'

'Noah, that's incredible!' I launched across the space between our bar stools, throwing my arms round him. He reflexively wrapped his round me and returned the hug. It felt so good to be captured against his chest that I couldn't move. Someday I'd have to face the reality that he belonged to another. But not tonight. We held each other until it wasn't about congratulations anymore. I didn't pull away until the sound of his cellphone jarred the mood.

'Hello?' Then his expression became strange. 'Beth.' He mouthed 'Excuse me' in my direction and hurried away from the bar, phone close to his mouth. After five minutes, he returned, seeming agitated.

'How's Beth?' I faked interest.

'Demanding,' he frowned. 'Maeve—'

'OK then, crab cakes for you?' The bartender interrupted him, placing a dish in front of us. Beth might be dominant in Noah's life, but I didn't want to hear about it. I seized my fork and took a bite. Noah opened his mouth, then closed it. After a pause, he picked up his fork as well. Diversion successful. 'So tell me more about it.'

'My agent called a few weeks ago with an offer. It happened that the conference was coming up, so I suggested this week. They're footing the bill for my trip to meet them and I get a free ride to the conference. But it doesn't mean they'll actually make the movie,' he warned. 'It just means they've bought the right to be the only ones who can decide to make the movie for the next two years.'

I swatted him. 'I *have* learned about Hollywood since I got here.'

'You've really taken to LA. I was impressed with your social savvy, suggesting all the places we could go.' I couldn't read his expression. 'You definitely don't miss Unknown.' Noah's voice was funny.

Oh but I do, I wanted to say. Instead I said, 'How's that Ronnie Two Shoes been behaving?'

After a while our main courses arrived. We salted and peppered and somewhere in there a second bottle of wine appeared. Noah asked me about life in LA. I couldn't tell him the truth—that I had no job, no friends, and lived on a futon in a dumpy squat. I told him about Marion and the characters on the boardwalk.

'And are you happy?'

'Yeah, sure.' I didn't meet his eyes.

Noah shook his head and looked at his watch. It was midnight. He looked at me regretfully. 'I should probably get to bed. I have an early flight tomorrow.'

'Wait,' I said, desperate. 'I haven't told you about Laura-Lola and Perez Hilton.' I launched into an expanded version of my story, anxious not to lose my lifeline. After that, I babbled about anything I could think of. I was recapping the weather for each of the forty-eight days I'd been in town when Noah's face split into a wide yawn.

'Maeve, I'm sorry. I love your company, but I've got to go to bed.'

'But you haven't been to the beach yet! Let's go.'

'Now?' he asked in disbelief.

'Yes. It'll be perfect. Santa Monica by moonlight.' I was already rising from my stool when he stopped me with a hand on my arm.

'Maeve, what's going on?' His face was concerned.

'What do you mean? Nothing's going on. Hey, I know! Let's stay up all night and watch the sunrise!'

'Unfortunately, I'll practically see the sunrise if I want to make my flight. So I'm going to have to put you in a taxi, I'm afraid.'

'Taxi? Oh, no. I'm not taking a taxi.' I accepted defeat, but refused to have him know the mess I was in. 'I prefer to walk.'

'That's it.' He crossed his arms. 'What's going on?'

I opened my mouth. Then I closed it. Exhaustion washed over me. I was tired of taking care of myself. 'I have nowhere to go,' I confessed.

'What do you mean?' He looked confused. I explained, bracing myself for his upbraid at getting myself into this predicament. Instead, he broke into a laugh. 'You silly goose, you can stay with me. Why didn't you say something hours ago?'

I shook my head, bemused.

'C'mon.' He stood, and I followed him, like a puppy.

The room he let us into was spacious and attractive, and dominated by a king-sized bed. I felt awkward. Noah caught my hesitation, and tugged my hand. 'C'mon, settle in. We'll watch TV until you're sleepy.'

We flopped onto the bed, burrowing in against the pillows.

'Where's the remote?' I feigned casual, trying not to be aware of his body stretched out next to mine. We both looked round.

'Uh-oh.' The remote was across the room, on top of the TV.

'Well, go get it,' I said.

'You go get it,' he said.

'I'm the guest,' I argued.

'I rescued you,' he disputed. 'You should show me gratitude.'

I turned on my side, propped up on my elbow. 'Oh yeah? Well I res-cued you from being that lonely guy at the bar drinking and eating alone. You should show *me* gratitude.'

'I paid for that dinner.'

'No you didn't. The studio did,' I countered.

'Well I gave you a job when you were broke and desperate.'

'Oh please. You were a mess. I saved that place for you.'

His look was incredulous. 'Cheeky monkey. I graciously hired your unemployable self, *and* I chauffeured you round Arizona.'

'I made you sandwiches when you would have starved to death, *and* organised your life, *and* made sure you paid your taxes.'

He shook his head, smiling. 'It figures that I finally get you into my bed and we're arguing.'

I frowned at him. Surely he didn't mean . . .

Noah laughed and pressed his index finger on the crease between my eyebrows. 'Watch out,' he teased. 'Your divot is showing.'

'I see London, I see Kent, I see someone's forehead dent.' I para-phrased childhood lyrics. I thrilled at his touch.

'You seem unperturbed.' He was surprised.

I flopped on my back. 'It's funny,' I said. 'I worried so much about that divot.' I let the truth come out. 'Lotions, creams, massages, never frown-ing. If I'd known about Botox, I'd have bought it by the gallon. Did you know, "Botox" isn't in spellcheck for Microsoft Word? It's that new.'

Noah tugged my nose. 'Stay on target, Red 5.'

'Some days they were pumping chemicals in my body designed to kill half my cells and I directed all my energy to maintaining a placid facial expression. I'm not sure why I thought I could control that one wrinkle when I couldn't control my cells, my hair, my dry skin, my chapped lips. But I was going to block that furrow, no matter what. And you know why?' I looked up at him again. 'Because I knew I was going to die,' I said out loud. And paused to catch my breath. The statement reverberated through my system like a bouncing gong. Right to home plate. Noah's gaze stayed steady. 'I knew I was going to die and I didn't want to be lying in my coffin with a divot on my forehead. I don't know if I didn't want my parents to think I was worried about going to . . . well, wherever you go. Maybe it was pure vanity. I wanted to be a good-looking corpse.' My laugh was a bark.

'And now?' Were Noah's eyes shimmering? I'd had a lot of wine.

'And now I'm going to live a *long* time,' I gloated. '*I* won. I have a life. And this,' I pointed at my forehead, 'this is the first stamp on my passport.'

I smiled up at him. He leaned down and kissed me. It was so sudden I didn't realise it was happening until it was. The moment his lips touched mine, we locked in an embrace, pent-up longing coursing between us as we kissed intensely. Time suspended as the kiss went on and on. It was beyond anything I had dreamed of in all my imagined Noah fantasies. His warm skin, solid body, searching lips were real. He kissed my eyelids, my cheeks, before capturing my mouth again. I gave myself completely to the kiss.

He pulled back at last, and gently brushed my fringe off my forehead. 'Thank God for you,' he murmured.

Emotions were raging through me. They must have reflected on my face, because Noah frowned and jerked back. His expression became frozen. 'I'm sorry. You weren't expecting to get jumped. I promised you a safe place to stay—here you were opening up to me and I leaped on you. God, what's wrong with me? I'm so sorry, Maeve.' He released me and rolled on his back, looking wretched.

I stared at the man I loved. I wanted him so badly. 'Stop talking,' I commanded against his mouth, unbuttoning his shirt. He looked in my eyes for a beat, then our lips locked hungrily.

I stared at him in the semi-dark of predawn. His face was beautiful, with its sharp cheekbones and precise mouth. His whole body was beautiful, naked next to me beneath the sheet. I knew it now. The finally discovered tattoo was an old friend, a sun symbol spreading between his shoulder blades. But I wanted to know more. The scar on his jaw, below his left ear. How did he get that? Part of me wanted to wake him, to gobble every second before he left tomorrow. I glanced at the clock and winced. Today.

It had been the most amazing night of my life. We'd alternated between lovemaking and intimate conversation, pillowed heads facing. I'd told him what it'd been like to be sick, and to feel life return in Unknown, like the pins and needles you feel after your foot's fallen asleep. He'd told me about trying to hold his family together as a boy, and the invented characters he escaped into. After a while he said it was my turn to stop talking, that he was going to worship every inch of my skin. And when he'd joined our bodies, something clicked in me, and my body and soul became one unit again, reunited at last after breaking so many years ago. Climaxed and satisfied, Noah had gathered me close and fallen asleep holding me to him. It was a perfect fit.

'I love you,' I sighed, and closed my eyes.

The whisper was so low it could have been part of a dream.

'I'll never regret this night. It will be the treasure I keep in a safe place to take out on dark days and bask in the glow of how beautiful you are and that I was with you. It's beyond belief. You're a miracle.'

Write it down, my sluggish mind urged, *write it down so I don't forget come daylight*. But nothing came out of my sleep-weighted mouth.

'Sleep, perchance to dream.' Gentle pressure. Kiss on my temple. Absence. The click of a door.

I awoke to a boxing match between disorientation and cottonmouth. Disorientation had an early advantage as I absorbed a bed too comfortable to be Laura-Lola's futon and the fact that I was naked. Shock flooded my system, along with the memory that last night I'd slept with another woman's boyfriend. The nausea of horrifying recollection trounced both cottonmouth and disorientation.

I leaped for the bathroom, and reached the toilet just in time to heave into the bowl.

I'd slept with Noah. He was Beth's boyfriend and I'd practically torn his clothes off. Fleetingly I rose on a magic-carpet memory of our tangled limbs and whispered words, but quickly fell back to the cold tiles with a bump. It had been sex, and I'd acted like a cheap whore.

I began to cry. Noah hadn't behaved above reproof, but I was worse, keeping him at the bar long after he intended to go to bed, attacking him when he'd only given me a kiss. He was the wrong 'wrong person' for me. I couldn't fix the ways I wasn't perfect, but I could avoid what made me imperfect in ways I couldn't live with.

I wiped my cheeks. Enough was enough. I'd been waiting for Los Angeles to fix itself for me, and that hadn't happened. It was time to get off my ass. Things were going to be different, starting today.

I dragged on last night's clothes, and was heading for the door, when I saw the $20 bill on the dresser with a note that said: 'For a cab—N.' I froze in shock. I'd never felt like more of a whore. Tears started again and I was pulling out my phone to call my sister, when another wave of nausea hit. I raced to the bathroom, stumbling as I reached to brace myself on the toilet. The porcelain knocked my phone into the toilet, and I had only a moment to watch it sink to the bottom before I threw up on top of it.

For once I didn't curse my bad luck. This punishment was deserved. I turned to go, pausing only to take the $20, and crumple the note. I was going to need a new cellphone after all. So Noah could call and explain why he left me money after cheating on his girlfriend.

When I got back to Venice, Laura was sitting on the sofa, listlessly flipping channels. I tried to gauge her mood. I'd have bet my whole twenty dollars on Not Good. 'Hey,' I said. 'How was last night?'

She looked about to break into tears. 'I'm a complete idiot.'

'Oh, hey! Lau— *Lola*, no.'

She gave a snotty burble of a laugh. 'You can call me Laura.' Her lip started to tremble. 'But really, I think I'm not very smart.'

'Hey.' I scooted over and put my arm round her. 'You are plenty smart. You have a heart of gold, sister, and don't you forget it. Look at how you've taken care of me.'

'Taken care of you?' she scoffed. 'You're the last person in the world that needs taking care of. You're not afraid of anything. You came all the way out here by yourself. In about a minute you'll have it all figured out and be way more successful than I'll ever be.' From where her head rested on my shoulder, she couldn't see my fly-catching mouth. 'Besides,' she was sniffling again, 'I was awful to you last night.'

'No . . .'

'Yes, I was. Can you believe I thought I was going to hook up with Perez Hilton?' Her tone rose to a wail. I was about to say that I would never have guessed Marion was gay, when she cried, 'He had a *million* girls with him. He didn't even *look* at me. I'm so stupid.' I shut my mouth. 'The worst was this crazy photographer following me round and recording everything! It was so humiliating!' I had to fight my smile. 'So where'd you stay last night? I'm really sorry I kicked you out.'

I opened my mouth to make a dismissive joke and turn the conversation back to her. Then I paused. And changed my mind.

'You won't believe it,' I said, and began to tell her the story.

A week later, Judd sifted through the photos spread on the desk before him. I'd spent most of the week creating a portfolio for him.

'I'm impressed.' He looked at me. 'We all were. A little too impressed. I'm not sure you'll find the work we do . . . artistically stimulating.'

'There's an art to paying rent,' I said. 'Remember the girl chasing Perez Hilton at Lisa Kline's party? I'm dependent on her.'

'You're hired.'

I exhaled in relief. This had been my last shot. Even Taco Loco didn't want me. 'Now I can replace the cellphone I dropped in the toilet.'

'I wondered about your, er, complicated messaging system.' Judd raised an eyebrow.

I snorted. It'd been a nightmare since I'd lost my phone. I had no money for a new one. Until I could afford a replacement, I was dependent on Laura to field messages and let me use her phone to return calls. It was my penance. Not that it mattered. He hadn't called. It hurt.

'Anyway, your missions for Woot Prints,' Judd went on, 'should you choose to accept them, are mostly charity events where no one remembers the charity, exclusive private parties that exist merely to be crashed by those higher in the Hollywood food chain—who never do—and promotional launches that attempt to convince meaningless twits that their indistinguishable product is indispensable.'

'So what do I actually do?'

'Every gig is swarming with the B-and-lower list. You're there to catch their good side. I try to catch them with chewed-up food in their mouth. Consider it a challenge. If you can catch one of these creatures showing genuine self without artifice, that'll be a masterpiece.'

I brightened. This would be fun. 'What's my first assignment?'

We decided that I would shadow Judd for a few events, learn the dance steps, then start solo with some small gigs.

'Fantastic. See you Wednesday!'

'Just out of curiosity . . .' Judd stopped me as I gathered my things. He tapped a print. 'Who's this?'

Stab of pain. I glanced away from the picture of Noah, chin resting on his hands as he stared at his computer. 'No one,' I said.

'Right.' Judd didn't buy it. 'See you Wednesday.'

It was the truth. Noah didn't exist for me anymore. Despite me making very sure that Tuesday had Laura's number, with strict instructions to give it to '*everyone*', he hadn't called, making it very clear what he thought of me—or, rather, that he didn't. I had too much pride to call him. When people had bailed on me when I got cancer I was smart enough to blame the cancer, not myself. Noah hadn't called because he didn't feel like it.

When I walked into Do You Tattoo, Marion didn't even look up from the *Semper Fi* he was inking on a Marine. 'Go ahead,' he grunted.

I headed for the phone. 'Tuesday?'

'Ay-yi, Maeve! Oh, I miss you!'

'Me, too. I got a job! I'm paparazzi now! I mean, I'm an event photographer. There'll be celebrities, of course, but it will be about the events themselves. The challenge will be catching people unawares, you know, food in their mouths . . .' I trailed off. What Judd had made sound artistic, I made sound creepy. 'It's hard to explain,' I concluded lamely. 'You kind of have to know LA.'

'I'm happy for you. Well, sort of happy. I kind of hoped you'd come back. Noah refuses to hire anyone—'

'Tuesday,' I cut her off. If Noah didn't care to talk to me himself, I didn't want to hear about him.

'Sorry. I've been working a lot of hours, and we're also trying to get ready for the Monkey Flower Festival. It doesn't help that Ronnie Two Shoes backed into the bandstand and now it's collapsed on one side . . . Noah was a bear about me taking only *one* day off. Of course, he's a bear all the time these days . . .'

'Tuesday.'

'Ugh, sorry. I swear, the two of you. That must have been one humdinger of a fight that neither of you will talk about.'

'Tuesday.'

'OK, Miss Avoidance, what else is new?'

I told her about connecting with Laura, and about what I now dubbed the Costco Moment, but soon I ran dry, because there was this giant thing I couldn't tell her, what had happened with Noah.

'Things sound good,' she said. 'I'm half astonished you got my message. It took me for ever to convince your friend that I was *named* Tuesday, instead of wanting you to call me *on* Tuesday.'

'I'm glad you did. It's good to talk to you,' I was reluctant to end the call, but was without the means of extending it.

'Aloha, love,' she said, before cutting my connection to Unknown.

The next call was to my brother. 'Yo!' I said.

'Yo!' he said.

'I'm calling you back,' I reminded him.

'Oh, right. Man, that secretary of yours is whack. It took me for ever to explain that I was "Brick, your brother" and not "Your black lover".'

I laughed. 'So what's up?'

'Hey, yeah, I met that old boss of yours, you know, the writer.'

Shock made my lips numb. I sucked in air. 'What?'

'I went to check out the Atlantic Book Festival, and what do you know, he was giving a talk. So I thought I'd introduce myself.'

'You met him?'

'Couldn't get near him. Interesting lecture, but he was mobbed by about a hundred boys afterwards. Though they may have been angling for the girlfriend. She was *hot*.'

My hand clenched the phone. 'If you like that sort of thing.'

'I've always been partial to redheads.' Brick's tone was approving.

I felt a wave of nausea wash over me. 'Redhead?' Beth was no ginger.

'Halfway down to her endless legs. I mean, I know you didn't like her that much, but you might want to think before tangling with an Amazon. I bet she's taller than Jules.' Beth was not taller than Jules. I felt seriously ill. How could I have been completely wrong about Noah? I knew from personal experience that he was a cheater, but I'd imagined it was because of our connection. I'd prayed there was an explanation for his silence. And now I had it—he had a girl in every port. I was nothing more than his Los Angeles girl.

I managed a goodbye to my oblivious brother, gave a halfhearted wave to Marion, and walked like a zombie back to Laura's.

When I let myself into the apartment, my heart jolted at the sight of the envelope Laura had left on the coffee table for me. It was old-fashioned snail mail, my name in Noah's familiar handwriting. I held it for a few beats, then my hurt bubbled up and I hurled it in the trash. I couldn't bear the thought of the lies—or truths—the letter would hold. I put on my sweats, and was heading for the door when Laura came in.

'Oh, hey!' she said, then her smile faded. 'Are you OK?'

I could only nod as I passed her and headed out of the door.

I don't remember running, or how long I was gone, but I registered a change immediately when I walked back into Laura's place. The living room was spotless. A note said, *I thought I'd improve on your room!!! Hope you feel better!!!* I didn't have to look to know the trash can had been emptied. I had no idea where the rubbish went. I didn't care.

Chapter 9: Welcome to the Z-List

HYPERTHYMESIA SYNDROME *A condition where the affected individual 1) spends an abnormally large amount of time thinking about his or her past, and 2) has an extraordinary capacity to recall specific events.*

I was hot, sweaty and irritated.

'I'm not sure you got my best side on that one.' The fake acrylic nails swept the bleached hair off the Botoxed forehead. I dutifully snapped a picture identical to the first. When the 'reality' star turned away,

I paused and waited. Within five seconds I was rewarded; her gorgeous manicure grasped the expensive silk fabric she wore and unglamorously dug it out of her butt. Click.

Instead of heading home after the midday party, I walked down Pacific to a small Venice street, paper clutched in hand. I found the sign for Ozone, double-checked the address and hurried to number 21. The draping fuchsia bougainvillea reminded me of home.

Ruby's home, I corrected myself. The buzzer sounded, and I took an old-time elevator with a folding iron cage door up to the fourth floor.

When the woman came to the door, I was startled by how pretty she was. Elegant was the word that came to mind. 'Dimple?'

'Maeve? Nice to meet you.' We shook hands. 'Please come in.' Her smile was warm, gesture graceful. I noticed she had a crooked tooth. Everyone should have a flaw, I thought.

'Thanks for seeing me,' I said.

'It's no problem. My schedule is flexible. I think this might work out.'

I stepped into the apartment and was instantly in love. This was definitely going to work out. I staged a thoughtful hand to my chin to keep from blurting, 'I'll take it!' The rent wasn't decided yet. Plus I hadn't seen the shower. An icky shower is a deal-breaker.

I took in the front room. It would have to be a seriously icky shower. The space was all light. The woodwork was bare cedar, walls vanilla. The kitchen wall had inlaid tiles. The corner bedroom was all windows on two walls. The bathroom was anything but icky, tiled in white octagonal tiles with a decorative black pattern.

We walked back into the airy bedroom. I absorbed the peace of it.

Dimple gave a nervous laugh. 'Don't think this is weird, but if you want to see the room's best feature, lie on the bed.'

I didn't skip a beat. I stretched out. 'What's the feature?'

'Look towards the ocean.'

Without lifting my head from the pillow, I could see an incredible ocean panorama. 'Holy guacamole, was that a dolphin?'

'Yeah.' She grinned. 'You can see them most mornings. As soon as you open your eyes.' Smile splitting my face, I lay back down.

'So you want to sublet it furnished?' I started the negotiation.

'Mmm-hmm. And you're OK with month to month so long as I give you reasonable notice that I'd like to come back?'

'Yep.'

'What can you afford?'

'What do you need?'

She looked over at me and giggled. 'Men would tear their hair out if they saw how women negotiate.'

As it turned out, we had exactly the same price in mind.

'A true meeting of minds.' I grinned.

'I found a place to live,' I reported to Tuesday without preamble when she answered her phone later that day. Relying on Laura's phone had made my calls efficient.

'That's great,' she said, but her tone was subdued.

'Is everything OK?'

'No. Yes. I mean . . . I'm just tired.' She sighed. 'I'm heading home from the hospital.' My heart stopped. Then kicked back on in overdrive. Tuesday. Or Noah. Or Ruby. 'It's Child.'

'What?' I croaked. My heart now thundered. It physically hurt.

'It's OK. He's OK. God, I'm crap at this.' I could see her biting her lip. 'I was about to call you. We were waiting for definite news. He's going to be fine. He was having chest pains.'

I was immobile, hand pressed to my eyes, world pulsating.

'He went to see Samuel. The ECG revealed a significant blockage, so they hustled him to the hospital. They had him on the table within thirty minutes and put in a stent.' Her voice caught a little. 'It was a ninety-eight per cent blockage.'

My breath came easier. 'OK. That's OK. My dad has a stent. In a way this is better. Now we're on alert, and we monitor.'

'I know. The doctors said he's fine. It was a little scary, that's all.'

'God. You're telling *me*.' My relieved laugh was shaky. 'That was almost as bad as when I thought Noah and Beth had got married!' It slipped out before I could stop it.

'Ha!' Tuesday's snigger was equally relieved. 'Married? As if. Holy vitriol, those two can barely pass a civil word since they broke up.'

There it was again. That moment when time shimmers a beat, like passing through a membrane to another world.

'They broke up?'

'Of course! Before you left.' My world spun again. Tuesday sucked in some air. 'Are you telling me you didn't know?' she demanded. 'He was going to tell you when you went to the store to say goodbye. I don't know what the hell happened, since neither one of you will talk about it, but afterwards he moped round like a kicked dog.'

I swallowed. 'But then he—'

'Noah ran into Primrose Tarquin at the Wagon Wheel. She was waiting for Samuel and he was waiting for Bruce, so they got to talking. He did the maths and realised you had to have broken up with Samuel before you left. Quite coincidentally, all of a sudden he's got meetings and a conference in Los Angeles and is off.'

'But Beth called him. When he was here.'

'Probably to tell him she was keeping his Jeff Buckley records.'

I made a strangled sound.

'My friends are two morons,' she muttered. To me, 'I don't know what happened out there, but after he got back he went from being a kicked dog, to being a neurotic teenager asking if there'd been any calls every two seconds, to being an aaaaangry bear.'

'So.' I licked my lips. 'So when he was here, in LA, he wasn't . . . he and Beth weren't . . .'

'Weren't even speaking. She was so spitting mad that he dumped her just when she'd got rid of you and thought she had a clear shot at her meal ticket that she was speaking in tongues. It was scary.'

'And now?'

'The good news is you can always get advice from Liz Goldberg on how to avoid a hatchet in your back or a horse's head in your bed.'

'That's not funny,' I muttered.

'Oh, I think it's funny. I think you're both ridiculous.'

'It's not as if he's a saint,' I defended. 'I know for a fact that he's seeing someone already. Maybe he wasn't cheating but that's pretty fast.'

'If you're so *akamai* and *niele*, you can explain how you, in California, know better than me, in Noah's house *and* store every day. *E kala mai!*' In her agitation, she peppered me with Hawaiian.

'My brother saw him, with a girl, at the Atlantic Book Festival.'

'Ooooh, *that* girl. Was she tall, with auburn hair, really pretty? That's Jan, his publicist.' Tuesday's voice resumed its disgusted tone.

'Mixing business with pleasure then.' Mine matched hers.

'Next time I see her, I'll be sure to ask Jan if she broke up with her *live-in girlfriend of seven years, Kristin,* so she could swing the other way with her long-time client,' she said, with a snort. 'You and Noah, and your rampant imaginations, are *perfect* for each other. You think he's married to Beth yet screwing his publicist. And every time he calls you, he gets some girl hyperventilating about the fact that you're out at some fabulous party so exclusive she can't get in. He's convinced you're living the glamorous socialite's life and want nothing to do with a small-town hick like him—his words, not mine.'

'What? That's ridiculous.' I protested. Noah had called?

'I don't get it. You return everyone's calls but Noah's. And he was horribly worried about you being too broke for a cab when he saw you. He was ready to wire you every penny he had to make sure you had enough to eat. He almost went mad when he heard you'd lost your phone. It really hurt him to find out you were partying every night.'

'I was working! I was photographing events.'

'Good luck getting that through his thick head. After fifty-seven unreturned calls, I can't blame him. Why didn't you just call back?'

'I never got any messages!' I was going to strangle Laura-Lola. 'I had no idea! I thought he was blowing *me* off.'

'You're the only person on the planet who can't see that Noah only has *maka* for you.'

'I hope "maka" means "eyes",' I muttered as my brain ricocheted. On the one hand, it felt like a huge boulder had rolled off my heart. Noah was who I thought he was. On the other hand, did I want to run backwards to a relationship based on making sure I ate enough? Or did I want to stand fully on my own two feet?

'So now that you know, what are you going to do?' Tuesday demanded. My lack of answer was notable.

'Don't tell him anything about this while I try to figure it out.'

After we hung up, I crossed to Laura's room in two steps. 'DidsomeonenamedNoahcallme?' The words tumbled out so fast they made no sense.

'What?' Her brow furrowed.

'Did. I. Get. Any. Calls. From. A. Man. Named. Noah.'

Laura's face cleared. 'Oooohhh. You mean No One? There was this guy that called, like, a *million* times, but every time I asked who was calling, he said, "No one," or "No-one-thanks," like it was one word.' She giggled. 'He was really polite, but never left his name. I didn't think it was worth mentioning.' She shrugged, smile bright. 'Mr No One!'

I sagged against the door frame. 'Oh. Thanks.'

I rolled back into the living room. So Noah had called. Noah wasn't a cheater. My relief was intense. But, I frowned, was it about Noah? I was over being 'taken care of'. I was finally doing a pretty good job on my own. Tuesday's question echoed in my mind. What are you going to do? 'I don't know,' I murmured.

Two weeks later, 'Enjoy,' Dimple said, as she handed me the key. Was I really about to become an official resident of Venice Beach, California? I closed my fingers round the key. Yes, I was.

I tripped over a box in the dark living room, and cursed as my shin collided with the coffee table. I'd been living out of suitcases for a month, and I seriously needed to unpack, but September was the busy season at work, and I'd had no time. All the television premieres held launch parties packed with people craving to be photographed. This was the eighth night in a row I'd got home after 2 a.m. Too tired to turn on the light, I wanted only to fall into bed.

When I awoke, I experienced the daily spurt of pleasure I'd known since getting my own place. I was exhausted from the amount of work I had to take on to make the rent, but, despite the cost, it was worth it. Every morning I remembered I was living in my own apartment, with my own job, in California, completely self-sufficient. I'd done what I set out to do

'Howdy, pardner,' Oliver greeted me when I entered the living room.

'Howdy yourself,' I said. It felt good to speak aloud. Last week, four days had gone by where I hadn't spoken a word beyond 'Hi' and 'Thank you' to clerks providing me with goods in exchange for money. I resolved to drop by Marion's tattoo parlour for an overdue visit. Being so busy, I barely saw the few friends I had.

I didn't have a job until evening, so I spent the morning sorting out the apartment. The bruise on my shin demanded it. I hung up clothes, and put books on the shelves. I wasn't ready to put nails in the walls, even though Dimple had assured me it was fine. Though I'd left over two months ago, I was still too homesick for Unknown to put up my pictures. The one thing I displayed in pride of place was the card I'd received from my parents when I'd sent them my new address. It read: *We couldn't be more proud of you.*

At five I had to get ready for that night's job. The event wasn't until eight, but it was in Studio City, so I had to allow two hours to get there in traffic.

'**E**xcuse me, honey.' Fake nails were snapped in front of my face. 'You need to step up the shutter action. You've barely taken any pictures.'

'Of course.' I lifted the camera to my eye.

'Hold on.' She repositioned herself. 'That's better.'

When I got home that night, a wave of tiredness washed over me, yet I was too restless for sleep. It was too late to call Vi or Tuesday, so even though it was two in the morning, I decided to finish unpacking.

By three, I was down to the last box. I sat on the floor and pulled it towards me. It was labelled 'Miscellaneous'. At the very bottom, under a jumble of pens and pencils, was *The Girl Who Could*. I carefully extracted the beautiful book. I opened it to the dedication, and slowly turned the pages. By the time I came to the end, I'd made a decision.

'Oliver,' I told the sleeping bird. 'We're going home.'

'I'm glad,' Vi said.

'I had to come here, though, to be able to make the choice.'

'I get you. When are you going to leave?'

'As soon as I can. I want to find someone trustworthy to take over the apartment sublet. I don't want to screw Dimple. I think Clark might take it. I also want to do all the jobs Judd assigned to me. He took a chance on me, so I owe it to him, especially during the busy season. And I want to build a comfortable financial cushion, so I don't get myself stranded like I did on the way out.'

'Let me send you some money,' Vi offered. 'You're still calling me from Marion's phone.'

'No.' I shook my head. 'I can do this on my own. I have a plan.'

A week and a few borrowed phone calls later, I put my plan into action. First was a trip to Michael's craft supply store to buy photo paper and inexpensive mattes and frames. Next, an all-night after-hours printing binge at the Woot Prints darkroom, permission of Judd. Finally, setting up my booth on the boardwalk one busy Saturday.

I displayed for sale both framed and unframed photos of Venice and Unknown. By sunset, I'd sold all my stock.

Three weeks later, Clark and Dimple had agreed on the sublet, I'd had several successful weekends on the boardwalk and amassed a substantial nest egg, and I'd finished my last job for Judd.

I smiled as I sold my last photo of palm trees to a tourist in a Hard Rock Los Angeles T-shirt. LA had helped get me where I belonged in more ways than one.

Marion looked up when I walked into the tattoo parlour. I'd said goodbye to Judd, Clark and Laura. My last stop was Marion and Jacob.

'How'd it go?' he asked.

'I sold 'em all again.' I was flush with profit. 'Check it out.' I waved my shiny new iPhone at him.

'Nice. But I hate to lose you,' he said.

'You're not losing me,' I said. 'You just have to drive farther.'

He handed me a bag. 'I got you these.' Inside were several pairs of touristy Los Angeles knee socks. 'So you remember us.'

'I love you too,' I said. 'I got you this.' I handed him a miniature Oscar statue that said *Best Friend Award*. With my plans, I was out of kachinas.

Jacob wandered out. 'Hey'ya, chicken.'

My smile broadened. 'Not this time.' I slapped $60 on the counter and tapped the page I'd found in the book. 'This one. Right here.' I tapped my neck behind my ear.

'Rock on!' Jacob exclaimed. We high fived.

Marion pulled the book to him and looked at the design. 'That's a good one,' was all he said, but his voice was gruff.

I knotted my hair and tilted my head so he could ink me with the Chinese symbol for Life. My decision was permanent.

Afterwards, Oliver and I walked over the soft white sand down to the water. I sat cross-legged and watched the mesmerising roll of the waves. I felt the sun on my face, smelled the salt. Oliver tugged strands from my braids: I breathed. I didn't take a picture. I didn't frame the scene. I *was* the scene. Breath, light, warm sand. I wasn't on the outside. I was the centre of everything. Breathing. Feeling.

When it was time, I reached into my pack. There was one last thing I needed to do. I couldn't go back in time and give Cameron this last kachina, but I could say goodbye.

I was perched on the side of Cameron's bed. For a change, it was just the two of us.

'No more,' she begged. We'd been playing 'Would You Rather . . .?' for almost an hour.

'You just don't want to choose between a hairy mole and a third nipple,' I chided.

'Hairy mole! It'd be the only hair I've got.' Her laugh turned to a cough that turned to gasping for air. She was pallid as onionskin, except for purple shadows bruising beneath her eyes.

She leaned her head back as she regained control of her breathing. 'I think I'm ready for this to be over,' she croaked, without opening her eyes.

A flash of agreement, then revolt. Cameron had been the gift God handed me when I needed it the most. I wasn't ready to give her back.

'Does it hurt?' I asked.

'Don't ask me that.' She silenced me, eyes open now.

'Are you afraid?' I asked.

'No.' Her head was almost comically too large for her twiglike neck, and her shake was more wobble. 'You know how it is.'

I nodded, but I didn't. I'd never got to that place where fear let go. When death had danced close, I'd been afraid. But even when they'd asked if we wanted a priest, they hadn't stopped the fight; chemicals continued to flow. And worked a miracle. Cameron was off the tubes. No more battling. This was a different kind of waiting.

'Tell them,' she made me pledge. 'Tell them I wasn't afraid. Coming from you, they might believe it.'

Again I nodded, wondering what I could possibly say to her family, a twenty-two-year-old girl trying to comfort broken sixty-year-olds.

Cameron went on. 'For years I was the manic, melodramatic cancer-won't-get-the-best-of-me person. But you know what? It's horseshit. Cancer sometimes will get the best of you, and that's why it sucks. I'm not saying permanently, just sometimes. Remember that.'

'Are you giving me a parting lecture?'

She rolled her head to look at me. 'I don't know what I would say for my last lecture.' We held eyes, wondering what wisdom we could give one another in our diverging journeys. When she spoke at last, she simply said, 'Live.'

'As long as I can.' I made the only promise I could keep.

She made a feeble gesture to her long-abandoned desk. 'Get that envelope. It's for you.'

'What is it?' I drew out a thick sheet of watercolour paper. Cameron was incredibly talented. She had been an art student.

It was a watercolour comic map of the United States, scattered with caricature icons—a cowboy galloping across Texas, an Amish buggy cantering through Pennsylvania, Mount Rushmore dominating South Dakota, surfers cresting California's coast. In the middle, hanging out of a bright red convertible, waved a blonde girl with a wide smile, driving, with Cameron's grinning freckled face on the passenger's side.

'It's all the places we said we'd go when we got better.'

'I can't do it alone.' I wasn't talking about the road trip.

'Not to sound like Dr Phil,'—we both hated the TV doctor with a passion—'but you're only as alone as you want to be.'

'I think I might want to be.' My throat was tight. 'For a while.'

'That's a choice.' Her voice was fading as she tired, but she managed a smile. 'But when you're ready,' she indicated the colourful map, 'take me with you.'

I'd cried a normal amount once—skinned knee, dead dog, broken heart. But when I got sick and had a well of legitimate causes, the tears had dried up. I hadn't wanted to wash away in them. In that moment, the valve burst, and every single tear I'd ever held back erupted. I put my head on her knees and sobbed. The watercolour still bears the blotch that stained the corn palace in Iowa before Cameron extracted the map to safety. She made shushing noises, hand on my head.

'I'm going to miss you,' I burbled through the snot.

She feebly tapped the map. 'I'm right here.'

I pulled myself together, and mopped my face. 'If you live, I'll get you a corndog and funnel cake at the Minnesota State Fair,' I begged.

She laughed. 'How did you know what I wanted for my last meal?'

'Crazy in the brains!' I scolded. 'You need to shop on the right-hand side of the menu. Get the lobster Thermidor and baked Alaska.'

'How about snow crab legs and artichokes . . .'

We bantered until her parents arrived. I would not be alone with Cameron again before her death three days later. It was years before I was able to say 'I love you' to anyone, because I hadn't said it to her.

I extracted the jar from my bag. I'd been carrying it with me a long time. 'I hope you enjoyed the trip,' I said to Cameron. 'I'm sorry it took so long.'

I unsealed my portion of Cameron's ashes and gently shook her into the breeze. Soon, I would write to her parents and tell them what I had done. I could stop avoiding them.

When the jar was empty, I filled it with Venice Beach sand. In the resulting hollow from my scooping, I nestled a kachina for Cameron. While her ashes continued her exploration of the world, the seventh kachina would stay on the California beach she'd dreamed of seeing. The statue intertwined a bird, nest, fish and wave. I wondered if my mom had been thinking of my friend when she created it. It reminded me of Cameron's own drawings. To me, the seamless joining of elements and animals meant belonging. I didn't belong to Los Angeles, but I belonged to myself at last, body and spirit. I was grateful to this place for giving that to me. I didn't need to stay until October. This particular marathon was over, though surely there would be others. I was ready for my new home.

The eighth kachina, the mother-figure with the owl, would return with me. It was mine to keep, to remind me of where I began, and of the seven others that marked my journey to where I was now. With a last gaze at the ocean, I walked to where Elsie was waiting to take me to the desert.

'Where're you headed?' The parking attendant looked at my packed car. 'You're loaded.'

What he didn't know was how free I finally was. 'Destination Unknown.' I smiled.

When I pulled into Unknown it was a far different scene from my shadowy arrival many months before. Though it was after dark, the town square was bustling with preparations for the Monkey Flower Festival. I could see Bruce and Ronnie bickering over how to erect the tent. Liz Goldberg and Jenny Up were hanging paper lanterns on the bandstand, while Helen Rausch skulked nearby, ready to pounce on flaws in their work. I could see Tuesday's work in clusters of mis-shapen paper flowers. I didn't see Noah's tall frame among the crowd, but that didn't worry me. I headed home to Ruby's. I had all the time in the world.

Epilogue

ELEVATED MOOD *An exaggerated feeling of well-being, euphoria or elation. A person with elevated mood may describe feeling 'high', 'ecstatic', 'on top of the world' or 'up in the clouds'.*

'**R**ed wine?'

'Yes, thanks. Did you get the popcorn?'

Pause.

'You remembered to get the popcorn, right?'

Cough.

'Are you kidding me? You forgot the popcorn! What's movie night without popcorn?'

'I had a deadline! I was focused on getting chapters out.'

'Spare me. You spent the entire day distracting me while I was trying to research the impact of Indonesian imports on domestic cement production for *Cement Times: Solid Facts*.'

'I didn't notice you complaining.'

'*Whatever*, clever. Let's watch the movie. Where's the remote?'

Silence. 'It's on the TV.'

'Well, go get it.'

'You go get it.'

'I'm the guest.'

'Right. You have more stuff here than I do. There's no room for *my* socks any more!'

'If you can call those socks.'

'There is nothing wrong with black socks.'

Snort. 'Fine. If you won't get the remote, we'll just sit here.'

'Fine.' Quiet. 'I can think of something to do . . .'

Giggle. 'That tickles.'

Pause. 'Want me to stop?'

'Not on your life. C'mere . . .'

Long silence. 'Maeve?'

'Yes, Noah?'

'What's this I hear about you opening a tattoo parlour in the corner of the bookstore?'

Kerry Reichs

Can you tell us a little about yourself and where you live and work?

I'm a southern girl who moved north a few states and now calls Washington, DC my home. A graduate of Oberlin College, Duke University School of Law, and Sanford Institute of Public Policy, I'm a 'recovering attorney'! I practised law in DC for six years before taking a sabbatical and moving to Venice Beach, California, to write my first book, *The Best Day of Someone Else's Life*. I returned to DC after selling the manuscript, but enjoy the flexibility and travel opportunities that life as a writer allows. You'll often find me on the road, tapping keys in Los Angeles, London, or wherever my fancy might take me.

What persuaded you to give up the law to become a full-time writer?

I always intended to write, but thought it would be when I was older. I felt that some nadir in my life had to occur to give me a sadness and wisdom to write anything meaningful. As I approached thirty-five, and a partnership in a large law firm, I questioned why I was waiting. I realised that I did have something to say. You don't have to be James Joyce to write something that people will want to read. You simply have to tell a story people can connect to.

Where did the idea for *The Good Luck Girl* come from?

After experiencing the loss of someone far too young to leukemia, I became deeply involved with fundraising through the Leukemia & Lymphoma Society. Through their Team in Training programme, participants undertake a physically challenging endeavour to raise funds for cancer research. I chose to bike 100 miles in one day and, in the course of doing these 'century rides', I've had the pleasure of meeting many current fighters and survivors. I've also known some who did not survive their illnesses. I've become passionate about the struggle of cancer patients, and I wanted to write about how such struggles impact all of our lives. Like a ripple effect, a single loss has a far-reaching consequence. I explore this through Maeve, who has suffered herself and lost her best friend to cancer, experiences that permanently alter her life.

Do you enjoy taking road trips?

I love driving across country in my beloved red Mini Cooper convertible, and I have learned that you can even sleep in it comfortably, as I did in the West Texas desert when I didn't plan ahead and there was no room at the inn. My two cats, Beatrice and Cedric, have also become fairly seasoned travellers and, while it is not their favourite pastime, they have at least settled into routines—and they enjoy exploring unfamiliar hotel rooms! I love driving across the northern route, experiencing the vastness of the middle of America, and swerving around alligators lazing on bayou roads in the south, and we often detour to visit the quirkily named towns. It's a never-ending pleasure to explore the incredible breadth of American landscape and life—and there is always more to see.

Have you ever, like Maeve, wanted to run a marathon?

I do run, but not marathons. I stick to cycling the century rides to raise money for the Leukemia & Lymphoma Society. That's exhausting enough!

Oliver, the cockatiel, is a wonderful character in the novel. Do you own one?

Oliver is a real cockatiel and quite a character, though with a slimmer—and cleaner—vocabulary than the bird in the novel! My brother and I bought Oliver as a birthday gift for my sister and he is part of our family.

Are you, like Maeve, a lover of brightly coloured knee socks?

I am very fond of knee socks and my current favourite pair is rainbow striped.

Are Maeve's desert island books the same choice as you would make: *Pride and Prejudice*, *Catch 22*, *A Bear Called Paddington*?

Not only are those books precisely the three that I would choose, I also had the exact conversation that occurs between Maeve and Noah about them, which resulted in someone giving me the Paddington Bear locket.

Your mother is Kathy Reichs, the best-selling crime writer. Your genres are very different, do you enjoy each other's work?

Yes. She's my biggest fan and manages to be supportive while still letting me do my own thing, which I think, as a mother, is the hard part! As for me, I read all her books and think they get better every time.

stILL Life

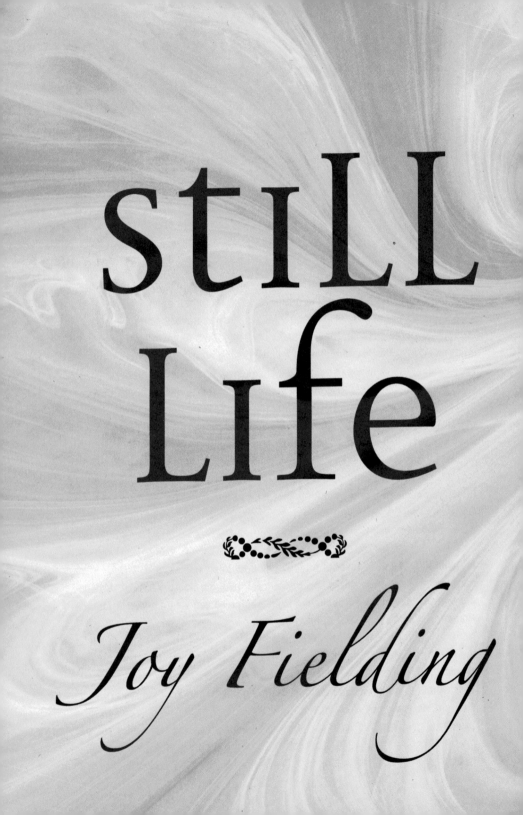

Joy Fielding

I've always been interested in exploring my own worst nightmares in my fiction, and a lot of my novels examine the dark side of human nature: murder, sexual abuse, rape . . . the feeling of being trapped, or of not knowing who you are. My latest novel, Still Life, combines a lot of those nightmares—the idea of being trapped in your own body, the realisation that your life is in danger and that you're helpless to save yourself.

It has been said that as parents, we get the children we need. I think this is true about writers as well. We write the books we need to write. I think I work out my personal demons in my fiction. Hopefully, these demons will prove both edifying and entertaining to you, the reader.

Joy

1

LESS THAN AN HOUR BEFORE the car slammed into her at a speed of almost fifty miles an hour, throwing her ten feet into the air, breaking nearly every bone in her body and cracking her head against the hard concrete, Casey Marshall was sitting in the elegant, narrow dining room of Southwark, one of South Philadelphia's more popular white-tablecloth restaurants, finishing lunch with her two closest friends and stealing glances at the beautiful, secluded courtyard behind their heads. She was wondering how long the unnaturally warm March weather was going to last, whether she'd have time to go for a run before her next appointment, and whether she should tell Janine the truth about what she really thought of her new haircut. She'd already lied and said she liked it.

Casey smiled at the thought of an early spring and allowed her gaze to drift over Janine's right shoulder, past a luminous still-life painting of pink peonies.

'You hate it, don't you?' she heard Janine say.

'The painting?' Casey asked, although she doubted Janine had even noticed it. 'I think it's fabulous.'

'My hair. You think it's awful.'

'I don't think it's awful.'

'You think it's too severe.'

Casey looked directly into Janine's intense blue eyes, several shades darker than her own. 'A little, yes,' she agreed, thinking that the blunt cut's sharp, geometric angles put too much emphasis on Janine's already exaggerated chin.

'I was just so tired of the same old thing all the time,' Janine explained, looking to their mutual friend, Gail, for confirmation.

Gail nodded obligingly. 'A change is as good as a rest,' she said.

'I mean, we're not in college any more,' Janine continued. 'We're over thirty. It was just time to do away with the Alice in Wonderland hairdo.' Her eyes settled pointedly on the naturally blonde hair that fell softly across Casey's shoulders.

'I liked your hair long,' Casey demurred.

'So did I,' Gail agreed, tucking a few frizzy brown curls behind her right ear. Gail never had a problem with her hair. It always looked as if she'd just stepped on an electrical current. 'Although I like it this way, too.'

'Yeah, well, it was time to move on. That's what you always say, isn't it?' The question was accompanied by such a sweet smile that it was difficult to know whether or not to take offence.

'Time for more coffee,' Gail announced, signalling to the waiter.

Casey ignored the deeper implications of Janine's remark. What was the point in reopening old wounds? Instead, she offered up her white china cup to the handsome waiter. While Casey knew Janine had never quite got over Casey's decision to leave the legal placement service they'd cofounded fresh out of college, to start her own interior design business, she'd talked herself into believing that, after almost a year, Janine had made peace with it. What complicated things was that Casey's new business had taken off running, while Janine's had ground to a halt. And who wouldn't resent that? 'It's amazing how everything you touch turns to gold,' Janine regularly observed, always with the dazzling smile that accompanied the vaguely unpleasant undertone in her voice.

Casey took a long sip of her black coffee. She and Janine had been friends since their sophomore year at Brown. Janine had just made the switch from prelaw to honours English; Casey was majoring in English and psychology. Despite the obvious differences in their personalities— Casey generally softer, more flexible, Janine more brittle and outgoing— they'd clicked immediately. Perhaps it was a case of opposites attracting, of sensing something in the other that was lacking in oneself. Casey had never tried too hard to analyse why their friendship had endured, despite myriad changes that included the dissolution of their business partnership and Casey's marriage to a man Janine described as 'Perfect, of course'. Casey chose to be grateful instead.

Just as she was grateful for her other close friend, Gail. Casey had known Gail since grade school, and although more than twenty years had passed, Gail was the same guileless, open-faced girl she'd always been. Despite much hardship, she still ended almost every sentence with a giggle. Casey considered it the auditory equivalent of a puppy offering up its stomach to be stroked.

Unlike Janine, there were no pretences where Gail was concerned, no hidden agendas. She generally waited until she knew how you felt about something before offering up an opinion. Occasionally Janine grumbled about Gail's naiveté, but Casey admired the skill involved in making each side believe you were on their side. It was probably what made her a good saleswoman.

'Everything OK?' Casey asked, turning to Janine.

'Everything's fine. Why?'

'I don't know. You just seem a little . . . I don't know.'

'Of course you do. You know everything.'

'You see—that's exactly what I mean.'

'Am I missing something here?' Gail asked, large brown eyes darting nervously between the two women.

'Are you angry at me?' Casey asked Janine.

'Why would I be angry at you?'

'I don't know.'

'I honestly don't know what you're talking about,' Janine said, adjusting the collar of her crisp, white Valentino blouse. Casey knew it was Valentino because she'd seen it on a recent cover of *Vogue*. She also knew that Janine couldn't afford to pay almost $2,000 for a blouse.

'OK,' Casey said. 'That's good.'

'So maybe I *am* a little irritated,' Janine conceded with a shake of her geometric blue-black hair. 'Not at you,' she added quickly.

'What's the problem?'

'It's just that little twerp, Richard Mooney—remember him?'

'The guy we set up at Haskins, Farber?'

'The one and only. Jerk finishes in the bottom third of his graduating class,' Janine explained to Gail. 'Has zero social skills. Can't get a job to save his life. He comes to us. I tell Casey he's a loser, we shouldn't take him on, but she says we should give him a shot. Sure. Why not? She's leaving soon anyway, as it turns out.'

'Whoa,' Casey exclaimed, raising her palms in protest.

Janine dismissed Casey's objection with a megawatt smile. 'I'm just teasing you. Besides, a few months later you *were* gone.' Janine returned her attention to Gail. 'Sure enough, Casey batted her eyelashes at one of the Haskins partners and he agreed to give Mooney a try.'

'That was hardly the reason,' Casey interjected.

'Anyway, Mooney goes to work at Haskins, lasts barely a year, then gets canned. Of course, by now, Casey's in her new role as decorator to the stars. And who's left to deal with the fallout?'

'What fallout?' Gail asked.

'What stars?' asked Casey.

'Well, I can't imagine Haskins, Farber beating down my door, looking for a replacement. But guess who *does* show up at my door this morning? The little twerp himself! He wants a job, says we screwed up the first time in sending him to Haskins, we should have known it would be a bad fit, and that it's up to me to find him a more suitable position. When I suggested he go elsewhere, he got quite upset and raised a ruckus. I almost had to call security.'

'That's awful,' Gail said.

'I'm so sorry,' Casey apologised. Janine was right—it *had* been her idea to take Richard Mooney on; maybe she *had* batted her eyelashes at Sid Haskins a few times.

'It's not your fault,' Janine conceded. 'I don't know why I let him get to me. I must be PMS-ing.'

'Speaking of which . . . well, not exactly . . .' Casey said, stopping to debate with herself whether or not to continue, then plunging ahead. 'Warren and I have been talking about having a baby.'

'You're kidding,' said Janine, long chin dropping.

'You waited until the end of the meal to tell us?' said Gail.

'I'm going to stop taking the pill at the end of the month.'

'That's fantastic!' Gail said.

'Are you sure this is the best timing?' Janine questioned. 'I mean, you haven't been married all that long, and you've just started a new business.'

'The business is doing great, my marriage couldn't be better, and as you pointed out earlier, we're not in college any more. I'm going to be thirty-three on my next birthday.'

'Good for you.' Gail reached across the table to pat Casey's hand. 'I think it's great. You'll be a terrific mom.'

'You really think so? I didn't have a very good example.'

'You practically raised your sister,' Gail pointed out.

'Yeah, and look how well that turned out.'

'How *is* Drew anyway?' Janine asked.

'Haven't heard in weeks. She doesn't return my messages.'

'Typical.' Janine signalled to the waiter. 'Sure you want to give up that perfect body?' she asked Casey as he brought the bill to the table. 'It'll never be the same, you know.'

'That's all right. It's . . .'

'. . . time to move on?' Janine quipped. She divided the amount. 'Fifty-five apiece, including tip.'

'So, what are you up to this weekend?' Casey asked, handing her the appropriate amount of cash.

'I have a date with that banker I went out with last week.' Janine's blue eyes grew opaque with boredom. 'He has tickets for *Jersey Boys*. You know how hard it is to get tickets.'

'Oh, you'll love it,' Casey said. 'It's fabulous. I saw the original on Broadway a few years ago.'

'Of course you did.' Janine smiled as she pushed herself off her chair and onto her feet. 'And this week you'll be with your fabulous husband, making fabulous babies together. I'm sorry,' she said in the same breath. 'I'm being a real bitch. I'm sure I'm PMS-ing.'

'Where are you off to now?' Gail asked Casey as they retrieved their coats from the maître d'.

'I was debating going for a run, but I don't think I have time.' Casey checked her Cartier watch, a second-anniversary gift from her husband.

'Save your energy for tonight,' Janine advised, kissing Casey on the cheek. 'Come on, Gail, I'll give you a ride to work.'

Casey watched her two friends walk down South Street arm in arm, thinking them an interesting study in contrasts: Janine tall and contained, Gail short and spilling out in all directions at once.

Which made her—what? Casey wondered. Maybe she *should* try a more current hairstyle. Although when had long blonde hair ever gone out of fashion? And it suited the soft oval of her face, her fair complexion and delicate features. 'Don't even try to tell me you weren't prom queen,' Janine had said shortly after they met, and Casey had laughed and kept silent. She *had* been prom queen. She'd also been captain of the swimming team, and scored near perfect on her SATs. And her family was almost obscenely wealthy. But her father had been a notorious ladies' man and her mother an alcoholic; then they were killed when their private jet crashed, and her younger sister, a drug-fuelled party girl, became a total screw-up.

It was these thoughts that were absorbing Casey's attention as she walked along South Street and headed towards the parking garage on Washington Avenue. That was the problem with having lunch in this area—it was almost impossible to find a place to park, and once you got away from South Street, you were pretty much in *Rocky* territory.

Casey entered the indoor garage, took the elevator to the fifth floor, and walked to the far end of the platform. She heard the gunning of an engine and looked over her shoulder, but aside from rows of automobiles, she saw nothing. The place was deserted.

She didn't hear the car until it was almost on top of her. She was approaching her Lexus, thumb on the button of the remote, when a silver-coloured SUV came careening round the corner. She had no time to get out of the way. One minute she was walking towards her car, the next she was in the air. Seconds later, she came crashing down, a limp repository of broken bones, her head slamming against the concrete.

Shortly after that, the SUV disappeared into the streets of South Philadelphia, and Casey Marshall slipped into oblivion.

She opened her eyes to darkness.

And not just ordinary darkness, Casey thought, straining to catch even a glimmer of light. It was the blackest black she'd ever seen, as if she'd fallen into a deep underground cave.

Where was she? Why was it so dark?

'Hello? Is anybody there?'

Was she alone? Could anybody hear her?

There was no answer. Casey tried to control the bubble of panic materialising inside her chest. There had to be a logical explanation, she assured herself, refusing to give in to her fear.

'Hello? Can anybody hear me?'

She squinted, then heard Janine's reprimand in the back of her head that squinting caused wrinkles. 'Janine,' she whispered, vaguely recalling their lunch together . . . How long ago?

Not long, Casey decided. Hadn't she just left her? Yes, she'd had lunch with Janine and Gail on South Street—she'd had warm chicken and papaya salad and a glass of pinot grigio—then headed over to retrieve her car. And then what?

And then . . . nothing.

At that precise moment Casey realised she couldn't move. 'What . . . ?' she began, and then the bubble in her chest metastasised into her throat, robbing her of her voice.

She tried to lift her hands but she couldn't feel them. She tried kicking her feet, but she couldn't locate them either. It was as if she was a head without a body. She didn't even know if she was lying down or sitting up, she realised, trying and failing to turn her head.

I've been kidnapped, she thought, still trying to make sense of her situation. Some lunatic had snatched her from the parking garage and buried her alive in his back yard. Hadn't she seen a movie like that a long time ago?

Oh God. Stay calm. Stay calm. Stay calm.

Casey fought to control her ragged breathing. She didn't feel a lack of air, she realised. Nor did she feel cold. Or hot. Or anything.

She felt nothing at all.

Was she dead?

'This can't be happening. It can't be.'

Of course it wasn't happening, she realised with a rush of relief. It was a dream. A nightmare. Now all she had to do was wake herself up. Except she couldn't remember having gone to bed.

'But I must have. I must have.' Obviously, the whole day had been a dream. She hadn't met Rhonda Miller this morning to discuss decorating the Millers' new condominium. She hadn't met her friends for lunch. They hadn't talked about Janine's hair or Richard Mooney. The little twerp, Janine had called him.

Since when had she ever been able to recall her dreams in such vivid detail? Casey wondered. Especially while she was still dreaming them. What kind of nightmare was this?

Wake up, she urged. Then again, aloud, 'Wake up.' She'd read somewhere that you could sometimes jolt yourself awake with a loud scream, which would literally push you to another level of consciousness. '*Wake up!*' she screamed at the top of her lungs, hoping that she wouldn't frighten Warren, who was undoubtedly sleeping beside her in their bed.

Maybe that was why she couldn't move. Maybe Warren had draped his body across her side. Warren Marshall was almost six feet tall and 185 pounds of muscle.

No, she realised, Warren wasn't here. Nobody was here. And she wasn't dreaming. 'Somebody, please help me,' she cried.

Her words echoed in her ears, causing only a few ripples in the overwhelming silence that surrounded her. Casey lay in her black hole, waiting, and cried into the void.

She fell asleep and dreamed she was a child playing golf with her father. She was only ten the first time he'd taken her to Merion Golf Club, the exclusive private course where he'd spent hours working to perfect her swing. She was twelve the first time she broke a hundred, fifteen the first time she broke ninety, twenty when she got the first of her two hole-in-ones. She offered to help her younger sister with her game, but Drew had turned her down flat, preferring to storm off the course in a snit. 'Let her go,' she could hear her father say. 'You're the athlete in the family, Casey.'

'OK, can somebody bring me up-to-date, please?' Casey heard her father say now.

Casey felt the air around her head begin to swirl.

'Yes, Dr Peabody,' her father said.

Who was Dr Peabody? Dr Marcus was their family physician, and had been ever since she could remember. So who was this Dr Peabody? And what was he doing in her dream?

It was then that Casey realised she was no longer asleep, and that the voice she'd been hearing belonged not to her deceased father but to someone who was alive and well and standing not very far away. She opened her eyes. It was still pitch-black. But at least she wasn't alone, and the voices were definitely close at hand.

'I'm over here,' she shouted.

'The patient,' someone answered, ignoring her outburst, 'is a thirty-two-year-old woman who was the victim of a hit-and-run accident three weeks ago. March the 26th to be exact.'

'Hey, you,' Casey called out. 'Dr Peabody! I'm over here.'

'She's on life support, having suffered multiple traumas, including multiple fractures of the pelvis, legs and arms, all of which required extensive surgeries,' the doctor continued. 'The external fixators in her bones will be in place for at least another month, as will the casts on her arms. Doctors discovered a ruptured spleen, and a splenectomy was performed.'

Who was he talking about? Casey wondered. And why was his voice strong one minute, then weak the next? And why did it sound so heavy, as if it were covered in molasses? 'Hey,' she called out.

'Luckily, an MRI determined there was no spinal fracture—'

'"Luck" being an odd choice of words in this case, wouldn't you say, Dr Peabody?' the first voice interrupted. 'Considering the patient might be in a coma for the rest of her life.'

What patient? Casey wondered. Who were these people? Was she in a hospital? How had she got here? And why couldn't anybody hear her?

'Yes, sir. I didn't mean to suggest—'

'Dr Benson, would you like to continue?'

Dr Benson? Who is Dr Benson?

'The patient had a subdural haemorrhage,' another voice said, 'and Dr Jarvis drilled a burr hole into the skull to remove the blood from just beneath the skull bone, in order to let it drain.'

'And the prognosis?'

'Generally good, especially when the patient is young and in as good physical condition as Mrs Marshall . . .'

Mrs Marshall? 'Excuse me, but that's *my* name.' Who were they talking about? Was there another Mrs Marshall?

'. . . But the patient sustained a major concussion, which led to a coma. MRIs show the subdural haemorrhaging is clearing up, but the shock to the brain continues. It's too early to know if the damage is permanent. The patient's brain has been rocked, as they say.'

'Who says that?' Casey demanded, indignant at the casual brutality of the assessment. Some poor woman was in a coma.

'How long do you estimate she'll remain on life support?'

'The patient's body is functioning, so we know her brain is functioning, albeit at a decreased level. Casey Marshall could be on the ventilator for years or she could wake up tomorrow.'

'Casey Marshall?' Casey repeated incredulously.

'Is the fact she opened her eyes yesterday of any significance?'

'Unfortunately not. It's an involuntary action, as is blinking. She can't see anything, despite the fact her pupils are reacting to light.'

'And the trach tube, Dr Zarb?'

'She's been on it for more than a couple of weeks. A tracheotomy should be performed, or the tube will erode the trachea.'

Dr Zarb? Dr Benson? Dr Peabody? How many doctors were there? Why couldn't she see any of them? She wasn't the woman they were talking about, this poor unfortunate in a coma. Possibly for years. Possibly for the rest of her life. *No! It can't be.* It was too awful to think about. *How can I be in a coma if I can hear you?*

'We do an incision in the neck,' Dr Zarb continued. 'If the patient is later able to breathe without the ventilator, we remove the tube and let the trach close up.'

'Is there much chance of that happening in this case, Dr Ein?'

'Impossible to say at this point. As we've said, the patient has several things going for her: Casey Marshall is young. She's very fit. And don't forget she's Ronald Lerner's daughter. For those of you too young to remember, he was a businessman of dubious moral character who died in a plane crash a number of years back. He left the bulk of his very sizable estate to the woman you see before you. Casey Marshall will be able to afford the best in private medical care.'

This isn't happening. I have to get out of here.

'Any more questions?' someone asked. Casey thought it might be Dr

Ein, but the voices were getting difficult to distinguish from one another.

'When can the peg tube come out?'

'Not until the patient can eat on her own,' came the response, so Casey concluded there must be some kind of feeding tube connected to her stomach.

I want to go home. Please, just let me go home.

'And the antibiotic drip?'

'Not for at least another week. The patient is very susceptible to infection. Any other questions before we move on?'

Yes! You have to explain everything: the accident, how I got here, what's going to happen to me. You can't just walk away and leave me alone in the dark. I can hear you! You have to come back.

'Dr Ein,' someone said.

'Yes, Dr Benson.'

'The patient seems to be in distress. Her heart rate is up.'

'It's possible she's experiencing some pain. We'll increase the Dilaudid, Demerol and Ativan. That should make her more comfortable. All right, let's go.'

No. Wait—there's been a huge mistake. I have to make you understand that I'm not in a coma. God, please, make these people understand that I can hear them. If you do that, I promise I'll be a better person. A better wife, a better friend, a better sister. Please. I'm so afraid. I don't want to spend the rest of my life lying here, not being able to see, or move, or speak. Please.

Casey felt her thoughts begin to wobble and disperse. She was suddenly very woozy. Dilaudid, Demerol, Ativan. She felt her eyes close. Seconds later, she was asleep.

'Casey,' she heard someone say softly. 'Wake up, sweetheart.'

Reluctantly, Casey felt herself being dragged into consciousness. She opened her eyes, saw her husband looming over her, his handsome features distorted by the proximity of his face to hers. 'What's going on?' she asked, trying to clear her mind of the dream she'd been having, and noting that the clock beside their bed said 3:00 a.m.

'There's someone in the house,' Warren whispered, casting a worried glance over his shoulder. 'They might have got in through a window. I tried calling 911, but the lines are dead.'

'Oh God.' Casey followed his gaze through the darkness.

'It's all right. I have the gun.' He held it up, its barrel glistening in the reflection of the half-moon outside their window.

Casey sat up, her pulse quickening. 'What do we do?'

'We hide in the closet and lock the door. If anyone opens it, I shoot first and ask questions later.'

'That's awful,' Casey said, in Gail's voice. 'Does anybody really talk like that?'

'They do on TV,' Warren answered.

What? What's going on? What TV?

'I don't think I saw this one,' Gail said.

What is Gail doing in our bedroom?

'I don't think anybody did. Looks like one of those straight-to-video numbers. But the doctors seem to think keeping the TV on might stimulate Casey's brain, and frankly, it helps pass the time.'

'It's almost one,' Gail said. 'Have you had any lunch?'

'One of the nurses brought me coffee. I'm not very hungry.'

'You have to eat, Warren. You have to keep up your strength.'

'They're getting closer. I hear them on the stairs. We don't have time.'

Who's on the stairs? What's happening?

'Get under the bed. Hurry.'

'I'm not going anywhere without you.'

Who are these people?

'Enough of that crap,' Warren said.

A clicking sound. Then silence.

What was happening? Casey wondered, startled to realise she didn't know whether her eyes were open or closed. Had she been asleep? Why couldn't she distinguish between what was real and what wasn't? Were these people *her* Warren, *her* Gail?

'Her colour's better,' Gail said. 'Has there been any change?'

'The doctors think she might be experiencing more pain. Patients in deep comas still experience pain,' Warren said, his voice flat. 'How fair is that?'

This was definitely *her* Warren, Casey thought, recognising the familiar rhythms of his voice. *Oh, Warren. You've found me. I knew you wouldn't let me stay in this awful, dark place.*

'I can't believe this is Casey,' Gail was saying. 'The last time I saw her, she looked so beautiful, so full of life.'

'She's still the most beautiful girl in the world,' he said.

Casey pictured his eyes filling with tears and knew he was fighting to keep them from falling.

'I don't even remember what we talked about at lunch that day,' Gail said. 'I didn't realise it might be our last time together.'

'This must bring back painful memories,' Warren said.

Casey pictured Gail lifting both shoulders in a gentle shrug, then tucking a few wayward curls behind her right ear. 'Mike was in a hospice for two months before he died,' Gail said, talking about the husband she'd lost to leukaemia five years earlier. 'There wasn't anything anybody could do but watch him fade away.'

'Casey isn't going to die,' Warren insisted. 'I won't even consider taking her off life support.'

'Taking her off life support? When did the doctors suggest that?'

'They haven't. They agree it's way too early to be thinking that way.'

'Of course it is. Then who?'

'Who do you think?'

'Oh. I didn't realise Drew had been here lately.'

My sister's been here?

'Are you kidding? She hasn't been here since right after the accident. Says she can't bear seeing her sister in this condition. She called last night for an update, then demanded to know how long I was going to let Casey suffer. She said there's no way Casey would want to be a vegetable, kept alive by tubes and ventilators.'

'That's only until she starts breathing on her own,' Gail said forcefully. 'Casey will get through this. Her body will repair itself. We should be grateful that she doesn't know what's going on . . .'

Except she did know, Casey was forced to acknowledge, as the direness of her predicament suddenly reasserted itself, spreading through the dark space around her like a nasty stain.

'No! No! No!' she shouted, unable to block out the horrifying truth that she was trapped in a coma that cruelly enabled her to hear but not see, to think but not communicate, to exist but not act. Hell, she couldn't even breathe without the help of a machine. Was she doomed to spend the rest of her days in this dark, free-floating limbo, unable to distinguish between what was real and imagined? How many days, weeks, months, years—God forbid, years!—could she lie here, not being able to reach out to those she loved?

The patient's brain has been rocked.

For that matter, how long would it be before her friends stopped visiting her, before even her husband moved on? Gail rarely talked about Mike any more. And Warren was only thirty-seven. He might hover over her for a year or two, but eventually he'd be lulled back into everyday life. She'd be carted off to some rehab facility, abandoned in a distant corner of a stale-smelling corridor, propped up in a wheelchair. How long before she went mad from frustration and rage?

Or she could wake up tomorrow.

'I could wake up tomorrow,' Casey repeated. Maybe the fact she could hear was a sign that she was on the road to recovery. Her eyes had opened. Maybe tomorrow the darkness would lift. Maybe once the tube was out of her mouth—Was it out already? Had the doctors performed the tracheotomy?—she'd regain the use of her vocal cords. She was already getting better at being able to distinguish between outside voices. Maybe she was really improving.

Or maybe this was as good as it was ever going to get. In which case, her sister was right. She'd rather be dead.

'Do the police have any new leads?' she heard Gail ask.

'Not that I know of,' Warren said. 'No auto-body shops reporting vehicles brought in with the kind of damage you'd expect. No witnesses. It seems the car that hit her has vanished into thin air.'

'How could somebody do something so awful? I mean, it was bad enough he hit her, but to just leave her like that . . .'

Casey imagined Warren shaking his head. She saw his soft brown hair fall across his forehead and into his darker brown eyes. 'Maybe the driver had been drinking. Probably he panicked. Who knows?'

A silence.

'I remember something we talked about at lunch,' Gail said suddenly, her voice tinged with sadness. 'Casey said the two of you had been talking about having a baby.'

'Yeah, she was all excited. A little nervous, too, of course. I guess because of her mother.'

'Yes, her mother was quite something.'

'Casey almost never talks about her.'

'There wasn't much to say. Alana Lerner was the kind of woman who never should have had children. It's a wonder Casey turned out so well,' Gail said, and then started to cry. 'I'm sorry.'

'Don't be. I know how much you love her.'

'Did you know she was my maid of honour? I married right out of high school, and Mike was ten years older, just diagnosed with leukaemia. Everybody told me I was going to ruin my life, everybody except Casey.'

'She's going to get better, Gail.'

'You promise?' Gail asked.

Before Warren could answer, Casey heard the sudden opening of a door, the approach of sturdy shoes. 'I'm afraid we're going to have to ask you to leave for a few minutes,' a female voice announced. 'We have to give the patient a sponge bath, adjust her position so she doesn't get bedsores.'

'We shouldn't be more than ten minutes,' a second voice added.

'Why don't we eat something in the cafeteria,' Gail said.

'All right,' Warren agreed, reluctance in his voice.

'Don't worry, Mr Marshall,' the first nurse told him. 'Patsy and I will take good care of your wife.'

'I'll be back soon, Casey,' Warren said.

'Donna, that is one lovely man,' Patsy proclaimed as the door shut behind them. 'My heart goes out to him. OK, Mrs Marshall, let's get you all cleaned up for that handsome husband of yours.'

Casey heard the rustle of sheets and, although she felt nothing, she'd never felt more exposed. Was she wearing a hospital gown? Was she wearing anything at all?

'How long do you think he's going to stick around?' Donna said. 'Soon as he realises she's not going to get any better . . .'

'Ssh. Don't say that,' Patsy admonished.

'What? She can't hear me.'

'You don't know that for sure. She opened her eyes, didn't she?'

'That doesn't mean anything. I heard one of the doctors say when they open their eyes, it's often a bad sign. It could signify the beginning of a profound vegetative state.'

To them she was already an inanimate object, Casey thought. A body to be rotated regularly so it didn't develop bedsores, and washed, so that it didn't start to smell. No more, no less.

'You want to help me turn her on her side?' Donna said.

Casey felt her body being manipulated, her head placed at a different angle, although she couldn't be sure if this was really happening or just part of her imagination.

'OK, I'm finished,' Donna said after several minutes.

'I think I'll brush her hair. You don't have to stay.'

'Suit yourself.'

'We'll just get you all prettied up for that devoted husband of yours,' Patsy said as Donna left the room. 'Although, you gotta wonder,' she continued, her voice shedding its softness with the closing of the door. 'I mean, he is a man, after all. A drop-dead gorgeous man at that. Not to mention a very rich, drop-dead gorgeous man.' She laughed. 'How long do you think it'll take me to get him into bed? Wanna bet? Ten bucks? A hundred? Hell, let's make it a thousand. You can afford it.'

'Patsy,' Donna called from the door. 'They need us in 307.'

'Sure thing,' Patsy responded cheerily. 'I'm done.'

2

CASEY WAS THREE years old when she found out that the beautiful lady with the waist-length blonde hair was her mother and not just a mysterious woman named Alana who always had a glass in her hand, and who slept in her father's bed.

'Here, Casey, sweetheart. Can you take this drink upstairs to your mama? I'm on the phone, and they've got me on hold.'

'My mama?' the child asked. Who was Maya talking about? Maya hadn't been living with them very long. It was possible she still didn't know everyone.

'The pretty blonde lady who's married to your father?' Maya said, as if Casey should know. 'The one who stays in bed all day?' she added with a laugh. Then her normally pale complexion reddened. 'Don't you dare tell your mother I said that.'

Casey took the glass of clear liquid and ice cubes and raised it to her nose. 'What is it?'

'Water.'

Casey lifted the glass to her mouth.

Maya quickly snatched it back. 'What are you doing? I'll get you your own drink.' She was instantly at the sink, pouring Casey a small glass of tepid water.

'Why can't I have some of *that* water?' Casey said pointing.

'Because it's not good to drink from anybody else's glass.'

Even at the tender age of three, Casey knew she was being lied to. Just as she knew Maya was making up what she'd said about the beautiful woman upstairs being her mother. Not that Casey knew what a mother was exactly. Her only experience had come at the park, when a woman with messy brown hair had played in the sandbox with a little boy.

'Are you new around here?' Maya had said to the woman, leading Casey over to the sandbox. 'Who do you work for?'

The woman looked puzzled. 'I'm not his nanny. I'm his mother.'

'Really?' Maya sounded very surprised. 'I think you're the first actual mother I've ever seen in this park.'

'What's an "actual mother"?' Casey asked later, struggling to keep up with her nanny as they made their way home. Maya laughed and said nothing, so Casey let the question die. But she knew the woman who slept in her father's bed couldn't be an actual mother. She had sweet-smelling yellow hair she was always combing, and she never set foot in a sandbox. She rarely left her room, and when she did, it was at night. 'Come kiss Alana good night,' her father would instruct Casey as they prepared to go out for the evening.

'You look pretty,' she'd say to the woman offering her smooth cheek to be pecked. Once Casey had made the mistake of throwing her arms round the woman's neck, and the woman had gasped and quickly pushed her aside. 'Watch my hair,' she'd cautioned.

'What are you waiting for?' Maya was asking now. 'Take this upstairs.' Once again, she deposited the cold glass in Casey's hand. 'And don't take a sip. You understand?'

Casey nodded, walking slowly to the giant circular staircase in the main foyer. It was very quiet as she made her way up to the bedroom door. She knocked gently.

'It's about time,' the woman inside snapped. 'What the hell have you been doing all morning?'

Casey stepped inside. The woman named Alana was sitting up in her dark oak four-poster bed, surrounded by lace pillows. The heavy brocade curtains were closed. Alana was wearing a pink negligee and her hair fell past her shoulders. 'Oh,' she said. 'It's you.'

'I have your water.' Casey extended the glass.

'Well, bring it over here. Do you think my arms are eight feet long?'

'Are you sick?' Casey watched her take a long sip.

Alana said nothing, not even 'Thank you.'

'Are you my mother?'

'Of course I'm your mother. What's the matter with you?'

Her mother finished the remaining liquid in her glass. Then she pushed away her blankets and swung her feet off the bed. 'Help me to the bathroom,' she said.

Casey noted her expanded, round belly. 'You're fat!'

'Don't be a smart-ass.'

Casey led her to the bathroom. 'What's a smart-ass?'

'It's little girls who say stupid things.'

Casey felt stung by the rebuke, so she said nothing further.

Alana proceeded to throw up in the toilet, then she returned to her bed. 'Send Maya up with another drink,' she said.

'Your mother's going to have a baby,' Maya explained later. 'I don't think she's too happy about it.'

'Why not?'

'I don't think motherhood's exactly her thing.'

'What's her thing?' Casey asked, not sure what they were talking about, as was often the case when she talked to Maya. Still, Maya was the only adult in the house who regularly paid her any attention at all, so Casey hoped the question wasn't too stupid.

'Your mother is a very complicated woman,' Maya said, refusing to elaborate.

'I wish you were my mother,' Casey told her.

And then suddenly, Maya was gone, replaced by Shauna, a teenager whose job it was to tend to Casey, and Lesley, a bosomy ex-barmaid who was supposed to look after the new baby, but who spent more time looking after Casey's father. Lesley was quickly replaced by Rosie, and she, too, soon disappeared, to be replaced by Kelly, then Misha, and finally Daniela.

'Your father's a lot older than your mother,' Shauna remarked one day as she was walking Casey to her private preschool.

'Seventeen years.' Casey wasn't sure how she knew this. Probably she'd overheard grown-ups whispering as if she weren't there. That was how she learned from Kelly her father was a 'scoundrel' who 'ran after anything that moved', and that her parents were 'filthy rich', despite the fact they bathed every day.

'You wouldn't think someone in a coma could get so dirty,' Casey heard someone say now, the remark jolting her out of her reveries. How long had she been asleep?

'It's just dead skin,' another voice said. Donna and Patsy. Hadn't they just bathed her? Hadn't they just left?

'Where's your handsome husband today?' Donna asked her.

'I haven't seen him in two days,' Patsy said.

Two days? Casey repeated silently. She'd lost two days?

Better than lying here day after endless day, she acknowledged. Although at least her days were filled with activity—people coming in and out, fussing over her, discussing her condition, gossiping about assorted friends and celebrities. Nights were mostly silent, punctuated only by the occasional laugh from the nurses' station or a cry from a nearby room. 'Please, somebody,' she screamed silently, 'just pull the plug. Do something to end this torment. Please.'

'Careful of the tube in her neck,' Patsy said.

OK, calm down. Calm down, Casey told herself, realising the doctors must have performed the tracheotomy.

'It's not the most attractive thing in the world,' Donna said.

'I don't think anybody's too concerned with the way it looks,' Patsy admonished, managing to sound as if she cared.

Was it possible, Casey wondered, that she'd imagined the earlier scene with Patsy, that the young woman hadn't said any of those hateful things?

'She's in good shape, considering what she's been through,' Donna remarked. 'Look at these biceps. She must lift weights.'

'Wish I had the time to work out,' Patsy said.

'You don't need to work out. You have a great body.'

'You really think so?' Patsy said, a smile in her voice.

'You look fantastic, and you know it.'

Casey heard a door open.

'I'm sorry, you can't come in right now,' Donna said sharply.

'Can I help you?' Patsy asked in the next beat.

'I'm looking for Warren Marshall,' a man answered.

'I haven't seen him today,' Donna said.

'I can leave him a message,' Patsy volunteered.

'No, thanks,' the man said brusquely. 'I'll wait a while.'

'Visitors' lounge is down the hall,' Patsy instructed, then said after he was gone, 'I wonder what he wants. He looks like trouble. I wouldn't want to see him upsetting Mr Marshall.'

'You're too sensitive,' Donna commented.

'Nurses are supposed to be sensitive.'

'We're not nurses. We're nurses' aides. OK, I'm finished.'

'OK. All through,' Patsy said as someone knocked on the door. 'You can come in,' she called out. 'We're done.'

Casey wondered what Patsy meant when she said that the man looked like trouble.

'Oh, hi, Mr Marshall,' Patsy said. 'How're you doing today?'

'I'm fine, thank you,' Warren replied. 'How's my wife?'

'About the same.'

'She seems more comfortable,' Donna said, 'since they put that tube in her throat.'

'Yeah.' He approached the bed. 'Hopefully, she'll start breathing on her own soon, and they can take it out.'

'We're rooting for her,' Patsy said.

Casey felt the women gathering their things and heading for the door.

'Oh, there was a man here looking for you,' Donna said. 'We sent him to the visitors' lounge.'

'I can tell him you're here, if you'd like,' Patsy offered.

'I wouldn't want to put you to any trouble.'

'It's no trouble at all, Mr Marshall.' She paused. 'If there's anything you need, anything at all . . .'

'Thank you. You're very kind.'

'I'd be happy to volunteer my services if you require any help once your wife leaves the hospital. My job here is just temporary.'

Oh, you're good. You're good.

'Thank you. I'll certainly consider your offer . . .'

'Patsy,' she told him.

'Patsy,' he repeated. 'Thank you. I know how much Casey would appreciate the kindness you've shown her.'

I wouldn't be too sure about that.

Warren thanked her again as Patsy left the room.

Don't even think about hiring that woman, Casey all but screamed. *I don't want her near me. Can't you see the only thing she wants is you? Even I can see that much, and* I'm *in a coma!*

What was it with men? Were they really so blind when it came to women? 'Men are basically very simple creatures,' Janine had once remarked, and Casey had dismissed it as the cynicism of someone who'd had her hopes dashed one too many times. Was it possible she was right?

'We marry our fathers,' Janine had also pronounced, a remark that had given Casey pause when she felt herself falling in love with Warren. Women made no secret of their attraction to him. She'd actually seen one brazen young woman slip a piece of paper into his hand as he walked past her to the washroom in a crowded restaurant. But seconds later, he'd tossed that paper into a nearby wastepaper basket without even glancing at it. So Warren Marshall was nothing like Ronald Lerner. Nothing like her father at all.

Which meant women like Patsy were of no consequence.

'Let's put the TV on, shall we?' Warren said, clicking it on.

Immediately, other voices filled the room.

'You never loved me,' a woman was saying. 'You've been lying to me from the very beginning.'

'Maybe not from the *very* beginning,' a man answered, a cruel laugh in his voice.

'How're you doing, sweetheart?' Warren asked, back at her side. She wondered if he was patting her hand. She wondered if she'd ever be able to feel again the gentleness of his touch. 'The nurse said you seem more comfortable since they put the tube in.'

They're not nurses. They're nurses' aides. And that one named Patsy. Watch out for her.

'She seems very nice,' he said with a sigh.

He sounds exhausted, Casey thought. As if someone had reached inside his chest and pulled out his heart. How different from the first time he'd walked into the small downtown offices of Lerner, Pegabo, wearing a dark grey suit with a silk burgundy tie, looking tanned and lean, and exuding confidence and energy. 'I have an appointment with Janine Pegabo,' he'd announced.

'You're Warren Marshall?' Casey asked, trying to ignore the quickening of her pulse. 'I'm sorry, but Janine had to leave rather suddenly. She broke a tooth, and the only time the dentist could squeeze her in was . . .' Why was she rambling on? 'I'm Casey Lerner, her partner. She asked me to fill in for her. I hope that's all right.'

'More than all right.' Warren sat in the red velvet chair across from her desk. 'Interesting room,' he said, penetrating brown eyes casually absorbing the leopard-print carpeting, the dark walnut desk, the taupe walls lined with black-and-white photographs of flowers and fruit. 'Who did you use?'

'I'm sorry?'

'The decorator,' he explained with a smile.

'Oh. No decorator. Just me. I did the whole office. It's always been kind of a hobby of mine. How can I help you, Mr Marshall?'

'Well, as I explained to Ms Pegabo on the phone, I've been with Miller, Sheridan for the last five years and I'm looking to make a move. I faxed over a copy of my résumé . . .'

'Yes, it's very impressive. I don't imagine we'll have much trouble finding you a new position. Do you mind me asking you why you want to leave Miller, Sheridan?'

'I'm looking for a firm with more vision, more guts,' he said. 'And I don't want to wait the requisite ten years before being made a full partner.'

Casey glanced back at his résumé: Warren Marshall had attended Princeton on a full scholarship and graduated Columbia in the top third of his class; his area of expertise was corporate and commercial law; he was pulling in a salary of several hundred thousand dollars a year. 'I'm not sure I can get you more money than you're getting now, at least to start out.'

'Sure you can,' he said with a smile.

He was a little arrogant, but that was all right, Casey decided. Providing there was something to be arrogant about. She found herself checking out his ring finger and was happy to see it was empty, although that didn't necessarily mean anything. What was she doing? This wasn't like her.

'Look. Nobody becomes a lawyer to get rich,' Warren was saying. 'You make more than a decent living, but factor in expenses and taxes and overheads, you're certainly not retiring at forty.'

'Is that what you want to do? Retire at forty?'

'No, that's not me. But sixty doesn't sound so unreasonable.'

They spent the next half-hour talking about his preferences and his politics, his goals and his dreams, all of which were compatible with hers. More than once, they had finished each other's sentences. Surprised at their easy camaraderie, Casey wished she could think of a way to prolong the interview further.

'So, you think you can do something for me?' he asked, pushing back his chair and standing up.

'I can't imagine I'll have too much trouble,' Casey said.

'By the way, will you marry me?' he asked in the next breath.

'What?'

'Sorry. We can start with dinner, if you'd prefer.'

'I don't believe it,' Janine had wailed when she returned to the office an hour later. 'I get a broken tooth; you get a date.'

She got more than that, Casey was thinking now. She got the man of her dreams. Ten months later, they were married.

The door to her hospital room suddenly swung open.

'I found him,' Patsy said, an irritating chirp to her voice.

'Mr Marshall,' a male voice said. 'I'm Detective Spinetti, with the Philadelphia Police Department. How is your wife doing?'

'About the same,' Warren answered. 'You have some news regarding her accident?'

'I'd like to ask you a few questions, if you wouldn't mind.'

'What sort of questions?'

'Do you know what your wife was doing in South Philly the day of the accident?' Detective Spinetti asked immediately.

'She was meeting friends for lunch.'

'Do you know who those friends were?'

'Of course I do. Janine Pegabo and Gail MacDonald.'

Casey listened to the scribbling of a pen.

'They're her best friends,' Warren said. 'I have to ask, how is this relevant to my wife's accident?'

'Actually, we're no longer convinced it *was* an accident.'

'What? What are you saying?'

What do you mean? Someone deliberately ran me down?

'We have reason to believe that your wife might have been deliberately targeted. In reviewing the garage's surveillance tapes—'

'Were you able to get a better look at the driver's face?' Warren interrupted. 'Was it someone you recognise?'

'No, I'm afraid not. The driver wore a hoodie and dark glasses. There was no way to make any positive identification.'

'Then I don't understand. What makes you think someone would have deliberately targeted my wife?' Warren's voice cracked.

'If you'll let me explain,' the detective began.

'I'm sorry. Of course. Go ahead.' Warren apologised.

Casey heard the sound of chairs being adjusted and occupied, Warren in one, the police officer right beside him.

'Unfortunately, the parking garage has been around for ever,' Detective Spinetti said, 'and the security cameras are on their last legs. So all we knew for certain was that the vehicle was a late-model Ford SUV, probably silver in colour. We were able to get a partial plate, as you know. But after we ran the plates, we discovered they were phoney. That, plus the fact your wife's father ruffled more than a few feathers in his day . . . It got us thinking this might not have been a simple case of hit-and-run. So we looked at the tapes again, both at the exit *and* the entrance to the garage, to see if we could spot the SUV when it arrived. We saw your wife drive in just before noon and the car that hit her drive in within seconds.'

Within seconds. What does that mean?

'You're saying you think she was being followed?'

'It's an awfully big coincidence if she wasn't. Think about it, Mr Marshall. Your wife enters the parking garage at noon, followed immediately by the same SUV that runs her down several hours later.'

'Good God,' Warren whispered.

'Can you think of anyone who might have wanted to hurt your wife, Mr Marshall?'

'No one. Casey is a wonderful woman. Everybody loves her.'

'Perhaps a jealous former boyfriend . . .'

Casey felt Warren shaking his head.

'Your wife's an interior decorator. Any unhappy customers?'

'You fire your decorator if you're unhappy, Detective. You don't run her down.'

'Still, I'd appreciate a list of all her clients.'

'I'll have it for you first thing in the morning,' Warren said.

'What about the people who work for her? Any disgruntled employees, someone she had to let go recently?'

'Casey worked alone. The business was relatively new. She used to run a lawyer placement service with Janine Pegabo, but they went their separate ways about a year ago.'

'Why was that?'

'Casey just wanted to try other things. She'd always been interested in design . . . Janine was understandably upset, but she certainly wouldn't have tried to kill Casey because of it.'

'Do you know what kind of car she drives, Mr Marshall?'

'Uh, a Toyota, I think.'

It's a Nissan. But it's red, not silver.

'And it's red. Janine always drives a red car.'

'What about Gail MacDonald?'

'I have no idea what kind of car she drives.'

It's a Ford Malibu, and it's white.

'Gail is the gentlest person on earth,' Warren said. 'I've actually seen her scoop up an ant in a tissue and carry it outside rather than kill it. There's no way she'd hurt Casey.'

'I'm just covering all the bases,' the detective replied obliquely. 'You said that your wife ran a lawyer placement service. Any lawyers she might have angered?'

'I honestly can't think of anyone who'd have been angry enough to try to kill her. Maybe you should talk to Janine about that.'

Wait a minute. There was the little twerp, Richard Mooney. But would he really try to kill me because his job placement hadn't worked out?

'Is there anyone who would profit by your wife's death? It's no secret your wife is a very wealthy woman,' said Spinetti.

'Her sister probably inherits her estate,' Warren answered after a moment's thought. 'To tell you the truth, I'm not sure.'

'You're not sure? You're a lawyer . . .'

'I'm not Casey's lawyer, Detective.'

'You mention a sister . . .'

'Casey's younger sister, Drew.'

'Were they close?'

'Not especially.'

'Mind my asking why?'

Another moment's thought, then, 'Even though she was extremely well provided for,' Warren said carefully, 'Drew resented her father naming Casey executor of his estate. Drew isn't the most responsible person on the planet. She's had her share of problems with drugs and alcohol.'

'Do you know what kind of car she drives?'

'I have no idea. She trades them in almost as often as she changes boyfriends. But look, although Drew may be a flake, and she has issues, there's no way she'd hurt Casey.'

'Any idea who she's seeing now?' the detective asked.

'I think his name is Sean. Sorry, his last name escapes me.'

'So you wouldn't know what kind of car this Sean drives.'

'Sorry, no. But again, you can't think . . .'

'I'm just gathering information, Mr Marshall.'

'In that case, I imagine you'll want to know *my* whereabouts on the afternoon my wife was run down.'

What? No!

'You understand I have to ask.'

I understand no such thing.

'I also understand the husband is always the prime suspect in cases like this. But I'm on the verge of being made a full partner with one of the city's premier law firms, and I make a very substantial living. I've never been interested in my wife's fortune. And I was in my office at the time, conferring with a client. I'll be happy to provide you with a list of people who will verify I didn't leave my desk all day, not even for lunch. I was there when the hospital called . . .' His voice cracked again.

'Do you hold any life insurance policies on your wife?'

'No.'

'That doesn't sound very lawyerly.'

'Lawyers are notoriously lax when it comes to their own affairs. Besides, Casey is young, she was in excellent health, and we don't have children. I guess we both assumed there was lots of time to talk about those things.' His voice drifted into the air. 'Detective, if I could change places with her, I would. I love her so much.'

Oh, Warren. I love you, too. More than you'll ever know.

Warren pushed back his chair. The sound of another chair being pushed back.

'You'll keep me informed?' Warren said.

'Count on it. We'll just take it one day at a time.'

One day at a time, Casey thought after they were both gone. One day at a time, she repeated wordlessly as the noises of the day dimmed into the whimpers of the night.

Someone deliberately ran me down, she was thinking as sleep began circling her brain. *Someone is trying to kill me.*

Somebody wants me dead. Who?

'Where were you on the night in question?' a man asked suddenly.

Detective Spinetti?

'I was home all night,' another man answered.

Who's that? Is someone here?

'Was anyone with you?'

'No. I was alone.'

I don't understand. Who are you? What are you talking about?

Then suddenly she did understand. There was no one in the room. She was alone, just like the man being questioned on her TV.

She'd imagined everything.

The entire episode had been nothing but a combination of dreams and television reruns, something her mind had cooked up. No one had tried to kill her. There was no Detective Spinetti. Her brain had been rocked! That's what the doctors had said. Or maybe that was something else her imagination had invented.

How could she be sure of anything?

Wake up. This stopped making sense a long time ago.

A car didn't run me down. I'm not lying, broken and comatose, in some hospital. There is no tube in my trachea. I did not hear a nurse's aide confide she intended to seduce my husband. I did not hear a police detective speculate that everyone I hold dear, even the husband I adore, is a suspect.

I did not. I did not. I did not. Casey lay in her bed, unseeing eyes open towards the ceiling.

'**S**o you missed the film festival this year,' Janine said, jolting Casey back to consciousness.

How long had she been asleep? When had Janine arrived? What was she talking about?

'But not to worry. You picked a good time to be brain-dead. The movies were crap. I saw one last night, and you would not believe how bad it was,' Janine said.

Casey tried to focus. If the city's modest attempt at a film festival had just ended, it meant it was still April. How much time had she lost since Janine's last visit?

'Anyway, I brought a newspaper. The doctors said it would be a good idea to read to you, that it might stimulate your brain. But there doesn't seem to be a whole lot going on that's very stimulating.'

Don't worry. I've been having the most extraordinary hallucinations.

'Let's see. Did you know that since the 1960s, Philadelphia has lost approximately six hundred thousand residents, due to urban blight, and there are sixty thousand derelict buildings throughout the city? Is this stimulating? Blink twice if the answer is yes.'

I'm blinking. Once. Twice. Did you see that?

'Not seeing any blinks, so not very stimulating. Let's see, what amazing things are you going to miss in May if you don't snap out of this ridiculous coma?'

Casey heard the rustling of paper. Or was her imagination providing the sound effects? Was Janine even there?

'OK, so there's the Dad Vail Regatta, which draws thousands of rowers and spectators to the Schuylkill River every year. Something I'm sure you wouldn't want to miss. And May is the month Philadelphia opens up its historic homes for public viewing. Your house is pretty historic, wouldn't you say? Ever consider all those people wanting to see exactly where and how Ronald Lerner lived? Although the truth is never as exciting as one's imagination, is it?'

Believe me, Janine. You have no idea.

'Anyway, I spoke to that police detective again. How come the policemen on TV all look like the guy off *Sex and the City*, and in real life they look like Detective Spinetti?'

He's real? I didn't dream him?

'He told me he questioned Richard Mooney, who claims he was visiting his mother at the time of your accident. Although Spinetti clearly doesn't think it *was* an accident. Anyway, Mooney's mother backs him up, although Spinetti says the police don't exactly trust mothers when it comes to alibis. They still haven't eliminated him as a suspect, especially since—get this—he owns a silver SUV. Although you'd think if he was going to kill anyone, it would have been me. I'm the one he had the fight with. But then, you always were the chosen one, weren't you?'

Casey pictured Janine's dazzling smile.

'Anyway, Spinetti asked a million questions about Drew. Apparently he's left a dozen messages on her voicemail, but she hasn't answered them. I said welcome to the club. He asked if I thought she was capable of trying to kill you. I told him, honestly, who knows with Drew? And, of course, he asked about Warren.'

'Are you talking about that detective?' Gail asked from the doorway.

'Oh, hi,' Janine said, her voice receding as she swivelled round in her chair. 'How long have you been standing there?'

'Just a few seconds. How's Casey doing today?'

'Not much change.'

The sound of footsteps approaching, the air growing heavy above Casey's head, a gentle laugh.

'Her colour's good,' said Gail.

'If you like the colour of skimmed milk. Has he talked to you?'

'Spinetti? I assume he's talking to everyone close to Casey.'

'He ask you about Warren?'

'I told him he was way off base. I said the same thing when he asked about your relationship with Casey.'

'What a jerk. Anyway, how was your date last night?'

'It was nice,' Gail said shyly, giggling softly. 'You know.'

'I don't know. "Nice" is not part of my vocabulary.'

'I had a good time. You're worse than Detective Spinetti.'

'How good a time?' Janine pressed.

'Really nice.' Gail sighed. 'But I feel like such a traitor.'

'Why would you feel like a traitor?'

'Because our best friend is lying here in a coma . . .'

'The last thing she'd want is for us to sit at home moping. If nothing else, what happened to Casey proves that we never know how long we've got on this earth, and that we have a duty to enjoy ourselves when we have the chance.'

Is that what it proved? Casey wondered, before deciding Janine was probably right.

'So, tell me about this guy,' continued Janine. 'What's he like?'

'He's just a guy.'

'Does he have a name?'

'Does it matter? You don't know him.'

'You're being very opaque. Did you meet him at work?'

'No.'

'Why won't you tell me who he is?'

'Because . . .'

'Because you *like* him, don't you?' Janine pounced.

Casey felt the burn in Gail's cheeks as if she herself were the one blushing. 'I don't know. We've only been on one date. He probably won't even call me again.'

'Why wouldn't he call you again? Were you too easy? Did you sleep with him already?'

'Of course not. Honestly, Janine. Can we talk about something else?'

'You're such a prude sometimes,' Janine said.

'I'm not a prude.'

'Are too.'

'Am not.'

Both women laughed, the tension in the room dissipating.

'Anyway, I should get going,' Janine said, jumping to her feet. 'Maybe next time I come, I'll bring a book so I can read to Casey. I think I'll bring *Middlemarch*. She hated that book in college.'

'Then why on earth would you bring it?'

'Because maybe if she has to listen to it again, she'll wake up, just so she can tell me to shut up.'

'You're crazy.'

'No argument there. Anyway I'm off. See you, Casey.'

'**H**i, sweetheart. How are you feeling today? Did you have a good sleep?'

Casey felt Warren's velvety voice curling up against her eardrum, like a kitten in a basket. How long had she been asleep this time? she wondered, coming fully awake, her heart pounding as the familiar panic overtook her, although she remained outwardly still. She heard him pull up a chair.

'The doctors think you might be ready to start breathing on your own,' he said. 'They're going to start trying to wean you off the ventilator, which is really wonderful news.'

Is it? Casey wondered. What difference did it make if she was breathing on her own if she still couldn't see or move or talk?

'Everybody keeps calling. Friends, neighbours, business associates.'

Except for one rather glaring exception.

'I think you're single-handedly keeping the florists in this city in business. Janine and Gail send a fresh arrangement every week. This week it's a bunch of white and pink tulips. And there's a vase of spectacular spring flowers from the partners at my firm. Not to mention a dozen red roses from yours truly, which are beautiful.'

There was a gentle knock on the door.

'Sorry for interrupting,' Patsy apologised sweetly. 'I saw you come in, and I thought I'd see how you were doing.'

'I'm OK, thanks,' Warren said.

'You look a little tired.'

'Not getting much sleep these days.'

'It doesn't get any easier, does it? Seeing her this way,' Patsy continued, as Casey felt the nurse's aide edging her way into the room, the scent of lavender following her.

Could she really smell lavender? Casey wondered, sniffing madly at the air. Or was it just all that talk about flowers triggering her already overactive imagination?

'That Detective Spinetti was back again,' Patsy went on, 'asking a lot of questions.'

'Such as?'

'Who comes to visit, if we've observed anything suspicious. I told him the only thing I've seen is a lot of really sad people with love in their hearts. Casey must have been a very special woman.'

'She still is,' Warren corrected.

'Of course. I'm so sorry. I didn't mean . . .'

'I know you didn't. I'm sorry. I didn't mean to snap at you. It's just that this whole thing was bad enough when we thought it was an accident. To think that someone might have deliberately . . . It's just so unbeliev-able, seeing her so still. Casey is always so animated, so full of life.'

'Tell me about her.' Patsy managed to sound as if she cared.

Warren laughed softly. 'Well, she's beautiful. You can see that, even in her condition. And I don't mean just on the outside. And she's funny, too. We used to laugh so much.'

It's true, Casey thought. We used to laugh all the time.

'And she's sensitive. Strong, smart, sexy. I miss her so much.'

Casey felt Patsy approach, pictured her laying a gentle hand on War-ren's shoulder. 'If she's half as strong and smart as you think she is, she'll find her way back to you.'

'Thank you,' Warren said.

'Can I get you anything? A cup of coffee? Something to eat?'

'Coffee would be wonderful. Let me give you some money.'

'No, don't be silly. It's my treat. Be right back.'

Casey wondered what kind of uniform Patsy was wearing, if the fabric flattered her figure. She wondered how young she was, and if Warren thought she was pretty.

'Nice girl,' Warren said after she was gone. 'Not bad-looking, although clearly her mother never taught her the fine art of applying mascara.' Casey heard him swivel in his chair. 'Let's see. What else can I tell you? You're missing a beautiful day. Sunshine, about seventy-four degrees. Everyone keeps trying to talk me into playing some golf. I can't quite bring myself to play, what with you lying here like this. "You can't stay at the hospital all day," they tell me. But everything seems so frivolous.'

Although she doubted any tears actually formed, Casey felt her eyes fill with tears.

'Anyway, Ted Bates—you remember him, we had dinner with him and his wife a few months back—he's trying to get me out to play a few holes. I said I'd think about it. God knows I could use the exercise. I haven't been to the gym since . . . Hell. What am I talking about? I'm not going near a golf course until you can go with me. Although this would probably be a good time for me to practise.' He tried to laugh. 'That way when you wake up, I can surprise you with my newfound prowess.' The laugh emerged as a strangled cry. 'Casey. I miss you.'

I miss you, too.

Another gentle knock on the door.

'I'm sorry,' Warren said. 'I didn't realise you were there.'

'I didn't want your coffee to get cold,' Patsy said.

So now even her most intimate moments with her husband were no longer hers alone, Casey thought. Her heart sank.

I *will* find my way back to you, she cried silently. *I will. I will.*

3

'I CAN'T BELIEVE you told that cop you think I tried to kill my sister!' Drew cried loudly.

What?

'I told him no such thing,' Warren protested.

'I get home from my holiday to find half the damn police force camped out in the lobby of my condominium. You'd think I was Osama bin Laden, for Pete's sake. And then to be practically accused of trying to kill my own sister! My sister!'

'I'm really sorry . . .'

'How could you accuse me of such a thing?'

'Drew,' Warren said, 'I didn't accuse you of anything.'

Casey heard the resignation in his voice. You could never win an argument with Drew. She thought back to the day, three months shy of her fourth birthday, when her sister was born.

'What kind of name is Drew anyway?' Lesley had scoffed when they brought her home from the hospital. Lesley was the new baby's recently hired nanny, a young woman with round, ruddy cheeks and spiky brown hair.

'She was supposed to be Andrew,' came the knowing response from Shauna, the girl hired to take care of Casey after Maya's abrupt departure. Casey wasn't overly fond of Shauna.

'Instead they got another stinking girl,' Lesley remarked carelessly, as if Casey weren't in the room.

Casey stood between the two young women in Drew's blue-and-white nursery. 'She isn't stinky,' Casey protested. 'She smells better than you do.'

Lesley laughed. 'You saying you don't like my perfume?'

'It smells yucky.'

'It smells *musky*. And your father likes it just fine.'

'Careful,' Shauna warned. 'That kind of talk can get a girl fired.'

Lesley shrugged dismissively, laying Drew on her back in her crib. Casey watched two tiny arms and legs immediately shoot into the air. The baby's face contorted, and her mouth opened in a shrill scream that pierced the air. 'What an awful sound,' Lesley said.

'Maybe she's hungry,' Casey volunteered.

'I just gave her a bottle. Maybe it's time for your nap.'

'I don't take naps any more.'

'What is the matter with this baby?' Lesley said to Shauna. 'She cries all the time.'

'I think she might be suffering from foetal alcohol syndrome. It's something babies get from their mother's drinking,' Shauna whispered, although Casey had no trouble hearing every word.

'Yeah, that mother's a real piece of work, isn't she? No wonder her husband plays around.'

'Shhh,' Shauna warned, eyes lowering towards Casey.

'I think she wants to be held,' Casey said to Lesley.

'Oh, you do, do you? Do you want to hold her, then?' She lifted the screaming infant from her crib and handed her to Casey.

Casey carried her baby sister, whose wet face was now a furious red ball, into a corner of the room, and gingerly lowered herself onto the soft blue carpeting, Drew's loud wails rising, like steam, towards the ceiling. 'It's OK, baby,' she said softly. 'I'm here. You don't have to cry.' She rocked Drew until the baby's roar dropped to a whimper. 'You feel better now, don't you? I'm your big sister, and I'll take care of you. You won't have to cry any more.'

Except she did cry. Constantly. 'Morning, noon and night,' Lesley proclaimed wearily. And then Lesley was gone, and it was a dark-haired girl named Rosie who was doing the complaining. 'I don't think I've ever heard a baby cry so much,' she said. 'Colic is colic, but this is . . .'

'It's a syndrome,' Casey explained.

And Rosie had laughed. Rosie had a kind face and big, dark eyes that Casey had overheard her father telling her were like two large pools of chocolate syrup. Rosie had laughed when he'd said that, too.

'I can't believe you told that cop I tried to kill my sister.' Drew was crying now.

'I specifically told Detective Spinetti that I didn't believe you had anything to do with what happened to Casey.'

'Then what's he doing snooping around, asking questions, insinuating that I skipped town . . .?'

'You didn't return his calls. Nobody knew where you were.'

'I was in the Bahamas for a few weeks. Sue me.'

'You were in the Bahamas,' Warren repeated dully.

'I needed a break. Is that a crime?'

'Your sister's in a coma, Drew.'

'Yeah, and she's been in one for almost two months.'

'During which you've been here how many times?'

'I told you, it's very hard on me, seeing her like this. I thought the doctors said she was improving.'

'She *is* improving. Her casts are off. Her injuries have pretty much healed. They're weaning her off the ventilator. They've even started her on physical therapy.'

'Why, for Pete's sake? It's not like she's going anywhere.'

Silence.

'I'm sorry,' Drew apologised. 'I'm just upset. It's that detective. What's he talking about anyway? Who would want to kill Casey?'

'You've known her longer than anyone, Drew. Is there anyone from her past, anyone you can think of who . . .?'

'We didn't exactly run in the same circles.'

'Is there anyone from *your* circle . . .?'

'What's that supposed to mean? You wouldn't be referring to my scumbag, drug-dealing acquaintances, would you?'

'I'm just trying to figure things out, Drew. Look. I don't want to argue. Especially in front of your sister.'

'Why? You think she can hear us?'

'No, of course not.'

'Can you hear us, Casey?' Drew asked, drawing closer, her breath brushing against Casey's cheek. 'Do you understand what we're saying?'

Yes. Yes, I understand everything.

'Ain't nobody home,' Drew pronounced, backing away.

'Watch your elbow,' Warren warned. 'She's bruised enough.'

Drew made a dismissive sound. 'So, what happens now?'

'Well, hopefully, now that she's started therapy, her muscles will get stronger. And the doctors will keep reducing the number of breaths the ventilator is providing. They're optimistic that in another week or two, she might be able to start breathing on her own.'

'You're saying she'll regain consciousness?'

'No. Nobody's saying that.'

'What *are* they saying? That she could be this way for ever?'

No, no. Warren, tell her that's not going to happen.

Silence.

'So, I repeat, what happens now?' Drew pressed.

A long sigh escaped Warren's lips. 'Once Casey is able to breathe without the respirator, I can start thinking about taking her home, hiring the right people—'

'I mean, what happens to me?' Drew interrupted.

Casey might have laughed had she been able to. Some things never changed. A rose is a rose is a rose, she thought. And Drew was Drew. Could she blame her?

Her sister had learned from a very early age that the only person who would be there to take care of her was herself. Casey had tried to fill the parental role, but Drew had reminded her vehemently, 'You're not my mother.' So she'd backed off.

'What happens to *you*?' Warren repeated.

'Yes, it's a reasonable question, under the circumstances.'

'A question I'm afraid I can't answer. I'm not an estate lawyer.'

'I'm sure you've been speaking to one.'

'Actually I haven't, no.'

'You haven't spoken to anyone about what happens to your wife's fortune if she remains in a vegetative state? I find that very hard to believe.'

'I've had a few other things on my mind.'

Casey could hear the click of her sister's heels as she paced around the bed and tried to imagine what she was wearing. Probably a pair of black leggings and a loose-fitting jersey, her dark blonde hair pulled into a high ponytail. No doubt, her dark green eyes were flashing daggers at Warren.

'I thought that if anything happened to Casey, my father's estate would automatically transfer to me.'

'Casey isn't dead, Drew,' Warren reminded her.

'She might as well be.'

'OK, that's enough. I'm afraid you'll just have to be patient.'

'Easy for you to say. You don't have to worry about money.'

'Maybe if you got a job,' Warren suggested.

'Do I have to remind you I have a child to look after?'

Casey felt a knot beginning to form in the pit of her stomach at the mention of her five-year-old niece, who was her mother's tiny clone in almost every respect. Casey wondered if Lola would be the beauty her sister predicted she'd be when she got older. She remembered the same predictions having been made about Drew. But while Drew had matured into an undeniably pretty young woman, she stopped short of being beautiful.

'Where is Lola?' Warren asked.

'Sean took her to the cafeteria for some ice cream.'

'Who is this guy anyway? How long have you known him exactly?'

'What's that supposed to mean, exactly?'

'It doesn't mean anything. I was just wondering.'

'What are you wondering, Warren? You wonder if I asked my boyfriend to run over my sister? Is that what you're wondering?'

Of course he isn't. You don't think that. Do you, Warren?

'Mommy!' a little voice called, footsteps dashing into the room.

'Oh God. Get her out of here. No. Go on. I thought you were taking her for ice cream,' Drew said all in one breath.

'She *had* ice cream,' a male voice protested.

'Then get her some more.'

'What's the matter with Auntie Casey?' the little girl asked.

'She's not feeling well,' Drew answered impatiently.

'Is she sleeping?'

'She was in a car accident,' Warren explained.

'Will she be OK?'

'We're keeping our fingers crossed,' Warren said.

'Can I cross mine, too?'

'I think that would be very helpful.'

'Good. See, Mommy? My fingers are crossed.'

'Great,' Drew said. 'Now, Sean, if you don't mind. A hospital room is no place for a child.'

'OK, OK. Come on, Lola. You can have that piece of cake you had your eye on.'

'I'm not hungry any more.'

'You know what?' Warren said. 'I think they have a kids' playroom downstairs. How about I show Lola? I think we've discussed enough for one afternoon.'

'You can go, too, Sean,' Drew said dismissively. 'Warren, I'll wait here till you get back.'

'Suit yourself.'

The door closed, leaving Casey alone with her sister.

'So, here we are again,' Drew said, as Casey pictured her sister walking over to the window. 'Just like old times. Except in those days, I was the one pretty much in a coma, and you were the one pacing back and forth, trying to figure out what to do with me.'

True enough, Casey thought, her mind racing back through all the years they'd shared the same house, the nights she'd spent waiting anxiously for her sister to come home, the days she'd spent watching her sleeping off a drunken bender.

'You kept telling me if I didn't straighten out, I wouldn't live to see my thirtieth birthday.' Drew laughed. 'And now look at us.' Casey felt her plop down on the bed. 'I can't bear to look at you. Not that you look awful for a member of the undead. The doctors stitched you up pretty good. Look, Casey,' Drew said angrily. 'Enough is enough. You've made your point. I'm a total screw-up who can't manage without you. Now snap out of this ridiculous coma and come back to us. Come on. I know you're in there.'

Do you? Do you really?

'You have to wake up. It's not fair. What you're doing just isn't right. And don't give me this bull about not having any choice in the matter, because how many times have you told me that we *always* have a choice? I need you to get better. By Friday a bunch of cheques are going to start bouncing all over town if you don't wake up and transfer some money—which is rightfully mine, anyway, in case you've forgotten—into my account.'

Oh, Drew.

'I mean, I'm sorry to have to lay this on you in your condition, but I'm in a bind here—a bind, I point out, that could have been avoided if Dad hadn't named you sole executor, or if you hadn't gone along with it. The current problem being that I haven't received my monthly stipend since you went into hibernation, and what with taking Sean to the Bahamas and shopping for my new spring wardrobe, I've maxed out my credit cards. Pretty soon, I'm not going to be able to feed my kid. And I know you love Lola to pieces, even if you weren't happy about my pregnancy. And yes, I *do* know who the father is. So, what am I supposed to do, huh? I need money, your husband says I have to be patient, and all this is your fault because you control the purse strings. I hate to say it, but this situation would have been a lot easier if you'd just died.'

Oh, Drew. Do you really hate me so much?

Casey felt Drew push herself off the bed. She'd never been able to sit still for more than a minute, Casey thought. Too many years of addictive white powder, although when she'd found herself pregnant she'd agreed to go into rehab, and managed to stay clean and sober until after Lola's birth. Casey had moved her sister into a larger apartment, hired a responsible woman to look after Lola, and paid for Drew's repeated rehab attempts. Occasionally it looked as if Drew was about to turn a corner, only to disappear round it altogether. Just before her accident, Casey hadn't spoken to her sister in almost a month.

'My feet are killing me,' Drew said now, and Casey heard her dragging a chair towards the bed. 'Don't let anybody tell you Manolos are comfortable. Hey, you have to admit these are great-looking shoes.' Casey pictured her sister showing off her footwear. 'Yes, I realise seven hundred dollars is an outrageous amount to pay for a strap of leather and a three-inch heel, but they're really a work of art.' She took a breath. 'Too bad you can't see them,' she continued. 'Too bad you can't see how good they look on my feet. Too bad you can't see how good I look, period. I've started sweating up a storm on one of those bicycles that go nowhere, which you'd probably say is a metaphor for the way I live my life.'

Would she? Casey wondered. *Was she really so judgmental?*

'Anyway, I really am looking pretty good. Not as good as Sleeping Beauty here, of course. Even in a coma, you're still the sister to beat. What the hell am I saying? I'm pretty sure it isn't what the doctors had in mind when they said to talk to you as much as possible. But it's not like you can hear me. Can you? Can you hear me? I get this feeling sometimes you can.'

Yes. You're right. You're right.

'No. I guess it's too ridiculous,' Drew said with a sigh. 'So, what do you think of Sean?' she asked in the next breath.

Sean?

'The guy who was just here. I can't remember if you two ever met. Wavy blond hair, little pug nose, nice brown eyes.' Drew giggled. 'Sean's OK. Not too bright. I kind of like that. But he's definitely not a keeper, so you don't have to worry. You have more than enough to worry about right now.'

Casey felt Drew lean in closer. 'Casey?' she heard her ask, her voice lowering, filling with concern. 'Casey, what's going on in there? Why do I think you can hear me?'

Because you know me better than anyone. Because you're my sister, and despite everything, there's an unbreakable bond.

'She can't hear you,' a male voice said gently.

Who's that?

'I know,' Drew concurred. 'There was just something about her expression all of a sudden. I thought for a moment that maybe . . . I don't know. Are you her doctor?'

'No. I'm her physical therapist. Jeremy Ross.'

'Drew Lerner,' Drew said. 'Casey's sister.'

'Yes, I can see the family resemblance. Nice to meet you, Drew. Casey's coming along well.' The therapist approached and took Casey's hand in his, squeezing it gently.

Was he? Or was she just imagining it? Could she actually feel him manipulating her fingers up and down?

'I can definitely feel an improvement.'

'You can?'

'She's getting a lot stronger. I can feel a difference in her fingers from even a few days ago. And once the doctors get rid of this ventilator, we can move her around a lot more.'

'What if she's not able to breathe on her own?'

'The doctors won't remove it until they're sure it's safe.'

'Do you think she'll regain consciousness?'

'Hard to say. Some do. Some don't.' Jeremy began manipulating Casey's wrist, rotating it in tiny circles. 'Generally, the longer the coma, the worse the chances for a complete recovery. But you never know. You can't give up hope.'

Casey felt the strength in his fingers as they applied gentle pressure to her own. She felt a pleasant tingle working its way up her arm. Were her senses coming back to her, a little at a time? Or was her brain simply projecting her desire to feel these things?

'Thatta girl, Casey. You're doing great,' Jeremy told her.

'Do you want me to leave?' Drew asked.

'No, that's all right. You can watch. Learn how to do some of these things yourself so you can do them with her the next time you visit.'

'Oh, no. I wouldn't want to hurt her. I can't. Really.'

'Sure you can. I promise you won't hurt her. Go on.'

Casey felt her right hand being passed from Jeremy's sure grip to

Drew's less steady palm. I can feel that, she thought giddily. I can feel that.

'That's good. Now, slowly and carefully, start moving her fingers up and down, one at a time, real slow, real gentle. See? And now rotate the wrist. Good. See? You're a natural.'

Drew scoffed. 'I don't think so.'

'Don't sell yourself short. Casey needs you right now.'

'Trust me. I'm the last thing she needs.' She quickly returned Casey's hand to the therapist.

'And why is that?' Jeremy began massaging Casey's forearms.

This isn't my imagination. I can really feel that.

'Does the phrase "black sheep of the family" ring any bells?' Drew asked. 'And my family's a pretty screwed-up bunch. Except for Casey. She was always perfect.'

'I guess it's hard trying to compete with perfection.'

'I stopped competing early. What about you? Any brothers and sisters?'

'Two of each.'

'Wow. Big family. Any children of your own?'

'My wife and I thought about it, but then we divorced. You?'

'I have a daughter. No husband,' Drew added quickly.

'Hello, Jeremy,' Warren said from the doorway. 'Drew, maybe you should leave and let the therapist do his job.'

'That's all right. She's not bothering—'

'Sean and Lola are waiting for you downstairs.'

'We need to talk,' Drew protested.

'Not now.'

'That's all right,' Jeremy interjected. 'I can come back in a few minutes. Nice meeting you, Drew.'

'You, too.'

'Please tell me you weren't flirting with your sister's therapist,' Warren said as soon as Jeremy was gone.

'What's the big deal? It's not like she can see me. He looks a bit like Tiger Woods, don't you think?'

'Look, your boyfriend's downstairs with Lola. Here's some money to tide you over.'

'What am I supposed to do with five hundred dollars?'

'It's for the time being. It's a complicated situation.'

'Then simplify it.'

'My hands are tied.'

'Untie them.'

'Don't you understand? It's not up to me.'

Please. I can't listen to any more of this.

'Oh, no, look at her,' Drew said suddenly. 'Look at her face.'

'What's wrong with her face?'

'She can hear us.'

'What are you talking about?'

'She can hear us, Warren. I know she can.'

Casey felt Warren inch closer. 'You're crazy, Drew,' he said after a long pause. 'Now please. Do us all a favour and go home.' After a deep, weary sigh, his voice was softer. 'Look. I'll talk to someone in my firm. Hopefully, we'll work something out.'

'I'd appreciate that.'

'Sorry if I said anything to upset you. I'll call.'

Casey listened to the click of her sister's Manolos as she walked briskly from the room without saying goodbye.

4

'. . . MIRACLE SHE DIDN'T DIE,' a voice was saying. 'If I were a betting man, I'd have wagered her chance of survival at less than ten per cent.'

'She's a fighter, all right,' a second voice confirmed.

Casey fought back the wave of panic she always felt upon awakening to total darkness. Would she ever get used to it?

'When they first asked me to consult, I took one look at her and thought, "Consult about what? This poor woman's a goner,"' the first voice continued. 'Her injuries were so horrific.'

'Nobody thought she'd make it through that first night,' the second voice concurred. Warren's voice, Casey realised.

'But she surprised everyone,' the first man said, his deep voice filled with admiration. 'Now that we've taken her off the respirator successfully and she's breathing on her own—'

'Still . . .' Warren interrupted, obviously wrestling with his thoughts. 'Her quality of life . . . I know there's no way she'd want to spend the rest of her life in this condition.'

'I know how hard this must be for you, Mr Marshall. We still don't know when or if your wife is going to regain consciousness.'

'You're the top neurologist in the city. When *will* you know, Dr Keith? A year from now? Five years? Fifteen?'

Fifteen years? Even five years? Dear God, no. Five months is more than I can bear to think about. Warren's right, I'd rather be dead than go on living like this.

But not until I know who did this to me.

It was this mystery, she realised, as much as the various tubes to which she was connected, which was keeping her alive. It was more engrossing than anything on TV, more stimulating than her friends' conversations, more riveting than her doctors' reports. The fact that someone had tried to kill her had begun to fill her waking thoughts.

'I know this is difficult,' Dr Keith said. 'But there's every reason to be optimistic. Your wife's bones are healing nicely. Her heart is strong. She's off the respirator and breathing normally. Her brain is functioning, albeit at a slowed rate of activity.'

'Is there any chance she's more aware than we think? That she can see or hear?'

Casey felt herself holding her breath. Could they tell?

'Highly unlikely,' the doctor responded. 'But we could test for corneal sensation, I suppose.'

'Meaning what?'

'We put a wisp of cotton on the cornea. It will produce a very powerful blink, and tell us whether sensation to the eye is being received. It's very hard to suppress a blink.'

'But she *does* blink.'

'A purely reflexive act. What I'm talking about is blinking in response to a direct stimulus.' Casey felt the doctor leaning over her. She heard a click. 'You see,' Dr Keith continued, 'I'm shining this light directly into your wife's eyes. A normal person would blink. A person in a coma doesn't. Which doesn't mean she might not see tomorrow.'

'And to find out if she can hear? Dr Keith, the idea that my wife could be conscious but unable to communicate, that she could be a prisoner of her own body, trapped inside her head, desperate to let us know . . .'

'I understand your frustration. I'll order a BSAEP. That stands for brain stem auditory evoked potential.'

'How does that work?'

'We put earphones over the patient's ears, present a series of tones—clicks mostly—and record the brain's response with electrodes. We can actually see waveforms responding to the stimuli. This can be a bit tricky because the computer has to separate the microvolts the brain is producing from the ones put out by the heart, lungs and other organs.'

'Fine. Do it.'

Do it.

'Mr Marshall, we've already performed this test, though not lately. Tell me, has something happened to make you think your wife's condition has changed?'

'No. Not really. It's just my wife's sister said something last week I can't get out of my head. She said that sometimes Casey gets this look on her face, almost like she's been listening . . .'

Casey felt the doctor move in again to examine her more closely. 'Frankly, I don't see anything in her expression to indicate that. But you know her much better than I do. And anything's possible. So why don't I schedule the test. But be prepared that even if the test indicates your wife *can* hear, that doesn't mean she necessarily understands what she's hearing.'

'I understand. I just have to know.'

'Try not to make yourself too crazy, Mr Marshall. If your wife *can* hear, then that means her condition is improving. It could even mean she's on the road to a full recovery.'

A full recovery, Casey repeated. *Was it possible?*

'Have you thought about where you'll send her for rehab?'

'I'm taking Casey home,' Warren said.

'You might want to reconsider that,' Dr Keith advised. 'Casey is going to require round-the-clock care for at least another two to three months. She'll still be connected to an IV; she'll have the feeding tube; she'll need to be moved every few hours so she doesn't develop bed-sores. It's much too much for you to handle. If you'd like, my secretary can give you a list of places . . .'

'I've already arranged for a nurse and a physical therapist. And one of those special beds to rotate her electronically. I think my wife would prefer to be at home, Doctor.'

'I'm sure she would. Well, then, good luck, Mr Marshall.'

Casey listened as Dr Keith walked from the room.

'Well, did you hear that, Casey?' Warren pulled a chair close to her head and sat down. 'We're going to find out if Drew was right, if maybe you can hear. Wouldn't that be something?' He hesitated briefly. 'If you *are* listening, I want you to know how much these last two years have meant to me. You've been such a great wife, Casey, the best lover and companion any man could hope for. Our time together has been the happiest time of my life. It's important to me that you know that.'

I do know that. I feel the same way.

'Mr Marshall,' a voice interrupted from the doorway.

Oh, for Pete's sake, Patsy.

'I'm sorry to intrude. Is everything all right? You look so sad.'

'Everything's fine. I'm fine. And please, call me Warren.'

'Warren,' Patsy repeated softly. 'How's Mrs Marshall today?'

'No real change.'

Casey felt a shift in the air as Patsy approached. Once again, the scent of lavender swirled around her head.

'I see her hair's growing back nicely where they had to shave it,' Patsy remarked, propping up the pillows behind Casey's head. Then, 'Is something the matter with your neck?'

'Oh, it's just a little stiff. I must have slept on it funny.'

'Here, let me have a look. I took a course in massage therapy.'

Of course you did, Casey thought.

'A woman of many talents.'

'I like to think so. Where is it bothering you?'

'Right here. Yeah, that's the spot.'

'You're really tight,' Patsy said. 'This shoulder, too.'

'I didn't realise I was so tense.'

'Are you kidding? You're here every day, in this uncomfortable chair, worrying yourself sick over your wife. I bet you're not getting enough sleep. Your whole back's probably a mess.'

Warren groaned.

'Just relax into my fingers. That's right. Now take a deep breath. Release it slowly. Good. What you need is a proper massage.'

'What I need is for my wife to get well,' Warren said.

'You getting sick isn't going to make her any better. You have to take care of yourself, Mr Mar—Warren. Otherwise, how are you going to manage when she comes home?'

'Well, I'm counting on you to help me there. That is, if that offer you made earlier is still open.'

Oh, no. This is not a good idea.

Casey didn't need eyes to see the smile that spread across Patsy's face. 'Of course it is. My bags are packed and ready to go. As soon as you know Mrs Marshall's release date, tell me and I'll be there.'

'It's a big house. You'll have a very nice room. Oh, that feels good. Anybody ever tell you that you have magic—'

'What's going on here?' a voice interrupted. 'I was under the impression the one in the bed was the patient.'

'Janine,' Warren stated. 'I had a bit of a stiff neck. Patsy—'

'Patsy can go,' Janine said pointedly.

A hurried movement. The scent of lavender retreating.

'I could use some coffee,' Warren said tersely. 'You want me to bring you anything back?'

'No, thank you.' Janine sat down in the chair, brushed her long fingers soothingly across Casey's forehead. 'What was that all about?' she said.

'**W**hat's this all about?' Casey heard herself cry, a tearful sixteen-year-old waving the morning newspaper in front of her father's bemused face. 'How can you let them write these things? Why don't you sue?'

Her father laughed. 'Let them say whatever they want. Sticks and stones. They have no proof of anything illegal.'

'Illegal?' Drew repeated from her place at the kitchen table. 'You did something illegal?'

Ronald Lerner ignored her, as if she wasn't there.

Casey groaned silently in her sleep, distant memories of her father brushing up against her hospital bed. She'd always thought that if there was one word to best describe him, it was 'too'. Too handsome, too rich, too charming, too athletic, too successful. His voice too smooth, his smile too seductive. Women, money, accolades—everything had always been his for the taking.

Casey's paternal grandfather had been a successful trader in the stock market and had left his only child an inheritance of several million dollars, which the son had parlayed into a serious fortune approaching a billion. Along the way, Ronald Lerner had acquired the well-earned reputation of being shrewd, savvy, and not averse to cutting corners. There were constant rumours of his womanising and occasional whispers of somewhat shadier shenanigans, which he always dismissed as the grumblings of jealous, small minds.

'You notice he didn't deny it,' Drew pointed out after their father had finished his coffee and left the house.

'Shut up, Drew.'

'You shut up.'

'You really think he knew that company was about to go under?' Casey demanded of her twelve-year-old sister. 'How could he possibly know that?'

'How should I know?'

'You don't know anything,' Casey insisted forcefully.

'Neither do you.'

'I know our father.'

'Yeah, right.' Gulping down the last of her orange juice, Drew had stomped from the room.

Casey had sat there for several seconds, not moving, then lowered her head to the glass tabletop and burst into tears. Because she knew Drew was right: despite their father's feigned indifference and his too-easy smile, he'd not denied doing anything illegal.

Something else Casey realised Drew was right about: she didn't know her father. She'd given her fantasies power over her instincts. A difficult habit to break, she thought now, opening her eyes.

It took a few seconds for Casey to realise the darkness wasn't quite as black as it had been before she'd fallen asleep. It took even less time to realise that she could make out shapes—the chair in the corner, the dim light of the moon sneaking in between the slats of the venetian blinds, casting an eerie light on the tiny TV suspended overhead.

She could see.

Slowly, Casey worked her eyes from side to side. There was a chair at the side of her bed, another against the far wall. A small bathroom was located to the right. The door to the hallway was closed, although a thin band of light was visible at the bottom.

Casey heard footsteps approaching and saw a shadow interrupt the line of light. Was someone standing there? What did they want with her in the middle of the night?

The door opened. Casey flinched from the sudden flash of light. A figure entered the room. Was it one of her doctors?

'Well, well, aren't you a mess,' a voice said.

Who was here? Panic washed over her as the figure drew close.

'All these tubes and wires. Not exactly flattering. But what goes around comes around. You put me through hell, you know.'

What's going on? Who is this man?

'Did you know the police have questioned me three times since you got yourself run over? Apparently, a mother's word isn't enough for our esteemed men in blue. Apparently, mothers lie for their sons all the time, an officer actually had the gall to tell me, as if I might not be familiar with the concept. I'm only a lawyer, after all, albeit unemployed.'

Dear God—Richard Mooney. What are you doing here?

'I thought I'd see for myself what sort of shape you were in. And I see you're still breathing. I guess we'll just have to take care of that. My mother always said to finish what you start.'

He pulled the pillow out from behind Casey's head and pressed it down against her nose and mouth.

And suddenly Casey was screaming, screaming as loud and as long as she could, screaming until she felt the last of her breath seep from her broken body even as she heard Warren's footsteps racing down the corridor, too late to save her.

Casey lay in her bed, unseeing eyes staring at the ceiling, and understood she'd been dreaming. Richard Mooney wasn't there. Warren wasn't rushing to her rescue. There was only darkness.

Nights were the worst. That's when the dreams came, the nightmares surfaced and the ghosts visited. How many times had she dreamed she could see, only to wake up in the same black hole into which she tumbled that late-March afternoon? Dreamed she could speak, only to awaken to silence? How many times had she fantasised she could move, only to find her once strong, vibrant body a dungeon from which there was no escape? How long before she willingly sacrificed her sanity in order to escape this hell on earth?

'That's the way, Casey,' she heard her father say now, his voice filtering through the night air. 'Shift your weight. Get that right hip dropping before you swing the club.'

How easy it had been—the effortless shifting of her weight, the instinctive dropping of her hip, the graceful swinging of the five-wood as her hands brought it up and over her left shoulder.

'It's a stupid game,' Drew had complained, watching Casey on the practise range, home from Brown for the summer vacation.

'Dad always says golf isn't a game—'

'Oh, please,' Drew groaned. 'If I have to listen to any more crap about golf being a symbol for life, I'll throw up.'

Drew's fifteen-year-old body was just starting to fill out and take shape. Soon the oversize sweatshirts and ratty jeans would be replaced by low-cut T-shirts and shorts so short they were banned from the clubhouse. As was one of the junior pros, who was subsequently caught with Drew in a decidedly non-golfing position.

Ronald Lerner was duly embarrassed. 'Remember,' he'd chastised his younger daughter, 'boys will be boys, but girls will be sluts, if they're not careful.' Drew wasn't careful, but she'd finally found a way to get her father's attention.

Not that anything held Ronald Lerner's attention for long.

'Where's your father?' Casey heard her mother ask, Alana's voice coming at her from the far corner of her hospital room.

'I think he went out.' Casey stopped packing up her things and turned towards her mother, who was standing in the doorway. It was unusual for her mother to leave her room, although the drink in her hand was as constant as ever.

'What are you doing? Are you going somewhere?'

'I'm moving into the city,' Casey reminded her. 'Into my own apartment.' She didn't elaborate. There was no point. Her mother wouldn't remember. She'd already told her several times.

'Everyone always leaves me,' Alana said.

'I'm sure Dad will be home soon.'

'How come we never do things together?' There was more than a hint of recrimination in the slur of her mother's words.

Because you never ask, Casey replied silently. Because you're always drunk or asleep or out of town. Because you've never shown the slightest interest in me. Ever. In all these years.

'You hate me,' her mother said.

Casey said nothing. She was thinking that it was the longest conversation she'd ever had with her mother. It was also the last. Three months later, Alana and Ronald Lerner were dead.

'So, what now?' Drew asked, pulling up a chair beside Casey's hospital bed. 'We divvy up the spoils?'

'Not exactly.' Casey braced for the explosion she knew would follow.

'Why don't I like the sound of that?' Drew leaned forward in the chair. She was almost four months' pregnant with Lola and not yet starting to show. 'You're saying he left everything to you?'

'No, of course not. The estate's pretty evenly divided. But there are conditions for your protection . . .'

'Get to the point.'

'The point is that Dad appointed me executor of the estate.'

'He appointed *you*,' Drew acknowledged, her foot tapping restlessly on the floor. She jumped up and began pacing back and forth. 'So, you can just release my money, right?'

'Dad wanted you put on a monthly allowance,' Casey sidestepped. 'It's a pretty substantial amount.'

'An allowance,' Drew repeated. 'Like a child.'

'You're only twenty-one, Drew.'

'You're barely twenty-five. What kind of allowance did he put you on?' Drew's eyes filled with bitter tears. 'This stinks, and you know it. This whole situation would be easier if you'd just died.'

'Whoa,' Janine said, coming out of the bathroom, fresh lipstick on her lips. 'What kind of thing is that to say to your sister?'

'She has every right to be angry,' Casey said as Drew melted into the far wall.

'Why don't you just give her the money?' Gail suggested, materialising by the windowsill to deadhead a pot of geraniums.

'I tried that,' Casey reminded her friend. 'I gave her over a hundred thousand dollars to buy into that gym franchise she was so desperate to have. It went belly-up in less than a year.'

'Maybe you could make her a partner in your new business,' Janine suggested, bitterness clinging to her bright smile.

'Come on, Janine. I thought we were past this.'

'And I thought we were friends.'

'We *are* friends.'

'Don't be so sure.'

No, no, no. I don't want to hear this.

'The patient is a thirty-two-year-old woman, the victim of a hit-and-run accident approximately three weeks ago,' Dr Peabody announced suddenly, reading from his clipboard as he entered the room trailed by Warren and Drew.

'How is the patient doing today?' Warren asked.

Wake up. Please, wake up.

'We should clear out,' Gail said. 'Let the doctors do their job.'

'This test could take a while,' the doctor explained.

'We'll grab some coffee. Want any, Warren?' Janine asked.

Casey heard her husband release a deep breath. 'No, thanks.'

'Try not to worry,' Gail urged. 'Like the doctor said, if she can hear, it could mean she's on the road to recovery.'

Wait. What are you talking about?

Seconds later, Casey heard equipment being wheeled into the room, the drone of doctors' voices, the scribbling of notes. She felt hands at her head, and earphones being fitted over her ears.

In that instant, she understood that it was no longer night, and the ghosts had all gone home. It was morning, and she was fully awake. This was really happening.

'"**W**ho that cares much to know the history of man, and how the mysterious mixture behaves under the varying experiments of Time, has not dwelt, at least briefly, on the life of Saint Theresa, has not smiled with some gentleness at the thought of the little girl walking forth one morning hand-in-hand with her still smaller brother, to go and seek martyrdom in the country of the Moors?" Huh? Say that again?' Janine asked. 'OK, no wonder you always hated this book. I've only read the first sentence and I'm totally confused. Is it even in English? I thought George Eliot was from England.'

The sound of pages being turned.

'Yes. It says right here in the introduction that Eliot was born in Warwickshire. And some professor says *Middlemarch* is "easily the best of the half-dozen best novels in the world". Anyway, to continue: "Out they toddled from rugged Avila, wide-eyed and helpless-looking as two fawns, but with human hearts, already beating to a national idea." Oh, dear. You'd better wake up soon, Casey, or I'll be in a coma right beside you. You don't really want to listen to six hundred pages of this, do you?'

A laugh, followed by footsteps. Someone approaching the bed. A giggle. 'What are you doing?' Gail asked.

'Making good on my threat.'

'Do you think she understands what you're reading?'

Deep sigh. 'The tests indicate Casey can definitely hear, but dammit, I don't know if this is good news or bad.'

'What do you mean?'

Janine lowered her voice. 'I know it means her condition has definitely improved, and she could be coming back to us. But at the same time'— her voice became a whisper—'how awful to have been lying here, unable to see or talk or move, but able to hear. What if she *can* understand? What if she knows someone might have tried to kill her?'

'What are you getting at?'

'Do you think there's any chance she'd think it's me?'

'Don't be ridiculous.'

'We both know Casey and I haven't always seen eye to eye. Things were pretty tense when she decided to dissolve our partnership. I actively prayed her new business would go under, that she'd lose all her money, even that her hair would fall out.'

'You prayed her hair would fall out?' Gail was incredulous.

'Shh! I didn't mean it. I wouldn't have wished this on my worst enemy,' Janine said.

Is it possible that's exactly what you are? That you're somehow responsible for this hell I'm living in?

'Casey, you know I love you,' Janine said plaintively.

Do I?

'I think we have to stay positive,' Gail was saying. 'Casey, if you *can* understand, as scary and as frustrating as that must be, then at least you know how much we all care about you, and how much Warren adores you, so hurry up and get well.'

'But what if years go by,' Janine broached quietly, 'and there's no further change, and she's trapped like this for ever?'

'She won't be. Casey's strong. She's been through a lot—'

'Oh, please,' Janine interrupted. 'Yes, Casey didn't have the best parents in the world, but at least hers had the decency to die and leave her obscenely wealthy. Plus, she wasn't exactly dealt a bad hand in the looks department. Not to mention, she's smart and educated and—'

'In a coma.'

'Yes, in a coma. I'm sorry, Casey. I didn't mean it the way it came out. It probably sounded like a bunch of sour grapes, and that's not how I really feel.'

Isn't it?

'She knows that,' Gail said.

'Do you remember the first time we met?' Janine asked.

'Of course,' Gail answered. 'It was hate at first sight.'

'You hated me?'

'*You* hated *me*,' Gail corrected.

'Yeah, well, I guess I felt threatened,' Janine admitted. 'I mean, you and Casey had been friends for ever.'

Gail giggled. 'I guess everyone wants Casey to themselves.'

'So, how did you and I ever end up as friends?'

'I don't think Casey gave us much choice. She was so persistent. Weren't you, Casey? All those lunches, girls' nights out.'

'Excruciating.'

'So, when did your feelings change?' Gail asked.

'I guess it was during Mike's final stay in the hospice. You were so loving and strong, unlike me, it was kind of hard not to admire you. Under the frizzy hair and shy smile, a real powerhouse. When did you realise you'd been wrong about me?'

'Around the same time,' Gail admitted. 'After the funeral, you were the one in my kitchen, putting together a plate of sandwiches, then loading the dishwasher while I talked to the guests.'

'I just didn't want Casey to get all the credit.'

'Why are you so afraid of letting people see the real you?'

Who is the real you, Janine?

'Maybe because they'll discover there isn't that much to see.'

The sound of a chair pushing back. 'I've had enough great literature for one day. I should get going.' A whiff of expensive French perfume. The feel of Janine's lips on Casey's cheek.

It's all coming back, Casey thought, almost bursting with excitement. She could hear. She could smell. She could feel. Surely any day now, she'd be able to move, to talk, to shout from the rooftops.

'Call me later?' Janine asked.

'Sure thing.'

A muffled embrace, a door opening and closing. 'I hope you didn't take any of that to heart, Casey,' Gail said. 'You know Janine's been here every day since your accident.'

According to Detective Spinetti, it wasn't an accident.

'Why would she come every day if she didn't love you?'

Maybe to look for an opportunity to finish the job?

Casey felt a soft hand brush across her forehead. 'Anyway, we're all so excited about the news. Warren called everybody last night. "She can hear," he shouted when I picked up the phone. The doctors say there's reason to be guardedly optimistic. That's better than guardedly pessimistic, right? Anyway . . .'

Her voice drifted to a halt.

'I'm not going to read to you. I'll just sit here, if that's OK, and tell you what's been going on in my life. Trust me, you won't want to miss a word. It's pretty juicy stuff. Well, juicy for me.'

She took a deep breath. 'I met this guy.' Another pause. 'His name is Stan. You might have heard me mention him to Janine. I really haven't told her much. You know Janine—she'd want to know everything, and it's still so early, I'm afraid to jinx it. Am I making any sense? His name is Stan Leonard, and he's thirty-eight. His wife died of breast cancer, and he has two children. He's a computer programmer, owns a house in Chestnut Hill.

'Let's see. He's maybe an inch taller than I am, and he could probably stand to lose a few pounds. I like him the way he is—not so perfect. His hair is thinning, but he has beautiful grey-green eyes. And he works out, so he's got these amazing biceps. Certainly more than you'd expect from a computer nerd. That's how he describes himself, although I don't think he's nerdy. You'd think he's cute.

'And, Casey, I can tell him things I haven't told anyone other than you, you know, stuff about Mike, and he understands, because his wife died so young, too. Does that sound maudlin? It's not like we sit around commiserating all the time. In fact, we laugh constantly. Does that make me sound callous?

'At first I felt really guilty. You know, like I was being disloyal to Mike, even after all this time. Anyway, on the third date, Stan finally kissed me good night. And it was great. Casey, it was so great. I can't believe I'm actually saying this. Do I sound really pathetic?'

You sound like a woman falling in love.

'But now he's talking about maybe going away for the weekend, which means he's probably expecting me to sleep with him. Not that I don't want to sleep with him. Don't get me wrong. I think about almost nothing else. But it's been years since I've been with a man. What if he takes one look at me naked and jumps into the Schuylkill River?

'So I need you, my best friend on earth, to tell me what to do. And I can't believe I'm going on and on, because I know it's all so trivial compared to what you're going through. And I feel kind of like I did with Mike. I keep thinking, how can I go out and have a good time while you're lying here in a coma?'

Because you deserve it. Because life goes on.

'Just know that I love you, and I need you, and I miss you.'

Oh, Gail. I love you, too.

'Please come back.' The sounds of sniffling. 'Casey, please.'

5

'LESTER WHITMORE, come on down!' the announcer brayed. 'You're the next contestant on *The Price Is Right*.'

'Would you just look at that guy,' Drew squealed from beside Casey's head. 'Oh, sorry. I keep forgetting you can't see. Shoot, I smeared my nails.'

The pungent smell of fresh polish. Casey wondered how long Drew had been in the room, giving herself a manicure.

'You should see this guy,' Drew continued. 'He looks like he's going to have a heart attack, he's so excited. He's sweating right through this ugly Hawaiian shirt, jumping up and down like a lunatic, and hugging the other contestants.'

The Price Is Right, Casey thought. She'd grown up with that show. That it was still on the air was strangely comforting.

'Oh, look. They have to guess the price of a set of golf clubs, including the bag.'

'Four hundred dollars,' the first contestant offered.

'Four hundred dollars?' Drew echoed. 'Are you crazy? Even I know they're worth way more than that.'

'Seven hundred and fifty dollars,' came the second bid.

'One thousand,' came the third.

'A thousand and one,' said Lester Whitmore.

'What do you say, Casey? I bet you know the answer.'

Assuming they're good clubs, I'd guess sixteen hundred.

'The answer is one thousand, six hundred and twenty dollars!' the host announced. 'Lester Whitmore, you're the winner on *The Price Is Right*.'

'So how close were you?' Drew asked. 'Pretty close, I bet. There's no beating you when it comes to anything golf, is there?'

'Wow, that's some shot,' Casey heard Warren marvel from a distant recess of her brain, his voice full of unbridled admiration. She watched him emerge from the darkness in her head and step into the bright sun of a brilliant spring day. 'Where'd you learn to hit a golf ball like that?'

'My father taught me,' Casey said.

'Who's your father—Arnold Palmer?'

Casey laughed and pulled her golf cart up the fairway.

'I think you might actually have outdriven me,' Warren said as they approached the two white balls, sitting inches from each other, 200 yards from the tee box.

Casey had, in fact, outdriven her handsome date.

'What—you aren't even going to tell me it was just a lucky shot? Soothe my wounded male ego?'

'Does it need soothing?'

'Perhaps a few kind words.'

'You're so cute when you're insecure,' Casey said in response, and was relieved when Warren laughed. She didn't want to come off as either mean-spirited or smug. When Warren had called several days earlier to ask her out, and enquired timidly whether she played golf, she'd refrained from telling him she belonged to the smartest course in the city and had a nine handicap.

Casey watched as Warren prepared for his next shot with a series of laborious half swings and waggles, then watched him slice the ball into the creek. What would be the harm in letting him win? It would be so easy to collapse her left elbow, or take her eye off the ball. Instead, she assumed her proper stance and swung. Seconds later, the ball flew across the creek to land ten feet from the pin.

'Why do I get the feeling you've done this before?' Warren asked, his third shot landing just outside hers.

'Actually I'm a pretty good golfer,' she admitted.

'No kidding.'

'I turned down a golf scholarship at Duke,' she told him two holes—and two pars—later.

'Because . . .?'

'Because I think sports should be fun, not work.'

'Instead of spending your days golfing in the glorious outdoors, you'd rather spend them finding jobs for disgruntled lawyers?'

'I'd rather be decorating their offices,' Casey replied.

'Then why aren't you?'

Casey retrieved her ball from the cup and dropped it into her pocket, then walked briskly towards the next hole. 'My father considered things like interior decorating to be frivolous, which is how I ended up majoring in psychology and English. Still, the last few years I've been taking night courses in interior design.'

'And what does your father think about that?'

'My father's dead. He and my mother were killed when his private plane crashed five years ago.'

'I'm sorry, that must have been awful for you.'

'It was hard. Especially with the press hounding us.'

'Why would the press hound you?' Warren asked.

'Because my father was Ronald Lerner,' Casey said, watching for Warren's reaction. There was none. Was it possible he didn't know who her father was? 'You never heard of Ronald Lerner?'

'Should I have?'

Casey made a face that said he probably should have.

'I grew up in New Jersey and went to law school in New York,' he reminded her. 'I just moved to Philly when I joined Miller, Sheridan. Maybe you could fill me in on what I missed.'

'Maybe later,' Casey said.

'Damn,' Drew swore again, snapping Casey from her reveries. 'This is what happens when you have to resort to doing your own nails. Normally, Amy does them for me. You remember Amy—over on Pine Street? Anyway, she's the best manicurist in the city, and I've been going there once a week since for ever, until, of course, you ended up in here, and it seems I can no longer afford to spend a measly *twenty-five dollars a week*! No more manicures for me, unless I want my daughter to go hungry.' Drew made a snort of derision. 'Guess if only you'd looked both ways, we wouldn't be in this mess.'

'Angela Campbell, come on down! You're the next contestant on *The Price Is Right!*'

Drew continued prattling on, her voice competing with the shrieks of the latest lucky contestant, and Casey found herself tuning out. She was exhausted from the stream of chatter coming at her nonstop since the doctors had announced it would be beneficial if everyone talked to her as much as possible. The noise started first thing in the morning, with the arrival of doctors and nurses, then family and friends. If they weren't talking *at* her, they were reading *to* her. And then there was the television, with its parade of moronic morning talk shows, hysteria-filled game shows, and sex-crazed afternoon soaps.

And, of course, there was Warren.

He came every day. Always, he'd kiss her forehead and stroke her hand. Then he'd pull up the chair next to her bed and talk softly, telling her about his day, reporting his conversations with various doctors. Surely there was a way of gauging her brain capacity, she'd heard him arguing with Dr Zarb. How long before she regained the use of her arms and legs? he'd questioned Jeremy. How long before he could take her home?

Of course Janine thought nothing of barging in on them regularly. As did Drew, who was oblivious to everything that didn't directly concern her.

Was it possible that Drew was less oblivious than she let on?

Was it possible her sister had tried to kill her, in order to lay claim to the fortune she believed was rightfully hers?

No, I won't do this. I won't allow Detective Spinetti's suspicions to poison my mind. Warren is still convinced it was an accident. Trust his instincts. Concentrate on something more pleasant. Listen to the damn TV. Find out how much that king-size tube of toothpaste is really worth.

'So, tell me something about yourself,' the TV host prompted the newest shrieking contestant.

'So, tell me more about Casey Lerner,' she heard Warren say, his soft voice caressing the nape of her neck, beckoning her back to the not-so-distant past when their relationship was unfolding.

'What would you like to know?'

They were spending the morning at the farmers' market in Lancaster, a pleasant little town sixty miles west of Philadelphia. The redbrick building where local Amish farmers brought their meat, fruit, vegetables and baked goods to be sold housed one of the oldest covered markets in America.

'I want to know everything,' Warren said.

Casey smiled. 'I'm not very complicated. What you see is generally what you get.'

They spent the night—their first night together—at a Spanish-style mansion B & B with private baths, antique furniture and large, comfortable beds. They had made love many times over the course of that night and the weeks that followed. Each time was magical, as Casey later confided to Janine and Gail.

'It's like he can read my mind,' she told them.

'It's so romantic,' Gail said.

'Excuse me while I go throw up,' Janine said.

The subject of children came up during a weekend getaway to Gettysburg. They were just nearing the end of the mile-long hike along the Big Round Top Loop Trail when three boys raced past them. 'So, how many children would you like?' Warren asked.

'I don't know. I've never really thought about it,' Casey lied. In fact, having children was something she'd thought about a lot. 'I guess two would be nice. What about you?'

'Well, I'm an only child, remember, so I've always pictured a house full of kids, but two sounds good.' He smiled, as if they'd just compromised on an important point.

Casey pretended not to notice. 'What were your parents like?'

'I never really knew my dad,' Warren said easily. 'He died when I was a kid. My mother, on the other hand . . .' He laughed. 'She was a force to be reckoned with. According to family legend, she divorced husband number one after he threw her down a flight of stairs, and number two when he went to prison for embezzlement. Number three, my dad, died of a heart attack at forty-nine. I don't remember much about four or five, since I was away at school, but my mother managed to come away from those last fiascoes with enough money to keep her in the style to which she'd always aspired. Speaking of which, I'm going to have to insist on a prenup.'

'What?'

'Before we go any further with this marriage talk . . .'

'What marriage talk?'

'In your office, the day we met. You've forgotten already?'

'You weren't serious,' Casey said, although she knew—had always known—that he was.

'I want you to have a lawyer draw up a foolproof prenup. In the event of a divorce, which is never going to happen, I want your assets completely protected. Nobody is ever going to question my motives where you're concerned, or accuse me of having married you for your money.'

'So, do you have my money?' Drew was asking now.

Instantly, Casey snapped back into the present. Who was Drew talking to?

'As I've explained, this is a complicated situation,' Warren said.

'How complicated can it be? It's *my* money.'

'Yes, but it was under Casey's control, and now Casey is—'

'Napping with the fishes. Tell me something I don't know, Counsellor.' Casey pictured her sister crossing one arm over the other, fingers extended so as not to smear her freshly polished nails. 'Give it your best shot.'

'I spoke to William Billy, one of my partners . . .'

'That's his real name?'

'William Billy, yes.'

'His name is Willy Billy?' Drew laughed.

'You find that funny?'

'Don't you?'

'Not particularly. William happens to be one of the best estate and trust lawyers in the city.'

'He'd have to be.'

'Can I continue? I thought you were in a hurry for this.'

'I am. Please proceed.' She laughed again.

'Are you high?'

'What?'

'You're stoned, aren't you? What are you on? Coke? Ecstasy?'

'Oh, please. I wish.'

'You're certainly high on something.'

'I'm not on trial here, Warren. Don't treat me like I'm one of those witnesses . . . What are they called?'

'Jehovah's?' Warren deadpanned.

More laughter. 'Now, see, I knew you had a sense of humour . . . Hostile! That's the word I'm looking for. I'm not a hostile witness.'

'I'm not going to talk to you when you're in this condition.'

'I'm not stoned, Warren. So I might have smoked a little weed before I got here. Can you blame me for wanting to take the edge off things? It's not exactly pleasant, coming down here, seeing my sister in this condition. Let me guess what you're going to tell me. You spoke to William

Billy, one of Philadelphia's top lawyers—Philly's Willy Billy! How perfect is that?' She laughed again. 'Sorry. I couldn't resist. Besides, Casey thinks it's funny, too.'

'What?'

'Look at her face,' Drew said. 'She's laughing. I can tell.'

She was right, Casey realised. 'Philly's Willy Billy' had done the trick. Despite everything, her sister had managed to make her laugh, even if Drew was the only person who could see it.

'You don't know what you're talking about,' Warren said.

'I was right about Casey being able to hear, and I'm right about this. Casey's laughing. She understands. So, you'd better be nice to me, because when she regains consciousness, she's going to be plenty pissed if you don't treat me well.'

'I'm trying to help you, you little twit.'

'How? By stealing my money?'

'Look, I don't want to argue. I spoke to my partner . . .'

'And you're the new executor of my parents' estate, right?'

'It's not that simple. In Casey's *absence*, I've been made *temporary* executor of the estate. Until we have a clearer understanding of what's happening with Casey, at which time a court will decide—'

'So we could be talking years,' Drew interrupted. 'Years with you *temporarily* in charge of *my* money.'

'You'll get your money, Drew. I intend to follow your sister's wishes to the letter. You'll continue to get your allowance.'

'This sucks, and you know it.'

'Nothing has changed.'

'*Everything's* changed. My sister is in a coma. You're the one calling the shots. Why do you get any part in the decision-making process?'

'Because I'm Casey's husband.'

'You've been her husband for what . . . all of two years? My father might not have trusted me with his precious estate, but he sure as hell wouldn't want you in charge of it.'

'This is getting us nowhere. It's a moot point anyway.'

'You're full of it. I'm talking to Willy Billy myself . . .'

'I'd be happy to make an appointment for you.'

'I don't need you to do anything for me. I'm going to hire my own Silly Billy, and then I'm going to sue your ass.'

'You do that, Drew. And while you're busy suing my ass, remember that it's very expensive to go to court. You also might want to think about the outcome of such a suit, considering the fact I'm a damn good lawyer. And *you* are an unwed single mother with a long history of drug abuse and promiscuity.'

'Whoa. That's some closing argument, Counsellor. Casey ever see this side of you?'

'Look, do what you have to do. Take me to court if you want to waste your money. I guess it beats shoving it up your nose.'

Silence, except for the sound of ragged breathing.

Casey couldn't tell who was breathing harder, Warren or Drew. She found herself actually feeling sorry for her younger sister. She was no match for Warren. He wouldn't allow himself to be steamrollered the way Casey had so often been by her younger sister.

'Who are you to tell me what I can or can't do?' Casey remembered Drew shouting at her one afternoon from across the living room of Drew's dark one-bedroom apartment in Penn's Landing. Heavy, mustard-coloured drapes, the stale odour of marijuana buried inside their deep folds, kept the late-day sun from the crowded, unkempt space, although Casey had no trouble making out the assorted drug paraphernalia spread across the glass coffee table.

'You're using again,' Casey stated plainly. 'How can you even think of having a baby?'

'You think I'll be such a horrible mother?'

'I think you'll be a great mother,' Casey said sincerely, 'when you're clean and sober and ready to settle down. Remember the problems you had because of the alcohol Alana drank when she—'

'You're comparing me to our mother? Not nice, Casey. Not nice at all. For Pete's sake, I'll do whatever it takes to get clean. And I'll take such good care of this baby. I know you don't think I can do it . . .' Drew wiped the tears away from her cheeks.

'I think you can do anything you set your mind to,' Casey argued, hearing the obvious lack of conviction in her voice, and knowing Drew could hear it, too. 'I just don't think now is the best time to be making this kind of decision.'

'I'm not interested in what you think,' Drew shouted. 'You know what *I* think? I think you should go to hell!'

And less than a year later, her sister was pacing back and forth across that same room, a squalling baby in her arms. 'What am I going to do, Casey? She hates me.'

'She doesn't hate you.'

'She cries all the time. I try so hard, Casey. I hold her. I sing to her. I feed her. She cries all day. She cries all night.'

'That's what babies do. Lola's fine, Drew. She's beautiful.'

'She *is* beautiful, isn't she?'

'Just like her mother.'

'I love her so much. Why does she hate me?'

'She doesn't hate you.'

'All I wanted was for her to love me. She knows I'm a fraud.'

'You're not a fraud. You're her mother.'

'I'm a horrible mother. Sometimes when she cries, I get so mad, I want to smother her with a pillow. Not that I'd do that.'

'I know that. You're exhausted,' Casey offered.

'I haven't slept in days. Every time I lie down, she starts to cry. It's like she's doing it on purpose.'

'She isn't.'

'I'm so tired.'

'How about hiring a baby nurse?' Casey broached carefully.

'You mean a nanny?' Drew spat out the word as if it were a curse. 'I won't have my child raised by strangers.'

'Nobody's saying it has to be for ever.'

'I can't afford a nanny.'

Casey shook her head. 'I'll pay for it.'

'I don't want your charity.'

'It's not charity.'

'Only because it'll come out of the estate. Because it's *my* money!'

'This is ridiculous, Drew. Can't you see I'm just trying to help? Why do you always have to make it about money?'

'Because that's what it's always about! Are you really so blind, or are you just stupid?'

'Oh, for Pete's sake. Why don't you just shut up?'

'Why don't you go to hell?' Drew snapped in return.

'So, when can I have my money?' Drew was asking now, her voice muffled, as if her chin were pressed against her throat.

'I can write you a cheque right now,' Warren said. Casey heard the scribbling of a ballpoint pen. 'Check it. Make sure it's the right amount.'

'It's fine.' A second's pause. 'Take care of yourself, Casey.'

And then Drew was gone.

'**N**ice to see you haven't lost your touch with the ladies,' a voice said from the doorway only seconds later.

Casey felt Warren jump to his feet. 'What the hell are you doing here?'

Who is it?

'Thought I'd check on how the patient is coming along.'

'Are you crazy?' Warren was clearly flustered.

'Relax. Take a few deep breaths. You're overreacting. If someone walks in, I'm just a friend from the gym, paying my respects.'

Who is this man? What's wrong? Why is Warren so upset?

'You need to leave right now.'

'I'm not going anywhere,' the man said calmly, walking towards the bed as the door swung shut behind him. 'It's been two months, Warren. You don't phone. You don't return calls.'

'I've been a little busy these days.'

'The dutiful, loving husband.'

'You didn't leave me a whole lot of choice,' Warren said.

What does that mean? What kind of choice?

'So how's Sleeping Beauty doing?' the man asked.

'I would think that's pretty self-evident.'

'She actually looks better than I expected. Are the police any closer to finding out what happened?'

Warren scoffed. 'No. They're clueless. Look, can we talk about this later? This is neither the time nor the place . . .'

'What is? You know this isn't my fault.'

'My wife might be in a coma, connected to a feeding tube, for the rest of her life, and you don't think it's your fault?'

I don't understand. What are you talking about?

'Hey,' the man protested. 'I'm really sorry for the way things turned out. But I ploughed into her at almost fifty miles an hour. A normal person would be dead after a hit like that.'

What? What! WHAT?!

'Would you shut up!'

Is this real? Did I drift off to sleep? Is it a TV movie?

'Look,' Warren whispered hoarsely. 'You have to keep your voice down. They've done tests. Casey can hear . . .'

'She can?' Casey felt the man's weight as he leaned across her bed. 'Can you hear me, Sleeping Beauty?' She felt him retreat. 'You're saying she understands what we're saying?'

'Probably not. But it's possible.'

A cluck of reluctant admiration. 'Hats off to you, Beauty,' the man said. 'You're a tough one.'

'Look,' Warren implored. 'You've got to get out of here.'

'Not until we come to an understanding.'

'An understanding about what?'

'Don't play dumb, Warren. It doesn't suit you. About fifty thousand dollars, to be precise.'

Fifty thousand dollars? For what?

'I don't give fifty thousand dollars to people who screw up.'

'I didn't screw up. It's obviously just a matter of time.'

'A matter of time,' Warren repeated wearily. 'According to the doctors, she could outlive us all.'

A long pause. 'Then we'll just have to speed things up.'

'How do you propose we do that?'

'Hey, man, I'm just a personal trainer. You're the one with the expensive degrees.'

'Yeah, well, when we talked at the gym, you gave me the distinct impression you'd done this kind of thing before. I thought I was dealing with an expert.'

The man laughed. 'Ever think of unplugging a couple of these tubes, maybe injecting an air bubble into her IV?'

Oh God. Somebody help me! Somebody!

'Yeah, right, moron. Nobody would suspect anything.'

'Hey, man, I know you're upset. No need to get testy.'

'I tend to get testy when people I hire don't do their jobs.'

Warren hired this man to kill me? It can't be. It can't be.

'It'll get done.' A sigh of resignation. 'So is she in here for good?'

'No. I should be able to take her home pretty soon.'

'And anything could happen after that.'

'It won't be easy,' Warren said. 'The police already suspect it wasn't an accident. I have to be very careful.'

'Don't worry, man. Nothing ties you to any of this.'

'Except if Casey understands and if she regains consciousness.'

Casey felt two sets of eyes burn into her flesh like acid.

'Then we'll just have to make sure that doesn't happen.'

Dear God. This is not happening.

'And how exactly do we do that?'

'You're a smart guy,' the man said. 'Call me when you think of something.' Casey felt the man's mouth inches from her own, his breath against her lips. 'Bye, Beauty. Take care of yourself.'

Footsteps receding. A door opening and closing.

This can't be happening, Casey thought again. She hadn't overheard her husband and another man discuss their failed attempt to murder her, and their plan to try again. *It hadn't happened.*

There was no way Warren would do anything to hurt her, let alone hire someone to kill her. It was ridiculous. What was the matter with her? First she'd been suspicious of Janine, then Drew. Now Warren? How could she think such insane thoughts?

What's the matter with me? Warren loves me.

She felt motion, a body moving towards her. Who? Was Warren still here? Was anybody?

'That was Nick,' Warren said casually. 'I'm sure you've heard me mention him. Great trainer. Lousy human being. Mean streak a mile wide. The kind of guy who likes pulling the wings off butterflies. I was joking around one day, told him he was wasting his time torturing jerks like me, said he should consider a career as a contract killer. He told me to name the time and place.' Warren scoffed. 'I shouldn't be talking about this, but the cat's out of the bag. Why couldn't you have died when you were supposed to?'

And then everything was still. It was as if the air in the room had suddenly ceased to circulate, and she was poised to stop breathing altogether. Panic surged through her veins.

'I'm gonna get a cup of coffee,' Warren said, his voice fading as he walked to the door. 'Don't suppose you want anything?'

So the mystery was solved.

How could it be? They'd been so happy. They never fought, rarely argued. And all the while, he was planning her death.

But why? Why would he want to kill her?

Why do you think? she asked herself. Money.

But Warren's the one who'd insisted on a prenup, Casey argued. And there are no insurance policies . . .

He doesn't need any of that, she realised. As her husband, he stood to inherit a good portion of her estate, even without a will. He'd probably walk away with a hundred million dollars.

'Nobody becomes a lawyer to get rich,' she heard him say. 'You're certainly not retiring at forty.'

Was that what he wanted after all? To retire at forty? *No. No way.* Warren had a thriving career that he loved. They had a terrific life together. There was no way he would do this.

He loves me.

A hundred million dollars could buy an awful lot of love.

'So how's our patient doing today?' someone asked.

What? Who said that?

'I see you're watching *Gaslight*. Great old movie.'

'I never saw that one,' a second voice said. 'What's it about?'

'The usual—unscrupulous husband tries to convince his wife she's losing her mind. That Ingrid Bergman was some beauty.'

Bye, Beauty.

'Her blood pressure's a little higher than normal. What's going on, Mrs Marshall? Are you in pain?'

You have to help me. I'm having these wild, horrible thoughts.

'Let's increase her meds.'

No. Please don't increase anything. I'm dopey enough, believe me. You should only know the weird things that have been going on in my rocked brain. If I weren't in a coma, I'd recommend I be committed.

'I have a favour to ask you,' one doctor said to the other.

'What's that?'

'If I ever get wheeled in here in that condition, just put a pillow over my face and end it right then and there, OK?'

'Only if you promise to do the same for me.'

They left the room.

Don't go. Somebody please help me before I lose my mind.

I trusted you, she thought. *I trusted you with my life.*

6

'"HE HAD BEEN LEFT an orphan when he was fresh from a public school,"' Janine read. '"His father, a military man, had made but little provision for three children, and when the boy Tertius asked to have a medical education, it seemed easier to his guardians to grant his request by apprenticing him to a country practitioner than to make any objections on the score of family dignity."'

'What's that you're reading her?' Patsy asked, adjusting Casey's pillow. The scent of lavender buzzed around Casey's face.

'*Middlemarch.*'

'*Middlemarch?* What's that mean?'

'It's the name of the town where the story is set.'

'What's it about?'

'Life.'

Patsy made a sound between a snort and a laugh. 'Any good?'

'It's considered a masterpiece.'

'It looks long,' Patsy said. 'Way too long for me. And look at the size of that print. I'd go blind.'

'You like big print, do you?' Casey pictured Janine's smile.

'I don't read that much,' Patsy confessed. 'I do like murder mysteries. They're always good for a laugh.'

'You find murder funny?'

'Well, not funny, no. But interesting. Like what's going on with Mrs Marshall.' Patsy drew an audible breath. 'Do you think somebody really tried to kill her?'

'Well, the police have pretty much eliminated all their major suspects. Apparently, none of their leads panned out,' Janine said.

What? Are you saying they've closed their investigation?

'Anyway, sorry to interrupt. Go on. Read some more.'

Casey pictured Janine's back stiffening. She always hated anyone telling her what to do. '"Most of us who turn to any subject with love,"' she continued, after a prolonged pause, '"remember some morning or evening hour when we got on a high stool to reach down an untried volume, or sat with parted lips listening to a new talker, or for very lack of books began to listen to the voices within, as the first traceable beginning of our love."'

'What's that mean?' Patsy asked.

'I guess it's about remembering the first time we realised we loved something or someone.'

'Why doesn't he just say that, then?'

'She,' Janine corrected.

'Huh?'

'Never mind.'

I knew I was in love with Warren the minute I laid eyes on him, Casey thought. Although the experts would no doubt insist that was just physical attraction. The love, they would argue, came later, after she got to know him.

Except she hadn't got to know him. Not really.

Who was this man she'd married? Was Warren Marshall even his real name? Had his mother really been married five times? Was it from her that Warren had inherited his taste for the finer things in life? All those wonderful things he'd told Patsy about her, had he meant any of them? Or had he merely been like any true sociopath, Casey thought, giving people what they needed to hear?

'I want you to know how much these last two years have meant to me,' he'd told her. 'You've been such a great wife, Casey, the best lover and companion any man could hope for.'

Had he meant any of it? Or did he lie in bed at night wondering, as she did, what his next move would be.

'You and Mrs Marshall have been friends a long time, huh?'

'Since college.'

And I doubted you. What kind of friend does that make me?

'Mr Marshall said you used to be in business together.'

'Really? So what else did Mr Marshall say about me?'

'That was pretty much it.'

'Pretty much it,' Janine repeated absently. 'So how does he seem to you? How is he holding up?'

'He's amazing. I guess they were really crazy about each other.'

'What makes you say that?'

'Oh, the way he's always holding her hand and whispering to her. It's got to be so hard, don't you think? I mean, one minute, you're a happily married man, and the next, well . . .'

'Life's just full of unpleasant little surprises,' Janine said.

'So, what kind of lawyer is he?' Patsy asked.

'Why? You in some sort of trouble?'

'Me? No. Of course not. I was just making conversation.'

'Not really necessary,' Janine said.

Patsy cleared her throat. 'I guess I should go.'

Casey felt Janine smile brightly. 'Don't let me keep you.'

'Well, it was nice talking to you,' Patsy said, lingering nonetheless.

'Have a good day,' came the quick retort.

'Oh, hello, Mr Marshall,' Patsy exclaimed suddenly. 'You're late today.'

So that's why you've been hanging around.

'I had a meeting with Casey's doctors,' Warren said, approaching the bed. Sitting down, he kissed Casey's forehead. 'Hi, sweetheart. How are you feeling this morning?'

Improving every day. Isn't that what you're afraid of?

'Hi, Janine. How are things in Middlemarch?'

'Marching steadily towards the middle,' Janine quipped.

Patsy laughed. 'Your friend's very funny.'

'Yes, she is,' Warren said. 'Casey looks pretty good today.'

'Her trach's healing nicely. Now that the ventilator's gone and the tubes are all out, I'd say it's just a matter of time,' said Patsy.

'Time for what?' Janine asked.

'I'm planning to take Casey home,' Warren answered.

'Really? You think that's a good idea?'

'I can't think of anything better than Casey in her own home.'

'But she still has a feeding tube,' Janine reminded him. 'And she's still unconscious.'

'That's irrelevant at this point.' A trace of impatience whisked through Warren's voice.

Irrelevant?

'Irrelevant?'

'The doctors have done all they can here, and they desperately need the bed. It becomes a question of whether Casey goes into a rehab clinic or whether she comes home.'

Don't let him take me home. Please, Janine. He only wants to get me home so he can finish what he started.

'But she'll need nurses round the clock.'

'She'll have them. I've also hired a housekeeper and arranged for her physical therapist to come three times a week.'

'And I'll be there,' Patsy chirped.

'You?' Janine asked.

'Casey's going to need all the care she can get,' Warren said.

'Well,' Janine said. 'You seem to have thought of everything. So when is the big move scheduled?'

'As soon as the paperwork can be processed. God willing, I might be able to take my wife home as early as tomorrow.'

Warren leaned closer. Casey felt his eyes boring into hers.

'Isn't that wonderful, Casey? You're going home.'

They came for her at ten o'clock the next morning.

'Well, this is a very big day for you,' one of the interns said, radiating the fake cheer they all seemed to adopt when talking to her, as if she were a not-very-bright three-year-old.

Casey thought the voice belonged to Dr Slotnick, but she couldn't be sure. A new batch of interns had arrived last week.

'I bet you can't wait to get out of here.'

No, please, don't let them take me. I need more time.

But all morning, nurses and orderlies had been filing in to say goodbye. Interns, residents, surgeons and specialists alike had all dropped by to pay their respects.

As if I've already died, Casey thought.

'Good luck, Casey,' another intern offered, touching her arm.

'Well, I think that's everything,' Warren suddenly announced, bounding into the room. 'Everything is ready to go.'

'You'll keep us apprised of her progress?' Dr Keith asked.

Has anybody called the police? Does Detective Spinetti know I'm about to be released?

'Of course,' Warren answered. 'Every little improvement, you'll be the first to hear about it.'

'If at any point you feel you've taken on too much, Lankenau Hospital in Wynnewood has a wonderful rehab—'

'I'm sure that won't be necessary, but thank you. Thank you all,' Warren said. 'You've been so kind to Casey, and to me. Words can never express how grateful I am.'

Casey heard sniffling. People were fighting back tears.

'But now it's my turn to take care of Casey,' Warren continued. 'Here's hoping that next time I see any of you, my wife will be able to thank each of you in person.'

'Here's hoping,' several voices around her bed agreed.

She heard the squeal of a stretcher racing down the hall to her room. 'Well, here we are,' Warren said.

'Be careful with her head,' someone cautioned, as strong hands gripped her ankles, hips and shoulders.

Casey's body slid effortlessly from the bed that had been her home for the last three months onto the narrow stretcher. In the next second, she was being strapped in and wheeled from the room.

'Can I get you anything, Mr Marshall?' Patsy was asking. 'I can have the housekeeper put on a fresh pot of coffee.'

'How about something a little stronger? A gin and tonic sounds pretty good right now.'

'Then a gin and tonic it shall be.'

'Why don't you fix yourself a glass as well. It's been a hectic day. I think we both deserve a break.'

'Really? Thank you, Mr Marshall. I'll be right back.'

'Patsy . . . didn't we agree to dispense with formalities? I insist you call me Warren.'

A satisfied sigh. 'I'll be right back, Warren.'

'The gin's in the cabinet beside the bar,' Warren called after her. 'And there should be lots of tonic in the fridge.'

'I'll find it.' Patsy's footsteps retreated down the stairs.

'And how about you, sweetheart?' Warren asked, a solicitous hand brushing across Casey's forehead. 'I wish there was something I could get you. Are you OK? Do you even know where you are?'

Casey felt her heart quicken at his touch, the way it always had. Except before, desire fuelled its pace. Now it was fear.

'You must be exhausted,' he continued. 'All that moving. All that jostling around. But you're as snug as a bug in a rug now. I hope you like your new bed. It looks comfortable. It should be—it cost a small fortune. I let the delivery guys take away the old bed. I figured we wouldn't need it any more. It was always a little girly for my taste anyway. Once you're all better, we can sell this mausoleum, start hunting for that perfect family house you wanted. Then we'll just buy everything new. Lots of bright colours. How does that sound?'

Sounds wonderful, Casey thought, wondering why her husband was being so nice to her. Was someone else there?

'I've moved into your parents' bedroom,' he continued. 'It doesn't have the same memories for me that it has for you, so I transferred my stuff there, temporarily.'

You've moved into my parents' bedroom?

'I thought you should have your own space. Your bed faces the window, and if you stretch your neck a bit, you can see the creek behind the weeping willow. So that's something to aspire to. Can you hear me, Casey? Do you understand what I'm saying?'

She was home. That much she understood. In her lilac-and-white bedroom, the same room she and Warren had been sharing since the day they'd moved here.

Except he'd got rid of their queen-size bed and moved into the master bedroom.

Where would Patsy be sleeping? she wondered.

The phone rang. Casey felt Warren rise from his chair beside the bed. Which chair? she wondered. The mauve-and-cream-striped armchair or one of the floral tub chairs?

'Hello?' Warren said. 'Oh, Gail. Yes, Casey's fine. We got home about lunchtime, and I'm sorry, I know I said I'd call, but it's been very hectic.'

It has?

Actually, it had been pretty quiet, Casey thought. She'd been left pretty much on her own during the afternoon. Patsy had checked in on her regularly, turning on the large flat-screen TV and monitoring her blood pressure. Warren had stuck his head in the door occasionally to say hello, but she'd fallen asleep in the middle of *Guiding Light* and only awakened to the sound of sirens from the five o'clock news.

'Yes, her blood pressure spiked a little bit when we first got her home, but it's pretty much back to normal. That's why I'd like to hold off on any visitors for a few days. I know how anxious you are to see her, and the flowers you and Janine sent are lovely. I have them sitting on the table beside Casey's bed.'

Casey sniffed, detected the fragrance of lilies of the valley.

'I'd just like to give Casey some time to adjust, you know . . . Thanks. Of course I will. And if you wouldn't mind calling Janine . . . OK. Great. Of course. Goodbye.' He hung up the phone. 'Gail sends you her love, says she has *lots* to tell you. Whatever that means. She also asked me to give you a kiss.' Warren planted a kiss on the side of her cheek. 'Any excuse to kiss my girl,' he said, as the sound of tinkling ice cubes echoed through the room.

'Everything OK?' Patsy asked, approaching.

'Everything's fine. Casey seems to be resting comfortably.'

'How about you?'

'Me? I'll be fine once I have a sip of this. Thank you.'

'I hope it's not too strong.'

'No such thing.' Casey heard him take a sip. 'Perfect.'

'Mrs Singer says dinner's in the oven. I told her she could go home.'

'Thanks. I didn't realise it was so late.'

Who's Mrs Singer?

'Has she been with you long?' Patsy asked.

'Just since Casey's accident. I was having trouble managing on my own.'

'I don't doubt it. This is an enormous house. You didn't have full-time help before?'

'Casey never wanted it. She grew up with a houseful of servants. It conjures up bad memories for her.'

'I see,' Patsy said, although, clearly, she didn't.

'We had a cleaning lady come in twice a week,' Warren said.

'Who did the cooking?'

'Well, we ate out a lot, especially when we were both working in the city. Other times, if Casey was home, she'd whip up some pasta. If I got off work early, I'd throw steaks on the barbecue.'

'And how do you like your steaks?' Patsy asked.

'Rare,' Warren said. 'Almost blue.'

'Yikes.'

'You'll have to try one of my steaks. But only on condition that you have it rare. I hope you like garlic.'

'I love it.'

Well, isn't this nice and cosy.

'Good. Because my steaks are loaded with it. It'll be days before you can kiss your boyfriend.'

'Then I guess it's a good thing I don't have one. It's not that easy to meet people in this city. Trust me.'

Oh, this just keeps getting better.

'Yeah. I guess you have to be lucky.'

'Like you were,' Patsy said. 'I was married once. It was annulled,' she added quickly. 'I think he moved to LA. Everyone was always saying how he should be an actor or something.'

The phone rang again.

'Excuse me,' Warren said, answering it. 'Hello?' A slight pause. 'Janine, hi. How are you?'

'Would you like me to refresh your drink?' Patsy whispered.

'That would be great, thank you,' Warren said. 'Yes, Janine, that was indeed Patsy. She just offered to get me a cup of tea. It's been a long day . . . Yes, I know I said I'd call. Gail phoned here earlier. I asked her to tell you . . . Yes, that's right . . . Because I think Casey needs time to acclimatise herself to her new surroundings. Her blood pressure was a little high . . . Yes, Saturday would be perfect. Oh, and thanks for the flowers. They're lovely . . . OK, we'll see you and Gail on Saturday. Bye.' He hung up the phone.

Patsy re-entered the room. 'Here you go,' she said. Again, the sound of ice cubes.

'Mmm. Even better than the first.'

'Thank you. How's Janine?'

'Indestructible. Come Armageddon, all that will be left are the cockroaches and Janine.'

'It doesn't sound as if you like her very much.'

'Let's just say a little of her goes a long way.' The phone rang again. 'It's like Grand Central Station in here.'

'Would you like me to get it?' Patsy offered.

'No, that's all right. Hello,' he barked into the receiver. A long pause, then, 'Oh, yes, Steve. Sorry. I forgot all about the meeting. If you'll just give me half a minute to locate that file . . .'

'Can I help?' Patsy volunteered.

'My briefcase is in my office downstairs,' he whispered. 'The room with the large oak desk and leather furniture.'

'I'll be right back.'

'Yes, someone's just gone to get my briefcase . . . What the hell do you think you're doing, calling here?' Warren suddenly snapped. 'Don't you know calls can be traced?'

What's going on?

'Yes, she's here,' Warren continued. 'I'm with her right now, as a matter of fact. She's getting stronger every day.'

'Here it is,' Patsy exclaimed as she re-entered the room.

'Thank you.'

'Would you like me to leave?'

'Sorry, yes. This is highly confidential. If you wouldn't mind closing the door . . . Yes, sorry about that, Steve. Thanks for your patience. If you'll allow me a minute to look over the contract . . .'

The door closed. Warren's tone changed instantly. 'Look, I can't talk to you now. I'll have to get back to you. It won't be long, that's all I can say right now. In the meantime, don't even think of dropping by. Do you understand?' He slammed down the receiver. 'People are so stupid!' he exclaimed.

That was the man who visited you at the hospital, wasn't it?

She listened to him pace back and forth in front of the bed.

Somebody help me. Get me out of here. Somebody, please.

'Her blood pressure's spiking again,' she heard Patsy say. 'One-seventy over a hundred.'

When had Patsy come back?

'Should we call the doctor?' Warren said.

'I don't think that's necessary. Dr Keith said this was to be expected. If it goes any higher, I'll call the hospital. I'm sure it should sort itself out by morning.'

'I feel so useless.'

'You're doing everything humanly possible to help Casey. No one could be more supportive.'

'I thought moving her home would help her get better.'

'It will. You just have to give it time.'

'You believe that? Thank you. You're very sweet.'

The phone rang.

'Let voicemail take it,' Warren said wearily. 'It's probably Drew.' The phone stopped after three rings.

'Why don't you get something to eat. I'll stay with Casey.'

Casey felt Warren's hesitation. 'That's probably a good idea. I'll be back soon, sweetheart,' he said reassuringly. A pause, then, 'Do you think she has any idea how much I love her?'

'I'm sure she knows,' came Patsy's unequivocal response.

7

'Jeez, MORE FLOWERS,' Patsy said, sweeping into the room.

What day is it? Casey wondered, snapping awake. Where am I?

'It's like a funeral parlour in here.' The sound of a heavy vase being deposited on a table. 'Which I guess it is, in a way,' Patsy continued cheerily. 'Don't tell your husband I said that.' She giggled. 'Anyway, this latest batch is from the good doctors and nurses at Pennsylvania Hospital. I guess they miss you.'

So she was home, Casey realised. She hadn't dreamed the move. She was really here.

'That was very thoughtful of them to send you flowers, if you ask me. Not that there was any mention of nurses' aides on the card. Nobody ever thinks to include us. Guess I should have stayed in school, got my nurse's diploma, but I thought . . . Hell, I probably wasn't thinking at all. That's what my mother would say.' The sound of drapes being pulled back. 'Let's say we get some light in here. Such a pretty view you've got.'

Casey agreed. She'd always loved the view from this window. It was the reason she'd selected this bedroom over any of the seven others. Drew had wanted it, too, but Casey had got here first. She always did, Casey recognised, with the sharp stab of guilt she always felt when she thought of her younger sister.

'I guess I can't really fault her,' Patsy continued. 'My mom, I mean. I've made some pretty stupid decisions. Dropping out of school at sixteen. Marrying Jeff at eighteen. Not getting my nursing diploma. Wasting two whole years waiting for Johnny Tuttle to leave his wife, which, of course, he never intended to do.' She laughed. 'Mothers—there ain't nothing like them.'

You'll get no argument from me there.

Visions of Alana Lerner circled Casey's head like buzzing flies: Alana with a crystal champagne glass in her hand; Alana impatiently pushing Casey aside when she snuggled up against her; Alana all dolled up and ready to go out; Alana's bloated corpse when they pulled her from the waters of Chesapeake Bay.

Still, Casey had cried when she'd been called on to identify her mother's body. Unlike Drew. 'Oh, come on, Casey. You expect me to be a hypocrite?' she'd said.

'I expect you to show a little respect.'

'Then you expect too much.'

Had she expected too much of Drew? Was she still expecting too much? Or maybe she'd never expected enough.

'Your mother was quite the beauty,' Patsy was saying, roughly lifting Casey's head to fluff out her pillow. 'Warren showed me some old picture where she's wearing a long, beaded gown and a diamond tiara, like the queen of England. A drama queen is more like it, I understand.'

Another image flashed across the dark screen of Casey's eyes: Alana, her long, beaded gown stained with champagne, her tiara slightly askew, streaks of mascara wobbling across her cheeks as she stumbled towards her bed, Ronald Lerner behind her, the child Casey behind them, unnoticed.

'For goodness' sake, just listen to yourself!' he was saying.

'Don't you dare tell me I'm imagining things. The whole room saw it. Does everyone have to know about your latest conquest? Do you always have to humiliate me in front of my friends?'

'You do a good job of that all by yourself,' Ronald Lerner said.

'You're so damn smug.'

'You're so damn drunk.'

'Miserable bastard.'

'Pathetic bitch.'

Casey watched her mother lurch to the night table, tripping over her silver stilettos as she struggled to open the drawer.

'What the hell are you doing now?' her father demanded.

'So I'm pathetic, am I?' her mother countered, her right hand rifling blindly through the drawer's contents. 'How pathetic is this?'

'Alana, put that gun away before you hurt someone.'

'I'll show you who's pathetic. I'll kill us. I'll kill us both!'

And suddenly Casey's father was knocking the gun from her hand and slapping her hard across the face.

'Pathetic bitch!' he kept saying, wrestling Alana to the bed, Alana punching at his head as he fought to secure her hands. And then he was fumbling with her gown, and she was tugging on his jacket, and soon their angry shouts had turned to squeals and laughter. Casey backed slowly out of the room.

The next morning Casey had passed by her parents' bedroom and seen them having breakfast together in bed. Her father had waved with his free arm, his other arm draped across her mother's shoulders. They were smiling. Casey thought the entire episode had been a bad dream.

Until now. Had she really seen a gun in her mother's hand? Casey wondered. And if she had, where was it now? Had they taken it when they moved? Was it possible it was here, in this house?

'Not that I'm not a bit of a drama queen myself,' Patsy was saying. 'I have my moments. Just not the wardrobe.' She made an exaggerated sigh. 'Bet your closet is just stuffed with expensive designer clothes, like the kind your friend wears. What's her name? The bitchy one . . . Janine? Can I have a peek?'

Casey heard Patsy clomp towards the large walk-in closet to the right of her bed and open the door.

'You don't mind, do you? I've been wanting to have a look since I arrived, but I didn't want Warren to think I was being presumptuous. You don't mind me calling your husband Warren, do you? Not that it matters what you mind.'

Casey heard the flip of a light switch.

'Well, isn't this a disappointment. You're not a clothes horse, are you, Casey? And it's all a little conservative for my taste, not exactly what I was expecting. I mean, this is a nice little Armani jacket, and these are nice enough trousers—Prada—but honestly, Casey, what on earth are these? The Gap? And does everything have to be black or brown? Don't you know that colour is all the rage for spring? Although I guess you missed the change in the seasons this year. Didn't have time to switch your closet around before getting mowed down. You probably keep all your summer clothes in one of the other bedrooms. I'll have to do some exploring next time Warren goes to the gym, where he is now, incidentally. Said he was feeling all flabby. I told him he's in great shape, but I also told him it wasn't healthy to stay glued to your side twenty-four hours a day.

'Oh, this is nice,' she said in the next breath. 'A Hermès scarf. Is it real? Of course it is. You'd never buy one of those awful knockoffs, would you? No, you wouldn't have to. You don't mind if I wear it for a while, do you? Yellow and black aren't exactly my colours, but hey, it doesn't look half bad. What do you think? Oh, sorry. You can't think, can you? But don't you worry your empty little head. I'm thinking enough for both of us. And I'm thinking I'm making headway, as far as your husband is concerned.

'I mean, he's always spouting off about how much he loves you and everything, but I'm not blind. I see the way he looks at me. And he's a man, for heaven's sake. He can only go so long without a little . . . comfort. Do you understand anything I'm saying?' She chuckled. 'I kind of hope you do.'

The sound of the front door opening. Thank goodness, Casey thought. An end to this torture. Patsy scurried back to close the closet as the sound of angry voices reached Casey's ears.

'What were you doing? Hiding in the bushes all morning, waiting to ambush me?' Warren demanded from downstairs.

'You don't take my phone calls. You won't answer the door.'

Who's that? Is that Drew?

'Sounds like your sister's here,' Patsy said.

'I told you your cheque's in the mail. If you'd prefer to pick it up in person, I can arrange that with my office. Now, if you'll excuse me, I'd like to say hello to my wife.'

'Which, strangely enough, happens to be why *I'm* here. I didn't even know she was out of the hospital.'

'Maybe because you haven't visited her in over a month. She's the same as the last time you saw her, Drew. Go home.'

'This is my home,' Drew told him. 'At least half of it.'

'Not until your thirtieth birthday.'

'Which, in case you've forgotten, is fourteen months off.'

'A lot can happen in fourteen months,' Warren said.

What does that mean?

'What does that mean?' Drew asked. 'Are you threatening me?'

'I don't have to threaten you, Drew. I don't have to do anything. You're doing a great job of messing up your life all by yourself.'

'Are you actually going to physically stop me from going upstairs?' Drew demanded. 'I'll get a court order.'

'Be my guest,' Warren said.

'How about I tell the papers you won't let me see my sister?'

'You don't think this family's had enough bad press? What is this? A grab at the spotlight? Your fifteen minutes?'

'I just want to see my sister.'

A brief silence. Casey pictured her husband motioning towards the staircase in the centre of the circular hallway.

'Thank you,' Drew said.

Seconds later, she came bursting into the room.

Casey pictured her younger sister, arms waving, long legs striding purposefully across the threshold, dark blonde hair flying behind her,

her cheeks glowing with anger. *Oh, Drew. I'm so glad you're here. You have to help me. You have to get me out of here.*

'Who are you?' Drew demanded.

'I'm Casey's nurse,' Patsy replied. 'I'm Patsy Lukas.'

'Why are you wearing my sister's scarf?'

'What?' Casey envisioned Patsy's hand quickly floating towards her neck, an embarrassed flush spreading across her face.

'Take it off,' Drew instructed.

'I didn't mean anything by it. I was just . . .'

'. . . helping yourself to my sister's belongings?'

'No. Of course not. I was just—'

'What's going on here?' Warren asked from the doorway.

'It seems the hired help wears Hermès. My sister's Hermès, no less,' Drew told him.

'I'm so sorry,' Patsy said. 'I was trying to find something to brighten Casey up a bit for when you came home. I was just about to put it on her. Honestly, Warren. I wasn't—'

'Warren?' Drew said. 'So, we're on a first-name basis?'

'You're being very rude,' Warren told her. 'This is really none of your business. Casey is being very well looked after.'

'Is she?'

The scent of lavender suddenly swirled around Casey's head. Sturdy hands gripped the back of her neck as a swatch of silk slithered across her skin, before curling over itself at the base of her throat.

'There,' Patsy said. 'That's better.'

'You think so?' Drew asked. 'She looks awfully pale to me.'

'Your sister's fine,' Warren said. 'Her blood pressure spiked a bit the other day, but it's back to normal. The doctor said it was probably the move from the hospital.'

'Was he here? Did he check her himself?'

'There was no need. Patsy had everything under control.'

'Well, aren't you just the greatest thing since sliced bread?' Drew expelled a deep breath and plopped down in the nearest chair. 'You know, I could really use a cup of coffee.'

'There's a Starbucks not far from here.'

'The kitchen's closer. Patsy, dear, would you mind . . .?'

'OK, Drew, enough,' said Warren.

'It's all right,' Patsy said. 'I'm happy to do it. I'll ask Mrs Singer to put on a fresh pot.'

'Who the hell is Mrs Singer?'

'I hired a housekeeper to help out with Casey,' said Warren.

'How do you take your coffee, Drew?' Patsy asked.

'Hot and black.'

'Can I bring you a cup?' she asked Warren.

'No, thanks,' Warren said. After Patsy had gone, he cautioned, 'Drew, you could lose the attitude.'

'The woman was stealing from my sister's closet.'

'I'm sure she was doing no such thing.'

'Right. OK. Just what *does* she do?'

'You want the gory details? She monitors your sister's blood pressure, inserts and removes her feeding tube, bathes her, checks her for bedsores, adjusts her catheter. Do you want me to go on?'

No. Please, no more.

'No,' Drew said softly.

'It's not exactly anyone's idea of a good time, and I was very lucky— *we* were very lucky—that Patsy agreed to take it on.'

'Who takes over when Patsy goes home?'

Warren sighed. 'She doesn't go home. She's living here.'

'How convenient. And Mrs Singer? Does she live here as well?'

'No. I have no idea where she lives.'

'But Patsy lives *here*.'

'What are you getting at, Drew?'

'I just don't like the kind of vibes I'm getting. Those my-sister's-in-a-coma-and-some-tart's-wearing-her-clothes kind of vibes,' Drew said.

Casey laughed silently.

'That would be funny if it weren't so pathetic,' Warren said. 'I love your sister, Drew.'

No, don't believe him. He sounds sincere, but don't believe him.

'I know you do. You really believe she's going to get better?'

'I *have* to believe it.'

Don't believe anything he tells you. It's all a con.

'Have the police been in touch with you lately?' Drew asked.

'No. You?'

'No. I think they've lost interest. Look, I hate to bring this up again—'

'You want answers about your money,' Warren stated.

'I think I've been pretty patient.'

'I'm sorry, but things are going to take more time . . .'

'How much more time? Months? Years?' Casey could hear the anger edging back into Drew's voice.

'I don't know.'

'I don't like this, Warren. I don't like this one bit.'

'Look. I know you're upset, but it wasn't my idea to name your sister executor of the estate. It wasn't my idea that you be kept on a short leash and put on a strict allowance. Those were your father's instructions, and I'm just making sure those wishes are respected. If you could be patient a little longer, I might be able to get you a little extra something until everything's resolved.'

'That would be nice.'

'I'll call my office Monday, see what I can arrange.'

Don't be placated so easily. Don't make this just about the money.

'But I'm still picking up some peculiar vibes,' Drew said.

Way to go, Drew. That's the baby sister I know and love.

Warren sighed. 'OK. Whatever. Have it your way. Now, if you'll excuse me, I have some work to do for Monday.'

'Would you mind if I opened a window in here?' Drew called after him. 'The smell of cheap perfume is suffocating.'

'Just show yourself out when you're ready to leave.'

The sound of a squeaky brass handle being rotated. 'There. That's better. I always find lavender so cloying, don't you? It's supposed to make you feel relaxed, but it sets my teeth on edge.'

Casey felt a gentle hand slide the scarf from her throat.

'That's better,' Drew said. 'You need something with a little more zip. I know—you can wear this.' Casey felt Drew manoeuvre something over her head. 'It's a necklace,' Drew explained. 'Nothing much, just a silver chain with a tiny silver high-heeled shoe dangling from it. It reminded me of my Manolos. Anyway, it looks better on you. What do you think?' she asked, almost as if she expected an answer.

'So, what's up?' she asked after a pause of at least thirty seconds. 'Yeah, nothing much happening with me, either. Oh, except I got rid of Sean. You remember Sean. Anyway, I dumped him. He was starting to get on my nerves.' She laughed. 'To be honest, he didn't seem upset. The only one who was sad was Lola. Turns out she liked him. I know I'm not the greatest mother in the world, but am I terrible?' Drew asked. She paused, as if giving Casey a chance to respond. 'It's just that she's always *there*. Do you understand what I'm saying? Every time I turn round, there she is. And I want to say to her, look, can I just have a few days to myself? But how can I do that? And she's always looking at me, like she's expecting me to do something. It's an awful feeling when you think you're constantly disappointing everyone. Although I guess I should be used to it by now.'

Oh, Drew.

'I guess I thought it would be different, you know? I thought if I had a baby, she'd have to love me.'

She does love you, Drew.

A sigh trembled in the air between them. 'She loves *you*, though. Before your accident, she was always asking when we could go visit her aunt Casey.'

The disparate smells of coffee and lavender fought for supremacy as they entered the room like a pair of hostile, conjoined twins.

'Here's your coffee,' Patsy said.

'Thank you.'

'Careful. It's hot. Listen, I'm sorry about the misunderstanding earlier. I appreciate how it must have looked to you.'

'Well, I appreciate your appreciation. Let's leave it at that.'

The doorbell rang.

'That's probably her therapist,' Patsy said.

A few seconds later, Jeremy strode into the bedroom. 'Well, hello there,' he said. 'Haven't seen you in a while. How've you been?'

'Fine,' Drew answered. 'Nice to see you again.' Casey recognised the strained attempt to sound casual in her sister's voice.

'You're a little late,' Patsy told him. 'Everything OK?'

'There was an accident on the expressway, and I was stuck for twenty minutes. Sorry about that. The good news is I'm here now, and that coffee smells great. Think you could spare another cup?'

'How do you take it?'

'Cream, lots of sugar.'

Patsy exited the room, and Casey absorbed the intensity of Jeremy's gaze as he approached her bed. 'Hello, Casey. How are you feeling? Happy to be back home?'

No, I'm not happy. You have to get me out of here.

'Apparently her blood pressure spiked some,' Drew told him, 'but it's back to normal now.'

'She does look a little pale. Well, we'll see if a little exercise can't bring some colour back to her cheeks.'

'Do you want me to leave? I don't want to be in the way.'

'I'm sure Casey appreciates the company. I know I do.'

Casey felt his hand on her forehead. Could he feel her mind working? *Listen to me*, she thought, as hard as she could. *My husband did this to me. He tried to kill me, and he's going to try again. You have to get me away from here.*

'She doesn't have a fever, does she?' Drew asked.

'No. Her forehead's nice and cool. And speaking of nice and cool, that's a cool little necklace she's wearing. You give her that?'

'Yes. How d'you know?'

''Cause it looks like you.'

'I look like a shoe?' Drew laughed.

'You know what I mean.'

'Well, thank you. I think. I mean, I'll take that as a compliment.'

'Good. That's the way it was intended.' Jeremy took Casey's right hand in his own and started to manipulate her fingers.

'Can I ask you a question?' Drew asked.

'Fire away.'

A moment's hesitation. 'What's your opinion of Patsy?'

A brief pause. 'Personally, I don't know her well. Professionally, I'd say she's competent, knowledgeable, compassionate. Patients like her. She's certainly dedicated to your sister.'

'You think so?'

'You don't? Did something happen?'

'I'm not sure. When I got here, she was wearing one of Casey's expensive scarves, and I got mad and said a few things I shouldn't have. She said she was about to put it on Casey when I came in.'

Jeremy lowered Casey's right hand, picked up her left. 'Well, if your instincts are telling you she was trying to pull a fast one, I'd say she was trying to pull a fast one.'

Casey could actually feel Drew's grateful smile. 'Thank you.'

'For what? What does Mr Marshall think?'

'I'm afraid he doesn't share your faith in my instincts. I guess the important thing is that she's a good nurse, right?'

Jeremy began massaging the muscles in the palm of Casey's hand with his thumb. If only she could grab that thumb, Casey thought. If only she could let him know . . .

'She's not actually a nurse,' Jeremy said. 'She's a nurse's aide.'

'I don't understand. Why would Warren hire her if she's not a nurse? It's not like he doesn't have the money . . .'

'Don't go getting all upset. Patsy's more than qualified. Your sister doesn't really need an RN at this point. And like I said, Patsy is knowledgeable and competent. She tends to go the extra mile. Plus, she's very familiar with Casey's condition. Frankly, I thought Mr Marshall was lucky to get her.' He rotated Casey's wrist. 'But you don't like her.'

'I don't like her,' Drew said quietly.

Footsteps on the stairs. The smell of fresh coffee.

'Cream, lots of sugar,' Patsy said cheerily from the doorway.

'If you wouldn't mind putting it on the nightstand for me. Thank you,' Jeremy said. Patsy's steps crossed the room to the small table beside the bed. 'That's great.'

'What about you, Drew? You ready for another cup?'

'I'm fine, thank you,' Drew said. 'Jeremy's shown me some exercises I can do with Casey. Maybe you'd like to stay so he can show you, too.'

'How about you show me later? Mr Marshall needs me to take care of a few things. Just holler when you're done, Jeremy.'

Patsy left the room.

Please. You have to help me. You have to get me out of here.

'So, OK. I'm a total bitch, right?' Drew stated. 'I mean, could she be any sweeter?'

'I don't know,' Jeremy said. 'I tend to be a little suspicious of people who are too sweet.'

Again, Casey felt Drew smile. 'So, just how *is* Casey doing?'

'Well, she has good flexibility and an excellent muscle base. Here, why don't you start on her other arm . . . That's right . . . just do what I showed you last time.'

'How realistic are her chances of being able to walk again?'

'There's no physical reason why she shouldn't walk again once she wakes up and her brain starts sending out the correct messages.'

I am awake, *dammit. Why isn't my brain sending them? Come on, brain. Concentrate. Do something. Do anything.*

'So have you been doing this sort of work long?' Drew asked.

'Not that long,' Jeremy replied. 'A little over four years.'

'And before that?'

'The army.'

'The army?'

'Long, sad story.' He sighed. 'My wife and I were struggling to make ends meet. I had student loans the army offered to repay if I enlisted. The recruiting officer said I'd probably never be sent overseas, and that in the very unlikely event that I was, I'd be assigned to the medical unit and almost certainly wouldn't see any direct combat.'

'Where'd they send you?'

'Afghanistan.'

'The recruiting officer lied to you about everything?'

'Well, that's the thing. He didn't exactly lie. He was very careful in his choice of words.'

'Were you scared?'

'Yes.'

Drew's voice fell to a whisper. 'Did you kill anybody?'

A long pause. 'Yes.'

'How awful. I don't think I could kill anyone.'

Casey felt Jeremy reach across her for his coffee, heard him take a tentative sip. 'You'd be amazed at what you're capable of doing. Especially when someone's trying to kill you.'

'How long were you over there?'

'Twenty-three months, one week and five days. But who's counting? By the time I got home, my wife had pretty much moved on. Anyway, what's done is done.' He turned his attention to Casey's legs. 'How about you?'

'Me?'

'How are things working out for you?'

Casey felt Drew shrug. 'I guess I'm still a work in progress.'

'Haven't decided what you want to be when you grow up?'

'Is that awful? I mean, I'm almost thirty. I have a child.'

'I know you'll figure it out.'

'Well, I appreciate the vote of confidence. Thank you. Do you mind if I ask you another question?' Drew asked.

'Go ahead.'

'What's it like to kill somebody?'

Silence. Then, 'I'm not sure I can answer that.'

'Sorry. I shouldn't have asked.'

'The problem is I'm really not sure how it felt, to be honest. I was so scared.' He took another sip of coffee. 'You're in a strange country, you don't speak the language. All you know is that bombs and land mines are exploding. Your adrenaline is pumping, and when you fire that weapon and you see that body drop, you don't have time to feel anything, except maybe relief it wasn't you. I don't know. All that destruction. All that blood. Sooner or later, you don't feel anything. That's probably the worst part. To kill another human being and not feel anything at all.'

Was that how Warren felt? Casey wondered. Had he felt nothing while plotting her death? Nothing at all?

'Sometimes it feels great not feeling anything. Isn't that why most people do drugs, so that they don't have to feel?'

'Is that why *you* do them?'

'People think you do drugs to get high,' Drew answered. 'But it's not to get high so much as to get where you're *so* high that you're floating above all the crap and don't feel anything at all.'

'I tried cocaine a couple of times,' Jeremy said. 'Hated the coming down. Decided it just wasn't worth it.'

'Yeah, I've decided that a couple of times myself.'

'What about your sister?' Jeremy asked, bending Casey's leg.

'Oh, no. Casey would never do drugs. Never. Ever. She was such a straight arrow. Always in control.'

'She's not in control now,' Jeremy stated.

'No, she's not. How fair is that?' Drew squeezed Casey's hand. 'She spends her whole life being the good daughter and the perfect wife and the consummate professional, and look how she ends up. You join the army to pay off a few loans and end up killing people. I spend half my life shoving drugs up my nose, yet here I sit, alive and relatively healthy. So, what's the point of anything?'

The point is that we have no control. The point is that there are no guarantees, but we can't give up. The point is that, fallible as we all are, we have to reach out to others . . .

'Oh my God!' Drew exclaimed. 'She just squeezed my hand.'

'What? Are you sure?'

I did? I squeezed your hand?

'I'm telling you—she just squeezed my hand!'

Casey felt Jeremy remove her hand from Drew's. 'I'm not feeling anything,' he said after several seconds.

'I wasn't imagining things, I swear,' Drew insisted.

'Can you do it again, Casey?' Jeremy squeezed her fingers, as if to show her how.

Yes, I can. I can. There. I'm squeezing. I'm squeezing.

'Anything?' Drew asked.

'I'm not sure.'

What do you mean? I'm squeezing your fingers hard.

'Come on, Casey. You can do it,' Drew urged.

'Even if she did squeeze your hand,' Jeremy said, 'that doesn't mean she was reacting to anything specific.'

'What *does* it mean?' another voice asked. Warren, Casey realised, a sinking sensation in the pit of her stomach.

'It was most likely a muscle spasm,' Jeremy explained.

'But it could be more than that,' Drew said. 'It could mean Casey's starting to regain the use of her hands. Couldn't it?'

'It could,' Jeremy said. 'But we shouldn't get our hopes up just yet.'

'Jeremy's right,' Warren said, lifting Casey's hand to his lips and gently kissing each finger. 'We'll just have to wait and see.'

$$8$$

IT WAS THE MIDDLE of the night, and the house was completely still.

Casey lay in her bed, wide awake. How much time had elapsed since she'd squeezed her sister's hand? How many hours had she spent going over every detail of what had transpired? Had she really squeezed Drew's hand, and if so, had it been a deliberate act?

Warren was certainly curious to know the answer. He hadn't left her side all afternoon. He'd monitored her for the slightest twitch, eating lunch in his chair and forgoing his dinner, taking her hand and coaxing her to squeeze his fingers.

Jeremy had left when he'd concluded his session. Drew had stayed until the end of *Guiding Light*, and promised to return the following afternoon. Patsy had been in and out of the room, mostly fussing over Warren, until she retired for the night at eleven o'clock. Warren had remained until the end of the David Letterman show, then pressed the TV remote and plunged the room into silence.

It had been that way ever since, Casey thought now, listening to the assorted squeaks and clicks a house makes when everyone is asleep.

Had she squeezed Drew's hand, or had it been wishful thinking on her sister's part? she wondered, sensing a slight shift in the air.

Someone was coming. Casey felt her heartbeat quicken. Someone was watching her from the doorway.

'Casey,' her husband said. 'Are you awake?'

What was he doing here? Casey wondered. Had he come to finish the job he'd started? How? By holding a pillow over her nose and mouth? By injecting an air bubble into her veins?

'I couldn't sleep,' Warren told her now, as he crossed the floor to stand by the window. 'How about you?'

Had he been having trouble sleeping, as he sometimes did, and reflexively turned to her, as he often had, for comfort?

Why are you here?

'It's really beautiful out. The sky is full of stars. The moon's almost full. You'd love it.'

I loved you. With all my heart. How could you have done this to me?

'So, is it true?' he asked, moving to the bed. 'Did you squeeze Drew's hand?' He took her palm in his. 'And if it wasn't your sister's overwrought imagination, was it simply a muscle spasm, or were you trying to communicate?'

So they'd spent the last several hours kept awake by the same gnawing questions, Casey thought, tortured by the same things. They were still in sync, even now.

Except they were never really in sync. It had all been an act.

Warren squeezed Casey's fingers. 'You can tell me, Casey,' he whispered seductively. 'You know you've never been able to keep anything from me. What do you think about, lying here all day and night? Do you think about me? About how happy we were?' He perched on the side of her bed, began absently stroking her thigh through the thin blanket.

Oh, Warren, she thought. We *were* happy, weren't we?

'I have to admit, I do miss you. I miss the interesting conversations we used to have. I miss how you used to snuggle up against me in bed. The way you touched me.' He took Casey's hand, moved it slowly to his leg. 'It's been so long,' he said. 'And I've been such a good boy. I actually think I've been a better husband since the accident. More attentive, more thoughtful. Certainly more faithful.'

What are you saying?

'You never had any idea, I'll bet. It was one of your greatest charms—your naiveté. Despite your upbringing, you still believed in marriage and monogamy. You still believed in fairy tales.'

Casey realised with an unseen shudder that her husband was talking about her in the past tense.

'Although, unlike your father, I was very discreet.'

Warren leaned in closer, his lips grazing her mouth. Casey wished she could turn her head aside, that she could pull her hand away, use it to slap him, hard, across the face.

He stood up, letting her hand flop down against the mattress like a dead fish. 'So, what to do, what to do,' he muttered. 'You're a real conundrum, Casey. What am I going to do with you?'

Haven't you done enough already?

He suddenly swooped closer, grabbed her chin roughly with his hand, forced her head up. 'Can you see this light? Can you?'

What was he doing?

'No blinks, powerful or otherwise,' he said with obvious relief. Casey heard fumbling and surmised he was returning a flashlight to the pocket of his robe. 'So, we know you still can't see. But it's just a matter of time, isn't it? And timing is everything. Right? *Right?* Dammit, Casey. Are you in there?'

'Is something wrong?' Patsy asked from the doorway.

Casey felt Warren jump. 'How long have you been there?'

'Just a few seconds. I thought I heard voices.'

'Unfortunately just mine,' Warren said, punctuating his sentence with a slight laugh of embarrassment.

Nice touch, thought Casey.

'Is something wrong?' Patsy asked. 'Is Casey all right?'

'She's fine. I just couldn't sleep,' Warren explained. 'I thought I might as well get up and see how she was doing.'

'Can I make you something to eat? You didn't have any dinner. You must be starving.'

'Not really.'

'How about some tea?'

'No. Thank you. You should go back to bed. It's going to be pretty hectic tomorrow—Casey's having lots of visitors. I'm sorry if I woke you.'

'Don't be. I'm a light sleeper. You actually saved me from a very unpleasant dream.'

'Really? What was it about?'

'Standard nightmare stuff. Faceless, knife-wielding man chasing me down a dark alley . . . Like I said, you saved me.'

'Glad to be of service.'

'How about something nice and simple like a cup of hot chocolate?' Patsy offered. 'It might help you sleep.'

'I don't want to put you to any trouble.'

'It's no trouble. Honestly.'

'Sure, hot chocolate sounds . . .' A sob caught in Warren's throat. 'I'm sorry,' he said, his voice suddenly awash with tears.

Casey felt Patsy rush to Warren's side and gather him in her arms as he cried. 'It's all right. Let it out. Let it out,' Patsy said.

'It's so awful. I'm so sorry. I'm trying to stay strong for Casey.'

'Nobody can be strong twenty-four hours a day.'

'But it's not enough. Sometimes I feel like such a failure.'

'You're not a failure. You're the best man I know.'

And suddenly the room fell silent, and Casey could see even without the benefit of sight that Patsy was now in Warren's arms, and that his lips were pressing tenderly against hers.

'Oh God, I'm sorry,' Warren apologised immediately, pulling back.

'I don't know what came over me. How could I do something like that?'

'Nothing happened, Warren. It's all right.'

'It's *not* all right. I've put you in an untenable position. I'll understand completely if you want to leave.'

'I'm not going anywhere. You were upset.'

'That's no excuse. I had no right.'

Another silence. Then Warren's voice: 'You're so sweet. Casey's lucky to have you. We're both lucky,' he added.

'How about I go make that hot chocolate?'

'I think I should just get some sleep,' Warren said, walking to the door. 'Clearly, I'm not thinking straight.'

'I'll see you in the morning, then. Good night, Warren.'

'Good night, Patsy. I'm really so sorry . . .'

Seconds later, Casey heard the doors to Warren's and Patsy's respective rooms close. Seconds after that, she felt a stirring in her fingers and realised her hands were curled into fists at her sides.

'"**D**orothea rang and asked Tantripp to bring her some wraps. She had been sitting still for a few minutes, but not in any renewal of the former conflict: she simply felt that she was going to say 'Yes' to her own doom: she was too full of dread at the thought of—"'

'OK,' Janine said, interrupting her own reading. 'That's all I can take for one day. I'm afraid poor Dorothea's starting to get on my nerves. How about we shift our attention to something more forceful, such as the current *Vogue*, which I happen to have.' The shuffling of objects, the turning of pages. 'Did you know that the hippie look—how awful—is making a comeback for autumn? Autumn! It's barely summer, and they're talking about fall?' She lowered the magazine to the bed, her hand grazing Casey's.

Slowly, carefully, Casey stretched her fingers towards Janine's.

'We have a visitor,' Warren announced, coming into the room.

Immediately Casey's fingers retreated. Had he seen them move?

'Detective Spinetti,' Janine said, her surprise evident.

Detective Spinetti? Thank goodness you're here.

'Ms Pegabo,' the detective replied. 'Nice to see you.'

'Have there been any new developments?'

'No, I'm afraid not.'

'What happened with Richard Mooney?' Janine asked.

'The doorman at his mother's building remembered seeing him around the time of Casey's accident, so . . .'

'Casey's *accident?*' Warren stressed.

'We're still not completely satisfied . . . but we have no proof it was anything else.'

'You never found the SUV that hit her?' Janine asked.

'We're still looking. But it's probably scrap metal by now.'

'And I take it there are no new suspects,' Warren stated.

'I'm afraid not. But don't get the impression we're dropping the case. Sometimes we have to be patient, hope for a break.'

'So, why *are* you here, Detective?' Warren asked.

'I heard Mrs Marshall was out of the hospital, and I thought I'd drop by to see how she was doing.'

'Well, that was very thoughtful,' Warren said. 'As you can see, there's been no real change.'

On the contrary. Look at me, Detective. Look at me.

'How are you managing?'

'We're doing OK. Casey has a nurse and a therapist, plus her friends stop by almost every day.'

'And her sister? Has she been here lately?'

'Yes. Why?'

'Just asking.'

You're asking about the wrong person.

'Well, I just wanted to pay my respects.'

No, don't leave. Look at me. Grab my hand.

'I can show Detective Spinetti out,' Patsy said. The scent of lavender suddenly tickled Casey's nose.

'Good luck, Casey,' Detective Spinetti said.

'Goodbye, Detective,' Janine said.

'Ms Pegabo, Mr Marshall,' Detective Spinetti said, then quickly exited the room.

No! Come back. Come back!

'What was that all about?' Janine asked. 'It sounded like he still considers Drew a suspect. What do you think?'

'I don't know what to think any more.' Warren released a long, deep breath. 'So, how are things at work? Doesn't seem as if you've been spending much time there.'

'No. I've kind of let things slide.'

'Nobody expects you to visit every day, you know.'

'I know.'

Another sigh. 'You have nothing to feel guilty about.'

'Who says I feel guilty? Do you?'

What are you talking about?

'Life's too short for regrets,' Warren said.

The doorbell rang. 'Busy morning,' Janine remarked.

Seconds later, a clumping on the stairs was followed by gleeful shouts. 'Auntie Casey, wait till you see what I made for you.'

'Easy there, Lola,' Warren cautioned as the little girl bounded into the room.

Casey pictured her niece in shorts and a T-shirt, her hair pulled into a high ponytail like her mother's. 'I painted a picture for Auntie Casey. It's a zebra.'

'I thought zebras were black and white,' Warren said.

'This one is special. It's black and white and orange and red.'

'It's very beautiful,' Janine said. 'Aunt Casey will love it.'

'Can I show it to her?'

'She can't see anything right now, sweetheart,' Warren explained. 'How about I tape it to the wall, and she'll see it as soon as she wakes up. I'll go get the tape.'

'Don't leave on my account,' Drew said, entering the room.

'He's getting tape for my picture,' Lola explained as she climbed onto the bed, arranging herself at Casey's feet.

Casey felt a stirring in her toes.

'Hi, Janine,' Drew said. 'Nice to see you again.'

'You just missed Detective Spinetti. Apparently he wanted to see how Casey was doing.'

Drew approached the bed. 'And how *is* she doing?'

'About the same.'

Casey began wiggling her toes beneath her blanket. *Look at my feet, Drew. Please, look at my feet.*

'I have a book,' Lola said. 'Where's my book, Mommy?'

'It's in my handbag somewhere. Handbags are so big these days, you can put your whole life in them. Omigod . . .'

Did you see that? Did you see my toes moving?

'Are my eyes deceiving me?' Drew asked. 'Is that really the new *Vogue*? Can I see it?'

Look at me, for goodness' sake.

'Careful. It's almost as heavy as your bag.'

'I want my book,' Lola demanded.

'Sorry, Lola. It looks like I forgot to bring it. Can't you make something up?' Drew started to flip through the pages of the magazine. 'Oh, great. The hippie look is coming back again. I love that.'

'OK,' Lola said. 'Since Auntie Casey's still asleep, I'll tell her the story of Sleeping Beauty.'

'How very appropriate,' Janine said.

'Once upon a time,' Lola began, 'there was a king and a queen who loved each other very much. Right, Mommy?'

'What?'

'You aren't listening.'

'Mommy's reading her magazine. Go on. Tell the story.'

'The king and queen just had a baby, so they decided to have a big celebration. They invited all the people in the kingdom, and all the fairies. Except the king forgot to invite one of the fairies, and she was so mad she crashed the party, and when it was her turn to give the baby a blessing, she gave a curse instead. She said that when the princess was sixteen years old, she would prick her finger on a spinning wheel and die. That was very mean, wasn't it, Mommy?'

'It certainly was,' Janine said when Drew failed to respond.

'But a good fairy was able to change the curse, so the princess wouldn't die. She'd just fall asleep for a hundred years.'

'Look what I found,' Warren said, re-entering the room. 'Some tape. Let me have your picture.'

'Can we put it right next to Auntie Casey's head?'

'We can put it close. How about right here?'

'That's good. Do you think she'll like it?'

'I think she'll love it,' Warren said.

The doorbell rang again. 'I'll get it,' Patsy called upstairs.

'So the king had all the spinning wheels in the land destroyed,' Lola recited, picking up the threads of her story. 'But he missed one.'

'First he forgot to invite the fairy, then he missed the spinning wheel. That's one careless king,' Janine remarked.

'Hi, everyone,' Gail said from the doorway.

'Hi, stranger,' Janine said pointedly. 'She's so busy with her new boyfriend, I don't get to see her any more.'

'That's not true,' Gail demurred with a shy giggle. 'How's Casey?'

'Pretty good,' Warren said. 'Gail, you remember Casey's sister, don't you?'

'Of course. How are you, Drew?'

'Fine. Catching up on the latest fashion.'

'I'm Lola,' Drew's daughter announced. 'I'm telling Auntie Casey the story of Sleeping Beauty.'

'Very nice to meet you. You look just like your mother.'

'I'm at the part where the baby grows into a beautiful princess. And how on her sixteenth birthday, she found a little room at the top of the stairs, and there sat a spinning wheel.'

'And then what happened?' Gail asked.

'Well, she didn't know what it was, so she touched it. And sure enough, she pricked her finger and fell fast asleep.'

Casey felt the toes of both her feet curl under to grip at the bedsheet. She began moving them back and forth.

'Then the king and queen fell asleep, and the servants and all the people. And vines started growing on the castle walls and . . . Hey!'

'What's the matter, sweetheart?' Warren asked.

'Auntie Casey poked me.'

Oh my God.

'What?' four voices asked as Casey held her breath.

'Where did she poke you?' Warren asked.

'On my bum,' Lola said.

Lola was lifted off the bed and Casey's blanket pushed aside.

'She grabbed my hand yesterday,' Drew said.

'She did?' Janine and Gail asked simultaneously.

'It was probably just a muscle spasm,' Warren said.

'Casey,' Drew urged, 'if you hear us, wiggle your toes.'

Casey didn't know what to do. If Warren knew she was regaining control of her muscles, that she was on the verge of being able to communicate, would that speed up his plans?

'Can you hear us, Casey?' Drew asked. 'Wiggle your toes.'

'Nothing,' Warren said after several seconds.

'You sure you didn't just sit on her toes?' Drew asked Lola.

'I don't know,' Lola admitted, her voice a whine. 'Maybe.'

'Casey, can you wiggle your toes for us?' Janine asked.

'Still nothing,' Gail said.

'You know what I think?' Warren returned the blanket to Casey's feet. 'This would be a good time to break for milk and cookies. What do you think, Lola? Peanut butter crunch?'

'They're my favourite.'

'I thought they might be. Why don't we go get some.'

'Why don't you bring a few back up here,' Drew suggested as Warren led Lola from the room.

Casey breathed a deep sigh of relief.

'So, what's going on with you?' Janine asked her friend. 'How are things going with Stan the man?'

'Good,' Gail said shyly. 'Everything's good.'

'When am I going to meet him?'

'Soon.'

'She's been saying that for weeks now,' Janine told Drew. 'I'm not convinced this guy even exists.'

'He exists,' Gail said, a nervous giggle bracketing her words.

'Let's all have dinner together next Saturday. You too, Drew.'

'I can't,' Gail said quickly. 'I'll be away next weekend.'

'You never go anywhere. You mean with Stan?'

Gail's breath trembled into the air. 'Yes.'

'I don't believe it! How long have you been sleeping with him?'

'Will you just listen to her,' Gail said, embarrassed laughter replacing the nervous giggle. 'I haven't . . . we haven't . . .'

'I can't stand it!' Janine snapped. 'What are you waiting for?'

'Next weekend?' came Gail's response.

This time everybody laughed.

Later, after everyone had left, Warren returned to Casey's bedside. 'Busy day,' he commented, once again pulling back the blanket from her feet. 'You must be exhausted. All that exertion.'

Casey felt his fingers tickle the underside of her foot, her foot reflexively withdrawing from his touch.

'So, tell me, Sleeping Beauty. Was that just another muscle spasm?' He squeezed her toes, hard. 'You aren't fooling me. I know you understand every word I say. Beauty never sleeps, does she?' he asked, kissing her.

His words remained in the room long after he'd left.

Beauty never sleeps, the walls whispered. Beauty never sleeps.

9

'WELL, WELL,' Patsy trilled, entering the room and circling the bed, pulling the covers from Casey's body in one continuous swoop. 'How are we feeling? Did we sleep well?'

We didn't sleep at all, Casey thought, feeling the young woman tugging on her blanket and top sheet, until she succeeded in freeing them from the mattress.

'It's Monday,' Patsy announced cheerily. 'Which means it's laundry day, according to Mrs Singer. Considerate employee that I am, I told the old bag I'd get your sheets for her. Although to get at that bottom sheet, we'll have to get you into this chair.' She sighed, as if exhausted. 'Think I'll wait for Warren to give me a hand.' Another sigh, this one decidedly more lusty. 'He's just finishing up in the shower, getting nice and clean after his workout. So dedicated, that husband of yours. Did I tell you he brought me a cappuccino from Starbucks? Anyway, I'm in a good mood. Let's get that pillowcase.' Without further warning, she pulled the pillow out from behind Casey's head, letting her neck snap back to the mattress. Casey lay on the bed, wondering if Patsy was going to whip the bottom sheet right out from under her, as if it were a tablecloth and Patsy a magician. Which made Casey . . . what exactly?

A place setting? A bowl of fruit?

Still life, she thought. That's all I am.

Except no longer quite so still, she thought, feeling a renewed surge of excitement. She had no doubt her senses were growing stronger every day. She could hear; she could smell; she could tell hot and cold, hard and soft; she could distinguish between Patsy's indifferent touch and Gail's caring caress.

And now she could stretch her fingers and wiggle her toes. She could form fists and rotate her ankles. In another week, she might be able to swing her feet out of bed. After that, she might even be able to walk, and then to see, to speak.

To tell everyone what had really happened.

Every day brought some improvement. She was gradually being returned to the body she'd been so violently torn from. But would she be able to save herself?

Casey heard footsteps approaching from down the hall.

'What are you doing?' Warren asked, entering the room.

Casey froze. Had her thoughts betrayed her? Had she been clenching her fingers, wiggling her toes?

'Do you need some help with that?' he asked.

Now Casey wondered if he was referring to her or the bedsheets. Had she become a 'that'?

'I'll need help getting your wife into the chair,' Patsy said.

Casey felt Warren's strong arms reach beneath her torso and the underside of her knees. 'Careful,' Patsy said. 'Don't strain yourself.'

'I'm used to much heavier weights than this,' Warren said.

So now she was a 'this'.

A this and a that. Casey laughed, although no sound emerged.

Warren suddenly loosened his grip, so that her body slipped to the bed. 'I thought I felt Casey . . . No. It's too crazy.'

'What is?'

A slight pause, then, 'There was this slight rumble. It was almost, I don't know, as if Casey was laughing.'

You felt that?

'Laughing? It was probably just her stomach,' Patsy said.

'Probably.' Warren tightened his grip on Casey's waist.

What did it mean? Casey wondered. Did the fact that Warren had been able to detect the laughter stirring inside her mean she was closer to actually laughing out loud?

'We should change her nightgown while we're at it,' Patsy said.

She listened as Patsy rifled through the top drawer of her dresser, like a thief in the night. She felt her muscles tense with indignation and wondered if Warren could feel it, too. She'd have to be so careful. At any second, her body—already a foreign object—could betray her without warning.

'Here's a pretty one, Casey. What do you think?'

Warren deposited her gently in the chair, carefully arranging pillows around her to support her. It feels like the striped chair, Casey thought, adjusting to its contours as her arms were lifted over her head and whatever nightgown she'd been wearing was pulled off.

Leaving her naked, Casey realised. In front of her husband and his soon-to-be lover. A wave of revulsion washed over her as she felt Patsy's eyes travel across her body. 'Would you like a sponge bath?' Patsy asked.

The thought of this woman's hands touching her while her husband watched was too horrible to contemplate.

'I don't think there's enough time for that now,' Warren said. 'Jeremy should be here any minute.'

Casey felt a fresh nightgown being lowered over her head, the silk dropping like a parachute towards the floor.

The doorbell rang as Patsy pulled the bottom sheet off. 'Speak of the devil . . . I'll take these sheets to Mrs Singer.'

'She's a good kisser,' Warren confided as soon as Patsy was gone. 'How long do you think I should wait before I sleep with her? I guess I really shouldn't be talking to you about these things, but I've got used to using you as a sounding board.'

The front door opened and closed.

'Casey?' her sister's voice called up from the foyer.

Drew!

'Crap,' Warren said. 'What's she doing here?'

'Casey,' Drew shouted again, racing up the stairs and into the room. 'Omigod, look at you! Sitting up in a chair. Wow. You look great. Look, Jeremy, she's sitting up in the chair!'

'Jeremy?' Warren asked as the therapist followed Drew into the room. 'Well, isn't this interesting. You two come together?'

'We pulled up at the same time,' Jeremy explained.

'You're back so soon, Drew. You're usually not so constant.'

'Constant . . . don't think I've ever been called that. I think I like it.' Drew dropped to her knees in front of her sister. 'You look so pretty. Although your hair's a bit of a mess. Where's her brush? Casey used to brush my hair all the time when we were kids. I know just how she likes it.'

'Here's the brush,' Jeremy offered.

Drew gathered Casey's long, silky hair into her hands.

'Casey always had such beautiful hair. Although it could use a touch-up. Maybe next time I come, I'll bring some colouring. What—Warren, you thought she was a natural blonde?'

'I think we should get out of here and let Jeremy work.'

'I'm not in your way. Am I, Jeremy?'

'She really isn't,' Jeremy said.

'In that case, you don't mind if I stay, too,' Warren said.

'Not at all.'

'The more the merrier,' Drew said, running a brush delicately through Casey's hair. 'She actually is a natural blonde,' she explained, as Jeremy began massaging Casey's fingers. 'Until she was about twelve, her hair was like spun gold. Daddy's golden girl, he used to call her, even after her hair started getting darker. Remember that, Casey?'

I remember, Casey thought, breathing in echoes of the past, finding them surprisingly close at hand, and understanding they'd never strayed too far away.

Drew continued expertly drawing the brush through her hair. That feels wonderful, Casey thought, as the soft bristles gently scraped across her scalp like hundreds of tiny fingers. She felt each hair being stretched and separated with each successive stroke. At the same time, Jeremy was massaging her forearms. Casey gave herself over to the mixture of pleasant sensations.

'She closed her eyes,' Warren said.

What?

'Now they're open again.' Casey felt him inch closer.

'It's a reflex action,' Jeremy said. 'It doesn't mean anything.'

'So everyone keeps saying.'

'Certain functions are automatic. She has no control over—'

'What if she does?' Warren asked.

'What do you mean?' Drew stopped her brushing. 'You think she's trying to tell us something? Is that what you're trying to do, Casey? Can you hear me? Blink once for yes.'

Casey kept her eyes resolutely still. Could she blink, even if she wanted to?

'Nothing,' Drew said, the sadness clearly audible in her voice.

The phone rang. Seconds later, Patsy appeared in the doorway. 'It's for you, Mr Marshall. He says it's very important.'

'I'll take it in my office,' Warren said, standing up. 'I'll be back.'

'Take your time,' Drew said, and took Casey's hand in hers.

Casey listened as Patsy followed Warren down the stairs.

'Something's a little off with him,' Drew said.

'What do you mean?' Jeremy asked.

'I can't put my finger on it. He's just got too comfortable as lord of the manor. I know he's dealing with a lot, and I haven't been much help—'

'I find you extremely helpful. Don't sell yourself short.'

'Thank you,' Drew said, then burst into tears.

'Hey, there,' Jeremy said. 'What's happening?'

'I'm sorry. I'm just not used to people being nice to me.'

'Wait. I'll get you a tissue.' Jeremy crossed to the bathroom.

'I'm sorry,' Drew apologised again, inadvertently squeezing Casey's hand.

Slowly, using all her strength, Casey squeezed back.

'Oh my God!' Drew exclaimed. She jumped to her feet, although her hand remained in her sister's. 'Jeremy!'

Casey squeezed her sister's fingers a second time, even harder than the first. *No! You can't tell him. You can't tell anyone.*

'Something wrong?' Jeremy asked from the bathroom doorway.

Casey squeezed a third time. *Please don't say anything. He'll tell Warren. You mustn't say anything to anyone. Not until I find a way to tell you what's happened.*

'Did you find a Kleenex?' Drew asked, as if she somehow understood.

'Got a handful right here.' Jeremy returned to her side. 'What's the matter? You look a little pale. Are you OK?'

'I don't know. I got a little dizzy for a few seconds there.'

'You'd better sit down.'

'I'm fine now. Really.'

'Don't argue. Come on.'

Drew reluctantly relinquished her grip on Casey's hand, which immediately slid into her lap. Casey heard Jeremy pull up a chair.

'Take a few deep breaths,' Jeremy instructed, and Drew complied. 'Can I get you some water? Maybe some tea?'

'Tea sounds wonderful.'

'I'll be right back.'

'Thank you.' As soon as he was gone, Drew grabbed her sister's hand. 'That was no accident. You're here, aren't you? You can understand me.'

Casey squeezed her sister's fingers.

'OK, OK, OK,' Drew muttered. 'This is amazing. I don't believe this. You understand what's going on, but for some reason, you don't want me to tell Jeremy. Is that right?'

Another squeeze.

'OK. I'm gonna assume that means yes. Why don't you want me to tell Jeremy? No, way too complicated. Do you want me to tell Warren? Of course you want me to tell Warren!'

Casey squeezed Drew's fingers as hard as she could.

'Are you saying you don't want me to tell him or you do?'

Casey squeezed several times in rapid succession.

'OK, this isn't working. We need a system. Can you blink? That might be easier. Blink once for yes, twice for no.'

Casey transferred all her energy to her eyelids. *Blink*, she urged. *Blink.*

'Nothing's happening. Squeeze once for yes, twice for no. Do you want me to tell Warren?'

Casey squeezed once, then tried a second time, but her fingers refused to cooperate. *Oh God.* Would Drew think she meant yes when she meant no?

'I couldn't tell whether that was once or twice. Try it again?'

'Try what again?' Warren asked suddenly from the door.

Instantly, Drew released Casey's hand. 'Oh, Warren! You scared me half to death. I didn't see you there.'

Don't tell him. Please don't tell him.

Warren entered the room. 'Where's Jeremy?'

'He went downstairs to get me some tea. I got a little dizzy.'

'If you're dizzy, perhaps you should go home and lie down.'

'That's all right. I'm starting to feel better.'

'Interesting. Try what again?'

'What?'

'When I got here, you were asking Casey to try something again.'

'I was?' Drew cleared her throat. 'Oh, that. I was just thinking out loud, asking Casey whether she thought I should give Sean another chance. You remember Sean? Anyway, he's been calling lately, asking me to give our relationship another try.'

'Really? And what was Casey's advice?'

A pause. 'She thinks I should err on the side of caution.'

'I'm not sure I agree,' Warren said. 'Sean struck me as a nice guy. He might be worth another shot.'

'You think so?'

'Well, things have been pretty tense around here since Casey's accident. It might even be a good idea for you and Sean to get away for a couple of weeks. Take a nice, romantic cruise.'

'A cruise? Now? With my sister in a coma?'

'It wouldn't be the first time, Drew,' he reminded her.

'It's different now. I think Casey needs me.'

'Casey wants you to be happy. I'm sure she'd understand.'

Jeremy re-entered the room. The aroma of blueberry-flavoured tea wafted towards Casey's nose.

'Unless something else is keeping you here,' Warren said.

'Careful,' Jeremy warned. 'It's hot.'

'Thank you,' Drew said.

'Feeling any better?' Jeremy asked.

'Drew's fine,' Warren answered in Drew's stead. 'My wife, on the other hand, is feeling a tad neglected.'

Jeremy sat down, lifting one of Casey's legs into his lap and gently rotating her ankle. 'Well, we'll try to rectify that right now.' He worked for several seconds in concentrated silence.

'Maybe we should ask Jeremy what he thinks,' Warren said.

'Thinks about what?' Jeremy asked.

'One of Drew's ex-boyfriends is after her to give their relationship another shot. I think he's a pretty decent guy. Certainly better than most of the low lifes she's been involved with. So, I think she should go for it. What do you think?'

Casey felt Jeremy's hand tense. 'I think Drew is the only person who can make that decision,' he said evenly.

'Yeah, well, Drew's never been very good at deductive reasoning.' Warren laughed. 'Anyway, I think it would be a good idea if she got away for a while. She's feeling weak enough that you saw fit to abandon my wife in order to fetch her a cup of tea, and we wouldn't want her coming down with anything, possibly transferring any of those nasty viruses going around to Casey.'

'I'm not coming down with anything.'

'Lola's in contact with lots of kids, all of them seething little incubators of disease. Where is your daughter, by the way?'

'At school. Just one more week of classes.'

'And then what? Ship her off to sleepaway camp, like last year? Most parents don't send their kids off so young. Lola was the youngest camper in the history of Camp Arrowroot.'

'Arrow*head*,' Drew corrected. 'And no, she won't be going back there this year. Actually, I was thinking the two of us might move in here for the summer. How would you like that?'

This time it was Jeremy who laughed.

'Something funny?' Warren asked.

Jeremy said nothing as he switched to Casey's other leg.

'I think that's enough therapy,' Warren announced abruptly.

'We've just started,' Jeremy told him.

'On the contrary, I think your work is finished here.'

'I'm not sure I understand. You're firing me?'

'That's ridiculous,' Drew said. 'You're firing him because he went to get me some tea?'

'I'm firing him because I hired him to take care of my wife, not to use her condition to get into her sister's pants.'

'Hey, wait a minute—' Jeremy said.

'No, you wait a minute. I hired you to do a job, and you haven't been doing it. You've been late, you're neglectful, you're rude—'

'You're out of line.'

'You've got attitude. You're out of my house,' Warren said.

'This is my house, too,' Drew reminded him. 'My sister is making progress. I want Jeremy to stay.'

'Your sister will make progress with someone else. I suggest you go with him, Drew. Please leave.'

'Warren, I'm staying right here. Go to hell,' Drew said.

Warren released a deep breath. 'Believe me, I'm already there.'

Silence. 'I believe you owe me some money,' Jeremy said.

'Well, then, follow me, Jeremy. I'll write you a cheque.'

'Wait . . .' Drew called after Jeremy.

'Bye, Drew,' came his response. 'Take care of your sister.'

Casey listened as footsteps retreated down the stairs.

'What was that all about?' Drew cried.

OK, Drew. Grab my hand. We don't have a lot of time.

'You heard all that, didn't you? You heard what just happened!' Drew took Casey's hand.

Casey squeezed Drew's fingers. Once. Hard.

'Once for yes,' Drew said. 'OK. So, what do we do now? Tell me what to do. I don't know what to do.'

Casey held her hand tightly. *You have to calm down.*

'OK. So I have to think of simple questions. What questions? OK. Think. First question. Do you want me to tell Warren?'

Casey squeezed her sister's hand twice. Had Drew felt it?

'That was twice. So you *don't* want Warren to know. Granted he's acting a little strange, but he's under a lot of stress.'

Casey squeezed Drew's hand.

'Why not? What's going on? Oh, hell. That was stupid. OK. All right. We're going to spell things out. I saw that once on TV. This guy was paralysed, but he spelled things out by blinking. Except you can't blink. Can you tap? With your finger against my hand?' Drew positioned her hand directly under Casey's fingers.

Casey threw all her concentration into her right index finger. Her mind lifted it, brought it down once. Twice. Three times.

Drew literally squealed. 'Great. Casey, that's so great. OK, so one tap is A, two is B, et cetera. I don't know how long we've got, but why don't you want Warren to know?'

Casey tapped twice on Drew's hand, then five times.

'OK, so we have B and E. Be . . . because?'

Casey squeezed Drew's hand. Then she tapped eight times for the letter H, followed by five more taps for the letter E.

'H . . . E . . . Because he . . .?'

Because he tried to kill me! Casey squeezed her sister's hand, then began tapping out the letter T.

'Wait,' Drew wailed, after a moment. 'I lost count. We have to do it again. Sorry, Casey.' She counted the taps out loud. 'T!' she exclaimed, dropping Casey's hand with excitement, then scooping it up again.

Casey began tapping out the letter R.

'O . . . P . . . Q . . . R . . . S?'

Casey squeezed twice. *No!*

'Not S?'

The sound of the front door closing reverberated up the stairs, followed immediately by Warren's footsteps on the stairs.

'Damn. Is there anybody I can tell about this?'

Who could she trust not to tell Warren? Casey wondered.

The footsteps were getting closer.

'Warren?' Patsy suddenly called out from downstairs.

The footsteps stopped. 'Yes?' he called back.

'Mrs Singer wants to know what you'd like for dinner.'

Jeremy. Warren had just fired him. She could certainly trust Jeremy not to tell Warren. Casey began tapping furiously.

'Wait. How about I say the letters, and you squeeze my hand when I say the right one. Ready? A . . . B . . . C . . . D.'

Faster. Faster.

'Tell her anything she wants to make is fine,' Warren called.

'H . . . I . . . J . . . J?'

Casey squeezed Drew's fingers.

'Jeremy? Oh, wait. Janine? Which is it, Janine or Jeremy?'

Footsteps on the stairs. Drew let Casey's hand drop.

'Looks like Jeremy has left the building,' Warren said, his presence filling the room.

'OK, time to go.' Drew said, pushing herself off her chair. She leaned in, buried her face in Casey's hair. 'Don't worry, Casey,' she whispered. 'I'll be back soon.'

'**A**re you OK?'

Patsy's voice was warm, solicitous. Casey knew immediately she wasn't talking to her.

'I don't know,' came Warren's response from the chair next to Casey's bed. 'It's been a very trying day.'

'You hardly touched your supper,' Patsy remarked. 'Casey's sister really gets under your skin.'

'Drew's been a selfish mess her entire life, and suddenly she turns into sister of the year. I'm not sure what to make of it.'

'Maybe it's just a phase, something she'll get tired of.'

'You don't think she'd do anything to hurt Casey, do you?'

What?

'What do you mean?'

'No, it's too crazy. Forget I said anything.'

'You think Drew had something to do with what happened to Casey?'

'No. Of course not. The police obviously still consider it a possibility, but . . . At the very least, I think her visits upset Casey. You saw how her blood pressure spiked after Drew left.'

'You think there's a connection?'

'I don't know. Part of me would like to bar Drew from the house, but she's such a loose cannon, she might go to the press. Which is the last thing this family needs. We'll just have to be vigilant when she's around. Make sure she's never alone with Casey.'

'I'll do my best. Have you thought about who you'll get to replace Jeremy?' Patsy asked.

'Actually I've already hired someone from my gym.'

Casey felt her entire body go numb.

'He's dropping by this evening.'

What? Had she run out of time already?

'Should I put some coffee on?' Patsy asked.

'I don't think he's a coffee drinker. Look, why don't you take the rest of the night off, go to a movie or something?'

No, don't go. Don't go.

'I'm kind of tired. Think I'll just go to my room, watch some TV, maybe go to bed early. Just shout if you want anything.'

'I will.'

Patsy made a show of fluffing up Casey's pillow. 'Good night, Casey.' She walked to the door. 'Good night, Warren.'

'Sweet dreams.'

'You too.'

Casey felt Patsy hovering in the doorway for several seconds before making her exit. So, what happens now? Casey wondered, hearing her husband pull his chair closer to the bed.

'So, what happens now?' he echoed.

He sat there, saying nothing, his eyes burning quarter-size holes in her skin. 'How did everything get so complicated?' he asked finally.

The doorbell rang.

'Well, what do you know? Your new therapist is early.'

'Do you want me to get that?' Patsy called out.

'No, that's OK,' Warren called back. 'I'll get it.' He touched Casey's arm. 'Don't get up,' he said before leaving her side.

I *have* to get up, Casey thought. There's no time left.

She projected all her energy into her feet. *Move, damn you. Move.* Miraculously, she felt an almost immediate stirring in her legs. Her arms stretched to their full length, her hands flexed. Her body was garnering all its reserves to propel her out of bed.

And then . . . nothing.

Her back lay flat against the mattress. Her head remained still on her pillow. She wasn't going anywhere.

What had she been thinking? Even if she'd been able to move, she couldn't see. She couldn't scream for help. Besides, did she really think Patsy would come to her rescue?

Casey heard voices talking softly in the downstairs foyer, followed by the sound of more than one set of footsteps. 'Casey,' Warren announced seconds later, 'Gail is here to see you.'

'How's my girl?' Gail asked, approaching the bed.

'No real change,' Warren said.

'Her colour's better than it was.' Gail took a deep breath. It trembled upon release. 'I feel guilty about going away this weekend. Maybe I shouldn't.'

'Where are you off to?' Warren asked.

'Martha's Vineyard. Believe it or not, I've never been.'

'You'll love it. It's beautiful.'

'So Stan keeps telling me, but . . .'

'But nothing. Go and have a good time. It's what Casey would want.'

'I'm a little nervous,' Gail confided.

'About what?'

'You know,' Gail said. 'Janine talked me into buying a new nightgown. It's lacy and low-cut, a bit out of my comfort zone, and I really wish Casey was here to advise me.'

'If I might offer a little advice in Casey's stead,' Warren said gently, 'just be yourself.'

'You think that'll be enough?'

'If it isn't, he's a fool who doesn't deserve you.'

Gail's grateful sigh filled the room. 'Thank you.' She kissed Casey's cheek. 'See you in a couple of days, Casey. Bye for now.'

'I'll show you out.'

So what do I do now? Casey thought as they left the room. She tried lifting one foot up, feeling it strain against the sheet. She attempted to turn her head. Had she moved at all?

'Oh, my,' Patsy said from the doorway. 'Looks like your friend got a little too close for comfort. Look what she's done to your poor head.' She walked over and readjusted Casey's head. 'That can't have been comfortable. Good thing I thought to look in on you.'

I moved my head? I actually moved my head?

Patsy took a step back, as if surveying her handiwork. 'That was a pretty quick visit. Although that's what happens, isn't it? Visits get shorter and shorter, with longer and longer intervals. Soon it'll be once a week for five minutes, then once a month for two, then maybe once a year, until you won't even be able to remember the last time anyone dropped by.'

I moved my head, Casey thought.

'Although, personally, I hate when people just drop over. My mother's always showing up at my door unexpectedly. Wonder what she'd make of this place.' Patsy laughed. 'Oh, well. Maybe one day I'll find out. I could be the new mistress of the manor. Stranger things have happened.'

'Everything all right?' Warren asked from somewhere behind her.

Patsy quickly spun around. Casey imagined her hand flying to her hair in an effort to hide her embarrassment. 'Everything's fine. Casey's head was tilted a bit to one side. Probably Gail hugged her when she said goodbye.'

'Her head was tilted to one side?'

'It's okay now.'

The doorbell rang. Who was here now? Casey wondered.

'You want me to answer that?' Patsy asked.

'If you wouldn't mind.'

The front door opened and closed. Then came a man's muffled hello and a muted exchange of pleasantries, followed by footsteps on the stairs.

The door opened. 'Hello, Warren.'

Dear God. There was no mistaking that voice.

Help me. Somebody, please help me.

'Hello, Beauty,' the man said.

10

'HOW ARE YOU DOING tonight?' the man continued, looming over Casey like a giant king cobra, body swaying and poised to strike.

Casey felt the man lower her blankets to her knees.

'I gotta say, Warren, she's lookin' pretty good for a corpse. Let's see what we've got.' The man took Casey's hand in his, moving it up and down, bending her elbow, then rotating her wrist.

'Well?' Warren asked.

'I'm not feeling much of anything, to tell you the truth. No resistance.

It's dead weight.' His fingers slid slowly down Casey's legs. She had to summon all her strength to keep her body from recoiling at his touch.

'So tell me what you want me to do. I'll do it.'

'Something simple: you come in, you put a pillow over her face, you leave without anybody seeing you,' Warren said calmly, as if he were reading from a recipe book.

You come in, you put a pillow over her face, Casey repeated silently, feeling tears form in the corners of her eyes. Were they real? Would Warren see them?

'Think you can do that?' Warren was asking.

'When did you have in mind?'

A tear traced a thin line down Casey's cheek.

'This weekend,' Warren said, his attention clearly focused on his murderous thoughts. 'Things are happening faster than I expected. I can't waste time. I'll make sure everybody's out of the house. While we're gone, you come in, do the deed, and get the hell out.'

'Sounds like a plan.'

'**W**endy Jackson, come on down. You're the next contestant on *The Price Is Right!*'

Casey pictured Wendy Jackson as a forty-year-old woman with bottle-blonde hair and a roll of flesh that jiggled beneath the bottom of her sweatshirt with each bounce of excitement.

Where was Drew? Why wasn't she here yet?

'I can't believe it! I can't believe it!' Wendy Jackson cried, no doubt jumping up and down.

'Hello, Wendy,' the host said.

Hello, Beauty.

'OK, try to settle down, Wendy, and pay close attention,' the host urged. 'Here's the next item coming up for bids.'

Where are you, Drew? What's keeping you?

'A new dining-room set!' the announcer exclaimed to an escalating chorus of oohs and aahs.

'What a pile of junk!' Patsy pronounced from the chair beside Casey's bed, as the announcer began his hyperbolic description of the items. 'I can't believe how excited she's getting over that ratty table and chairs.'

'Twenty-five hundred dollars,' came the bid from Wendy.

'Three thousand,' came the second bid.

'Did you know they sign an agreement not to sell the stuff they win?' Patsy asked. 'So if they don't like it, they're screwed.'

Where are you, Drew? I'm running out of time.

A loud buzzer sounded. 'That buzzer means you've all overbid,' the host explained cheerily.

The four contestants quickly offered up new bids, and this time one of them won, although it wasn't Wendy Jackson.

Bye, Beauty.

'Poor Wendy. She has loser written all over her,' Patsy said.

She can see, she can move, she can talk, hell, she can scream. That makes her a winner in my book, Casey thought.

'I liked Bob Barker better than this guy. Did he die or something?'

'You come in, you put a pillow over her face, you leave,' Casey had heard her husband say.

Had she cried? And if tears had fallen, had Warren seen them?

The doorbell rang.

'Can you get that, Mrs Singer?' Patsy called down the stairs. Seconds later, Drew hollered up hello.

Drew, thank God! Where have you been? We have so little time.

Seconds later, Drew bounded into the room, then stopped abruptly. 'Oh, hi, Patsy. I didn't realise you'd be here.'

'Where else would I be?'

'How's Casey doing today?' Drew took Casey's hand, gave it a con-spiratorial squeeze. 'Sorry I'm late. There was a minor crisis at Lola's school. Seems I forgot to sign this permission slip to let her go on some field trip. And when I showed up at the school, nobody knew who I was. Can you believe it? I actually had to show them my driver's licence. Which, of course, had expired. Anyway, do you think I could get a cup of coffee?' she asked Patsy.

'You'll have to go downstairs and ask Mrs Singer,' Patsy said. 'I'm under strict instructions not to leave Casey's side.'

'Really? Why is that? Did something happen?'

'Her blood pressure's been a little erratic. And she's been having spasms.'

'What do you mean, spasms? Since when?'

'Since last night. First her head was tilted and later I found her slumped on her side.' Patsy laughed. 'Mr Marshall said it almost looked like she was trying to get out of bed.'

'Casey was trying to get out of bed?'

'What? No! Of course not. This morning her doctor said maybe she was experiencing muscle spasms, which can be quite painful, so he gave her a shot and prescribed painkillers and a muscle relaxant, which is where Warren is now—picking up the medication.'

'Well, I can watch Casey now,' Drew said. 'I'm sure Warren wouldn't mind if you took a half-hour break.'

'It's time for the final showcase on *The Price Is Right!*' the announcer excitedly declared.

'I'd better not. Wouldn't want to miss that final showcase.'

Drew pulled up a chair and reached under the covers for her sister's hand. 'Casey? Are you in pain?'

Casey squeezed her sister's thumb twice, as the announcer began his description of the first showcase. 'It's a set of encyclopedias!' he said. 'You can use these handsome *Britannica* encyclopedias to learn everything from A to Z, starting with . . . the Acropolis. Information that might come in handy on your trip to . . . Greece!'

A prolonged series of oohs and aahs. A burst of applause.

'Yes, you and a companion will fly first-class to Athens, where you'll visit the Acropolis and many other amazing ancient sites. Then it's off for a spectacular cruise of the Greek islands.'

'You like cruises, don't you?' Patsy asked Drew. 'Have you ever been to Greece?'

'A few years ago,' Drew answered. 'It's pretty amazing.'

'I've never been anywhere. But who knows?' Patsy chuckled. 'Maybe one day.'

'I tried contacting Jeremy,' Drew said. 'The hospital wouldn't give out his personal information. So I left him a note there last night, but he hasn't got back to me yet.'

'Why would you want to contact him?' Patsy asked.

'Just to see if he's OK.' Drew's squeeze of Casey's hand said, *To tell him about Casey.* 'Warren was pretty brutal with him.'

'No more than he deserved.'

'Anyway, I could do some of the exercises he showed me.'

'I'm not sure that's such a good idea,' Patsy said. 'Casey's new therapist probably has his own way of doing things.'

'Warren hired a new therapist already? Who is he?'

'His name's Nick something-or-other. Margolin . . . Margolis? He's a trainer at the gym where Warren works out.'

'Warren hired a personal trainer to look after my sister?'

'He's very qualified. Mr Marshall would never hire anyone who wasn't highly qualified to look after his wife.'

'He hired you,' Drew said.

'I'm taking excellent care of Casey.' Patsy bristled.

'I'm concerned about my sister.'

'You have no idea how good he is to her. Warren is a wonderful man. If Casey were conscious, I bet she'd be pissed at the way you treat him.'

'Do you think so?' Drew's fingers wrapped around Casey's under the blankets. 'Is Warren a wonderful man, Casey?'

Casey grasped Drew's fingers.

Casey squeezed once. Then again. Twice for no.

'That's what I thought,' Drew said.

'You thought what?' Patsy asked.

'I thought that contestant's bid was too low. Now the other lady has to go to Greece to see some old ruins she couldn't care less about. Look, I owe you an apology,' Drew said in the same breath.

'You do?'

You do?

'I've been rude and I'm sorry.' Drew squeezed Casey's fingers, as if to say *Bear with me.* 'I know you're doing your best. It's just so hard seeing Casey in this condition, and I've been taking out my frustration on you and Warren.'

'He deserves better.'

'I know he does.'

Casey recognised the mock sincerity in her sister's voice.

'Wow. I'm not used to apologising. That took a lot out of me. I don't suppose you'd reconsider getting me that coffee.'

'Not a chance.'

The front door opened and closed. 'I'm back,' Warren called from the foyer. In the next minute, he was up the stairs. 'Drew, hi. Nice to see you.' Casey felt him lean forward to give her sister a kiss on the cheek. Clearly, he was trying a new approach.

'I understand Casey had a bit of a rough night,' Drew said.

'The doctor thinks she's experiencing muscle spasms. We'll give her a shot later, make sure she has a restful night.'

No, I don't want a shot of anything. I need my head clear.

'Do you really think drugs are a good idea?' Drew asked. 'Won't they just interfere with her progress?'

'I'm really not seeing a lot of progress, Drew. I don't want her in pain. Patsy, I'm dying for a cup of coffee. Would you mind?'

'Of course not. What about you, Drew?'

'Thank you, Patsy,' Drew said. 'You're so kind.'

'So, how's my niece?' Warren asked Drew as Patsy left the room. 'I was thinking maybe I could take the two of you to Gettysburg this Sunday. If that works for you.'

'You want to take us to Gettysburg?'

'I thought you might enjoy it. I know I would. Casey and I had such a good time when we went there. And it would give me the chance to make up for being such a jerk lately.'

No. Don't fall for this. He wants an alibi.

'I haven't exactly been all sweetness and light myself.'

'So, how about it? Think you could give me another chance?'

No. Please, no. Don't do it.

'Sunday would be great,' Drew said.

'"**D**orothea seldom left home without her husband, but she did occasionally drive into Middlemarch alone, on little errands of shopping or charity such as occur to every lady of any wealth when she lives within three miles of a town,"' Janine read. 'Dorothea needs to get a life.'

Where am I? What's happening?

Was she back in the hospital? Had the last week been a dream?

'"Two days after that scene in the Yew-tree Walk, she determined to use such an opportunity in order if possible to see Lydgate, and learn from him whether her husband had really felt any depressing change of symptoms which he was concealing."'

'Almost finished that book?' Patsy asked, her voice swimming somewhere above Casey's head.

'Page three fifteen.'

'Still a long way to go.'

'Guess I could say the same thing about Casey,' Janine said. 'She hasn't opened her eyes since I've been here.'

'At least she's not in pain any more,' Patsy said.

When was I in pain?

Casey fought through the fog in her brain to piece together what was happening. How long had she been floating in and out of consciousness. What day was it?

'Casey,' she heard her sister whisper. 'Casey, can you hear me? If you can hear me, squeeze my hand.'

How long ago was that? Had she mustered the strength?

'Casey, listen to me,' Drew had said on another occasion.

Or had it been the same occasion?

'Tap once for yes, twice for no.'

What day is it? How much time do I have left?

'Warren's taking Lola and me to Gettysburg on Sunday. He's being awfully nice to me all of a sudden. It's hard to tell if he's really trying to make up for being such a jerk lately, or if he's up to something.'

He's going to kill me.

'You come in, you put a pillow over her face, you leave without anybody seeing you,' Warren had said.

When had he said that?

'I love your T-shirt,' Patsy was saying now. 'Who's Ed Hardy anyway?'

'The designer,' Janine said.

'Designer T-shirts. Wow. Guess it was expensive, huh?'

'Reasonably. Two hundred dollars.'

A buzzer sounded. 'That buzzer means you've all overbid.'

What?

'What's that?' Patsy asked.

'My BlackBerry. Another message from Richard Mooney. I'm going to call him back. Is there a room I can use?'

'Only about eighty of them.'

'I'll be just down the hall.'

What time is it?

How much time had she lost? Casey wondered. How much time before she was sedated again? She tried moving her fingers beneath the covers, but she felt nothing.

'Casey, squeeze my hand,' she heard her sister urge.

When had she said that? Today? Yesterday? The day before that? When was the last time Drew had been here?

'It's nice that Janine comes over so often,' Patsy was saying.

The front door opened and closed. Was it Drew?

'I'm back,' Warren called up the stairs.

Not Drew. Warren. Where had he been?

'How's Casey?' he said from the doorway moments later.

'Resting peacefully,' Patsy said. 'How was your workout?'

'Not great. I might have pulled something in my shoulder.'

'Oh, no. Let me have a look at it.'

'No, that's all right.'

'Come on, I'm the one with the magic hands, remember? Now sit your ass down and let me have a look. Sorry,' she apologised immediately. 'I didn't mean to overstep—'

'You haven't.' Warren plopped down in the nearest chair.

'Where is it sore?' Patsy asked.

'There. And a bit there.'

'Take a deep breath and release it into my fingers. That's right.'

'That feels good. You really *do* have magic hands.'

'In more ways than one,' Janine said, returning to the room.

'Janine,' Warren said. 'I didn't realise you were here.'

'Clearly. We need to talk,' Janine said. 'In private.'

'I'll be in my room,' Patsy said.

Seconds later, Casey heard the door to Patsy's room close.

'Is there a problem?' Warren asked Janine.

'You tell me. What's with you and Florence Nightingale?'

'If you're insinuating . . .'

'I'm not insinuating anything. I'm asking flat out. Are you sleeping with her?'

'Of course I'm not sleeping with her. I hurt my shoulder at the gym. Patsy was just being kind . . .'

'Kind of what? Kind of available?'

'Really, Janine, what exactly did you see that was so awful?'

'Whatever it was, it was the second time I saw it. I don't like it one bit and, more importantly, Casey wouldn't like it.'

'Casey wouldn't have liked my sleeping with you either, but that didn't concern you a whole lot at the time.'

What?

Silence. Then, 'This is neither the time nor the place to talk about that.'

'Maybe it is.'

Janine closed the bedroom door, took an audible breath. 'What happened between us happened a long time ago.'

'Less than a year,' Warren corrected.

What? No, this can't be. I'm having a nightmare. It's the drugs the doctor gave me. I'm hallucinating again.

'It should never have happened,' Janine said.

I don't believe it. I won't believe it.

It wasn't Warren's betrayal she was having such a hard time processing, she realised. It was Janine's.

'Look. I'm not proud of what I did,' Janine said. 'I was going through a hard time, with Casey opting out of our partnership. I was angry, I was spiteful, I let myself be seduced . . .'

'As I recall, you did the seducing,' Warren corrected again.

'I was flirting. I didn't think you'd take me up on it.'

'You're fooling yourself, Janine.'

'Maybe. You fooled Casey, that's for sure.'

'I love Casey.'

'You have an interesting way of showing it.'

'I can't change what happened. It's time to move on.'

'You're unbelievable.'

'You're jealous.'

Janine took a deep breath. 'What I am is sick at heart. Sick that I betrayed my best friend, sick that her husband isn't the man she thought he was, sick she's the one in a coma when I'm the one who deserves to be.'

'Oh, please. Give it up. Nobility doesn't become you.'

'And most of all, I'm sick that you have so little decency that you could carry on with another woman while your wife is lying there in front of you.'

'Bull,' Warren said coldly. 'The only thing bothering you is that the woman is no longer you.'

'I want her out of here, Warren. I want her out of here this afternoon. Either she goes, or I swear I'll tell everyone all about us. And that includes Detective Spinetti.'

'Now why on earth would you do a stupid thing like that?'

'Because it's all I *can* do for Casey now. She needs the very best of care and, frankly, Patsy isn't the one to give it to her.'

There was a silence of several long seconds. 'You might be right about that,' Warren said finally. 'Whether you believe it or not, I want what's best for Casey. I'll tell Patsy her services are no longer required.'

'When?'

'Right after you leave,' he said pointedly. 'Oh, and, Janine, I think we could use a time-out. Call the next time you decide to drop by. I'll arrange to be elsewhere.'

Casey heard Patsy sniffling as she carried her suitcase from her room to the top of the stairs.

'I want you to take this,' Warren said outside Casey's door.

'What is it?'

'Just a little something to tide you over until you find another position. It's only fair. Please. I want you to have it.'

Warren picked up Patsy's suitcase and carried it downstairs.

And then she was gone.

'Well, that worked out rather well,' Warren was saying minutes later, pulling up a chair. 'Mrs Singer's gone for the weekend, Patsy's out of the picture, Gail's out of town, and I don't have to worry about Janine. So it's all systems go for Sunday. That's the day after tomorrow, in case you're keeping track.'

The day after tomorrow, Casey repeated. Where was Drew? She had one day left to get through to her.

'I've arranged for a private nurse to come in tomorrow, and the doctor's going to drop by later to give you your shot. So you won't get too frisky when Drew comes to visit,' Warren said. 'So, let's just try to relax, shall we? It'll all be over soon.'

She dreamed she was in the passenger seat of a twin-engine Cessna when it crashed into a wall of turbulence and spun out of control, propelling its passengers into the thin, cold air, as if they'd been shot from a cannon.

'Daddy!' Casey screamed, as she watched her mother somersault through the sky in her pink chiffon gown, a drunken Alice disappearing into the rabbit hole below.

'Try to relax, golden girl,' her father's voice urged from behind an ash-coloured cloud. 'Grab my hand.'

Casey stretched her arm as far as it would reach, her fingers waving frantically in the void for his reassuring grasp. They touched nothing. Her father wasn't there, she realised. He never had been.

He couldn't save her. Nobody could.

Casey lay in her bed, slowly drifting back into consciousness. Even through the wooziness that occupied her head, she understood that although she was no longer plummeting through the air to her doom, she was no less at risk. She was going to die, she realised, trying to imagine how her parents must have felt the afternoon their plane had plunged into Chesapeake Bay.

She'd never really thought about it before, never permitted herself the necessary introspection to board that doomed plane, to feel what her parents must have felt as the plane careened wildly through the sky before disappearing into the sea. Had her mother been flailing about helplessly, berating her husband in a panic-fuelled fury, or had she tried to embrace him one last time, even as the waves rose up to welcome them? Or had she passed out from a surfeit of alcohol and fatigue as Casey's father fought frantically with the controls? Had he been too drunk to fully comprehend the danger? In his last seconds, had he thought about his daughters at all? Had either of them?

Did it matter? Casey thought now.

Did anything?

Had she ever really meant anything to anyone?

Crying silently, she tried to project two days ahead, to imagine how it would feel to have someone put a pillow over her nose and mouth until she stopped breathing. Would she gasp for air? Would it take a long time to die or be mercifully quick? Would there be an angel waiting to greet her? What would death be like?

Could it be any worse than this?

And yet, despite the horror of the past few months, despite the lies and the betrayals, the loss of everything that made her who she was, Casey realised she wasn't ready to die. Not when she was so close to recovering all she'd lost. Not without a fight.

Some fight, she thought, as dizziness washed over her, the result of the powerful drugs in her system. Not exactly a fair fight.

'What's the point of fighting if you're going to fight fair?' she heard her father ask, his too-big laugh trailing after him as he strode into the room to peer out of the window.

'Daddy, hi,' Casey told him, pushing herself up in bed.

'What are you doing still in bed?' He pivoted round on his heels and stared at Casey with disapproval.

'I'm not feeling very well.'

'Nonsense. You're just feeling sorry for yourself. Mind over matter, Casey. Put one foot in front of the other. See where it takes you.'

'But I can't see.'

'Then open your eyes,' her father said simply, before disappearing into the night.

Casey opened her eyes.

The first thing she saw was the light of the moon coming in through the window at which her father had been standing.

She blinked once, twice, a third time.

Each time the light grew stronger.

OK, try not to get too excited, she warned herself. You're obviously still dreaming, like the last time. *You're hallucinating.*

Except this didn't feel like any of her hallucinations.

It's the drugs. They're playing tricks on your mind.

I can see, she thought, blinking again. The powerful blink.

Don't be ridiculous, she told herself. You're just imagining the curve of the moon in the bay window. You can't really make out the lilac-coloured drapery or the floral tub chairs. You can't see the striped chair beside the bed or the TV. You can't see the fireplace or the white bed-sheets. You can't see the mauve blanket lying at your feet.

I can't. It's impossible.

Casey's eyes shot frantically from side to side, elation spreading through her body like a fire through dry wood.

It's the drugs. Any minute now, you'll wake up.

'Relax,' she heard Warren say. 'It'll all be over soon.'

No. Not now. Not when I'm so close. She lay in her bed, feeling her breath grow increasingly ragged, and staring up at the round overhead light fixture, trying to calm herself down.

I will get out of this. I will. I will.

She heard Warren's footsteps and knew he was coming to check on her. She told herself that even in the dim light, he would spot immediately that she could see, yet she couldn't close her eyes, so terrified was she that all would be blackness again when she reopened them.

Warren stepped into the room.

Casey took a breath, uttered a silent prayer, and closed her eyes.

'Hi, sweetheart. How're you doing?' He perched on the side of the bed, and Casey could smell the liquor on his breath. 'I was having trouble sleeping again, so I thought I'd see what you were up to. Seems I'm missing our little chats already.' He rubbed her leg. 'Your breathing seems a little laboured. What's with that? You're not going to die on me, are you?' He laughed. 'Your sister called earlier. She was thinking of stopping by tomorrow with Lola. I told her I'd send out for pizza and we'd have a back-yard picnic. She thought that was great, and you know what? So do I. Why waste energy fighting when we all know I'm a lover, not a fighter.' He laughed again. 'I didn't see it, I was just so pissed off at everything. But now I see that Drew's like this sad little puppy everybody's always kicking to the kerb. So instead of treating her like a Gucci-clad piece of crap, I've decided to treat her like a princess in one of Lola's fairy tales. I'm going to ride in on my white horse, and sweep her off her feet.

'How, you may ask? Well, you're not going to be around past Sunday, and once you're dead and gone, it'll be up to me to provide your sister with a sturdy shoulder to cry on. The grieving widower comforting his distraught sister-in-law. A love born of shared loss, it's perfect, don't you think? We'll take it slow, of course, wait a year before a tasteful wedding, Lola serving as flower girl, Gail and Janine as bridesmaids. Well, maybe not Janine.

'Anyway, Drew and I live happily ever after, at least a year or two, and then another horrifying twist of fate. Mother and child lose their lives; distraught husband tries to save them. While I expect that Detective Spinetti will come snooping, his investigation will hit the same brick wall his last one did. I think I can put up with a few months of suspicion for a lifetime of luxury. This time, it'll *all* be mine. Everything your father worked for. And cheated for. And stole for. Because your father wasn't a nice man, Casey. I followed his career for years. I can't tell you how much I admired him. I don't think I told you, but I wrote a paper on him in law school.'

Casey felt her eyelids flutter with indecision. She wanted to see this man, this man she'd loved who'd played and used her. If nothing else, she had to look at his face—to see the grotesque ogre behind the Prince Charming mask—one last time before she died.

It was risky, she knew. Could she fool him into thinking her eyes saw nothing? Slowly, cautiously, she opened her eyes.

He was standing by the window, staring out at the night, his handsome profile lit by the moon.

He looks exactly the same, Casey thought, suppressing a sigh of longing, so deep she almost gasped out loud. Longing for what? How could she long for a man who longed only for her death?

And yet, there it was—longing, albeit mixed with fear and anger and loathing. Was there any doubt at all that Drew would succumb to that same magnetic pull? They were Ronald Lerner's daughters, after all, and he'd prepared them all too well.

Warren sighed and tightened the belt of the silk bathrobe Casey had given him last Christmas. Casey closed her eyes.

'OK, then.' He walked to the side of the bed and sighed again. 'All this patting myself on the back has proved quite exhausting.' He kissed the side of her lips. 'Think I'll go back to bed now.'

Casey lay awake for the balance of the night, her eyes open and refusing to give in to fatigue. She watched the moon grow dimmer. She watched the pale blue early morning turn to steel-grey clouds. By the time she heard Warren in the shower, lightning was streaking across the sky, and thunder was shaking the room.

A sound-and-light show just for me, Casey thought, enjoying the spectacle in spite of everything. Or maybe because of it. When was the last time she'd derived such pleasure from the sight of rain slamming against the window?

Drew had always been terrified of storms. When they were little, she used to come into Casey's room in the middle of the night and crawl into Casey's bed as the thunder raged. Casey would kiss the top of her head, and invariably Drew would fall asleep, while Casey would remain awake until the storm had passed. In the morning, Drew would return to her own room without a word. As they grew older and increasingly estranged, Drew had stopped coming into Casey's room altogether. Eventually, she found other arms to comfort her, other beds to share.

The phone rang.

Casey heard Warren answer it in his bedroom. 'Oh, hello, Drew,' he said, his voice warm. 'Yes, it's pretty awful. According to the weatherman, it's going to get worse. But it's supposed to clear tonight, so we should be all right for Gettysburg tomorrow . . . No, I wouldn't drive today if I were you . . . Of course . . . I understand completely. I'll call you later with a full report. Try not to worry, and give Lola a big kiss from me . . .' He hung up the phone.

Moments later, he was standing in Casey's doorway. 'That was your sister,' he said. 'She won't be coming today.'

11

'WELL, WELL,' a soft female voice was saying. 'How are you this beautiful Sunday morning, Mrs Marshall? Did yesterday's storm upset you? Your blood pressure's still a little high, I see.'

Casey recognised Nurse Harriet Friedlander's voice from the previous afternoon and welcomed her gentle touch. How different it was from Patsy's, she thought, as Harriet continued with her ministrations, running a warm washcloth over Casey's face and hands, and then tending to her feeding tube. 'There,' she said when she was done. 'Now you're all set to face the day.'

To face my death, Casey amended.

'How's my wife this morning?' Entering the room and approaching the bed, Warren took both of Casey's hands, which Mrs Friedlander had left lying on top of the covers, in his.

'Her blood pressure is still higher than I'd like. You might want to consult with her doctor.'

'I'll call him first thing tomorrow morning. Unless you think I should take her to the hospital right now . . .'

'No, I don't think that's necessary. Sunday's never a good day to go to hospital. All you get are interns and residents. I'll be back to change her feeding tube at five o'clock.'

'Perfect. See you then,' Warren said. 'Let me show you out.'

As soon as they were gone, Casey opened her eyes. A spectacular summer sun was blasting through the bedroom window. It was a breathtaking day, the kind they put on the covers of brochures. A shame to waste it by dying, Casey thought, flexing her fingers and toes, and rotating her ankles and wrists, stopping only when she heard the front door close.

'Now, that's one nice lady,' Warren commented, reappearing in the doorway. 'She's going to be very upset when she comes back and finds out you passed away. Oh, well. What can you do? Nick'll be here in a couple of hours. Hopefully I'm sending you to a better place, so take care of yourself. I'd love to stay and chat, but I have to get going for my date. Wouldn't want to keep your sister waiting.' Warren leaned forward and kissed her full on the mouth. 'Goodbye, Casey.'

She felt him pause in the doorway for one last look. Did he have any regrets at all? she wondered. Seconds later, the front door closed. Only then did Casey risk opening her eyes. The room came into immediate, sharp focus.

I have to get out of here.

How? What could she do?

Casey tried turning on her side. But her body refused to cooperate, allowing her only limited movement as she fought to bring her right arm towards her left side. Tears filled her eyes. If she could just get to the phone to call 911.

Except how was she supposed to get out of bed when all her larger muscles had atrophied from months of inactivity, and she was as powerless as a newborn baby?

There has to be a way. She couldn't just lie here and wait passively for a cold-hearted stranger to smother her to death.

After what felt like an eternity, Casey succeeded in turning her head several inches to the left. Slowly, she watched the room slide across her line of vision, the intense blue sky disappearing into the soft mauve of the wall, her eyes scanning the plasma TV, the striped chair, the night table beside her bed. I did it, she thought, catching sight of the large red numbers on the digital clock: 11:15.

I have lots of time, Casey reassured herself, fighting dizziness. All I have to do is get out of this bed and grab the phone.

Her fingers were already tapping at the air as Casey painstakingly brought her head towards the phone on the night table. She pictured the night table beside her mother's bed and wondered if her mother's gun was still in its top drawer. Was it possible? No one had used that room until Warren.

Oh, no, Casey thought as her eyes settled again on the clock: 11:52. No way could it have taken her this long to do so little.

What am I supposed to do?

You keep trying, she told herself as the phone started ringing. Once, twice, three times. You reach over and answer. Four times. Five. *Hello? Hello?* Except that even as Casey was stretching her hand towards the sound, the ringing stopped.

This isn't fair. This isn't fair.

'Oh, grow up,' she heard Janine admonish from a distant corner of her brain. 'Who said life was fair?'

'You think I was ready to die?' her father asked.

'Mike died of leukaemia,' Gail said. 'How fair was that?'

You're right, Casey acknowledged silently, bringing her head back to its original position. Fairness had never been part of the equation. If you asked 'Why me?' when times were bad, you had to ask the same question when times were good. The bottom line was that you had to play the hand you'd been dealt.

So, she started the exercises Jeremy had done with her, bending her arms and trying to bend her knees. Except that she was tucked in so tightly, her legs had almost no room to manoeuvre. Still, after ten minutes, she felt the sheets finally start to give way. She closed her eyes, exhausted.

When she opened them again, it was ten minutes past twelve.

No, it can't be. It can't be.

Again, Casey tried lifting her legs. This time she succeeded in bringing her knees halfway up. Her heart was pounding erratically in her chest. Her blood pressure must be through the roof.

I have to get up. I have to get out of bed.

'I haaat . . .'

Casey heard the strange sound as if it was emanating from somewhere across the room. Who was here? Slowly she brought her head round. A careful scan confirmed she was alone.

'Whaaa . . .?'

Oh my God. The sounds were coming from her own mouth, Casey realised, quickly pushing out more grunts and hoarse whispers. *I can't die now. I can't.*

'I caaaaa . . .'

The phone rang again. Casey's head moved towards the sound. Not quite as slowly as the last time.

Keep moving. Keep moving.

The phone stopped after only four rings.

You don't have time for this, Casey castigated herself, forcing one knee back to her chest, then the other. *Keep trying.*

'Keeeee . . .'

The next time she looked at the clock it said 12:30.

Keep trying. Keep trying.

12:35. 12:42. 12:47.

The phone rang again.

Four more rings. Maybe someone would get suspicious that no one was answering. Maybe they'd alert the police.

Five minutes later, it was the doorbell that was ringing, followed by a loud pounding on the door.

'Hellll . . .' Casey sighed, the faint sound riding the wave of her breath as the front door opened and closed.

He's here, she realised. Her killer was in the house.

Except why would he ring the bell and knock on the door?

'Hello?' a female voice called out. 'Anybody home?'

Patsy? What was Patsy doing here?

'Warren? Are you home?' Patsy reached the top of the stairs.

Casey brought her legs down as her hands returned to the top of the covers, her head finding its familiar groove in the middle of the pillow. She kept her eyes open and stared straight ahead.

'Well, well, well,' Patsy said, walking into the room and dropping her large canvas bag on the floor. 'I thought maybe they'd taken you back to the hospital or something. I can't believe everyone left you all alone. That wasn't very nice of them, was it?' She laughed, leaning over the end of the bed.

She was prettier than Casey had expected. Her eyes were a rich brown, somewhat dulled by her lavish mascara. Her reddish blonde hair was twisted into a bun at the top of her head. Lush breasts spilled out from the deep V of her purple jersey. Her belly button, pierced by a small gold loop, was visible above her tight white jeans.

'Where's Warren? Working out?' Patsy asked. 'Maybe he shouldn't have been so quick to let me go. Hard finding someone of my calibre.' She laughed again, a bitter laugh. 'You're looking a bit flushed.' Patsy leaned in closer, then pulled back sharply.

Does she realise I can see her? Should I let her know?

'What am I doing?' Patsy asked, backing away. 'You're not my job any more. Oh, well.' She sighed. 'You're probably wondering what I'm doing here. I *accidentally* left a sweater at the back of a drawer, so my plan was to ask Warren to help me find it and tempt him with a little cleavage. I tried phoning, but nobody picked up. I even called right outside the front door. And I knocked and knocked. Then I thought, what's the point of coming all this way and leaving empty-handed? I *accidentally* still have my key. Anyway, like I said, I figured you must be back in the hospital. But here you are, and here *I* am. I might as well leave with a few parting gifts.'

She walked to Casey's closet, opened the door, then stepped inside.

'Like this, for example,' she said, returning moments later with the yellow-and-black Hermès scarf and wrapping it loosely round her neck. 'I mean, what are you gonna do with it? Besides, it looks much better on me, don't you think?'

You can take whatever you want. Just get me out of here.

'Help me,' Casey cried softly, the barely audible plea tumbling from her mouth like a leaf from a tree.

Patsy froze. Her lower lip dropped. 'What?'

Casey tried to form the words again, but their letters floundered on her tongue, unable to regroup.

Patsy stared at her. 'You scared the hell out of me. I actually thought you said something. Damn, I've gotta get out of here.'

No. No, wait. Please.

'I'll just grab a few more things,' Patsy said, once again disappearing inside the closet. 'I like this Armani jacket, although I'll have to let it out at the bust.'

You have to help me. You can't leave me here. Casey began frantically kicking her feet beneath the covers. She pushed her head off the pillow and lifted her right hand, grabbing at the air as if it were a lifeline. *Help me. You have to help me.*

'OK, I think that's everything.' Patsy emerged from the closet, her arms filled with Casey's belongings. 'Oh my God!' she said as her eyes connected with Casey's.

Casey fell back, overwhelmed by the effort of what she'd just accomplished, as Patsy crumpled to the floor.

Patsy? Patsy? Where are you? Had she run away? Casey tried to raise her torso to get a better look, but her body refused to cooperate.

Patsy, for God's sake, where are you? Get me out of here.

Several minutes passed before Casey was able to lift her head again. At first, all she saw were her clothes spread, like loosely raked leaves, across the carpet. And then she saw her, half lying on the floor, her back against the closet door, her eyes closed.

Don't you dare faint on me, you thieving little twit. Wake up!

Patsy groaned. The groan became a moan. 'Oh God,' she whispered. In the next minute, she was scrambling to her feet, her eyes with obvious reluctance travelling to Casey. 'I don't believe this. You can see me, can't you? You're conscious. Has anyone called the hospital?' She walked towards the phone.

And then the unmistakable click of a key turning in a lock. The front door opening.

'Warren?' Patsy gasped, confusion shooting through her eyes.

The sound of footsteps as they ascended the staircase.

'Hell,' Patsy muttered, running back and scooping up all of Casey's clothes from the floor and hurling them into the closet. 'What'll I tell him? How am I going to explain . . .?'

'Beauty?' the voice purred from the hallway. 'Your prince has arrived.'

Casey watched Patsy grab her bag from the floor, then run into the closet with no time to close the door after her.

Was she watching? Casey wondered. Would she see what happened? Was there a chance she might come to her rescue?

Out of the corner of her eye, Casey saw Nick's muscular frame appear in the doorway. He walked to the foot of the bed. 'You sure are a pretty thing,' he said. 'It's a shame I gotta do this.'

Casey found herself staring at a man of average height with a barrel chest and notable biceps. His dark hair was cropped short.

Her eyes widening in fear, she watched him put on a pair of latex gloves, although the man was too preoccupied to notice. 'Can't go leaving any telltale DNA,' he said, coming round to stand next to her head. 'Now you just lie still, and I'll make this quick.' Without any delay, he gripped Casey's nose, squeezing her nostrils with his right hand while covering her mouth with his left.

Casey fought desperately for breath, and the room began spinning. Her arms shot reflexively from her sides. She heard a loud gasp escape her lips.

Except the gasp hadn't come from her, she realised, as the pressure on her nose and mouth suddenly weakened.

'What was that?' the man asked, leaving Casey's side.

Casey's mouth flew open, sucking air into her lungs like a powerful vacuum as Nick walked into the closet, then re-emerged, dragging a sobbing Patsy. 'What the hell are you doing here?'

'Please,' she was crying. 'Don't hurt me. Don't hurt me.'

He slammed her against Casey's bed. 'You gotta be kidding me,' he snarled, slapping her hard across the face.

Patsy screamed as she grabbed the striped armchair, trying to drag it between them, but Nick pushed it aside, then grabbed her by the throat, twisting the Hermès scarf tight. Patsy's hands shot up, her fingernails clawing at his face, drawing blood. In an obvious rage, he pulled the scarf tight.

Casey watched in horror as Patsy's feet lifted off the floor to kick frantically at the air, her fingers straining to loosen the deadly silk at her throat. *No, please, no.*

And then something snapped, and suddenly Patsy stopped struggling. Casey closed her eyes, understanding she was dead.

When she opened them again, Nick was loosening his hold, allowing Patsy's body to slide clumsily to the floor. 'Hell,' he cursed repeatedly, dabbing at his cheek with the back of his hand. He tore the gloves from his hands and glared at Casey.

Casey forced her face to go blank, her eyes to stare ahead.

Nick stood absolutely still for two full minutes, clearly weighing his options. 'OK,' he said. 'Looks like you get a reprieve, Beauty. I'm bleeding. The bitch has my DNA under her fingernails. And there's no way in hell I'm doing two for the price of one.'

Casey watched as he straightened the room, then looked around, his eyes sweeping across the floor on his way to the closet. Seconds later he returned, Patsy's big canvas bag in his hands. He then took a minute to straighten Casey's covers. 'Catch you later, Beauty.' Returning to Patsy, he scooped up her dead body and tossed it over his shoulder. Without so much as a backwards glance, Death strode from the room.

Only when she heard the front door slam and knew he was gone did Casey unleash a low, guttural wail, as primal as life itself.

Two hours later, the front door opened and Lola burst through, followed by Drew and Warren, laughing at some shared private joke. Already a happy little family unit, Casey thought.

'Auntie Casey,' Lola called out. 'Auntie Casey, I'm here!'

'Me, too,' Drew said, laughing as she followed her daughter.

Was Warren right behind them? What would he do when he saw her? Casey was actually looking forward to finding out.

Her niece raced towards the bed, clambering up its side and burrowing in against her. 'We've been to Gettysburg. It was so fun. Wasn't it, Mommy?'

'It was so fun,' Drew agreed. 'Oh, good. Your eyes are open.'

'Is Auntie Casey awake?'

'I don't know, sweetie. Are you awake, Casey?' Drew took Casey's hand.

Casey squeezed as hard as she could.

'You know what, Lola?' Drew said. 'I have an idea. Why don't you go downstairs to the kitchen and paint your aunt a picture of some of the things we saw in Gettysburg.'

'We saw big, big rocks. What are they called, Mommy?'

'Boulders.'

'Can I paint the boulders green and blue?'

'I don't see why not.'

Lola jumped down from the bed and ran to the door, colliding with Warren's legs. 'Is something wrong?' he asked.

'I'm going to paint a picture of boulders for Auntie Casey.'

Casey could feel Warren's confusion. Had they not realised his wife was dead? she could almost hear him thinking.

'How's Casey?' he asked tentatively.

'Her eyes are open again,' Drew said. 'I know they say it doesn't mean anything, but . . .'

Warren took Casey's hand away from Drew's, surreptitiously checking her pulse. 'But you think it's a good sign?'

'Maybe it just makes me feel better.'

'Me, too.' Warren stared directly into Casey's eyes.

Casey stared back, unblinking.

'Where's Patsy?' Drew asked suddenly.

'I had to let her go.' Warren's eyes never wavered from Casey's. 'She wasn't working out.'

'Wow. First Jeremy, then Patsy. You've been doing some major house-keeping. So who's looking after Casey?'

'I hired a temporary nurse.'

'Where is she?'

'I told her to come back at five.' Warren said, as if he'd just dismissed her. 'Would you excuse me for a few minutes? I have to make a phone call.'

'Take your time,' Drew said, reaching for Casey's hand as Warren left the room. 'OK, are you still there?'

Casey squeezed Drew's hand. 'Help me,' she managed to whisper, the words blurring together like sticky rice.

'Oh my God. Did you just say something?'

'Help me,' Casey said, the words murky again.

'Warren!' Drew cried. 'Get back here!'

'No!' Casey said. This time the word was crystal clear.

'I don't understand. Why don't you want me to tell Warren? He loves you so much, Casey. He didn't stop talking about you all day. And he was so great with Lola. I've been unfair to him.'

'No!' Casey said again. *He's going to kill me. Call the police.*

'Why don't you want me to tell Warren?'

Because he tried to kill me. Because you're next.

But the words refused to form, tumbling from her lips as a series of disconnected vowels and consonants.

'Is Auntie Casey singing?' Lola skipped back into the room.

'Go paint your aunt a picture,' Drew said, clearly flustered.

'I couldn't find the paints.'

'Look in the cupboard under the sink.'

'I looked there. I want Auntie Casey to sing me a song.'

'She can't sing, sweetheart.'

'Yes, she can. I heard her.' Lola climbed back on the bed.

'Did you call me?' Warren asked from the hallway.

'Auntie Casey is singing!'

No!

'Lola . . . She wasn't singing,' Drew said.

'What exactly *was* she doing?' Warren crossed to the bed.

'It was really more of a groan.' Drew glanced at Casey.

'Why are you looking at her that way? Do you think she can see you?' Warren suddenly ripped Lola's zebra painting off the wall, waving the colourful stripes back and forth in front of Casey's eyes. 'Can you see this? Can you?'

'You're ruining my picture!' Lola cried.

'You blinked,' Warren said. 'Dear God, you can see.'

'Is that true? Casey, can you see?' Drew grabbed Casey's hand. 'Squeeze once for yes.'

'What are you doing?' Warren's face registered shock. 'Are you saying she's responsive? Drew, if you know something about my wife's condition that I don't, tell me.'

There was a long pause. *Don't tell him. Please, don't tell him.*

'Casey is conscious,' Drew said finally.

'What? For how long?'

'Probably just a few days. She's been spelling out words.'

'Spelling out words?' Warren repeated dully. He sank into a chair and lowered his head to his hands.

'This is such great news,' Drew said. 'Casey can see. She's starting to communicate. Soon she'll be walking and talking. Isn't that wonderful, Warren? Casey's come back to us.'

12

'Is Lola asleep?' Warren asked several hours later.

Drew stepped to Casey's bedside. 'Out like a light. I guess she was pretty exhausted, what with Gettysburg and then all the excitement with my sister.'

'It's been quite the day,' Warren agreed. 'Casey seems to be resting comfortably. Looks like the Valium the nurse gave her is finally starting to take effect.'

'You really think it was necessary? I mean, it seems a shame to knock her out when she's starting to come round.'

'Casey was awfully agitated when Mrs Friedlander was here, Drew. She's confused and terrified. I don't want her falling out of bed and hurting herself.'

'I guess you're right. Were you able to reach her doctors?'

'Not yet. I called the hospital; I've left messages all over the city. It's Sunday night—what can you expect? I'll keep trying.'

'I'm so sorry I didn't tell you earlier.'

'How could you keep something like that from me?' Warren asked, his voice incredulous.

'I don't know. I was just so mad at you, I guess. I wasn't thinking straight. And then today, we were having such a good time, and I wanted to tell you, I was *going* to tell you . . .'

'It's all right,' Warren said. 'What's important is I know now.' He paused. 'So, you think a little champagne is in order?'

'Champagne?'

'To celebrate the great news.'

Drew hesitated. 'I don't know. I really shouldn't . . .'

'Come on. You're sleeping here tonight. You won't be driving. One glass. I won't let you have any more than that.'

'You really think it's a good idea?'

'I think Casey deserves a toast in her honour.'

Drew laughed happily. 'I guess she does.'

'Be right back.'

As soon as he was gone, Casey reached through the dense fog enveloping her head and grabbed Drew's hand.

Drew gasped with fright. 'Casey, you scared me.'

'Help me,' Casey said, opening her eyes, not sure whether she'd said anything at all.

'What? I don't understand.'

He's trying to kill me.

'You're not making any sense. Do you want me to get Warren?'

Casey twisted from side to side, squeezing Drew's hand. *No!*

'OK, OK. Please try to calm down. Warren's right. You're going to hurt yourself if you keep thrashing around like this.'

Warren didn't call the hospital. He's going to get you good and drunk, then he's going to kill me and put the blame on you.

'I'm so sorry. I can't understand what you're telling me.'

He's going to kill me!

'Please calm down, Casey. I know this is frustrating, but you're not making any sense. Get some sleep, and in the morning I promise you'll feel better.' Drew looked towards the door. 'Oh, I think I hear Warren coming with the champagne.'

Casey closed her eyes.

'Is there a problem?' Warren asked, entering the room.

'Casey was groaning a bit, but she seems OK now. Here, let me help you with those glasses.'

Please, Drew, Casey thought, refusing to give in to the sleep hovering over her head like a plastic bag. Don't drink.

'Dom Pérignon,' Drew said. 'How nice.'

'I've been saving this bottle for a special occasion.'

'Which this definitely is,' Drew agreed, as Casey heard a loud pop, followed by the sound of her sister's high-pitched laughter. 'Careful. It's spilling on the carpet.'

'So we'll buy new carpet,' Warren said, laughing now as well. 'Hold out your glass.'

No. Don't. Please don't take a sip. One sip will lead to another. You know it will. You know what will happen.

'Well? What's the verdict?' Warren asked.

'Absolutely fabulous.'

'You hear that, Casey? It's absolutely fabulous,' Warren said. 'To the love of my life.'

'Welcome back, Casey,' Drew seconded.

Casey pictured her husband and sister raising their glasses.

'Hurry up and get better,' Drew urged, emptying her glass. 'Oh, man, I forgot just how good great champagne can be.'

'Let's have another toast. Your turn,' Warren suggested.

'My turn? I think I need a little more champagne first. Thank you. Well, let's see. To my sister, whom I love with all my heart, even if I don't always know how to show it.'

'Hear, hear. And to health, wealth and the American way.'

'I don't suppose I could tempt you into topping off my glass again,' Drew said moments later.

No, Drew. Please, don't do this.

'I guess I can let you have just a little bit more.'

'You're a real sport. Aw, come on, Warren. You can do better than that, can't you? My sister's come back from the dead.'

'All right. But this is it.'

Casey listened to the sound of liquid being poured into a glass and felt sleep gently massaging her temples. It took all her concentration to keep from drifting off.

'To true love,' Drew said.

'True love,' Warren echoed.

'Think I'll ever find it?' Drew asked wistfully.

'True love? I don't see why not. You're a beautiful girl . . .'

'A *rich*, beautiful girl,' Drew amended.

Warren laughed. 'And you're funny and feisty and . . .'

'Fabulous, like this champagne,' Drew said, giggling. 'How about one more glass? I promise I won't ask for more.'

'All right. But absolutely no more.'

'It goes down very smoothly for something with so many bubbles.' Drew giggled again.

'That it does, Drew. Now then,' Warren's voice grew warmly concerned. 'Whatever happened with you and Sean?'

'Who?'

'Sean? Your old boyfriend who wanted to get back together?'

'He did?'

'He didn't?' Warren asked.

'He probably did,' Drew said, and laughed again. 'I mean, why wouldn't he? I'm funny and feisty and . . . what else?'

'You're fabulous. And you're a very fast drinker. I can't believe your glass is empty already.'

'That's because you're a very slow pourer.'

'Well, then, let me correct that.'

'You're a kind and generous man.'

'And you are a sweet and sensitive woman.'

'Thank you. But I have a very low tolerance for alcohol, you know. Don't let me drink too much.'

'I wouldn't dream of it.'

Drew laughed as if this was the most hilarious thing she'd ever heard. 'You're very funny. You know that? And feisty.'

'What happened to fabulous?'

'You're pretty fabulous, actually.'

'Thank you.' Again the sound of liquid filling a glass. 'So, have you heard anything from Jeremy?'

'Who?' said Drew.

'Jeremy. Casey's therapist. I was sure he'd get in touch.'

'Oh, right. Him. Actually he did call. Yesterday, as a matter of fact.'

'He didn't waste much time.'

'I guess you had him pegged.'

'What did he want?'

'I'd left a note at the hospital, asking him to call. You know. Just to see if he was all right.'

'Drink up,' Warren said.

'You're a good man.'

Warren laughed. 'Where's he taking you on your first date?'

'He said think of something unusual. I'm supposed to call.'

'Are you going to?'

'Maybe.'

'Have another drink.' Warren filled her glass again.

'Don't tell me that bottle's almost empty?'

'I have another one. He's not good enough for you, you know.'

'What? Who?'

'Jeremy.'

'Probably not. But you have to admit he's pretty cute.'

'Not exactly my type. You can do better.'

Drew laughed. 'You have anyone particular in mind?'

'I might.'

'Wait—don't tell me. Could his name by any chance be Willy Billy?' Drew shrieked with laughter.

'I promise you his name is definitely *not* Willy Billy. Something tells me you've had enough champagne.'

'Come on, Uncle Warren. Might as well finish the bottle.'

'Looks like this is the last of it.'

'But you said you had another one.' Drew jumped to her feet. 'Where is it? I'll go get it. We're celebrating.'

'That we are. It's in the fridge. Be careful on the stairs.'

'I'm fine. Don't worry.' Drew's voice faded as she went downstairs.

'I won't.' Warren sank down into the chair beside Casey's bed. 'I have enough to worry about at the moment. Wouldn't you say, Casey? What with old Nick screwing up again.' He began stroking her hair. 'I called him earlier. He was full of excuses; he'd had no choice but to kill Patsy.' His hand stilled. 'And now he expects to be paid double. Can you beat that? What the hell was Patsy doing here anyway? Stupid girl.'

Casey opened her eyes, saw Warren staring back at her. Who is this man? she wondered, watching his image split in two, then double up and circle round her head.

'Stop trying to fight it, Casey,' Warren was saying, his voice warm as a kitten's fur. 'You're only making things harder for everybody.' He leaned over. 'This really has to be the last of our little chats, I'm afraid.' Casey watched two Warrens kiss the backs of two pairs of hands as her eyelids grew increasingly heavy, her will no longer enough to sustain them.

'Thatta girl,' Warren said as her eyes closed.

Casey fought to remain conscious. Stay awake, she told herself. Don't make it so easy for him. He'll just wait until Drew passes out, and then . . . what? Throw her down the stairs and somehow make it look like an accident? Or would he smother her with a pillow, all the while finding a way to place the blame on Drew?

I'm so tired.

Drew didn't stand a chance against him.

Warren suddenly walked to the door. 'Drew,' he called out. 'What are you doing? Drinking the whole bottle yourself?'

'Ready or not,' Drew sang out from the stairway. 'Here I am.' She chortled as she walked into the room. 'Did you miss me?'

'I missed Mr Pérignon.'

'A good thing I found him. It wasn't easy either. Here you go.'

'Stand back.' A loud pop followed. 'How about toasting world peace?'

'Always a favourite. To world peace. And Madonna,' Drew said. 'She's my idol, the way she keeps reinventing herself.'

'To Madonna,' Warren said, with a laugh. 'Here. Let me pour you some more.' Then, 'Drew, what's that on your nose?'

'My nose?'

'What exactly were you doing downstairs?' There was a smile in Warren's voice.

'You know what I was doing,' Drew said defensively. 'I was getting the champagne.'

'Champagne produces bubbles, not white powder.'

Casey felt her sister pull back as her husband reached his hand towards Drew's face. No, Casey thought. *No, no, no.*

'It's just baking soda,' Drew said, sniffling loudly. 'Maybe I was baking a cake.'

'Baking soda? You really expect me to believe that?'

'OK, so it's a little something to take the edge off. A lot's happened. What is it they say? Things go better with . . .?'

Oh, Drew. You signed my death warrant.

'How much did you do?'

'Just a couple of lines. It's no big deal. Come on. Let's have another glass of champagne.'

'I think maybe you've had enough.'

'Are you kidding? This is nothing. Don't be a party-pooper.'

Warren sighed. 'You're sure this is what you want?'

'I'm sure. And pour yourself a glass while you're at it.'

Sometime in the next hour, her sister and her husband still noisily toasting her recovery, Casey gave in to the inevitable, and surrendered to unconsciousness.

When Casey woke up some time later, she was alone.

What time is it? she wondered groggily, turning her head towards her nightstand: 2:07, the red clock numbers announced.

Two in the morning, she thought, allowing the numbers to sink in and wondering what had woken her up.

And then she heard it—the gentle squeak on the stairs.

Who would it be this time? Casey wondered, stiffening beneath the sheets. Warren, or the man he'd hired to do his dirty work? Was her husband even now asleep in his bed, waiting for Death to hurl her down the stairs like so much soiled laundry? Or maybe it was Warren, having easily seduced Drew into a drugged and drunken stupor, come to finish the job himself.

Casey strained through the darkness, the light of the moon through the window cloaking the room in a gentle mist. A male figure appeared in the doorway, filling the frame. He paused for an instant, then crept quickly across the carpet. Tears filled her eyes. Would she have enough strength to scream? Would it do any good?

'No!' Casey heard herself cry, her heart thumping wildly, threatening to explode in her chest, as a large palm covered her mouth. Her eyes opened wide.

'Shh,' the man whispered.

Was she dreaming? How was this possible?

'It's OK,' the man said soothingly, slowly alleviating the pressure on her mouth. 'Don't scream. It's OK.' He pulled back her covers and lifted her carefully out of bed.

Jeremy.

'We're going to get you out of here,' he said.

We? It was only then that Casey became aware of a second figure watching from the doorway. *Drew. My God. It's Drew.*

'Hurry. I'll get Lola,' Drew whispered, leaving their side as Jeremy carried Casey into the hall and headed for the stairs.

But suddenly there was a third figure, blocking their path.

'Going somewhere?' Warren asked, almost casually. Even through the darkness, Casey could make out the gun in his hand.

She recognised her mother's gun. He'd found it.

'Put my wife down,' he directed Jeremy. 'Now.'

Slowly, Jeremy lowered Casey to the floor, resting her back against the wall at the top of the stairs. 'Easy, man . . .'

'Shut up. What the hell do you think you're doing?'

'We're taking my sister out of here,' Drew said defiantly.

'You're kidnapping my wife? Why would you want to do that?'

'Because it's what Casey wants. And because I know you're up to something. I don't know what it is, but I know you deliberately tried to get me drunk.'

'I don't recall twisting your arm.'

'You almost had me fooled, you know. I was actually feeling guilty about having given such a sweet guy such a hard time. But then I thought, why is he offering me champagne when he knows what will happen if I start drinking? Although what you obviously *don't* know is that it takes a whole lot more than a couple of bottles of champagne to knock *me* out. And it really *was* baking soda, incidentally.'

'Put the gun down,' Jeremy urged. 'We leave. Nobody gets hurt.'

Warren aimed the gun at Drew's head. 'I don't think so.'

'You're going to shoot us all?' Drew asked. 'You'll never—'

'I'll never what? Please tell me you weren't going to say I'll never get away with it. How's this? Jealous cokehead enlists the help of a disgruntled former employee to help murder her sister. Brave and selfless husband confronts the killers and is forced to shoot them dead. Think the good detective will buy it? It's not perfect, I know, but by the time the cops get here, it will be.'

'Oh my God,' Drew muttered, her eyes travelling between Warren and her sister. 'Detective Spinetti was right—what happened to Casey was no accident. That's what she's been trying to tell me.'

'Not very nice, Casey, keeping things from your husband,' Warren said, waving the gun in her direction.

'Come on,' Jeremy said. 'Put the gun away before you hurt somebody.'

'That's the general idea, isn't it?' Warren pointed the gun at Jeremy and squeezed the trigger.

'No!' Drew screamed, Casey's cries echoing hers as Jeremy collapsed, bleeding, to the floor. Drew ran to his side as Warren calmly pointed the gun at her head.

'Mommy?' a little voice asked from somewhere behind Warren. 'What was that noise?'

Warren swung round. In the next second, Casey watched her sister leap off the floor and propel herself towards Warren, her hands thrashing out, her feet kicking at his shins, her fingers clawing at his eyes and throat. The gun flew from his hands, landing several feet from Casey. Slowly, her fingers stretched towards it.

You can do this. You can do this.

After several failed attempts, she managed to make contact with the cold metal handle, her fingertips dragging the weapon closer. At the same time, Warren succeeded in pinning Drew's hands behind her back. Lifting her into the air, he hurled her against the wall. Drew crumpled to the floor in a shapeless heap.

'Mommy!' Lola cried, rushing to her mother's side.

Warren strode to Casey just as her fist closed round the handle. 'Give me the gun,' he said, lowering himself down and balancing on the balls of his feet.

Casey lifted the gun from her side, pointing it directly at her husband's heart. Does he even have one? she wondered.

'You don't have the strength to pull the trigger,' Warren said.

Was he right?

'Tap once for yes, twice for no,' she heard Drew say.

'Even if you had the strength, you couldn't do it,' Warren said, his voice soothing and hypnotic. 'I'm your husband, Casey. I love you. You know that. And you love me. You know you do. I'm so sorry for everything I've put you through. You know that in your heart, don't you? It's not too late. We can start over. Please.'

'Tap once for yes, twice for no,' she heard Drew say again.

'You don't really want to shoot me, do you, Casey?'

Casey looked into her husband's warm brown eyes, seeing the cold-blooded monster behind them. As he reached for the gun, she tapped her finger forcefully against the trigger.

Once for yes.

13

'"SHE DID NOT MOVE, and he came towards her with more doubt and timidity in his face than she had ever seen before,"' Janine read. '"He was in a state of uncertainty which made him afraid lest some look or word of his should condemn him to a new distance from her; and Dorothea was afraid of her own emotion. She looked as if there were a spell upon her." Are you OK?' Janine lay the book across her lap and took Casey's hand.

'She's great,' Gail said from her chair next to the fireplace. 'Aren't you, Casey?'

'She just wants to get the hell out of Middlemarch,' Drew said, leaning over to stoke the fire, several errant sparks shooting to her living-room floor. Drew stamped them out with her high-heeled Manolo boots. 'I can't believe you still haven't finished that book.'

'Just twenty-three more pages to go. Come on, you want to find out what happens. Admit it.'

'You mean something happened in the first six hundred pages?' Drew said. 'OK, I admit it. I'm enjoying it. Does that mean I'm maturing?'

'It happens to the best of us.'

'I'm far from the best.'

'And far from the worst,' Gail said.

'So my therapist tells me. Thanks for noticing.'

'Casey says she's really helping the two of you reconnect.'

The women turned as one to Casey, smiles filling their faces.

'We're working things out,' Drew said. 'Aren't we, Casey?'

'How about some tea?' Gail asked.

'Sounds great,' Janine said.

'I'll make it,' Drew offered.

'No, I'll do it. Just tell me where you keep everything,' Gail said.

'Tea bags are in the pantry, mugs are in the first cupboard,' Drew said. 'Can you believe I'm so domestic?'

'What I can't believe is the cold weather,' Janine said.

'It always gets cold for Halloween.' Gail headed for the kitchen. 'Those kids freeze every year. Stan says his kids end up wearing coats over their costumes, and nobody knows what they're supposed to be.'

'Are you taking Lola trick-or-treating?' Janine asked Drew.

'Yup. She's going as a cat.'

'A cat? I would have thought she'd be a fairy princess.'

'Fairy princesses are so last year. This year she wants to be a cat.' Drew's proud smile filled her face. 'Like her mother. I always used to be a cat on Halloween. Remember, Casey?'

Casey smiled at the distant memory.

'So when Lola gets home from school, we'll make cat ears.'

'Sounds like fun,' Janine deadpanned.

'Gail's coming. And Casey. They're going to be cats, too.'

Janine turned to Casey. 'Is that the price you have to pay for staying here until you're all better?'

'She loves it here. Don't you, Casey?' Drew said.

'Are you sure you're up for so much activity?'

'Jeremy thinks she is,' Drew answered in Casey's stead. 'We're only going to go a couple of blocks.'

'How is Jeremy?'

'He's great. His shoulder's almost healed. He hopes to be back working in the new year.'

'And the two of you?'

'Still going strong,' Drew replied, borrowing Gail's giggle.

'That's nice.' Janine sounded genuinely pleased. 'I'm really happy for you. And for you,' she told Gail as she re-entered the room. 'Even if all this sex is making her quite unbearable.'

'You'll meet someone,' Gail said.

'Not high on my list of priorities at the moment,' Janine said, squeezing Casey's hand.

'How's your business doing?' Drew asked.

'Seems to be picking up. Oh—you'll never guess who I ran into the other day. Richard Mooney! Apparently he got a job over at Goodman and Francis.'

'Aren't they the guys who represented Warren?' Gail asked.

'That was Goodman, Latimer. They're better than Goodman and Francis. Not that it did Warren any good.'

'I guess their hands were tied once Nick Margolis agreed to testify in exchange for taking the death penalty off the table.'

'I still can't believe he tried to kill Casey, and then strangled that poor Patsy,' Gail said. 'At least Warren got what he deserved.'

'Not really,' Drew countered. 'He's still alive, isn't he?'

'If you call spending life behind bars any kind of life.'

'Beats spending it in a coma. Right, Casey?' Drew asked. 'Too bad my sister's such a lousy shot. If that bullet had been another two inches to the right, we wouldn't be having this conversation.'

The kettle started whistling from the kitchen.

'That's my cue,' Gail said, exiting the room.

'I'll help you,' Drew said, going with her.

'You're very quiet today,' Janine told Casey after a pause. 'Does it upset you? Listening to us talk about what happened?'

'Not really,' Casey said slowly, still adjusting to the sound of her voice, just as her body was still adjusting to its growing range of movement.

'I guess I sounded pretty insensitive before.'

'I know,' Casey said.

'I'm sorry. I didn't mean . . .'

'About you and Warren,' Casey qualified. 'I know.'

Janine nodded, as if she wasn't surprised. 'Do you hate me?'

'No.'

'*I'd* hate *you*,' Janine said.

'I know you would.'

'Do you want me to leave?'

'How can you leave? You still have twenty-three pages to go.'

Janine smiled sadly. 'You don't need me to read them to you.'

'I don't think I could get through them without you.'

Janine lowered her head and burst into tears. 'Oh, Casey. I'm so sorry. I was so stupid. And I *hate* stupid.'

Casey smiled. 'Warren fooled everybody, Janine.'

'If only I could go back . . .'

'You can't. We have to move forward.'

'If I could make it up to you, you know I would.'

'You can come trick-or-treating with us tonight.'

'What?'

'Lola will be happy to make another set of cat ears.'

'You really *do* hate me,' Janine said.

Casey laughed out loud.

'Now, that's a beautiful sound,' Drew said, returning to the living room, holding a tray containing a plate of pumpkin-shaped cookies and four mugs, Gail following right behind with the teapot. Drew deposited the tray on the ottoman in front of the sofa and knelt on the shag carpet. Gail sank down beside her. Casey pushed herself off her overstuffed velvet chair to join them on the floor.

'Careful,' Janine said.

'Watch yourself,' Gail echoed.

'I'm OK,' Casey told them, crossing one leg over the other.

Gail poured the sweet-smelling herbal tea into each mug.

'Here,' Drew said. 'Try my cookies. I made them myself.'

'Is there anything worse than a reformed junkie?' Janine asked rhetorically, biting into a cookie. 'These *are* good.'

'It's my own recipe,' Drew told her. 'Peanut butter, sugar, a little hashish. Just kidding,' she said to laughter. 'Honestly, Casey. Just kidding.'

Casey joined in the women's laughter, feeling the fire from the fireplace warm against her back. 'To my sister,' she said, securing the mug in her right hand and raising it, 'who saved my life.'

'To my sister,' Drew echoed softly, 'who saved mine.'

Casey rubbed the tiny silver shoe dangling from the chain round her neck, wishing she could always feel this safe. She sipped slowly at her tea. She took a deep breath, her eyes floating lovingly between her sister and her two closest friends, and breathed again.

Joy Fielding

How did you do your research into what it's like to be in a coma?

I spoke to a neurologist about what goes on in the brain of someone who's in a coma, and he was very helpful in outlining the various tests that are performed to determine a coma victim's state of awareness. I also spoke at length to an internist about the kind of injuries a person might sustain during a car accident, and the range of tests and operations that might be performed. But the happy truth, for a novelist anyway, is that most people who emerge from a coma don't remember very much, so I had complete freedom to make up whatever I wanted, within reason.

Have you ever spoken to a patient who has emerged from a coma?

No, but I did have a friend, now deceased, who was involved in an accident and fell into a coma. When she emerged, after a few months, she was like a two-year-old and she never got any better. It was tragic, and I often wondered, when I went to visit her in hospital, how aware she was of what was happening around her. It's interesting, because until I started to answer your question, I didn't realise that she might have played a part in the writing of *Still Life*. I'd kind of divorced myself from that painful time and certainly was never consciously writing about my friend. Casey's story is definitely not my friend's story, but the coma part . . . maybe that was my subconscious at work.

Do you know, or have you met, a victim of a hit-and-run accident?
When I was at a writers' convention in British Columbia a few years ago, I met a young woman who'd been hit by a car. I can't remember if it was a hit-and-run, but she did tell me about being hit and what she went through afterwards—the various tests and operations and how she felt both mentally and physically, all of which was very helpful in the writing of *Still Life*.

Casey and her sister were both deeply traumatised by the complete lack of a mother's love. Is this life-affecting situation something you set out to explore?
The mother–daughter relationship is at the heart of virtually all my novels. It's not something I've deliberately set out to explore, but no matter how determined I am not to get into it, it always reappears. It's especially interesting to me because I had a great relationship with my own mother, who was the best anyone could have hoped for. When I had my daughters—I have two, the youngest of whom has just become a mother herself—all I wanted was to have the same kind of relationship with them that I'd enjoyed with my mother. Luckily, I think that's proved to be the case, although I've learned that it's much easier to be a daughter! My beloved mother died at the relatively young age of sixty-two, just four months after my elder daughter was born, and I think I've been searching for her ever since.

Do you think it was inevitable that once Drew felt that her sister Casey needed her, the natural sibling love she had was able to develop?
Yes, once Casey is in trouble, Drew is finally able to grow up and blossom. She's been in the unfortunate position of being the younger sibling to the perfect older sister. She feels she can't measure up and so she stops trying.

Did you find that Drew began to take off in an unexpected direction, or had you planned it all from the start?
It was always my intention that Drew should grow as the book progressed, although her precise role in what happens was not defined at the outset. Some of the best things about the writing process are the surprises that happen along the way. Drew was a very pleasant surprise indeed.

Do you believe it's possible to be immensely rich, and to find true inner happiness, too?
Yes, I do. The trick is to be happy with yourself. If you like yourself, and are good to others, money can be a bonus.

We are hugely grateful to Joy, who took time out to answer our questions when she was looking after her daughter, who had just given birth to Hayden. She sent us this gorgeous photo, taken when he was just three days old.